HEART AND SCIENCE

HEART AND SCIENCE:
A Story of the Present Time

Wilkie Collins

edited by Steve Farmer

broadview literary texts

Canadian Cataloguing in Publication Data

Collins, Wilkie, 1824–1889
    Heart and science: a story of the present time

(Broadview literary texts)
Includes bibliographical references.
ISBN 1-55111-124-1

I. Farmer, Steve, 1957-   . II. Title. III. Series.

PR4494.H4 1996   823′.8   C96-932118-X

Broadview Press
Post Office Box 1243, Peterborough, Ontario, Canada K9J 7H5

in the United States of America:
3576 California Road, Orchard Park, NY 14127

in the United Kingdom:
B.R.A.D. Book Representation & Distribution Ltd., 244A, London Road, Hadleigh, Essex SS7 2DE

Broadview Press gratefully acknowledges the support of the Canada Council, the Ontario Arts Council, and the Ministry of Canadian Heritage.

Typesetting and assembly: True to Type Inc., Mississauga, Canada.

PRINTED IN CANADA

Contents

Acknowledgements

I am grateful to Ms. Lyn Farmer, Mr. Andrew Gasson, Mr. Barry Pike, Dr. Lesley Gordon, Dr. Jean Valk, Dr. Neil Nehring, Ms. Nicola Freshwater, Ms. Sharon Migotsky, Dr. Nicholas Salerno, Ms. Deb Person, and the staff at the Harry Ransom Research Library, University of Texas at Austin for their generous help during the preparation of this text.

Introduction

I. Wilkie Collins and Heart and Science: A Story of the Present Time

In the past decade Wilkie Collins's fiction has undergone a literary reassessment that has led some scholars to place him nearer the first tier of Victorian novelists than he has ever been. Two new biographies, a number of recent book-length critical studies, and several re-issues of novels long out of print have drawn much deserved attention to Collins, but for most casual readers of Victorian fiction, his success as a novelist is still measured primarily by the two novels he wrote relatively early in his career, *The Woman in White* (1859-60) and *The Moonstone* (1868). Because of the continuing popularity of these two novels, many readers still recognize in Collins only a figure instrumental in the development and growth of English detective, mystery, and sensation fiction, reading his novels because they have heard that *The Woman in White* is a top shelf mystery, or because they have been told by the likes of T.S. Eliot that *The Moonstone* is "the first and greatest of English detective novels."[1] But with new attention being paid to his later fiction, new generations of readers are being introduced to Collins as a multi-faceted novelist whose many other works deserve individual recognition.

Collins was himself initially touchy about the role his most popular novels would play in future analyses of his literary career. As early as 1869, twenty years and a dozen novels before his death, he lamented to a publisher: "[D]on't let us encourage the public ... in its one everlasting cry to me: 'Ah! He may write what he pleases! He will never do anything again like *The Woman in White.*'"[2] At the end of his life, however, this anxiety had mellowed to acceptance. Anticipating the direction popular and critical evaluation of his novels would take, he gave instructions that the inscription on his gravestone in Kensal Green cemetery should read, "In Memory of Wilkie Collins, Author of *The Woman in White* and Other Works of Fiction."

We have only recently begun to recognize the value of these "other works of fiction," of which there are many. Collins wrote more novels in the last twenty years of his life than he had written in the first forty-five, most of them popular successes at the time and most still very lively reading today.[3] By 1882, in fact, the year he began *Heart and Science*, he had already completed eight post-*The Moonstone* novels. He was by this time the lonely survivor among the handful of British novelists who had commanded centre stage at mid-century, those whose names enter immediately into any discussion of Victorian fiction. Dickens, the Brontës, George Eliot, and Thackeray were all dead, and Anthony Trollope would pass away in December of 1882. But rather than live as a literary *doyen* to a new generation of writers, as an old-timer content to sell reminiscences about his heyday, Collins quietly but industriously continued to write, publishing *Heart and Science* between August 1882 and June 1883, and five more popular novels before his death in October 1889. And it is to *Heart and Science*, one of these long-hidden gems, that we now turn our attention.

In October 1889, A.C. Swinburne, recruited by the *Fortnightly Review* to write an obituary notice, unwittingly provided for generations of future critics an easy prescription to evaluate *Heart and Science* with a carelessness that it simply does not deserve. Near the close of the obituary, in which he elsewhere praises Collins's "remarkable genius ... for invention and construction," and in which he labels the novelist a "genuine artist," Swinburne singles out *Heart and Science* as representing a problematic shift away from the page turners that had brought Collins fame and fortune in 1860s. His memorable pronouncement became the battle-cry for critics who have wanted to find fault with the novel:

> What brought good Wilkie's genius nigh perdition?
> Some demon whispered—'Wilkie! have a mission.' (See Appendix E, for more of Swinburne's commentary on *Heart and Science*).

The lines are humorous, to be certain, but they are unfair and too easy to use. All of Collins's six biographers reproduce the couplet, most seemingly satisfied that it somehow effectively summarizes *Heart and Science*.[4] Such cursory treatment stereotypes the novel, for in the wink of a couplet *Heart and Science* suddenly exists solely as one of Collins's "mission" novels, as a "thesis" novel, as a "propaganda" novel, as a "purpose" novel, or as his "anti-vivisection" novel. Such designations have the potential to do a grave disservice, for they may discourage readers by leading them to anticipate either some sort of mouldy lecture on animal rights or some unreasonable and emotional rant. But *Heart and Science*, as even its title suggests, is not a two-dimensional novel. It is, as we will see, a delightfully multi-layered work, one that rewards all readers in a variety of ways.

Collins's preface to *Heart and Science* reveals that he knew he was writing for a large and varied audience. An inveterate preface writer his whole career, he created a two-part preface for the novel—one section for his faithful "Readers in General," another for "Readers in Particular"—in which he assures his audience that his novel has much to offer everyone: character and humour, incident and dramatic situation, even an accurate depiction of the world of modern science.

To his "Readers in General" Collins wrote, "In the present story you will find the scales inclining, on the whole, in favour of character and humour" (37). Perhaps stung by such remarks as Anthony Trollope's— "The construction [of a Collins novel] is most minute and wonderful. But I can never lose the taste of the construction"[5]—Collins set out to downplay plot while paying special attention to character in *Heart and Science*, and the results are remarkable. Rather than depending on incident and dramatic situation to shape "gross caricature," as he had done in many of his earlier works, he made a concerted effort to create round characters who shaped incident.

Of course there are some stock characters in the novel. In fact, the story's two key figures—Ovid Vere and Carmina Graywell, the young hero and heroine—are, all in all, rather static and conventional Victorian pictures of goodness, faith, and love. But Collins's skill with the novel's other characters provides the two with a vitality they would not otherwise have. Among these fascinating characters is the governess, Miss Minerva, who seems ready early in the story to assume the role of a conventional villainess, but who develops dramatically and quite convincingly over the course of the novel, influencing the course of events and becoming one of the work's most complex and memorable figures. Her suicidal self-loathing, her intense struggle to overcome her past, her repeated warnings to the innocent Carmina—"don't trust me"—even as she determines to help the poor girl, and her keen ability to do intellectual battle with Mrs. Gallilee and to see through the deceptions being practised by those around her, make her one of Collins's darkest and most fascinating psychological studies.

Mrs. Gallilee, the aloof and hardened ambassadress of modern science, is another of the novel's more intriguing character studies. She cares only for her tadpoles, for the "Diathermancy of ebonite," for the interspatial regions, for Thomson's theory of atoms; in her world poetry is laughable, flowers exist to be dissected, music serves to test a concert hall's acoustics, children are born and raised only to insure the future of scientific inquiry. Though she shares many of the characteristics of Collins's other villains—the calculated eccentricities just noted, a cold and cunning intellect, a driving will to overcome adversity, and a penchant for a chillingly effective manipulation of people she considers her inferiors—she transcends caricature to become the embodiment of her creator's fears of contemporary science. She becomes one of the central elements of Collins's broad commentary on the malaise he saw creeping into his world as a result of the blind and indiscriminate rush for knowledge on the part of the scientific community.

The reader witnesses Mrs. Gallilee change over the course of the novel from a keen and calculating intellect into a paranoid psychopath who refuses to recognize her son, her daughters, even her kindly husband. The words with which she ends the novel are both ironic, in light of all the familial damage she has caused, and unsettlingly ominous. As she sits in her room after having hosted an evening of scientific discussion, she proclaims, "At last, I'm a happy woman!" The steady march of Scientific Inquiry, Collins knows, cannot be halted, but though we leave Mrs. Gallilee ostensibly happy at the end of the tale, we find ourselves consciously tallying her many losses. She is alienated from her husband, her son, her daughters, in fact, from all who once loved her. Science, for all its superficial benefits, exacts a personal toll.

Within the vivisectionist Benjulia, the dark genius in whose character Collins took particular pride, we see an involved and remarkably successful attempt, as Collins himself claims, to trace "the moral influence of those cruelties [of vivisection] on the nature of the man who practices them, and the result as to his social relations with the persons about him." (See Appendix D, 1.) To make Benjulia full and convincing, Collins had to paint him as "a man not infinitely wicked and cruel, and to show the efforts made by his better instincts to resist the inevitable hardening of the heart, the fatal stupefying of all the finer sensibilities, produced by the deliberately merciless occupations of his life." (Again, see Appendix D, 1.) To this end, Collins gives him a poignant humanity, as expressed in his affection for the idiot-child, Zoe, as well as a vicious streak of cruelty, as we see in his sadistic treatment of his cook. His schizophrenia becomes apparent on the rare occasion when he discusses vivisection. In an unsettlingly passionate outburst, Benjulia reveals the two sides of his soul as he admits to his stunned brother that an unfettered quest for knowledge is all that drives his life. His willingness to take vivisection to its horrible extreme, juxtaposed as it is in the following passage with his pitiful lament for a monkey he has recently vivisected, offers a dramatic portrait of a man not altogether evil but one certainly tormented by personal demons:

> Knowledge sanctifies cruelty. ... In that sacred cause, if I could steal a living man without being found out, I would tie him on my table, and grasp my grand discovery in days, instead of months. ... Have I no feeling, as you call it? My last experiments on a monkey horrified me. His cries of suffering, his gestures of entreaty, were like the cries and gestures of a child. I would have given the world to put him out of his misery. But I went on. In the glorious cause I went on. My hands turned cold—my heart ached—I thought of a child I sometimes play with—I suffered—I resisted—I went on. All for Knowledge! all for Knowledge! (190-91)

Heart and Science is also peopled with intriguing minor figures, among them Teresa, Carmina's faithful and ferocious duenna; Mr. Gallilee, Ovid's foolish but golden-hearted stepfather; Mr. Mool, the weak but honest Gallilee family lawyer; Mr. Null, the buffoonish family doctor; and Mr. LeFrank the sycophantic music-master. Most memorable of the minor figures, though, is Zoe, Ovid's dull-witted but loving half-sister, whom Swinburne calls "a capital child ... nothing less than delicious." (See Appendix E.) Zoe provides the novel with much of its comic relief, but she also becomes the agent who delivers one of Collins's intended messages, for by unwittingly saving the day near the novel's end, she reinforces the notion that the simple love of a simple child is powerful enough to conquer the dark and cold world of modern science.[6]

Of course, the novel offers much more than several intriguing character studies, and though Collins suggested in his preface that he had intentionally de-emphasized "incident and dramatic situation," those who appreciate his better-known fiction for its masterful plotting and precision of construction will be pleased with *Heart and Science*. The novel has dual villains and dual heroines, and the complex action stretches from the suburbs of London to the relative wilds of the prairies of western Canada. The story quickly envelops its readers in a series of intricate cabals whose successes and failures are dependent on a number of riveting scenes of eavesdropping, spying, chance meetings, and general skulking about. Collins heightens the tension by implanting in his story a number of false leads, and he provides his readers with a series of memorably lurid climaxes near the novel's conclusion.

We may also recognize in *Heart and Science* many of the plotting strategies that drive Collins's better known novels, and some of the parallels are fascinating. Aside from containing a familiar, rather conventional Victorian love story, *Heart and Science* emphasizes the strength of a woman left alone by a rather ineffectual lover to fend off villainy by herself, as do *The Woman in White, No Name*, and *Man and Wife*. Much of the action of the novel is generated by an unfortunate and problematic inheritance, as is the case in *The Woman in White* and *The Moonstone*. There is also for a time in *Heart and Science* a crucial question of legitimacy and its effect on the inheritance, as there is in *The Dead Secret, The Woman in White*, and *No Name*.

Much of the story is driven forward by a parade of household servants, who play key roles as spies, messengers, and accomplices of various sorts. Collins was fascinated by domestic servants and what he saw to be their major roles in the Victorian household, and we see them in *Heart and Science* playing parts they also take in *The Dead Secret, The Woman in White, No Name, Armadale, Man and Wife*, and several of the shorter works of fiction.[7] Collins also calls on the epistolary form he had perfected in such novels as *The Woman in White, No Name*, and *Armadale* to forward the plot of *Heart and Science*, devoting long sections in the middle of the book to important exchanges—and even more important interceptions—of letters among various parties.

We must not get the impression, though, that Collins was simply falling back on time-tested but stale strategies and tactics as if his inventive powers were waning late in life, for he manages to manipulate these devices in new and vital ways. In her recent biography of Collins, Catherine Peters admits sensing in *Heart and Science* a refreshing return of its creator's "old energy" (399). And Collins himself felt this resurgence of the old vigour as he composed. He labelled it the old "blood and dynamite." (See Appendix D, 3.)

Aside from his concerns for character and plot, Collins realized that he was writing a novel for another audience, one distinct from the "Readers in General" he mentions in the first part of his preface. He knew that his work would be scrutinized as a social/political document by "Readers in Particular," including not only professional reviewers but activists on both sides of the vivisection controversy of the day. With them in mind, Collins took care with the presentation of his anti-vivisection arguments, making certain to remain reasonable while also making very apparent his indignation.

This is not to suggest that the discussion of animal rights and the cruelties of animal experimentation in *Heart and Science* is didactic or aggressively partisan. In fact, Collins took great pains to remain a temperate advocate for the cause. In a letter to Frances Power Cobbe—London's most vocal and most powerful anti-vivisectionist—as he prepared to write his novel, he assured her that he did not wish his book to be "terrifying and revolting [to] the ordinary reader" and thus would make certain to "leave the detestable cruelties of the laboratory to be merely inferred." (See Appendix D, 1, for the complete text of this letter.) And in his novel's preface, he claims to have achieved the desired effect: "From first to last, [readers] are purposely left in ignorance of the hideous secrets of Vivisection. The outside of the laboratory is a necessary object in my landscape—but I never once open the door and invite [them] in" (38). And to a large degree this is true. In fact, we do not learn of the vivisectionist Benjulia's devotion to animal experimentation until chapter XXXI, and it is not until XXXII that Collins lays out with splendid precision, and a great deal of passion, the heart of his anti-vivisection argument.

Chapter XXXII takes the form of an interrogation, becoming at points a fascinating Socratic dialogue containing a tight summary of several key anti-vivisection arguments of the day. Visited at his home by his brother, Lemuel—the only person who knows the horrible secrets of the vivisector's laboratory—Dr. Nathan Benjulia learns that his sibling has joined a society for suppressing vivisectionists. Initially amused, Dr. Benjulia allows himself to be drawn into an involved and detailed discussion of the central moral and utilitarian issues of the animal experimentation debate. Collins skilfully manipulates the exchange of ideas between the brothers, allowing Lemuel's line of inquiry to trap the sceptical vivisectionist at every turn. By the time Dr. Benjulia's exasperation finally turns to rage, Collins's point has become clear—there is no adequate moral ground on which the vivisectionist can stand.

Near the close of the novel, Collins bolsters his arguments against animal experimentation rather dramatically by having his hero, Ovid Vere, return from the wilds of Canada with a manuscript concerning "brain disease," a work that allows him both to treat Carmina's illness and prove the uselessness of scientific inquiry via vivisection. After reading the work and determining its legitimacy, Benjulia realizes the futility of his occupation. Again, the message is clear, and rather cleverly made: there is always a more appealing alternative to vivisection.

But if the presentation of the anti-vivisection theme is not overbearing, neither is it completely subtle. There are at least a couple of notable occasions when Collins lets the heavy hand of his thesis get the better of him. Early in the novel, we puzzle over Carmina's odd, almost comical, reaction to witnessing a dog being killed under the wheels of a cab: "She shrank from the bare idea of getting into a cab. 'We may run over some other poor creature,' she said. 'If it isn't a dog, it may be a child next time'" (58). Her sensitivity here seems rather morbid, but is rivalled by Ovid's when, later in the story, he shrieks with horror as Benjulia accidentally crushes a beetle underfoot. On another occasion, we witness Ovid's rescue of an abandoned and starving cat, and on still another Mrs. Gallilee's unpleasant suggestion that her son simply poison his pet rather than make arrangements for its care while he is out of the country. Such passages serve to remind us that Collins occasionally succumbed to the temptations of melodrama, but that there are only a few of them is solid enough evidence that he succeeds, as he claims in his preface, in holding his personal indignation in check, leaving the facts to speak for themselves.

Heart and Science, then, is much more than Swinburne would have us believe. More than a two-dimensional "mission" statement, it offers lively and rewarding reading on a number of levels. It is, among other things, an interesting Victorian love story, a fast-paced and tightly-woven tale of intrigue and suspense, a sardonic condemnation of the world of modern science, an engaging study of character and its ability to shape people and events, an occasionally lurid melodrama, and a unique and provocative document of a nineteenth-century controversy that remains a volatile issue even today. And, finally, it is a pleasure.

II. Historical Background: The English Vivisection Controversy in the 1870s and 1880s

The Victorian vivisection debate—the moral/medical conflict that prompted Wilkie Collins to write *Heart and Science*—raged primarily in several popular British periodicals from the mid-1870s to the mid-1880s. The often bitter exchanges occasionally boiled over into London courtrooms, and the issues frequently found their way into numerous discussions in both houses of Parliament. The ebb and flow of this decade of engagement offer fascinating drama, and a brief history at this point will help to contextualize Collins's important contribution.

In August 1874, a continental physiologist, Eugene Magnan, punctuated a lecture at the British Medical Association's annual meeting in Norwich by injecting absinthe into the thigh of a dog. The cries of pain from the dog led to cries of anger from some in the audience and to charges of cruelty to animals in violation of Martin's Act (1822 and 1835), a law that forbade unwarranted cruelty to domestic animals. The Royal Society for the Prevention of Cruelty to Animals (R.S.P.C.A) investigated the incident, deciding late in the year that there was enough evidence to prosecute. Charges were filed against Magnan, who was safely in France by the time, as well as against three others present at the late-summer experiment. However, the Norwich Petty Sessions in December 1874 struck a blow for science and physiology by finding that there was not enough evidence to convict Magnan or his fellow scientists (French 55-59).[8]

The December 1874 ruling led to a call from angry anti-vivisectionists for a Parliamentary bill to restrict animal experimentation dramatically, and the movement gained momentum early in February 1875 when the respected anti-vivisectionist George Hoggan wrote an impassioned letter to the editor of the *Morning Post* decrying vivisection as a heartless and cold blooded business and condemning its practitioners as loathsome sadists. (See Appendix B, 1, for the complete letter.) When Hoggan's letter was reprinted in the *Spectator* by R. H. Hutton, the weekly magazine's anti-vivisectionist editor, the animal rights activists began to mobilize, realizing their cause could be taken to an sympathetic general public.

London anti-vivisection organizations began to form in earnest early in 1875 (with the *International Association for the Total Suppression of Vivisection*, founded in February; the *Victoria Street Society*, headed by Frances Power Cobbe, later in the year; and the *London Anti-Vivisection Society*, in March 1876), and by the end of the decade there were nearly a dozen major organizations whose purpose was to push for the abolition of live animal experimentation.[9] Eventually, the various societies established their own journals—first the *Home Chronicler* (1876), and later the *Anti-Vivisectionist* (1879) and the *Zoophilist* (1881)—but the Hoggan letter in early 1875 signalled the beginning of the public debate in popular forums. The *Spectator* published nearly thirty discussions of the issue in 1875 alone, another twenty-five in 1876, and the *Fortnightly Review*, the *Contemporary Review*, *Macmillan's*, the *Nineteenth Century*, *Punch*, even the *Cornhill* all provided much space for debate. (See Appendix B, 1-5, for several of these letters and articles.)

In May 1875, anti-vivisectionists felt they had gained the momentum necessary to accomplish their goals through legislative action. They recruited Lord Henniker to sponsor a bill in the House of Lords requesting strict regulation of animal experimentation and stiff penalties for violations. A little more than a week later, the voices of science and physiology countered the Henniker bill by having their own spokesperson, Lyon Playfair, sponsor the Darwin-Burdon Sanderson bill in the House of Commons. Playfair's bill sought to keep animal experimentation legal and relatively unregulated by proposing limitations on experiments conducted without anaesthesia. Both Henniker's and Playfair's bills were eventually withdrawn in favour of a board of inquiry, a Royal Commission, established to discuss the necessity of legislation. The Commission sat for over five months—from July to December of 1875—questioning scores of people and producing hundreds of pages of transcripts (French 96) before recommending, in early 1876, limitations on animal experimentation.

As the Commission met over the last half 1875, the debate intensified in London journals, and with the shifting of the battle to these more public arenas—to journals available and accessible to England's growing middle class—the anti-vivisection movement became a true *cause célèbre*. The ranks of the crusaders began to swell with many influential literary figures, among them Lewis Carroll (see Appendix B, 2), Thomas Carlyle, Robert Browning (see appendix H, 1 and 2), Alfred Lord Tennyson, John Ruskin, Christina Rossetti, and George Bernard Shaw (MacEachen 23). The scientific community, both in England and on the continent, countered with the powerful voices of Charles Darwin, Louis Pasteur, and Thomas Henry Huxley, among others.

By early 1876, the Royal Commission reached the decision that vivisection was at least in need of regulation through the stricter licensing of practising physiologists. Lord Carnarvon, sympathetic to the anti-vivisectionist movement, presented a bill to the House of Lords in mid-May, a bill that proposed the strict licensing of physiologists who practised live animal experimentation. After three months of Parliamentary debate, lengthy and effective stonewalling by the conservatives in Disraeli's government, and closed-door lobbying on the part of the medical community, a watered-down version of Carnarvon's bill, known thereafter as the Cruelty to Animals Act of 1876, passed into law in August. Anti-vivisectionists expressed ambivalence on passage of Carnarvon's bill into law. They recognized that they had gained a partial victory, but they also felt the need to push for the total abolition of vivisection. The wave of public fervour they had ridden through 1875-76 had crested, however, and between 1876 and 1881 the movement saw its annual, and less publicized, attempts to push for the end of animal experimentation rebuffed by an increasingly stubborn Parliament.

It was not again until mid-1881 that the vivisection debate flared publicly, and this time rather dramatically. The International Medical Congress (IMC) met in London in August 1881 and drafted as its official position an aggressive statement professing live animal experimentation to be "indispensable" to the future of medicine. Less than a week after the Congress concluded its business, the annual meeting of the British Medical Association continued the offensive by proclaiming that further restrictions on vivisection would "demoraliz[e] and damage ... the community."[10] The lines were drawn for further, and more volatile, debate.

The most important event of 1881 occurred late in the year with the trial of David Ferrier. A celebrated London physiologist, Professor of Forensic Medicine at King's College Hospital and Medical School, London, and author of *The Localization of Cerebral Disease* (1878), Ferrier had attended the IMC in August and either witnessed or participated in a vivisection—the cerebral dissection of a living monkey. Anti-vivisectionists cried foul and used Ferrier as a test case for the Act of 1876 by causing him to be charged with practising animal experimentation without a proper licence. Ferrier's prominence in the medical community gave the case the national attention and notoriety that the anti-vivisectionists believed would aid their cause. But the trial, held on November 17, 1881, at Bow Street, was brief and ended in Ferrier's acquittal. His defence—that he had merely witnessed a certain Professor Yeo perform the surgery and had not actually participated in the experimentation—infuriated his opponents, who came finally to realize with the verdict that the Act of 1876 could be ignored with relative impunity by the scientific community. (See France Power Cobbe's bitter account of the trial in Appendix C.)

The euphoria that the scientific community felt after a year's worth of unchecked successes in congresses, conventions, and courtrooms spilled over into the journals of the day. No longer did the medical community feel that it was on the defensive, and its published attacks on what William Stanley Jevons called the "sentimental frenzy"[11] of the anti-vivisection movement set off a year-long exchange of often very ugly *ad hominem* arguments. In December 1881, the *Nineteenth Century* published "Vivisection: Its Pains and Its Uses," an attack on anti-vivisectionists, who were labelled representatives of "an ignorant majority" who "lack a sense of the ludicrous."[12] Anti-vivisectionists countered with strong words of their own in 1882, Frances Power Cobbe unabashedly pronouncing physiologists dishonest by likening them to the "two-faced Janus" in "Vivisection and Its Two-Faced Advocates," her article for the *Contemporary Review*. (See Appendix B, 4.) Sir John Simon called Cobbe and her compatriots "mere screamers,"[13] and physiologist Professor Gerald Yeo countered Cobbe's attack with one of his own, a letter to the editor of the *Contemporary Review* in which he concluded sardonically that "it would be a mere waste of time to expose the numerous fallacies" of some of Cobbe's assertions. (See Appendix C.)

But the most aggressive (and at times vicious) attacks came from continental physiologist M. de Cyon, who contributed "The Anti-vivisection Agitation" to the *Contemporary Review* in April 1883. Calling into question the femininity of any women involved in the anti-vivisectionist movement,[14] M. de Cyon asked, "Is it necessary to repeat that women—or rather, old maids—form the most numerous contingent of this group? Let my adversaries contradict me, if they can show among the leaders of the agitation one young girl, rich, beautiful, and beloved, or one young wife who has found in her home the full satisfaction of her affections!"[15] This is clearly a thinly veiled reference to the unmarried Frances Power Cobbe. M. de Cyon's article at times also bristles with sarcasm, especially in one pointed reference to anti-vivisectionists as sentimentalists "who shed tears over the sad fate of some poor rabbit snatched too early from household joys, or of some kitten whose brilliant future has been cut short by the pitiless biologist!"[16] But the low blows weren't limited to M. de Cyon, or to continental vivisectionists; even Charles Darwin was not above the personal attack, claiming at one point that the rather slight-of-stature anti-vivisectionist R. H. Hutton "seems to be a kind of female Miss Cobbe" (Rupke 264).

The debate continued in this fashion for another year or so, with the anti-vivisectionists taking an increasingly hard-line position in their call for the total abolition of live animal experimentation. The first five years of the 1880s saw one bill after another introduced into the House of Commons, but after R. T. Reid's bill was defeated in 1884,[17] legislative attempts to ban vivisection came to an end until after the turn of the century, and much of the public debate that accompanied those attempts quieted as well (French 164-65).

III. Wilkie Collins and the Vivisection Debate

It was to the contentious debate of the early 1880s that Wilkie Collins decided to add his voice. Though not a formal member of any of the many anti-vivisectionist societies that flourished in metropolitan London at the time, Collins did share their beliefs, was on friendly terms with some of the activists, and felt that he could aid the cause by addressing the issue in his fiction. The incentive to write may have been provided by the bitter defeat suffered by the movement in the Ferrier case or by the sharp personal attacks he saw being levelled at people he considered friends. Whatever the trigger, Collins decided to take up the mantle of the animal rights activists and began planning his own contribution to the discussion. He had struck a deal with his publishers, Chatto & Windus, in late 1881, but it is not until mid-1882 that we see from Collins's letters his careful plans for a novel concerning vivisection. In a July 13, 1882 letter to Surgeon-General Charles Alexander Gordon thanking him for helpful research material, he spells out his belief that fiction, by appealing to a large and general audience, could indeed have an impact: "I am endeavouring to add my small contribution in aid of this good cause. ... The little I may be able to do will at least have a large audience." (See Appendix D, 2, for the entire text of this letter.)

With all his fiction, Collins prepared himself carefully for the task of writing *Heart and Science*, a care he was quick to proclaim. In one portion of his preface to *Heart and Science*, he assures his readers that he has researched his subject thoroughly, that his knowledge of the facts of modern science, as expressed in the novel primarily by his villainness, Mrs. Gallilee, is unassailable: "On becoming acquainted with 'Mrs. Gallilee,' you will find her talking—and you will sometimes even find the author talking—of scientific subjects in general. You will naturally concluded that it is 'all gross caricature.' No; it is all promiscuous reading. Let me spare you a long list of books consulted, and of newspapers and magazines mutilated for 'cuttings' " (39). He then refers sceptical readers to a particular article in *The Times* (see Appendix F) for verification of certain of these facts, to Chambers's Encyclopædia, to David Ferrier's "writing on the 'Localization of Cerebral Disease,'" and he claims also to have had the details of his discussion of medical practices checked by "an eminent London surgeon, whose experience extends over a period of forty years" (39).

Implicit in these several careful claims about the accuracy of his knowledge of science is also some strong indication of the pains Collins took to research the anti-vivisectionist philosophy that he expresses in his novel. Though we get a general sense throughout the novel of his feelings for animals and animal rights, midway through the story Collins promotes quite specifically the three basic anti-vivisectionist tenets of the day: 1) that vivisection had a hardening effect on the moral character of the practitioner, 2) that the motives behind the practice of vivisection were morally questionable, at best, and 3) that Man had neither a moral nor a medical right to assume a superiority over the "lower animals" that might fall prey to vivisection.

These three arguments find voice in the character of Dr. Benjulia. First, we see in him a brilliant man cruelly hardened by his abhorrent practice; he portrays on occasion some shreds of compassion, as we see in his odd relationship with Zoe, but by the end of the tale we witness him abandon his humanity altogether when he quite eagerly involves Carmina in his study of "brain disease" by intentionally letting her illness worsen solely to study its progress. We see also in his actions the questionable motives behind vivisection, for Benjulia is far more interested in securing the recognition of his peers in the scientific community and in gaining knowledge for its own sake than he is using his expertise for the good of the community of Man. In fact, at one point he chillingly admits the driving force behind his interest in vivisection: "*I* do it because I like it" (189). Finally, we see in Benjulia a man utterly unable to recognize Man's moral obligation to protect all living creatures. He is confounded by his brother's declaration that "If the Law ... protects any living creatures, it is bound, in reason and in justice, to protect all" (188), to which he responds rather impotently, "I am not a lawyer" (188).

These three arguments had been promoted in print by anti-vivisectionists throughout the 1870s and early 1880s. We find Collins's concerns about the soul-deadening effect of vivisection expressed by Lewis Carroll, in his "Some Popular Fallacies about Vivisection": "It is a humiliating but undeniable truth, that man has something of the wild beast in him, that thirst for blood can be aroused in him by witnessing a scene of carnage, and that the infliction of torture, when the first instincts of horror have been deadened by familiarity, may become, first, a matter of indifference, then a subject of morbid interest, then a positive pleasure, then a ghastly and ferocious delight." (See Appendix B, 2, 8.) A similar view appears in George Hoggan's proclamation, "Were the feelings of experimental physiologists not blunted, they could not long continue the practice of vivisection." (See Appendix B, 1.)

Collins's attack of the questionable motives of vivisectionists, who often attempted to argue their position from a rather utilitarian vantage point—that animal experimentation saved human lives in the long run, that the necessary infliction of pain was ultimately good for humanity— rises directly out of several published anti-vivisectionist arguments: of his experiences in the laboratory, George Hoggan bluntly stated, "The idea of the good of humanity was simply out of the question, and would have been laughed at, the great aim being to keep up with, or get ahead of, one's contemporaries in science. . . ." (See Appendix B, 1); Lewis Carroll wrote, "The lust for scientific knowledge is [the scientist's] real guiding principle." (See Appendix B, 2, 4); Francis Power Cobbe echoed this opinion, claiming that "the *raison d'être* of most experiments appears to be the elucidation of points of purely scientific interest" and that "the experiments [discussed in scientific journals] are generally described as showing that ... Professor A.'s theory has been disproved and that of Professor B. (temporarily) established." (See Appendix B, 4, 1); and Lord Chief Justice Coleridge voiced a similar concern for "experiment *in vacuo*, experiment on chance, experiment in pursuit of nothing in particular, but of anything which may turn up." He continued, "I deny that the pursuit of knowledge is in itself always lawful; still more do I deny that the gaining of knowledge justifies all means of getting it." (See Appendix B, 3.)

The third prong of Collins's argument—that Man has a moral obligation to care for his fellow creatures, an obligation neglected by physiologists—is an echo of Lord Chief Justice Coleridge's perturbation with a vivisector's "assumption that ... we [have] no duties to the lower creatures when science [is] in question, and that the animal world [is] to a man of science like clay to the potter, or marble to the sculptor, to be crushed or carved at his will with no more reference to pain in animals than if they were clay or marble." (See Appendix B, 3.) The same claims were put forth in Frances Power Cobbe's simple yet powerful dictum, "we owe it to God to be kind to His creatures ... [and] we owe to every sentient creature to spare it pain, simply because it is sentient."

The parallels, then, seem apparent. Collins, in his ambitious attempt to strike the heaviest blow in his power for the anti-vivisection movement with which he felt such a close kinship, believed it was crucial to adopt the very arguments they took to the English public. The result, his "small contribution ... to this good cause," exists as a testament to his skill as an artist, for within *Heart and Science* Collins admirably blends the world of his fiction with the very real world of the Victorian animal rights movement.

IV. *Heart and Science*: A Brief Review of the Literary and Critical Background

The critical history of *Heart and Science* is a relatively brief one. Since the initial flurry of primarily friendly reviews (See Appendix A, 1-5 for five of these reviews) appeared in mid-1883 upon the release of the first volume edition of the novel, and perhaps owing partly to Swinburne's 1889 couplet condemning the book as an anti-vivisectionist "mission" statement, critical interest has, at least until recently, been limited and rather cursory.

Collins's six biographers seems content to mention the book only in passing, some with words of praise, others with condemnation. Robert Ashley (*Wilkie Collins*, 1952), Nuell Pharr Davis (*The Life of Wilkie Collins*, 1956), and Catherine Peters (*The King of Inventors: A Life of Wilkie Collins*, 1991) briefly comment on the skill with which Collins has drawn unique and memorable characters, Davis suggesting that the novel "approaches the status of a major novel" (296) and Peters proclaiming it to be "one of the best and liveliest of his later novels" (399). On the other hand, Kenneth Robinson (*Wilkie Collins: A Biography*, 1952) and William Marshall (*Wilkie Collins*, 1970) offer only disparaging remarks, Robinson stating curtly that the novel is "yet another failure" whose "plain narrative is handled clumsily and fails to grip" (302) and Marshall labelling it an "unfortunate work" whose author had "ventured into an area of dispute, the controversy over vivisection, in which his opinions were based upon sentiment and inclination rather than upon understanding" (104-05). William Clarke, in his *The Secret Life of Wilkie Collins* (1988), had as his primary goal the uncovering of the shadowy and mysterious aspects of Collins's rather bohemian life, and because his interests were strictly biographical, he chose not to provide any grist for the critical mill.

Dougald MacEachen's "Wilkie Collins' *Heart and Science* and the Vivisection Controversy"[18] offers much valuable information concerning the social/political climate in England in the early 1880s, but MacEachen's main concern is not literary. He places Collins within the arena of the vivisection controversy, and he summarizes *Heart and Science* skilfully, but he chose not to offer critical analysis of any sort.

Within several recent book-length critical studies devoted to Collins's fiction, measured discussions of *Heart and Science* are also scarce. Philip O'Neill's *Wilkie Collins: Women, Property, and Propriety* (1988) ignores *Heart and Science*, as does Peter Thoms's *The Windings of the Labyrinth: Quest and Structure in the Major Novels of Wilkie Collins* (1992). Sue Lonoff's *Wilkie Collins and His Victorian Readers* (1980) briefly discusses characterization and character names and then cursorily dismisses the book to the "deserved obscurity" into which it retreated soon after publication (78). Tamar Heller's *Dead Secrets: Wilkie Collins and the Female Gothic* (1992) mentions *Heart and Science* in passing, using the work, along with other of Collins's late novels, only as a springboard to her conclusion that Collins's last several works failed to achieve "the careful balance ... between female Gothic and male detection, marginality and professionalism, resistance and suppression" (168) that we see in *The Moonstone*.

One of the long studies that does devote some critical attention to *Heart and Science* is Coral Lansbury's *The Old Brown Dog: Women, Workers, and Vivisection in Edwardian England* (1985), which offers a chapter-long—

and quite fascinating—feminist reading of the novel. Lansbury argues that the connections between "sexuality and vivisection ... were made blindingly clear in Wilkie Collins's febrile and complex work" (133). She posits that Collins, rather than burdening his novel with conventional anti-vivisectionist propaganda, strikes a double blow by accomplishing "a translation of the general repugnance people felt towards vivisection into an abhorrence for the illicit sexual gratification that the vivisector derived from his work" (141).

Going so far as to claim that the "title of Collins' work in a less inhibited age would possibly have been *Sex and Science*," Lansbury argues rather interestingly that Collins uses his novel to link the cruelties of vivisection with the horrors of sexual sadism. She begins by noting that "animals and their relationship with people are a continuing figure in the novel" (138), suggesting that the reader becomes aware over the course of the novel that Benjulia's sadistic—and often sexually provocative—treatment of people clearly parallels his hideous treatment of the poor beasts he keeps locked in his laboratory. We see his tickling of Zoe—which Lansbury suggests is "a synonym for flogging or sexual intercourse" (140)—to be an experiment in cerebral paralysis; we see his sadistic treatment of his own cook become an experiment in measuring the boundaries of hysteria; and we see his medical treatment of the novel's heroine, Carmina, near the end of the story become quite literally a part of the research that he has been conducting via animal experimentation in his laboratory. Zoe, the cook, and Carmina are all as much a part of Benjulia's world of cruel experimentation as the dogs and cats that flee in horror from his laboratory at the novel's close. Lansbury concludes, then, that Collins's anti-vivisectionist argument is rather more provocative than many have noted; Benjulia, a man whose often-bloody walking stick "we have met ... before in all its manifestations of whip and male organ" (140), "a man who tickles little girls and tortures animals" (141), becomes by the end of the novel the embodiment of "the psychological truth ... which Collins valued more than the profit-and-loss arguments of the antivivisectionists" (141).

Jenny Bourne Taylor's *In the Secret Theatre of the Home: Wilkie Collins, sensation narrative, and nineteenth-century psychology* (1988) also offers interesting material for the reader of *Heart and Science*. Taylor's intriguing study of Collins's connection with nineteenth-century psychology argues that Collins often consciously polarized the worlds of medicine and morality in much of his fiction. After recalling for the reader the asylums of *The Woman in White*, *Armadale*, and *Jezebel's Daughter*, as well as the pseudo-scientific experiments that play a role in *The Moonstone* and *Armadale*, Bourne discusses *Heart and Science* as a novel that "depends on the dichotomy implied by its title even as it attempts to redraw its boundaries within science by invoking a moralized physiology" (231). The polarity is blurred in this novel, though, where the world of science offers not only the problem but the solution, not only the villain but the hero. As Bourne puts it, "the story ... revolves around the opposition between the good and the bad physiologist" (231). These ambivalences create the overriding tensions of the novel, and she claims finally that in the novel "the split between morality and medicine is amplified and finally modified as physiological investigation into the brain and nervous system becomes a source of both horror and reconciliation" (230).

The most recent critical consideration of *Heart and Science* appears in Nelson Smith's and R. C. Terry's *Wilkie Collins to the Forefront: Some Reassessments* (1995). Christine S. Wiesenthal's feminist reading "From Charcot to Plato: The History of Hysteria in *Heart and Science* points to the novel's "fascinating awareness of the medical and mythical past" and to its "depth and richness of historical allusiveness which is no where better illustrated than in the text's conceptual construction of hysteria" (258).

Wiesenthal's reading of the novel has three sections. First, she catalogues the novel's scientific language, especially those passages which refer to Carmina's mysterious "brain disease," and suggests that it offers a "fairly sound reflection of the physiological bent of Darwinian psychiatrists" (259) of Collins's day. In response to those critics of the novels who have long criticized the "technical superficiality" of the novel's scientific language, she argues that "Carmina's dramatic symptoms ... represent a plausible repertoire of the types of hysterical conversion symptoms being studied at the time by great theorists of the disease, such as Charcot, Freud, and Josef Breuer" (258-59).

More provocative still is Wiesenthal's expansion of her discussion to include all the other women in the novel. In addition to Carmina's spells, Miss Minerva's excited jealousy, Mrs. Gallilee's frenzies of rage, Teresa's hot-bloodedness, and even the hysterics of Benjulia's's cook compel the reader to see the novel unfold "as a drama of uncontrolled female passions" wherein "Collins' women reveal themselves as essentially creatures of the 'heart,' beings defined against both the uncannily dispassionate Dr. Benjulia, the representative of a hyper-rational realm of modern 'science,' and against the hero, Ovid Vere, who as both a humanistic physician and a man in love is intended to embody the novel's normative ideal of 'Heart *in* Science'" (260-61). In other words, Wiesenthal argues that in *Heart and Science*, indeed, in much of Collins's fiction, the "well-being of women is ... dependent on the state of the heart and not of the head" (261).

Wiesenthal's final point rather inventively, though somewhat tenuously, links the ancient notion of hysteria as a "disease of the migratory womb," a disease once known as "Suffocation of the Mother," to the climactic moment of the novel, when Mrs. Gallilee labels Carmina an "impudent bastard" and is attacked and nearly choked to death by Carmina's fierce protector, Teresa. Wiesenthal, seemingly a little sceptical herself, concludes that it is "not implausible for Collins to have expected his readers to be able to recognize and reconstitute the metaphor of the 'suffocation of the mother'" (263).

V. Chatto & Windus, *Belgravia*, Wilkie Collins, and *Heart and Science*

In 1873, Andrew Chatto and W.E. Windus (a partner in little more than name) purchased the publishing firm that bears their name from the estate of John Cambden Hotten, who had established the company in 1855. Almost immediately, Chatto & Windus, labelled "hustlers" of the industry by Michael Sadleir,[19] set out to challenge such publishing firms as Chapman and Hall and W.H. Smith and Sons for supremacy in the world of the cheap re-issue. They purchased the copyrights of fiction from several novelists and began to reprint inexpensive editions of popular fiction. They followed Chapman and Hall's lead with "Yellowback" or "Railway Fiction"—cheap and flashy volumes mass-marketed for the general public, readers Wilkie Collins labelled the "Unknown Public"[20]—and began to make fortunes for themselves.

In April 1876, looking to expand their publishing empire, Chatto & Windus seized the opportunity presented to them by the sale of *Belgravia: An Illustrated London Magazine*.[21] The magazine had been in existence for ten years since 1866. Founded by publisher John Maxwell to accommodate his companion and future wife, the prolific and wildly popular sensation novelist Mary Elizabeth Braddon,[22] *Belgravia* did well throughout Maxwell's ownership, reaching a regular audience of more than 10,000 a month and providing a forum for such popular second-tier novelists as Charles Reade, G.A. Sala, and J.S. LeFanu. But Maxwell, notoriously reckless with money, fell on hard times and sold to Chatto & Windus.

The partners hoped to take the magazine, which had a monthly circulation of a respectable 12,000 at the time of their purchase, and make it a worthy competitor of the *Cornhill Magazine*, a journal that John Sutherland calls "the premier fiction-carrying magazine of the century" (Sutherland 150) and which occasionally achieved a monthly readership numbering an incredible 110,000. Similar in appearance, price, and format to the *Cornhill*, *Belgravia* also began to reflect its new owners' desires to emulate its competitor's philosophy of presenting its audience with a periodical consisting almost entirely of serialized fiction.

To compete with the *Cornhill*, Chatto & Windus had to acquire the services of popular authors, and succeeded in doing so quite impressively for quite some time. They secured such contributors as Collins, Charles Reade, Mark Twain, Conan Doyle, Julian Hawthorne (Nathaniel's son), Bret Harte, Ouida, even Thomas Hardy, whose *Return of the Native* (1878) clearly ranks as the best known work to appear in the magazine.

It was also in the mid-70s that Chatto & Windus struck a deal with Collins, paying £2000 for the British rights to most of his earlier fiction, and they wasted little time publishing it. But paying Collins for his past works accomplished much more for the shrewd partners, for they gained from him an agreement to allow them to publish all his future work. They printed cheap editions of *The Law and the Lady* in 1875 after its serial run in the *Graphic*; *The Two Destinies* in 1876 after its serial run in *Temple Bar*; *Fallen Leaves* in 1879 after its serial run in the *World* and *Canadian Monthly*; and *Jezebel's Daughter* in 1880 and *The Black Robe* in 1881 after their serial runs in several provincial newspapers.

This secured relationship also made it easier for Collins to be a regular contributor to their magazine. He contributed a substantial amount of short fiction beginning in 1876. His stories "The Captain's Last Love," "The Duel in Herne Wood," and "A Shocking Story" ran in 1876, 1877, and 1878, respectively; his novella *The Haunted Hotel* appeared over the course of six months in 1878 and 1879; and his stories "How I Married Him," "Your Money or Your Life," "She Loves and Lies," and "An Old Maid's Husband" appeared between 1881 and 1887.

After Hardy's *Return of the Native*, *Belgravia* offered its readers a run of mediocre fiction, and circulation began to dip, to close to 5,000 by mid-1881. Chatto & Windus realized they must attempt to bolster sales by securing for their magazine a novel by a popular writer. Collins was a known commodity to them, and they were pleased with the sales of his re-issued fiction, so they offered him the opportunity to write a novel for serialization in *Belgravia*. They secured the deal in autumn of 1881, almost a year before *Heart and Science* began to appear in *Belgravia*, and though he was ill through much 1881 and the early part of 1882, Collins began to research his topic and outline his strategies with some care.

It is unclear what immediate effect *Heart and Science* had on circulation when it began to appear in the late summer of 1882. Collins was quietly enthusiastic about his book, likening his feelings for it to those he had once had for his masterpiece *The Woman in White*, and by the end of its serial run, it had begun to meet with modest critical praise. But the novel did not have the permanent positive effect on circulation that Chatto & Windus had hoped. Sales of *Belgravia* continued to slide, bottoming out at 3,000-3,500 in the mid-1880s and remaining low until Chatto & Windus decided to sell, a sale which took place in September 1889, the month of Collins's death. F.V. White and Co. purchased the magazine and attempted to rejuvenate it, but after the initial flurry of success that often comes with new ownership, the magazine settled once again into its circulation rut and never recovered. White and Co. sold it in 1897, after which *Belgravia* began its death throes. It was sold a second time in 1897; it was resold in 1898; and it ceased circulation altogether in April 1899. The last three owners seem either to have been impatient or practical businessmen.

An interesting sidelight on the publishing history of *Heart and Science* concerns the American pirates who so often managed to upset Collins by beating the legitimate presses to publication. In March 1883, as he and

Chatto & Windus were readying the novel for publication in three-volume form, Collins wrote to W.M. Laffan, a representative of the American publishing house Harper Brothers, with whom Collins had published previously, to cancel arrangements for an authorized American edition: "I have been too thoroughly disgusted with the thefts committed on *Heart and Science* during its periodical publication in the United States to make any arrangements for its publication in book-form." (See Appendix D, 4.) While Collins's bitterness toward pirates was nothing new, his willingness to forego a battle with them is intriguing. Whatever the case, in March 1883, a full month before Chatto & Windus published the first volume edition of the novel, George Munro, the Canadian-born New York publisher (and pirate) whose *Seaside Library* series made him rich at the expense of many a British novelist, published *Heart and Science* without thought of compensation to Collins. One Collins biographer, Nuell Pharr Davis, believes that the ease with which Munro printed the earliest edition of the novel may suggest that the pirate actually had Collins's blessing (296), but there is another explanation; Collins's letters reveal that he suffered a debilitating attack of the gout upon finishing the *Heart and Science* and remained ill during much of 1882. His reluctance to fight the copyright wars he had fought most of his career may simply have resulted from physical exhaustion. (See Appendix D, 3 and 5, for Collins's discussion of his illness.)

Notes

1   Eliot's essay "Wilkie Collins and Dickens" (Rpt. in *T. S. Eliot: Selected Essays, 1917-1932*. New York: Harcourt, Brace, 1932, 373-82) is often credited with re-popularizing Collins in the first quarter of the twentieth century.

2   William Coleman's dissertation (*The University of Texas Collection of the Letters of Wilkie Collins, Victorian Novelist*, Austin: The University of Texas at Austin, 1975) is an edition of 262 Collins letters housed in the Harry Ransom Research Center, The University of Texas at Austin. Coleman numbered the letters; the passage quoted here appears in letter 85. Complete texts of *Heart and Science*-related letters from the University of Texas Collection may be found in Appendix D, 3-7. The complete text of Collins's letter to Francis Power Cobbe concerning *Heart and Science* may be found in Appendix D, 1. The complete text of Collins's letter to C. A. Gordon concerning *Heart and Science* may be found in Appendix D, 2.

3   During these last years, Collins remained popular among the novel-reading public and—more importantly as far as he and his publishers were concerned—the novel-buying public. In fact, most of his late fiction sold well—one of his last novels, *The Evil Genius* (1886), earned him more money than any of his other works—and often received kind notices from reviewers. Collins's last novel, *Blind Love*, exists as a testament to his diligence and sense of authorial responsibility. Realizing that he would die before he completed the novel, he made arrangements for his friend Walter Besant to finish the work after he was gone.

4 See the *Select Bibliography* for the titles and authors of these six biographies. Catherine Peters's *The King of Inventors: A Life of Wilkie Collins* is now considered the standard Collins biography. The Sayers biography listed in the *Select Bibliography* is a fragment, left incomplete at her death.

5 This passage appears in Trollope's 1882 *An Autobiography* (Michael Sandleir and Frederick Page, eds, Oxford UP, 1980). In the same passage, Trollope continues: "[Collins] seems always to be warning me to remember that something happened at exactly half-past two o'clock on Tuesday morning; or that woman disappeared from the road just fifteen yards beyond the fourth milestone" (257).

6 Collins's message echoes Dickens's in *Hard Times* (1854), where the innocence and purity of Sissy Jupe ultimately saves the day by helping to convince Mr. Thomas Gradgrind that his coldly utilitarian system does not work.

7 Collins realized the pivotal role played in the typical British household by its domestic servants. He used them often in his long fiction, and more often in the short essays—fiction and nonfiction—that he published in Dickens's weekly periodicals *Household Words* and *All the Year Round*. Here are some essays that show Collins's legitimate interest in the Victorian domestic servant.: "Laid up in Lodgings" (*Household Words*, 7-14 June 1856), "Mrs. Badgery" (*Household Words*, 26 September 1857), "Mrs. Bullwinkle" (*Household Words*, 17 April 1858), "Bold Words by a Bachelor" (*Household Words*, 13 December 1856), "Deep Design on Society" (*Household Words*, 2 January 1858), "Save Me from My Friends" (*Household Words*, 16 January 1858), "A Shockingly Rude Article" (*Household Words*, 28 August 1858), and "Cooks at College (*All the Year Round*, 29 October 1859)."

8 Richard French's *Antivivisection and Medical Science in Victorian Society* (Princeton, NJ: Princeton UP, 1975) provides much of the information found in this section of the introduction and is an extremely valuable resource for the researcher who needs information on any aspect of the vivisection debate in Victorian England.

9 Until the mid-1870s, the many anti-vivisectionist societies that existed in and around London chose to operate independently of one another, often, it seems, in competition with one another. In fact, two of the most powerful advocates for animal rights, Frances Power Cobbe and Anna Kingsford, engaged in personal feuding that some say damaged the cause. An account of their clashes may be found in John Vyvyan's *In Pity and in Anger: A Study of the Use of Animals in Science* (London: Michael Joseph, 1969).

10 From James Paget, Richard Owens, and Samuel Wilks's three-part "Vivisection: Its Pains and Its Uses," in the *Nineteenth Century* X (December 1881), pages 920-48.

11 William Stanley Jevons, who sympathized with the vivisectionist cause, coined this phrase in his article "Cruelty to Animals: A Study in Sociology," which appeared in the *Fortnightly Review* on May 1, 1876, 670-84.

12 From James Paget, Richard Owens, and Samuel Wilks's three-part "Vivisection: Its Pains and Its Uses," in the *Nineteenth Century* X (December 1881), pages 920-48.

13 In his article "The Nineteenth Century Defenders of Vivisection," Lord Chief Justice Coleridge quotes his adversary, Sir John Simon, as labelling vocal anti-vivisectionists "mere screamers." (See Appendix B, 3 for the full text of Coleridge's article.)

14 Women were not the only targets of the vivisectionist attacks; often the mas-

culinity of the men who supported animal rights was also maligned—see Darwin's comments concerning R.H. Hutton.

15   From the *Contemporary Review*, April 1883, vol. 43, pp. 498-516.

16   From the *Contemporary Review*, April 1883, vol. 43, pp. 498-516.

17   R.T. Reid, M.P., sponsor of the 1882, 1883, and 1884 failed bills, was later to become Lord Chancellor (French 164).

18   MacEachen's article appears in *Victorian Newsletter*, Spring 1966, 22-25.

19   From John Sutherland's *The Stanford Companion to Victorian Fiction* (Stanford, CA: Stanford UP, 1989) 119.

20   Collins discusses this "Unknown Public" in an article of the same name printed in *Household Words* on 21 August 1858, 217-22. In it he numbers the readers of fiction in England by considering the circulation of five weeklies he terms "penny-novel-journals." He writes:

The weekly circulation of the most successful of the five, is now publicly advertised ... at half a Million. Taking the other four as attaining altogether to a circulation of another half million ... we have a sale of a Million weekly for five penny journals. Reckoning only three readers to each copy sold, the result is a *public of three millions*—a public unknown to the literary world; unknown, as disciples, to the whole body of professed critics; unknown, as customers, at the great libraries and the great publishing-houses; unknown, as an audience, to the distinguished English writers of our own time." (218)

21   Much of the information concerning *Belgravia* in this section comes from P.D. Edwards, I.G. Sibley, and Margaret Versteeg's *Indexes to Fiction in* Belgravia. Department of English, U of Queensland: *Victorian Fiction Research Guides*, XIV, 1988. Though it does contain some minor inaccuracies, this resource is quite valuable to the researcher who works with *Belgravia*.

22   Braddon, best known today for her lurid sensation novel *Lady Audley's Secret* (1862), took advantage of Maxwell's offer of a new vehicle for her fiction, naming herself chief editor and serializing fourteen her own novels in the magazine between 1866 and 1875.

A Note on the Text

Heart and Science was first issued in serial form in the monthly magazine *Belgravia: An Illustrated London Magazine* in eleven episodes between August 1882 and June 1883. (See Appendix G.) At the same time, it appeared in various provincial weeklies. A pirated single-volume edition was published in America in Munro's *Seaside Library* series in March 1883, and the authorized British three-volume edition was published by Chatto & Windus, the publishing firm which owned *Belgravia*, in April 1883.

Though Collins fell very ill with the gout soon after completing *Heart and Science* in February 1883, he managed to use his period of convalescence to amend his text for publication; the serial version of *Heart and Science* was much revised for the three-volume edition . The revisions are mainly stylistic, and most are minor enough to have no bearing on the plot of the novel. The complete holograph manuscript is held by the Harry Ransom Research Library, the University of Texas, Austin, Texas. It consists of 299 leaves, is marked for both weekly and monthly divisions, is heavily edited and quite difficult to read. (See Photographs 1 and 2 for some indication of Collins's writing and editing practices.)

The text of this edition is a reproduction of the first Chatto & Windus three-volume edition of 1883. The only changes made have been silent corrections of typographical errors that appeared in the first edition.

[First Weekly Part]

Heart and Science;

A Story of the Present Time.

By Wilkie Collins.

[The Right of Translation is Reserved.]

Chapter I.

The weary old ~~nineteenth~~ nineteenth century had advanced into the last twenty years of its life.

Towards two o'clock in the afternoon, Ovid Vere (of the Royal College of Surgeons) stood at the window of his consulting-room in London, looking out at the summer sunshine, and the quiet dusty street.

He had received a warning, familiar to the busy men of our time — the warning from overwrought Nature, which counsels rest after excessive work. With a prosperous career before him, he had been compelled (at only thirty one years of age) to ask a colleague to take charge of his practice, and to give the brain which he had cruelly wearied a rest of some months to come. On the next day, he had arranged to sail back for the Mediterranean in a friend's yacht.

An active man, devoted heart and soul to his profession, is not a man who can learn the happy knack of being idle, at a moment's notice. Ovid found the mere act of looking out of window, and wondering what he should do next, more than he had patience to endure.

He turned to his study-table. If he had possessed a wife to look after him, he would have been reminded that he and his study-table had nothing in common, under present circumstances. Being deprived of conjugal superintendence, he let slip through his own rules. His restless hand unlocked a drawer, and took out a manuscript work on medicine of his own writing. "Surely," he thought, "I may finish a chapter, before I go to sea tomorrow?"

His head, steady enough while he was only looking out of window, began to swim before he had got to the bottom of a page. The last sentences of the unfinished chapter alluded to a matter of fact which he had not yet verified. In emergencies of any sort, he was a patient man and a man of resource. The necessary verification could be accomplished by a visit to the College of Surgeons, situated in the great square called Lincoln's Inn Fields. Here was a motive for a walk — with an occupation at the end of it, which only involved a question to a Curator and an examination of a specimen. He locked up his manuscript, and set forth for Lincoln's Inn Fields.

[Chapter II.]

When two friends happen to meet in the street, do they ever look back along the procession of small circumstances which has led them both, from starting from their own houses, to the same spot, at the same time? Not one man in ten thousand has probably ever thought of making such a fantastic inquiry as this. And consequently, not one man in ten thousand, living in the midst of reality, has discovered that he is also living in the midst of romance.

William Wilkie Collins: A Brief Chronology

1824   Born January 8 at 11 New Cavendish Street, St. Marylebone, London, to William Collins (1788-1847) and Harriet Collins (1790-1868).

1826   Family moves to Pond Street, Hampstead.

1828   Brother, Charles Allston Collins, born.

1829   Family moves to Hampstead Square.

1830   Family moves to Porchester Terrace, Bayswater.

1835   Briefly attends school at the Maida Hill Academy.

1836   Family begins to travel in France and Italy.

1838   Family returns to England and settles at 20 Avenue Road, Regent's Park; begins to attend Mr. Cole's private school at Highbury Place.

1840   Family moves to 85 Oxford Terrace, Bayswater.

1841   Begins apprenticeship at Antrobus & Co., tea importers, The Strand.

1842   Travels with father to Scottish Highlands and Shetland Islands.

1843   "The Last Stage Coachman," first signed publication, appears in the *Illuminated Magazine*; family moves to 1 Devonport Street, Bayswater.

1844   Travels to Paris.

1845   First novel, with a Polynesian setting, rejected by Chapman & Hall, among other publishers; the novel was never published but is currently being prepared for publication.

1846   Enters Lincoln's Inn as law student.

1847   Father, William Collins, dies.

1848   Family moves to 38 Blandford Square, St. Marylebone; first book, *Memoirs of the Life of William Collins, Esq., RA*, published in two volumes by Longmans.

1850   First novel, *Antonina, or the Fall of Rome*, published in three volumes by Bentley; family moves to 17 Hanover Terrace, Regent's Park.

1851   *Rambles Beyond Railways* published by Bentley; meets Dickens; acts with Dickens in Bulwer Lytton play *Not So Bad As We Seem*; called to Bar but never practices.

1852   *Mr.Wray's Cash Box* published by Bentley; first contribution to *Household Words*, the short story "A Terribly Strange Bed," published; tours provinces with Dickens; second novel, *Basil*, published by Bentley.

1853   Tours Switzerland and Italy with Dickens and Augustus Egg.

1854   *Hide and Seek* published in three volumes by Bentley.

1855   First play, *The Lighthouse*, performed by Dickens's theatrical company at Tavistock House.

1856   *After Dark* published in two volumes by Smith, Elder; *A Rogue's Life* serialized in *Household Words*; travels to Paris with Dickens; joins staff of *Household Words*; *Wreck of the Golden Mary*, a Christmas story written in collaboration with Dickens, published in *Household Words*.

1857   *The Dead Secret* published in two volumes by Bradbury & Evans following serialization in *Household Words*; The play *The Frozen Deep* performed by Dickens's company at Tavistock House. *The Lazy Tour of Two Idle Apprentices* and *The Perils of Certain English Prisoners*, both written in collaboration with Dickens, published in *Household Words*.

1858   The play *The Red Vial* produced at The Olympic Theatre.

1859   Moves to 124 Albany Street, Regent's Park; moves to 2a New Cavendish Street, Marylebone; moves to 12 Harley Street, Marylebone; *The Queen of Hearts* published in three volumes by Hurst & Blackett; *The Woman in White* serialized in *All the Year Round* (November-August 1860); begins living with Caroline Graves.

1860   *The Woman in White* published in three volumes by Sampson Low. Brother, Charles Collins, marries Kate Dickens, Dickens's daughter.

1861   Resigns from staff of *All the Year Round*.

1862   *No Name* serialized in *All the Year Round* and published in three volumes by Sampson Low.

1863   *My Miscellanies* published in two volumes by Sampson Low; visits Germany and Italy with Caroline Graves.

1864   Moves to 9 Melcombe Place, Dorset Square; *Armadale* serialized in *The Cornhill* (November-June 1866).

1866   *Armadale* published in two volumes by Smith Elder.

1867 Moves to 90 Gloucester Place, Portsman Square; *No Thoroughfare*, written in collaboration with Dickens, published in *All the Year Round*; dramatic version of *No Thoroughfare* produced at the Adelphi Theatre.

1868 *The Moonstone* published in three volumes by Tinsley after serialization in *All the Year Round*; mother, Harriet Collins, dies; temporarily ends relationship with Caroline Graves; begins relationship with Martha Rudd (alias Mrs. Dawson); attends wedding of Caroline Graves and Joseph Charles Clow.

1869 *The play Black and White*, written in collaboration with Charles Fechter, produced at the Adelphi Theatre; daughter, Marian Dawson, by Martha Rudd, born.

1870 *Man and Wife* published in three volumes by F. S. Ellis, following serialization in *Cassell's Magazine*; Dickens dies.

1872 Second daughter, Harriet Constance Dawson, by Martha Rudd; resumes cohabitation with Caroline Graves; dramatic version of *No Name* produced in New York; dramatic version of *The Woman in White* performed at the Olympic Theatre; *Poor Miss Finch* serialized in *Cassell's Magazine* (October–March 1872).

1872 *Poor Miss Finch* published in three volumes by Bentley; *The New Magdalen* serialized in *Temple Bar*.

1873 Brother, Charles Allston Collins, dies; *The New Magdalen* published in two volumes by Bentley; dramatic version of *Man and Wife* produced at the Prince of Wales Theatre; dramatic version of *The New Magdalen* produced at the Olympic Theatre; *Miss or Mrs? and Other Stories in Outline* published by Bentley; begins six-month reading tour of United States and Canada.

1874 *The Law and the Lady* serialized in the *Graphic* (September–March 1875); *The Frozen Deep and Other Tales* published in two volumes by Bentley; son, William Charles Collins Dawson, born to Martha Rudd.

1875 Copyrights for most of Collins's works transferred to Chatto & Windus, who become his primary British publisher; *The Law and the Lady* published in three volumes by Chatto & Windus.

1876 *Miss Gwilt*, a dramatic version of *Armadale*, produced at the Globe Theatre; *The Two Destinies* published in two volumes by Chatto & Windus following serialization in *Temple Bar*.

1877 Dramatic version of *The Dead Secret* produced at the Lyceum Theatre; dramatic version of *The Moonstone* produced at the Olympic Theatre; *My Lady's Money* published in the *Illustrated London News*; travels in France, Germany, and Italy with Caroline Graves.

1878   *The Haunted Hotel* serialized in *Belgravia*; *My Lady's Money* and *The Haunted Hotel* published together in two volumes by Chatto & Windus; *The Fallen Leaves—First Series* serialized in both *The World* and *Canadian Monthly*.

1879   *The Fallen Leaves* published in three volumes by Chatto & Windus; *Jezebel's Daughter* syndicated by Tillotson & Son's newspaper chain and appears in thirteen Northern newspapers.

1880   *Jezebel's Daughter*, a novel based on the play *The Red Vial*, published in three volumes by Chatto & Windus.

1881   *The Black Robe* published in three volumes by Chatto & Windus following serialization in the *Sheffield Independent* and other provincial newspapers; A. P. Watt becomes Collins's literary agent; contracts with Chatto & Windus to write *Heart and Science* and begins research.

1882   *Heart and Science* serialized in *Belgravia* (August-June 1883).

1883   *Heart and Science* published in three volumes by Chatto & Windus (April 1883); the play *Rank and Riches* is produced at the Adelphi Theatre and proves to be an immediate failure.

1884   *"I Say No"* published in three volumes by Chatto & Windus following serialization in the *London Society*.

1886   *The Evil Genius* published in three volumes by Chatto & Windus following serial syndication by Tillotson & Son in the *Leigh Journal & Times* and other provincial papers; *The Guilty River* published in *Arrowsmith's Christmas Annual*.

1887   *Little Novels*, fourteen reprinted short stories, published in three volumes by Chatto & Windus.

1888   *The Legacy of Cain* published in three volumes by Chatto & Windus following serial syndication by Tillotson & Son; moves to 82 Wimpole Street, Marylebone.

1889   Collins dies on September 23 at 82 Wimpole Street and is buried at Kensal Green Cemetery.

1890   *Blind Love*, completed by Walter Besant after Collins's death, published in three volumes by Chatto & Windus following serialization in the *Illustrated London News*.

1895   Caroline Graves dies and is buried in Collins's grave.

1913   Son, William Charles Collins Dawson, dies.

1919   Martha Rudd dies.

HEART AND SCIENCE:
A Story of the Present Time

By Wilkie Collins

In Three Volumes
London: Chatto & Windus, Piccadilly, 1883[1]

---

1   *Chatto & Windus, Piccadilly, 1883*: Chatto & Windus, primarily interested in
sales to lending libraries, published *Heart and Science* in three volumes in April
1883, two months before the end of the novel's serial run in the *Belgravia: An
Illustrated London Magazine* (also owned by Chatto & Windus at the time of
the novel's publication). The *Seaside Library*, an American series created by
George Munro, pirated *Heart and Science*, publishing it on March 1, 1883. The
text of this edition follows the text of the Chatto & Windus three-volume first
edition.

TO

SARONY

(OF NEW YORK)

ARTIST, PHOTOGRAPHER,

AND

GOOD FRIEND[1]

---

1   *To Sarony ... Good Friend*: Napoleon Sarony (1821-1896) was a New York portrait photographer for whom Collins sat during his 1873 visit to the United
States. The two remained friends for the rest of Collins's life.

Preface[1]

I.

TO READERS IN GENERAL.[2]

You are the children of Old Mother England, on both sides of the Atlantic; you form the majority of buyers and borrowers of novels; and you judge of works of fiction by certain inbred preferences, which but slightly influence the other great public of readers on the continent of Europe.

The two qualities in fiction which hold the highest rank in your estimation are: Character and Humour. Incident and dramatic situation only occupy the second place in your favour. A novel that tells no story, or that blunders perpetually in trying to tell a story—a novel so entirely devoid of all sense of the dramatic side of human life, that not even a theatrical thief can find anything in it to steal[3]—will nevertheless be a work that wins (and keeps) your admiration, if it has Humour which dwells on your memory, and characters which enlarge the circle of your friends.

I have myself always tried to combine the different merits of a good novel, in one and the same work; and I have never succeeded in keeping an equal balance. In the present story you will find the scales inclining, on the whole, in favour of character and Humour. This has not happened accidentally.

Advancing years, and health that stands sadly in need of improvement, warn me—if I am to vary my way of work—that I may have little time to lose.[4] Without waiting for future opportunities, I have kept your standard of merit more constantly before my mind, in writing this book, than on some former occasions.

Still persisting in telling you a story—still refusing to get up in the pulpit and preach, or to invade the platform and lecture, or to take you by the buttonhole in confidence and make fun of my Art—it has been my chief effort to draw the characters with a vigour and breadth of treatment, derived from the nearest and truest view that I could get of the one model, Nature. Whether I shall at once succeed in adding to the circle of your friends in the world of fiction—or whether you will hurry through the narrative, and only discover on a later reading that it is the characters which have interested you in the story—remains to be seen. Either way, your sympathy will find me grateful; for, either way, my motive has been to please you.

During its periodical publication correspondents, noting certain passages in "Heart and Science," inquired how I came to think of writing this book. The question may be readily answered in better words than mine.

My book has been written in harmony with opinions which have an indisputable claim to respect. Let them speak for themselves.

SHAKESPEARE'S OPINION.[5]—"It was always yet the trick of our English nation, if they have a good thing, to make it too common." (*King Henry IV., Part II.*)

WALTER SCOTT'S OPINION.[6]—"I am no great believer in the extreme degree of improvement to be derived from the advancement of Science; for every study of that nature tends, when pushed to a certain extent, to harden the heart." (*Letter to Miss Edgeworth.*)

FARADAY'S OPINION.[7]—"The education of the judgment has for its first and its last step—Humility." (*Lecture on Mental Education, at the Royal Institution.*)

Having given my reasons for writing the book, let me conclude by telling you what I have kept out of the book.

It encourages me to think that we have many sympathies in common; and among them, that most of us have taken to our hearts domestic pets. Writing under this conviction, I have not forgotten my responsibility towards you, and towards my Art, in pleading the cause of the harmless and affectionate beings of God's creation. From first to last, you are purposely left in ignorance of the hideous secrets of Vivisection.[8] The outside of the laboratory is a necessary object in my landscape—but I never once open the door and invite you to look in. I trace, in one of my characters, the result of the habitual practice of cruelty (no matter under what pretence) in fatally deteriorating the nature of man—and I leave the picture to speak for itself. My own personal feeling has throughout been held in check. Thankfully accepting the assistance rendered to me by Miss Frances Power Cobbe,[9] by Mrs. H. M. Gordon,[10] and by Surgeon-General Gordon, C.B.,[11] I have borne in mind (as they have borne in mind) the value of temperate advocacy to a good cause.

With this, your servant withdraws, and leaves you to the story.

II.

TO READERS IN PARTICULAR.

If you are numbered among those good friends of ours, who are especially capable of understanding us and sympathising with us, be pleased to accept the expression of our gratitude, and to pass over the lines that follow.

But if you open our books with a mind soured by distrust; if you habitually anticipate inexcusable ignorance where the course of the story happens to turn on matters of fact; it is you, Sir or Madam, whom I now want. Not to dispute with you—far from it! I own with sorrow that your severity does occasionally encounter us on assailable ground. But there are exceptions, even to the stiffest rules. Some of us are not guilty of wilful carelessness: some of us apply to competent authority, when we write on subjects beyond the range of our own experience. Having thus far ventured to speak for my colleagues, you will conclude that I am paving the way for speaking next of myself. As our cousins in the United States say— that is so.

In the following pages, there are allusions to medical practice at the bedside; leading in due course to physiological questions which connect themselves with the main interest of the novel. In traversing this delicate ground, you have not been forgotten. Before the manuscript went to the printer, it was submitted for correction to an eminent London surgeon, whose experience extends over a period of forty years.[12]

Again: a supposed discovery in connection with brain disease, which occupies a place of importance, is not (as you may suspect) the fantastic product of the author's imagination. Finding his materials everywhere, he has even contrived to make use of Professor Ferrier[13]—writing on the "Localisation of Cerebral Disease," and closing a confession of the present result of post-mortem examination of brains in these words: "We cannot even be sure, whether many of the changes discovered are the cause or the result of the Disease, or whether the two are the conjoint results of a common cause." Plenty of elbow room here for the spirit of discovery.

On becoming acquainted with "Mrs. Gallilee," you will find her talking—and you will sometimes even find the author talking—of scientific subjects in general. You will naturally conclude that it is "all gross caricature." No; it is all promiscuous reading. Let me spare you a long list of books consulted, and of newspapers and magazines mutilated for "cuttings"—and appeal to examples once more, and for the last time.

When "Mrs. Gallilee" wonders whether "Carmina has ever heard of the Diathermancy of Ebonite," she is thinking of proceedings at a conversazione in honour of Professor Helmholtz[14] (reported in the "Times" of April 12, 1881), at which "radiant energy" was indeed converted into "sonorous vibrations." Again: when she contemplates taking part in a discussion on Matter, she has been slily looking into Chambers's Encyclopædia, and has there discovered the interesting conditions on which she can "dispense with the idea of atoms." Briefly, not a word of my own invention occurs, when Mrs. Gallilee turns the learned side of her character to your worships' view.

I have now only to add that the story has been subjected to careful revision,[15] and I hope to consequent improvement, in its present form of publication. Past experience has shown me that you have a sharp eye for slips of the pen, and that you thoroughly enjoy convicting a novelist, by post, of having made a mistake.[16] Whatever pains I may have taken to disappoint you, it is quite likely that we may be again indebted to each other on this occasion. So, to our infinite relief on either side, we part friends after all.

W.C.

London: April *1883*[17]

Notes

1   *Preface*: Despite suggestions from Dickens "that a book (of all things) should speak for and explain itself" (Walter Dexter, ed., *The Letters of Charles Dickens*. 3 volumes. London: Nonesuch, 1938, II, 436), Collins remained an inveterate preface writer throughout his career. Often his prefaces attempted to explain or defend his tactics as a writer of fiction. The preface to *Heart and Science* does both.

2   *To Readers in General*: Collins divided his preface into two parts, "To Readers in General" and "To Readers in Particular," feeling the need to explain himself and his motives to *all* his readers, those of his largely uneducated but faithful general public as well as those of the professional literary community, whom he distrusted. See Collins's article, "The Unknown Public," (*Household Words*, July 21, 1858, 217-22) and Sue Lonoff's *Wilkie Collins and His Victorian Readers* (New York: AMS, 1982) for detailed discussions of his opinions of his readership.

3   *A novel ... steal*: There is more to this statement than the obvious surface humour. Collins, like his friend Dickens, fought a lifelong losing battle against literary piracy, both of his fiction and of the stage adaptations of several of his novels. The case of *Heart and Science* shows that Collins had good reason for his bitter opinions. A month before Chatto & Windus published the three-volume edition of the novel in April 1883, the Canadian-born New York publisher George Munro (1825-1896) pirated the novel, putting it out in his cheap *Seaside Library* series (a series that specialized in British fiction and eventually included nearly two thousand titles) without any thought of compensation for Collins. Of the piracy of *Heart and Science*, Collins wrote to a Harper Brothers' representative on February 24,1883:

> I have been too thoroughly disgusted with the thefts committed on *Heart and Science* during its periodical publication in the United States to make any arrangements for its publication there in book form. Under the sanction of the President and Congress, the honest American citizen who purchased my advance-sheets for "Frank Leslie's" newspaper was robbed of them three days afterward, in each week, by the publication of another New York newspaper—to say nothing of other thefts committed in other places. (See Appendix D, 4 for the complete text of this letter.)

4   *Advancing years ... little time to lose*: Collins was very much aware of his chronic poor health. He claims in a letter to a friend to have forestalled a vicious attack of the gout just long enough to finish *Heart and Science*:

> For six months—while I was writing furiously, without cessation, one part sane and three parts mad—I had no gout. I finished my story [*Heart and Science*]—discovered one day that I was half dead with fatigue—and the next

day that the gout was in my right eye. (See Appendix D, 5 for the complete text of this letter.)

5 *Shakespeare's Opinion*: Falstaff gives voice to this opinion in *The Second Part of King Henry IV* (I, ii, 239-41). With this passage, as well as with the two quotations that follow it, Collins suggests that he fears the dramatic and unchecked advances in the world of science.

6 *Scott's Opinion*: (Sir Walter Scott, 1771-1832) Collins admired Scott as one of the "Kings of Fiction" (Coleman 291). Here, "Scott's Opinion" comes from a letter of February 4, 1829 to friend and fellow-novelist Maria Edgeworth (1767-1849).

7 *Faraday's Opinion*: (Michael Faraday, 1791-1867) Faraday is most noteworthy for his discovery of magneto-electricity, but he was known also for his remarkable power as a lecturer. The "Lecture on Mental Education" from which this passage was taken was presented to the Royal Institution, Albemarle Street, where Faraday conducted his experiments on electricity, and where he was Professor of Chemistry from 1833 until his death.

8 *From first to last ... the hideous secrets of Vivisection*: Swinburne created his famous couplet—"What brought good Wilkie's genius nigh perdition?/Some demon whispered-'Wilkie! have a mission'"—in response to Collins's anti-vivisection theme in *Heart and Science*. But the attack on Collins and "thesis novels" seems unfair. Vivisection is scarcely mentioned until the thirty-first and thirty-second chapters, which contains the bulk of Collins's propaganda, and then not again until the novel's conclusion. Nor does the vivisection theme overshadow the novel's main story—Carmina's struggle to change those around her for the better.

At least some of the novel's reviewers (see Appendix A, 1-5) expressed surprise that the novel had less to do with vivisection than its preface suggested.

9 *Miss Frances Power Cobbe*: Frances Power Cobbe (1822-1904) was foundress of the *Victoria Street Society for Protection of Animals from Vivisection* and author of many articles and pamphlets on the vivisection controversy that raged in Britain during the last half of the nineteenth century. Collins corresponded with her as he prepared to write *Heart and Science*. Cobbe's autobiography, *Life of Francis Power Cobbe, As Told by Herself* (London: Swan Sonnenschein, 1904), provides a detailed account of the vivisection controversy, as well as a brief discussion of her correspondence with Collins.

10 *Mrs. H.M. Gordon*: Mrs. H.M. Gordon remains unidentified but seems not to have been a relation of Surgeon-General Charles Alexander Gordon, whose wife's name was Annie. She may have been related to a Frederick Gordon, Esq., who attended a dinner party with Collins at the home of Edmund Yates in May 1885. In any event, it is probably safe to assume that she was a participant in the anti-vivisection movement and provided Collins with information he sought while preparing to write.

11 *Surgeon-General Gordon, C.B.*: Surgeon-General Charles Alexander Gordon, Companion of the Bath (1821-1899), an eminent physician to whom Collins turned for advice on the medical particulars mentioned in his novel. (See Appendix D, 2 for a letter from Collins to Gordon.)

12 *Before the manuscript ... forty years*: Collins may have been referring here to his personal physician, Francis Carr Beard, who served as his advisor on physical and mental disorders. Through his career, Collins often relied on unnamed authorities for the accuracy of his material. In a preface to *The Woman and White*, Collins suggests that his legal facts have been legitimized by "a solicitor

of great experience." In a preface to *The Moonstone*, Collins tells his readers that he has "ascertained, not only from books, but from living authorities as well, what the result of that experiment would really have been."

13   *Professor Ferrier*: David Ferrier (1843-1928) was Professor of Forensic Medicine at King's College Hospital and Medical School, London, and author of *The Localisation of Cerebral Disease* (1878); he was charged in 1881 under the Cruelty to Animals Act of 1876 for practising vivisection without a license. He was acquitted at his trial, at Bow Street, in November 1881. (See Appendix C for Frances Power Cobbe's discussion of the trial.)

14   *Professor Helmholtz*: True enough, Collins secured information from *The Times* (April 12, 1881) about a *conversazione* (see Note 2, p. 88 and Appendix F) given in honour of the visiting Professor Hermann von Helmholtz (1821-1894), of Berlin. *The Times* information, as well as much of the other scientific language that Collins employs in the novel, serves little or no function except, as one reviewer suggested, to provide Collins "with a phrase here and there to round off a sentence and raise a laugh. ..." (See Appendix A, 2.) Collins biographer Kenneth Robinson agrees, claiming that the author's "immersion in the scientific literature of his day ... enable (sic) him to sprinkle his pages with the current jargon of science" (302).

15   *I have now only to add ... careful revision*: In a March 9, 1883 letter to the editor of the *Belgravia* magazine, Collins claims that "there is hardly a page of this periodical publication which has not been revised, altered, abridged, in one place, or enlarged in another, for the English reprint" (See Appendix D, 6 for the complete text of this letter). And Collins was true to his word. He revised *Heart and Science* more vigorously than any of his other novels. (See Photographs 1 and 2 for samples of Collins's penmanship and editing tactics.)

16   *Past experience ... made a mistake*: Stung early in his career by a critic who discovered an error in chronology in *The Woman in White*, Collins thereafter became both defensive and insistent about maintaining the accuracy of even seemingly unimportant details in his fiction. He researched postal routes, train and steamer schedules, even theatre registers, in an effort to out-duel his detective critics.

17   *London, April 1883*: Collins penned this preface at his residence, 90 Gloucester Place, Portman Square West, London, days before the book was released in three volumes by Chatto & Windus in April, 1883.

VOLUME ONE

CHAPTER I.

The weary old nineteenth century had advanced into the last twenty years of its life.

Towards two o'clock in the afternoon, Ovid Vere[1] (of the Royal College of Surgeons)[2] stood at the window of his consulting-room in London, looking out at the summer sunshine, and the quiet dusty street. He had received a warning, familiar to the busy men of our time—the warning from overwrought Nature, which counsels rest after excessive work. With a prosperous career before him, he had been compelled (at only thirty-one years of age) to ask a colleague to take charge of his practice, and to give the brain which he had cruelly wearied a rest of some months to come. On the next day he had arranged to embark for the Mediterranean in a friend's yacht.[3]

An active man, devoted heart and soul to his profession, is not a man who can learn the happy knack of being idle at a moment's notice. Ovid found the mere act of looking out of window, and wondering what he should do next, more than he had patience to endure.

He turned to his study table. If he had possessed a wife to look after

---

1   *Ovid Vere*: Collins often used provocative or suggestive character names, and those employed in *Heart and Science* are no exception: Ovid Vere brings to mind the exiled Roman poet of love poetry, whose "Art of Love" explores the folly of turning love into a science; the volatile governess, Miss Frances Minerva, owes her name to the Roman goddess of Wisdom and of War; Mrs. Maria Gallilee, the modern "Muse of Science," brings to mind of Galilei Galileo (1564-1642), Italian pioneer of modern physics and astronomy. At least one of the novel's reviewers took exception to Collins's use of such names (See Appendix A, 3).

2   *Royal College of Surgeons*: Located in Lincoln's Inn Fields, the Royal College was given its first Royal Charter in 1800 and housed various laboratories and teaching facilities, as well as a museum and world famous collections of scientific specimens. The reader should also note here the distinction between Victorian surgeons and physicians. Ovid Vere, Mr. Morphew, and Mr. Null are all surgeons. Nathan Benjulia and Sir Richard are physicians. A surgeon, usually addressed as Mister, generally administered to external injuries such as cuts and bruises; he also delivered babies and set broken bones. A physician, usually addressed as Doctor, most often treated internal illnesses and was allowed to prescribe medicine. Surgeons did not need a license to practice, while a physician had to be licensed by the Royal College of Physicians of London.

3   *On the next day ... a friend's yacht*: Collins yachted frequently, and he often included yachting in both his fiction and nonfiction. Allan Armadale, the title character of *Armadale*, is a skilled yachtsman; and Collins reported his own high seas adventure in "The Cruise of the TomTit" (*Household Words*, December 22, 1855, 490-99).

him, he would have been reminded that he and his study table had nothing in common, under present circumstances. Being deprived of conjugal superintendence, he broke though his own rules. His restless hand unlocked a drawer, and took out a manuscript work on medicine of his own writing. "Surely," he thought, "I may finish a chapter, before I go to sea to-morrow?"

His head, steady enough while he was only looking out of window, began to swim before he had got to the bottom of a page. The last sentences of the unfinished chapter alluded to a matter of fact which he had not yet verified. In emergencies of any sort, he was a patient man and a man of resource. The necessary verification could be accomplished by a visit to the College of Surgeons, situated in the great square called Lincoln's Inn Fields.[1] Here was a motive for a walk—with an occupation at the end of it, which only involved a question to a Curator, and an examination of a Specimen. He locked up his manuscript, and set forth for Lincoln's Inn Fields.

CHAPTER II.

When two friends happen to meet in the street, do they ever look back along the procession of small circumstances which has led them both, from the starting-point of their own houses, to the same spot, at the same time? Not one man in ten thousand has probably ever thought of making such a fantastic inquiry as this. And consequently not one man in ten thousand, living in the midst of reality, has discovered that he is also living in the midst of romance.

From the moment when the young surgeon closed the door of his house, he was walking blindfold on his way to a patient in the future who was personally still a stranger to him. He never reached the College of Surgeons. He never embarked on his friend's yacht.

What were the obstacles which turned him aside from the course that he had in view? Nothing but a series of trivial circumstances, occurring in the experience of a man who goes out for a walk.[2]

---

1   *Lincoln's Inn Fields*: Bordered by High Holborn on the north and the Strand on the south, Chancery Lane on the east and Kingsway on the west, Lincoln's Inn Fields—which had long been a playground for the students of close-by Lincoln's Inn, where Collins studied the law in the 1840s—housed, among other noteworthy landmarks, Sir John Soane's Museum and the Royal College of Surgeons.

2   *Nothing but a series ... goes out for a walk*: Much of Collins's fiction depends on coincidence, but not simply to drive the plot, for Collins was fascinated by the notions of fate and destiny, which play a role in many of his novels, including *Basil, The Dead Secret, Armadale,* and *Heart and Science.*

He had only reached the next street, when the first of the circumstances presented itself in the shape of a friend's carriage, which drew up at his side. A bright benevolent face encircled by bushy white whiskers, looked out of the window, and a hearty voice asked him if he had completed his arrangements for a long holiday. Having replied to this, Ovid had a question to put, on his side.

"How is our patient, Sir Richard?"

"Out of danger."

"And what do the other doctors say now?"

Sir Richard laughed: "They say it's my luck."

"Not convinced yet?"

"Not in the least. Who has ever succeeded in convincing fools? Let's try another subject. Is your mother reconciled to your new plans?"

"I can hardly tell you. My mother is in a state of indescribable agitation. Her brother's Will has been found in Italy.[1] And his daughter may arrive in England at a moment's notice."

"Unmarried?" Sir Richard asked slyly.

"I don't know."

"Any money?"

Ovid smiled—not cheerfully. "Do you think my poor mother would be in a state of indescribable agitation if there was *not* money?"

Sir Richard was one of those obsolete elderly persons who quote Shakespeare. "Ah, well," he said, "your mother is like Kent in King Lear—she's too old to learn.[2] Is she as fond as ever of lace? and as keen as ever after a bargain?" He handed a card out of the carriage window. "I have just seen an old patient of mine," he resumed, "in whom I feel a friendly interest. She is retiring from business by my advice; and she asks me, of all the people in the world, to help her in getting rid of some wonderful 'remnants,' at 'an alarming sacrifice!' My kind regards to your mother—and there's a chance for her. One last word, Ovid. Don't be in too great a hurry to return to work; you have plenty of spare time before you. Look at my wise dog here, on the front seat, and learn from him to be idle and happy."

---

1   *Her brother's Will has been found in Italy*: The Will (whose details we learn in Chapter VIII), the lawyer, and the perplexities of laws governing legitimacy and inheritance are staples in Collins's fiction, including his four best-known novels—*The Woman in White*, *No Name*, *Armadale*, and *The Moonstone*. Collins entered Lincoln's Inn to study law in 1846 and was called to the Bar in 1851; he never practised law, but he remained intrigued by it and its practitioners throughout his life.

2   *Your mother is ... too old to learn*: Sir Richard quotes Shakespeare's *King Lear*. Kent tells Cornwall: "Sir, I am too old to learn" (II, ii, 134). Sir Richard, who drives the plot forward with essential family history, does not appear in the novel again; he seems to have been a character Collins contemplated developing but abandoned as he serialized.

The great physician had another companion, besides his dog. A friend, bound his way, had accepted a seat in the carriage. "Who is that handsome young man?" the friend asked as they drove away.

"He is the only son of a relative of mine, dead many years since," Sir Richard replied.

"Don't forget that you have seen him."

"May I ask why?"

"He has not yet reached the prime of life; and he is on the way—already far on the way—to be one of the foremost men of his time. With a private fortune, he has worked as few surgeons work who have their bread to get by their profession. The money comes from his late father. His mother has married again. The second husband is a lazy, harmless old fellow, named Gallilee; possessed of one small attraction—fifty thousand pounds, grubbed up in trade. There are two little daughters, by the second marriage. With such a stepfather as I have described, and, between ourselves, with a mother who has rather more than her fair share of the jealous, envious, and money-loving propensities of humanity, my friend Ovid is not diverted by family influences from the close pursuit of his profession. You will tell me, he may marry. Well! if he gets a good wife she will be a circumstance in his favour. But, so far as I know, he is not that sort of man. Cooler, a deal cooler, with women than I am—though I am old enough to be his father. Let us get back to his professional prospects. You heard him ask me about a patient?"

"Yes."

"Very good. Death was knocking hard at that patient's door, when I called Ovid into consultation with myself and with two other doctors who differed with me. It was one of the very rare cases in which the old practice of bleeding was, to my mind, the only treatment to pursue. I never told him that this was the point in dispute between me and the other men—and they said nothing, on their side, at my express request. He took his time to examine and think; and he saw the chance of saving the patient by venturing on the use of the lancet as plainly as I did—with my forty years' experience to teach me? A young man with that capacity for discovering the remote cause of disease, and with that superiority to the trammels of routine in applying the treatment, has no common medical career before him. His holiday will set his health right in next to no time. I see nothing in his way, at present—not even a woman! But," said Sir Richard, with the explanatory wink of one eye peculiar (like quotation from Shakespeare) to persons of the obsolete old time, "*we* know better than to forecast the weather if a petticoat influence appears on the horizon. One prediction, however, I do risk. If his mother buys any of that lace—I know who will get the best of the bargain!"

The conditions under which the old doctor was willing to assume the character of a prophet never occurred. Ovid remembered that he was going away on a long voyage—and Ovid was a good son. He bought some of the lace, as a present to his mother at parting; and, most assuredly, he got the worst of the bargain.

His shortest way back to the straight course, from which he had deviated in making his purchase, led him into a by-street, near the flower and fruit market of Covent Garden.[1] Here he met with the second in number of the circumstances which attended his walk. He found himself encountered by an intolerably filthy smell.

The market was not out of the direct way to Lincoln's Inn Fields. He fled from the smell to the flowery and fruity perfumes of Covent Garden, and completed the disinfecting process by means of a basket of strawberries.

Why did a poor ragged little girl, carrying a big baby, look with such longing eyes at the delicious fruit, that, as a kind-hearted man, he had no alternative but to make her a present of the strawberries? Why did two dirty boyfriends of hers appear immediately afterwards with news of Punch in a neighbouring street, and lead the little girl away with them? Why did these two new circumstances inspire him with a fear that the boys might take the strawberries away from the poor child, burdened as she was with a baby almost as big as herself? When we suffer from overwrought nerves we are easily disturbed by small misgivings. The idle man of wearied mind followed the friends of the street drama to see what happened, forgetful of the College of Surgeons, and finding a new fund of amusement in himself.

Arrived in the neighbouring street, he discovered that the Punch performance had come to an end—like some other dramatic performances of higher pretensions—for want of a paying audience. He waited at a certain distance, watching the children. His doubts had done them an injustice. The boys only said, "Give us a taste." And the liberal little girl rewarded their good conduct. An equitable and friendly division of the strawberries was made in a quiet corner.

Where—always excepting the case of a miser or a millionaire—is the man to be found who could have returned to the pursuit of his own affairs, under these circumstances, without encouraging the practice of the social virtues by a present of a few pennies? Ovid was not that man.

Putting back in his breast-pocket the bag in which he was accustomed to carry small coins for small charities, his hand touched something which felt like the envelope of a letter. He took it out—looked at it with an expression of annoyance and surprise—and once more turned aside from the direct way to Lincoln's Inn Fields.

The envelope contained his last prescription. Having occasion to consult the "Pharmacopoeia," he had written it at home, and had promised

---

1   *Covent Garden*: A block from Lincoln's Inn Fields, Covent Garden was, and is, a bustling central city market area.

to send it to the patient immediately. In the absorbing interest of making his preparations for leaving England, it had remained forgotten in his pocket for nearly two days. The one means of setting this unlucky error right, without further delay, was to deliver his prescription himself, and to break through his own rules for the second time by attending to a case of illness—purely as an act of atonement.

The patient lived in a house nearly opposite to the British Museum.[1] In this northward direction he now set his face.

He made his apologies, and gave his advice—and, getting out again into the street, tried once more to shape his course for the College of Surgeons. Passing the walled garden of the British Museum, he looked towards it—and paused. What had stopped him, this time? Nothing but a tree, fluttering its bright leaves in the faint summer air.

A marked change showed itself in his face.

The moment before he had been passing in review the curious little interruptions which had attended his walk, and had wondered humorously what would happen next. Two women, meeting him, and seeing a smile on his lips, had said to each other, "There goes a happy man." If they had encountered him now, they might have reversed their opinion. They would have seen a man thinking of something once dear to him, in the far and unforgotten past.

He crossed over the road to the side-street which faced the garden. His head drooped; he moved mechanically. Arrived in the street, he lifted his eyes, and stood (within nearer view of it) looking at the tree.

Hundreds of miles away from London, under another tree of that gentle family, this man—so cold to women in after life—had made child-love, in the days of his boyhood, to a sweet little cousin long since numbered with the dead. The present time, with its interests and anxieties, passed away like the passing of a dream. Little by little, as the minutes followed each other, his sore heart felt a calming influence, breathed mysteriously from the fluttering leaves. Still forgetful of the outward world, he wandered slowly up the street; living in the old scenes; thinking, not unhappily now, the old thoughts.

Where, in all London, could he have found a solitude more congenial to a dreamer in daylight?

The broad district, stretching northward and eastward from the British Museum, is like the quiet quarter of a country town set in the midst of the roaring activities of the largest city in the world. Here, you can cross the road, without putting limb or life in peril. Here, when you are idle, you can saunter and look about, safe from collision with merciless straight-walkers whose time is money, and whose destiny is business. Here, you

---

1   *British Museum*: The British Museum lies a half-mile north of Covent Garden, in Great Russell Street. It opened in 1759, but the general public did not have open access to its vast collections until 1879.

may meet undisturbed cats on the pavement, in the full glare of noontide, and may watch, through the railings of the squares, children at play on grass that almost glows with the lustre of the Sussex Downs.[1] This haven of rest is alike out of the way of fashion and business; and is yet within easy reach of the one and the other. Ovid paused in a vast and silent square. If his little cousin had lived, he might perhaps have seen his children at play in some such secluded place as this.

The birds were singing blithely in the trees. A tradesman's boy, delivering fish to the cook, and two girls watering flowers at a window, were the only living creatures near him, as he roused himself and looked around.

Where was the College? Where were the Curator and the Specimen? Those questions brought with them no feeling of anxiety or surprise. He turned, in a half-awakened way, without a wish or a purpose—turned, and listlessly looked back.

Two foot-passengers, dressed in mourning garments, were rapidly approaching him. One of them, as they came nearer, proved to be an aged woman. The other was a girl.

He drew aside to let them pass. They looked at him with the lukewarm curiosity of strangers, as they went by. The girl's eyes and his met. Only the glance of an instant—and its influence held him for life.[2]

She went swiftly on, as little impressed by the chance meeting as the old woman at her side. Without stopping to think—without being capable of thought—Ovid followed them. Never before had he done what he was doing now; he was, literally, out of himself. He saw them ahead of him, and he saw nothing else.

Towards the middle of the square, they turned aside into a street on the left. A concert-hall was in the street—with doors open for an afternoon performance. They entered the hall. Still out of himself, Ovid followed them.

CHAPTER III.

A room of magnificent size; furnished with every conventional luxury that money can buy; lavishly provided with newspapers and books of reference; lighted by tall windows in the day-time, and by gorgeous chandeliers at night, may be nevertheless one of the dreariest places of rest and

---

1   *Sussex Downs:* Collins knew this part of the city well. He lived in various apartments within a mile or so of the Downs, west of the central city, for over forty years.

2   *Only the glance of an instant—and its influence held him for life:* Collins employed the notion of "love at first sight" in much of his fiction, including *Basil* and *The Woman in White.* In fact, Ovid Vere uses the very phrase "love at first sight" in Chapter XIV of *Heart and Science.*

shelter that can be found on the civilised earth. Such places exist, by hundreds, in those hotels of monstrous proportions and pretensions, which now engulf the traveller who ends his journey on the pier or the platform. It may be that we feel ourselves to be strangers among strangers—it may be that there is something innately repellent in splendid carpets and curtains, chairs and tables, which have no social associations to recommend them—it may be that the mind loses its elasticity under the inevitable restraint on friendly communication, which expresses itself in lowered tones and instinctive distrust of our next neighbour; but this alone is certain: life, in the public drawing-room of a great hotel, is life with all its healthiest emanations perishing in an exhausted receiver.

On the same day, and nearly at the same hour, when Ovid had left his house, two women sat in a corner of the public room, in one of the largest of the railway hotels latterly built in London.[1]

Without observing it themselves, they were objects of curiosity to their fellow-travellers. They spoke to each other in a foreign language. They were dressed in deep mourning—with an absence of fashion and a simplicity of material which attracted the notice of every other woman in the room. One of them wore a black veil over her gray hair. Her hands were brown, and knotty at the joints; her eyes looked unnaturally bright for her age; innumerable wrinkles crossed and re-crossed her skinny face; and her aquiline nose (as one of the ladies present took occasion to remark) was so disastrously like the nose of the great Duke of Wellington[2] as to be an offensive feature in the face of a woman.

The lady's companion, being a man, took a more merciful view. "She can't help being ugly," he whispered. "But see how she looks at the girl with her. A good old creature, I say, if ever there was one yet." The lady eyed him, as only a jealous woman can eye her husband, and whispered back, "Of course you're in love with that slip of a girl!"

She *was* a slip of a girl—and not even a tall slip. At seventeen years of age, it was doubtful whether she would ever grow to a better height.

But a girl who is too thin, and not even so tall as the Venus de' Medici,[3] may still be possessed of personal attractions. It was not altogether a matter of certainty, in this case, that the attractions were sufficiently remark-

---

1   *one of the largest of the railways hotels latterly built in London*: Collins may have been thinking of the large *Euston Railway Station* hotel that had just opened in 1881. But since his characters left the hotel, "crossed the Strand" and headed "out of it towards the North," Collins may also have been recalling the *Charing Cross Hotel*, built in 1863-4 at the same time that *Charing Cross Station* was opened to rail travel from south London and beyond.

2   *The nose of the great Duke of Wellington*: The Duke of Wellington (1769-1852), the Iron Duke and Prime Minister (1828-1830), had a markedly Roman nose.

3   *Venus de' Medici*: Venus is the Roman goddess of love and beauty, so the comparison with Carmina is thematically appropriate. The sculpture, 3rd century B.C., is housed in the Uffizi Gallery, Florence.

able to excite general admiration. The fine colour and the plump healthy cheeks, the broad smile, and the regular teeth, the well-developed mouth, and the promising bosom which form altogether the average type of beauty found in the purely bred English maiden, were not among the noticeable charms of the small creature in gloomy black, shrinking into a corner of the big room. She had very little colour of any sort to boast of. Here hair was of so light a brown that it just escaped being flaxen; but it had the negative merit of not being forced down to her eyebrows, and twisted into the hideous curly-wig which exhibits a liberal equality of ugliness on the heads of women in the present day. There was a delicacy of finish in her features—in the nose and the lips especially—a sensitive changefulness in the expression of her eyes (too dark in themselves to be quite in harmony with her light hair), and a subtle yet simple witchery in her rare smile, which atoned, in some degree at least, for want of complexion in the face and of flesh in the figure. Men might dispute her claims to beauty—but no one could deny that she was, in the common phrase, an interesting person. Grace and refinement; a quickness of apprehension and a vivacity of movement, suggestive of some foreign origin; a childish readiness of wonder, in the presence of new objects—and perhaps, under happier circumstances, a childish playfulness with persons whom she loved—were all characteristic attractions of the modest stranger who was in the charge of the ugly old woman, and who was palpably the object of that wrinkled duenna's devoted love.[1]

A travelling writing-case stood open on a table near them. In an interval of silence the girl looked at it reluctantly. They had been talking of family affairs—and had spoken in Italian, so as to keep their domestic secrets from the ears of the strangers about them. The old woman was the first to resume the conversation.

"My Carmina, you really ought to write that letter," she said; "the illustrious Mrs. Gallilee is waiting to hear of our arrival in London."

Carmina took up the pen, and put it down again with a sigh. "We only arrived last night," she pleaded. "Dear old Teresa, let us have one day in London by ourselves!"

Teresa received this proposal with undisguised amazement and alarm. "Jesu Maria! a day in London—and your aunt waiting for you all the time! She is your second mother, my dear, by appointment; and her house is your new home. And you propose to stop a whole day at an hotel, instead of going home. Impossible! Write, my Carmina—write. See, here is the address on a card:—'Fairfield Gardens.'[2] What a pretty place it must be to live in, with such a name as that! And a sweet lady, no doubt. Come! come !"

---

1   *that wrinkled duenna's devoted love*: A duenna is usually an elderly woman acting as companion and chaperon.

2   *Fairfield Gardens*: Fairfield Gardens is a fictional address.

But Carmina still resisted. "I have never even seen my aunt," she said. "It is dreadful to pass my life with a stranger. Remember, I was only a child when you came to us after my mother's death. It is hardly six months yet since I lost my father. I have no one but you, and, when I go to this new home, *you* will leave me. I only ask for one more day to be together, before we part."

The poor old duenna drew back out of sight, in the shadow of a curtain—and began to cry. Carmina took her hand, under cover of a tablecloth; Carmina knew how to console her. "We will go and see sights," she whispered "and, when dinner-time comes, you shall have a glass of the Porto-porto-wine."[1]

Teresa looked round out of the shadow, as easily comforted as a child. "Sights!" she exclaimed—and dried her tears. "Porto-porto-wine!" she repeated—and smacked her withered lips at the relishing words. "Ah, my child, you have not forgotten the consolations I told you of, when I lived in London in my young days. To think of you, with an English father, and never in London till now! I used to go to museums and concerts sometimes, when my English mistress was pleased with me. That gracious lady often gave me a glass of the fine strong purple wine. The Holy Virgin grant that Aunt Gallilee may be as kind a woman! Such a head of hair as the other one she cannot hope to have. It was a joy to dress it. Do you think I wouldn't stay here in England with you if I could? What is to become of my old man in Italy, with his cursed asthma, and nobody to nurse him? Oh, but those were dull years in London! The black endless streets—the dreadful Sundays—the hundreds of thousands of people, always in a hurry; always with grim faces set on business, business, business! I was glad to go back and be married in Italy. And here I am in London again, after God knows how many years. No matter. We will enjoy ourselves to-day; and when we go to Madam Gallilee's to-morrow, we will tell a little lie, and say we only arrived on the evening that has not yet come."

The duenna's sense of humour was so tickled by this prospective view of the little lie, that she leaned back in her chair and laughed. Carmina's rare smile showed itself faintly. The terrible first interview with the unknown aunt still oppressed her. She took up a newspaper in despair. "Oh, my old dear!" she said, "let us get out of this dreadful room, and be reminded of Italy!" Teresa lifted her ugly hands in bewilderment. "Reminded of Italy—in London?"

"Is there no Italian music in London?" Carmina asked suggestively.

---

1   *Porto-porto-wine*: Porto, or port, is a sweet wine, fortified by brandy, that English wine merchants in Oporto, Portugal developed and exported beginning in the eighteenth century. Porto was a very popular drink in England during the nineteenth century.

The duenna's bright eyes answered this in their own language. She snatched up the nearest newspaper.

It was then the height of the London concert season. Morning performances of music were announced in rows. Reading the advertised programmes, Carmina found them, in one remarkable respect, all alike. They would have led an ignorant stranger to wonder whether any such persons as Italian composers, French composers, and English composers had ever existed. The music offered to the English public was music of exclusively German (and for the most part modern German) origin. Carmina held the opinion—in common with Mozart and Rossini,[1] as well as other people—that music without melody is not music at all. She laid aside the newspaper.

The plan of going to a concert being thus abandoned, the idea occurred to them of seeing pictures. Teresa, in search of information, tried her luck at a great table in the middle of the room, on which useful books were liberally displayed. She returned with a catalogue of the Royal Academy Exhibition[2] (which someone had left on the table), and with the most universally well-informed book, on a small scale, that has ever enlightened humanity—modestly described on the title-page as an Almanac.

Carmina opened the catalogue at the first page, and discovered a list of Royal Academicians. Were all these gentlemen celebrated painters? Out of nearly forty names, three only had made themselves generally known beyond the limits of England. She turned to the last page. The works of art on show numbered more than fifteen hundred. Teresa, looking over her shoulder, made the same discovery. "Our heads will ache, and our feet will ache," she remarked, "before we get out of that place." Carmina laid aside the catalogue.

Teresa opened the Almanac at hazard, and hit on the page devoted to Amusements. Her next discovery led her to the section inscribed "Museums." She scored an approving mark at that place with her thumbnail—and read the list in fluent broken English.

---

1 *Mozart and Rossini*: Wolfgang A. Mozart (1756-1791) and Gioachino Rossini (1792-1868) were among Collins's favourite composers, though, as we learn by the end of the chapter, Collins had a poor opinion of most modern continental composers.

2 *Royal Academy Exhibition*: The Royal Academy, founded by George III in 1768, is the official institute of painting in England and offers an annual summer exhibition (Collins's father, William, was a Royal Academician). Collins often expressed dismay at the state of the Royal Academy, and art in general, in England. The following three articles, written by Collins for Dickens's *Household Words*, provide representative discussions of this dismay: "To Think, or Be Thought For?" (September 13, 1856, 193-98), "The National Gallery and the Old Masters" (October 25, 1856, 347-48), and "The Royal Academy in Bed" (May 28, 1859, 105-09).

The British Museum? Teresa's memory of that magnificent building recalled it vividly in one respect. She shook her head. "More headache and footache, there!" Bethnal Green; Indian Museum; College of Surgeons; Practical Geology; South Kensington; Patent Museum—all unknown to Teresa.[1] "The saints preserve us! what headaches and footaches in all these, if they are as big as that other one!" She went on with the list—and astonished everybody in the room by suddenly clapping her hands. Sir John Soane's Museum,[2] Lincoln's Inn Fields. "Ah, but I remember that! A nice little easy museum in a private house, and all sorts of pretty things to see. My dear love, trust your old Teresa. Come to Soane!"

In ten minutes more they were dressed, and on the steps of the hotel. The bright sunlight, the pleasant air, invited them to walk. On the same afternoon, when Ovid had set forth on foot for Lincoln's Inn Fields, Carmina and Teresa set forth on foot for Lincoln's Inn Fields. Trivial obstacles had kept the man away from the College. Would trivial obstacles keep the women away from the Museum?

They crossed the Strand, and entered a street which led out of it towards the North; Teresa's pride in her memory forbidding her thus far to ask their way.

Their talk—dwelling at first on Italy, and on the memory of Carmina's Italian mother—reverted to the formidable subject of Mrs. Gallilee. Teresa's hopeful view of the future turned to the cousins, and drew the picture of two charming little girls, eagerly waiting to give their innocent

---

1   *Bethnal Green; Indian Museum; College of Surgeons; Practical Geology; South Kensington; Patent Museum—all unknown to Teresa*: The Bethnal Green Museum was essentially a doll and toy museum established at mid-century. Bethnal Green proper, north-east of the central city, was among the very poorest sections of London in the 1880s; the Indian Museum, established in 1867, was initially housed in the India Office Library and Records building at Blackfriars Road. The contents of the museum were later transferred to the Victoria and Albert Museum; the College of Surgeons, at Lincoln's Inn Fields, housed, in addition to the medical school, a medical museum; the Museum of Practical Geology, established in 1851 at Jermyn Street, later moved and became part of what is now the Science Museum at Exhibition Road; the South Kensington Museum, established in 1851 and located where Victoria and Albert Museum now stands at Cromwell Road, was also absorbed by the Science Museum; the Patent Office Museum opened in 1857 and displayed locomotives, engines, and various machinery. By 1884, the Patent Office Museum, like the Museum of Practical Geology and the South Kensington Museum, had become part of the Science Museum, which today stands just across Exhibition Road from the Victoria and Albert Museum.

2   *Sir John Soane's Museum*: Sir John Soane (1753-1837), Professor of Architecture at the Royal Academy, was an avid collector of antiques. He obtained an Act of Parliament that established his houses at Lincoln's Inn Fields as a public museum, which has been open since the 1830s.

hearts to their young relative from Italy. "Are there only two?" she said. "Surely you told me there was a boy, besides the girls?" Carmina set her right. "My cousin Ovid is a great doctor," she continued with an air of importance. "Poor papa used to say that our family would have reason to be proud of him." "Does he live at home?" asked simple Teresa. "Oh, dear, no! He has a grand house of his own. Hundreds of sick people go there to be cured, and give hundreds of golden guineas." Hundreds of golden guineas gained by only curing sick people, represented to Teresa's mind something in the nature of a miracle: she solemnly raised her eyes to heaven. "What a cousin to have! Is he young? is he handsome? is he married?"

Instead of answering these questions, Carmina looked over her shoulder. "Is this poor creature following us?" she asked.

They had now turned to the right, and had entered a busy street leading directly to Covent Garden. The "creature" (who was undoubtedly following them) was one of the starved and vagabond dogs of London. Every now and then, the sympathies of their race lead these inveterate wanderers to attach themselves, for the time, to some human companion, whom their mysterious insight chooses from the crowd. Teresa, with the hard feeling towards animals which is one of the serious defects of the Italian character, cried, "Ah, the mangy beast!" and lifted her umbrella. The dog started back, waited a moment, and followed them again as they went on. Carmina's gentle heart gave its pity to this lost and hungry fellow-creature. "I must buy that poor dog something to eat," she said—and stopped suddenly as the idea struck her.

The dog, accustomed to kicks and curses, was ignorant of kindness. Following close behind her, when she checked herself, he darted away in terror into the road. A cab was driven by rapidly at the same moment. The wheel passed over the dog's neck. And there was an end, as a man remarked looking on, of the troubles of a cur.

This common accident struck the girl's sensitive nature with horror. Helpless and speechless, she trembled piteously. The nearest open door was the door of a music-seller's shop. Teresa led her in, and asked for a chair and a glass of water. The proprietor, feeling the interest in Carmina which she seldom failed to inspire among strangers, went the length of offering her a glass of wine. Preferring water, she soon recovered herself sufficiently to be able to leave her chair.

"May I change my mind about going to the museum?" she said to her companion. "After what has happened, I hardly feel equal to looking at curiosities."

Teresa's ready sympathy tried to find some acceptable alternative. "Music would be better, wouldn't it?" she suggested.

The so-called Italian Opera was open that night, and the printed announcement of the performance was in the shop. They both looked at it. Fortune was still against them. A German opera appeared on the bill. Carmina turned to the music-seller in despair. "Is there no music, sir, but

German music to be heard in London?" she asked. The hospitable shop-keeper produced a concert programmed for that afternoon—the modest enterprise of an obscure piano-forte teacher, who could only venture to address pupils, patrons, and friends. What did he promise? Among other things, music from "Lucia," music from "Norma," music from "Ernani."[1] Teresa made another approving mark with her thumb-nail; and Carmina purchased tickets.

The music-seller hurried to the door to stop the first empty cab that might pass. Carmina showed a deplorable ignorance of the law of chances. She shrank from the bare idea of getting into a cab. "We may run over some other poor creature," she said. "If it isn't a dog, it may be a child next time."[2] Teresa and the music-seller suggested a more reasonable view as gravely as they could. Carmina humbly submitted to the claims of common sense—without yielding, for all that. "I know I'm wrong," she confessed. "Don't spoil my pleasure; I can't do it!"

The strange parallel was now complete. Bound for the same destination, Carmina and Ovid had failed to reach it alike. And Carmina had stopped to look at the garden of the British Museum, before she overtook Ovid in the quiet square.

CHAPTER IV.

If, on entering the hall, Ovid had noticed the placards, he would have found himself confronted by a coincidence. The person who gave the concert was also the person who taught music to his half-sisters. Not many days since, he had himself assisted the enterprise, by taking a ticket at his mother's request. Seeing nothing, remembering nothing—hurried by the fear of losing sight of the two strangers if there was a large audience—he impatiently paid for another ticket, at the doors.

The room was little more than half full, and so insufficiently ventilated that the atmosphere was oppressive even under those circumstances. He easily discovered the two central chairs, in the midway row of seats, which she and her companion had chosen. There was a vacant chair

---

1   *music from "Lucia," music from "Norma," music from Ernani": Lucia di Lammermoor* (1835) is an opera in three acts by Donizetti; *Norma* (1831) is an opera, originally in two acts, by Bellini; *Ernani* (1844) is an opera in four acts by Verdi.

2   *We may run over ... a child next time*: Carmina's reaction to the dog's death marks Collins's initial and somewhat heavy-handed attempt to express the sensitivity of his heroine, especially in relation to the animal world. Collins plays a virtu-ally identical card with his hero, Ovid Vere, in Chapter XIII, having him express horror when Benjulia accidentally crushes a common beetle.

(among many others) at one extremity of the row in front of them. He took that place. To look at her, without being discovered—there, so far, was the beginning and the end of his utmost desire.

The performances had already begun. So long as her attention was directed to the singers and players on the platform, he could feast his eyes on her with impunity. In an unoccupied interval, she looked at the audience—and discovered him.

Had he offended her?

If appearances were to be trusted, he had produced no impression of any sort. She quietly looked away, towards the other side of the room. The mere turning of her head was misinterpreted by Ovid as an implied rebuke. He moved to the row of seats behind her. She was now nearer to him than she had been yet. He was again content, and more than content.

The next performance was a solo on the piano. A round of applause welcomed the player. Ovid looked at the platform for the first time. In the bowing man, with a prematurely bald head and a servile smile, he recognized Mrs. Gallilee's music-master. The inevitable inference followed. His mother might be in the room.

After careful examination of the scanty audience, he failed to discover her—thus far. She would certainly arrive, nevertheless. My money's-worth for my money was a leading principle in Mrs. Gallilee's life.

He sighed as he looked towards the door of entrance. Not for long had he revelled in the luxury of a new happiness. He had openly avowed his dislike of concerts, when his mother had made him take a ticket for *this* concert. With her quickness of apprehension what might she not suspect, if she found him among the audience?

Come what might of it, he still kept his place; he still feasted his eyes on the slim figure of the young girl, on the gentle yet spirited carriage of her head. But the pleasure was no longer pleasure without alloy. His mother had got between them now.

The solo on the piano came to an end.

In the interval that followed, he turned once more towards the entrance. Just as he was looking away again, he heard Mrs. Gallilee's loud voice. She was administering a maternal caution to one of the children. "Behave better here than you behaved in the carriage, or I shall take you away."

If she found him in his present place—if she put her own clever construction on what she saw—her opinion would assuredly express itself in some way. She was one of those women who can insult another woman (and safely disguise it) by an inquiring look. For the girl's sake, Ovid instantly moved away from her to the seats at the back of the hall.

Mrs. Gallilee made a striking entrance—dressed to perfection; powdered and painted to perfection; leading her daughters, and followed by her governess. The usher courteously indicated places near the platform. Mrs. Gallilee astonished him by a little lecture on acoustics, delivered with the sweetest condescension. Her Christian humility smiled, and call the usher, Sir. "Sound, sir, is most perfectly heard towards the centre of the auditorium."[1] She led the way towards the centre. Vacant places invited her to the row of seats occupied by Carmina and Teresa. She, the unknown aunt, seated herself next to the unknown niece.

They looked at each other.

Perhaps, it was the heat of the room. Perhaps, she had not perfectly recovered the nervous shock of seeing the dog killed. Carmina's head sank on good Teresa's shoulder. She had fainted.

CHAPTER V.

"May I ask for a cup of tea, Miss Minerva?"

"Delighted, I'm sure, Mr. Le Frank."

"And was Mrs. Gallilee pleased with the Concert?"

"Charmed."

Mr. Le Frank shook his head. "I am afraid there was a drawback," he suggested. "You forget the lady who fainted. So alarming to the audience. So disagreeable to the artists."

"Take care, Mr. Le Frank! These new houses are flimsily built; they might hear you upstairs. The fainting lady is upstairs. All the elements of a romance are upstairs. Is your tea to your liking?"

In this playfully provocative manner, Miss Minerva (the governess) trifled with the curiosity of Mr. Le Frank (the music-master),[2] as the proverbial cat trifles with the terror of the captive mouse. The man of the

---

1   *Sound, sir, is ... centre of the auditorium*: This passage serves to introduce Mrs. Gallilee and provides humour, of course, but Collins had strong opinions about the design problems of English concert halls and theatres. His article, "'The Use of Gas in Theatres' or 'The Air and the Audience: Considerations on the Atmospheric Influences of Theatres'" (1881, 1885), considered the ill effects of a theatre-goer's trip to a typically unhealthy and comfortless English theatre. An earlier condemnation of the English theatre appeared in his article "A Breach of British Privilege," written for Dickens's *Household Words* (March 19, 1859, 361-64).

2   *Miss Minerva (the governess) ... Mr. Le Frank (the music-master)*: Collins was intrigued by the various roles played by domestic servants in the upper-middle-class Victorian household. Several of his articles for Dickens's *Household Words* and *All the Year Round* are devoted to domestic servants, who also often emerge as key characters in his fiction. *Heart and Science* introduces us to an unusual number of these various servants and offers us some fascinating insight into their individual household duties. We meet here the governess (the children's live-in teacher) and the music-master (their in-house teacher of pianoforte). Later in the novel we meet or hear mention of, among other domestics, a dancing-master; a footman (an indoor servant whose jobs usually

bald head and the servile smile showed a polite interest in the coming disclosure; he opened his deeply-sunk eyes, and lazily lifted his delicate eyebrows.

He had called at Mrs. Gallilee's house, after the concert, to get a little tea (with a large infusion of praise) in the schoolroom. A striking personal contrast confronted him, in the face of the lady who was dispensing the hospitalities of the table. Mr. Le Frank's plump cheeks were, in colour, of the obtrusively florid sort. The relics of yellow hair, still adhering to the sides of his head, looked as silkily frail as spun glass. His noble beard made amends for his untimely baldness. The glossy glory of it exhaled delicious perfumes; the keenest eyes might have tried in vain to discover a hair that was out of place. Miss Minerva's eager sallow face, so lean, and so hard, and so long, looked, by contrast, as if it wanted some sort of discreet covering thrown over some part of it. Her coarse black hair projected like a penthouse over her bushy black eyebrows and her keen black eyes. Oh, dear me (as they said in the servants' hall), she would never be married—so yellow and so learned, so ugly and so poor! And yet, if mystery is interesting, this was an interesting woman. The people about her felt an uneasy perception of something secret, ominously secret, in the nature of the governess which defied detection. If Inquisitive Science, vowed to medical research, could dissect firmness of will, working at its steadiest repressive action—then, the mystery of Miss Minerva's inner nature might possibly have been revealed. As it was, nothing more remarkable exposed itself to view than an irritable temper; serving perhaps as safety-valve to an underlying explosive force, which (with strong enough temptation and sufficient opportunity) might yet break out.

"Gently, Mr. Le Frank! The tea is hot—you may burn your mouth. How am I to tell you what has happened?" Miss Minerva dropped the playfully provocative tone, with infinite tact, exactly at the right moment. "Just imagine," she resumed, "a scene on the stage, occurring in private life. The lady who fainted at your concert, turns out to be no less a person that Mrs. Gallilee's niece!"

The general folly which reads a prospectus and blindly speculates in shares, is matched by the equally diffused stupidity, which is incapable of discovering that there can be any possible relation between fiction and

included cleaning, waiting tables, and announcing visitors); a housemaid (who usually cleaned bedrooms, carried water, and washed floors); a housekeeper (usually the head female servant, in charge of all other female servants in a household); a parlour-maid (who performed the duties of a butler in households without a butler); a manservant (a master's personal attendant or valet); a cook (the preparer of a family's meals); a kitchen-maid (a maid who helped the cook with meals by preparing the kitchen fire and cleaning up afterwards); and a coachman (a man who maintained and drove the family's carriages or coaches).

truth. Say it's in a novel—and you are a fool if you believe it. Say it's in a newspaper—and you are a fool if you doubt it.[1] Mr. Le Frank, following the general example, followed it on this occasion a little too unreservedly. He avowed his doubts of the circumstance just related, although it was, on the authority of a lady, a circumstance occurring in real life! Far from being offended, Miss Minerva cordially sympathized with him.

"It *is* too theatrical to be believed," she admitted; "but this fainting young person is positively the interesting stranger we have been expecting from Italy. You know Mrs. Gallilee. Hers was the first smelling-bottle produced; hers was the presence of mind which suggested a horizontal position. 'Help the heart,' she said; 'don't impede it.' The whole theory of fainting fits, in six words! In another moment," proceeded the governess making a theatrical point without suspecting it—"in another moment, Mrs. Gallilee herself stood in need of the smelling-bottle."

Mr. Le Frank was not a true believer, even yet. "You don't mean *she* fainted!" he said.

Miss Minerva held up the indicative forefinger, with which she emphasized instruction when her pupils required rousing. "Mrs. Gallilee's strength of mind—as I was about to say, if you had listened to me—resisted the shock. What the effort must have cost her you will presently understand. Our interesting young lady was accompanied by a hideous old foreign woman who completely lost her head. She smacked her hands distractedly; she call on the saints (without producing the slightest effect)—but she mixed up a name, remarkable even in Italy, with the rest of the delirium; and *that* was serious. Put yourself in Mrs. Gallilee's place—"

"I couldn't do it," said Mr. Le Frank, with humility.

Miss Minerva passed over this reply without notice. Perhaps she was not a believer in the humility of musicians.

"The young lady's Christian name," she proceeded, "is Carmina; (put the accent, if you please, on the *first* syllable). The moment Mrs. Gallilee heard the name, it struck her like a blow. She enlightened the old woman, and asserted herself as Miss Carmina's aunt in an instant. 'I am Mrs. Gallilee:' that was all she said. The result"—Miss Minerva paused, and pointed to the ceiling; "the result is up there. Our charming guest was on the sofa, and the hideous old nurse was fanning her, when I had the honour of seeing them just now. No, Mr. Le Frank! I haven't done yet. There is a last act in this drama of private life still to relate. A medical gentleman was present at the concert, who offered his services in reviving Miss

---

1   *Say it's in a novel ... doubt it*: Collins often defended himself, usually in his novels's prefaces, against charges that his plots and characters were improbable. In the preface to *Basil*, perhaps anticipating a career that would involve defending the untenable, he hedged his bets: "I have not thought it either politic or necessary, while adhering to realities, to adhere to every-day realities."

Carmina. The same gentleman is now in attendance on the interesting patient. Can you guess who he is?"

Mr. Le Frank had sold a ticket for his concert to the medical adviser of the family—one Mr. Null. A cautious guess in this direction seemed to offer the likeliest chance of success.

"He is a patron of music," the pianist began.

"He hates music," the governess interposed.

"I mean Mr. Null," Mr. Le Frank persisted.

"*I* mean—" Miss Minerva paused (like the cat with the mouse again!)—"*I* mean, Mr. Ovid Vere."

What form the music-master's astonishment might have assumed may be matter for speculation, it was never destined to become matter of fact. At the moment when Miss Minerva overwhelmed him with the climax of her story, a little, rosy, elderly gentleman, with a round face, a sweet smile, and a curly gray head, walked into the room, accompanied by two girls. Persons of small importance—only Mr. Gallilee and his daughters.[1]

"How d'ye-do, Mr. Le Frank. I hope you got plenty of money by the concert. I gave away my own two tickets. You will excuse me, I'm sure. Music, I can't think why, always sends me to sleep. Here are your two pupils, Miss Minerva, safe and sound. It struck me we were rather in the way, when that sweet young creature was brought home. Sadly in want of quiet, poor thing—not in want of *us*. Mrs. Gallilee and Ovid, so clever and attentive, were just the right people in the right place. So I put on my hat—I'm always available, Mr. Le Frank; I have the great advantage of never having anything to do—and I said to the girls, 'Let's have a walk.' We had no particular place to go to—that's another advantage of mine—so we drifted about. I didn't mean it, but, somehow or other, we stopped at a pastry-cook's shop. What was the name of the pastry-cook?"

So far Mr. Gallilee proceeded, speaking in the oddest self-contradictory voice, if such a description is permissible—a voice at once high in pitch and mild in tone: in short, as Mr. Le Frank once professionally remarked, a soft falsetto. When the good gentleman paused to make his little effort of memory, his eldest daughter—aged twelve, and always ready to distinguish herself—saw her opportunity, and took the rest of the narrative into her own hands.

Miss Maria, named after her mother, was one of the successful new products of the age we live in—the conventionally-charming child (who has never been smacked); possessed of the large round eyes that we see in pictures, and the sweet manners and perfect principles that we read of in books. She called everybody "dear;" she knew to a nicety how much

---

1   *Mr. Gallilee and his daughters*: Collins biographer Catherine Peters suggests that Collins was painting a picture of himself in Mr. Gallilee, a "lazy, harmless old fellow," and that Maria and Zo are modelled after Collins's own daughters, Maria and Constance Harriet (Peters 400).

oxygen she wanted in the composition of her native air; and—alas, poor wretch!—she had never wetted her shoes or dirtied her face since the day when she was born.

"Dear Miss Minerva," said Maria, "the pastry-cook's name was Timbal. We have had ices."

His mind being now set at rest on the subject of the pastry-cook, Mr. Gallilee turned to his youngest daughter—aged ten, and one of the unsuccessful products of the age we live in. This was a curiously slow, quaint, self-contained child; the image of her father, with an occasional reflection of his smile; incurably stupid, or incurably perverse—the friends of the family were not quite sure which. Whether she might have been over-crammed with useless knowledge, was not a question in connection with the subject which occurred to anybody.

"Rouse yourself, Zo," said Mr. Gallilee. "What did we have besides ices?"

Zoe (known to her father, by vulgar abbreviation, as "Zo") took Mr. Gallilee's stumpy red hand, and held hard by it as if that was the one way in which a dull child could rouse herself, with a prospect of success.

"I've had so many of them," she said; "I don't know. Ask Maria."

Maria responded with the sweetest readiness. "Dear Zoe, you are *so* slow! Cheesecakes."

Mr. Gallilee patted Zoe's head as encouragingly as if she had discovered the right answer by herself. "That's right—ices and cheese-cakes," he said. "We tried cream-ice, and then we tried water-ice. The children, Miss Minerva, preferred the cream-ice. And, do you know, I'm of their opinion. There's something in a cream-ice—what do you think yourself of cream-ices, Mr. Le Frank?"

It was one among the many weaknesses of Mr. Gallilee's character to be incapable of opening his lips without, sooner or later, taking somebody into his confidence. In the merest trifles, he instinctively invited sympathy and agreement from any person within his reach—from a total stranger quite as readily as from an intimate friend. Mr. Le Frank, representing the present Court of Social Appeal, attempted to deliver judgment on the question of ices, and was interrupted without ceremony by Miss Minerva. She, too, had been waiting her opportunity to speak, and she now took it—not amiably.

"With all possible respect, Mr. Gallilee, I venture to entreat that you will be a little more thoughtful, where the children are concerned. I beg your pardon, Mr. Le Frank, for interrupting you—but it is really a little too hard on Me. I am held responsible for the health of these girls; I am blamed over and over again, when it is not my fault, for irregularities in their diet—and there they are, at this moment, chilled with ices and cloyed with cakes! What will Mrs. Gallilee say?"

"Don't tell her," Mr. Gallilee suggested.

"The girls will be thirsty for the rest of the evening," Miss Minerva persisted; "the girls will have no appetite for the last meal before bed-time. And their mother will ask Me what it means."

"My good creature," cried Mr. Gallilee, "don't be afraid of the girls' appetites! Take off their hats, and give them something nice for supper. They inherit my stomach, Miss Minerva—and they'll 'tuck in,' as we used to say at school. Did they say so in your time, Mr. Le Frank?"

Mrs. Gallilee's governess and vulgar expressions were anomalies never to be reconciled, under any circumstances. Miss Minerva took off the hats in stern silence. Even "Papa" might have seen the contempt in her face, if she had not managed to hide it in this way, by means of the girls.

In the silence that ensued, Mr. Le Frank had his chance of speaking, and showed himself to be a gentleman with a happily balanced charac-ter—a musician, with an eye to business. Using gratitude to Mr. Gallilee as a means of persuasion, he gently pushed the interests of a friend who was giving a concert next week. "We poor artists have our faults, my dear sir; but we are all earnest in helping each other. My friend sang for noth-ing at my concert. Don't suppose for a moment that he expects it of me! But I am going to play for nothing at his concert. May I appeal to your kind patronage to take two tickets?" The reply ended appropriately in musical sound—a golden tinkling, in Mr. Le Frank's pocket.

Having paid his tribute to art and artists, Mr. Gallilee looked furtively at Miss Minerva. On the wise principle of letting well alone, he perceived that the happy time had arrived for leaving the room. How was he to make his exit? He prided himself on his readiness of resource, in difficul-ties of this sort, and he was equal to the occasion as usual—he said he would go to his club.

"We really have a capital smoking-room at that club," he said. "I do like a good cigar; and—what do *you* think Mr. Le Frank?—isn't a pint of champagne nice drinking, this hot weather? Just cooled with ice—I don't know whether you feel the weather, Miss Minerva, as I do?—and poured, fizzing, into a silver mug. Lord, how delicious! Good-bye, girls. Give me a kiss before I go."

Maria led the way, as became the elder. She not only gave the kiss, but threw an appropriate sentiment into the bargain. "I do love you, dear papa!" said this perfect daughter—with a look in Miss Minerva's direc-tion, which might have been a malicious look in any eyes but Maria's.

Mr. Gallilee turned to his youngest child. "Well, Zo—what do *you* say?"

Zo took her father's hand once more, and rubbed her head against it like a cat. This new method of expressing filial affection seemed to inter-est Mr. Gallilee. "Does your head itch, my dear?" he asked. The idea was new to Zo. She brightened, and looked at her father with a sly smile. "Why do you do it?" Miss Minerva asked sharply. Zo clouded over again, and answered, "I don't know." Mr. Gallilee rewarded her with a kiss, and went away to champagne and the club.

Mr. Le Frank left the schoolroom next. He paid the governess the compliment of reverting to her narrative of events at the concert.

"I am greatly struck," he said, "by what you told me about Mr. Ovid Vere. We may, perhaps, have misjudged him in thinking that he doesn't like music. His coming to my concert suggests a more cheering view. Do you think there would be any impropriety in my calling to thank him? Perhaps it would be better if I wrote, and enclosed two tickets for my friend's concert? To tell you the truth, I've pledged myself to dispose of a certain number of tickets. My friend is so much in request—it's expecting too much to ask him to sing for nothing. I think I'll write. Good-evening!"

Left alone with her pupils, Miss Minerva looked at her watch. "Prepare your lessons for to-morrow," she said.

The girls produced their books. Maria's library of knowledge was in perfect order. The pages over which Zo pondered in endless perplexity were crumpled by weary fingers, and stained by frequent tears. Oh, fatal knowledge! mercifully forbidden to the first two of our race, who shall count the crimes and stupidities committed in your name?

Miss Minerva leaned back in her easy-chair. Her mind was occupied by the mysterious question of Ovid's presence at the concert. She raised her keenly penetrating eyes to the ceiling, and listened for sounds from above.

"I wonder," she thought to herself, "what they are doing upstairs?"

CHAPTER VI.

Mrs. Gallilee was as complete a mistress of the practice of domestic virtue as of the theory of acoustics and fainting fits. At dressing with taste, and ordering dinners with invention; at heading her table gracefully, and making her guests comfortable; at managing refractory servants and detecting dishonest tradespeople, she was the equal of the least intellectual woman that ever lived. Her preparations for the reception of her niece were finished in advance, without an oversight in the smallest detail. Carmina's inviting bedroom, in blue, opened into Carmina's irresistible sitting-room, in brown. The ventilation was arranged, the light and shade were disposed, the flowers were attractively placed, under Mrs. Gallilee's infallible superintendence. Before Carmina had recovered her senses she was provided with a second mother, who played the part to perfection.

The four persons, now assembled in the pretty sitting-room upstairs, were in a position of insupportable embarrassment towards each other.

Finding her son at a concert (after he had told her that he hated music) Mrs. Gallilee, had first discovered him hurrying to the assistance of a young lady in a swoon, with all the anxiety and alarm which he might have shown in the case of a near and dear friend. And yet, when this stranger was revealed as a relation, he had displayed an amazement equal to her own! What explanation could reconcile such contradictions as these?

As for Carmina, her conduct complicated the mystery.

What was she doing at a concert, when she ought to have been on her way to her aunt's house? Why, if she must faint when the hot room had not overpowered anyone else, had she failed to recover in the usual way? There she lay on the sofa, alternately flushing and turning pale when she was spoken to; ill at ease in the most comfortable house in London; timid and confused under the care of her best friends. Making all allowance for a sensitive temperament, could a long journey from Italy, and a childish fright at seeing a dog run over, account for such a state of things as this?

Annoyed and perplexed—but yet far too prudent to commit herself ignorantly to inquiries which might lead to future embarrassment—Mrs. Gallilee tried suggestive small talk as a means of enlightenment. The wrinkled duenna, sitting miserably on satin supported by frail gilt legs, seemed to take her tone of feeling from her young mistress, exactly as she took her orders. Mrs. Gallilee spoke to her in English, and spoke to her in Italian—and could make nothing of the experiment in either case. The wild old creature seemed to be afraid to look at her.

Ovid himself proved to be just as difficult to fathom, in another way.

He certainly answered when his mother spoke to him, but always briefly, and in the same absent tone. He asked no questions, and offered no explanations. The sense of embarrassment, on his side, had produced unaccountable changes. He showed the needful attention to Carmina, with a silent gentleness which presented him in a new character. His customary manner with ailing persons, women as well as men, was rather abrupt: his quick perception hurried him into taking the words out of their mouths (too pleasantly to give offence) when they were describing their symptoms. There he sat now, contemplating his pale little cousin, with a patient attention wonderful to see; listening to the commonplace words which dropped at intervals from her lips, as if—in his state of health, and with the doubtful prospect which it implied—there were no serious interests to occupy his mind.

Mrs. Gallilee could endure it no longer.

If she had not deliberately starved her imagination, and emptied her heart of any tenderness of feeling which it might once have possessed, her son's odd behaviour would have interested instead of perplexing her. As it was, her scientific education left her as completely in the dark, where questions of sentiment were concerned, as if her experience of humanity, in its relation to love, had been experience in the cannibal islands.[1] She decided on leaving her niece to repose, and on taking her son away with her.

---

1   *cannibal islands*: These were the Caribbean islands of Cuba and Haiti, so named by Christopher Columbus, who claimed to have witnessed man-eating tribes there.

"In your present state of health, Ovid," she began, "Carmina must not accept your professional advice."

Something in those words stung Ovid's temper.

"My professional advice?" he repeated. "You talk as if she was seriously ill!"

Carmina's sweet smile stopped him there.

"We don't know what may happen," she said, playfully.

"God forbid *that* should happen!" He spoke so fervently that the women all looked at him in surprise.

Mrs. Gallilee turned to her niece, and proceeded quietly with what she had to say.

"Ovid is so sadly overworked, my dear, that I actually rejoice in his giving up practice, and going away from us to-morrow. We will leave you for the present with your old friend. Pray ring, if you want anything." She kissed her hand to Carmina, and, beckoning to her son, advanced towards the door.

Teresa looked at her, and suddenly looked away again. Mrs. Gallilee stopped on her way out, at a chiffonier,[1] and altered the arrangement of some of the china on it. The duenna followed on tiptoe—folded her thumb and two middle fingers into the palm of her hand—and, stretching out the forefinger and the little finger, touched Mrs. Gallilee on the back, so softly that she was unaware of it. "The Evil Eye,"[2] Teresa whispered to herself in Italian, as she stole back to her place.

Ovid lingered near his cousin: neither of them had seen what Teresa had done. He rose reluctantly to go. Feeling his little attentions gratefully, Carmina checked him with innocent familiarity as he left his chair. "I must thank you," she said, simply; "it seems hard indeed that you, who cure others, should suffer from illness yourself."

Teresa, watching them with interest, came a little nearer.

She could now examine Ovid's face with close and jealous scrutiny. Mrs. Gallilee reminded her son that she was waiting for him. He had some last words yet to say. The duenna drew back from the sofa, still looking at Ovid: she muttered to herself, "Holy Teresa, my patroness, show me that man's soul in his face!" At last, Ovid took his leave. "I shall call and see how you are to-morrow," he said, "before I go." He nodded kindly to Teresa. Instead of being satisfied with that act of courtesy, she wanted something more. "May I shake hands?" she asked. Mrs. Gallilee was a Liberal in politics; never had her principles been tried, as they were tried when she heard those words. Teresa wrung Ovid's hand with tremulous energy—still intent on reading his character in his face. He asked her, smiling, what she saw to interest her. "A good man, I hope," she

---

1   *chiffonier*: A chiffonier is a narrow chest of drawers or a bureau.
2   *The Evil Eye*: Teresa's beliefs provide humour and help to characterize her as a superstitious old lady of strong will.

answered, sternly. Carmina and Ovid were amused. Teresa rebuked them, as if they had been children. "Laugh at some fitter time," she said, "not now."

Descending the stairs, Mrs. Gallilee and Ovid met the footman. "Mr. Mool is in the library, ma'am," the man said.

"Have you anything to do, Ovid, for the next half-hour?" his mother asked.

"Do you wish me to see Mr. Mool? If it's law-business, I am afraid I shall not be of much use."

"The lawyer is here by appointment, with a copy of your late uncle's Will," Mrs. Gallilee answered. "You may have some interest in it. I think you ought to hear it read."

Ovid showed no inclination to adopt this proposal. He asked an idle question. "I heard of their finding the Will—are there any romantic circumstances?"

Mrs. Gallilee surveyed her son with an expression of good-humoured contempt. "What a boy you are, in some things! Have you been reading a novel lately? My dear, when the people in Italy made up their minds, at last, to have the furniture in your uncle's room taken to pieces, they found the Will. It had slipped behind a drawer, in a rotten old cabinet, full of useless papers. Nothing romantic (thank God!), and nothing (as Mr. Mool's letter tells me) that can lead to misunderstandings or disputes."

Ovid's indifference was not to be conquered. He left it to his mother to send him word if he had a legacy. "I am not as much interested in it as you are," he explained. "Plenty of money left to you, of course?" He was evidently thinking all the time of something else.

Mrs. Gallilee stopped in the hall, with an air of downright alarm.

"Your mind is in a dreadful state," she said.

"Have you really forgotten what I told you, only yesterday? The Will appoints me Carmina's guardian."

He had plainly forgotten it—he started, when his mother recalled the circumstance. "Curious," he said to himself, "that I was not reminded of it, when I saw Carmina's rooms prepared for her." His mother, anxiously looking at him, observed that his face brightened when he spoke of Carmina. He suddenly changed his mind.

"Make allowances for an overworked man," he said. "You are quite right. I ought to hear the Will read—I am at your service."

Even Mrs. Gallilee now drew the right inference at last. She made no remark. Something seemed to move feebly under her powder and paint. Soft emotion trying to find its way to the surface? Impossible!

As they entered the library together, Miss Minerva returned to the schoolroom. She had lingered on the upper landing, and had heard the conversation between mother and son.

End of the August 1882 *Belgravia* Serial Number

CHAPTER VII.

The library at Fairfield Gardens possessed two special attractions, besides the books. It opened into a large conservatory; and it was adorned by an admirable portrait of Mrs. Gallilee, painted by her brother.

Waiting the appearance of the fair original, Mr. Mool looked at the portrait, and then mentally reviewed the history of Mrs. Gallilee's family. What he did next, no person acquainted with the habits of lawyers will be weak enough to believe. Mr. Mool blushed.

Is this the language of exaggeration, describing a human anomaly on the roll of attorneys? The fact shall be left to answer the question. Mr. Mool had made a mistake in his choice of a profession. The result of the mistake was—a shy lawyer.

Attended by such circumstances as these, the history of the family assumes, for the moment, a certain importance. It is connected with a blushing attorney. It will explain what happened on the reading of the Will. And it is sure beforehand of a favourable reception—for it is all about money.

Old Robert Graywell began life as the son of a small farmer. He was generally considered to be rather an eccentric man; but prospered, nevertheless, as a merchant in the city of London. When he retired from business, he possessed a house and estate in the country, and a handsome fortune safely invested in the Funds.[1]

His children were three in number:—his son Robert, and his daughters Maria and Susan.

The death of his wife, to whom he was devotedly attached, was the first serious calamity of his life. He retired to his estate a soured and broken man. Loving husbands are not always, as a necessary consequence, tender fathers. Old Robert's daughters afforded him no consolation on their mother's death. Their anxiety about their mourning dresses so disgusted him that he kept out of their way. No extraordinary interest was connected with their prospects in life: they would be married—and there would be an end of them. As for the son, he had long since placed himself beyond the narrow range of his father's sympathies. In the first place, his refusal to qualify himself for a mercantile career had made it necessary to dispose of the business to strangers. In the second place, young Robert Graywell proved—without any hereditary influence, and in the face of the strongest discouragement—to be a born painter! One of the greatest

---

1   *he possessed ... a handsome fortune safely invested in the Funds*: The government issued securities against the national debt. Investors could purchase the securities, which were referred to as "funds." Paying 3% interest, they were also known as "three-per-centres."

artists of that day saw the boy's first efforts, and pronounced judgment in these plain words: "What a pity he has not got his bread to earn by his brush!"

On the death of old Robert, his daughters found themselves (to use their own expression) reduced to a trumpery legacy of ten thousand pounds each. Their brother inherited the estate, and the bulk of the property—not because his father cared about founding a family, but because the boy had always been his mother's favourite.

The first of the three children to marry was the eldest sister.

Maria considered herself fortunate in captivating Mr. Vere—a man of old family, with a high sense of what he owed to his name. He had a sufficient income, and he wanted no more. His wife's dowry was settled on herself. When he died, he left her a life-interest in his property amounting to six hundred a year.[1] This, added to the annual proceeds of her own little fortune, made an income of one thousand pounds. The remainder of Mr. Vere's property was left to his only surviving child, Ovid.

With a thousand a year for herself, and with two thousand a year for her son, on his coming of age, the widowed Maria might possibly have been satisfied—but for the extraordinary presumption of her younger sister.

Susan, ranking second in age, ranked second also in beauty; and yet, in the race for a husband, Susan won the prize!

Soon after her sister's marriage, she made a conquest of a Scotch nobleman, possessed of a palace in London, and a palace in Scotland, and a rent-roll of forty thousand pounds.[2] Maria, to use her own expression, never recovered it. From the horrid day when Susan became Lady Northlake, Maria became a serious woman. All her earthly interests centred now in the cultivation of her intellect. She started on that glorious career, which associated her with the march of science. In only a year afterwards—as an example of the progress which a resolute woman can make—she was familiar with zoophyte fossils,[3] and had succeeded in dissecting the nervous system of a bee.

Was there no counter-attraction in her married life?

Very little. Mr. Vere felt no sympathy with his wife's scientific pursuits. On her husband's death, did she find no consolation in her son? Let her speak for herself. "My son fills my heart. But the school, the university,

---

1   *When he died ... a life-interest in his property amounting to six hundred a year.* His widow drew six hundred pounds a year generated by the interest on his property for the rest of her life.

2   *Soon after ... rent-roll of forty thousand pounds:* A rent-roll was a landlord's list of properties and rental income. In other words, Lord Northlake received forty thousand pounds annually from his various tenants.

3   *zoophyte fossils:* A zoophyte is an invertebrate animal that attaches itself to a surface and resembles a plants. Collins provides Mrs. Gallilee with scientific interests and a scientific vocabulary to accentuate her heartlessness.

and the hospital have all in turn taken his education out of my hands. My mind must be filled, as well as my heart." She seized her exquisite instruments, and returned to the nervous system of the bee.

In course of time, Mr. John Gallilee—"drifting about," as he said of himself—drifted across the path of science.

The widowed Mrs. Vere (as exhibited in public) was still a fine woman. Mr. Gallilee admired "that style"; and Mr. Gallilee had fifty thousand pounds. Only a little more, to my lord and my lady, than one year's income. But, invested at four percent, it added an annual two thousand pounds to Mrs. Vere's annual one thousand. Result, three thousand a year, encumbered with Mr. Gallilee. On reflection, Mrs. Vere accepted the encumbrance—and reaped her reward. Susan was no longer distinguished as the sister who had her dresses made in Paris; and Mrs. Gallilee was not now subjected to the indignity of getting a lift in Lady Northlake's carriage.

What was the history of Robert, during this interval of time? In two words, Robert disgraced himself.

Taking possession of his country house, the new squire was invited to contribute towards the expense of a pack of hounds kept by subscription[1] in the neighbourhood, and was advised to make acquaintance with his fellow-sportsmen by giving a hunt-breakfast. He answered very politely; but the fact was not to be concealed—the new man refused to encourage hunting: he thought that noble amusement stupid and cruel. For the same reason, he refused to preserve game.[2] A last mistake was left to make, and he made it. After returning the rector's visit,[3] he failed to appear at church. No person with the smallest knowledge of the English character, as exhibited in an English county, will fail to foresee that Robert's residence on his estate was destined to come, sooner or later, to an untimely end. When he had finished his sketches of the picturesque aspects of his landed property, he disappeared. The estate was

---

1   *Taking possession ... a pack of hounds kept by subscription*: Hunting was an expensive and time-consuming proposition, so neighbourhood sportsmen would often collectively subscribe to a pack of hounds, who were then bred, boarded, and trained by local working-class men.

2   *he refused to preserve game*: Young Robert Graywell refused to allow his land to be used to breed and keep animals hunted for sport. It makes sense in this novel that Collins's sympathetic characters would reject any perceived cruelty to animals. Victorian supporters of vivisection argued that anti-vivisectionists should direct their scorn at the cruelties of the sport of hunting and not at the legitimate studies of physiologists. This passage is as close as Collins gets to that aspect of the vivisection debate.

3   *After returning the rector's visit*: The rector was the clergyman in charge of a parish.

not entailed.[1] Old Robert—who had insisted on the minutest formalities and details in providing for his dearly-loved wife—-was impenetrably careless about the future of his children. "My fortune has no value now in my eyes," he said to judicious friends; "let them run through it all, if they please. It would do them a deal of good if they were obliged to earn their own living, like better people than themselves." Left free to take his own way, Robert sold the estate merely to get rid of it. With no expensive tastes, except the taste for buying pictures, he became a richer man than ever.

When their brother next communicated with them, Lady Northlake and Mrs. Gallilee heard of him as a voluntary exile in Italy. He was building a studio and a gallery; he was contemplating a series of pictures; and he was a happy man for the first time in his life.

Another interval passed—and the sisters heard of Robert again.

Having already outraged the sense of propriety among his English neighbours, he now degraded himself in the estimation of his family, by marrying a "model." The letter announcing this event declared, with perfect truth, that he had chosen a virtuous woman for his wife. She sat to artists, as any lady might sit to any artist, "for the head only."[2] Her parents gained a bare subsistence by farming their own little morsel of land; they were honest people—and what did brother Robert care for rank? His own grandfather had been a farmer.

Lady Northlake and Mrs. Gallilee felt it due to themselves to hold a consultation, on the subject of their sister-in-law. Was it desirable, in their own social interests, to cast Robert off from that moment?

Susan (previously advised by her kind-hearted husband) leaned to the side of mercy. Robert's letter informed them that he proposed to live, and die, in Italy. If he held to this resolution, his marriage would surely be an endurable misfortune to his relatives in London. "Suppose we write to him," Susan concluded, "and say we are surprised, but we have no doubt he knows best. We offer our congratulations to Mrs. Robert, and our sincere wishes for his happiness."

To Lady Northlake's astonishment, Mrs. Gallilee adopted this indulgent point of view, without a word of protest. She had her reasons—but they were not producible to a relative whose husband had forty thousand a year. Robert had paid her debts.

An income of three thousand pounds, even in these days, represents a handsome competence—provided you don't "owe a duty to society." In

---

1   *The estate was not entailed*: An entailed estate limited the inheritance of property to a specified succession of heirs. After the death of his wife, Old Robert Graywell lost interest in his fortune and left it un-entailed.

2   *She sat ... "for the head only"*: Young Robert Graywell's Italian wife sat for busts but never modeled in the nude.

Mrs. Gallilee's position, an income of three thousand pounds represented genteel poverty. She was getting into debt again; and she was meditating future designs on her brother's purse. A charming letter to Robert was the result. It ended with, "Do send me a photograph of your lovely wife!" When the poor "model" died, not many years afterwards, leaving one little daughter, Mrs. Gallilee implored her brother to return to England. "Come, dearest Robert, and find consolation and a home, under the roof of your affectionate Maria."

But Robert remained in Italy, and was buried in Italy. At the date of his death, he had three times paid his elder sister's debts. On every occasion when he helped her in this liberal way, she proved her gratitude by anticipating a larger, and a larger, and a larger legacy if she outlived him.

Knowing (as the family lawyer) what sums of money Mrs. Gallilee had extracted from her brother, Mr. Mool also knew that the advances thus made had been considered as representing the legacy, to which she might otherwise have had some sisterly claim. It was his duty to have warned her of this, when she questioned him generally on the subject of the Will; and he had said nothing about it, acting under a most unbecoming motive—in plain words, the motive of fear. From the self-reproachful feeling that now disturbed him, had risen that wonderful blush which made its appearance on Mr. Mool's countenance. He was actually ashamed of himself. After all, is it too much to have suggested that he was a human anomaly on the roll of attorneys?

CHAPTER VIII.

Mrs. Gallilee made her appearance in the library—and Mr. Mool's pulse accelerated its beat. Mrs. Gallilee's son followed her into the room—and Mr. Mool's pulse steadied itself again. By special arrangement with the lawyer, Ovid had been always kept in ignorance of his mother's affairs. No matter how angry she might be in the course of the next few minutes, she could hardly express her indignation in the presence of her son.

Joyous anticipation has the happiest effect on female beauty. Mrs. Gallilee looked remarkably well, that day. Having rather a round and full face, she wore her hair (coloured from youthful nature) in a fringe across her forehead, balanced on either side by clusters of charming little curls. Her mourning for Robert was worthy of its Parisian origin; it showed to perfect advantage the bloom of her complexion and the whiteness of her neck—also worthy of *their* Parisian origin. She looked like a portrait of the period of Charles the Second, endowed with life.[1]

---

1   *Her mourning ... endowed with life:* French, especially Parisian, imports were the
     rage in mid- and late-Victorian England, so it is socially imperative that Mrs.
     Gallilee receive her facial powders, her perfumes, and her clothing from Paris.

"And how do you do, Mr. Mool? Have you been looking at my ferns?" The ferns were grouped at the entrance, leading from the library to the conservatory. They had certainly not escaped the notice of the lawyer, who possessed a hot-house of his own, and who was an enthusiast in botany. It now occurred to him—if he innocently provoked embarrassing results—that ferns might be turned to useful and harmless account as a means of introducing a change of subject. "Even when she hasn't spoken a word," thought Mr. Mool, consulting his recollections, "I have felt her eyes go through me like a knife."

"Spare us the technicalities, please," Mrs. Gallilee continued, pointing to the documents on the table. "I want to be exactly acquainted with the duties I owe to Carmina. And, by the way, I naturally feel some interest in knowing whether Lady Northlake has any place in the Will."

Mrs. Gallilee never said "my sister," never spoke in the family circle of "Susan." The inexhaustible sense of injury, aroused by that magnificent marriage, asserted itself in keeping her sister at the full distance implied by never forgetting her title.

"The first legacy mentioned in the Will," said Mr. Mool, "is a legacy to Lady Northlake." Mrs. Gallilee's face turned as hard as iron. "One hundred pounds," Mr. Mool continued, "to buy a mourning ring."[1] Mrs. Gallilee's eyes became eloquent in an instant, and said as if in words, "Thank Heaven!"

"So like your uncle's unpretending good sense," she remarked to her son. "Any other legacy to Lady Northlake would have been simply absurd. Yes, Mr. Mool? Perhaps my name follows?"

Mr. Mool cast a side-look at the ferns. He afterwards described his sensations as reminding him of previous experience in a dentist's chair, at the awful moment when the operator says "Let me look," and has his devilish instrument hidden in his hand. The "situation," to use the language of the stage, was indeed critical enough already. Ovid added to the horror of it by making a feeble joke. "What will you take for your chance, mother?"

Before bad became worse, Mr. Mool summoned the energy of despair. He wisely read the exact words of the Will, this time: "'And I give and bequeath to my sister, Mrs. Maria Gallilee, one hundred pounds.'"

Ovid's astonishment could only express itself in action. He started to his feet.

Mr. Mool went on reading. "'Free of legacy duty, to buy a mourning ring—'"

By comparing her with a portrait from the age of Charles II (1630-1685), Collins suggests that Mrs. Gallilee has overused the make-up and looks ghoulishly pale.

1   *to buy a mourning ring*: The Victorians took their mourning very seriously and ceremoniously. Any mourning jewellery, the ring in this case, would probably have been fashioned out of jet, a dense black coal that takes on a high polish.

"Impossible!" Ovid broke out.

Mr. Mool finished the sentence. "'And my sister will understand the motive which animates me in making this bequest.'" He laid the Will on the table, and ventured to look up. At the same time, Ovid turned to his mother, struck by the words which had been just read, and eager to inquire what their meaning might be.

Happily for themselves, the two men never knew what the preservation of their tranquillity owed to that one moment of delay.

If they had looked at Mrs. Gallilee, when she was first aware of her position in the Will, they might have seen the incarnate Devil self-revealed in a human face. They might have read, in her eyes and on her lips, a warning hardly less fearful than the unearthly writing on the wall, which told the Eastern Monarch of his coming death.[1] "See this woman, and know what I can do with her, when she has repelled her guardian angel, and her soul is left to ME."

But the revelation showed itself, and vanished. Her face was composed again, when her son and her lawyer looked at it. Her voice was under control; her inbred capacity for deceit was ready for action. All those formidable qualities in her nature, which a gentler and wiser training than hers had been might have held in check—by development of preservative influences that lay inert—were now driven back to their lurking-place; leaving only the faintest traces of their momentary appearance on the surface. Her breathing seemed to be oppressed; her eyelids drooped heavily—and that was all.

"Is the room too hot for you?" Ovid asked.

It was a harmless question, but any question annoyed her at that moment. "Nonsense!" she exclaimed irritably.

"The atmosphere of the conservatory is rich in reviving smells," Mr. Mool remarked. "Do I detect, among the delightful perfumes which reach us, the fragrant root-stock of the American fern? If I am wrong, Mrs. Gallilee, may I send you some of the sweet-smelling Maidenhair[2] from my own little hot-house?" He smiled persuasively. The ferns were already justifying his confidence in their peace-making virtues, turned discreetly to account. Those terrible eyes rested on him mercifully. Not even a covert allusion to his silence in the matter of the legacy escaped her. Did the lawyer's artlessly abrupt attempt to change the subject warn her to be on her guard? In any case, she thanked him with the readiest

---

1   *They might have read ... which told the Eastern Monarch of his coming death*: Belshazzar, king of the Chaldeans, saw the writing on the wall, called for Daniel to interpret it, and learned the following, "Thou art weighed in the balances, and art found wanting" (Daniel, 5:27). Belshazzar was slain that night.

2   *sweet-smelling Maidenhair*: The maidenhair fern is of the genus Adiantum and has light-green feathery fronds.

courtesy for his kind offer. Might she trouble him in the meantime to let her see the Will?

She read attentively the concluding words of the clause in which her name appeared—"My sister will understand the motive which animates me in making this bequest"—and then handed back the Will to Mr. Mool. Before Ovid could ask for it, she was ready with a plausible explanation. "When your uncle became a husband and a father," she said, "those claims on him were paramount. He knew that a token of remembrance (the smaller the better) was all I could accept, if I happened to outlive him. Please go on, Mr. Mool."

In one respect, Ovid resembled his late uncle. They both belonged to that high-minded order of men, who are slow to suspect, and therefore easy to deceive. Ovid tenderly took his mother's hand.

"I ought to have known it," he said, "without obliging you to tell me."

Mrs. Gallilee did *not* blush. Mr. Mool did.

"Go on!" Mrs. Gallilee repeated. Mr. Mool looked at Ovid. "The next name, Mr. Vere, is yours."

"Does my uncle remember me as he has remembered my mother?" asked Ovid.

"Yes, sir—and let me tell you, a very pretty compliment is attached to the bequest. 'It is needless' (your late uncle says) 'to leave any more important proof of remembrance to my nephew. His father has already provided for him; and, with his rare abilities, he will make a second fortune by the exercise of his profession.' Most gratifying, Mrs. Gallilee, is it not? The next clause provides for the good old housekeeper Teresa, and for her husband if he survives her, in the following terms—"

Mrs. Gallilee was becoming impatient to hear more of herself. "We may, I think, pass over that," she suggested, "and get to the part of it which relates to Carmina and me. Don't think I am impatient; I am only desirous—"

The growling of a dog in the conservatory interrupted her. "That tiresome creature!" she said sharply; "I shall be obliged to get rid of him!"

Mr. Mool volunteered to drive the dog out of the conservatory. Mrs. Gallilee, as irritable as ever, stopped him at the door.

"Don't, Mr. Mool! That dog's temper is not to be trusted. He shows it with Miss Minerva, my governess—growls just in that way whenever he sees her. I dare say he smells you. There! Now he barks! You are only making him worse. Come back!"

Being at the door, gentle Mr. Mool tried the ferns as peace-makers once more. He gathered a leaf, and returned to his place in a state of meek admiration. "The flowering fern!" he said softly.

"A really fine specimen, Mrs. Gallilee, of the Osmunda Regalis.[3]

---

3   *Osmunda Regalis*: Mr Mool here refers to the Regal Fern, a fern from the genus Osmunda.

What a world of beauty in this bipinnate frond![1] One hardly knows where the stalk ends and the leaf begins!"

The dog, a bright little terrier, came trotting into the library. He saluted the company briskly with his tail, not excepting Mr. Mool. No growl, or approach to a growl, now escaped him. The manner in which he laid himself down at Mrs. Gallilee's feet completely refuted her aspersion on his temper. Ovid suggested that he might have been provoked by a cat in the conservatory.

Meanwhile, Mr. Mool turned over a page of the Will, and arrived at the clauses relating to Carmina and her guardian.

"It may not be amiss," he began, "to mention, in the first place, that the fortune left to Miss Carmina amounts, in round numbers, to one hundred and thirty thousand pounds. The Trustees—"[2]

"Skip the Trustees," said Mrs. Gallilee.

Mr. Mool skipped.

"In the matter of the guardian," he said, "there is a preliminary clause, in the event of your death or refusal to act, appointing Lady Northlake—"

"Skip Lady Northlake," said Mrs. Gallilee.

Mr. Mool skipped.

"You are appointed Miss Carmina's guardian, until she comes of age," he resumed. "If she marries in that interval—"

He paused to turn over a page. Not only Mrs. Gallilee, but Ovid also, now listened with the deepest interest.

"If she marries in that interval, with her guardian's approval—"

"Suppose I don't approve of her choice?" Mrs. Gallilee interposed.

Ovid looked at his mother—and quickly looked away again. The restless little terrier caught his eye, and jumped up to be patted. Ovid was too pre-occupied to notice this modest advance. The dog's eyes and ears expressed reproachful surprise. His friend Ovid had treated him rudely for the first time in his life.

"If the young lady contracts a matrimonial engagement of which you disapprove," Mr. Mool answered, "you are instructed by the testator to assert your reasons in the presence of—well, I may describe it, as a family council; composed of Mr. Gallilee, and of Lord and Lady Northlake."

---

1   *What a world of beauty in this bipinnate frond!*: He is fawning here over the compound leaves of a fern. Again, the language is Collins's attempt to show that people can only communicate with Mrs. Gallilee in the cold language of science, and that science can reduce even the simple beauty of a fern to something unpleasant.

2   *The Trustees*: The trustees, in whom Mrs. Gallilee has no interest, are the agents, probably of a bank, who hold the estate in escrow to administer to the beneficiary.

"Excessively foolish of Robert," Mrs. Gallilee remarked. "And what, Mr. Mool, is this meddling council of three to do?"

"A majority of the council, Mrs. Gallilee, is to decide the question absolutely. If the decision confirms your view, and if Miss Carmina still persists in her resolution notwithstanding—"

"Am I to give way?" Mrs. Gallilee asked.

"Not until your niece comes of age, ma'am. Then, she decides for herself."

"And inherits the fortune?"

"Only an income from part of it—if her marriage is disapproved by her guardian and her relatives."

"And what becomes of the rest?"

"The whole of it," said Mr. Mool, "will be invested by the Trustees, and will be divided equally, on her death, among her children."

"Suppose she leaves no children?"

"That case is provided for, ma'am, by the last clause. I will only say now, that you are interested in the result."

Mrs. Gallilee turned swiftly and sternly to her son. "When I am dead and gone," she said, "I look to you to defend my memory."

"To defend your memory?" Ovid repeated, wondering what she could possibly mean.

"If I do become interested in the disposal of Robert's fortune—which God forbid!—can't you foresee what will happen?" his mother inquired bitterly. "Lady Northlake will say, 'Maria intrigued for this!' "

Mr. Mool looked doubtfully at the ferns. No! His vegetable allies were not strong enough to check any further outpouring of such family feeling as this. Nothing was to be trusted, in the present emergency, but the superior authority of the Will.

"Pardon me," he said; "there are some further instructions, Mrs. Gallilee, which, as I venture to think, exhibit your late brother's well-known liberality of feeling in a very interesting light. They relate to the provision made for his daughter, while she is residing under your roof. Miss Carmina is to have the services of the best masters, in finishing her education."

"Certainly!" cried Mrs. Gallilee, with the utmost fervour.

"And the use of a carriage to herself, whenever she may require it."

"No, Mr. Mool! *Two* carriages—in such a climate as this. One open, and one closed."

"And to defray these and other expenses, the Trustees are authorized to place at your disposal one thousand a year."

"Too much! too much!"

Mr. Mool might have agreed with her—if he had not known that Robert Graywell had thought of his sister's interests, in making this excessive provision for expenses incurred on his daughter's account.

"Perhaps, her dresses and her pocket money are included?" Mrs. Gallilee resumed.

Mr. Mool smiled, and shook his head. "Mr. Graywell's generosity has no limits," he said, "where his daughter is concerned. Miss Carmina is to have five hundred a year for pocket-money and dresses."

Mrs. Gallilee appealed to the sympathies of her son. "Isn't it touching?" she said. "Dear Carmina! my own people in Paris shall make her dresses. Well, Mr. Mool?"

"Allow me to read the exact language of the Will next," Mr. Mool answered. "'If her sweet disposition leads her into exceeding her allowance, in the pursuit of her own little charities, my Trustees are hereby authorized, at their own discretion, to increase the amount, within the limit of another five hundred pounds annually.' It sounds presumptuous, perhaps, on my part," said Mr. Mool, venturing on a modest confession of enthusiasm, "but one can't help thinking, What a good father! what a good child!"

Mrs. Gallilee had another appropriate remark ready on her lips, when the unlucky dog interrupted her once more. He made a sudden rush into the conservatory, barking with all his might. A crashing noise followed the dog's outbreak, which sounded like the fall of a flower-pot.

Ovid hurried into the conservatory—with the dog ahead of him, tearing down the steps which led into the back garden.

The pot lay broken on the tiled floor. Struck by the beauty of the flower that grew in it, he stooped to set it up again. If, instead of doing this, he had advanced at once to the second door, he would have seen a lady hastening into the house; and, though her back view only was presented, he could hardly have failed to recognize Miss Minerva. As it was, when he reached the door, the garden was empty.

He looked up at the house, and saw Carmina at the open window of her bedroom.

The sad expression on that sweet young face grieved him. Was she thinking of her happy past life? or of the doubtful future, among strangers in a strange country? She noticed Ovid—and her eyes brightened. His customary coldness with women melted instantly: he kissed his hand to her. She returned the salute (so familiar to her in Italy) with her gentle smile, and looked back into the room. Teresa showed herself at the window. Always following her impulses without troubling herself to think first, the duenna followed them now. "We are dull up here," she called out. "Come back to us, Mr. Ovid." The words had hardly been spoken before they both turned from the window. Teresa pointed significantly into the room. They disappeared.

Ovid went back to the library.

"Anybody listening?" Mr. Mool inquired.

"I have not discovered anybody, but I doubt if a stray cat could have upset that heavy flower-pot." He looked round him as he made the reply. "Where is my mother?" he asked.

Mrs. Gallilee had gone upstairs, eager to tell Carmina of the handsome allowance made to her by her father. Having answered in these terms, Mr. Mool began to fold up the Will—and suddenly stopped.

"Very inconsiderate, on my part," he said; "I forgot, Mr. Ovid, that you haven't heard the end of it. Let me give you a brief abstract. You know, perhaps, that Miss Carmina is a Catholic? Very natural—her poor mother's religion. Well, sir, her good father forgets nothing. All attempts at prose-lytizing are strictly forbidden."

Ovid smiled. His mother's religious convictions began and ended with the inorganic matter of the earth.

"The last clause," Mr. Mool proceeded, "seemed to agitate Mrs. Gallilee quite painfully. I reminded her that her brother had no near relations living, but Lady Northlake and herself. As to leaving money to my lady, in my lord's princely position—"

"Pardon me," Ovid interposed, "what is there to agitate my mother in this?"

Mr. Mool made his apologies for not getting sooner to the point, with the readiest good-will. "Professional habit, Mr. Ovid," he explained. "We are apt to be wordy—paid, in fact, at so much a folio, for so many words!—and we like to clear the ground first. Your late uncle ends his Will, by providing for the disposal of his fortune, in two possible events, as follows: Miss Carmina may die unmarried, or Miss Carmina (being married) may die without offspring."

Seeing the importance of the last clause now, Ovid stopped him again. "Do I remember the amount of the fortune correctly?" he asked. "Was it a hundred and thirty thousand pounds?"

"Yes."

"And what becomes of all that money, if Carmina never marries, or if she leaves no children?"

"In either of those cases, sir, the whole of the money goes to Mrs. Gallilee and her daughters."[1]

CHAPTER IX.

Time had advanced to midnight, after the reading of the Will—and Ovid was at home.

---

1   *In either of those cases ... Mrs. Gallilee and her daughters*: It may strike the reader that the conditions of the Will—especially those that make Mrs. Gallilee wealthy if her niece dies unmarried or without issue—are rather strained, that they exist only to turn the rather squeaky gears of this part of the novel's plot. Collins, himself, must have realized the heavy-handedness of the conditions, for he goes to some length to explain Graywell's motives much later in his novel.

The silence of the quiet street in which he lived was only disturbed by the occasional rolling of carriage wheels, and by dance-music from the house of one of his neighbours who was giving a ball. He sat at his writing-table, thinking. Honest self-examination had laid out the state of his mind before him like a map, and had shown him, in its true proportions, the new interest that filled his life.

Of that interest he was now the willing slave. If he had not known his mother to be with her, he would have gone back to Carmina when the lawyer left the house. As it was, he had sent a message upstairs, inviting himself to dinner, solely for the purpose of seeing Carmina again—and he had been bitterly disappointed when he heard that Mr. and Mrs. Gallilee were engaged, and that his cousin would take tea in her room. He had eaten something at this club, without caring what it was. He had gone to the Opera afterwards, merely because his recollections of a favourite singing-lady of that season vaguely reminded him of Carmina. And there he was, at midnight, on his return from the music, eager for the next opportunity of seeing his cousin, a few hours hence—when he had arranged to say good-bye at the family breakfast-table.

To feel this change in him as vividly as he felt it, could lead to but one conclusion in the mind of a man who was incapable of purposely deceiving himself. He was as certain as ever of the importance of rest and change, in the broken state of his health. And yet, in the face of that conviction, his contemplated sea-voyage had already become one of the vanished illusions of his life!

His friend had arranged to travel with him, that morning, from London to the port at which the yacht was waiting for them. They were hardly intimate enough to trust each other unreservedly with secrets. The customary apology for breaking an engagement was the alternative that remained. With the paper on his desk and with the words on his mind, he was yet in such a strange state of indecision that he hesitated to write the letter!

His morbidly-sensitive nerves were sadly shaken. Even the familiar record of the half-hour by the hall clock startled him. The stroke of the bell was succeeded by a mild and mournful sound outside the door—the mewing of a cat.

He rose, without any appearance of surprise, and opened the door.

With grace and dignity entered a small black female cat; exhibiting, by way of variety of colour, a melancholy triangular patch of white over the lower part of her face, and four brilliantly clean white paws. Ovid went back to his desk. As soon as he was in his chair again, the cat jumped on his shoulder, and sat there purring in his ear. This was the place she occupied, whenever her master was writing alone. Passing one day through a suburban neighbourhood, on his round of visits, the young surgeon had been attracted by a crowd in a by-street. He had rescued his present companion from starvation in a locked-up house, the barbarous inhabitants of which had gone away for a holiday, and had forgotten the cat. When Ovid took the poor creature home with him in his carriage, popular feeling decided that the unknown gentleman was "a rum 'un." From that moment, this fortunate little member of a brutally-slandered race attached herself to her new friend, and to that friend only. If Ovid had owned the truth, he must have acknowledged that her company was a relief to him, in the present state of his mind.

When a man's flagging purpose is in want of a stimulant, the most trifling change in the circumstances of the moment often applies the animating influence. Even such a small interruption as the appearance of his cat rendered this service to Ovid. To use the common and expressive phrase, it had "shaken him up." He wrote the letter—and his patient companion killed the time by washing her face.

His mind being so far relieved, he went to bed—the cat following him upstairs to *her* bed in a corner of the room. Clothes are unwholesome superfluities not contemplated in the system of Nature. When we are exhausted, there is no such thing as true repose for us until we are freed from our dress. Men subjected to any excessive exertion—fighting, rowing, walking, working—must strip their bodies as completely as possible, or they are not equal to the call on them. Ovid's knowledge of his own temperament told him that sleep was not to be hoped for, that night. But the way to bed was the way to rest notwithstanding, by getting rid of his clothes.

With the sunrise he rose and went out.

He took his letter with him, and dropped it into the box in his friend's door. The sooner he committed himself to the new course that he had taken, the more certain he might feel of not renewing the miserable and useless indecision of the past night. "Thank God, that's done!" he said to himself, as he heard the letter fall into the box, and left the house.

After walking in the Park until he was weary, he sat down by the ornamental lake, and watched the waterfowl enjoying their happy lives.

Wherever he went, whatever he did, Carmina was always with him. He had seen thousands of girls, whose personal attractions were far more remarkable—and some few among them whose manner was perhaps equally winning. What was the charm in the little half-foreign cousin that had seized on him in an instant, and that seemed to fasten its subtle hold more and more irresistibly with every minute of his life? He was content to feel the charm without caring to fathom it. The lovely morning light took him in imagination to her bedside; he saw here sleeping peacefully in her new room. Would the time come when she might dream of him? He looked at his watch. It was seven o'clock. The breakfast-hour at Fairfield Gardens had been fixed for eight, to give him time to catch the morning train. Half an hour might be occupied in walking back to his own house. Add ten minutes to make some change in his dress—and he might set forth for his next meeting with Carmina. No uneasy anticipation of what the family circle might think of his sudden change of plan troubled his mind. A very different question occupied him. For the first time in his life, he wondered what dress a woman would wear at break-fast time.

He opened his house door with his own key. An elderly person, in a coarse black gown, was seated on the bench in the hall. She rose, and advanced towards him. In speechless astonishment, he confronted Carmina's faithful companion—Teresa.

"If you please, I want to speak to you," she said, in her best English.

Ovid took her into his consulting-room. She wasted no time in apologies or explanations. "Don't speak!" she broke out. "Carmina has had a bad night."

"I shall be at the house in half an hour!" Ovid eagerly assured her.

The duenna shook her forefinger impatiently. "She doesn't want a doctor. She wants a friend, when I am gone. What is her life here? A new life, among new people. Don't speak! She's frightened and miserable. So young, so shy, so easily startled. And I must leave her—I must! I must! My old man is failing fast; he may die, without a creature to comfort him, if I don't go back. I could tear my hair when I think of it. Don't speak! It's *my* business to speak. Ha! I know, what I know. Young doctor, you're in love with Carmina! I've read you like a book. You're quick to see, sudden to feel—like one of my people. *Be* one of my people. Help me."

She dragged a chair close to Ovid, and laid her hand suddenly and heavily on his arm.

"It's not my fault, mind; *I* have said nothing to disturb her. No! I've made the best of it. I've lied to her. What do I care? I would lie like Judas Iscariot[1] himself to spare Carmina a moment's pain. It's such a new life for her—try to see it for yourself—such a new life. You and I shook hands yesterday. Do it again. Are you surprised to see me? I asked your mother's servants where you lived; and here I am—with the cruel teeth of anxiety gnawing me alive when I think of the time to come. Oh, my lamb! my angel! she's alone. Oh, my God, only seventeen years old, and alone in the world! No father, no mother; and soon—oh, too soon, too soon—not even Teresa! What are you looking at? What is there so wonderful in the tears of a stupid old fool? Drops of hot water. Ha! ha! if they fall on your fine carpet here, they won't hurt it. You're a good fellow; you're a dear fellow. Hush! I know the Evil Eye when I see it. No more of that! A secret in your ear—I've said a word for you to Carmina already. Give her time; she's not cold; young and innocent, that's all. Love will come—I know, what I know—love will come."

She laughed—and, in the very act of laughing, changed again. Fright looked wildly at Ovid out of her staring eyes. Some terrifying remembrance had suddenly occurred to her. She sprang to her feet.

"You said you were going away," she cried. "You said it, when you left

---

1   *Judas Iscariot:* Judas was one of the twelve Apostles and the betrayer of Christ (Matthew 26: 47-50; Mark 14: 42-6; Luke 22: 47-8).

us yesterday. It can't be! it shan't be! *You're* not going to leave Carmina, too?"

Ovid's first impulse was to tell the whole truth. He resisted the impulse. To own that Carmina was the cause of his abandonment of the sea-voyage, before she was even sure of the impression she had produced on him, would be to place himself in a position from which his self-respect recoiled. "My plans are changed," was all he said to Teresa. "Make your mind easy; I'm not going away."

The strange old creature snapped her fingers joyously. "Good-bye! I want no more of you." With those cool and candid words of farewell, she advanced to the door—stopped suddenly to think—and came back. Only a moment had passed, and she was as sternly in earnest again as ever.

"May I call you by your name?" she asked.

"Certainly!"

"Listen, Ovid! I may not see you again before I go back to my husband. This is my last word—never forget it. Even Carmina may have enemies!"

What could she be thinking of? "Enemies—in my mother's house!" Ovid exclaimed. "What can you possibly mean?"

Teresa returned to the door, and only answered him when she had opened it to go.

"The Evil Eye never lies," she said. "Wait—and you will see."

CHAPTER X.

Mrs. Gallilee was on her way to the breakfast-room, when her son entered the house. They met in the hall. "Is your packing done?" she asked.

He was in no humour to wait, and make his confession at that moment. "Not yet," was his only reply.

Mrs. Gallilee led the way into the room. "Ovid's luggage is not ready yet," she announced; "I believe he will lose his train."

They were all at the breakfast table, the children and the governess included. Carmina's worn face, telling its tale of a wakeful night, brightened again, as it had brightened at the bedroom window, when she saw Ovid. She took his hand frankly, and made light of her weary looks. "No, my cousin," she said, playfully; "I mean to be worthier of my pretty bed to-night; I am not going to be your patient yet." Mr. Gallilee (with this mouth full at the moment) offered good advice. "Eat and drink as I do, my dear," he said to Carmina; "and you will sleep as I do. Off I go when the light's out—flat on my back, as Mrs. Gallilee will tell you—and wake me if you can, till it's time to get up. Have some buttered eggs, Ovid. They're good, ain't they, Zo?" Zo looked up from her plate, and agreed with her father, in one emphatic word, "Jolly!" Miss Minerva, queen of governesses, instantly did her duty. "Zoe! how often must I tell you not to talk slang? Do you ever hear your sister say 'Jolly?'" That highly-cultivated child, Maria, strong in conscious virtue, added her authority in support of the protest. "No young lady who respects herself, Zoe, will ever talk slang." Mr. Gallilee was unworthy of such a daughter. He muttered under his breath, "Oh, bother!" Zo held out her plate for more. Mr. Gallilee was delighted. "My child all over!" he exclaimed. "We are both of us good feeders. Zo will grow up a fine woman." He appealed to his stepson to agree with him. "That's your medical opinion, Ovid, isn't it?"

Carmina's pretty smile passed like rippling light over her eyes and her lips. In her brief experience of England, Mr. Gallilee was the one exhilarating element in family life.

Mrs. Gallilee's mind still dwelt on her son's luggage, and on the rigorous punctuality of railway arrangements.

"What is your servant about?" she said to Ovid. "It's his business to see that you are ready in time."

It was useless to allow the false impression that prevailed to continue any longer. Ovid set them all right, in the plainest and fewest words.

"My servant is not to blame, " he said. "I have written an apology to my friend—I am not going away."

For the moment, this astounding announcement was received in silent dismay—excepting the youngest member of the company. After her father, Ovid was the one other person in the world who held a place in Zo's odd little heart. *Her* sentiments were now expressed without hesitation and without reserve. She put down her spoon, and she cried, "Hooray!" Another exhibition of vulgarity. But even Miss Minerva was too completely preoccupied by the revelation which had burst on the family to administer the necessary reproof. Her eager eyes were riveted on Ovid. As for Mr. Gallilee, he held his bread and butter suspended in mid-air, and stared open-mouthed at his stepson, in helpless consternation.

Mrs. Gallilee always set the right example. Mrs. Gallilee was the first to demand and explanation.

"What does this extraordinary proceeding mean?" she asked.

Ovid was impenetrable to the tone in which that question was put. He had looked at his cousin, when he declared his change of plan—and he was looking at her still. Whatever the feeling of the moment might be, Carmina's sensitive face expressed it vividly. Who could mistake the faintly-rising colour in her cheeks, the sweet quickening of light in her eyes, when she met Ovid's look? Still hardly capable of estimating the influence that she exercised over him, her sense of the interest taken in her by Ovid was the proud sense that makes girls innocently bold. Whatever the others might think of his broken engagement, her artless eyes said plainly, "My feeling is happy surprise."

Mrs. Gallilee summoned her son to attend her, in no friendly voice. She, too, had looked at Carmina—and had registered the result of her observation privately.

"Are we to hear your reasons?" she inquired.

Ovid had made the one discovery in the world, on which his whole heart was set. He was so happy, that he kept his mother out of his secret, with a masterly composure worthy of herself.

"I don't think a sea-voyage is the right thing for me," he answered.

"Rather a sudden change of opinion," Mrs. Gallilee remarked.

Ovid coolly agreed with her. It *was* rather sudden, he said.

The governess still looked at him, wondering whether he would provoke an outbreak.

After a little pause, Mrs. Gallilee accepted her son's short answer—with a sudden submission which had a meaning of its own. She offered Ovid another cup of tea; and, more remarkable yet, she turned to her eldest daughter, and deliberately changed the subject. "What are your lessons, my dear, to-day?" she asked, with bland maternal interest.

By this time, bewildered Mr. Gallilee had finished his bread and butter. "Ovid knows best, my dear," he said cheerfully to his wife. Mrs. Gallilee's sudden recovery of her temper did not include her husband. If a look could have annihilated that worthy man, his corporal presence must have vanished into air, when he had delivered himself of his opinion. As it was, he only helped Zo to another spoonful of jam. "When Ovid first thought of that voyage," he went on, "I said, Suppose he's sick? A dreadful sensation isn't it, Miss Minerva? First you seem to sink into your shoes, and then it all comes up—eh? You're *not* sick at sea? I congratulate you! I most sincerely congratulate you! My dear Ovid, come and dine with me to-night at the club." He looked doubtfully at his wife, as he made that proposal. "Got the headache, my dear? I'll take you out with pleasure for a walk. What's the matter with her, Miss Minerva? Oh, I see! Hush! Maria's going to say grace.—Amen! Amen!"

They all rose from the table.

Mr. Gallilee was the first to open the door. The smoking-room at Fairfield Gardens was over the kitchen; he preferred enjoying his cigar in the garden of the Square. He looked at Carmina and Ovid, as if he wanted one of them to accompany him. They were both at the aviary, admiring the birds, and absorbed in their own talk. Mr. Gallilee resigned himself to his fate; appealing, on his way out, to somebody to agree with him as usual. "Well!" he said with a little sigh, "a cigar keeps one company." Miss Minerva (absorbed in her own thoughts) passed near him, on her way to the school-room with her pupils. "You would find it so yourself, Miss Minerva—that is to say, if you smoked, which of course you don't. Be a good girl, Zo; attend to your lessons."

Zo's perversity in the matter of lessons put its own crooked construction on this excellent advice. She answered in a whisper, "Give us a holiday."

The passing aspirations of idle minds, being subject to the law of chances, are sometimes fulfilled, and so exhibit poor human wishes in a consolatory light. Thanks to the conversation between Carmina and Ovid, Zo got her holiday after all.

Mrs. Gallilee, still as amiable as ever, had joined her son and her niece at the aviary. Ovid said to his mother, "Carmina is fond of birds. I have been telling her she may see all the races of birds assembled in the Zoological Gardens.[1] It's a perfect day. Why shouldn't we go!"

The stupidest woman living would have understood what this proposal really meant. Mrs. Gallilee sanctioned it as composedly as if Ovid and Carmina had been brother and sister. "I wish I could go with you," she said, "but my household affairs fill my morning. And there is a lecture this afternoon, which I cannot possibly lose. I don't know, Carmina, whether you are interested in these things. We are to have the apparatus, which illustrates the conversion of radiant energy into sonorous vibrations. Have you ever heard, my dear, of the Diathermancy of Ebonite?[2] Not in your way, perhaps?"

Carmina looked as unintelligent as Zo herself. Mrs. Gallilee's science seemed to frighten her. The Diathermancy of Ebonite, by some incomprehensible process, drove her bewildered mind back on her old companion. "I want to give Teresa a little pleasure before we part," she said timidly; "may she go with us?"

"Of course!" cried Mrs. Gallilee. "And, now I think of it, why shouldn't the children have a little pleasure too? I will give them a holiday. Don't be alarmed, Ovid; Miss Minerva will look after them. In the meantime, Carmina, tell your good old friend to get ready."

Carmina hastened away, and so helped Mrs. Gallilee to the immediate object which she had in view—a private interview with her son.

Ovid anticipated a searching inquiry into the motives which had led him to give up the sea voyage. His mother was far too clever a woman to waste her time in that way. Her first words told him that his motive was as plainly revealed to her as the sunlight shining in at the window.

"That's a charming girl," she said, when Carmina closed the door behind her. "Modest and natural—quite the sort of girl, Ovid, to attract a clever man like you."

Ovid was completely taken by surprise, and owned it by his silence. Mrs. Gallilee went on in a tone of innocent maternal pleasantry.

"You know you began young," she said; "your first love was that poor little wizen girl of Lady Northlake's who died. Child's play, you will tell me, and nothing more. But, my dear, I am afraid I shall require some persuasion, before I quite sympathize with this new—what shall I call it?— infatuation is too hard a word, and 'fancy' means nothing. We will leave it a blank. Marriages of cousins are debatable marriages, to say the least of

---

1   *Zoological Gardens*: The London Zoo, located in Regent's Park, opened in 1828 and remains one of the premier zoos in the world.

2   *We are to have the apparatus ... Diathermancy of Ebonite?*: Collins has taken the language here directly from *The Times* article that he mentions in the novel's preface. (See Note 15 and Appendix F.)

them; and Protestant fathers and Papist mothers[1] do occasionally involve difficulties with children. Not that I say, No. Far from it. But if this is to go on, I do hesitate."

Something in his mother's tone grated on Ovid's sensibilities. "I don't at all follow you," he said, rather sharply; "you are looking a little too far into the future."

"Then we will return to the present," Mrs. Gallilee replied—still with the readiest submission to the humour of her son.

On recent occasions, she had expressed the opinion that Ovid would do wisely—at his age, and with his professional prospects—to wait a few years before he thought of marrying. Having said enough in praise of her niece to satisfy him for the time being (without appearing to be meanly influenced, in modifying her opinion, by the question of money), her next object was to induce him to leave England immediately, for the recovery of his health. With Ovid absent, and with Carmina under her sole super-intendence, Mrs. Gallilee could see her way to her own private ends.

"Really," she resumed, "you ought to think seriously of change of air and scene. You know you would not allow a patient, in your present state of health, to trifle with himself as your are trifling now. If you don't like the sea, try the Continent. Get away somewhere, my dear, for your own sake."

It was only possible to answer this, in one way. Ovid owned that his mother was right and asked for time to think. To his infinite relief, he was interrupted by a knock at the door. Miss Minerva entered the room—not in a very amiable temper, judging by appearances.

"I am afraid I disturb you," she began.

Ovid seized the opportunity of retreat. He had some letters to write—he hurried away to the library.

"Is there any mistake?" the governess asked, when she and Mrs. Gallilee were alone.

"In what respect, Miss Minerva?"

"I met your niece, ma'am, on the stairs. She says you wish the children to have a holiday."

"Yes, to go with my son and Miss Carmina to the Zoological Gardens."

"Miss Carmina said I was to go too."

"Miss Carmina was perfectly right."

The governess fixed her searching eyes on Mrs. Gallilee. "You really wish me to go with them?" she said.

"I do."

---

1   *Protestant fathers and Papist mothers*: Collins painted Jesuits as villains in *The Black Robe*, the novel published the year before *Heart and Science*, and Collins biographer Catherine Peters claims that he purposely makes Carmina Catholic and half-Italian "to counteract accusations of anti-Catholic bias, raised after *The Black Robe*" (Peters 400).

"I know why."

In the course of their experience, Mrs. Gallilee and Miss Minerva had once quarrelled fiercely—and Mrs. Gallilee had got the worst of it. She learnt her lesson. For the future she knew how to deal with her governess. When one said, "I know why," the other only answered, "Do you?"

"Let's have it out plainly, ma'am," Miss Minerva proceeded. "I am not to let Mr. Ovid" (she laid a bitterly strong emphasis on the name, and flushed angrily)—"I am not to let Mr. Ovid and Miss Carmina be alone together."

"You are a good guesser," Mrs. Gallilee remarked quietly.

"No," said Miss Minerva more quietly still; "I have only seen what you have seen."

"Did I tell you what I have seen?"

"Quite needless, ma'am. Your son is in love with his cousin. When am I to be ready?"

The bland mistress mentioned the hour. The rude governess left the room.

Mrs. Gallilee looked at the closing door with a curious smile. She had already suspected Miss Minerva of being crossed in love. The suspicion was now confirmed, and the man was discovered.

"Soured by a hopeless passion," she said to herself. "And the object is—my son."

End of the September 1882 *Belgravia* Serial Number

CHAPTER XI.

On entering the Zoological Gardens, Ovid turned at once to the right, leading Carmina to the aviaries, so that she might begin by seeing the birds. Miss Minerva, with Maria in dutiful attendance, followed them. Teresa kept at a little distance behind; and Zo took her own erratic course, now attaching herself to one member of the little party, and now to another.

When they reached the aviaries the order of march became confused; differences in the birds made their appeal to differences in the taste of the visitors. Insatiably eager for useful information, that prize-pupil Maria held her governess captive at one cage; while Zo darted away towards another, out of reach of discipline, and good Teresa volunteered to bring her back. For a minute, Ovid and his cousin were left alone. He might have taken a lover's advantage even of that small opportunity. But Carmina had something to say to him—and Carmina spoke first.

"Has Miss Minerva been your mother's governess for a long time?" she inquired.

"For some years," Ovid replied. "Will you let me put a question on my side? Why do you ask?"

Carmina hesitated—and answered in a whisper, "She looks ill-tempered."

"She is ill-tempered," Ovid confessed. "I suspect," he added with a smile, "you don't like Miss Minerva."

Carmina attempted no denial; her excuse was a woman's excuse all over: "She doesn't like *me*."

"How do you know?"

"I have been looking at her. Does she beat the children?"

"My dear Carmina! do you think she would be my mother's governess if she treated the children in that way? Besides, Miss Minerva is too well-bred a woman to degrade herself by acts of violence. Family misfortunes have very materially lowered her position in the world."

He was reminded, as he said those words, of the time when Miss Minerva had entered on her present employment, and when she had been the object of some little curiosity on his own part. Mrs. Gallilee's answer, when he once asked why she kept such an irritable woman in the house, had been entirely satisfactory, so far as she herself was concerned: "Miss Minerva is remarkably well informed, and I get her cheap." Exactly like his mother! But it left Miss Minerva's motives involved in utter obscurity. Why had this highly cultivated woman accepted an inadequate reward for her services, for years together? Why—to take the event of that morning as another example—after plainly showing her temper to her employer, had she been so ready to submit to a suddenly decreed holiday, which disarranged her whole course of lessons for the week? Little did Ovid think that the one reconciling influence which adjusted these contradictions, and set at rest every doubt that grew out of them, was to be found in himself. Even the humiliation of watching him in his mother's interest, and of witnessing his devotion to another woman, was a sacrifice which Miss Minerva could endure for the one inestimable privilege of being in Ovid's company.

Before Carmina could ask any more questions a shrill voice, at its high- est pitch of excitement, called her away. Zo had just discovered the most amusing bird in the Gardens—the low comedian of the feathered race— otherwise known as the Piping Crow.[1]

Carmina hurried to the cage as if she had been a child herself. Seeing Ovid left alone, the governess seized *her* chance of speaking to him. The first words that passed her lips told their own story. While Carmina had been studying Miss Minerva, Miss Minerva had been studying Carmina. Already, the same instinctive sense of rivalry had associated, on a common ground of feeling, the two most dissimilar women that ever breathed the breath of life.

"Does your cousin know much about birds?" Miss Minerva began.

The opinion which declares that vanity is a failing peculiar to the sex

---

1   *Piping Crow*: The Piping Crow is a common crow.

is a slander on women. All the world over, there are more vain men in it than vain women. If Ovid had not been one of the exceptions to a general rule among men, or even if his experience of the natures of women had been a little less limited, he too might have discovered Miss Minerva's secret. Even her capacity for self-control failed, at the moment when she took Carmina's place. Those keen black eyes, so hard and cold when they looked at anyone else—flamed with an all-devouring sense of possession when they first rested on Ovid. "He's mine. For one golden moment he's mine!" They spoke—and, suddenly, the every-day blind was drawn down again; there was nobody present but a well-bred woman, talking with delicately implied deference to a distinguished man.

"So far, we have not spoken of the birds," Ovid innocently answered.

"And yet you seemed to be both looking at them!" She at once covered this unwary outbreak of jealousy under an impervious surface of compliment. "Miss Carmina is not perhaps exactly pretty, but she is a singularly interesting girl."

Ovid cordially (too cordially) agreed. Miss Minerva had presented her better self to him under a most agreeable aspect. She tried—struggled—fought with herself—to preserve appearances. The demon in her got possession again of her tongue. "Do you find the young lady intelligent?" she inquired.

"Certainly!"

Only one word—spoken perhaps a little sharply. The miserable woman shrank under it. "An idle question on my part," she said, with the pathetic humility that tries to be cheerful. "And another warning, Mr. Vere, never to judge by appearances." She looked at him, and returned to the children.

Ovid's eyes followed her compassionately. "Poor wretch!" he thought. "What an infernal temper, and how hard she tries to control it!" He joined Carmina, with a new delight in being near her again. Zo was still in ecstasies over the Piping Crow. "Oh, the jolly little chap! Look how he cocks his head! He mocks me when I whistle. Buy him," cried Zo, tugging at Ovid's coat tails in the excitement that possessed her; "buy him, and let me take him home with me!"

Some visitors within hearing began to laugh. Miss Minerva opened her lips; Maria opened her lips. To the astonishment of both of them the coming rebuke proved to be needless.

A sudden transformation to silence and docility had made a new creature of Zo, before they could speak—and Ovid had unconsciously worked the miracle. For the first time in the child's experience, he had suffered his coat tails to be pulled without immediately attending to her. Who was he looking at? It was only too easy to see that Carmina had got him all to herself. The jealous little heart swelled in Zo's bosom. In silent perplexity she kept watch on the friend who had never disappointed her before. Little by little, her slow intelligence began to realise the discovery of something in his face which made him look handsomer than ever, and which she had never seen in it yet. They all left the aviaries, and turned to the railed paddocks in which the larger birds were assembled. And still Zo followed so quietly, so silently, that her elder sister—threatened with a rival in good behaviour—looked at her in undisguised alarm.

Incited by Maria (who felt the necessity of vindicating her character) Miss Minerva began a dissertation on cranes, suggested by the birds with the brittle-looking legs hopping up to her in expectation of something to eat. Ovid was absorbed in attending to his cousin; he had provided himself with some bread, and was helping Carmina to feed the birds. But one person noticed Zo, now that her strange lapse into good behaviour had lost the charm of novelty. Old Teresa watched her. There was something plainly troubling the child in secret; she had a mind to know what it might be.

Zo approached Ovid again, determined to understand the change in him if perseverance could do it. He was talking so confidentially to Carmina, that he almost whispered in her ear. Zo eyed him, without daring to touch his coat tails again. Miss Minerva tried hard to go on composedly with the dissertation on cranes. "Flocks of these birds, Maria, pass periodically over the southern and central countries of Europe"— Her breath failed her, as she looked at Ovid: she could say no more. Zo stopped those maddening confidences; Zo, in desperate want of information, tugged boldly at Carmina's skirts this time.

The young girl turned round directly. "What is it, dear?"

With big tears of indignation rising in her eyes, Zo pointed to Ovid. "I say!" she whispered, "is he going to buy the Piping Crow for *you?*"

To Zo's discomfiture they both smiled. She dried her eyes with her fists, and waited doggedly for an answer. Carmina set the child's mind at ease very prettily and kindly; and Ovid added the pacifying influence of a familiar pat on her cheek. Noticed at last, and satisfied that the bird was not to be bought for anybody, Zo's sense of injury was appeased; her jealousy melted away as the next result. After a pause—produced, as her next words implied, by an effort of memory—she suddenly took Carmina into her confidence.

"Don't tell!" she began. "I saw another man look like Ovid."

"When, dear?" Carmina asked—meaning, at what past date.

"When his face was close to yours," Zo answered—meaning, under what recent circumstances.

Ovid, hearing this reply, knew his small sister well enough to foresee embarrassing results if he allowed the conversation to proceed. He took Carmina's arm, and led her a little farther on.

Miss Minerva obstinately followed them, with Maria in attendance, still imperfectly enlightened on the migration of cranes. Zo looked round, in search of another audience. Teresa had been listening; she was present, waiting for events. Being herself what stupid people call "an oddity," her sympathies were attracted by this quaint child. In Teresa's opinion, seeing the animals was very inferior, as an amusement, to exploring Zo's mind. She produced a cake of chocolate, from a travelling bag which she carried with her everywhere. The cake was sweet, it was flavoured with vanilla, and it was offered to Zo, unembittered by advice not to be greedy and make herself ill. Staring hard at Teresa, she took an experimental bite. The wily duenna chose that propitious moment to present herself in the capacity of a new audience.

"Who was that other man you saw, who looked like Mr. Ovid?" she asked; speaking in the tone of serious equality which is always flattering to the self-esteem of children in intercourse with elders. Zo was so proud of having her own talk reported by a grown-up stranger, that she even forgot the chocolate. "I wanted to say more than that," she announced. "Would you like to hear the end of it?" And this admirable foreign person answered, "I should very much like."

Zo hesitated. To follow out its own little train of thought, in words, was no easy task to the immature mind which Miss Minerva had so mercilessly overworked. Led by old Dame Nature (first of governesses!) Zo found her way out of the labyrinth by means of questions.

"Do you know Joseph?" she began.

Teresa had heard the footman called by his name: she knew who Joseph was.

"Do you know Matilda?" Zo proceeded.

Teresa had heard the housemaid called by her name: she knew who Matilda was. And better still, she helped her little friend by a timely guess at what was coming, presented under the form of a reminder. "You saw Mr. Ovid's face close to Carmina's face," she suggested.

Zo nodded furiously—the end of it was coming already.

"And before that," Teresa went on, "you saw Joseph's face close to Matilda's face."

"I saw Joseph kiss Matilda!" Zo burst out, with a scream of triumph. "Why doesn't Ovid kiss Carmina?"

A deep bass voice, behind them, answered gravely: "Because the governess is in the way." And a big bamboo walking-stick pointed over their heads at Miss Minerva. Zo instantly recognised the stick, and took it into her own hands.

Teresa turned—and found herself in the presence of a remarkable man.

CHAPTER XII.

In the first place, the stranger was almost tall enough to be shown as a giant; he towered to a stature of six feet six inches, English measure.[1] If

---

1   *he towered ... English measure*: A six-and-a-half foot man was considered gigantic in 1883, when the average height was little more than five-and-a-half feet.

his immense bones had been properly covered with flesh, he might have presented the rare combination of fine proportions with great height. He was so miserably—it might almost be said, so hideously—thin that his enemies spoke of him as "the living skeleton." His massive forehead, his great gloomy gray eyes, his protuberant cheek-bones, overhung a flesh-less lower face naked of beard, whiskers, and moustache. His complexion added to the startling effect which his personal appearance produced on strangers. It was of the true gipsy-brown, and, being darker in tone than his eyes, added remarkably to the weird look, the dismal thoughtful scrutiny, which it was his habit to fix on persons talking with him, no matter whether they were worthy of attention or not. His straight black hair hung as gracelessly on either side of his hollow face as the hair of an American Indian. His great dusky hands, never covered by gloves in the summer time, showed amber-coloured nails on bluntly-pointed fingers, turned up at the tips. Those tips felt like satin when they touched you. When he wished to be careful, he could handle the frailest objects with the most exquisite delicacy. His dress was of the recklessly loose and easy kind. His long frock-coat descended below his knees; his flowing trousers were veritable bags; his lean and wrinkled throat turned about in a wide-ly-opened shirt-collar, unconfined by any sort of neck-tie. He had a theory that a head-dress should be solid enough to resist a chance blow—a fall from a horse, or the dropping of a loose brick from a house under repair. His hard black hat, broad and curly at the brim, might have graced the head of a bishop, if it had not been secularised by a queer resemblance to the bell-shaped hat worn by dandies in the early years of the present century. In one word he was, both in himself and in his dress, the sort of man whom no stranger is careless enough to pass without turning round for a second look. Teresa, eyeing him with reluctant curiosity, drew back a step, and privately reviled him (in the secrecy of her own language) as an ugly beast! Even his name startled people by the outlandish sound of it. Those enemies who called him "the living skeleton" said it revealed his gipsy origin. In medical and scientific circles he was well and widely known as—Doctor Benjulia.[1]

Zo ran away with his bamboo stick. After a passing look of gloomy indifference at the duenna, he called to the child to come back.

She obeyed him in an oddly indirect way, as if she had been returning against her will. At the same time she looked up in his face, with an absence of shyness which showed, like the snatching away of his stick, that she was familiarly acquainted with him, and accustomed to take lib-

---

1   *Doctor Benjulia*: Collins often enjoyed providing his villains with physical characteristics and odd behavioral traits designed to make them memorable. *The Woman in White*'s huge Count Fosco with his mice, *No Name*'s cold-blooded Mrs. Lecount with her reptiles, and *Armadale*'s seductive Lydia Gwilt with her astonishing red hair are three examples. Benjulia, as we see here, is another.

erties. And yet there was an expression of uneasy expectation in her round attentive eyes. "Do you want it back again?" she asked, offering the stick.

"Of course I do. What would your mother say to me, if you tumbled over my big bamboo, and dashed out your brains on this hard gravel walk?"

"Have you been to see Mama?" Zo asked.

"I have *not* been to see Mama—but I know what she would say to me if you dashed out your brains, for all that."

"What would she say?"

"She would say—Doctor Benjulia, your name ought to be Herod."[1]

"Who was Herod?"

"Herod was a Royal Jew, who killed little girls when they took away his walking-stick. Come here, child. Shall I tickle you?"

"I knew you'd say that," Zo answered.

When men in general thoroughly enjoy the pleasure of talking nonsense to children, they can no more help smiling than they can help breathing. The doctor was an extraordinary exception to this rule; his grim face never relaxed—not even when Zo reminded him that one of his favourite recreations was tickling her. She obeyed, however, with the curious appearance of reluctant submission showing itself once more. He put two of his soft big finger-tips on her spine, just below the back of her neck, and pressed on the place. Zo started and wriggled under his touch. He observed her with as serious an interest as if he had been conducting a medical experiment. "That's how you make our dog kick with his leg," said Zo, recalling her experience of the doctor in the society of the dog. "How do you do it?"

"I touch the Cervical Plexus,"[2] Doctor Benjulia answered as gravely as ever.

This attempt at mystifying the child failed completely. Zo considered the unknown tongue in which he had answered her as being equivalent to lessons. She declined to notice the Cervical Plexus, and returned to the little terrier at home. "Do you think the dog likes it?" she asked.

"Never mind the dog. Do *you* like it?"

" I don't know."

Doctor Benjulia turned to Teresa. His gloomy gray eyes rested on her, as they might have rested on any inanimate object near him—on the railing that imprisoned the birds, or on the pipes that kept the monkey-house

---

1   *Herod*: Herod Antipas (son of Herod the Great), tetrarch of Galilee (4 B.C.-A.D. 40), ordered the deaths of all male infants under the age of two years in Bethlehem after Christ's birth.

2   *Cervical Plexus*: The cervical plexus is a network of nerves near the top of the spine, and thus Benjulia is pinching Zoe's neck. Even the simple act of tickling a child becomes experimental for Benjulia.

warm. "I have been playing the fool, ma'am, with this child," he said; "and I fear I have detained you. I beg your pardon." He pulled off his episcopal hat, and walked grimly on, without taking any further notice of Zo.

Teresa made her best courtesy in return. The magnificent civility of the ugly giant daunted, while it flattered her. "The manners of a prince," she said, "and the complexion of a gipsy. Is he a nobleman?"

Zo answered, "He's a doctor,"—as if that was something much better.

"Do you like him?" Teresa inquired next.

Zo answered the duenna as she had answered the doctor: "I don't know."

In the meantime, Ovid and his cousin had not been unobservant of what was passing at a little distance from them. Benjulia's great height, and his evident familiarity with the child, stirred Carmina's curiosity.

Ovid seemed to be disinclined to talk of him. Miss Minerva made herself useful, with the readiest politeness. She mentioned his odd name, and described him as one of Mrs. Gallilee's old friends. "Of late years," she proceeded, "he is said to have discontinued medical practice, and devoted himself to chemical experiments. Nobody seems to know much about him. He has built a house in a desolate field[1]—in some lost suburban neighbourhood that nobody can discover. In plain English, Dr. Benjulia is a mystery."

Hearing this, Carmina appealed again to Ovid.

"When I am asked riddles," she said, "I am never easy till the answer is guessed for me. And when I hear of mysteries, I am dying to have them revealed. You are a doctor yourself. Do tell me something more!"

Ovid might have evaded her entreaties by means of an excuse. But her eyes were irresistible: they looked him into submission in an instant.

"Doctor Benjulia is what we call a Specialist," he said. "I mean that he only professes to treat certain diseases. Brains and nerves are Benjulia's diseases. Without quite discontinuing his medical practice, he limits himself to serious cases—when other doctors are puzzled, you know, and want him to help them. With this exception, he has certainly sacrificed his professional interests to his mania for experiments in chemistry. What those experiments are, nobody knows but himself. He keeps the key of his laboratory about him by day and by night. When the place wants cleaning, he does the cleaning with his own hands."

Carmina listened with great interest: "Has nobody peeped in at the windows?" she asked.

---

1   *He has built a house in a desolate field*: Collins used dark, strange old houses and laboratories in his fiction so often that one critic, H.J.W. Milley, designated the "sinister house" theme a major aspect of several of the novels. *A Rogue's Life*, *The Dead Secret*, *Armadale*, and *Man and Wife* all include secluded and mysterious houses with dark secrets like Benjulia's home and laboratory, whose horrors are exposed late in the novel.

"There are no windows—only a skylight in the roof."

"Can't somebody get up on the roof, and look in through the skylight?"

Ovid laughed. "One of his men-servants is said to have tried that experiment," he replied.

"And what did the servant see?"

"A large white blind, drawn under the skylight, and hiding the whole room from view. Somehow, the doctor discovered him—and the man was instantly dismissed. Of course there are reports which explain the mystery of the doctor and his laboratory. One report says that he is trying to find a way of turning common metals into gold. Another declares that he is inventing some explosive compound, so horribly destructive that it will put an end to war. All I can tell you is, that his mind (when I happen to meet him) seems to be as completely absorbed as ever in brains and nerves. But, what they can have to do with chemical experiments, secretly pursued in a lonely field, is a riddle to which I have thus far found no answer."

"Is he married?" Carmina inquired.

The question seemed to amuse Ovid. "If Doctor Benjulia had a wife, you think we might get at his secrets? There is no such chance for us—he manages his domestic affairs for himself."

"Hasn't he even got a housekeeper?"

"Not even a housekeeper!"

While he was making that reply, he saw the doctor slowly advancing towards them. "Excuse me for one minute," he resumed; "I will just speak to him, and come back to you."

Carmina turned to Miss Minerva in surprise.

"Ovid seems to have some reason for keeping the tall man away from us," she said. "Does he dislike Doctor Benjulia?"

But for restraining motives, the governess might have gratified her hatred of Carmina by a sharp reply. She had her reasons—not only after what she had overheard in the conservatory, but after what she had seen in the Gardens—for winning Carmina's confidence, and exercising over her the influence of a trusted friend. Miss Minerva made instant use of her first opportunity.

"I can tell you what I have noticed myself," she said confidentially. "When Mrs. Gallilee gives parties, I am allowed to be present—to see the famous professors of science. On one of these occasions they were talking of instinct and reason. Your cousin, Mr. Ovid Vere, said it was no easy matter to decide where instinct ended and reason began. In his own experience, he had sometimes found people of feeble minds, who judged by instinct, arrive at sounder conclusions than their superiors in intelligence, who judged by reason. The talk took another turn—and, soon after, Doctor Benjulia joined the guests. I don't know whether you have observed that Mr. Gallilee is very fond of his stepson?"

Oh, yes! Carmina had noticed that. "I like Mr. Gallilee," she said warmly; "he is such a nice, kind-hearted, natural old man."

Miss Minerva concealed a sneer under a smile. Fond of Mr. Gallilee? what simplicity! "Well," she resumed, "the doctor paid his respects to the master of the house, and then he shook hands with Mr. Ovid; and then the scientific gentlemen all got round him, and had learned talk. Mr. Gallilee came up to his stepson, looking a little discomposed. He spoke in a whisper—you know his way?—'Ovid, do you like Doctor Benjulia? Don't mention it; I hate him.' Strong language for Mr. Gallilee, wasn't it? Mr. Ovid said, 'Why do you hate him?' And poor Mr. Gallilee answered like a child, 'Because I do.' Some ladies came in, and the old gentleman left us to speak to them. I ventured to say to Mr. Ovid, 'Is that instinct or reason?' He took it quite seriously. 'Instinct,' he said—'and it troubles me.' I leave you, Miss Carmina, to draw your own conclusion."

They both looked up. Ovid and the doctor were walking slowly away from them, and were just passing Teresa and the child. At the same moment, one of the keepers of the animals approached Benjulia. After they had talked together for a while, the man withdrew. Zo (who had heard it all, and had understood a part of it) ran up to Carmina, charged with news.

"There's a sick monkey in the gardens, in a room all by himself!" the child cried. "And, I say, look there!" She pointed excitedly to Benjulia and Ovid, walking on again slowly in the direction of the aviaries. "There's the big doctor who tickles me! He says he'll see the poor monkey, as soon as he's done with Ovid. And what do you think he said besides? He said perhaps he'd take the monkey home with him."

"I wonder what's the matter with the poor creature?" Carmina asked.

"After what Mr. Ovid has told us, I think I know," Miss Minerva answered. "Doctor Benjulia wouldn't be interested in the monkey unless it had a disease of the brain."

CHAPTER XIII.

Ovid had promised to return to Carmina in a minute. The minutes passed, and still Doctor Benjulia held him in talk.

Now that he was no longer seeking amusement, in his own dreary way, by mystifying Zo, the lines seemed to harden in the doctor's fleshless face. A scrupulously polite man, he was always cold in his politeness. He waited to have his hand shaken, and waited to be spoken to. And yet, on this occasion, he had something to say. When Ovid opened the conversation, he changed the subject directly.

"Benjulia! what brings You to the Zoological Gardens?"

"One of the monkeys has got brain disease; and they fancy I might like to see the beast before they kill him. Have you been thinking lately of that patient we lost?"

Not at the moment remembering the patient, Ovid made no immediate reply. The doctor seemed to distrust his silence.

"You don't mean to say you have forgotten the case?" he resumed. "We called it hysteria, not knowing what else it was. I don't forgive the girl for slipping through our fingers; I hate to be beaten by Death, in that way. Have you made up your mind what to do, on the next occasion? Perhaps you think you could have saved her life if you had been sent for, now?"

"No, indeed, I am just as ignorant—"

"Give ignorance time," Benjulia interposed, "and ignorance will become knowledge—if a man is in earnest. The proper treatment might occur to you to-morrow."

He held to his idea with such obstinacy that Ovid set him right, rather impatiently. "The proper treatment has as much chance of occurring to the greatest ass in the profession," he answered, "as it has of occurring to me. I can put my mind to no good medical use; my work has been too much for me. I am obliged to give up practice, and rest—for a time."

Not even a formal expression of sympathy escaped Doctor Benjulia. Having been a distrustful friend so far, he became an inquisitive friend now. "You're going away, of course," he said. "Where to? On the Continent? Not to Italy—if you really want to recover your health!"

"What is the objection to Italy?"

The doctor put his great hand solemnly on his young friend's shoulder. "The medical schools in that country are recovering their past reputation," he said. "They are becoming active centres of physiological inquiry. You will be dragged into it, to a dead certainty. They're sure to try what they can strike out by collision with a man like you. What will become of that overworked mind of yours, when a lot of professors are searching it without mercy? Have you ever been to Canada?"[1]

"No. Have you?"

"I have been everywhere. Canada is just the place for you, in this summer season. Bracing air; and steady-going doctors who leave the fools in Europe to pry into the secrets of Nature. Thousands of miles of land, if you like riding. Thousands of miles of water, if you like sailing. Pack up, and go to Canada."

What did all this mean? Was he afraid that his colleague might stumble on some discovery which he was in search of himself? And did the discovery relate to his own special subject of brains and nerves? Ovid made an attempt to understand him.

"Tell me something about yourself, Benjulia," he said. "Are you returning to your regular professional work?"

---

1   *Have you ever been to Canada?*: Collins visited Canada in 1873 and enjoyed the trip. The dry climate of the Prairies seemed to invigorate him, as it does his hero.

Benjulia struck his bamboo stick emphatically on the gravel-walk. "Never! Unless I know more than I know now."

This surely meant that he was as much devoted to his chemical experiments as ever? In that case, how could Ovid (who knew nothing of chemical experiments) be an obstacle in the doctor's way? Baffled thus far, he made another attempt at inducing Benjulia to explain himself.

"When is the world to hear of your discoveries?" he asked.

The doctor's massive forehead gathered ominously into a frown. "Damn the world!" That was his only reply.

Ovid was not disposed to allow himself to be kept in the dark in this way. "I suppose you are going on with your experiments?" he said.

The gloom of Benjulia's grave eyes deepened: they stared with a stern fixedness into vacancy. His great head bent slowly over his broad breast. The whole man seemed to be shut up in himself. "I go on a way of my own," he growled. "Let nobody cross it."

After that reply, to persist in making inquiries would only have ended in needlessly provoking an irritable man. Ovid looked back towards Carmina. "I must return to my friends," he said.

The doctor lifted his head, like a man awakened. "Have I been rude?" he asked. "Don't talk to me about my experiments. That's my raw place, and you hit me on it. What did you say just now? Friends? who are your friends?" He rubbed his hand savagely over his forehead—it was a way he had of clearing his mind. "I know," he went on. "I saw your friends just now. Who's the young lady?" His most intimate companions had never heard him laugh: they had sometimes seen his thin-lipped mouth widen drearily into a smile. It widened now. "Whoever she is," he proceeded, "Zo wonders why you don't kiss her."

This specimen of Benjulia's attempts at pleasantry was not exactly to Ovid's taste. He shifted the topic to his little sister. "You were always fond of Zo," he said.

Benjulia looked thoroughly puzzled. Fondness for anybody was, to all appearance, one of the few subjects on which he had not qualified himself to offer an opinion. He gave his head another savage rub, and returned to the subject of the young lady. "Who is she?" he asked again.

"My cousin," Ovid replied as shortly as possible.

"Your cousin? A girl of Lady Northlake's?"

"No: my late uncle's daughter."

Benjulia suddenly came to a standstill. "What!" he cried, "has that misbegotten child grown up to be a woman?"[1]

Ovid started. Words of angry protest were on his lips, when he per-

---

1   *"What!" he cried, "has that misbegotten child grown up to be a woman?"*: This slip of the tongue foreshadows one of the novel's major crises. It also marks another instance of Collins's fascination with adultery and illegitimacy, which lie at the heart of much of his fiction.

ceived Teresa and Zo on one side of him, and the keeper of the monkeys on the other. Benjulia dismissed the man, with the favourable answer which Zo had already reported. They walked on again. Ovid was at liberty to speak.

"Do you know what you said of my cousin, just now?" he began.

His tone seemed to surprise the doctor. "What did I say?" he asked.

"You used a very offensive word. You called Carmina a 'misbegotten child.' Are you repeating some vile slander on the memory of her mother?"

Benjulia came to another standstill. "Slander?" he repeated—and said no more.

Ovid's anger broke out. "Yes!" he replied. "Or a lie, if you like, told of a woman as high above reproach as your mother or mine!"

"You are hot," the doctor remarked, and walked on again. "When I was in Italy—" he paused to calculate, "when I was at Rome, fifteen years ago, your cousin was a wretched little rickety child. I said to Robert Graywell, 'Don't get too fond of that girl; she'll never live to grow up.' He said something about taking her away to the mountain air. I didn't think, myself, the mountain air would be of any use. It seems I was wrong. Well! it's a surprise to me to find her—" he waited, and calculated again, "to find her grown up to be seventeen years old." To Ovid's ears, there was an inhuman indifference in his tone as he said this, which it was impossible not to resent, by looks, if not in words. Benjulia noticed the impression that he had produced, without in the least understanding it. "Your nervous system's in a nasty state," he remarked; "you had better take care of yourself. I'll go and look at the monkey."

His face was like the face of the impenetrable sphinx; his deep bass voice droned placidly. Ovid's anger had passed by him like the passing of the summer air. "Good-bye!" he said; "and take care of those nasty nerves. I tell you again—they mean mischief."

Not altogether willingly, Ovid made his apologies. "If I have misunderstood you, I beg your pardon. At the same time, I don't think I am to blame. Why did you mislead me by using that detestable word?"

"Wasn't it the right word?"

"The right word—when you only wanted to speak of a poor sickly child! Considering that you took your degree at Oxford—"[1]

---

1   *Considering that you took your degree at Oxford*: Part of Collins's anti-vivisection thesis, and part of the anti-vivisection movement's most important argument, suggests that the sustained practice of cruelty hardens the heart and soul. Collins wanted to show in Benjulia such a figure, a man of potential ruined by his profession; in order to avoid the argument that Benjulia was simply a foreign-born gypsy and thus hardened and cruel from the start, Collins provides him with a proper British education.

"You could expect nothing better from the disadvantages of my education," said the doctor, finishing the sentence with the grave composure that distinguished him. "When I said 'misbegotten,' perhaps I ought to have said 'half-begotten?' Thank you for reminding me. I'll look at the dictionary when I get home."

Ovid's mind was not set at ease yet. "There's one other thing," he persisted, "that seems unaccountable." He started, and seized Benjulia by the arm. "Stop!" he cried, with a sudden outburst of alarm.

"Well?" asked the doctor, stopping directly. "What is it?"

"Nothing," said Ovid, recoiling from a stain on the gravel walk, caused by the remains of an unlucky beetle, crushed under his friend's heavy foot. "You trod on the beetle before I could stop you."

Benjulia's astonishment at finding an adult male human being (not in a lunatic asylum) anxious to spare the life of a beetle, literally struck him speechless. His medical instincts came to his assistance. "You had better leave London at once," he suggested. "Get into pure air, and be out of doors all day long." He turned over the remains of the beetle with the end of his stick. "The common beetle," he said; "I haven't damaged a Specimen."

Ovid returned to the subject, which had suffered interruption through his abortive little act of mercy. "You knew my uncle in Italy. It seems strange, Benjulia, that I should never have heard of it before."

"Yes; I knew your uncle; and," he added with especial emphasis, "I knew his wife."

"Well?"

"Well, I can't say I felt any particular interest in either of them. Nothing happened afterwards to put me in mind of the acquaintance till you told me who the young lady was, just now."

"Surely my mother must have reminded you?"

"Not that I can remember. Women in her position don't much fancy talking of a relative who has married"—he stopped to choose his next words. "I don't want to be rude; suppose we say married beneath him?"

Reflection told Ovid that this was true. Even in conversation with himself (before the arrival in England of Robert's Will), his mother rarely mentioned her brother—and still more rarely his family. There was another reason for Mrs. Gallilee's silence, known only to herself. Robert was in the secret of her debts, and Robert had laid her under heavy pecuniary obligations. The very sound of his name was revolting to his amiable sister: it reminded her of that humiliating sense, known in society as a sense of gratitude.

Carmina was still waiting—and there was nothing further to be gained by returning to the subject of her mother with such a man as Benjulia. Ovid held out his hand to say good-bye.

Taking the offered hand readily enough, the doctor repeated his odd question—"I haven't been rude, have I?"—with an unpleasant appearance of going through a form purely for form's sake. Ovid's natural generosity of feeling urged him to meet the advance, strangely as it had been made, with a friendly reception.

"I am afraid it is I who have been rude," he said. "Will you go back with me, and be introduced to Carmina?"

Benjulia made his acknowledgments in his own remarkable way. "No, thank you," he said, quietly, "I'd rather see the monkey."

CHAPTER XIV.

In the meantime, Zo had become the innocent cause of a difference of opinion between two no less dissimilar personages than Maria and the duenna.

Having her mind full of the sick monkey, the child felt a natural curiosity to see the other monkeys who were well. Amiable Miss Minerva consulted her young friend from Italy before she complied with Zo's wishes. Would Miss Carmina like to visit the monkey-house? Ovid's cousin, remembering Ovid's promise, looked towards the end of the walk. He was not returning to her—he was not even in sight. Carmina resigned herself to circumstances, with a little air of pique which was duly registered in Miss Minerva's memory.

Arriving at the monkey-house, Teresa appeared in a new character. She surprised her companions by showing an interest in natural history.

"Are they all monkeys in that big place?" she asked. "I don't know much about foreign beasts. How do they like it, I wonder?"

This comprehensive inquiry was addressed to the governess, as the most learned person present. Miss Minerva referred to her elder pupil with an encouraging smile. "Maria will inform you," she said. "Her studies in natural history have made her well acquainted with the habits of monkeys."

Thus authorised to exhibit her learning, even the discreet Maria actually blushed with pleasure. It was that young lady's most highly-prized reward to display her knowledge (in imitation of her governess's method of instruction) for the benefit of unfortunate persons of the lower rank, whose education had been imperfectly carried out. The tone of amiable patronage with which she now imparted useful information to a woman old enough to be her grandmother, would have made the hands of the bygone generation burn to box her ears.

"The monkeys are kept in large and airy cages," Maria began; "and the temperature is regulated with the utmost care. I shall be happy to point out to you the difference between the monkey and the ape. You are not perhaps aware that the members of the latter family are called 'Simiadae,'[1] and are without tails and cheek-pouches?"

---

1   '*Simiadae*': Maria is identifying a family of anthropoid apes that includes the gorilla, the orangutan, the chimpanzee, and the gibbon.

Listening so far in dumb amazement, Teresa checked the flow of information at tails and cheek-pouches.

"What gibberish is this child talking to me?" she asked. "I want to know how the monkeys amuse themselves in that large house?"

Maria's perfect training condescended to enlighten even this state of mind.

"They have ropes to swing on," she answered sweetly; "and visitors feed them through the wires of the cage. Branches of trees are also placed for their diversion; reminding many of them no doubt of the vast tropical forests in which, as we learn from travellers, they pass in flocks from tree to tree."

Teresa held up her hand as a signal to stop. "A little of You, my young lady, goes a long way," she said. "Consider how much I can hold, before you cram me at this rate."

Maria was bewildered, but not daunted yet. "Pardon me," she pleaded; "I fear I don't quite understand you."

"Then there are two of us puzzled," the duenna remarked. "*I* don't understand *you*. I shan't go into that house. A Christian can't be expected to care about beasts—but right is right all the world over. Because a monkey is a nasty creature (as I have heard, not even good to eat when he's dead), that's no reason for taking him out of his own country and putting him into a cage. If we are to see creatures in prison, let's see creatures who have deserved it—men and women, rogues and sluts. The monkeys haven't deserved it. Go in—I'll wait for you at the door."

Setting her bitterest emphasis on this protest, which expressed inveterate hostility to Maria (using compassion for caged animals as the readiest means at hand), Teresa seated herself in triumph on the nearest bench.

A young person, possessed of no more than ordinary knowledge, might have left the old woman to enjoy the privilege of saying the last word. Miss Minerva's pupil, exuding information as it were at every pore in her skin, had been rudely dried up at a moment's notice. Even earthly perfection has its weak places within reach. Maria lost her temper.

"You will allow me to remind you," she said, "that intelligent curiosity leads us to study the habits of animals that are new to us. We place them in a cage—"

Teresa lost *her* temper.

"You're an animal that's new to me," cried the irate duenna. "I never in all my life met with such a child before. If you please, madam governess, put this girl into a cage. My intelligent curiosity wants to study a monkey that's new to me."

It was fortunate for Teresa that she was Carmina's favourite and friend, and, as such, a person to be carefully handled. Miss Minerva stopped the growing quarrel with the readiest discretion and good-feeling. She patted Teresa on the shoulder, and looked at Carmina with a pleasant smile.

"Worthy old creature! how full of humour she is![1] The energy of the people, Miss Carmina. I often remark the quaint force with which they express their ideas. No—not a word of apology, I beg and pray. Maria, my dear, take your sister's hand, and we will follow." She put her arm in Carmina's arm with the happiest mixture of familiarity and respect, and she nodded to Carmina's old companion with the cordiality of a good-humoured friend.

Teresa was not further irritated by being kept waiting for any length of time. In a few minutes Carmina joined her on the bench.

"Tired of the beasts already, my pretty one?"

"Worse than tired—driven away by the smell! Dear old Teresa, why did you speak so roughly to Miss Minerva and Maria?"

"Because I hate them! because I hate the family! Was your poor father demented in his last moments, when he trusted you among these detestable people?"

Carmina listened in astonishment. "You said just the contrary of the family," she exclaimed, "only yesterday!"

Teresa hung her head in confusion. Her well-meant attempt to reconcile Carmina to the new life on which she had entered was now revealed as a sham, thanks to her own outbreak of temper. The one honest alternative left was to own the truth, and put Carmina on her guard without alarming her, if possible.

"I'll never tell a lie again, as long as I live," Teresa declared. "You see I didn't like to discourage you. After all, I dare say I'm more wrong than right in my opinion. But it *is* my opinion, for all that. I hate those women, mistress and governess, both alike. There! now it's out. Are you angry with me?"

"I am never angry with you, my old friend; I am only a little vexed. Don't say you hate people, after only knowing them for a day or two! I am sure Miss Minerva has been very kind—to me, as well as to you. I feel ashamed of myself already for having begun by disliking her."

Teresa took her young mistress's hand, and patted it compassionately. "Poor innocent, if you only had my experience to help you! There are good ones and bad ones among all creatures. I say to you the Gallilees are bad ones! Even their music-master (I saw him this morning) looks like a rogue. You will tell me the poor old gentleman is harmless, surely. I shall not contradict that—I shall only ask, what is the use of a man who is as weak as water? Oh, I like him, but I distinguish! I also like Zo. But what is a child—especially when that beastly governess has muddled her unfortunate little head with learning? No, my angel, there's but one person

---

1   *how full of humour she is!*: Miss Minerva is not here referring to any inherent ability on Teresa's part to make others laugh but to her passionate, sanguine nature.

among these people who comforts me, when I think of the day that will part us. Ha! do I see a little colour coming into your cheeks? You sly girl! you know who it is. *There* is what I call a Man! If I was as young as you are, and as pretty as you are—"

A warning gesture from Carmina closed Teresa's lips. Ovid was rapidly approaching them.

He looked a little annoyed, and he made his apologies without mentioning the doctor's name. His cousin was interested enough in him already to ask herself what this meant. Did he really dislike Benjulia, and had there been some disagreement between them?

"Was the tall doctor so very interesting?" she ventured to inquire.

"Not in the least!" He answered as if the subject was disagreeable to him—and yet he returned to it. "By-the-by, did you ever hear Benjulia's name mentioned, at home in Italy?"

"Never! Did he know my father and mother?"

"He says so."

"Oh, do introduce me to him!"

"We must wait a little. He prefers being introduced to the monkey to-day. Where are Miss Minerva and the children?"

Teresa replied. She pointed to the monkey-house, and then drew Ovid aside. "Take her to see some more birds, and trust me to keep the governess out of your way," whispered the good creature. "Make love—hot love to her, doctor!"

In a minute more the cousins were out of sight. How are you to make love to a young girl, after an acquaintance of a day or two? The question would have been easily answered by some men. It thoroughly puzzled Ovid.

"I am so glad to get back to you!" he said, honestly opening his mind to her. "Were you half as glad when you saw me return?"

He knew nothing of the devious and serpentine paths by which love finds the way to its ends. It had not occurred to him to approach her with those secret tones and stolen looks which speak for themselves. She answered with the straightforward directness of which he had set the example.

"I hope you don't think me insensible to your kindness," she said. "I am more pleased and more proud than I can tell you."

"Proud!" Ovid repeated, not immediately understanding her.

"Why not?" she asked. "My poor father used to say you would be an honour to the family. Ought I not to be proud, when I find such a man taking so much notice of me?"

She looked up at him shyly. At that moment, he would have resigned all his prospects of celebrity for the privilege of kissing her. He made another attempt to bring her—in spirit—a little nearer to him.

"Carmina, do you remember where you first saw me?"

"How can you ask?—it was in the concert-room. When I saw you there, I remembered passing you in the large Square. It seems a strange coincidence that you should have gone to the very concert that Teresa and I went to by accident."

Ovid ran the risk, and made his confession. "It was no coincidence," he said. "After our meeting in the Square I followed you to the concert."

This bold avowal would have confused a less innocent girl. It only took Carmina by surprise.

"What made you follow us?" she asked.

Us? Did she suppose he had followed the old woman? Ovid lost no time in setting her right. "I didn't even see Teresa," he said. "I followed You."

She was silent. What did her silence mean? Was she confused, or was she still at a loss to understand him? That morbid sensitiveness, which was one of the most serious signs of his failing health, was by this time sufficiently irritated to hurry him into extremities. "Did you ever hear," he asked, "of such a thing as love at first sight?"

She started. Surprise, confusion, doubt, succeeded each other in rapid changes on her mobile and delicate face. Still silent, she roused her courage, and looked at him.

If he had returned the look, he would have told the story of his first love without another word to help him. But his shattered nerves unmanned him, at the moment of all others when it was his interest to be bold. The fear that he might have allowed himself to speak too freely—a weakness which would never have misled him in his days of health and strength—kept his eyes on the ground. She looked away again with a quick flush of shame. When such a man as Ovid spoke of love at first sight, what an instance of her own vanity it was to have thought that his mind was dwelling on *her*! He had kindly lowered himself to the level of a girl's intelligence, and had been trying to interest her by talking the language of romance. She was so dissatisfied with herself that she made a movement to turn back.

He was too bitterly disappointed, on his side, to attempt to prolong the interview. A deadly sense of weakness was beginning to overpower him. It was the inevitable result of his utter want of care for himself. After a sleepless night, he had taken a long walk before breakfast; and to these demands on his failing reserves of strength, he had now added the fatigue of dawdling about a garden. Physically and mentally he had no energy left.

"I didn't mean it," he said to Carmina sadly; "I am afraid I have offended you."

"Oh, how little you know me," she cried, "if you think that!"

This time their eyes met. The truth dawned on her—and he saw it.

He took her hand. The clammy coldness of his grasp startled her. "Do you still wonder why I followed you?" he asked. The words were so faintly uttered that she could barely hear them. Heavy drops of perspiration stood on his forehead; his face faded to a gray and ghastly whiteness—he staggered, and tried desperately to catch at the branch of a tree near them. She threw her arms round him. With all her little strength she tried to hold him up. Her utmost effort only availed to drag him to the grass plot by their side, and to soften his fall. Even as the cry for help passed her lips, she saw help coming. A tall man was approaching her—not running, even when he saw what had happened; only stalking with long strides. He was followed by one of the keepers of the gardens. Doctor Benjulia had his sick monkey to take care of. He kept the creature sheltered under his long frock-coat.

"Don't do that, if you please," was all the doctor said, as Carmina tried to lift Ovid's head from the grass. He spoke with his customary composure, and laid his hand on the heart of the fainting man, as coolly as if it had been the heart of a stranger. "Which of you two can run the fastest?" he asked, looking backwards and forwards between Carmina and the keeper. "I want some brandy."

The refreshment room was within sight. Before the keeper quite understood what was required of him, Carmina was speeding over the grass like Atalanta[1] herself.

Benjulia looked after her, with his usual grave attention. "That wench can run," he said to himself, and turned once more to Ovid. "In his state of health, he's been fool enough to over-exert himself." So he disposed of the case in his own mind. Having done that, he remembered the monkey, deposited for the time being on the grass. "Too cold for him," he remarked, with more appearance of interest than he had shown yet. "Here, keeper! Pick up the monkey till I'm ready to take him again." The man hesitated.

"He might bite me, sir."

"Pick him up!" the doctor reiterated; "he can't bite anybody, after what I've done to him." The monkey was indeed in a state of stupor. The keeper obeyed his instructions, looking half stupefied himself: he seemed to be even more afraid of the doctor than of the monkey. "Do you think I'm the Devil?" Benjulia asked with dismal irony. The man looked as if he would say "Yes," if he dared.

Carmina came running back with the brandy. The doctor smelt it first, and then took notice of her. "Out of breath?" he said.

"Why don't you give him the brandy?" she answered impatiently.

"Strong lungs," Benjulia proceeded, sitting down cross-legged by Ovid, and administering the stimulant without hurrying himself. "Some girls would not have been able to speak, after such a run as you have had. I didn't think much of you or your lungs when you were a baby."

"Is he coming to himself?" Carmina asked.

---

1 *Atalanta*: In Greek mythology, Atalanta was the maiden who agreed to marry any man who could outrun her. Hippomenes defeated her by dropping golden apples, which she paused to pick up.

"Do you know what a pump is?" Benjulia rejoined. "Very well; a pump sometimes gets out of order. Give the carpenter time, and he'll put it right again." He let his mighty hand drop on Ovid's breast. "*This* pump is out of order; and I'm the carpenter. Give me time, and I'll set it right again. You're not a bit like your mother."

Watching eagerly for the slightest signs of recovery in Ovid's face, Carmina detected a faint return of colour. She was so relieved that she was able to listen to the doctor's oddly discursive talk, and even to join in it. "Some of our friends used to think I was like my father," she answered.

"Did they?" said Benjulia—and shut his thin-lipped mouth as if he was determined to drop the subject for ever.

Ovid stirred feebly, and half opened his eyes.

Benjulia got up. "You don't want me any longer," he said. "Now, Mr. Keeper, give me back the monkey." He dismissed the man, and tucked the monkey under one arm as if it had been a bundle. "There are your friends," he resumed, pointing to the end of the walk. "Good-day!"

Carmina stopped him. Too anxious to stand on ceremony, she laid her hand on his arm. He shook it off—not angrily: just brushing it away, as he might have brushed away the ash of his cigar or a splash of mud in the street.

"What does this fainting fit mean?" she asked timidly. "Is Ovid going to be ill?"

"Seriously ill—unless you do the right thing with him, and do it at once." He walked away. She followed him, humbly and yet resolutely. "Tell me, if you please," she said, "what we are to do."

He looked back over his shoulder. "Send him away."

She returned, and knelt down by Ovid—still slowly reviving. With a fond and gentle hand, she wiped the moisture from his forehead.

"Just as we were beginning to understand each other!" she said to herself, with a sad little sigh.

CHAPTER XV.

Two days passed. In spite of the warnings that he had received, Ovid remained in London.

The indisputable authority of Benjulia had no more effect on him than the unanswerable arguments of Mrs. Gallilee. "Recent circumstances" (as his mother expressed it) "had strengthened his infatuated resistance to reason." The dreaded necessity for Teresa's departure had been hastened by a telegram from Italy: Ovid felt for Carmina's distress with sympathies which made her dearer to him than ever. On the second morning after the visit to the Zoological Gardens, her fortitude had been severely tried. She had found the telegram under her pillow, enclosed in a farewell letter. Teresa had gone.

"My Carmina,—I have kissed you, and cried over you, and I am writing good-bye as well as my poor eyes will let me. Oh, my heart's darling, I cannot be cruel enough to wake you, and see you suffer! Forgive me for going away, with only this dumb farewell. I am so fond of you—that is my only excuse. While he still lives, my helpless old man has his claim on me. Write by every post, and trust me to write back—and remember what I said when I spoke of Ovid. Love the good man who loves *you*; and try to make the best of the others. They cannot surely be cruel to the poor angel who depends on their kindness. Oh, how hard life is—"

The paper was blotted, and the rest was illegible.

The miserable day of Teresa's departure was passed by Carmina in the solitude of her room: gently and firmly, she refused to see anyone. This strange conduct added to Mrs. Gallilee's anxieties. Already absorbed in considering Ovid's obstinacy, and the means of overcoming it, she was now confronted by a resolute side in the character of her niece, which took her by surprise. There might be difficulties to come, in managing Carmina, which she had not foreseen. Meanwhile, she was left to act on her own unaided discretion in the serious matter of her son's failing health. Benjulia had refused to help her; he was too closely occupied in his laboratory to pay or receive visits. "I have already given my advice" (the doctor wrote). "Send him away. When he has had a month's change, let me see his letters; and then, if I have anything more to say, I will tell you what I think of your son."

Left in this position, Mrs. Gallilee's hard self-denial yielded to the one sound conclusion that lay before her. The only influence that could be now used over Ovid, with the smallest chance of success, was the influence of Carmina. Three days after Teresa's departure, she invited her niece to take tea in her own boudoir. Carmina found her reading. "A charming book," she said, as she laid it down, "on a most interesting subject, Geographical Botany. The author divides the earth into twenty-five botanical regions—but, I forget; you are not like Maria; you don't care about these things."

"I am so ignorant," Carmina pleaded. "Perhaps, I may know better when I get older." A book on the table attracted her by its beautiful binding. She took it up. Mrs. Gallilee looked at her with compassionate good humour.

"Science again, my dear," she said facetiously, "inviting you in a pretty dress! You have taken up the 'Curiosities of Coprolites.' That book is one of my distinctions—a presentation copy from the author."

"What are Coprolites?" Carmina asked, trying to inform herself on the subject of her aunt's distinctions.

Still good-humoured, but with an effort that began to appear, Mrs. Gallilee lowered herself to the level of her niece.

"Coprolites," she explained, "are the fossilised indigestions of extinct reptiles. The great philosopher who has written that book has discovered scales, bones, teeth, and shells—the undigested food of those interesting Saurians.[1] What a man! what a field for investigation! Tell me about your own reading. What have you found in the library?"

"Very interesting books—at least to me," Carmina answered. "I have found many volumes of poetry. Do you ever read poetry?"

Mrs. Gallilee laid herself back in her chair, and submitted patiently to her niece's simplicity. "Poetry?" she repeated, in accents of resignation. "Oh, good heavens!"

Unlucky Carmina tried a more promising topic. "What beautiful flowers you have in the drawing-room!" she said.

"Nothing remarkable, my dear. Everybody has flowers in their drawing-rooms—they are part of the furniture."[2]

"Did you arrange them yourself, aunt?"

Mrs. Gallilee still endured it. "The florist's man," she said, "does all that. I sometimes dissect flowers, but I never trouble myself to arrange them. What would be the use of the man if I did?" This view of the question struck Carmina dumb. Mrs. Gallilee went on. "By-the-by, talking of flowers reminds one of other superfluities. Have you tried the piano in your room? Will it do?"

"The tone is quite perfect!" Carmina answered with enthusiasm. "Did you choose it?" Mrs. Gallilee looked as if she was going to say "Good Heavens!" again, and perhaps to endure it no longer. Carmina was too simple to interpret these signs in the right way. Why should her aunt not choose a piano? "Don't you like music?" she asked.

Mrs. Gallilee made a last effort. "When you see a little more of society, my child, you will know that one *must* like music. So again with pictures— one *must* go to the Royal Academy Exhibition. So again—"

Before she could mention any more social sacrifices, the servant came in with a letter, and stopped her.

Mrs. Gallilee looked at the address. The weary indifference of her manner changed to vivid interest, the moment she saw the handwriting. "From the Professor!" she exclaimed. "Excuse me, for one minute." She

---

1   *those interesting Saurians*: Saurians are lizards. The entire scene, from Mrs. Gallilee's book on Geographical Botany and the twenty-five botanical regions to her autographed copy of the *Curiosities of Coprolites* (fossilized excrement, and thus, perhaps a quiet joke for Collins) and her discussion of the undigested food of Saurians, again reflects Collins's willingness to poke fun at science and at his rigidly scientific villainness.

2   *Everybody has flowers in their drawing-rooms—they are part of the furniture*: This conversation, where Mrs. Gallilee seems oblivious to the aesthetic appeal of flowers, recalls the eminently practical Thomas Gradgrind's lecture to Sissy Jupe concerning the absurdity of ornamental wall-paper and carpeting with floral patterns in the second chapter of Dickens's *Hard Times*. For another *Hard Times* parallel, see Note 1, p. 187.

read the letter, and closed it again with a sigh of relief. "I knew it!" she said to herself. "I have always maintained that the albuminoid substance of frog's eggs[1] is insufficient (viewed as nourishment) to transform a tadpole into a frog—and, at last, the Professor owns that I am right. I beg your pardon, Carmina; I am carried away by a subject that I have been working at in my stolen intervals for weeks past. Let me give you some tea. I have asked Miss Minerva to join us. What is keeping her, I wonder? She is usually so punctual. I suppose Zoe has been behaving badly again."

In a few minutes more, the governess herself confirmed this maternal forewarning of the truth. Zo had declined to commit to memory "the political consequences of the granting of Magna Charta"[2]—and now stood reserved for punishment, when her mother "had time to attend to it." Mrs. Gallilee at once disposed of this little responsibility. "Bread and water for tea," she said, and proceeded to the business of the evening.

"I wish to speak to you both," she began, "on the subject of my son."

The two persons addressed waited in silence to hear more. Carmina's head drooped: she looked down. Miss Minerva attentively observed Mrs. Gallilee. "Why am I invited to hear what she has to say about her son?" was the question which occurred to the governess. "Is she afraid that Carmina might tell me about it, if I was not let into the family secrets?"

Admirably reasoned, and correctly guessed!

Mrs. Gallilee had latterly observed that the governess was insinuating herself into the confidence of her niece—that is to say, into the confidence of a young lady, whose father was generally reported to have died in possession of a handsome fortune. Personal influence, once obtained over an heiress, is not infrequently misused. To check the further growth of a friendship of this sort (without openly offending Miss Minerva) was an imperative duty. Mrs. Gallilee saw her way to the discreet accomplishment of that object. Her niece and her governess were interested—diversely interested—in Ovid. If she invited them both together, to consult with her on the delicate subject of her son, there would be every chance of exciting some difference of opinion, sufficiently irritating to begin the process of estrangement, by keeping them apart when they had left the tea-table.

"It is most important that there should be no misunderstanding among us, Mrs. Gallilee proceeded. "Let me set the example of speaking without reserve. We all three know that Ovid persists in remaining in London—"

She paused, on the point of finishing the sentence. Although she *had*

---

1   *albuminoid substance of frog's eggs*: This substance is a water-soluble protein coagulated by heat and found in egg white.

2   *Magna Charta*: The Magna Charta is the great charter of English civil liberties granted by King John at Runnymede in 1215.

converted a Professor, Mrs. Gallilee was still only a woman. There did enter into her other calculations, the possibility of exciting some accidental betrayal of her governess's passion for her son. On alluding to Ovid, she turned suddenly to Miss Minerva. "I am sure you will excuse my troubling you with family anxieties," she said—"especially when they are connected with the health of my son."

It was cleverly done, but it laboured under one disadvantage. Miss Minerva had no idea of what the needless apology meant, having no suspicion of the discovery of her secret by her employer. But to feel herself baffled in trying to penetrate Mrs. Gallilee's motives was enough, of itself, to put Mrs. Gallilee's governess on her guard for the rest of the evening.

"You honour me, madam, by admitting me to your confidence"—was what she said. "Trip me up, you cat, if you can!"—was what she thought.

Mrs. Gallilee resumed.

"We know that Ovid persists in remaining in London, when change of air and scene are absolutely necessary to the recovery of his health. And we know why. Carmina, my child, don't think for a moment that I blame you! don't even suppose that I blame my son. You are too charming a person not to excuse, nay even to justify, any man's admiration. But let us (as we hard old people say) look the facts in the face. If Ovid had not seen you, he would be now on the health-giving sea, on his way to Spain and Italy. You are the innocent cause of his obstinate indifference, his most deplorable and dangerous disregard of the duty which he owes to himself. He refuses to listen to his mother, he sets the opinion of his skilled medical colleague at defiance. But one person has any influence over him now." She paused again, and tried to trip up the governess once more. "Miss Minerva, let me appeal to You. I regard you as a member of our family; I have the sincerest admiration of your tact and good sense. Am I exceeding the limits of delicacy, if I say plainly to my niece, Persuade Ovid to go?"

If Carmina had possessed an elder sister, with a plain personal appearance and an easy conscience, not even that sister could have matched the perfect composure with which Miss Minerva replied.

"I don't possess your happy faculty of expressing yourself, Mrs. Gallilee. But, if I had been in your place, I should have said to the best of my poor ability exactly what you have said now." She bent her head with a graceful gesture of respect, and looked at Carmina with a gentle sisterly interest while she stirred her tea.

At the very opening of the skirmish, Mrs. Gallilee was defeated. She had failed to provoke the slightest sign of jealousy, or even of ill-temper. Unquestionably the most crafty and most cruel woman of the two—possessing the most dangerously deceitful manner, and the most mischievous readiness of language—she was, nevertheless, Miss Minerva's inferior in the one supreme capacity of which they both stood in need, the capacity for self-restraint.

She showed this inferiority on expressing her thanks. The underlying malice broke through the smooth surface that was intended to hide it. "I am apt to doubt myself," she said; "and such sound encouragement as yours always relieves me. Of course I don't ask you for more than a word of advice. Of course I don't expect *you* to persuade Ovid."

"Of course not!" Miss Minerva agreed. "May I ask for a little more sugar in my tea?"

Mrs. Gallilee turned to Carmina.

"Well, my dear? I have spoken to you, as I might have spoken to one of my own daughters, if she had been of your age. Tell me frankly, in return, whether I may count on your help."

Still pale and downcast, Carmina obeyed. "I will do my best, if you wish it. But—"

"Yes? Go on."

She still hesitated. Mrs. Gallilee tried gentle remonstrance. "My child, surely you are not afraid of me?"

She was certainly afraid. But she controlled herself.

"You are Ovid's mother, and I am only his cousin," she resumed. "I don't like to hear you say that my influence over him is greater than yours."

It was far from the poor girl's intention; but there was an implied rebuke in this. In her present state of irritation, Mrs. Gallilee felt it.

"Come! come!" she said. "Don't affect to be ignorant, my dear, of what you know perfectly well."

Carmina lifted her head. For the first time in the experience of the two elder women, this gentle creature showed that she could resent an insult. The fine spirit that was in her fired her eyes, and fixed them firmly on her aunt.

"Do you accuse me of deceit?" she asked.

"Let us call it false modesty," Mrs. Gallilee retorted.

Carmina rose without another word—and walked out of the room.

In the extremity of her surprise, Mrs. Gallilee appealed to Miss Minerva. "Is she in a passion?"

"She didn't bang the door," the governess quietly remarked.

"I am not joking, Miss Minerva."

"I am not joking either, madam."

The tone of that answer implied an uncompromising assertion of equality. You are not to suppose (it said) that a lady drops below your level, because she receives a salary and teaches your children. Mrs. Gallilee was so angry, by this time, that she forgot the importance of preventing a conference between Miss Minerva and her niece. For once, she was the creature of impulse—the overpowering impulse to dismiss her insolent governess from her hospitable table.

"May I offer you another cup of tea?"

"Thank you—no more. May I return to my pupils?"

"By all means!"

Carmina had not been five minutes in her own room before she heard a knock at the door. Had Mrs. Gallilee followed her? "Who is there?" she asked. And a voice outside answered,

"Only Miss Minerva!"

End of October 1882 *Belgravia* Serial Number

CHAPTER XVI.

"I am afraid I have startled you?" said the governess, carefully closing the door.

"I thought it was my aunt," Carmina answered, as simply as a child.

"Have you been crying?"

"I couldn't help it, Miss Minerva."

"Mrs. Gallilee spoke cruelly to you—I don't wonder at your feeling angry."

Carmina gently shook her head. "I have been crying," she explained, "because I am sorry and ashamed. How can I make it up with my aunt? Shall I go back at once and beg her pardon? I think you are my friend, Miss Minerva. Will you advise me?"

It was so prettily and innocently said that even the governess was touched—for a moment. "Shall I prove to you that I am your friend?" she proposed. "I advise you not to go back yet to your aunt—and I will tell you why. Mrs. Gallilee bears malice; she is a thoroughly unforgiving woman. And I should be the first to feel it, if she knew what I have just said to you."

"Oh, Miss Minerva! you don't think that I would betray your confidence?"

"No, my dear, I don't. I felt attracted towards you, when we first met. You didn't return the feeling—you (very naturally) disliked me. I am ugly and ill-tempered: and, if there is anything good in me, it doesn't show itself on the surface. Yes! yes! I believe you are beginning to understand me. If I can make your life here a little happier, as time goes on, I shall be only too glad to do it." She put her long yellow hands on either side of Carmina's head, and kissed her forehead.

The poor child threw her arms round Miss Minerva's neck, and cried her heart out on the bosom of the woman who was deceiving her. "I have nobody left, now Teresa has gone," she said. "Oh, do try to be kind to me—I feel so friendless and so lonely!"

Miss Minerva neither moved nor spoke. She waited, and let the girl cry.

Her heavy black eyebrows gathered into a frown; her sallow face deepened in colour. She was in a state of rebellion against herself. Through all the hardening influences of the woman's life—through the fortifications against good which watchful evil builds in human hearts—

that innocent outburst of trust and grief had broken its way; and had purified for a while the fetid inner darkness with divine light. She had entered the room, with her own base interests to serve. In her small sordid way she, like her employer, was persecuted by debts—miserable debts to sellers of expensive washes, which might render her ugly complexion more passable in Ovid's eyes; to makers of costly gloves, which might show Ovid the shape of her hands, and hide their colour; to skilled workmen in fine leather, who could tempt Ovid to look at her high instep, and her fine ankle—the only beauties that she could reveal to the only man whom she cared to please. For the time, those importunate creditors ceased to threaten her. For the time, what she had heard in the conservatory, while they were reading the Will, lost its tempting influence. She remained in the room for half an hour more—and she left it without having borrowed a farthing.

"Are you easier now?"

"Yes, dear."

Carmina dried her eyes, and looked shyly at Miss Minerva. "I have been treating you as if I had a sister," she said; "you don't think me too familiar, I hope?"

"I wish I was your sister, God knows!"

The words were hardly out of her mouth before she was startled by her own fervour. "Shall I tell you what to do with Mrs. Gallilee?" she said abruptly. "Write her a little note."

"Yes! yes! and you will take it for me?"

Carmina's eyes brightened through her tears, the suggestion was such a relief! In a minute the note was written: "My dear Aunt, I have behaved very badly, and I am very much ashamed of it. May I trust to your kind indulgence to forgive me? I will try to be worthier of your kindness for the future; and I sincerely beg your pardon." She signed her name in breathless haste. "Please take it at once!" she said eagerly.

Miss Minerva smiled. "If I take it," she said,"I shall do harm instead of good—I shall be accused of interfering. Give it to one of the servants. Not yet! When Mrs. Gallilee is angry, she doesn't get over it so soon as you seem to think. Leave her to dabble in science first," said the governess in tones of immeasurable contempt. "When she has half stifled herself with some filthy smell, or dissected some wretched insect or flower, she may be in a better humour. Wait."

Carmina thought of the happy days at home in Italy, when her father used to laugh at her little outbreaks of temper, and good Teresa only shrugged her shoulders. What a change—oh, me, what a change for the worse! She drew from her bosom a locket, hung round her neck by a thin gold chain—and opened it, and kissed the glass over the miniature portraits inside. "Would you like to see them?" she said to Miss Minerva. "My mother's likeness was painted for me by my father; and then he had his photograph taken to match it. I open my portraits and look at them, while I say my prayers. It's almost like having them alive again, sometimes. Oh, if I only had my father to advise me now—!" Her heart swelled—but she kept back the tears: she was learning that self-restraint, poor soul, already! "Perhaps," she went on, "I ought not to want advice. After that fainting-fit in the Gardens, if I can persuade Ovid to leave us, I ought to do it—and I will do it!"

Miss Minerva crossed the room, and looked out of window. Carmina had roused the dormant jealousy; Carmina had fatally weakened the good influences which she had herself produced. The sudden silence of her new friend perplexed her. She too went to the window. "Do you think it would be taking a liberty?" she asked.

"No."

A short answer—and still looking out of window! Carmina tried again. "Besides, there are my aunt's wishes to consider. After my bad behaviour—"

Miss Minerva turned round from the window sharply. "Of course! There can't be a doubt of it." Her tone softened a little. "You are young, Carmina—I suppose I may call you by your name—you are young and simple. Do those innocent eyes of yours ever see below the surface?"

"I don't quite understand you."

"Do you think your aunt's only motive in wishing Mr. Ovid Vere to leave London is anxiety about his health? Do you feel no suspicion that she wants to keep him away from You?"

Carmina toyed with her locket, in an embarrassment which she was quite unable to disguise. "Are you afraid to trust me?" Miss Minerva asked. That reproach opened the girl's lips instantly.

"I am afraid to tell you how foolish I am," she answered. "Perhaps, I still feel a little strangeness between us? It seems to be so formal to call you Miss Minerva. I don't know what your Christian name is. Will you tell me?"

Miss Minerva replied rather unwillingly. "My name is Frances. Don't call me Fanny!"

"Why not?"

"Because it's too absurd to be endured! What does the mere sound of Fanny suggest? A flirting, dancing creature—plump and fair, and playful and pretty!" She went to the looking-glass, and pointed disdainfully to the reflection of herself. "Sickening to think of," she said, "when you look at that. Call me Frances—a man's name, with only the difference between an i and an e. No sentiment in it; hard, like me. Well, what was it you didn't like to say of yourself?"

Carmina dropped her voice to a whisper. "It's no use asking me what I do see, or don't see, in my aunt," she answered. "I am afraid we shall never be—what we ought to be to each other. When she came to that concert, and sat by me and looked at me—" She stopped, and shuddered over the recollection of it.

Miss Minerva urged her to go on—first, by a gesture; then by a suggestion:"They said you fainted under the heat."

"I didn't feel the heat. I felt a horrid creeping all over me. Before I looked at her, mind!—when I only knew that somebody was sitting next to me. And then, I did look round. Her eyes and my eyes flashed into each other. In that one moment, I lost all sense of myself as if I was dead. I can only tell you of it in that way. It was a dreadful surprise to me to remember it—and a dreadful pain—when they brought me to myself again. Though I do look so little and so weak, I am stronger than people think; I never fainted before. My aunt is—how can I say it properly?—hard to get on with since that time. Is there something wicked in my nature? I do believe she feels in the same way towards me. Yes; I dare say it's imagination, but it's as bad as reality for all that. Oh, I am sure your are right—she does want to keep Ovid out of my way!"

"Because she doesn't like you?" said Miss Minerva. "Is that the only reason you can think of?"

"What other reason can there be?"

The governess summoned her utmost power of self-restraint. She needed it, even to speak of the bare possibility of Carmina's marriage to Ovid, as if it was only a matter of speculative interest to herself.

"Some people object to marriages between cousins,"[1] she said. "You are cousins. Some people object to marriages between Catholics and Protestants. You are a Catholic—" No! She could not trust herself to refer to him directly; she went on to the next sentence. "And there might be some other reason," she resumed.

"Do you know what that is?" Carmina asked.

"No more than you do—thus far."

She spoke the plain truth. Thanks to the dog's interruption, and to the necessity of saving herself from discovery, the last clauses of the Will had been read in her absence.

"Can't you even guess what it is?" Carmina persisted.

"Mrs. Gallilee is very ambitious," the governess replied: "and her son has a fortune of his own. She may wish him to marry a lady of high rank. But—no—she is always in need of money. In some way, money may be concerned in it."

"In what way?" Carmina asked.

"I have already told you," Miss Minerva answered, "that I don't know."

Before the conversation could proceed, they were interrupted by the appearance of Mrs. Gallilee's maid, with a message from the schoolroom. Miss Maria wanted a little help in her Latin lesson. Noticing Carmina's letter, as she advanced to the door, it struck Miss Minerva that the woman

---

1   *Some people object to marriages between cousins*: Marriages between cousins were legal and not uncommon in Victorian England. They were very common in Victorian fiction. As a scientist, though, Mrs. Gallilee has Mendelian genetics to back her objection to such familial ties.

might deliver it. "Is Mrs. Gallilee at home?" she asked. Mrs. Gallilee had just gone out. "One of her scientific lectures, I suppose," said Miss Minerva to Carmina. "Your note must wait till she comes back."

The door closed on the governess—and the lady's-maid took a liberty. She remained in the room; and produced a morsel of folded paper, hitherto concealed from view. Smirking and smiling, she handed the paper to Carmina.

"From Mr. Ovid, Miss."

CHAPTER XVII.

"Pray come to me; I am waiting for you in the garden of the Square."

In those two lines, Ovid's note began and ended. Mrs. Gallilee's maid—deeply interested in an appointment which was not without precedent in her own experience—ventured on an expression of sympathy, before she returned to the servants' hall. "Please to excuse me, Miss; I hope Mr. Ovid isn't ill? He looked sadly pale, I thought. Allow me to give you your hat." Carmina thanked her, and hurried downstairs.

Ovid was waiting at the gate of the Square—and he did indeed look wretchedly ill.

It was useless to make inquiries; they only seemed to irritate him. "I am better already, now you have come to me." He said that, and led the way to a sheltered seat among the trees. In the later evening-time the Square was almost empty. Two middle-aged ladies, walking up and down (who considerately remembered their own youth, and kept out of the way), and a boy rigging a model yacht (who was too closely occupied to notice them), were the only persons in the enclosure besides themselves.

"Does my mother know that you have come here?" Ovid asked.

"Mrs. Gallilee has gone out. I didn't stop to think of it, when I got your letter. Am I doing wrong?"

Ovid took her hand. "Is it doing wrong to relieve me of anxieties that I have no courage to endure? When we meet in the house either my mother or her obedient servant, Miss Minerva, is sure to interrupt us. At last, my darling, I have got you to myself! You know that I love you. Why can't I look into your heart, and see what secrets it is keeping from me? I try to hope; but I want some little encouragement. Carmina! shall I ever hear you say that you love me?"

She trembled, and turned away her head. Her own words to the governess were in her mind; her own conviction of the want of all sympathy between his mother and herself made her shrink from answering him

"I understand your silence." With those words he dropped her hand, and looked at her no more.

It was sadly, not bitterly spoken. She attempted to find excuses; she showed but too plainly how she pitied him. "If I only had myself to think of—" Her voice failed her. A new life came into his eyes, the colour rose in his haggard face: even those few faltering words had encouraged him!

She tried again to make him understand her. "I am so afraid of distressing you, Ovid; and I am so anxious not to make mischief between you and your mother—"

"What has my mother to do with it?"

She went on, without noticing the interruption. "You won't think me ungrateful? We had better speak of something else. Only this evening, your mother sent for me, and—don't be angry!—I am afraid she might be vexed if she knew what you have been saying to me. Perhaps I am wrong? Perhaps she only thinks I am too young. Oh, Ovid, how you look at me! Your mother hasn't said in so many words—"

"What has she said?"

In that question she saw the chance of speaking to him of other interests than the interests of love.

"You must go away to another climate," she said; "and your mother tells me I must persuade you to do it. I obey her with a heavy heart. Dear Ovid, you know how I shall miss you; you know what a loss it will be to me, when you say good-bye—but there is only one way to get well again. I entreat you to take that way! Your mother thinks I have some influence over you. Have I any influence?"

"Judge for yourself," he answered. "You wish me to leave you?"

"For your own sake. Only for your own sake."

"Do you wish me to come back again?"

"It's cruel to ask the question!"

"It rests with you, Carmina. Send me away when you like, and where you like. But, before I go, give me my one reason for making the sacrifice. No change will do anything for me, no climate will restore my health—unless you give me your love. I am old enough to know myself; I have thought of it by day and by night. Am I cruel to press you in this way? I will only say one word more. It doesn't matter what becomes of me—if you refuse to be my wife."[1]

Without experience, without advice—with her own heart protesting against her silence—the restraint that she had laid on herself grew harder and harder to endure. The tears rose in her eyes. He saw them; they embittered his mind against his mother. With a darkening face he rose, and walked up and down before her, struggling with himself.

"This is my mother's doing," he said.

His tone terrified her. The dread, present to her mind all through the interview, of making herself a cause of estrangement between mother and

---

1   *if you refuse to be my wife*: Apparently, Collins not only believed in love at first sight but in love at fast pace, as well. A quick review tells the reader that Ovid here proposes to Carmina less than a day after meeting her for the first time.

son, so completely overcame her that she even made an attempt to defend Mrs. Gallilee! At the first words, he sat down by her again. For a moment, he scrutinised her face without mercy—and then repented of his own severity.

"My poor child," he said, "you are afraid to tell me what has happened. I won't press you to speak against your own inclinations. It would be cruel and needless—I have got at the truth at last. In the one hope of my life, my mother is my enemy. She is bent on separating us; she shall not succeed. I won't leave you."

Carmina looked at him. His eyes dropped before her, in confusion and shame.

"Are you angry with me?" she asked.

No reproaches could have touched his heart as that question touched it. "Angry with you? Oh, my darling, if you only knew how angry I am with myself! It cuts me to the heart to see how I have distressed you. I am a miserable selfish wretch; I don't deserve your love. Forgive me, and forget me. I will make the best atonement I can, Carmina. I will go away to-morrow."

Under hard trial, she had preserved her self-control. She had resisted him; she had resisted herself. His sudden submission disarmed her in an instant. With a low cry of love and fear she threw her arms round his neck, and laid her burning cheek against his face. "I can't help it," she whispered; "oh, Ovid, don't despise me!" His arms closed round her; his lips were pressed to hers. "Kiss me," he said. She kissed him, trembling in his embrace. That innocent self-abandonment did not plead with him in vain. He released her—and only held her hand. There was silence between them; long, happy silence.

He was the first to speak again. "How can I go away now?" he said.

She only smiled at that reckless forgetfulness of the promise, by which he had bound himself a few minutes since. "What did you tell me," she asked playfully, "when you called yourself by hard names, and said you didn't deserve my love?" Her smile vanished softly, and left only a look of tender entreaty in its place. "Set me an example of firmness, Ovid—don't leave it all to me! Remember what you have made me say. Remember"—she only hesitated for a moment—"remember what an interest I have in you now. I love you, Ovid. Say you will go."

He said it gratefully. "My life is yours; my will is yours. Decide for me, and I will begin my journey."

She was so impressed by her sense of this new responsibility, that she answered him as gravely as if she had been his wife. "I must give you time to pack up," she said.

"Say time to be with You!"

She fell into thought. He asked if she was still considering when to send him away. "No," she said; "it isn't that. I was wondering at myself. What is it that makes a great man like you so fond of me?"

His arm stole round her waist. He could just see her in the darkening twilight under the trees; the murmuring of the leaves was the only sound near them—his kisses lingered on her face. She sighed softly. "Don't make it too hard for me to send you away!" she whispered. He raised her, and put her arm in his. "Come," he said, "we will walk a little in the cool air."

They returned to the subject of his departure. It was still early in the week. She inquired if Saturday would be too soon to begin his journey. No: he felt it, too—the longer they delayed, the harder the parting would be.

"Have you thought yet where you will go?" she asked.

"I must begin with a sea-voyage," he replied. "Long railway journeys, in my present state, will only do me harm. The difficulty is where to go to. I have been to America; India is too hot; Australia is too far. Benjulia has suggested Canada."

As he mentioned the doctor's name, her hand mechanically pressed his arm

"That strange man!" she said. "Even his name startles one; I hardly know what to think of him. He seemed to have more feeling for the monkey than for you or me. It was certainly kind of him to take the poor creature home, and try what he could do with it. Are you sure he is a great chemist?"

Ovid stopped. Such a question, from Carmina, sounded strange to him. "What makes you doubt it?" he said.

"You won't laugh at me, Ovid?"

"You know I won't!"

"Now you shall hear. We knew a famous Italian chemist at Rome— such a nice old man! He and my father used to play piquet;[1] and I looked at them, and tried to learn—and I was too stupid. But I had plenty of opportunities of noticing our old friend's hands. They were covered with stains; and he caught me looking at them. He was not in the least offended; he told me his experiments had spotted his skin in that way, and not‐ ing would clean off the stains. I saw Doctor Benjulia's great big hands, while he was giving you the brandy—and I remembered afterwards that there were no stains on them. I seem to surprise you."

"You do indeed surprise me. After knowing Benjulia for years, I have never noticed, what you have discovered on first seeing him."

"Perhaps he has some way of cleaning the stains off his hands."

Ovid agreed to this, as the readiest means of dismissing the subject. Carmina had really startled him. Some irrational connection between the great chemist's attention to the monkey, and the perplexing purity of his hands, persisted in vaguely asserting itself in Ovid's mind. His unac-

---

1   *He and my father used to play piquet*: Piquet is a two-player card game played with a deck from which all cards below the seven are omitted. Players take tricks in their attempt to reach thirty points.

knowledged doubts of Benjulia troubled him as they had never troubled him yet. He turned to Carmina for relief.

"Still thinking, my love?"

"Thinking of you," she answered. "I want you to promise me something—and I am afraid to ask it."

"Afraid? You don't love me, after all!"

"Then I will say it at once! How long do you expect to be away?"

"For two or three months, perhaps."

"Promise to wait till you return, before you tell your mother—"

"That we are engaged?"

"Yes."

"You have my promise, Carmina; but you make me uneasy."

"Why?"

"In my absence, you will be under my mother's care. And you don't like my mother."

Few words and plain words—and they sorely troubled her.

If she owned that he was right, what would the consequence be? He might refuse to leave her. Even assuming that he controlled himself, he would take his departure harassed by anxieties, which might exercise the worst possible influence over the good effect of the journey. To prevaricate with herself or with him was out of the question. That very evening she had quarrelled with his mother; and she had yet to discover whether Mrs. Gallilee had forgiven her. In her heart of hearts she hated deceit—and in her heart of hearts she longed to set his mind at ease. In that embarrassing position, which was the right way out? Satan persuaded Eve; and Love persuaded Carmina. Love asked if she was cruel enough to make her heart's darling miserable when he was so fond of her? Before she could realise it, she had begun to deceive him. Poor humanity! poor Carmina!

"You are almost as hard on me as if you were Doctor Benjulia himself!" she said. "I feel your mother's superiority—and you tell me I don't like her. Haven't you seen how good she has been to me?"

She thought this way of putting it irresistible. Ovid resisted, nevertheless. Carmina plunged into lower depths of deceit immediately.

"Haven't you seen my pretty rooms—my piano—my pictures—my china—my flowers? I should be the most insensible creature living if I didn't feel grateful to your mother."

"And yet, you are afraid of her."

She shook his arm impatiently. "I say, No!"

He was as obstinate as ever. "I say, Yes! If you're not afraid, why do you wish to keep our engagement from my mother's knowledge?"

His reasoning was unanswerable. But where is the woman to be found who is not supple enough to slip through the stiff fingers of Reason? She sheltered herself from his logic behind his language.

"Must I remind you again of the time when you were angry?" she rejoined. "You said your mother was bent on separating us. If I don't want her to know of our engagement just yet—isn't that a good reason?" She rested her head caressingly on his shoulder. "Tell me," she went on, thinking of one of Miss Minerva's suggestions, "doesn't my aunt look to a higher marriage for you than a marriage with me?"

It was impossible to deny that Mrs. Gallilee's views might justify that inquiry. Had she not more than once advised him to wait a few years—in other words, to wait until he had won the highest honours of his profession—before he thought of marrying at all? But Carmina was too precious to him to be humiliated by comparisons with other women, no matter what their rank might be. He paid her a compliment, instead of giving her an answer.

"My mother can't look higher than you," he said. "I wish I could feel sure, Carmina—in leaving you with her—that I am leaving you with a friend whom you trust and love."

There was a sadness in his tone that grieved her. "Wait till you come back," she replied, speaking as gaily as she could. "You will be ashamed to remember your own misgivings. And don't forget, dear, that I have another friend besides your mother—the best and kindest of friends—to take care of me."

Ovid heard this with some surprise. "A friend in my mother's house?" he asked.

"Certainly!"

"Who is it?"

"Miss Minerva."

"What!" His tone expressed such immeasurable amazement, that Carmina's sense of justice was roused in defence of her new friend.

"If I began by wronging Miss Minerva, I had the excuse of being a stranger," she said, warmly. "You have known her for years, and you ought to have found out her good qualities long since! Are all men alike, I wonder? Even my kind dear father used to call ugly women the inexcusable mistakes of Nature. Poor Miss Minerva says herself she is ugly, and expects everybody to misjudge her accordingly. I don't misjudge her, for one. Teresa has left me; and you are going away next. A miserable prospect, Ovid, but not quite without hope. Frances—yes, I call her by her Christian name, and she calls me by mine!—Frances will console me, and make my life as happy as it can be till you come back."

Excepting bad temper, and merciless cultivation of the minds of children, Ovid knew of nothing that justified his prejudice against the governess. Still, Carmina's sudden conversion inspired him with something like alarm. "I suppose you have good reasons for what you tell me," he said.

"The best reasons," she replied, in the most positive manner.

He considered for a moment how he could most delicately inquire what those reasons might be. But valuable opportunities may be lost, even in a moment. "Will you help me to do justice to Miss Minerva?" he cautiously began.

"Hush!" Carmina interposed. "Surely, I heard somebody calling to me?"

They paused, and listened. A voice hailed them from the outer side of the garden. They started guiltily. It was the voice of Mrs. Gallilee.

CHAPTER XVIII.

"Carmina! are you in the Square?"

"Leave it to me," Ovid whispered. "We will come to you directly," he called back.

Mrs. Gallilee was waiting for them at the gate. Ovid spoke, the moment they were within sight of each other. "You will have no more cause to complain of me," he said cheerfully; "I am going away at the end of the week."

Mrs. Gallilee's answer was addressed to Carmina instead of to her son. "Thank you, my dear," she said, and pressed her niece's hand.

It was too dark to see more of faces than their shadowy outline. The learned lady's tone was the perfection of amiability. She sent Ovid across the road to knock at the house-door, and took Carmina's arm confidentially. "You little goose!" she whispered, "how could you suppose I was angry with you? I can't even regret your mistake, you have written such a charming note."

Ovid was waiting for them in the hall. They went into the library. Mrs. Gallilee enfolded her son in a fervent motherly embrace.

"This completes the enjoyment of a most delightful evening," she said. "First a perfect lecture—and then the relief of overpowering anxiety about my son. I suppose your professional studies, Ovid, have never taken you as high as the Interspacial Regions?[1] We were an immense audience to-night, to hear the Professor on that subject, and I really haven't recovered it yet. Fifty miles above us—only fifty miles—there is an atmosphere of cold that would freeze the whole human family to death in a second of time. Moist matter, in that terrific emptiness, would explode, and become stone; and—listen to this, Carmina—the explosion itself would be frozen, and produce no sound. Think of serious people looking up in that dreadful direction, and talking of going to Heaven. Oh, the insignificance of man, except—I am going to make a joke, Ovid—except when he pleases his old mother by going away for the benefit of his health! And where are you going? Has sensible Carmina advised you? I agree with her beforehand, whatever she has said."

Ovid informed his mother of Benjulia's suggestion, and asked her what she thought of it.

---

1   *Interspacial Regions*: This lecture represents still more of Collins's amateur fascination with the language—and especially the "sound"—of Victorian science.

Mrs. Gallilee's overflowing geniality instantly flooded the absent doctor. He was rude, he was ugly; but what an inestimable friend! what admirable advice! In Ovid's state of health he must not write letters; his mother would write and thank the doctor, and ask for introductions to local grandees who occupied a position in colonial society. She seized the newspaper: a steamer for Canada sailed from Liverpool on Saturday. Ovid could secure his cabin the next morning ("amidships, my dear, if you can possibly get it"), and could leave London by Friday's train. In her eagerness to facilitate his departure, she proposed to superintend the shutting up of his house, in his absence, and to arrange the disposal of the servants, if he considered it worth while to keep them. She even thought of the cat. The easiest way to provide for the creature would be of course to have her poisoned;[1] but Ovid was so eccentric in some things, that practical suggestions were thrown away on him. "Sixpence a week for cat's meat isn't much," cried Mrs. Gallilee in an outburst of generosity. "We will receive the cat!"

Ovid made his acknowledgments resignedly. Carmina could see that Mrs. Gallilee's overpowering vitality was beginning to oppress her son.

"I needn't trouble you, mother," he said. "My domestic affairs were all settled when I first felt the necessity of getting rest. My manservant travels with me. My housemaid and kitchenmaid will go to their friends in the country; the cook will look after the house; and her nephew, the little page, is almost as fond of the cat as I am. If you will send for a cab, I think I will go home. Like other people in my wretched state, I feel fatigued towards night-time."

His lips just touched Carmina's delicate little ear, while his mother turned away to ring the bell. "Expect me to-morrow," he whispered. "I love you!—love you!—love you!" He seemed to find the perfection of luxury in the reiteration of those words.

When Ovid had left them, Carmina expected to hear something of her aunt's discovery in the Square.

Mrs. Gallilee's innocence was impenetrable. Not finding her niece in the house, she had thought of the Square. What could be more natural than that the cousins should take an evening walk, in one of the prettiest enclosures in London? Her anticipation of Ovid's recovery, and her admiration of Carmina's powers of persuasion appeared, for the time, to be the only active ideas in that comprehensive mind. When the servant brought in the tray, with the claret and soda-water,[2] she sent for Miss Minerva to

---

1   *The easiest way ... have her poisoned*: Poisoning was at the time a relatively common way to dispose of unwanted pets. Collins, of course, wants his readers to recoil from Mrs. Gallilee's chilling practicality.

2   *claret and soda water*: Claret, a red wine originally from France, was a Victorian favourite. Claret and soda water were the ingredients of a summer drink known as a Badminton.

join them, and hear the good news; completely ignoring the interruption of their friendly relations, earlier in the evening. She became festive and facetious at the sight of the soda-water. "Let us imitate the men, Miss Minerva, and drink a toast before we go to bed. Be cheerful, Carmina, and share half a bottle of soda-water with me. A pleasant journey to Ovid, and a safe return!" Cheered by the influences of conviviality, the friend of Professors, the tender nurse of half-developed tadpoles, lapsed into learning again. Mrs. Gallilee improvised an appropriate little lecture on Canada—on the botany of the Dominion;[1] on the geology of the Dominion; on the number of gallons of water wasted every hour by the falls of Niagara.[2] "Science will set it all right, my dears; we shall make that idle water work for us, one of these days. Good-night, Miss Minerva! Dear Carmina, pleasant dreams!"

Safe in the solitude of her bedroom, the governess ominously knitted her heavy eyebrows.

"In all my experience," she thought, "I never saw Mrs. Gallilee in such spirits before. What mischief is she meditating, when she has got rid of her son?"

CHAPTER XIX.

The lapse of a few hours exercised no deteriorating influence on Mrs. Gallilee's amiability.

On the next day, thanks to his mother's interference, Ovid was left in the undisturbed enjoyment of Carmina's society. Not only Miss Minerva, but even Mr. Gallilee and the children, were kept out of the way with a delicately-exercised dexterity, which defied the readiest suspicion to take offence. In one word, all that sympathy and indulgence could do to invite Ovid's confidence, was unobtrusively and modestly done. Never had the mistress of domestic diplomacy reached her ends with finer art.

In the afternoon, a messenger delivered Benjulia's reply to Mrs. Gallilee's announcement of her son's contemplated journey—despatched by the morning's post. The doctor was confined to the house by an attack of gout.[3] If Ovid wanted information on the subject of Canada, Ovid must go to him, and get it. That was all.

---

1   *on the botany of the Dominion*: the Dominion refers to any of the self-governing nations within the British Commonwealth.
2   *Niagara*: Collins visited Niagara Falls late in 1873 during his stay in the United States and Canada.
3   *attack of gout*: Collins knew all too well the pain of gout, which plagued him most of his adult life. Benjulia may soothe his pain with "cooling lotions," but Collins turned to laudanum—a tincture of opium—to which he was addicted for nearly thirty years.

"Have you ever been to Doctor Benjulia's house?" Carmina asked.

"Never."

"Then all you have told me about him is mere report? Now you will find out the truth! Of course you will go?"

Ovid felt no desire to make a voyage of exploration to Benjulia's house—and said so plainly. Carmina used all her powers of persuasion to induce him to change his mind. Mrs. Gallilee (superior to the influence of girlish curiosity) felt the importance of obtaining introductions to Canadian society, and agreed with her niece. "I shall order the carriage," she said, assuming a playfully despotic tone; "and, if you don't go to the doctor—Carmina and I will pay him a visit in your place."

Threatened, if he remained obstinate, with such a result as this, Ovid had no alternative but to submit.

The one order that could be given to the coachman was to drive to the village of Hendon,[1] on the north-western side of London, and to trust to inquiries for the rest of the way. Between Hendon and Willesden, there are pastoral solitudes within an hour's drive of Oxford Street[2]—wooded lanes and wild-flowers, farms and cornfields, still unprofaned by the devastating brickwork of the builder of modern times. Following winding ways, under shadowing trees, the coachman made his last inquiry at a roadside public-house. Hearing that Benjulia's place of abode was now within half a mile of him, Ovid set forth on foot; leaving the driver and the horses to take their ease at their inn.

He arrived at an iron gate, opening out of a lonely lane.

There, in the middle of a barren little field, he saw Benjulia's house—a hideous square building of yellow brick, with a slate roof. A low wall surrounded the place, having another iron gate at the entrance. The enclosure within was as barren as the field without: not even an attempt at flower-garden or kitchen-garden was visible. At a distance of some two hundred yards from the house stood a second and smaller building, with a skylight in the roof, which Ovid recognised (from description) as the famous laboratory. Behind it was the hedge which parted Benjulia's morsel of land from the land of his neighbour. Here, the trees rose again, and the fields beyond were cultivated. No dwellings, and no living creatures appeared. So near to London—and yet, in its loneliness, so far away—there was something unnatural in the solitude of the place.

Led by a feeling of curiosity, which was fast degenerating into suspicion, Ovid approached the laboratory, without showing himself in front of

---

1   *Hendon, on the north-western side of London*: Hendon is north of the city and west of Hampstead Heath. Collins lived in Hampstead as a child and probably remembered Hendon as remote and rural.

2   *Between Hendon and Willesden ... within an hour's drive of Oxford Street*: The remoteness of Benjulia's home in 1882-83 shows how the city has grown since, for the address is only three or four miles from Oxford Street.

the house. No watch-dog barked; no servant appeared on the look-out for a visitor. He was ashamed of himself as he did it, but (so strongly had he been impressed by Carmina's observation of the doctor) he even tried the locked door of the laboratory, and waited and listened! It was a breezy summer-day; the leaves of the trees near him rustled cheerfully. Was there another sound audible? Yes—low and faint, there rose through the sweet woodland melody a moaning cry. It paused; it was repeated; it stopped. He looked round him, not quite sure whether the sound proceeded from the outside or the inside of the building. He shook the door. Nothing happened. The suffering creature (if it was a suffering creature) was silent or dead. Had chemical experiment accidentally injured some living thing? Or—?

He recoiled from pursuing that second inquiry. The laboratory had, by this time, become an object of horror to him. He returned to the dwelling-house.

He put his hand on the latch of the gate, and looked back at the laboratory. He hesitated.

That moaning cry, so piteous and so short-lived, haunted his ears. The idea of approaching Benjulia became repellent to him. What he might afterwards think of himself—what his mother and Carmina might think of him—if he returned without having entered the doctors' house, were considerations which had no influence over his mind, in its present mood. The impulse of the moment was the one power that swayed him. He put the latch back in the socket. "I won't go in," he said to himself.

It was too late. As he turned from the house a manservant appeared at the door—crossed the enclosure—and threw the gate open for Ovid, without uttering a word.

They entered the passage. The speechless manservant opened a door on the right, and made a bow, inviting the visitor to enter. Ovid found himself in a room as barren as the field outside. There were the plastered walls, there was the bare floor, left exactly as the builders had left them when the house was finished. After a short absence, the man appeared again. He might be depressed in spirits, or crabbed in temper: the fact remained that, even now, he had nothing to say. He opened a door on the opposite side of the passage—made another bow—and vanished.

"Don't come near me!" cried Benjulia, the moment Ovid showed himself.

The doctor was seated in an inner corner of the room; robed in a long black dressing-gown, buttoned round his throat, which hid every part of him below his fleshless face, except his big hands, and his tortured gouty foot. Rage and pain glared in his gloomy gray eyes, and shook his clenched fists, resting on the arms of an easy chair. "Ten thousand red-hot devils are boring ten thousand holes through my foot," he said. "If you touch the pillow on my stool, I shall fly at your throat." He poured some cooling lotion from a bottle into a small watering-pot, and irrigated his foot as if it had been a bed of flowers. By way of further relief to the pain, he swore ferociously; addressing his oaths to himself, in thunderous undertones which made the glasses ring on the sideboard.

Relieved, in his present frame of mind, to have escaped the necessity of shaking hands, Ovid took a chair, and looked about him. Even here he discovered but little furniture, and that little of the heavy old-fashioned sort. Besides the sideboard, he perceived a dining-table, six chairs, and a dingy brown carpet. There were no curtains on the window, and no pictures or prints on the drab-coloured walls. The empty grate showed its bleak black cavity undisguised; and the mantelpiece had nothing on it but the doctor's dirty and strong-smelling pipe. Benjulia set down his watering-pot, as a sign that the paroxysm of pain had passed away. "A dull place to live in, isn't it?" In those words he welcomed the visitor to his house.

Irritated by the accident which had forced him into the repellent presence of Benjulia, Ovid answered in a tone which matched the doctor on his own hard ground.

"It's your own fault if the place is dull. Why haven't you planted trees, and laid out a garden?"

"I dare say I shall surprise you," Benjulia quietly rejoined; "but I have a habit of speaking my mind. I don't object to a dull place; and I don't care about trees and gardens."

"You don't seem to care about furniture either," said Ovid.

Now that he was out of pain for awhile, the doctor's innate insensibility to what other people might think of him, or might say to him, resumed its customary torpor in its own strangely unconscious way. He seemed only to understand that Ovid's curiosity was in search of information about trifles. Well, there would be less trouble in giving him his information, than in investigating his motives. So Benjulia talked of his furniture.

"I dare say you're right," he said. "My sister-in-law—did you know I had a relation of that sort?—my sister-in-law got the tables and chairs, and beds and basins. Buying things at shops doesn't interest me. I gave her a cheque; and I told her to furnish a room for me to eat in, and a room for me to sleep in—and not to forget the kitchen and the garrets for the servants. What more do I want?

His intolerable composure only added to his guest's irritability.

"A selfish way of putting it," Ovid broke out. "Have you nobody to think of but yourself?"

"Nobody—I am happy to say."

"That's downright cynicism, Benjulia!"

The doctor reflected. "Is it?" he said. "Perhaps you may be right again. I think it's only indifference, myself. Curiously enough my brother looks at it from your point of view—he even used the same word that you used just now. I suppose he found my cynicism beyond the reach of reform. At any rate, he left off coming here. I got rid of *him* on easy terms. What do you say? That inhuman way of talking is unworthy of me? Really I don't think so. I'm not a downright savage. It's only indifference."

"Does your brother return your indifference? You must be a nice pair, if he does!"

Benjulia seemed to find a certain dreary amusement in considering the question that Ovid had proposed. He decided on doing justice to his absent relative.

"My brother's intelligence is perhaps equal to such a small effort as you suggest," he said. "He has just brains enough to keep himself out of an asylum for idiots. Shall I tell you what he is in two words? A stupid sensualist—that's what he is. I let his wife come here sometimes, and cry. It doesn't trouble *me*; and it seems to relieve *her*. More of my indifference—eh? Well, I don't know. I gave her the change out of the furniture-cheque, to buy a new bonnet with. You might call that indifference, and you might be right once more. I don't care about money. Will you have a drink? You see I can't move. Please ring for the man."

Ovid refused the drink, and changed the subject. "Your servant is a remarkably silent person," he said.

"That's his merit," Benjulia answered; "the women-servants have quarrelled with every other man I've had. They can't quarrel with this man. I have raised his wages in grateful acknowledgment of his usefulness to me. I hate noise."

"Is that the reason why you don't keep a watch-dog?"

"I don't like dogs. They bark."

He had apparently some other disagreeable association with dogs, which he was not disposed to communicate. His hollow eyes stared gloomily into vacancy. Ovid's presence in the room seemed to have become, for the time being, an impression erased from his mind. He recovered himself, with the customary vehement rubbing of his head, and turned the talk to the object of Ovid's visit.

"So you have taken my advice," he said. "You're going to Canada, and you want to get at what I can tell you before you start. Here's my journal. It will jog my memory, and help us both."

His writing materials were placed on a movable table, screwed to his chair. Near them lay a shabby-looking book, guarded by a lock. Ten minutes after he had opened his journal, and had looked here and there through the pages, his hard intellect had grasped all that it required. Steadily and copiously his mind emptied its information into Ovid's mind; without a single digression from beginning to end, and with the most mercilessly direct reference to the traveller's practical wants. Not a word escaped him, relating to national character or to the beauties of Nature. Mrs. Gallilee had criticized the Falls of Niagara as a reservoir of wasted power. Doctor Benjulia's scientific superiority over the woman asserted itself with magnificent ease. Niagara being nothing but useless water, he never mentioned Niagara at all.

"Have I served your purpose as a guide?" he asked. "Never mind thanking me. Yes or no will do. Very good. I have got a line of writing to give you next." He mended his quill pen, and made an observation.

"Have you ever noticed that women have one pleasure which lasts to the end of their lives?" he said. "Young and old, they have the same inexhaustible enjoyment of society; and, young and old, they are all alike incapable of understanding a man, when he says he doesn't care to go to a party. Even your clever mother thinks you want to go to parties in Canada." He tried his pen, and found it would do—and began his letter.

Seeing his hands at work, Ovid was again reminded of Carmina's discovery. His eyes wandered a little aside, towards the corner formed by the pillar of the chimney-piece and the wall of the room. The big bamboo-stick rested there. A handle was attached to it, made of light-coloured horn, and on that handle there were some stains. Ovid looked at them with a surgeon's practised eye. They were dry stains of blood. (Had he washed his hands on the last occasion when he used his stick? And had he forgotten that the handle wanted washing too?)

Benjulia finished his letter, and wrote the address. He took up the envelope, to give it to Ovid—and stopped, as if some doubt tempted him to change his mind. The hesitation was only momentary. He persisted in his first intention, and gave Ovid the letter. It was addressed to a doctor at Montreal.

"That man won't introduce you to society," Benjulia announced, "and won't worry your brains with medical talk. Keep off one subject on your side. A mad bull is nothing to my friend if you speak of Vivisection."

Ovid looked at him steadily, when he uttered the last word. Benjulia looked back, just as steadily at Ovid.

At the moment of that reciprocal scrutiny, did the two men suspect each other? Ovid, on his side, determined not to leave the house without putting his suspicions to the test.

"I thank you for the letter," he began; "and I will not forget the warning."

The doctor's capacity for the exercise of the social virtues had its limits. His reserves of hospitality were by this time near their end.

"Is there anything more I can do for you?" he interposed.

"You can answer a simple question," Ovid replied. "My cousin Carmina—"

Benjulia interrupted him again: "Don't you think we said enough about your cousin in the Gardens?" he suggested.

Ovid acknowledged the hint with a neatness of retort almost worthy of his mother. "You have your own merciful disposition to blame, if I return to the subject," he replied. "My cousin cannot forget your kindness to the monkey."

"The sooner she forgets my kindness the better. The monkey is dead."

"I am glad to hear it."

"Why?"

"I thought the creature was living in pain."

"What do you mean?"

"I mean that I heard a moaning—"

"Where?"

"In the building behind your house."

"You heard the wind in the trees."

"Nothing of the sort. Are your chemical experiments ever made on animals?"

The doctor parried that direct attack, without giving ground by so much as a hair's breadth.

"What did I say when I gave you your letter of introduction?" he asked. "I said, A mad bull is nothing to my friend, if you speak to him of Vivisection. Now I have something more to tell you. I am like my friend." He waited a little. "Will that do?" he asked.

"Yes," said Ovid; "that will do."

They were as near to an open quarrel as two men could be: Ovid took up his hat to go. Even at that critical moment, Benjulia's strange jealousy of his young colleague—as a possible rival in some field of discovery which he claimed as his own—showed itself once more. There was no change in his tone; he still spoke like a judicious friend.

"A last word of advice," he said. "You are travelling for your health; don't let inquisitive strangers lead you into talk. Some of them might be physiologists."

"And might suggest new ideas," Ovid rejoined, determined to make him speak out this time.

Benjulia nodded, in perfect agreement with his guest's view.

"Are you afraid of new ideas?" Ovid went on.

"Perhaps I am—in *your* head." He made that admission, without hesitation or embarrassment. "Good-bye!" he resumed. "My sensitive foot feels noises: don't bang the door."

Getting out into the lane again, Ovid looked at his letter to the doctor at Montreal. His first impulse was to destroy it.

As Benjulia had hesitated before giving him the letter, so he now hesitated before tearing it up.

Contrary to the usual practice in such cases, the envelope was closed. Under those circumstances, Ovid's pride decided him on using the introduction. Time was still to pass, before events opened his eyes to the importance of his decision. To the end of his life he remembered that Benjulia had been near to keeping back the letter, and that he had been near to tearing it up.

CHAPTER XX.

The wise ancient who asserted that "Time flies," must have made that remarkable discovery while he was in a state of preparation for a journey. When are we most acutely sensible of the shortness of life? When do we consult our watches in perpetual dread of the result? When does the night steal on us unawares, and the morning take us by surprise? When we are going on a journey.

The remaining days of the week went by with a rush. Ovid had hardly time to ask himself if Friday had really come, before the hours of his life at home were already numbered.

He had still a little time to spare when he presented himself at Fairfield Gardens late in the afternoon. Finding no one in the library, he went up to the drawing-room. His mother was alone, reading.

"Have you anything to say to me, before I tell Carmina that you are here?" Mrs. Gallilee put that question quietly, so far as her voice was concerned. But she still kept her eyes on her book. Ovid knew that she was offering him his first and last chance of speaking plainly, before he went away. In Carmina's interests he spoke.

"Mother," he said, "I am leaving the one person in the world who is most precious to me, under your care."

"Do you mean," Mrs. Gallilee asked, "that you and Carmina are engaged to be married?"

"I mean that; and I am not sure that you approve of the engagement. Will you be plainer with me than you were on the last occasion when we spoke on this subject?"

"When was that?" Mrs. Gallilee inquired.

"When you and I were alone for a few minutes, on the morning when I breakfasted here. You said it was quite natural that Carmina should have attracted me; but you were careful not to encourage the idea of a marriage between us. I understood that you disapproved of it—but you didn't plainly tell me why."

"Can women always give their reason?"

"Yes—when they are women like you."

"Thank you, my dear, for a pretty compliment. I can trust my memory. I think I hinted at the obvious objections to an engagement. You and Carmina are cousins; and you belong to different religious communities. I may add that a man with your brilliant prospects has, in my opinion, no reason to marry unless his wife is in a position to increase his influence and celebrity. I had looked forward to seeing my clever son rise more nearly to a level with persons of rank, who are members of our family. There is my confession, Ovid. If I did hesitate on the occasion to which you have referred, I have now, I think, told you why."

"Am I to understand that you hesitate still?" Ovid asked.

"No." With that brief reply she rose to put away her book.

Ovid followed her to the bookcase. "Has Carmina conquered you?" he said.

She put her book back in its place. "Carmina has conquered me," she answered.

"You say it coldly."

"What does that matter, if I say it truly?"

The struggle in him between hope and fear burst its way out. "Oh, mother, no words can tell you how fond I am of Carmina! For God's sake take care of her, and be kind to her!"

"For *your* sake," said Mrs. Gallilee, gently correcting the language of her excitable son, from her own protoplastic point of view. "You do me an injustice if you feel anxious about Carmina, when you leave her here. My dead brother's child, is *my* child. You may be sure of that." She took his hand, and drew him to her, and kissed his forehead with dignity and deliberation. If Mr. Mool had been present, during the registration of that solemn pledge, he would have been irresistibly reminded of the other ceremony, which is called signing a deed.

"Have you any instructions to give me?" Mrs. Gallilee proceeded. "For instance, do you object to my taking Carmina to parties? I mean, of course, parties which will improve her mind."

He fell sadly below his mother's level in replying to this. "Do everything you can to make her life happy while I am away." Those were his only instructions.

But Mrs. Gallilee had not done with him yet. "With regard to visitors," she went on, "I presume you wish me to be careful, if I find young men calling here oftener than usual?"

Ovid actually laughed at this. "Do you think I doubt her?" he asked. "The earth doesn't hold a truer girl than my little Carmina!" A thought struck him while he said it. The brightness faded out of his face; his voice lost its gaiety. "There is one person who may call on you," he said, "whom I don't wish her to see."

"Who is he?"

"Unfortunately, he is a man who has excited her curiosity. I mean Benjulia."

It was now Mrs. Gallilee's turn to be amused. Her laugh was not one of her foremost fascinations. It was hard in tone, and limited in range—it opened her mouth, but it failed to kindle any light in her eyes. "Jealous of the ugly doctor!" she exclaimed. "Oh, Ovid, what next?"

"You never made a greater mistake in your life," her son answered sharply.

"Then what is the objection to him?" Mrs. Gallilee rejoined.

It was not easy to meet that question with a plain reply. If Ovid asserted that Benjulia's chemical experiments were assumed—for some reason known only to himself—as a cloak to cover the atrocities of the Savage Science, he would only raise the doctor in his mother's estimation. If, on the other hand, he described what had passed between them when they met in the Zoological Gardens, Mrs. Gallilee might summon Benjulia to explain the slur which he had indirectly cast on the memory of Carmina's mother—and might find, in the reply, some plausible reason for objecting to her son's marriage. Having rashly placed himself in this dilemma, Ovid unwisely escaped from it by the easiest way. "I don't think Benjulia a fit person," he said, "to be in the company of a young girl."

Mrs. Gallilee accepted this expression of opinion with a readiness, which would have told a more suspicious man that he had made a mistake. Ovid had roused the curiosity—perhaps awakened the distrust—of his clever mother.

"You know best," Mrs. Gallilee replied; "I will bear in mind what you say." She rang the bell for Carmina, and left the room. Ovid found the minutes passing slowly, for the first time since the day had been fixed for his departure. He attributed this impression to his natural impatience for the appearance of his cousin—until the plain evidence of the clock pointed to a delay of five endless minutes, and more. As he approached the door to make inquiries, it opened at last. Hurrying to meet Carmina, he found himself face to face with Miss Minerva!

She came in hastily, and held out her hand without looking at him.

"Forgive me for intruding on you," she said, with a rapidity of utterance and a timidity of manner strangely unlike herself. "I'm obliged to prepare the children's lessons for to-morrow; and this is my only opportunity of bidding you good-bye. You have my best wishes—my heartfelt wishes—for your safety and your health, and—and your enjoyment of the journey. Good-bye! good-bye!

After holding his hand for a moment, she hastened back to the door. There she stopped, turned towards him again, and looked at him for the first time. "I have one thing more to say," she broke out. "I will do all I can to make Carmina's life pleasant in your absence." Before he could thank her, she was gone.

In another minute Carmina came in, and found Ovid looking perplexed and annoyed. She had passed Frances on the stairs—had there been any misunderstanding between Ovid and the governess?

"Have you seen Miss Minerva?" she asked.

He put his arm round her, and seated her by him on the sofa. "I don't understand Miss Minerva," he said. "How is it that she came here, when I was expecting You?"

"She asked me, as a favour, to let her see you first; and she seemed to be so anxious about it that I gave way. I didn't do wrong, Ovid—did I?"

"My darling, you are always kind, and always right! But why couldn't she say good-bye (with the others) downstairs? Do *you* understand this curious woman?"

"I think I do." She paused, and toyed with the hair over Ovid's forehead. "Miss Minerva is fond of you, poor thing," she said innocently.

"Fond of me?"

The surprise which his tone expressed, failed to attract her attention. She quietly varied the phrase that she had just used.

"Miss Minerva has a true regard for you—and knows that you don't return it," she explained, still playing with Ovid's hair. "I want to see how it looks," she went on, "when it's parted in the middle. No! it looks better as you always wear it. How handsome you are, Ovid! Don't you wish I was beautiful, too? Everybody in the house loves you; and everybody is sorry you are going away. I like Miss Minerva, I like everybody, for being so fond of my dear, dear hero. Oh, what shall I do when day after day passes, and only takes you farther and farther away from me? No! I won't cry. You shan't go away with a heavy heart, my dear one, if I can help it. Where is your photograph? You promised me your photograph. Let me look at it. Yes! it's like you, and yet not like you. It will do to think over, when I am alone. My love, it has copied your eyes, but it has not copied the divine kindness and goodness that I see in them!" She paused, and laid her head on his bosom. "I shall cry, in spite of my resolution, if I look at you any longer. We won't look—we won't talk—I can feel your arm round me—I can hear your heart. Silence is best. I have been told of people dying happily; and I never understood it before. I think I could die happily now." She put her hand over his lips before he could reprove her, and nestled closer to him. "Hush!" she said softly; "hush!"

They neither moved nor spoke: that silent happiness was the best happiness, while it lasted. Mrs. Gallilee broke the charm. She suddenly opened the door, pointed to the clock, and went away again.

The cruel time had come. They made their last promises; shared their last kisses; held each other in the last embrace. She threw herself on the sofa, as he left her—with a gesture which entreated him to go, while she could still control herself. Once, he looked round, when he reached the door—and then it was over.

Alone on the landing, he dashed the tears away from his eyes. Suffering and sorrow tried hard to get the better of his manhood: they had shaken, but had not conquered him. He was calm, when he joined the members of the family, waiting in the library.

Perpetually setting an example, Mrs. Gallilee ascended her domestic pedestal as usual. She favoured her son with one more kiss, and reminded him of the railway. "We understand each other, Ovid—you have only five minutes to spare. Write, when you get to Quebec. Now, Maria! say good-bye."

Maria presented herself to her brother with a grace which did honour to the family dancing-master. Her short farewell speech was a model of its kind.

"Dear Ovid, I am only a child; but I feel truly anxious for the recovery of your health. At this favourable season you may look forward to a pleasant voyage. Please accept my best wishes." She offered her cheek to be kissed—and looked like a young person who had done her duty, and knew it.

Mr. Gallilee—modestly secluded behind the window curtains—appeared, at a sign from his wife. One of his plump red hands held a bundle of cigars. The other clutched an enormous new travelling-flask—the giant of its tribe.

"My dear boy, it's possible there may be good brandy and cigars on board; but that's not my experience of steamers—is it yours?" He stopped to consult his wife. "My dear, is it yours?" Mrs. Gallilee held up the

"Railway Guide,"[1] and shook it significantly. Mr. Gallilee went on in a hurry. "There's some of the right stuff in this flask, Ovid, if you will accept it. Five-and-forty years old—would you like to taste it? Would *you* like to taste it, my dear?" Mrs. Gallilee seized the "Railway Guide" again, with a terrible look. Her husband crammed the big flask into one of Ovid's pockets, and the cigars into the other. "You'll find them a comfort when you're away from us. God bless you, my son! You don't mind my calling you my son? I couldn't be fonder of you, if I really was your father. Let's part as cheerfully as we can," said poor Mr. Gallilee, with the tears rolling undisguisedly over his fat cheeks. "We can write to each other—can't we? Oh dear! dear! I wish I could take it as easy as Maria does. Zo! come and give him a kiss, poor fellow. Where's Zo?"

Mrs. Gallilee made the discovery—she dragged Zo into view, from under the table. Ovid took his little sister on his knee, and asked why she had hidden herself.

"Because I don't want to say good-bye!" cried the child, giving her reason with a passionate outbreak of sorrow that shook her from head to foot. "Take me with you, Ovid, take me with you!" He did his best to console her, under adverse circumstances. Mrs. Gallilee's warning voice sounded like a knell—"Time! time!" Zo's shrill treble rang out louder still. Zo was determined to write to Ovid, if she was not allowed to go with him. "Pa's going to write to you—why shouldn't I?" she screamed through her tears. "Dear Zoe, you are too young," Maria remarked. "Damned nonsense!" sobbed Mr. Gallilee; "she *shall* write!" "Time, time!" Mrs. Gallilee reiterated. Taking no part in the dispute, Ovid directed two envelopes for Zo, and quieted her in that way. He hurried into the hall; he glanced at the stairs that led to the drawing-room. Carmina was on the landing, waiting for a farewell look at him. On the higher flight of stairs, invisible from the hall, Miss Minerva was watching the scene of departure. Reckless of railways and steamers, Ovid ran up to Carmina. Another and another kiss; and then away to the house-door, with Zo at his heels, trying to get into the cab with him. A last kind word to the child, as they carried her back to the house; a last look at the familiar faces in the doorway; a last effort to resist that foretaste of death which embitters all human partings—and Ovid was gone!

End of November 1882 *Belgravia* Serial Number

END OF THE FIRST VOLUME

---

1   *Mrs. Gallilee held up the "Railway Guide"*: Mrs. Gallilee probably waves *Bradshaw's Railway Guide* at her son; it was the standard timetable for all passenger trains of the day.

VOLUME TWO

CHAPTER XXI.

On the afternoon of the day that followed Ovid's departure, the three ladies of the household were in a state of retirement—each in her own room.

The writing-table in Mrs. Gallilee's boudoir was covered with letters. Her banker's pass-book and her cheque-book were on the desk; Mr. Gallilee's affairs having been long since left as completely in the hands of his wife, as if Mr. Gallilee had been dead. A sheet of paper lay near the cheque-book, covered with calculations divided into two columns. The figures in the right-hand column were contained in one line at the top of the page. The figures in the left-hand column filled the page from top to bottom. With her fan in her hand, and her pen in the ink-bottle, Mrs. Gallilee waited, steadily thinking.

It was the hottest day of the season. All the fat women in London fanned themselves on that sultry afternoon; and Mrs. Gallilee followed the general example. When she looked to the right, her calculations showed the balance at the bank. When she looked to the left, her calculations showed her debts: some partially paid, some not paid at all. If she wearied of the prospect thus presented, and turned for relief to her letters, she was confronted by polite requests for money; from tradespeople in the first place, and from secretaries of fashionable Charities in the second. Here and there, by way of variety, were invitations to parties, representing more pecuniary liabilities, incurred for new dresses, and for hospitalities acknowledged by dinners and conversaziones at her own house.[1] Money that she owed, money that she must spend; nothing but outlay of money—and where was it to come from?

So far as her pecuniary resources were concerned, she was equally removed from hope and fear. Twice a year the same income flowed in regularly from the same investments. What she could pay at any future time was far more plainly revealed to her than what she might owe. With tact and management it would be possible to partially satisfy creditors, and keep up appearances for six months more. To that conclusion her reflections led her, and left her to write cheques.

And after the six months—what then?

Having first completed her correspondence with the tradespeople, and

---

1   *Here and there ... dinners and conversaziones at her own house*. A conversazione was an Italian name for an evening assembly that came to be known in England as an "At Home." Thus, when Mrs. Gallilee is "At Home to Science" in the novel's final chapter, the reader may assume she is hosting an evening of enlightened scientific discussion.

having next decided on her contributions to the Charities, this iron matron took up her fan again, cooled herself, and met the question of the future face to face.

Ovid was the central figure in the prospect.

If he lived devoted to his profession, and lived unmarried, there was a last resource always left to Mrs. Gallilee. For years past, his professional gains had added largely to the income which he had inherited from his father. Unembarrassed by expensive tastes, he had some thousands of pounds put by—for the simple reason that he was at a loss what else to do with them. Thus far, her brother's generosity had spared Mrs. Gallilee the hard necessity of making a confession to her son. As things were now, she must submit to tell the humiliating truth; and Ovid (with no wife to check his liberal instincts) would do what Ovid's uncle (with no wife living to check *his* liberal instincts) had done already.

There was the prospect, if her son remained a bachelor. But her son had resolved to marry Carmina. What would be the result if she was weak enough to allow it?

There would be, not one result, but three results. Natural; Legal; Pecuniary.

The natural result would be—children.

The legal result (if only one of those children lived) would be the loss to Mrs. Gallilee and her daughters of the splendid fortune reserved for them in the Will, if Carmina died without leaving offspring.

The pecuniary result would be (adding the husband's income to the wife's) about eight thousand a year for the young married people.

And how much for a loan, applicable to the mother-in-law's creditors? Judging Carmina by the standard of herself—by what other standard do we really judge our fellow-creatures, no matter how clever we may be?— Mrs. Gallilee decided that not one farthing would be left to help her to pay debts, which were steadily increasing with every new concession that she made to the claims of society. Young Mrs. Ovid Vere, at the head of a household, would have the grand example of her other aunt before her eyes. Although her place of residence might not be a palace, she would be a poor creature indeed, if she failed to spend eight thousand a year, in the effort to be worthy of the social position of Lady Northlake. Add to these results of Ovid's contemplated marriage the loss of a thousand a year, secured to the guardian by the Will, while the ward remained under her care—and the statement of disaster would be complete. "We must leave this house, and submit to be Lady Northlake's poor relations—there is the price I pay for it, if Ovid and Carmina become man and wife."

She quietly laid aside her fan, as the thought in her completed itself in this form

The trivial action, and the look which accompanied it, had a sinister meaning of their own, beyond the reach of words. And Ovid was already on the sea. And Teresa was far away in Italy.

The clock on the mantelpiece struck five; the punctual parlour-maid appeared with her mistress's customary cup of tea. Mrs. Gallilee asked for the governess. The servant answered that Miss Minerva was in her room.

"Where are the young ladies?"

"My master has taken them out for a walk."

"Have they had their music lesson?"

"Not yet, ma'am. Mr. Le Frank left word yesterday that he would come at six this evening."

"Does Mr. Gallilee know that?"

"I heard Miss Minerva tell my master, while I was helping the young ladies to get ready."

"Very well. Ask Miss Minerva to come here, and speak to me."

Miss Minerva sat at the open window of her bedroom, looking out vacantly at the backs of houses, in the street behind Fairfield Gardens.

The evil spirit was the dominant spirit in her again. She, too, was thinking of Ovid and Carmina. Her memory was busy with the parting scene on the previous day.

The more she thought of all that had happened in that short space of time, the more bitterly she reproached herself. Her one besetting weakness had openly degraded her, without so much as an attempt at resistance on her part. The fear of betraying herself if she took leave of the man she secretly loved, in the presence of his family, had forced her to ask a favour of Carmina, and to ask it under circumstances which might have led her rival to suspect the truth. Admitted to a private interview with Ovid, she had failed to control her agitation; and, worse still, in her ungovernable eagerness to produce a favourable impression on him at parting, she had promised—honestly promised, in that moment of impulse—to make Carmina's happiness her own peculiar care! Carmina, who had destroyed in a day the hope of years! Carmina, who had taken him away from her; who had clung round him when he ran upstairs, and had kissed him—fervently, shamelessly kissed him—before the servants in the hall!

She started to her feet, roused to a frenzy of rage by her own recollections. Standing at the window, she looked down at the pavement of the courtyard—it was far enough below to kill her instantly if she fell on it. Through the heat of her anger there crept the chill and stealthy prompting of despair. She leaned over the window-sill—she was not afraid—she might have done it, but for a trifling interruption. Somebody spoke outside.

It was the parlour-maid. Instead of entering the room, she spoke through the open door. The woman was one of Miss Minerva's many enemies in the house. "Mrs. Gallilee wishes to see you," she said—and shut the door again, the instant the words were out of her mouth.

Mrs. Gallilee!

The very name was full of promise at that moment. It suggested hope—merciless hope.

She left the window, and consulted her looking-glass. Even to herself, her haggard face was terrible to see. She poured eau-de-cologne and water into her basin, and bathed her burning head and eyes. Her shaggy black hair stood in need of attention next. She took almost as much pains with it as if she had been going into the presence of Ovid himself. "I must make a calm appearance," she thought, still as far as ever from suspecting that her employer had guessed her secret, "or his mother may find me out." Her knees trembled under her. She sat down for a minute to rest.

Was she merely wanted for some ordinary domestic consultation? or was there really a chance of hearing the question of Ovid and Carmina brought forward at the coming interview?

She believed what she hoped: she believed that the time had come when Mrs. Gallilee had need of an ally—perhaps of an accomplice. Only let her object be the separation of the two cousins—and Miss Minerva was eager to help her, in either capacity. Suppose she was too cautious to mention her object? Miss Minerva was equally ready for her employer, in that case. The doubt which had prompted her fruitless suggestions to Carmina, when they were alone in the young girl's room—the doubt whether a clue to the discovery of Mrs. Gallilee's motives might not be found, in that latter part of the Will which she had failed to overhear—was as present as ever in the governess's mind. "The learned lady is not infallible," she thought as she entered Mrs. Gallilee's room. "If one unwary word trips over her tongue, I shall pick it up!"

Mrs. Gallilee's manner was encouraging at the outset. She had left her writing-table; and she now presented herself, reclining in an easy chair, weary and discouraged—the picture of a woman in want of a helpful friend.

"My head aches with adding up figures, and writing letters," she said. "I wish you would finish my correspondence for me."

Miss Minerva took her place at the desk. She at once discovered the unfinished correspondence to be a false pretence. Three cheques for charitable subscriptions, due at that date, were waiting to be sent to three secretaries, with the customary letters. In five minutes, the letters were ready for the post. "Anything more?" Miss Minerva asked.

"Not that I remember. Do you mind giving me my fan? I feel perfectly helpless—I am wretchedly depressed to-day."

"The heat, perhaps?"

"No. The expenses. Every year, the demands on our resources seem to increase. On principle, I dislike living up to our income—and I am obliged to do it."

Here, plainly revealed to the governess's experienced eyes, was another false pretence—used to introduce the true object of the interview, as something which might accidentally suggest itself in the course of conversation. Miss Minerva expressed the necessary regret with innocent readiness. "Might I suggest economy?" she asked with impenetrable gravity.

"Admirably advised," Mrs. Gallilee admitted; "but how is it to be done? Those subscriptions, for instance, are more than I ought to give. And what happens if I lower the amount? I expose myself to unfavourable comparison with other people of our rank in society."

Miss Minerva still patiently played the part expected of her. "You might perhaps do with only one carriage-horse," she remarked.

"My good creature, look at the people who have only one carriage-horse! Situated as I am, can I descend to that level? Don't suppose I care two straws about such things, myself. *My* one pride and pleasure in life is the pride and pleasure of improving my mind. But I have Lady Northlake for a sister; and I must not be entirely unworthy of my family connections. I have two daughters; and I must think of their interests. In a few years, Maria will be presented at Court.[1] Thanks to you, she will be one of the most accomplished girls in England. Think of Maria's mother in a one-horse chaise.[2] Dear child! tell me all about her lessons. Is she getting on as well as ever?"

"Examine her yourself, Mrs. Gallilee. I can answer for the result."

"No, Miss Minerva! I have too much confidence in you to do anything of the kind. Besides, in one of the most important of Maria's accomplishments, I am entirely dependent on yourself. I know nothing of music. You are not responsible for her progress in that direction. Still, I should like to know if you are satisfied with Maria's music?"

"Quite satisfied."

"You don't think she is getting—how can I express it?—shall I say beyond the reach of Mr. Le Frank's teaching?"

"Certainly not."

"Perhaps you would consider Mr. Le Frank equal to the instruction of an older and more advanced pupil than Maria?"

Thus far, Miss Minerva had answered the questions submitted to her with well-concealed indifference. This last inquiry roused her attention. Why did Mrs. Gallilee show an interest, for the first time, in Mr. Le Frank's capacity as a teacher? Who was this "older and more advanced pupil," for whose appearance in the conversation the previous questions had so smoothly prepared the way? Feeling delicate ground under her, the governess advanced cautiously.

---

1 *In a few years, Maria will be presented at Court*: The presentation at court, where participants met and were honoured by the Queen, was the ritual marking the "coming out" into society of young girls. Mrs. Gallilee, whose first husband, Vere, belonged to an old family, may meet the social requirements for her daughter's presentation, but her present social position and her husband's professional background may not be lofty enough to merit such an honour.

2 *Think of Maria's mother in a one-horse chaise*: A chaise was a two-wheeled carriage pulled by one horse. Mrs. Gallilee obviously shuns the ordinary and dreams of a four-wheeled, two-horse carriage.

"I have always thought Mr. Le Frank an excellent teacher," she said.

"Can you give me no more definite answer than that?" Mrs. Gallilee asked.

"I am quite unacquainted, madam, with the musical proficiency of the pupil to whom you refer. I don't even know (which adds to my perplexity) whether you are speaking of a lady or a gentleman."

"I am speaking," said Mrs. Gallilee quietly, "of my niece, Carmina."

Those words set all further doubt at rest in Miss Minerva's mind. Introduced by such elaborate preparation, the allusion to Carmina's name could only lead, in due course, to the subject of Carmina's marriage. By indirect methods of approach, Mrs. Gallilee had at last reached the object that she had in view.

CHAPTER XXII.

There was an interval of silence between the two ladies.

Mrs. Gallilee waited for Miss Minerva to speak next. Miss Minerva waited to be taken into Mrs. Gallilee's confidence. The sparrows twittered in the garden; and, far away in the schoolroom, the notes of the piano announced that the music lesson had begun.

"The birds are noisy," said Mrs. Gallilee.

"And the piano sounds out of tune," Miss Minerva remarked.

There was no help for it. Either Mrs. Gallilee must return to the matter in hand—or the matter in hand must drop.

"I am afraid I have not made myself understood," she resumed.

"I am afraid I have been very stupid," Miss Minerva confessed.

Resigning herself to circumstances, Mrs. Gallilee put the adjourned question under a new form. "We were speaking of Mr. Le Frank as a teacher, and of my niece as a pupil," she said. "Have you been able to form any opinion of Carmina's musical abilities?"

Miss Minerva remained as prudent as ever. She answered, "I have had no opportunity of forming an opinion."

Mrs. Gallilee met this cautious reply by playing her trump card. She handed a letter to Miss Minerva. "I have received a proposal from Mr. Le Frank," she said. "Will you tell me what you think of it?"

The letter was short and servile. Mr. Le Frank presented his best respects. If Mrs. Gallilee's charming niece stood in need of musical instruction, he ventured to hope that he might have the honour and happiness of superintending her studies. Looking back to the top of the letter, the governess discovered that this modest request bore a date of eight days since. "Have you written to Mr. Le Frank?" she asked.

"Only to say that I will take his request into consideration," Mrs. Gallilee replied.

Had she waited for her son's departure, before she committed herself to a decision? On the chance that this might be the case, Miss Minerva consulted her memory. When Mrs. Gallilee first decided on engaging a music-master to teach the children, her son had disapproved of employing Mr. Le Frank. This circumstance might possibly be worth bearing in mind. "Do you see any objection to accepting Mr. Le Frank's proposal?" Mrs. Gallilee asked. Miss Minerva saw an objection forthwith, and, thanks to her effort of memory, discovered an especially mischievous way of stating it. "I feel a certain delicacy in offering an opinion," she said modestly.

Mrs. Gallilee was surprised. "Do you allude to Mr. Le Frank?" she inquired.

"No. I don't doubt that his instructions would be of service to any young lady."

"Are you thinking of my niece?"

"No, Mrs. Gallilee. I am thinking of your son."

"In what way, if you please?"

"In this way. I believe your son would object to employing Mr. Le Frank as Miss Carmina's teacher."

"On musical grounds?"

"No; on personal grounds."

"What do you mean?"

Miss Minerva explained her meaning. "I think you have forgotten what happened, when you first employed Mr. Le Frank to teach Maria and Zoe. His personal appearance produced an unfavourable impression on your son; and Mr. Ovid made certain inquiries which you had not thought necessary. Pardon me if I persist in mentioning the circumstances. I owe it to myself to justify my opinion—an opinion, you will please to remember, that I did not volunteer. Mr. Ovid's investigations brought to light a very unpleasant report, relating to Mr. Le Frank and a young lady who had been one of his pupils."

"An abominable slander, Miss Minerva! I am surprised that you should refer to it."

"I am referring, madam, to the view of the matter taken by Mr. Ovid. If Mr. Le Frank had failed to defend himself successfully, he would of course not have been received into this house. But your son had his own opinion of the defence. I was present at the time, and I heard him say that, if Maria and Zoe had been older, he should have advised employing a music-master who had no false reports against him to contradict. As they were only children, he would say nothing more. That is what I had in my mind, when I gave my opinion. I think Mr. Ovid will be annoyed when he hears that Mr. Le Frank is his cousin's music-master. And, if any foolish gossip reaches him in his absence, I fear it might lead to mischievous results—I mean, to misunderstandings not easily set right by correspondence, and quite likely therefore to lead, in the end, to distrust and jealousy."

There she paused, and crossed her hands on her lap, and waited for what was to come next.

If Mrs. Gallilee could have looked into her mind at that moment, as well as into her face, she would have read Miss Minerva's thoughts in these plain terms: "All this time, madam, you have been keeping up appearances in the face of detection. You are going to use Mr. Le Frank as a means of making mischief between Ovid and Carmina. If you had taken me into your confidence, I might have been willing to help you. As it is, please observe that I am not caught in the trap you have set for me. If Mr. Ovid discovers your little plot, you can't lay the blame on your governess's advice."

Mrs. Gallilee felt that she had again measured herself with Miss Minerva, and had again been beaten. She had confidently reckoned on the governess's secret feeling towards her son to encourage, without hesitation or distrust, any project for promoting the estrangement of Ovid and Carmina. There was no alternative now but to put her first obstacle in the way of the marriage, on her own sole responsibility.

"I don't doubt that you have spoken sincerely," she said; "but you have failed to do justice to my son's good sense; and you are—naturally enough, in your position—incapable of estimating his devoted attachment to Carmina." Having planted that sting, she paused to observe the effect. Not the slightest visible result rewarded her. She went on. "Almost the last words he said to me expressed his confidence—his affectionate confidence—in my niece. The bare idea of his being jealous of anybody, and especially of such a person as Mr. Le Frank, is simply ridiculous. I am astonished that you don't see it in that light."

"I should see it in that light as plainly as you do," Miss Minerva quietly replied, "if Mr. Ovid was at home."

"What difference does that make?"

"Excuse me—it makes a great difference, as I think. He has gone away on a long journey, and gone away in bad health. He will have his hours of depression. At such times, trifles are serious things; and even well-meant words—in letters—are sometimes misunderstood. I can offer no better apology for what I have said; and I can only regret that I have made so unsatisfactory a return for your flattering confidence in me."

Having planted *her* sting, she rose to retire.

"Have you any further commands for me?" she asked.

"I should like to be quite sure that I have not misunderstood you," said Mrs. Gallilee. "You consider Mr. Le Frank to be competent, as director of any young lady's musical studies? Thank you. On the one point on which I wished to consult you, my mind is at ease. Do you know where Carmina is?"

"In her room, I believe."

"Will you have the goodness to send her here?"

"With the greatest pleasure. Good-evening!"

So ended Mrs. Gallilee's first attempt to make use of Miss Minerva, without trusting her.

CHAPTER XXIII.

The mistress of the house, and the governess of the house, had their own special reasons for retiring to their own rooms. Carmina was in solitude as a matter of necessity. The only friends that the poor girl could gather round her now, were the absent and the dead.

She had written to Ovid—merely for the pleasure of thinking that her letter would accompany him, in the mail-steamer which took him to Quebec. She had written to Teresa. She had opened her piano, and had played the divinely beautiful music of Mozart, until its tenderness saddened her, and she closed the instrument with an aching heart. For a while she sat by the window, thinking of Ovid. The decline of day has its melancholy affinities with the decline of life. As the evening wore on, her loneliness had become harder and harder to endure. She rang for the maid, and asked if Miss Minerva was at leisure. Miss Minerva had been sent for by Mrs. Gallilee. Where was Zo? In the schoolroom, waiting until Mr. Le Frank had done with Maria, to take her turn at the piano. Left alone again, Carmina opened her locket, and put Ovid's portrait by it on the table. Her sad fancy revived her dead parents—imagined her lover being presented to them—saw him winning their hearts by his genial voice, his sweet smile, his wise and kindly words. Miss Minerva, entering the room, found her still absorbed in her own little melancholy daydream; recalling the absent, reviving the dead—as if she had been nearing the close of life. And only seventeen years old. Alas for Carmina, only seventeen!

"Mrs. Gallilee wishes to see you."

She started. "Is there anything wrong?" she asked.

"No. What makes you think so?"

"You speak in such a strange way. Oh, Frances, I have been longing for you to keep me company! And now you are here, you look at me as coldly as if I had offended you. Perhaps you are not well?"

"That's it. I am not well."

"Have some of my lavender water![1] Let me bathe your forehead, and then blow on it to cool you this hot weather. No? Sit down, dear, at any rate. What does my aunt want with me?"

"I think I had better not tell you."

"Why?"

"Your aunt is sure to ask you what I have said. I have tried her temper; you know what her temper is! She has sent me here instead of sending a maid, on the chance that I may commit some imprudence. I give you her

---

1   *lavender water*: The flowers of the lavender produced an oil used in a popular perfume of the day. Carmina proposes using her lavender water as a balm for Miss Minerva, just as Miss Minerva does for herself with her eau-de-cologne and water in Chapter XXI.

message exactly as the servant might have given it—and you can tell her so with a safe conscience. No more questions!;"

"One more, please. Is it anything about Ovid?"

"No."

"Then my aunt can wait a little. Do sit down! I want to speak to you."

"About what?"

"About Ovid, of course!"

Carmina's look and tone at once set Miss Minerva's mind at ease. Her conduct, on the day of Ovid's departure, had aroused no jealous suspicion in her innocent rival. She refused to take the offered chair.

"I have already told you your aunt is out of temper," she said. "Go to her at once."

Carmina rose unwillingly. "There were so many things I wanted to say to you," she began—and was interrupted by a rapid little series of knocks at the door. Was the person in a hurry? The person proved to be the discreet and accomplished Maria. She made her excuses to Carmina with sweetness, and turned to Miss Minerva with sorrow.

"I regret to say that you are wanted in the schoolroom. Mr. Le Frank can do nothing with Zoe. Oh, dear!" She sighed over her sister's wickedness, and waited for instructions.

To be called away, under any circumstances, was a relief to Miss Minerva. Carmina's affectionate welcome had irritated her in the most incomprehensible manner. She was angry with herself for being irritated; she felt inclined to abuse the girl for believing her. "You fool, why don't you see through me? Why don't you write to that other fool who is in love with you, and tell him how I hate you both?" But for her self-command, she might have burst out with such mad words as those. Maria's appearance was inexpressibly welcome. "Say I will follow you directly," she answered.

Maria, in the language of the stage, made a capital exit. With a few hurried words of apology, Miss Minerva prepared to follow. Carmina stopped her at the door.

"Don't be hard on Zo!" she said.

"I must do my duty," Miss Minerva answered sternly.

"We were sometimes naughty ourselves when we were children," Carmina pleaded. "And only the other day she had bread and water for tea. I am so fond of Zo! And besides—" she looked doubtfully at Miss Minerva—"I don't think Mr. Le Frank is the sort of man to get on with children."

After what had just passed between Mrs. Gallilee and herself, this expression of opinion excited the governess's curiosity. "What makes you say that?" she asked.

"Well, my dear, for one thing Mr. Le Frank is so ugly. Don't you agree with me?"

"I think you had better keep your opinion to yourself. If he heard of it—"

"Is he vain? My poor father used to say that all bad musicians were vain."

"You don't call Mr. Le Frank a bad musician?"

"Oh, but I do! I heard him at his concert. Mere execution of the most mechanical kind. A musical box is as good as that man's playing. This is how he does it!"

Her girlish good spirits had revived in her friend's company. She turned gaily to the piano, and amused herself by imitating Mr. Le Frank.

Another knock at the door—a single peremptory knock this time—stopped the performance.

Miss Minerva had left the door ajar, when Carmina had prevented her from quitting the room. She looked through the open space, and discovered—Mr. Le Frank.

His bald head trembled, his florid complexion was livid with suppressed rage. "That little devil has run away!" he said—and hurried down the stairs again, as if he dare not trust himself to utter a word more.

"Has he heard me?" Carmina asked in dismay.

"He may only have heard you playing."

Offering this hopeful suggestion, Miss Minerva felt no doubt, in her own mind, that Mr. Le Frank was perfectly well acquainted with Carmina's opinion of him. It was easy enough to understand that he should himself inform the governess of an incident, so entirely beyond the reach of his own interference as the flight of Zo. But it was impossible to assume that the furious anger which his face betrayed, could have been excited by a child who had run away from a lesson. No: the vainest of men and musicians had heard that he was ugly, and that his pianoforte-playing resembled the performance of a musical box.

They left the room together—Carmina, ill at ease, to attend on her aunt; Miss Minerva, pondering on what had happened, to find the fugitive Zo.

The footman had already spared her the trouble of searching the house. He had seen Zo running out bare-headed into the Square, and had immediately followed her. The young rebel was locked up. "I don't care," said Zo; "I hate Mr. Le Frank!" Miss Minerva's mind was too seriously preoccupied to notice this aggravation of her pupil's offence. One subject absorbed her attention—the interview then in progress between Carmina and her aunt.

How would Mrs. Gallilee's scheme prosper now? Mr. Le Frank might, or might not, consent to be Carmina's teacher. Another result, however, was certain. Miss Minerva thoroughly well knew the vindictive nature of the man. He neither forgave nor forgot—he was Carmina's enemy for life.

CHAPTER XXIV.

The month of July was near its end.

On the morning of the twenty-eighth, Carmina was engaged in reply-ing to a letter received from Teresa. Her answer contained a record of domestic events, during an interval of serious importance in her life under Mrs. Gallilee's roof. Translated from the Italian, the letter was expressed in these terms:

"Are you vexed with me, dearest, for this late reply to your sad news from Italy? I have but one excuse to offer.

"Can I hear of your anxiety about your husband, and not feel the wish to help you to bear your burden by writing cheerfully of myself? Over and over again, I have thought of you and have opened my desk. My spirits have failed me, and I have shut it up again. Am I now in a happier frame of mind? Yes, my good old nurse, I am happier. I have had a letter from Ovid.

"He has arrived safely at Quebec, and he is beginning to feel better already, after the voyage. You cannot imagine how beautifully, how ten-derly he writes! I am almost reconciled to his absence, when I read his let-ter. Will that give you some idea of the happiness and the consolation that I owe to this best and dearest of men?

"Ah, my old granny, I see you start, and make that favourite mark with your thumb-nail under the word 'consolation'! I hear you say to yourself, 'Is she unhappy in her English home? And is Aunt Gallilee to blame for it?' Yes! it is even so. What I would not for the whole world write to Ovid, I may confess to you. Aunt Gallilee is indeed a hard, hard woman.

"Do you remember telling me, in your dear downright way, that Mr. Le Frank looked like a rogue? I don't know whether he is a rogue—but I do know that it is through his conduct that my aunt is offended with me.

"It happened three weeks ago.

"She sent for me, and said that my education must be completed, and that my music in particular must be attended to. I was quite willing to obey her, and I said so with all needful readiness and respect. She answered that she had already chosen a music-master for me—and then, to my astonishment, she mentioned his name. Mr. Le Frank, who taught her children, was also to teach me! I have plenty of faults, but I really think vanity is not one of them. It is only due to my excellent master in Italy to say, that I am a better pianoforte player than Mr. Le Frank.

"I never breathed a word of this, mind, to my aunt. It would have been ungrateful and useless. She knows and cares nothing about music.

"So we parted good friends, and she wrote the same evening to engage my master. The next day she got his reply. Mr. Le Frank refused to be my professor of music—and this, after he had himself proposed to teach me, in a letter addressed to my aunt! Being asked for his reasons, he made an excuse. The spare time at his disposal, when he had written, had been since occupied by another pupil. The true reason for his conduct is, that he heard me speak of him—rashly enough, I don't deny it—as an ugly man and a bad player. Miss Minerva sounded him on the subject, at my request, for the purpose of course of making my apologies. He affected not to understand what she meant—with what motive I am sure I don't know. False and revengeful, you may say, and perhaps you may be right. But the serious part of it, so far as I am concerned, is my aunt's behaviour to me. If I had thwarted her in the dearest wish of her life, she could hardly treat me with greater coldness and severity. She has not stirred again, in the matter of my education. We only meet at meal-times; and she receives me, when I sit down at table, as she might receive a perfect stranger. Her icy civility is unendurable. And this woman is my darling Ovid's mother!

"Have I done with my troubles now? No, Teresa; not even yet. Oh, how I wish I was with you in Italy!

"Your letters persist in telling me that I am deluded in believing Miss Minerva to be truly my friend. Do pray remember—even if I am wrong—what a solitary position mine is, in Mrs. Gallilee's house! I can play with dear little Zo; but whom can I talk to, whom can I confide in, if it turns out that Miss Minerva has been deceiving me?

"When I wrote to you, I refused to acknowledge that any such dreadful discovery as this could be possible; I resented the bare idea of it as a cruel insult to my friend. Since that time—my face burns with shame while I write it—I am a little, just a little, shaken in my own opinion.

"Shall I tell you how it began? Yes; I will.

"My good old friend, you have your prejudices. But you speak your mind truly—and whom else can I consult? Not Ovid! The one effort of my life is to prevent him from feeling anxious about me. And, besides, I have contended against his opinion of Miss Minerva, and have brought him to think of her more kindly. Has he been right, notwithstanding? and are you right? And am I alone wrong? You shall judge for yourself.

"Miss Minerva began to change towards me, after I had done the thing of all others which ought to have brought us closer together than ever. She is very poorly paid by my aunt, and she has been worried by little debts. When she owned this, I most willingly lent her the money to pay her bills—a mere trifle, only thirty pounds. What do you think she did? She crushed up the bank-notes in her hand, and left the room in the strangest headlong manner—as if I had insulted her instead of helping her! All the next day, she avoided me. The day after, I myself went to her room, and asked what was the matter. She gave me a most extraordinary answer. She said, 'I don't know which of us two I most detest—myself or you. Myself for borrowing your money, or you for lending it.' I left her; not feeling offended, only bewildered and distressed. More than an hour passed before she made her excuses. 'I am ill and miserable'—that was all she said. She did indeed look so wretched that I forgave her directly. Would you not have done so too, in my place?

"This happened a fortnight since. Only yesterday, she broke out again, and put my affection for her to a far more severe trial. I have not got over it yet.

"There was a message for her in Ovid's letter—expressed in the friendliest terms. He remembered with gratitude her kind promise, on saying good-bye; he believed she would do all that lay in her power to make my life happy in his absence; and he only regretted her leaving him in such haste that he had no time to thank her personally. Such was the substance of the message. I was proud and pleased to go to her room myself, and read it to her.

"Can you guess how she received me? Nobody—I say it positively—nobody could guess.

"She actually flew into a rage! Not only with me (which I might have pardoned), but with Ovid (which is perfectly inexcusable). 'How dare he write to *you*,' she burst out, 'of what I said to him when we took leave of each other? And how dare you come here, and read it to me? What do I care about your life, in his absence? Of what earthly consequence are his remembrance and his gratitude to Me!' She spoke of him, with such fury and such contempt, that she roused me at last. I said to her, 'You abominable woman, there is but one excuse for you—you're mad!' I left the room—and didn't I bang the door! We have not met since. Let me hear your opinion, Teresa. I was in a passion when I told her she was mad; but was I altogether wrong? Do you really think the poor creature is in her right senses?

"Looking back at your letter, I see that you ask if I have made any new acquaintances.

"I have been introduced to one of the sweetest women I ever met with. And who do you think she is? My other aunt—Mrs. Gallilee's younger sister, Lady Northlake! They say she was not so handsome as Mrs. Gallilee, when they were both young. For my part, I can only declare that no such comparison is possible between them now. In look, in voice, in manner there is something so charming in Lady Northlake that I quite despair of describing it. My father used to say that she was amiable and weak; led by her husband, and easily imposed upon. I am not clever enough to have his eye for character: and perhaps I am weak and easily imposed upon too. Before I had been ten minutes in Lady Northlake's company, I would have given everything I possess in the world to have had *her* for my guardian.

"She had called to say good-bye, on leaving London; and my aunt was not at home. We had a long delightful talk together. She asked me so kindly to visit her in Scotland, and be introduced to Lord Northlake, that I accepted the invitation with a glad heart.

"When my aunt returned, I quite forgot that we were on bad terms. I gave her an enthusiastic account of all that had passed between her sister and myself. How do you think she met this little advance on my part? She positively refused to let me go to Scotland.

"As soon as I had in some degree got over my disappointment, I asked for her reasons. 'I am your guardian,' she said; 'and I am acting in the exercise of my own discretion. I think it better you should stay with me.' I made no further remark. My aunt's cruelty made me think of my dead father's kindness. It was as much as I could do to keep from crying.

"Thinking over it afterwards, I supposed (as this is the season when everybody leaves town) that she had arranged to take me into the country with her. Mr. Gallilee, who is always good to me, thought so too, and promised me some sailing at the sea-side. To the astonishment of everybody, she has not shown any intention of going away from London! Even the servants ask what it means.

"This is a letter of complaints. Am I adding to your anxieties instead of relieving them? My kind old nurse, there is no need to be anxious. At the worst of my little troubles, I have only to think of Ovid—and his mother's ice melts away from me directly; I feel brave enough to endure anything.

"Take my heart's best love, dear—no, next best love, after Ovid!—and give some of it to your poor suffering husband. May I ask one little favour? The English gentleman who has taken our old house at Rome, will not object to give you a few flowers out of what was once my garden. Send them to me in your next letter."

CHAPTER XXV.

On the twelfth of August, Carmina heard from Ovid again. He wrote from Montreal; describing the presentation of that letter of introduction which he had once been tempted to destroy. In the consequences that followed the presentation—apparently harmless consequences at the time—the destinies of Ovid, of Carmina, and of Benjulia proved to be seriously involved.

Ovid's letter was thus expressed:[1]

"I want to know, my love, if there is any other man in the world who is as fond of his darling as I am of you? If such a person exists, and if adverse circumstances compel him to travel, I should like to ask a question. Is he

---

1   *Ovid's letter was thus expressed*: For the next three chapters, and at various points throughout the rest of the novel, Collins employs a literary device that had served him well in several of his earlier works: the epistolary furthering of the action. *The Woman in White*, *No Name*, *Armadale*, and *The Moonstone*—considered Collins's four best novels—are all dependent at certain points of the action on postal exchanges, diary entries, journals passages, notebook material, or written confessions.

perpetually calling to mind forgotten things, which he ought to have said to his sweetheart before he left her?

"This is my case. Let me give you an instance.

"I have made a new friend here—one Mr. Morphew. Last night, he was so kind as to invite me to a musical entertainment at his house. He is a medical man; and he amuses himself in his leisure hours by playing on that big and dreary member of the family of fiddles, whose name is Violoncello. Assisted by friends, he hospitably cools his guests, in the hot season, by the amateur performance of quartets. My dear, I passed a delightful evening. Listening to the music? Not listening to a single note of it. Thinking of You.

"Have I roused your curiosity? I fancy I can see your eyes brighten; I fancy I can hear you telling me to go on!

"My thoughts reminded me that music is one of the enjoyments of your life. Before I went away, I ought to have remembered this, and to have told you that the manager of the autumn concerts at the opera-house is an old friend of mine. He will be only too glad to place a box at your disposal, on any night when his programme attracts your notice; I have already made amends for my forgetfulness, by writing to him by this mail. Miss Minerva will be your companion at the theatre. If Mr. Le Frank (who is sure to be on the free list) pays you a visit in your box, tell him from me to put a wig on his bald head, and to try if *that* will make him look like an honest man!

"Did I forget anything else before my departure? Did I tell you how precious you are to me? how beautiful you are to me? how entirely worthless my life is without you? I dare say I did; but I tell it all over again— and, when you are tired of the repetition, you have only to let me know.

"In the meanwhile, have I nothing else to say? have I no travelling adventures to relate? You insist on hearing of everything that happens to me; and you are to have your own way before we are married, as well as after. My sweet Carmina, your willing slave has something more serious than common travelling adventures to relate—he has a confession to make. In plain words, I have been practising my profession again, in the city of Montreal!

"I wonder whether you will forgive me, when you are informed of the circumstances? It is a sad little story; but I am vain enough to think that my part in it will interest you. I have been a vain man, since that brightest and best of all possible days when you first made *your* confession— when you said that you loved me.

"Look back in my letter, and you will see Mr. Morphew mentioned as a new friend of mine, in Canada. I became acquainted with him through a letter of introduction, given to me by Benjulia.

"Say nothing to anybody of what I am now going to tell you—and be especially careful, if you happen to see him, to keep Benjulia in the dark. I sincerely hope you will not see him. He is a hard-hearted man—and he might say something which would distress you, if he knew of the result which has followed his opening to me the door of his friend's house.

"Mr. Morphew is a worthy busy old gentleman, who follows his professional routine, and whose medical practice consists principally in bringing infant Canadians into the world. His services happened to be specially in request, at the time when I made his acquaintance. He was called away from his table, on the day after the musical party, when I dined with him. I was the only guest—and his wife was left to entertain me.

"The good lady began by speaking of Benjulia. She roundly declared him to be a brute—and she produced my letter of introduction (closed by the doctor's own hand, before he gave it to me) as a proof. Would you like to read the letter, too? Here is a copy:—'The man who brings this is an overworked surgeon, named Ovid Vere. He wants rest and good air. Don't encourage him to use his brains; and give him information enough to take him, by the shortest way, to the biggest desert in Canada.' You will now understand that I am indebted to myself for the hospitable reception which has detained me at Montreal.

"To return to my story. Mr. Morphew's services were again in request, ten minutes after he had left the house. This time the patient was a man—and the messenger declared that he was at the point of death.

"Mrs. Morphew seemed to be at a loss what to do. 'In this dreadful case,' she said, 'death is a mercy. What I cannot bear to think of is the poor man's lonely position. In his last moments, there will not be a living creature at his bedside.'

"Hearing this, I ventured to make some inquiries. The answers painted such a melancholy picture of poverty and suffering, and so vividly reminded me of a similar case in my own experience, that I forgot I was an invalid myself, and volunteered to visit the dying man in Mr. Morphew's place.

"The messenger led me to the poorest quarter of the city, and to a garret in one of the wretchedest houses in the street. There he lay, without anyone to nurse him, on a mattress on the floor. What his malady was, you will not ask to know. I will only say that any man but a doctor would have run out of the room, the moment he entered it. To save the poor creature was impossible. For a few days longer, I could keep pain in subjection, and could make death easy when it came.

"At my next visit he was able to speak.

"I discovered that he was a member of my own profession—a mulatto from the Southern States of America, by birth. The one fatal event of his life had been his marriage. Every worst offence of which a bad woman can be guilty, his vile wife had committed—and his infatuated love clung to her through it all. She had disgraced and ruined him. Not once, but again and again he had forgiven her, under circumstances which degraded him in his own estimation, and in the estimation of his best friends. On the last occasion when she left him, he had followed her to Montreal. In a fit of drunken frenzy, she had freed him from her at last by self-destruction. Her death affected his reason. When he was discharged from the asylum, he spent his last miserable savings in placing a monument over her grave. As long as his strength held out, he made daily pilgrimages to the cemetery. And now, when the shadow of death was darkening over him, his one motive for clinging to life, his one reason for vainly entreating me to cure him, still centred in devotion to the memory of his wife. 'Nobody will take care of her grave,' he said, 'when I am gone.'

"My love, I have always thought fondly of you. After hearing this miserable story, my heart overflowed with gratitude to God for giving me Carmina.

"He died yesterday. His last words implored me to have him buried in the same grave with the woman who had dishonoured him. Who am I that I should judge him? Besides, I shall fulfil his last wishes as a thank-offering for You.

"There is still something more to tell.

"On the day before his death he asked me to open an old portmanteau—literally, the one thing that he possessed. He had no money left, and no clothes. In a corner of the portmanteau there was a roll of papers, tied with a piece of string—and that was all.

" 'I can make you but one return,' he said; 'I give you my book.'

"He was too weak to tell me what the book was about, or to express any wish relative to its publication. I am ashamed to say I set no sort of value on the manuscript presented to me—except as a memorial of a sad incident in my life. Waking earlier than usual this morning, I opened and examined my gift for the first time.

"To my amazement, I found myself rewarded a hundredfold for the little that I had been able to do. This unhappy man must have been possessed of abilities which (under favouring circumstances) would, I don't hesitate to say, have ranked him among the greatest physicians of our time. The language in which he writes is obscure, and sometimes grammatically incorrect. But he, and he alone, has solved a problem in the treatment of disease, which has thus far been the despair of medical men throughout the whole civilised world.

"If a stranger was looking over my shoulder, he would be inclined to say, This curious lover writes to his young lady as if she was a medical colleague! We understand each other, Carmina, don't we? My future career is an object of interest to my future wife. This poor fellow's gratitude has opened new prospects to me; and who will be so glad to hear of it as you?

"Before I close my letter, you will expect me to say a word more about my health. Sometimes I feel well enough to take my cabin in the next vessel that sails for Liverpool. But there are other occasions, particularly when I happen to over-exert myself in walking or riding, which warn me to be careful and patient. My next journey will take me inland, to the mighty plains and forest of this grand country. When I have breathed the health-giving air of those regions, I shall be able to write definitely of the blessed future day which is to unite us once more.

"My mother has, I suppose, given her usual conversazione at the end of the season. Let me hear how you like the scientific people at close quarters, and let me give you a useful hint. When you meet in society with a particularly positive man, who looks as if he was sitting for his photograph, you may safely set that man down as a Professor.

"Seriously, I do hope that you and my mother get on well together. You say too little of each other in your letters to me, and I am sometimes troubled by misgivings. There is another odd circumstance, connected with our correspondence, which sets me wondering. I always send messages to Miss Minerva; and Miss Minerva never sends any messages back to me. Do you forget? or am I an object of perfect indifference to your friend?

"My latest news of you all is from Zo. She has sent me a letter, in one of the envelopes that I directed for her when I went away. Miss Minerva's hair would stand on end if she could see the blots and the spelling. Zo's account of the family circle (turned into intelligible English), will I think personally interest you. Here it is, in its own Roman brevity—with your pretty name shortened to two syllables: 'Except Pa and Car, we are a bad lot at home.' After that, I can add nothing that is worth reading.[1]

"Take the kisses, my angel, that I leave for you on the blank morsel of paper below, and love me as I love you. There is a world of meaning, Carmina, even in those commonplace words. Oh, if I could only go to you by the mail steamer, in the place of my letter!"

CHAPTER XXVI.

The answers to Ovid's questions were not to be found in Carmina's reply. She had reasons for not mentioning the conversazione; and she shrank from writing to him of his mother. Her true position in Mrs. Gallilee's house—growing, day by day, harder and harder to endure; threatening, more and more plainly, complications and perils to come—was revealed in her next letter to her old friend in Italy. She wrote to Teresa in these words:

"If you love me, forget the inhuman manner in which I have spoken of Miss Minerva!

"After I had written to you, I would have recalled my letter, if it could

---

1   *Here it is, in its own Roman brevity ... I can add nothing that is worth reading:* Latin is a famously telescopic language. The Romans often used a very few words to convey even a complicated idea; and they were notorious abbreviators. Collins biographer Catherine Peters uses the text of Zoe's note to label her dyslexic (Peters 399).

have been done. I began, that evening, to feel ashamed of what I had said in my anger. As the hours went on, and bedtime approached, I became so wretched that I ran the risk of another harsh reception, by intruding on her once more. It was a circumstance in my favour that she was, to all appearance, in bad spirits too. There was something in her voice, when she asked what I wanted, which made me think—though she looks like the last person in the world to be guilty of such weakness—that she had been crying.

"I gave the best expression I could to my feelings of repentance and regret. What I actually said to her, has slipped out of my memory; I was frightened and upset—and I am always stupid in that condition. My attempt at reconciliation may have been clumsy enough; but she might surely have seen that I had no intention to mystify and distress her. And yet, what else could she have imagined?—to judge by her own actions and words.

"Her bedroom candle was on the table behind me. She snatched it up and held it before my face, and looked at me as if I was some extraordinary object that she had never seen or heard of before! 'You are little better than a child,' she said; 'I have ten times your strength of will—what is there in you that I can't resist? Go away from me! Be on your guard against me! I am false; I am suspicious; I am cruel. You simpleton, have you no instincts to protect you? Is there nothing in you that shrinks from me?'

"She put down the candle, and burst into a wretched mocking laugh. 'There she stands,' cried this strange creature, 'and looks at me with the eyes of a baby that sees something new! I can't frighten her. I can't disgust her. What does it mean?' She dropped into a chair; her voice sank almost to a whisper—I should have thought she was afraid of me, if such a thing had been possible. 'What do you know of me, that I don't know of myself?' she asked.

"It was quite beyond me to understand what she meant. I took a chair, and sat down by her. 'I only know what you said to me yesterday,' I answered.

" 'What did I say?'

" 'You told me you were miserable.'

" 'I told you a lie! Believe what I have said to you to-day. In your own interests, believe it to be the truth!'

"Nothing would induce me to believe it. 'No,' I said. 'You were miserable yesterday, and you are miserable to-day. *That* is the truth!'

"What put my next bold words into my head, I don't know. It doesn't matter; the thought was in me—and out it came.

" 'I think you have some burden on your mind,' I went on. 'If I can't relieve you of it, perhaps I can help you bear it. Come! tell me what it is.' I waited; but it was of no use—she never even looked at me. Because I am in love myself, do I think everybody else is like me? I thought she blushed. I don't know what else I thought. 'Are you in love?' I asked.

"She jumped up from her chair, so suddenly and so violently that she threw it on the floor. Still, not a word passed her lips. I found courage enough to go on—but not courage enough to look at her.

"'I love Ovid, and Ovid loves me,' I said. 'There is my consolation, whatever my troubles may be. Are you not so fortunate?' A dreadful expression of pain passed over her face. How could I see it, and not feel the wish to sympathise with her? I ran the risk, and said, 'Do you love somebody, who doesn't love you?'

"She turned her back on me, and went to the toilet-table. I think she looked at herself in the glass. 'Well,' she said, speaking to me at last, 'what else?'

"'Nothing else,' I answered—'except that I hope I have not offended you.'

"She left the glass as suddenly as she had approached it, and took up the candle again. Once more she held it so that it lit my face.

"'Guess who he is,' she said.

"'How can I do that?' I asked.

"She quietly put down the candle again. In some way, quite incomprehensible to myself, I seemed to have relieved her. She spoke to me in a changed voice, gently and sadly.

"'You are the best of good girls, and you mean kindly. It's of no use—you can do nothing. Forgive my insolence yesterday; I was mad with envy of your happy marriage engagement. You don't understand such a nature as mine. So much the better! ah, so much the better! Good-night!'

"There was such hopeless submission, such patient suffering, in those words, that I could not find it in my heart to leave her. I thought of how I might have behaved, of the wild things I might have said, if Ovid had cared nothing for me. Had some cruel man forsaken her? That was *her* secret. I asked myself what I could do to encourage her. Your last letter, with our old priest's enclosure, was in my pocket. I took it out.

"'Would you mind reading a short letter,' I said, 'before we wish each other goodnight?' I held out the priest's letter.

"She drew back with a dark look; she appeared to have some suspicion of it. 'Who is the writer?' she inquired sharply.

"'A person who is a stranger to you.'

"Her face cleared directly. She took the letter from me, and waited to hear what I had to say next. 'The person,' I told her, 'is a wise and good old man—the priest who married my father and mother, and baptised me. We all of us used to consult Father Patrizio,[1] when we wanted advice. My nurse Teresa felt anxious about me in Ovid's absence; she spoke to him about my marriage engagement, and of my exile—forgive me for using

---

1   *We all used to consult Father Patrizio*: The kindly and wise Father Patrizio may be another of Collins's attempts to answer the criticism he suffered as a result of his attack on Jesuits in *The Black Robe*.

the word!—in this house. He said he would consider, before he gave her his opinion. The next day, he sent her the letter which you have got in your hand.'

"There, I came to a full stop; having something yet to say, but not knowing how to express myself with the necessary delicacy.

" 'Why do you wish me to read the letter?' she asked, quietly.

" 'I think there is something in it which might—.'

"There, like a fool, I came to another full stop. She was as patient as ever; she only made a little sign to me to go on.

" 'I think Father Patrizio's letter might put you in a better frame of mind,' I said; 'it might keep you from despising yourself.'

"She went back to her chair, and read the letter. You have permitted me to keep the comforting words of the good Father, among my other treasures. I copy his letter for you in this place—so that you may read it again, and see what I had in my mind, and understand how it affected poor Miss Minerva.

" 'Teresa, my well-beloved friend,—I have considered the anxieties that trouble you, with this result: that I can do my best, conscientiously, to quiet your mind. I have had the experience of forty years in the duties of the priesthood. In that long time, the innermost secrets of thousands of men and women have been confided to me. From such means of observation, I have drawn many useful conclusions; and some of them may be also useful to you. I will put what I have to say, in the plainest and fewest words: consider them carefully, on your side. The growth of the better nature, in women, is perfected by one influence—and that influence is Love. Are you surprised that a priest should write in this way? Did you expect me to say, Religion? Love, my sister, *is* Religion, in women. It opens their hearts to all that is good for them; and it acts independently of the conditions of human happiness. A miserable woman, tormented by hopeless love, is still the better and the nobler for that love; and a time will surely come when she will show it. You have fears for Carmina—cast away, poor soul, among strangers with hard hearts! I tell you to have no fears. She may suffer under trials; she may sink under trials. But the strength to rise again is in her—and that strength is Love.'

"Having read our old friend's letter, Miss Minerva turned back, and read it again—and waited a little, repeating some part of it to herself.

" 'Does it encourage you?' I asked.

"She handed the letter back to me. 'I have got one sentence in it by heart,' she said.

"You will know what that sentence is, without my telling you. I felt so relieved, when I saw the change in her for the better—I was so inexpressibly happy in the conviction that we were as good friends again as ever—that I bent down to kiss her, on saying goodnight.

"She put up her hand and stopped me. 'No,' she said, 'not till I have done something to deserve it. You are more in need of help than you think. Stay here a little longer; I have a word to say to you about your aunt.'

"I returned to my chair, feeling a little startled. Her eyes rested on me absently—she was, as I imagined, considering with herself, before she spoke. I refrained from interrupting her thoughts. The night was still and dark. Not a sound reached our ears from without. In the house, the silence was softly broken by a rustling movement on the stairs. It came nearer. The door was opened suddenly. Mrs. Gallilee entered the room.

"What folly possessed me? Why was I frightened? I really could not help it—I screamed. My aunt walked straight up to me, without taking the smallest notice of Miss Minerva. 'What are you doing here, when you ought to be in your bed?' she asked.

"She spoke in such an imperative manner—with such authority and such contempt—that I looked at her in astonishment. Some suspicion seemed to be roused in her by finding me and Miss Minerva together.

"'No more gossip!' she called out sternly. 'Do you hear me? Go to bed!'

"Was it not enough to rouse anybody? I felt my pride burning in my face. 'Am I a child, or a servant?' I said. 'I shall go to bed early or late as I please.'

"She took one step forward; she seized me by the arm, and forced me to my feet. Think of it, Teresa! In all my life I have never had a hand laid on me except in kindness. Who knows it better than you! I tried vainly to speak—I saw Miss Minerva rise to interfere—I heard her say, 'Mrs. Gallilee, you forget yourself!' Somehow, I got out of the room. On the landing, a dreadful fit of trembling shook me from head to foot. I sank down on the stairs. At first, I thought I was going to faint. No; I shook and shivered, but I kept my senses. I could hear their voices in the room.

"Mrs. Gallilee began. 'Did you tell me just now that I had forgotten myself?'

"Miss Minerva answered, 'Certainly, madam. You *did* forget yourself.'

"The next words escaped me. After that, they grew louder; and I heard them again—my aunt first.

"'I am dissatisfied with your manner to me, Miss Minerva. It has latterly altered very much for the worse.'

"'In what respect, Mrs. Gallilee?'

"'In this respect. Your way of speaking to me implies an assertion of equality—'

"'Stop a minute, madam! I am not so rich as you are. But I am at a loss to know in what other way I am not your equal. Did you assert your superiority—may I ask—when you came into my room without first knocking at the door?'

"'Miss Minerva! Do you wish to remain in my service?'

"'Say employment, Mrs. Gallilee—if you please. I am quite indifferent in the matter. I am equally ready, at your entire convenience, to stay or to go.'

"Mrs. Gallilee's voice sounded nearer, as if she was approaching the door. 'I think we arranged,' she said, 'that there was to be a month's notice on either side, when I first engaged you?'

" 'Yes—at my suggestion.'

" 'Take your month's notice, if you please.'

" 'Dating from to-morrow?'

" 'Of course!'

"My aunt came out, and found me on the stairs. I tried to rise. It was not to be done. My head turned giddy. She must have seen that I was quite prostrate—and yet she took no notice of the state I was in. Cruel, cruel creature! she accused me of listening.

" 'Can't you see that the poor girl is ill?'

"It was Miss Minerva's voice. I looked round at her, feeling fainter and fainter. She stooped; I felt her strong sinewy arms round me; she lifted me gently. 'I'll take care of you,' she whispered—and carried me downstairs to my room, as easily as if I had been a child.

"I must rest, Teresa. The remembrance of that dreadful night brings it all back again. Don't be anxious about me, my old dear! You shall hear more to-morrow."

End of December 1882 *Belgravia* Serial Number

CHAPTER XXVII.

On the next day events happened, the influence of which upon Carmina's excitable nature urged her to complete her unfinished letter, without taking the rest that she needed. Once more—and, as the result proved, for the last time—she wrote to her faithful old friend in these words:

"Don't ask me to tell you how the night passed! Miss Minerva was the first person who came to me in the morning.

"She had barely said a few kind words, when Maria interrupted us, reminding her governess of the morning's lessons. 'Mrs. Gallilee has sent her,' Miss Minerva whispered; 'I will return to you in the hour before the children's dinner.'

"The next person who appeared was, as we had both anticipated, Mrs. Gallilee herself.

"She brought me a cup of tea; and the first words she spoke were words of apology for her conduct on the previous night. Her excuse was that she had been 'harassed by anxieties which completely upset her.' And—can you believe it?—she implored me not to mention 'the little misunderstanding between us when I next wrote to her son!' Is this woman made of iron and stone, instead of flesh and blood? Does she really think me such a wretch as to cause Ovid, under any provocation, a moment's anxiety while he is away? The fewest words that would satisfy her, and so send her out of my room, were the only words I said.

"After this, an agreeable surprise was in store for me. The familiar voice of good Mr. Gallilee applied for admission—through the keyhole!

"'Are you asleep, my dear? May I come in?' His kind, fat old face peeped round the door when I said Yes—and reminded me of Zo, at dinner, when she asks for more pudding, and doesn't think she will get it. Mr. Gallilee had something to ask for, and some doubt of getting it, which accounted for the resemblance. 'I've taken the liberty, Carmina, of sending for our doctor. You're a delicate plant, my dear—' (Here, his face disappeared, and he spoke to somebody outside)— 'You think so yourself, don't you, Mr. Null? And you have a family of daughters, haven't you?' (His face appeared again; more like Zo than ever.) 'Do please see him, my child; I'm not easy about you. I was on the stairs last night—nobody ever notices me, do they, Mr. Null?—and I saw Miss Minerva—good creature, and, Lord, how strong!—carrying you to your bed. Mr. Null's waiting outside. Don't distress me by saying No!'

"Is there anybody cruel enough to distress Mr. Gallilee? The doctor came in—looking like a clergyman; dressed all in black, with a beautiful frill to his shirt, and a spotless white cravat. He stared hard at me; he produced a little glass-tube; he gave it a shake, and put it under my arm; he took it away again, and consulted it;[1] he said, 'Aha!' he approved of my tongue; he disliked my pulse; he gave his opinion at last. 'Perfect quiet. I must see Mrs. Gallilee.' And there was an end of it.

"Mr. Gallilee observed the medical proceedings with awe. 'Mr. Null is a wonderful man,' he whispered, before he followed the doctor out. Ill and wretched as I was, this little interruption amused me. I wonder why I write about it here? There are serious things waiting to be told—am I weakly putting them off?

"Miss Minerva came back to me as she had promised. 'It is well,' she said gravely, 'that the doctor has been to see you.'

"I asked if the doctor thought me very ill.

"'He thinks you have narrowly escaped a nervous fever; and he has given some positive orders. One of them is that your slightest wishes are to be humoured. If he had not said that, Mrs. Gallilee would have prevented me from seeing you. She has been obliged to give way; and she hates me—almost as bitterly, Carmina, as she hates you.'

"This called to my mind the interruption of the previous night, when Miss Minerva had something important to tell me. When I asked what it was, she shook her head, and said painful subjects of conversation were not fit subjects in my present state.

"Need I add that I insisted on hearing what she had to say? Oh, how completely my poor father must have been deceived, when he made his horrible sister my guardian! If I had not fortunately offended the music-

---

1   *he produced a little glass-tube ... consulted it*: The mercury thermometer, which
     Mr. Null uses here, was invented by Gabriel Fahrenheit in 1718.

master, she would have used Mr. Le Frank as a means of making Ovid jealous, and of sowing the seeds of dissension between us. Having failed so far, she is (as Miss Minerva thinks) at a loss to discover any other means of gaining her wicked ends. Her rage at finding herself baffled seems to account for her furious conduct, when she discovered me in Miss Minerva's room.

"You will ask, as I did, what has she to gain by this wicked plotting and contriving, with its shocking accompaniments of malice and anger?

"Miss Minerva answered, 'I still believe that money is the motive. Her son is mistaken about her; her friends are mistaken; they think she is fond of money—the truer conclusion is, she is short of money. There is the secret of the hard bargains she drives, and the mercenary opinions she holds. I don't doubt that her income would be enough for most other women in her position. It is not enough for a woman who is jealous of her rich sister's place in the world. Wait a little, and you will see that I am not talking at random. You were present at the grand party she gave some week's since?'

"'I wish I had stayed in my own room,' I said. 'Mrs. Gallilee was offended with me for not admiring her scientific friends. With one or two exceptions, they talked of nothing but themselves and their discoveries—and, oh, dear, how ugly they were!'

"'Never mind that now, Carmina. Did you notice the profusion of splendid flowers, in the hall and on the staircase, as well as in the reception-rooms?'

"'Yes.'

"'Did you observe—no, you are a young girl—did you hear any of the gentlemen, in the supper-room, expressing their admiration of the luxuries provided for the guests, the exquisite French cookery and the delicious wine? Why was all the money which these things cost spent in one evening? Because Lady Northlake's parties must be matched by Mrs. Gallilee's parties. Lady Northlake lives in a fashionable neighbourhood in London, and has splendid carriages and horses. This is a fashionable neighbourhood. Judge what this house costs, and the carriages and horses, when I tell you that the rent of the stables alone is over a hundred pounds a year. Lady Northlake has a superb place in Scotland. Mrs. Gallilee is not able to rival her sister in that respect—but she has her marine villa in the Isle of Wight.[1] When Mr. Gallilee said you should have some sailing this autumn, did you think he meant that he would hire a boat? He referred to the yacht, which is part of the establishment at the sea-side. Lady Northlake goes yachting with her husband; and Mrs. Gallilee goes yachting with her husband. Do you know what it costs,

---

1   *her marine villa in the Isle of Wight:* Mrs. Gallilee and her husband own what amounts to a summer home on the island that sits off the south-central coast of England, in the English Channel.

when the first milliner in Paris[1] supplies English ladies with dresses? That milliner's lowest charge for a dress which Mrs. Gallilee would despise—ordinary material, my dear, and imitation lace—is forty pounds. Think a little—and even your inexperience will see that the mistress of this house is spending more than she can afford, and is likely (unless she has resources that we know nothing about) to be, sooner or later, in serious need of money.'

"This was a new revelation to me, and it altered my opinion of course. But I still failed to see what Mrs. Gallilee's extravagances had to do with her wicked resolution to prevent Ovid from marrying me. Miss Minerva's only answer to this was to tell me to write to Mr. Mool, while I had the chance, and ask for a copy of my father's Will. 'I will take the letter to him,' she said, 'and bring the reply myself. It will save time, if it does nothing else.' The letter was written in a minute. Just as she took it from me, the parlourmaid announced that the early dinner was ready.

Two hours later, the reply was in my hands. The old father had taken Maria and Zo for their walk; and Miss Minerva had left the house by herself—sending word to Mrs. Gallilee that she was obliged to go out on business of her own.

" 'Did Mrs. Gallilee see you come in?' I asked.

" 'Yes. She was watching for me, no doubt.'

" 'Did she see you go upstairs to my room?'

" 'Yes.'

" 'And said nothing?'

" 'Nothing.'

"We looked at each other; both of us feeling the same doubt of how the day would end. Miss Minerva pointed impatiently to the lawyer's reply. I opened it.

"Mr. Mool's letter was very kind, but quite incomprehensible in the latter part of it. After referring me to his private residence, in case I wished to consult him personally later in the day, he mentioned some proceeding, called 'proving the Will,' and some strange place called 'Doctors' Commons.'[2] However, there was the copy of the Will, and that was all we wanted.

---

1 *the first milliner in Paris*: Though milliners more often specialized in making ladies' hats, Lady Northlake's, the best in Paris, also supplies her with dresses that her sister can only dream of affording.

2 *called 'proving the Will,' and some strange place called 'Doctors' Commons'*: The Doctors' Commons is the colloquial name for the College of Advocates and Doctors of Law located near St. Paul's Cathedral. Wills and marriage licenses were stored here for scrutiny by the public. One of *Heart and Science*'s critics, though, claimed, "One of the characters is a solicitor, and if accuracy in legal matters is as important as correctness in science, it would have been well to have avoided the mistake of sending a person to look for a will at Doctors' Commons instead of Somerset House." (See Appendix A, 2). Somerset House, a building in the Strand, was home to various government offices, including the General Register of Births, Deaths and Marriages.

"I began reading it. How I pitied the unfortunate men who have to learn the law! My dear Teresa, I might as well have tried to read an unknown tongue. The strange words, the perpetual repetitions, the absence of stops, utterly bewildered me. I handed the copy to Miss Minerva. Instead of beginning on the first page, as I had done, she turned to the last. With what breathless interest I watched her face! First, I saw that she understood what she was reading. Then, after a while, she turned pale. And then, she lifted her eyes to me. 'Don't be frightened,' she said.

"But I *was* frightened. My ignorant imagination pictured some dreadful unknown power given to Mrs. Gallilee by the Will. 'What can my aunt do to me?' I asked.

"Miss Minerva composed me—without concealing the truth. 'In her position, Carmina, and with her intensely cold and selfish nature, there is no fear of her attempting to reach her ends by violent means. Your happiness may be in danger—and that prospect, God knows, is bad enough.'

"When she talked of *my* happiness, I naturally thought of Ovid. I asked if there was anything about him in the Will.

"It was no doubt a stupid thing to say at such a time; and it seemed to annoy her. '*You* are the only person concerned,' she answered sharply. 'It is Mrs. Gallilee's interest that you shall never be her son's wife, or any man's wife. If she can have her way, you will live and die an unmarried woman.'

"This did me good: it made me angry. I began to feel like myself again. I said, 'Please let me hear the rest of it.'

"Miss Minerva first patiently explained to me what she had read in the Will. She then returned to the subject of my aunt's extravagance; speaking from experience of what had happened in her own family. 'If Mrs. Gallilee borrows money,' she said, 'her husband will, in all probability, have to repay the loan. And, if borrowings go on in that way, Maria and Zoe will be left wretchedly provided for, in comparison with Lady Northlake's daughters. A fine large fortune would wonderfully improve these doubtful prospects—can you guess, Carmina, where it is to come from?' I could easily guess, now I understood the Will. My good Teresa, if I die without leaving children, the fine large fortune comes from Me.

"You see it all now—don't you? After I had thanked Miss Minerva, I turned away my head on the pillow overpowered by disgust.

"The clock in the hall struck the hour of the children's tea. Miss Minerva would be wanted immediately. At parting, she kissed me. 'There is the kiss that you meant to give me last night,' she said. 'Don't despair of yourself. I am to be in the house for a month longer; and I am a match for Mrs. Gallilee. We will say no more now. Compose yourself, and try to sleep.'

"She went away to her duties. Sleep was out of the question. My attention wandered when I tried to read. Doing nothing meant, in other words, thinking of what had happened. If you had come into my room, I should have told you all about it. The next best thing was to talk to you in this way. You don't know what a relief it has been to me to write these lines."

"The night has come, and Mrs. Gallilee's cruelty has at last proved too much even for my endurance.

"Try not to be surprised; try not to be alarmed. If my mind to-morrow is the same as my mind to-night, I shall attempt to make my escape. I shall take refuge with Lady Northlake.

"Oh, if I could go to Ovid! But he is travelling in the deserts of Canada. Until his return to the coast, I can only write to him to the care of his bankers at Quebec. I should not know where to find him, when I arrived; and what a dreadful meeting—if I did find him—to be obliged to acknowledge that it is his mother who has driven me away! There will be nothing to alarm him, if I go to his mother's sister. If you could see Lady Northlake, you would feel as sure as I do that she will take my part.

"After writing to you, I must have fallen asleep. It was quite dark, when I was awakened by the striking of a match in my room. I looked round, expecting to see Miss Minerva. The person lighting my candle was Mrs. Gallilee.

"She poured out the composing medicine which Mr. Null had ordered for me. I took it in silence. She sat down by the bedside.

"'My child,' she began, 'we are friends again now. You bear no malice, I am sure.'

"Distrust still kept me silent. I remembered that she had watched for Miss Minerva's return, and that she had seen Miss Minerva go up to my room. The idea that she meant to be revenged on us both for having our secrets, and keeping them from her knowledge, took complete possession of my mind.

"'Are you feeling better?' she asked.

"'Yes.'

"'Is there anything I can get for you?'

"'Not now—thank you.'

"'Would you like to see Mr. Null again, before to-morrow?'

"'Oh, no!'

"These were ungraciously short replies—but it cost me an effort to speak to her at all. She showed no signs of taking offence; she proceeded as smoothly as ever.

"'My dear Carmina, I have my faults of temper; and, with such pursuits as mine, I am not perhaps a sympathetic companion for a young girl. But I hope you believe that it is my duty and my pleasure to be a second mother to you?'

"Yes; she did really say that! Whether I was only angry, or whether I was getting hysterical, I don't know. I began to feel an oppression in my breathing that almost choked me. There are two windows in my room, and one of them only was open. I was obliged to ask her to open the other.

"She did it; she came back, and fanned me. I submitted as long as I could—and then I begged her not to trouble herself any longer. She put down the fan, and went on with what she had to say.

" 'I wish to speak to you about Miss Minerva. You are aware that I gave her notice, last night, to leave her situation. For your sake, I regret that I did not take this step before you came to England.'

"My confidence in myself returned when I heard Miss Minerva spoken of in this way. I said at once that I considered her to be one of my best and truest friends.

" 'My dear child, that is exactly what I lament! This person has insinuated herself into your confidence—and she is utterly unworthy of it.'

"Could I let those abominable words pass in silence? 'Mrs. Gallilee!' I said, 'you are cruelly wronging a woman whom I love and respect!'

" 'Mrs. Gallilee?' she repeated. 'Do I owe it to Miss Minerva that you have left off calling me Aunt? Your obstinacy, Carmina, leaves me no alternative but to speak out. If I had done my duty, I ought to have said long since, what I am going to say now. You are putting your trust in the bitterest enemy you have; an enemy who secretly hates you with the unforgiving hatred of a rival!'

"Look back at my letter, describing what passed between Miss Minerva and me, when I went to her room; and you will know what I felt on hearing her spoken of as 'a rival.' My sense of justice refused to believe it. But, oh, my dear old nurse, there was some deeper sense in me that said, as if in words, It is true!

"Mrs. Gallilee went on, without mercy.

" 'I know her thoroughly; I have looked into her false heart. Nobody has discovered her but me. Charge her with it, if you like; and let her deny it if she dare. Miss Minerva is secretly in love with my son.'

"She got up. Her object was gained: she was even with me, and with the woman who had befriended me, at last.

" 'Lie down in your bed again,' she said, 'and think over what I have told you. In your own interests, think over it well.'

"I was left alone.

"Shall I tell you what saved me from sinking under the shock? Ovid—thousands and thousands of miles away—Ovid saved me.

"I love him with all my heart and soul; and I do firmly believe that I know him better than I know myself. If his mother had betrayed Miss Minerva to him, as she has betrayed her to me, that unhappy woman would have had his truest pity. I am as certain of this, as I am that I see the moon, while I write, shining on my bed. Ovid would have pitied her. And I pitied her.

"I wrote the lines that follow, and sent them to her by the maid. In the fear that she might mistake my motives, and think me angry and jealous, I addressed her with my former familiarity by her christian name:—

" 'Last night, Frances, I ventured to ask if you loved some one who did not love you. And you answered by saying to me, Guess who he is. My aunt has just told me that he is her son. Has she spoken the truth?'

"I am now waiting to receive Miss Minerva's reply.

"For the first time since I have been in the house, my door is locked. I cannot, and will not, see Mrs. Gallilee again. All her former cruelties are, as I feel it, nothing to the cruelty of her coming here when I am ill, and saying to me what she has said.

"The weary time passes, and still there is no reply. Is Frances angry? or is she hesitating how to answer me—personally or by writing? No! she has too much delicacy of feeling to answer in her own person.

"I have only done her justice. The maid has just asked me to open the door. I have got my answer. Read it.

" 'Mrs. Gallilee has spoken the truth.

" 'How I can have betrayed myself so that she has discovered my miserable secret, is more than I can tell. I will not own it to her, or to any living creature but yourself. Undeserving as I am, I know that I can trust you.

" 'It is needless to dwell at any length on this confession. Many things in my conduct, which must have perplexed you, will explain themselves now. There has been, however, one concealment on my part, which it is due to you that I should acknowledge.

" 'If Mrs. Gallilee had taken me into her confidence, I confess that my jealousy would have degraded me into becoming her accomplice. As things were, I was too angry and too cunning to let her make use of me without trusting me.

" 'There are other acts of deceit which I ought to acknowledge—if I could summon composure enough to write about them. Better to say at once—I am not worthy of your pardon, not worthy even of your pity.

" 'With the same sincerity, I warn you that the wickedness in me, on which Mrs. Gallilee calculated, may be in me still. The influence of your higher and better nature—helped perhaps by that other influence of which the old priest spoke in his letter—has opened my heart to tenderness and penitence of which I never believed myself capable: has brought the burning tears into my eyes which make it a hard task to write to you. All this I know, and yet I dare not believe in myself. It is useless to deny it, Carmina—I love him. Even now, when you have found me out, I love him. Don't trust me. Oh, God, what torture it is to write it—but I *do* write it, I *will* write it—don't trust me!

" 'One thing I may say for myself. I know the utter hopelessness of that love which I have acknowledged. I know that he returns your love, and will never return mine. So let it be.

" 'I am not young; I have no right to comfort myself with hopes that I know to be vain. If one of us is to suffer, let it be that one who is used to suffering. I have never been the darling of my parents, like you; I have not been used at home to the kindness and the love that *you* remember. A life without sweetness and joy has well fitted me for a loveless future. And, besides, you are worthy of him, and I am not. Mrs. Gallilee is wrong, Carmina, if she thinks I am your rival. I am not your rival; I never can be your rival. Believe nothing else, but, for God's sake, believe that!

" 'I have no more to say—at least no more that I can remember now. Perhaps, you shrink from remaining in the same house with me? Let me know it, and I shall be ready—I might almost say, glad—to go.'

"Have you read her letter, Teresa? Am I wrong in feeling that this poor wounded heart has surely some claim on me? If I *am* wrong, oh, what am I to do? what am I to do?"

CHAPTER XXVIII.

The last lines addressed by Carmina to her old nurse were completed on the seventeenth of August, and were posted that night.

The day that followed was memorable to Carmina, and memorable to Mrs. Gallilee. Doctor Benjulia had his reasons also for remembering the eighteenth of August.

Still in search of a means to undermine the confidence which united Ovid and Carmina, and still calling on her invention in vain, Mrs. Gallilee had passed a sleepless night. Her maid, entering the room at the usual hour, was ordered to leave her in bed, and not to return until the bell rang. On ordinary occasions, Mrs. Gallilee was up in time to receive the letters arriving by the first delivery; the correspondence of the other members of the household being sorted by her own hands, before it was distributed by the servant. On this particular morning (after sleeping a little through sheer exhaustion), she entered the empty breakfast-room two hours later than usual. The letters waiting for her were addressed only to herself. She rang for the maid.

"Any other letters this morning?" she asked.

"Two, for my master."

"No more than that!"

"Nothing more, ma'am—except a telegram for Miss Carmina."

"When did it come?"

"Soon after the letters."

"Have you given it to her?"

"Being a telegram, ma'am, I thought I ought to take it to Miss Carmina at once."

"Quite right. You can go."

A telegram for Carmina? Was there some private correspondence going on? And were the interests involved too important to wait for the ordinary means of communication by post? Considering these questions, Mrs. Gallilee poured out a cup of tea and looked over her letters.

Only one of them especially attracted her notice in her present frame of mind. The writer was Benjulia. He dispensed as usual with the customary forms of address.

"I have had a letter about Ovid, from a friend of mine in Canada. There is an allusion to him of the complimentary sort, which I don't altogether understand. I want to ask you about it—but I can't spare the time to go a-visiting. So much the better for me—I hate conversation, and I like work. You have got your carriage—and your fine friends are out of town. If you want a drive, come to me, and bring your last letters from Ovid with you."

Mrs. Gallilee decided on considering this characteristic proposal later in the day. Her first and foremost interest took her upstairs to her niece's room.

Carmina had left her bed. Robed in her white dressing-gown, she lay on the sofa in the sitting-room. When her aunt came in, she started and shuddered. Those signs of nervous aversion escaped the notice of Mrs. Gallilee. Her attention had been at once attracted by a travelling bag, opened as if in preparation for packing. The telegram lay on Carmina's lap. The significant connection between those two objects asserted itself plainly. But it was exactly the opposite of the connection suspected by Mrs. Gallilee. The telegram had prevented Carmina from leaving the house.

Mrs. Gallilee paved the way for the necessary investigation, by making a few common-place inquiries. How had Carmina passed the night? Had the maid taken care of her at breakfast-time? Was there anything that her aunt could do for her? Carmina replied with a reluctance which she was unable to conceal. Mrs. Gallilee passed over the cold reception accorded to her without remark, and pointed with a bland smile to the telegram.

"No bad news, I hope?"

Carmina handed the telegram silently to her aunt. The change of circumstances which the arrival of the message had produced, made concealment superfluous. Mrs. Gallilee opened the telegram, keeping her suspicions in reserve. It had been sent from Rome by the old foreign woman, named "Teresa," and it contained these words:

"My husband died this morning. Expect me in London from day to day."

"Why is this person coming to London?" Mrs. Gallilee inquired.

Stung by the insolent composure of that question, Carmina answered sharply, "Her name is on the telegram; you ought to know!"

"Indeed?" said Mrs. Gallilee. "Perhaps, she likes London?"

"She hates London! You have had her in the house; you have seen us together. Now she has lost her husband, do you think she can live apart from the one person in the world whom she loves best?"

"My dear, these matters of mere sentiment escape my notice," Mrs. Gallilee rejoined. "It's an expensive journey from Italy to England. What was her husband?"

"Her husband was foreman in a manufactory till his health failed him."

"And then," Mrs. Gallilee concluded, "the money failed him, of course. What did he manufacture?"

"Artists' colours."[1]

"Oh! an artists' colourman? Not a very lucrative business, I should think. Has his widow any resources of her own?"

"My purse is hers!"

"Very generous, I am sure! Even the humblest lodgings are dear in this neighbourhood. However—with your assistance—your old servant may be able to live somewhere near you."

Having settled the question of Teresa's life in London in this way, Mrs. Gallilee returned to the prime object of her suspicion—she took possession of the travelling bag.

Carmina looked at her with the submission of utter bewilderment. Teresa had been the companion of her life; Teresa had been received as her attendant, when she was first established under her aunt's roof. She had assumed that her nurse would become a member of the household again, as a matter of course. With Teresa to encourage her, she had summoned the resolution to live with Ovid's mother, until Ovid came back. And now she had been informed, in words too plain to be mistaken, that Teresa must find a home for herself when she returned to London! Surprise, disappointment, indignation held Carmina speechless.

"This thing," Mrs. Gallilee proceeded, holding up the bag, "will only be in your way here. I will have it put with our own bags and boxes, in the lumber-room.[2] And, by-the-bye, I fancy you don't quite understand (naturally enough, at your age) our relative positions in this house. My child, the authority of your late father is the authority which your guardian holds over you. I hope never to be obliged to exercise it—especially, if you will be good enough to remember two things. I expect you to consult me in your choice of companions; and to wait for my approval before you make arrangements which—well! let us say, which require the bag to be removed from the lumber-room."

Without waiting for a reply, she turned to the door. After opening it, she paused—and looked back into the room.

"Have you thought of what I told you, last night?" she asked.

Sorely as they had been tried, Carmina's energies rallied at this. "I have done my best to forget it!" she answered.

"At Miss Minerva's request?"

Carmina took no notice of the question.

---

1   *Artists' colours*: Teresa's husband worked in a factory mixing paints for artists, Robert Graywell among them.

2   *in the lumber-room*: The lumber-room was not, as we might suspect, a wood shed of some sort; it was a room in which old furniture and other unused household items were stored.

Mrs. Gallilee persisted. "Have you had any communication with that person?"

There was still no reply. Preserving her temper, Mrs. Gallilee stepped out on the landing, and called to Miss Minerva. The governess answered from the upper floor.

"Please come down here," said Mrs. Galilee.

Miss Minerva obeyed. Her face was paler than usual; her eyes had lost something of their piercing brightness. She stopped outside Carmina's door. Mrs. Gallilee requested her to enter the room.

After an instant—only an instant—of hesitation, Miss Minerva crossed the threshold. She cast one quick glance at Carmina, and lowered her eyes before the look could be returned. Mrs. Gallilee discovered no mute signs of an understanding between them. She turned to the governess.

"Have you been here already this morning?" she inquired.

"No."

"Is there some coolness between you and my niece?"

"None, madam, that I know of."

"Then, why don't you speak to her when you come into the room?"

"Miss Carmina has been ill. I see her resting on the sofa—and I am unwilling to disturb her."

"Not even by saying good-morning?"

"Not even that!"

"You are exceedingly careful, Miss Minerva."

"I have had some experience of sick people, and I have learnt to be careful. May I ask if you have any particular reason for calling me downstairs?"

Mrs. Gallilee prepared to put her niece and her governess to the final test.

"I wish you to suspend the children's lesson for an hour or two," she answered.

"Certainly. Shall I tell them?"

"No; I will tell them myself."

"What do you wish me to do?" said Miss Minerva.

"I wish you to remain here with my niece."

If Mrs. Gallilee, after answering in those terms, had looked at her niece, instead of looking at her governess, she would have seen Carmina—distrustful of her own self-control—move on the sofa so as to turn her face to the wall. As it was, Miss Minerva's attitude and look silently claimed some explanation.

Mrs. Gallilee addressed her in a whisper. "Let me say a word to you at the door."

Miss Minerva followed her to the landing outside. Carmina turned again, listening anxiously.

"I am not at all satisfied with her looks, this morning," Mrs. Gallilee proceeded; "and I don't think it right she should be left alone. My household duties must be attended to. Will you take my place at the sofa, until

Mr. Null comes?" ("*Now*," she thought, "if there is jealousy between them, I shall see it!")

She saw nothing: the governess quietly bowed to her, and went back to Carmina. She heard nothing: although the half-closed door gave her opportunities for listening. Ignorant, she had entered the room. Ignorant, she left it.

Carmina lay still and silent. With noiseless step, Miss Minerva approached the sofa, and stood by it, waiting. Neither of them lifted her eyes, the one to the other. The woman suffered her torture in secret. The girl's sweet eyes filled slowly with tears. One by one the minutes of the morning passed—not many in number, before there was a change. In silence, Carmina held out her hand. In silence, Miss Minerva took it and kissed it.

CHAPTER XXIX.

Mrs. Gallilee saw her housekeeper as usual, and gave her orders for the day. "If there is anything forgotten," she said, "I must leave it to you. For the next hour or two, don't let me be disturbed."

Some of her letters of the morning were still unread, others required immediate acknowledgment. She was not as ready for her duties as usual. For once, the most unendurably industrious of women was idle, and sat thinking.

Even her unimaginative nature began to tremble on the verge of superstition. Twice, had the subtle force of circumstances defeated her, in the attempt to meddle with the contemplated marriage of her son. By means of the music-master, she had planned to give Ovid jealous reasons for doubting Carmina—and she had failed. By means of the governess, she had planned to give Carmina jealous reasons for doubting Ovid—and she had failed. When some people talked of Fatality, were they quite such fools as she had hitherto supposed them to be? It would be a waste of time to inquire. What next step could she take?

Urged by the intolerable sense of defeat to find reasons for still looking hopefully to the future, the learned Mrs. Gallilee lowered herself to the intellectual level of the most ignorant servant in the house. The modern Muse of Science unconsciously opened her mind to the vulgar belief in luck. She said to herself, as her kitchen-maid might have said, We will see what comes of it, the third time!

Benjulia's letter was among the other letters waiting on the table. She took it up, and read it again.

In her present frame of mind, to find her thoughts occupied by the doctor, was to be reminded of Ovid's strange allusion to his professional colleague, on the day of his departure. Speaking of Carmina, he had referred to one person whom he did not wish her to see in his absence; and that person, he had himself admitted to be Benjulia. He had been asked to state his objection to the doctor—and how had he replied? He had said, "I don't think Benjulia a fit person to be in the company of a young girl."

Why?

There are many men of mature age, who are not fit persons to be in the company of young girls—but they are either men who despise, or men who admire, young girls. Benjulia belonged neither to the one nor to the other of these two classes. Girls were objects of absolute indifference to him—with the one exception of Zo, aged ten. Never yet, after meeting him in society hundreds of times, had Mrs. Gallilee seen him talk to young ladies or even notice young ladies. Ovid's alleged reason for objecting to Benjulia stood palpably revealed as a clumsy excuse.

In the present posture of events, to arrive at that conclusion was enough for Mrs. Gallilee. Without stopping to pursue the idea, she rang the bell, and ordered her carriage to be ready that afternoon, at three o'clock.

Doubtful, and more than doubtful, though it might be, the bare prospect of finding herself possessed, before the day was out, of a means of action capable of being used against Carmina, raised Mrs. Gallilee's spirits. She was ready at last to attend to her correspondence.

One of the letters was from her sister in Scotland. Among other subjects, it referred to Carmina.

"Why won't you let that sweet girl come and stay with us?" Lady Northlake asked. "My daughters are longing for such a companion; and both my sons are ready to envy Ovid the moment they see her. Tell my nephew, when you next write, that I thoroughly understand his falling in love with that gentle pretty creature at first sight."

Carmina's illness was the ready excuse which presented itself in Mrs. Gallilee's reply. With or without an excuse, Lady Northlake was to be resolutely prevented from taking a foremost place in her niece's heart, and encouraging the idea of her niece's marriage. Mrs. Gallilee felt almost pious enough to thank Heaven that her sister's palace in the Highlands[1] was at one end of Great Britain, and her own marine villa at the other!

The marine villa reminded her of the family migration to the sea-side.

When would it be desirable to leave London? Not until her mind was relieved of the heavier anxieties that now weighed on it. Not while events might happen—in connection with the threatening creditors or the contemplated marriage—which would baffle her latest calculations, and make her presence in London a matter of serious importance to her own interests. Miss Minerva, again, was a new obstacle in the way. To take her to the Isle of Wight was not to be thought of for a moment. To dismiss her at once, by paying the month's salary, might be the preferable course to pursue—but for two objections. In the first place (if the friendly under-

---

1   *her sister's palace in the Highlands*: The Highlands are the mountainous northern and western parts of Scotland.

standing between them really continued) Carmina might communicate with the discarded governess in secret. In the second place, to pay Miss Minerva's salary before she had earned it, was a concession from which Mrs. Gallilee's spite, and Mrs. Gallilee's principles of paltry economy, recoiled in disgust. No! the waiting policy in London, under whatever aspect it might be viewed, was, for the present, the one policy to pursue.

She returned to the demands of her correspondence. Just as she had taken up her pen, the sanctuary of the boudoir was violated by the appearance of a servant.

"What is it now? Didn't the housekeeper tell you that I am not to be disturbed?"

"I beg your pardon, ma'am. My master—"

"What does your master want?"

"He wishes to see you, ma'am."

This was a circumstance entirely without parallel in the domestic history of the house. In sheer astonishment, Mrs. Gallilee pushed away her letters, and said "Show him in."

When the boys of fifty years since were naughty, the schoolmaster of the period was not accustomed to punish them by appealing to their sense of honour. If a boy wanted a flogging, in those days, the educational system seized a cane, or a birch-rod, and gave it to him. Mr. Gallilee entered his wife's room, with the feelings which had once animated him, on entering the schoolmaster's study to be caned. When he said "Good-morning, my dear!" his face presented the expression of fifty years since, when he had said, "Please, sir, let me off this time!"

"Now," said Mrs. Gallilee, "what do you want?"

"Only a little word. How well you're looking, my dear!"

After a sleepless night, followed by her defeat in Carmina's room, Mrs. Gallilee looked, and knew that she looked, ugly and old. And her wretched husband had reminded her of it. "Go on!" she answered sternly.

Mr. Gallilee moistened his dry lips. "I think I'll take a chair, if you will allow me," he said. Having taken his chair (at a respectful distance from his wife), he looked all round the room with the air of a visitor who had never seen it before. "How very pretty!" he remarked softly. "Such taste in colour. I think the carpet was your own design, wasn't it? How chaste!"

"*Will* you come to the point, Mr. Gallilee?"

"With pleasure, my dear—with pleasure. I'm afraid I smell of tobacco?"

"I don't care if you do!"

This was such an agreeable surprise to Mr. Gallilee, that he got on his legs again to enjoy it standing up. "How kind! Really now, how kind!" He approached Mrs. Gallilee confidentially. "And do you know, my dear, it was one of the most remarkable cigars I ever smoked." Mrs. Gallilee laid down her pen, and eyed him with an annihilating frown. In the extremity of his confusion Mr. Gallilee ventured nearer. He felt the sinister fascination of the serpent in the expression of those awful eyebrows. "How well you are looking! How amazingly well you are looking this morning!" He leered at his learned wife, and patted her shoulder!

For the moment, Mrs. Gallilee was petrified. At his time of life, was this fat and feeble creature approaching her with conjugal endearments? At that early hour of the day, had his guilty lips tasted his favourite champagne, foaming in his well-beloved silver mug, over his much-admired lump of ice? And was *this* the result?

"Mr. Gallilee!"

"Yes, my dear?"

"Sit down!"

Mr. Gallilee sat down.

"Have you been to the club?"

Mr. Gallilee got up again.

"Sit down!"

Mr. Gallilee sat down. "I was about to say, my dear, that I'll show you over the club with the greatest pleasure—if that's what you mean."

"If you are not a downright idiot," said Mrs. Gallilee, "understand this! Either say what you have to say, or—" she lifted her hand, and let it down on the writing-table with a slap that made the pens ring in the inkstand— "or, leave the room!"

Mr. Gallilee lifted *his* hand, and searched in the breast-pocket of his coat. He pulled out his cigar-case, and put it back in a hurry. He tried again, and produced a letter. He looked piteously round the room, in sore need of somebody whom he might appeal to, and ended in appealing to himself. "What sort of temper will she be in?" he whispered.

"What have you got there?" Mrs. Gallilee asked sharply. "One of the letters you had this morning?"

Mr. Gallilee looked at her with admiration. "Wonderful woman!" he said. "Nothing escapes her! Allow me, my dear."

He rose and presented the letter, as if he was presenting a petition. Mrs. Gallilee snatched it out of his hand. Mr. Gallilee went softly back to his chair, and breathed a devout ejaculation. "Oh, Lord!"

It was a letter from one of the tradespeople, whom Mrs. Gallilee had attempted to pacify with a payment "on account." The tradesman felt compelled, in justice to himself, to appeal to Mr. Gallilee, as master of the house (!). It was impossible for him (he submitted with the greatest respect) to accept a payment, which did not amount to one-third of the sum owing to him for more than a twelvemonth. "Wretch!" cried Mrs. Gallilee. "I'll settle his bill, and never employ him again!" She opened her cheque-book, and dipped her pen in the ink. A faint voice meekly protested. Mr. Gallilee was on his legs again. Mr. Gallilee said. "Please don't!"

His incredible rashness silenced his wife. There he stood; his round eyes staring at the cheque-book, his fat cheeks quivering with excitement. "You mustn't do it," he said, with a first and last outburst of courage. "Give me a minute, my dear—oh, good gracious, give me a minute!"

He searched in his pocket again, and produced another letter. His eyes wandered towards the door; drops of perspiration oozed out on his forehead. He laid the second letter on the table; he looked at his wife, and—ran out of the room.

Mrs. Gallilee opened the second letter. Another dissatisfied tradesman? No: creditors far more formidable than the grocer and the butcher. An official letter from the bankers, informing Mr. Gallilee that "the account was overdrawn."

She seized her pass-book, and her paper of calculations. Never yet had her rigid arithmetic committed an error. Column by column she revised her figures—and made the humiliating discovery of her first mistake. She had drawn out all, and more than all, the money deposited in the bank; and the next half-yearly payment of income was not due until Christmas.

There was but one thing to be done—to go at once to the bank. If Ovid had not been in the wilds of Canada, Mrs. Gallilee would have made her confession to him without hesitation. As it was, the servant called a cab, and she made her confession to the bankers.

The matter was soon settled to her satisfaction. It rested (exactly as Miss Minerva had anticipated) with Mr. Gallilee. In the house, he might abdicate his authority to his heart's content. Out of the house, in matters of business, he was master still.[1] His "investments" represented excellent "security;" he had only to say how much he wanted to borrow, and to sign certain papers—and the thing was done.

Mrs. Gallilee went home again, with her pecuniary anxieties at rest for the time. The carriage was waiting for her at the door.

Should she fulfil her intention of visiting Benjulia? She was not a person who readily changed her mind—and, besides, after the troubles of the morning, the drive into the country would be a welcome relief. Hearing that Mr. Gallilee was still at home, she looked in at the smoking-room. Unerring instinct told her where to find her husband, under present circumstances. There he was, enjoying his cigar in comfort, with his coat off and his feet on a chair. She opened the door. "I want you, this evening," she said—and shut the door again; leaving Mr. Gallilee suffocated by a mouthful of his own smoke.

Before getting into the carriage, she only waited to restore her face with a flush of health (from Paris), modified by a sprinkling of pallor (from London). Benjulia's humour was essentially an uncertain humour. It might be necessary to fascinate the doctor.

---

1   *In matters of business, he was master still:* The submissive Mr. Gallilee and his
    puzzlement with the law concerning his position as head of his own household
    recall a conversation between Mr. Bumble and Mr. Brownlow late in
    Dickens's *Oliver Twist:* Mr. Brownlow suggests to Bumble, "the law supposes
    that your wife acts under your direction," to which Bumble responds, "the law
    is a ass—a idiot."

CHAPTER XXX.

The complimentary allusion to Ovid, which Benjulia had not been able to understand, was contained in a letter from Mr. Morphew, and was expressed in these words:—

"Let me sincerely thank you for making us acquainted with Mr. Ovid Vere. Now that he has left us, we really feel as if we had said good-bye to an old friend. I don't know when I have met with such a perfectly unselfish man—and I say this, speaking from experience of him. In my unavoidable absence, he volunteered to attend a serious case of illness, accompanied by shocking circumstances—and this at a time when, as you know, his own broken health forbids him to undertake any professional duty. While he could preserve the patient's life—and he did wonders, in this way—he was every day at the bedside, taxing his strength in the service of a perfect stranger. I fancy I see you (with your impatience of letter-writing at any length) looking to the end. Don't be alarmed. I am writing to your brother Lemuel by this mail, and I have little time to spare."

Was this "serious case of illness" —described as being "accompanied by shocking circumstances"—a case of disease of the brain?

There was the question, proposed by Benjulia's inveterate suspicion of Ovid! The bare doubt cost him the loss of a day's work. He reviled poor Mr. Morphew as "a born idiot" for not having plainly stated what the patient's malady was, instead of wasting paper on smooth sentences, encumbered by long words. If Ovid had alluded to his Canadian patient in his letters to his mother, his customary preciseness of language might be trusted to relieve Benjulia's suspense. With that purpose in view, the doctor had written to Mrs. Gallilee.

Before he laid down his pen, he looked once more at Mr. Morphew's letter, and paused thoughtfully over one line: "I am writing to your brother Lemuel by this mail."

The information of which he was in search might be in *that* letter. If Mrs. Gallilee's correspondence with her son failed to enlighten him, here was another chance of making the desired discovery. Surely the wise course to take would be to write to Lemuel as well.

His one motive for hesitating was dislike of his younger brother—dislike so inveterate that he even recoiled from communicating with Lemuel through the post.

There had never been any sympathy between them; but indifference had only matured into downright enmity, on the doctor's part, a year since. Accident (the result of his own absence of mind, while he was perplexed by an unsuccessful experiment) had placed Lemuel in possession of his hideous secret. The one person in the world who knew how he was really occupied in the laboratory, was his brother.

Here was the true motive of the bitterly contemptuous tone in which Benjulia had spoken to Ovid of his nearest relation. Lemuel's character was certainly deserving of severe judgment, in some of its aspects. In his hours of employment (as clerk in the office of a London publisher) he steadily and punctually performed the duties entrusted to him. In his hours of freedom, his sensual instincts got the better of him; and his jealous wife had her reasons for complaint. Among his friends, he was the subject of a wide diversity of opinion. Some of them agreed with his brother in thinking him little better than a fool. Others suspected him of possessing natural abilities, but of being too lazy, perhaps too cunning, to exert them. In the office he allowed himself to be called "a mere machine"—and escaped the overwork which fell to the share of quicker men. When his wife and her relations declared him to be a mere animal, he never contradicted them—and so gained the reputation of a person on whom reprimand was thrown away. Under the protection of this unenviable character, he sometimes said severe things with an air of perfect simplicity. When the furious doctor discovered him in the laboratory, and said, "I'll be the death of you, if you tell any living creature what I am doing!"—Lemuel answered, with a stare of stupid astonishment, "Make your mind easy; I should be ashamed to mention it."

Further reflection decided Benjulia on writing. Even when he had a favour to ask, he was unable to address Lemuel with common politeness. "I hear that Morphew has written to you by the last mail. I want to see the letter." So much he wrote, and no more. What was barely enough for the purpose, was enough for the doctor, when he addressed his brother.

CHAPTER XXXI.

Between one and two o'clock, the next afternoon, Benjulia (at work in his laboratory) heard the bell which announced the arrival of a visitor at the house. No matter what the circumstances might be, the servants were forbidden to disturb him at his studies in any other way.

Very unwillingly he obeyed the call, locking the door behind him. At that hour it was luncheon-time in well-regulated households, and it was in the last degree unlikely that Mrs. Gallilee could be the visitor. Getting within view of the front of the house, he saw a man standing on the doorstep. Advancing a little nearer, he recognised Lemuel.

"Hullo!" cried the elder brother.

"Hullo!" answered the younger, like an echo.

They stood looking at each other with the suspicious curiosity of two strange cats. Between Nathan Benjulia, the famous doctor, and Lemuel Benjulia, the publisher's clerk, there was just family resemblance enough to suggest that they were relations. The younger brother was only a little over the ordinary height; he was rather fat than thin; he wore a moustache and whiskers; he dressed smartly—and his prevailing expression announced that he was thoroughly well satisfied with himself. But he inherited Benjulia's gipsy complexion; and, in form and colour, he had Benjulia's eyes.

"How-d'ye-do, Nathan?" he said.

"What the devil brings you here?" was the answer.

Lemuel passed over his brother's rudeness without notice. His mouth curled up at the corners with a mischievous smile.

"I thought you wished to see my letter," he said.

"Why couldn't you send it by post?"

"My wife wished me to take the opportunity of calling on you."

"That's a lie," said Benjulia quietly. "Try another excuse. Or do a new thing. For once, speak the truth."

Without waiting to hear the truth, he led the way into the room in which he had received Ovid. Lemuel followed, still showing no outward appearance of resentment.

"How did you get away from your office?" Benjulia inquired.

"It's easy to get a holiday at this time of year. Business is slack, old boy—"

"Stop! I don't allow you to speak to me in that way."

"No offence, brother Nathan!"

"Brother Lemuel, I never allow a fool to offend me. I put him in his place—that's all."

The distant barking of a dog became audible from the lane by which the house was approached. The sound seemed to annoy Benjulia. "What's that?" he asked.

Lemuel saw his way to making some return for his brother's reception of him.

"It's my dog," he said; "and it's lucky for you that I have left him in the cab."

"Why?"

"Well, he's as sweet-tempered a dog as ever lived. But he has one fault. He doesn't take kindly to scientific gentlemen in your line of business." Lemuel paused, and pointed to his brother's hands. "If he smelt *that*, he might try his teeth at vivisecting You."

The spots of blood which Ovid had once seen on Benjulia's stick, were on his hands now. With unruffled composure he looked at the horrid stains, silently telling their tale of torture.

"What's the use of washing my hands," he answered, "when I am going back to my work?"

He wiped his finger and thumb on the tail of his coat. "Now," he resumed, "if you have got your letter with you, let me look at it."

Lemuel produced the letter. "There are some bits in it," he explained, "which you had better not see. If you want the truth—that's the reason I brought it myself. Read the first page-and then I'll tell you where to skip."

So far, there was no allusion to Ovid. Benjulia turned to the second page—and Lemuel pointed to the middle of it. "Read as far as that," he went on, "and then skip till you come to the last bit at the end."

On the last page, Ovid's name appeared. He was mentioned, as a "delightful person, introduced by your brother,"—and with that the letter ended. In the first bitterness of his disappointment, Benjulia conceived an angry suspicion of those portions of the letter which he had been requested to pass over unread.

"What has Morphew got to say to you that I mustn't read?" he asked.

"Suppose you tell me first, what you want to find in the letter," Lemuel rejoined. "Morphew is a doctor like you. Is it anything medical?"

Benjulia answered this in the easiest way—he nodded his head.

"Is it Vivisection?" Lemuel inquired slyly.

Benjulia at once handed the letter back, and pointed to the door. His momentary interest in the suppressed passages was at an end. "That will do," he answered. "Take yourself and your letter away."

"Ah," said Lemuel, "I'm glad you don't want to look at it again!" He put the letter away, and buttoned his coat, and tapped his pocket significantly. "You have got a nasty temper, Nathan—and there are things here that might try it."

In the case of any other man, Benjulia would have seen that the one object of these prudent remarks was to irritate him. Misled by his profound conviction of his brother's stupidity, he now thought it possible that the concealed portions of the letter might be worth notice. He stopped Lemuel at the door. "I've changed my mind," he said; "I want to look at the letter again."

"You had better not," Lemuel persisted. "Morphew's going to write a book against you—and he asks me to get it published at our place. I'm on his side, you know; I shall do my best to help him; I can lay my hand on literary fellows who will lick his style into shape—it will be an awful exposure!" Benjulia still held out his hand. With over-acted reluctance, Lemuel unbuttoned his coat. The distant dog barked again as he gave the letter back. "Please excuse my dear old dog," he said with maudlin tenderness; "the poor dumb animal seems to know that I'm taking his side in the controversy. *Bow-wow* means, in his language, Fie upon the cruel hands that bore holes in our head and use saws on our backs. Ah, Nathan, if you have got any dogs in that horrid place of yours, pat them and give them their dinner! You never heard me talk like this before—did you? I'm a new man since I joined the Society for suppressing you.[1] Oh, if I only had the gift of writing!"

The effect of this experiment on his brother's temper, failed to fulfil

---

1   *I joined the Society for suppressing you*: Perhaps Benjulia's brother had joined the *Working Men's Association for the Suppression of Vivisection*. But there were many Victorian societies whose goal it was to realize the abolition of vivisection, among them the *British Union for the Abolition of Vivisection*, the *Church Anti-Vivisection League*, the *Electoral Anti-Vivisection League*, the *London Anti-Vivisection Society*, the *National Anti-Vivisection Society*, the *Society for the Abolition of Vivisection*, and the *Victoria Street Society*.

Lemuel's expectations. The doctor's curiosity was roused on the doctor's own subject of inquiry.

"You're quite right about one thing," said Benjulia gravely; "I never heard you talk in this way before. You suggest some interesting considerations, of the medical sort. Come to the light." He led Lemuel to the window—looked at him with the closest attention—and carefully consulted his pulse. Lemuel smiled. "I'm not joking," said Benjulia sternly. "Tell me this. Have you had headaches lately? Do you find your memory failing you?"

As he put those questions, he thought to himself—seriously thought—"Is this fellow's brain softening? I wish I had him on my table!"

Lemuel persisted in presenting himself under a sentimental aspect. He had not forgiven his elder brother's rudeness yet—and he knew, by experience, the one weakness in Benjulia's character which, with his small resources, it was possible to attack.

"Thank you for your kind inquiries," he replied. "Never mind my head, so long as my heart's in the right place.[1] I don't pretend to be clever—but I've got my feelings; and I could put some awkward questions on what you call Medical Research, if I had Morphew to help me."

"I'll help you," said Benjulia—interested in developing the state of his brother's brain.

"I don't believe you," said Lemuel—interested in developing the state of his brother's temper.

"Try me, Lemuel."

"All right, Nathan."

The two brothers returned to their chairs; reduced for once to the same moral level.

CHAPTER XXXII.

"Now," said Benjulia, "what is it to be? The favourite public bugbear? Vivisection?"[2]

"Yes."

---

1   *Never mind my head, so long as my heart's in the right place.* Here is another reminder of Dickens's *Hard Times*. Late in that book, Thomas Gradgrind addresses his suffering daughter Louisa in the following terms: "Some persons hold that ... there is a wisdom of the Head, and that there is a Wisdom of the Heart. I have not supposed so; but, as I have said, I mistrust myself. I have supposed the Head to be all-sufficient. It may not be all-sufficient."

2   *"NOW," said Benjulia, "what is it to be? The favourite public bugbear? Vivisection?"*: Benjulia's brother shows that Collins had prepared his case carefully, for Lemuel's several arguments in this chapter echo most of the common antivivisection opinions expressed in the 1870s and early 1880s.

"Very well. What can I do for you?"

"Tell me first," said Lemuel, "what is Law?"

"Nobody knows."

"Well, then, what *ought* it to be?"

"Justice, I suppose."

"Let me wait a bit, Nathan, and get that into my mind."

Benjulia waited with exemplary patience.

"Now about yourself," Lemuel continued. "You won't be offended—will you? Should I be right, if I called you a dissector of living creatures?"

Benjulia was reminded of the day when he had discovered his brother in the laboratory. His dark complexion deepened in hue. His cold gray eyes seemed to promise a coming outbreak. Lemuel went on.

"Does the Law forbid you to make your experiments on a man?" he asked.

"Of course it does!"

"Why doesn't the Law forbid you to make your experiments on a dog?"

Benjulia's face cleared again. The one penetrable point in his ironclad nature had not been reached yet. That apparently childish question about the dog appeared, not only to have interested him, but to have taken him by surprise. His attention wandered away from his brother. His clear intellect put Lemuel's objection in closer logical form, and asked if there was any answer to it, thus:

The Law which forbids you to dissect a living man, allows you to dissect a living dog. Why?

There was positively no answer to this.

Suppose he said, Because a dog is an animal? Could he, as a physiologist, deny that a man is an animal too?

Suppose he said, Because a dog is the inferior creature in intellect? The obvious answer to this would be, But the lower order of savage, or the lower order of lunatic, compared with the dog, is the inferior creature in intellect; and, in these cases, the dog has, on your own showing, the better right to protection of the two.

Suppose he said, Because a man is a creature with a soul, and a dog is a creature without a soul? This would be simply inviting another unanswerable question: How do you know?

Honestly accepting the dilemma which thus presented itself, the conclusion that followed seemed to be beyond dispute.

If the Law, in the matter of Vivisection, asserts the principle of interference, the Law has barred its right to place arbitrary limits on its own action. If it protects any living creatures, it is bound, in reason and in justice, to protect all.

"Well," said Lemuel, "am I to have an answer?"

"I'm not a lawyer."

With this convenient reply, Benjulia opened Mr. Morphew's letter, and read the forbidden part of it which began on the second page. There he found the very questions with which his brother had puzzled him—followed by the conclusion at which he had himself arrived!

"You interpreted the language of your dog just now," he said quietly to Lemuel; "and I naturally supposed your brain might be softening. Such as it is, I perceive that your memory is in working order. Accept my excuses for feeling your pulse. You have ceased to be an object of interest to me."

He returned to his reading. Lemuel watched him—still confidently waiting for results.

The letter proceeded in these terms:

"Your employer may perhaps be inclined to publish my work, if I can satisfy him that it will address itself to the general reader.

"We all know what are the false pretences, under which English physiologists practice their cruelties. I want to expose those false pretences in the simplest and plainest way, by appealing to my own experience as an ordinary working member of the medical profession.

"Take the pretence of increasing our knowledge of the curative action of poisons, by trying them on animals. The very poisons, the action of which dogs and cats have been needlessly tortured to demonstrate, I have successfully used on my human patients in the practice of a lifetime.

"I should also like to ask what proof there is that the effect of a poison on an animal may be trusted to inform us, with certainty, of the effect of the same poison on a man. To quote two instances only which justify doubt—and to take birds this time, by way of a change—a pigeon will swallow opium enough to kill a man, and will not be in the least affected by it; and parsley, which is an innocent herb in the stomach of a human being, is deadly poison to a parrot.

"I should deal in the same way, with the other pretence, of improving our practice of surgery by experiment on living animals.

"Not long since, I saw the diseased leg of a dog cut off at the hip joint. When the limb was removed, not a single vessel bled. Try the same operation on a man—and twelve or fifteen vessels must be tied as a matter of absolute necessity.

"Again. We are told by a great authority that the baking of dogs in ovens has led to new discoveries in treating fever. I have always supposed that the heat, in fever, is not a cause of disease, but a consequence. However, let that be, and let us still stick to experience. Has this infernal cruelty produced results which help us to cure scarlet fever? Our bedside practice tells us that scarlet fever runs it course as it always did. I can multiply such examples as these by hundreds when I write my book.

"Briefly stated, you now have the method by which I propose to drag the scientific English Savage from his shelter behind the medical interests of humanity, and to show him in his true character,—as plainly as the scientific Foreign Savage shows himself of his own accord. *He* doesn't shrink behind false pretences. *He* doesn't add cant to cruelty. *He* boldly proclaims the truth:—I do it, because I like it!"

Benjulia rose, and threw the letter on the floor.

"*I* proclaim the truth," he said; "*I* do it because I like it. There are some few Englishmen who treat ignorant public opinion with the contempt that it deserves—and I am one of them." He pointed scornfully to the letter. "That wordy old fool is right about the false pretences. Publish his book, and I'll buy a copy of it."

"That's odd," said Lemuel.

"What's odd?"

"Well, Nathan, I'm only a fool—but if you talk in that way of false pretences and public opinion, why do you tell everybody that your horrid cutting and carving is harmless chemistry? And why were you in such a rage when I got into your workshop, and found you out? Answer me that!"

"Let me congratulate you first," said Benjulia. "It isn't every fool who knows that he *is* a fool. Now you shall have your answer. Before the end of the year, all the world will be welcome to come into my workshop, and see me at the employment of my life. Brother Lemuel, when you stole your way through my unlocked door, you found me travelling on the road to the grandest medical discovery of this century. You stupid ass, do you think I cared about what *you* could find out? I am in such perpetual terror of being forestalled by my colleagues, that I am not master of myself, even when such eyes as yours look at my work. In a month or two more—perhaps in a week or two—I shall have solved the grand problem. I labour at it all day. I think of it, I dream of it, all night. It will kill me. Strong as I am, it will kill me. What do you say? Am I working myself into my grave, in the medical interests of humanity? *That* for humanity! I am working for my own satisfaction—for my own pride—for my own unutterable pleasure in beating other men—for the fame that will keep my name living hundreds of years hence. Humanity! I say with my foreign brethren—Knowledge for its own sake, is the one god I worship. Knowledge is its own justification and its own reward. The roaring mob follows us with its cry of Cruelty. We pity their ignorance. Knowledge sanctifies cruelty. The old anatomist stole dead bodies for Knowledge. In that sacred cause, if I could steal a living man without being found out, I would tie him on my table, and grasp my grand discovery in days, instead of months. Where are you going? What? You're afraid to be in the same room with me? A man who can talk as I do, is a man who would stick at nothing? Is that the light in which you lower order of creatures look at us? Look a little higher—and you will see that a man who talks as I do is a man set above you by Knowledge. Exert yourself, and try to understand me. Have I no virtues, even from your point of view? Am I not a good citizen? Don't I pay my debts? Don't I serve my friends? You miserable creature, you have had my money when you wanted it! Look at that letter on the floor. The man mentioned in it is one of those colleagues whom I distrust. I did my duty by him for all that. I gave him the information he wanted; I introduced him to a friend in a land of strangers.

Have I no feeling, as you call it? My last experiments on a monkey horrified me. His cries of suffering, his gestures of entreaty, were like the cries and gestures of a child. I would have given the world to put him out of his misery. But I went on. In the glorious cause I went on. My hands turned cold—my heart ached—I thought of a child I sometimes play with—I suffered—I resisted—I went on. All for Knowledge! all for Knowledge!"[1]

His brother's presence was forgotten. His dark face turned livid; his gigantic frame shuddered; his breath came and went in deep sobbing gasps—it was terrible to see him and hear him.

Lemuel slunk out of the room. The jackal had roused the lion; the mean spirit of mischief in him had not bargained for this. "I begin to believe in the devil," he said to himself when he got to the house door.

As he descended the steps, a carriage appeared in the lane. A footman opened the gate of the enclosure. The carriage approached the house, with a lady in it.

Lemuel ran back to his brother. "Here's a lady coming!" he said. "You're in a nice state to see her! Pull yourself together, Nathan—and, damn it, wash your hands!"

He took Benjulia's arm, and led him upstairs.

When Lemuel returned to the hall, Mrs. Gallilee was ascending the house-steps. He bowed profoundly, in homage to the well-preserved remains of a fine woman. "My brother will be with you directly, ma'am. Pray allow me to give you a chair."

His hat was in his hand. Mrs. Gallilee's knowledge of the world easily set him down at his true value. She got rid of him with her best grace. "Pray don't let me detain you, sir; I will wait with pleasure."

If she had been twenty years younger the hint might have been thrown away. As it was, Lemuel retired.

End of January 1883 *Belgravia* Serial Number

CHAPTER XXXIII.

An unusually long day's work at the office had fatigued good Mr. Mool. He pushed aside his papers, and let his weary eyes rest on a glass vase full of flowers on the table—a present from a grateful client. As a man, he enjoyed the lovely colours of the nosegay. As a botanist, he lamented the act which had cut the flowers from their parent stems, and doomed them

---

1   *All for Knowledge! all for Knowledge!*: Benjulia's monomania suggests another common anti-vivisectionist argument, that the physiologists were driven by selfish motives rather than by a desire to aid their fellow man.

to a premature death. "I should not have had the heart to do it myself," he thought; "but tastes differ."

The office boy came into the room, with a visiting card in his hand.

"I'm going home to dinner," said Mr. Mool. "The person must call to-morrow."

The boy laid the card on the table. The person was Mrs. Gallilee.

Mrs. Gallilee, at seven o'clock in the evening! Mrs. Gallilee, without a previous appointment by letter! Mr. Mool trembled under the apprehension of some serious family emergency, in imminent need of legal interference. He submitted as a matter of course. "Show the lady in."

Before a word had passed between them, the lawyer's mind was relieved. Mrs. Gallilee shone on him with her sweetest smiles; pressed his hand with her friendliest warmth; admired the nosegay with her readiest enthusiasm. "Quite perfect," she said—"especially the Pansy. The round flat edge, Mr. Mool; the upper petals perfectly uniform—there is a flower that defies criticism! I long to dissect it."

Mr. Mool politely resigned the Pansy to dissection (murderous mutilation, he would have called it, in the case of one of his own flowers), and waited to hear what his learned client might have to say to him.

"I am going to surprise you," Mrs. Gallilee announced. "No—to shock you. No—even that is not strong enough. Let me say, to horrify you."

Mr. Mool's anxieties returned, complicated by confusion. The behaviour of Mrs. Gallilee exhibited the most unaccountable contrast to her language. She showed no sign of those strong emotions to which she had alluded. "How am I to put it?" she went on, with a transparent affectation of embarrassment. "Shall I call it a disgrace to our family?" Mr. Mool started. Mrs. Gallilee entreated him to compose himself; she approached the inevitable disclosure by degrees. "I think," she said, "you have met Doctor Benjulia at my house?"

"I have had that honour, Mrs. Gallilee. Not a very sociable person—if I may venture to say so."

"Downright rude, Mr. Mool, on some occasions. But that doesn't matter now. I have just been visiting the doctor."

Was this visit connected with the "disgrace to the family?" Mr. Mool ventured to put a question.

"Doctor Benjulia is not related to you, ma'am—is he?"

"Not the least in the world. Please don't interrupt me again. I am, so to speak, laying a train of circumstances before you; and I might leave one of them out. When Doctor Benjulia was a young man—I am returning to my train of circumstances, Mr. Mool—he was at Rome, pursuing his professional studies. I have all this, mind, straight from the doctor himself. At Rome, he became acquainted with my late brother, after the period of his unfortunate marriage. Stop! I have failed to put it strongly enough again. I ought to have said, his disgraceful marriage."

"Really, Mrs. Gallilee—"

"Mr. Mool!"

"I beg your pardon, ma'am."

"Don't mention it. The next circumstance is ready in my mind. One of the doctor's fellow-students (described as being personally an irresistible man) was possessed of abilities which even attracted our unsociable Benjulia. They became friends. At the time of which I am now speaking, my brother's disgusting wife—oh, but I repeat it, Mr. Mool! I say again, his disgusting wife—was the mother of a female child."

"Your niece, Mrs. Gallilee."

"No!"

"Not Miss Carmina?"

"Miss Carmina is no more my niece than she is your niece. Carry your mind back to what I have just said. I mentioned a medical student who was an irresistible man. Miss Carmina's father was that man."

Mr. Mool's astonishment and indignation would have instantly expressed themselves, if he had not been a lawyer. As it was, his professional experience warned him of the imprudence of speaking too soon.

Mrs. Gallilee's exultation forced its way outwards. Her eyes glittered; her voice rose. "The law, Mr. Mool! what does the law say?" she broke out. "Is my brother's Will no better than waste-paper? Is the money divided among his only near relations? Tell me! tell me!"

Mr. Mool suddenly plunged his face into his vase of flowers. Did he feel that the air of the office wanted purifying? or was he conscious that his face might betray him unless he hid it? Mrs. Gallilee was at no loss to set her own clever interpretation on her lawyer's extraordinary proceeding.

"Take your time," she said with the most patronising kindness. "I know your sensitive nature; I know what I felt myself when this dreadful discovery burst upon me. If you remember, I said I should horrify you. Take your time, my dear sir—pray take your time."

To be encouraged in this way—as if he was the emotional client, and Mrs. Gallilee the impassive lawyer—was more than even Mr. Mool could endure. Shy men are, in the innermost depths of their nature, proud men: the lawyer had his professional pride. He came out of his flowery retreat, with a steady countenance. For the first time in his life, he was not afraid of Mrs. Gallilee.

"Before we enter on the legal aspect of the case—" he began.

"The shocking case," Mrs. Gallilee interposed, in the interests of virtue.

Under any other circumstances Mr. Mool would have accepted the correction. He actually took no notice of it now! "There is one point," he proceeded, "on which I must beg you to enlighten me."

"By all means! I am ready to go into any details, no matter how disgusting they may be."

Mr. Mool thought of certain "ladies" (objects of perfectly needless respect among men) who, being requested to leave the Court, at unmentionable Trials, persist in keeping their places.[1] It was a relief to him to feel—if his next questions did nothing else—that they would disappoint Mrs. Gallilee.

"Am I right in supposing that you believe what you have told me?" he resumed.

"Most assuredly!"

"Is Doctor Benjulia the only person who has spoken to you on the subject?"

"The only person."

"His information being derived from his friend—the fellow-student whom you mentioned just now?"

"In other words," Mrs. Gallilee answered viciously, "the father of the wretched girl who has been foisted on my care."

If Mr. Mool's courage had been in danger of failing him, he would have found it again now. His regard for Carmina, his respect for the memory of her mother, had been wounded to the quick. Strong on his own legal ground, he proceeded as if he was examining a witness in a police court.

"I suppose the doctor had some reason for believing what his friend told him?"

"Ample reason! Vice and poverty generally go together—*this* man was poor. He showed Doctor Benjulia money received from his mistress—her husband's money, it is needless to say."

"Her motive might be innocent, Mrs. Gallilee. Had the man any letters of hers to show?"

"Letters? From a woman in her position? It's notorious, Mr. Mool, that Italian models don't know how to read or write."

"May I ask if there are any further proofs?"

"You have had proofs enough."

"With all possible respect, ma'am, I deny that."

Mrs. Gallilee had not been asked to enter into disgusting details. Mrs. Gallilee had been contradicted by her obedient humble servant of other days. She thought it high time to bring the examination to an end.

"If you are determined to believe in the woman's innocence," she said, "without knowing any of the circumstances—"

Mr. Mool went on from bad to worse: he interrupted her now.

"Excuse me, Mrs. Gallilee, I think you have forgotten that one of my autumn holidays, many years since, was spent in Italy. I was in Rome, like

---

1   *Mr. Mool thought of certain "ladies" ... persist in keeping their places*: Mr. Mool may have been thinking of the relatively recent sensational murder trial of the Staunton brothers in 1877, a trial that drew to the courtroom a conspicuous and noteworthy number of society women. Richard Altick discusses the trial, as well as Victorian women's odd fascination with crimes and courtrooms, in his *Victorian Studies in Scarlet* (New York: Norton, 1970).

Doctor Benjulia, after your brother's marriage. His wife was, to my certain knowledge, received in society. Her reputation was unblemished; and her husband was devoted to her."

"In plain English," said Mrs. Gallilee, "my brother was a poor weak creature—and his wife, when you knew her, had not been found out."

"That is just the difficulty I feel," Mr. Mool rejoined. "How is it that she is only found out now? Years have passed since she died. More years have passed since this attack on her character reached Doctor Benjulia's knowledge. He is an old friend of yours. Why has he only told you of it to-day? I hope I don't offend you by asking these questions?"

"Oh, dear, no! your questions are so easily answered. I never encouraged the doctor to speak of my brother and his wife. The subject was too distasteful to me—and I don't doubt that Doctor Benjulia felt about it as I did."

"Until to-day," the lawyer remarked; "Doctor Benjulia appears to have been quite ready to mention the subject to-day."

"Under special circumstances, Mr. Mool. Perhaps, you will not allow that special circumstances make any difference?"

On the contrary, Mr. Mool made every allowance. At the same time, he waited to hear what the circumstances might be.

But Mrs. Gallilee had her reasons for keeping silence. It was impossible to mention Benjulia's reception of her without inflicting a wound on her self-esteem. To begin with, he had kept the door of the room open, and had remained standing. "Have you got Ovid's letters? Leave them here; I'm not fit to look at them now." Those were his first words. There was nothing in the letters which a friend might not read: she accordingly consented to leave them. The doctor had expressed his sense of obligation by bidding her get into her carriage again, and go. "I have been put in a passion; I have made a fool of myself; I haven't a nerve in my body that isn't quivering with rage. Go! go! go!" There was his explanation. Impenetrably obstinate, Mrs. Gallilee faced him—standing between the doctor and the door—without shrinking. She had not driven all the way to Benjulia's house to be sent back again without gaining her object: she had her questions to put to him, and she persisted in pressing them as only a woman can. He was left—with the education of a gentleman against him—between the two vulgar alternatives of turning her out by main force, or of yielding, and getting rid of her decently in that way. At any other time, he would have flatly refused to lower himself to the level of a scandal-mongering woman, by entering on the subject. In his present mood, if pacifying Mrs. Gallilee, and ridding himself of Mrs. Gallilee, meant one and the same thing, he was ready, recklessly ready, to let her have her own way. She heard the infamous story, which she had repeated to her lawyer; and she had Lemuel Benjulia's visit, and Mr. Morphew's contemplated attack on Vivisection, to thank for getting her information.

Mr. Mool waited, and waited in vain. He reminded his client of what she had just said.

"You mentioned certain circumstances. May I know what they are?" he asked.

Mrs. Gallilee rose, before she replied.

"Your time is valuable, and my time is valuable," she said. "We shall not convince each other by prolonging our conversation. I came here, Mr. Mool, to ask you a question about the law. Permit me to remind you that I have not had my answer yet. My own impression is that the girl now in my house, not being my brother's child, has no claim on my brother's property? Tell me in two words, if you please—am I right or wrong?"

"I can do it in one word, Mrs. Gallilee. Wrong."

"What!"

Mr. Mool entered on the necessary explanation, triumphing in the reply that he had just made. "It's the smartest thing," he thought, "I ever said in my life."

"While husbands and wives live together," he continued, "the Law holds that all children, born in wedlock, are the husband's children. Even if Miss Carmina's mother had not been as good and innocent a woman as ever drew the breath of life—"

"That will do, Mr. Mool. You really mean to say that this girl's interest in my brother's Will—"

"Remains quite unaffected, ma'am, by all that you have told me."

"And I am still obliged to keep her under my care?"

"Or," Mr. Mool answered, "to resign the office of guardian, in favour of Lady Northlake—appointed to act, in your place."

"I won't trouble you any further, sir. Good-evening!"

She turned to leave the office. Mr. Mool actually tried to stop her.

"One word more, Mrs. Gallilee."

"No; we have said enough already."

Mr. Mool's audacity arrived at its climax. He put his hand on the lock of the office door, and held it shut.

"The young lady, Mrs. Gallilee! I am sure you will never breathe a word of this to the pretty gentle, young lady? Even if it was true; and, as God is my witness, I am sure it's false—"

"Good-evening, Mr. Mool!"

He opened the door, and let her go; her looks and tones told him that remonstrance was worse than useless. From year's end to year's end, this modest and amiable man had never been heard to swear. He swore now. "Damn Doctor Benjulia!" he burst out, in the solitude of his office. His dinner was waiting for him at home. Instead of putting on his hat, he went back to his writing-table. His thoughts projected themselves into the future—and discovered possibilities from which they recoiled. He took up his pen, and began a letter. "To John Gallilee, Esquire: Dear Sir,— Circumstances have occurred, which I am not at liberty to mention, but which make it necessary for me, in justice to my own views and feelings, to withdraw from the position of legal adviser to yourself and family." He paused and considered with himself. "No," he decided; "I may be of some use to that poor child, while I am the family lawyer." He tore up his unfinished letter.

When Mr. Mool got home that night, it was noticed that he had a poor appetite for his dinner. On the other hand, he drank more wine than usual.

CHAPTER XXXIV.

"I don't know what is the matter with me. Sometimes I think I am going to be really ill."

It was the day after Mrs. Gallilee's interview with her lawyer—and this was Carmina's answer, when the governess entered her room, after the lessons of the morning, and asked if she felt better.

"Are you still taking medicine?" Miss Minerva inquired.

"Yes. Mr. Null says it's a tonic, and it's sure to do me good. It doesn't seem to have begun yet. I feel so dreadfully weak, Frances. The least thing makes me cry; and I put off doing what I ought to do, and want to do, without knowing why. You remember what I told you about Teresa? She may be with us in a few days more, for all I know to the contrary. I must find a nice lodging for her, poor dear—and here I am, thinking about it instead of doing it."

"Let me do it," Miss Minerva suggested.

Carmina's sad face brightened. "That's kind indeed!" she said.

"Nonsense! I shall take the children out, after dinner to-day. Looking over lodgings will be an amusement to me and to them."

"Where is Zo? Why haven't you brought her with you?"

"She is having her music lesson—and I must go back to keep her in order. About the lodging? A sitting-room and bedroom will be enough, I suppose? In this neighbourhood, I am afraid the terms will be rather high."

"Oh, never mind that! Let us have clean airy rooms—and a kind land-lady. Teresa mustn't know it, if the terms are high."

"Will she allow you to pay her expenses?"

"Ah, *you* put it delicately! My aunt seemed to doubt if Teresa had any money of her own. I forgot, at the time, that my father had left her a lit-tle income. She told me so herself, and wondered, poor dear, how she was to spend it all. She mustn't be allowed to spend it all. We will tell her that the terms are half what they may really be—and I will pay the other half. Isn't it cruel of my aunt not to let my old nurse live in the same house with me?"

At that moment, a message arrived from one of the persons of whom she was speaking. Mrs. Gallilee wished to see Miss Carmina immediate-ly.

"My dear," said Miss Minerva, when the servant had withdrawn, "why do you tremble so?"

"There's something in me, Frances, that shudders at my aunt, ever since—"

She stopped.

Miss Minerva understood that sudden pause—the undesigned allusion to Carmina's guiltless knowledge of her feeling towards Ovid. By unexpressed consent, on either side, they still preserved their former relations as if Mrs. Gallilee had not spoken. Miss Minerva looked at Carmina sadly and kindly. "Good-bye for the present!" she said—and went upstairs again to the schoolroom.

In the hall, Carmina found the servant waiting for her. He opened the library door. The learned lady was at her studies.

"I have been speaking to Mr. Null about you," said Mrs. Gallilee.

On the previous evening, Carmina had kept her room. She had breakfasted in bed—and she now saw her aunt for the first time, since Mrs. Gallilee had left the house on her visit to Benjulia. The girl was instantly conscious of a change—to be felt rather than to be realised—a subtle change in her aunt's way of looking at her and speaking to her. Her heart beat fast. She took the nearest chair in silence.

"The doctor," Mrs. Gallilee proceeded, "thinks it of importance to your health to be as much as possible in the air. He wishes you to drive out every day, while the fine weather lasts. I have ordered the open carriage to be ready, after luncheon. Other engagements will prevent me from accompanying you. You will be under the care of my maid, and you will be out for two hours. Mr. Null hopes you will gain strength. Is there anything you want?"

"Nothing—thank you."

"Perhaps you wish for a new dress?"

"Oh, no!"

"You have no complaint to make of the servants?"

"The servants are always kind to me."

"I needn't detain you any longer—I have a person coming to speak to me."

Carmina had entered the room in doubt and fear. She left it with strangely-mingled feelings of perplexity and relief. Her sense of a mysterious change in her aunt had strengthened with every word that Mrs. Gallilee had said to her. She had heard of reformatory institutions,[1] and of discreet persons called matrons who managed them. In her imaginary picture of such places, Mrs. Gallilee's tone and manner realised, in the strangest way, her idea of a matron speaking to a penitent.

As she crossed the hall, her thoughts took a new direction. Some indefinable distrust of the coming time got possession of her. An ugly model

---

1   *She had heard of reformatory institutions*: These institutions were privately sponsored and funded halfway-homes for the morally fallen or otherwise disadvantaged.

of the Colosseum, in cork, stood on the hall table.[1] She looked at it absently. "I hope Teresa will come soon," she thought—and turned away to the stairs.

She ascended slowly; her head drooping, her mind still preoccupied. Arrived at the first landing, a sound of footsteps disturbed her. She looked up—and found herself face to face with Mr. Le Frank, leaving the school-room after his music lesson. At that sudden discovery, a cry of alarm escaped her—the common little scream of a startled woman. Mr. Le Frank made an elaborately formal bow: he apologised with sternly stupid emphasis. "I *beg* your pardon."

Moved by a natural impulse, penitently conscious of those few foolish words of hers which he had so unfortunately overheard, the poor girl made an effort to conciliate him. "I have very few friends, Mr. Le Frank," she said timidly. "May I still consider you as one of them? Will you for-give and forget? Will you shake hands?"

Mr. Le Frank made another magnificent bow. He was proud of his voice. In his most resonant and mellifluous tones, he said, "You do me honour—" and took the offered hand, and lifted it grandly, and touched it with his lips.

She held by the baluster with her free hand, and controlled the sick-ening sensation which that momentary contact with him produced. He might have detected the outward signs of the struggle, but for an inter-ruption which preserved her from discovery. Mrs. Gallilee was standing at the open library door. Mrs. Gallilee said, "I am waiting for you, Mr. Le Frank."

Carmina hurried up the stairs, pursued already by a sense of her own imprudence. In her first confusion and dismay, but one clear idea pre-sented itself. "Oh!" she said, "have I made another mistake?"

Meanwhile, Mrs. Gallilee had received her music-master with the nearest approach to an indulgent welcome, of which a hardened nature is capable.

"Take the easy chair, Mr. Le Frank. You are not afraid of the open win-dow?"

"Oh, dear no! I like it." He rapidly unrolled some leaves of music which he had brought downstairs. "With regard to the song that I had the honour of mentioning—"

Mrs. Gallilee pointed to the table. "Put the song there for the present. I have a word to say first. How came you to frighten my niece? I heard something like a scream, and naturally looked out. She was making an apology; she asked you to forgive and forget. What does all this mean?"

---

1   *An ugly model of the Colosseum, in cork, stood on the hall table*: Whether this model, which causes Carmina to think of Rome and Teresa, belongs to Mrs. Gallilee or her children remains a mystery. This is Collins's only mention of this rather odd image.

Mr. Le Frank exhausted his ingenuity in efforts of polite evasion—without the slightest success. From first to last (if the expression may be permitted) Mrs. Gallilee had him under her thumb. He was not released, until he had literally reported Carmina's opinion of him as a man and a musician, and had exactly described the circumstances under which he had heard it. Mrs. Gallilee listened with an interest, which (under less embarrassing circumstances) would have even satisfied Mrs. Le Frank's vanity.

She was not for a moment deceived by the clumsy affectation of good humour with which he told his story. Her penetration discovered the vindictive feeling towards Carmina, which offered him, in case of necessity, as an instrument ready made to her hand. By fine degrees, she presented herself in the new character of a sympathising friend.

"I know now, Mr. Le Frank, why you declined to be my niece's music-master. Allow me to apologise for having ignorantly placed you in a false position. I appreciate the delicacy of your conduct—I understand, and admire you."

Mr. Le Frank's florid cheeks turned redder still. His cold blood began to simmer, heated by an all-pervading glow of flattered self-esteem.

"My niece's motives for concealment are plain enough," Mrs. Gallilee proceeded. "Let me hope that she was ashamed to confess the total want of taste, delicacy, and good manners which has so justly offended you. Miss Minerva, however, has no excuse for keeping me in the dark. Her conduct, in this matter, offers, I regret to say, one more instance of her habitual neglect of the duties which attach to her position in my house. There seems to be some private understanding between my governess and my niece, of which I highly disapprove. However, the subject is too distasteful to dwell on. You were speaking of your song—the last effort of your genius, I think?"

His "genius"! The inner glow in Mr. Le Frank grew warmer and warmer. "I asked for the honour of an interview," he explained, "to make a request." He took up his leaves of music. "This is my last, and, I hope, my best effort at composition. May I dedicate it—?"

"To me!" Mrs. Gallilee exclaimed with a burst of enthusiasm.

Mr. Le Frank felt the compliment. He bowed gratefully.

"Need I say how gladly I accept the honour?" With this gracious answer Mrs. Gallilee rose.

Was the change of position a hint, suggesting that Mr. Le Frank might leave her to her studies, now that his object was gained? Or was it an act of homage offered by Science to Art? Mr. Le Frank was incapable of placing an unfavourable interpretation on any position which a woman—and such a woman—could assume in his presence. He felt the compliment again. "The first copy published shall be sent to you," he said—and snatched up his hat, eager to set the printers at work.

"And five-and-twenty copies more, for which I subscribe," cried his munificent patroness, cordially shaking hands with him.

Mr. Le Frank attempted to express his sense of obligation. Generous Mrs. Gallilee refused to hear him. He took his leave; he got as far as the hall; and then he was called back—softly, confidentially called back to the library.

"A thought has just struck me," said Mrs. Gallilee."Please shut the door for a moment. About that meeting between you and my niece? Perhaps, I am taking a morbid view?"

She paused. Mr. Le Frank waited with breathless interest.

"Or *is* there something out of the common way, in that apology of hers?" Mrs. Gallilee proceeded. "Have you any idea what the motive might be?"

Mr. Le Frank's ready suspicion was instantly aroused. "Not the least idea," he answered. "Can you tell me?"

"I am as completely puzzled as you are," Mrs. Gallilee rejoined.

Mr. Le Frank considered. His suspicions made an imaginative effort, assisted by his vanity. "After my refusal to teach her," he suggested, "that proposal to shake hands may have a meaning—" There, his invention failed him. He stopped, and shook his head ominously.

Mrs. Gallilee's object being attained, she made no attempt to help him. "Perhaps, time will show," she answered discreetly. "Good-bye again—with best wishes for the success of the song."

CHAPTER XXXV.

The solitude of her own room was no welcome refuge to Carmina, in her present state of mind. She went on to the schoolroom.

Miss Minerva was alone. The two girls, in obedience to domestic regulations, were making their midday toilet before dinner. Carmina described her interview with Mrs. Gallilee, and her meeting with Mr. Le Frank. "Don't scold me," she said; "I make no excuse for my folly."

"If Mr. Le Frank had left the house, after you spoke to him," Miss Minerva answered, "I should not have felt the anxiety which troubles me now. I don't like his going to Mrs. Gallilee afterwards—especially when you tell me of that change in her manner towards you. Yours is a vivid imagination, Carmina. Are you sure that it has not been playing you any tricks?"

"Perfectly sure."

Miss Minerva was not quite satisfied. "Will you help me to feel as certain about it as you do?" she asked. "Mrs. Gallilee generally looks in for a few minutes, while the children are at dinner. Stay here, and say something to her in my presence. I want to judge for myself."

The girls came in. Maria's perfect toilet, reflected Maria's perfect character. She performed the duties of politeness with her usual happy choice of words. "Dear Carmina, it is indeed a pleasure to see you again in our schoolroom. We are naturally anxious about your health. This lovely weather is no doubt in your favour; and papa thinks Mr. Null a remarkably clever man." Zo stood by frowning, while these smooth conventionalities trickled over her sister's lips. Carmina asked what was the matter. Zo looked gloomily at the dog on the rug. "I wish I was Tinker," she said. Maria smiled sweetly. "Dear Zoe, what a very strange wish! What would you do, if you were Tinker?" The dog, hearing his name, rose and shook himself. Zo pointed to him, with an appearance of the deepest interest. "*He* hasn't got to brush his hair, before he goes out for a walk; *his* nails don't look black when they're dirty. And, I say!" (she whispered the next words in Carmina's ear) "*he* hasn't got a governess."

The dinner made its appearance; and Mrs. Gallilee followed the dinner. Maria said grace. Zo, always ravenous at meals, forgot to say Amen. Carmina, standing behind her chair, prompted her. Zo said "Amen; oh, bother!" the first word at the top of her voice, and the last two in a whisper. Mrs. Gallilee looked at Carmina as she might have looked at an obtrusive person who had stepped in from the street. "You had better dress before luncheon," she suggested, "or you will keep the carriage waiting." Hearing this, Zo laid down her knife and fork, and looked over her shoulder. "Ask if I may go with you," she said. Carmina made the request. "No," Mrs. Gallilee answered, "the children must walk. My maid will accompany you." Carmina glanced at Miss Minerva on leaving the room. The governess replied by a look. She too had seen the change in Mrs. Gallilee's manner, and was at a loss to understand it.

Mrs. Gallilee's maid Marceline belonged to a quick-tempered race: she was a Jersey woman.[1] It is not easy to say which of the two felt most oppressed by their enforced companionship in the carriage.

The maid was perhaps the most to be pitied. Secretly drawn towards Carmina like the other servants in the house, she was forced by her mistress's private instruction, to play the part of a spy.[2] "If the young lady changes the route which the coachman has my orders to take, or if she communicates with any person while your are out, you are to report it to me." Mrs. Gallilee had not forgotten the discovery of the travelling bag; and Mr. Mool's exposition of the law had informed her, that the superintendence of Carmina was as much a matter of serious pecuniary interest as ever.

But recent events had, in one respect at least, improved the prospect.

If Ovid (as his mother actually ventured to hope!) broke off his engagement, when he heard the scandalous story of Carmina's birth, there was surely a chance that she, like other girls of her sensitive tem-

---

1   *she was a Jersey woman*: Jersey is the largest of the nine Channel Islands, off the coast of Normandy, France. Norse mariners settled the islands, whose inhabitants were long considered rugged and wild by mainland Britons.

2   *she was forced ... to play the part of a spy*: Collins often employed domestic servants as household spies and saboteurs in his fiction, but Marceline is won over by Carmina before she can do any damage at Mrs. Gallilee's request.

perament, might feel the calamity that had fallen on her so acutely as to condemn herself to a single life. Misled, partly by the hope of relief from her own vile anxieties; partly by the heartless incapability of appreciating generous feeling in others, developed by the pursuits of her later life, Mrs. Gallilee seriously contemplated her son's future decision as a matter of reasonable doubt.

In the meanwhile, this detestable child of adultery—this living obstacle in the way of the magnificent prospects which otherwise awaited Maria and Zoe, to say nothing of their mother—must remain in the house, submitted to her guardian's authority, watched by her guardian's vigilance. The hateful creature was still entitled to medical attendance when she was ill, and must still be supplied with every remedy that the doctor's ingenuity could suggest. A liberal allowance was paid for the care of her; and the trustees were bound to interfere if it was not fairly earned.

Looking after the carriage as it drove away—Marceline on the front seat presenting the picture of discomfort; and Carmina opposite to her, unendurably pretty and interesting, with the last new poem on her lap—Mrs. Gallilee's reflections took their own bitter course. "Accidents happen to other carriages, with other girls in them. Not to my carriage, with that girl in it! Nothing will frighten *my* horses to-day; and, fat as he is, *my* coachman will not have a fit on the box!"

It was only too true. At the appointed hour the carriage appeared again—and (to complete the disappointment) Marceline had no report to make.

Miss Minerva had not forgotten her promise. When she returned from her walk with the children, the rooms had been taken. Teresa's London lodging was within five minutes' walk of the house.

That evening, Carmina sent a telegram to Rome, on the chance that the nurse might not yet have begun her journey. The message (deferring other explanations until they met) merely informed her that her rooms were ready, adding the address and the landlady's name. Guessing in the dark, Carmina and the governess had ignorantly attributed the sinister alteration in Mrs. Gallilee's manner to the prospect of Teresa's unwelcome return. "While you have the means in your power," Miss Minerva advised, "it may be as well to let your old friend know that there is a home for her when she reaches London."

CHAPTER XXXVI.

The weather, to Carmina's infinite relief, changed for the worse the next day. Incessant rain made it impossible to send her out in the carriage again.

But it was an eventful day, nevertheless. On that rainy afternoon, Mr. Gallilee asserted himself as a free agent, in the terrible presence of his wife!

"It's an uncommonly dull day, my dear," he began. This passed without notice, which was a great encouragement to go on. "If you will allows me to say so, Carmina wants a little amusement." Mrs. Gallilee looked up from her book. Fearing that he might stop altogether if he took his time as usual, Mr. Gallilee proceeded in a hurry. "There's an afternoon performance of conjuring tricks; and, do you know, I really think I might take Carmina to see it. We shall be delighted if you will accompany us, my dear; and they do say—perhaps you have heard of it yourself?—that there's a good deal of science in this exhibition." His eyes rolled in uneasy expectation, as he waited to hear what his wife might decide. She waved her hand contemptuously in the direction of the door. Mr. Gallilee retired with the alacrity of a young man. "Now we shall enjoy ourselves!" he thought as he went up to Carmina's room.

They were just leaving the house, when the music-master arrived at the door to give his lesson.

Mr. Gallilee immediately put his head out of the cab window. "We are going to see the conjuring!" he shouted cheerfully. "Carmina! don't you see Mr. Le Frank? He is bowing to you. Do you like conjuring, Mr. Le Frank? Don't tell the children where we are going! They would be disappointed, poor things—but they must have their lessons, mustn't they? Good-bye! I say! stop a minute. If you ever want your umbrella mended, I know a man who will do it cheap and well. Nasty day, isn't it? Go on! go on!"

The general opinion which ranks vanity among the lighter failings of humanity, commits a serious mistake. Vanity wants nothing but the motive power to develop into absolute wickedness. Vanity can be savagely suspicious and diabolically cruel. What are the two typical names which stand revealed in history as the names of the two vainest men that ever lived? Nero and Robespierre.[1]

In his obscure sphere, and within his restricted means, the vanity of Mrs. Gallilee's music-master had developed its inherent qualities, under her cunning and guarded instigation. Once set in action, his suspicion of Carmina passed beyond all limits. There could be no reason but a bad reason for that barefaced attempt to entrap him into a reconciliation. Every evil motive which it was possible to attribute to a girl of her age, no matter how monstrously improbable it might be, occurred to him when he recalled her words, her look, and her manner at their meeting on the

---

1   *Nero and Robespierre*: Nero, (A.D. 37-68) a Roman Emperor, was noted for his cruelty. He had his mother and wife murdered, was blamed for the Great Fire of Rome, 64 A.D., and committed suicide amid revolts resulting from his mistreatment of his subjects. Robespierre (1758-1794) was the architect of France's Reign of Terror. He was eventually guillotined, suffering the same fate as many of his victims.

stairs. His paltry little mind, at other times preoccupied in contemplating himself and his abilities, was now so completely absorbed in imagining every variety of conspiracy against his social and professional position, that he was not even capable of giving his customary lesson to two children. Before the appointed hour had expired, Miss Minerva remarked that his mind did not appear to be at ease, and suggested that he had better renew the lesson on the next day. After a futile attempt to assume an appearance of tranquillity—he thanked her and took his leave.

On his way downstairs, he found the door of Carmina's room left half open.

She was absent with Mr. Gallilee. Miss Minerva remained upstairs with the children. Mrs. Gallilee was engaged in scientific research. At that hour of the afternoon, there were no duties which called the servants to the upper part of the house. He listened—he hesitated—he went into the room.

It was possible that she might keep a journal: it was certain that she wrote and received letters. If he could only find her desk unlocked and her drawers open, the inmost secrets of her life would be at his mercy.

He tried her desk; he tried the cupboard under the bookcase. They were both locked. The cabinet between the windows and the drawer of the table were left unguarded. No discovery rewarded the careful search that he pursued in these two repositories. He opened the books that she had left on the table, and shook them. No forgotten letter, no private memorandum (used as marks) dropped out. He looked all round him; he peeped into the bedroom; he listened, to make sure that nobody was outside; he entered the bedroom, and examined the toilet-table, and opened the doors of the wardrobe—and still the search was fruitless, persevere as he might.

Returning to the sitting-room, he shook his fist at the writing-desk. "You wouldn't be locked," he thought, "unless you had some shameful secrets to keep! *I* shall have other opportunities; and *she* may not always remember to turn the key." He stole quietly down the stairs, and met no one on his way out.

The bad weather continued on the next day. The object of Mr. Le Frank's suspicion remained in the house—and the second opportunity failed to offer itself as yet.

The visit to the exhibition of conjuring had done Carmina harm instead of good. Her head ached, in the close atmosphere—she was too fatigued to be able to stay in the room until the performance came to an end. Poor Mr. Gallilee retired in disgrace to the shelter of his club. At dinner, even his perfect temper failed him for the moment. He found fault with the champagne—and then apologised to the waiter. "I'm sorry I was a little hard on you just now. The fact is, I'm out of sorts—you have felt in that way yourself, haven't you? The wine's first-rate; and, really the weather is so discouraging, I think I'll try another pint."

But Carmina's buoyant heart defied the languor of illness and the gloomy day. The post had brought her a letter from Ovid—enclosing a photograph, taken at Montreal, which presented him in his travelling costume.

He wrote in a tone of cheerfulness, which revived Carmina's sinking courage, and renewed for a time at least the happiness of other days. The air of the plains of Canada he declared to be literally intoxicating. Every hour seemed to be giving him back the vital energy that he had lost in his London life. He slept on the ground, in the open air, more soundly than he had ever slept in a bed. But one anxiety troubled his mind. In the roving life which he now enjoyed, it was impossible that his letters could follow him—and yet, every day that passed made him more unreasonably eager to hear that Carmina was not weary of waiting for him, and that all was well at home.

"And how have these vain aspirations of mine ended?"—the letter went on. "They have ended, my darling, in a journey for one of my guides—an Indian, whose fidelity I have put to the proof, and whose zeal I have stimulated by a promise of reward.

"The Indian takes these lines to be posted at Quebec. He is also provided with an order, authorising my bankers to trust him with the letters that are waiting for me. I begin a canoe voyage to-morrow; and, after due consultation with the crew, we have arranged a date and a place at which my messenger will find me on his return. Shall I confess my own amiable weakness? or do you know me well enough already to suspect the truth? My love, I am sorely tempted to be false to my plans and arrangements—to go back with the Indian to Quebec—and to take a berth in the first steamer that returns to England.

"Don't suppose that I am troubled by any misgivings about what is going on in my absence! It is one of the good signs of my returning health that I take the brightest view of our present lives, and of our lives to come. I feel tempted to go back, for the same reason that makes me anxious for letters. I want to hear from you, because I love you—I want to return at once, because I love you. There is longing, unutterable longing, in my heart. No doubts, my sweet one, and no fears!

"But I was a doctor, before I became a lover. My medical knowledge tells me that this is an opportunity of thoroughly fortifying my constitution, and (with God's blessing) of securing to myself reserves of health and strength which will take us together happily on the way to old age. Dear love, you must be my wife—not my nurse! There is the thought that gives me self-denial enough to let the Indian go away by himself."

Carmina answered this letter as soon as she had read it.

Before the mail could carry her reply to its destination, she well knew that the Indian messenger would be on the way back to his master. But Ovid had made her so happy that she felt the impulse to write to him at once, as she might have felt the impulse to answer him at once if he had been present and speaking to her. When the pages were filled, and the letter had been closed and addressed, the effort produced its depressing effect on her spirits.

There now appeared to her a certain wisdom in the loving rapidity of her reply.

Even in the fullness of her joy, she was conscious of an underlying distrust of herself. Although he refused to admit it, Mr. Null had betrayed a want of faith in the remedy from which he had anticipated such speedy results, by writing another prescription. He had also added a glass to the daily allowance of wine, which he had thought sufficient thus far. Without despairing of herself, Carmina felt that she had done wisely in writing her answer, while she was still well enough to rival the cheerful tone of Ovid's letter.

She laid down to rest on the sofa, with the photograph in her hand. No sense of loneliness oppressed her now; the portrait was the best of all companions. Outside, the heavy rain pattered; in the room, the busy clock ticked. She listened lazily, and looked at her lover, and kissed the faithful image of him—peacefully happy.

The opening of the door was the first little event that disturbed her. Zo peeped in. Her face was red, her hair was tousled, her fingers presented inky signs of a recent writing lesson.

"I'm in a rage," she announced; "and so is the Other One."

Carmina called her to the sofa, and tried to find out who this second angry person might be. "Oh, you know!" Zo answered doggedly. "She rapped my knuckles. I call her a Beast."

"Hush! you mustn't talk in that way."

"She'll be here directly," Zo proceeded. "You look out! She'd rap *your* knuckles—only you're too big. If it wasn't raining, I'd run away." Carmina assumed an air of severity, and entered a serious protest adapted to her young friend's intelligence. She might as well have spoken in a foreign language. Zo had another reason to give, besides the rap on the knuckles, for running away.

"I say!" she resumed—"you know the boy?"

"What boy, dear?"

"He comes round sometimes. He's got a hurdy-gurdy. He's got a monkey. He grins. He says, *Aha-gimmee-haypenny*. I mean to go to that boy!"

As a confession of Zo's first love, this was irresistible. Carmina burst out laughing. Zo indignantly claimed a hearing. "I haven't done yet!" she burst out. "The boy dances. Like this." She cocked her head, and slapped her thigh, and imitated the boy. "And sometimes he sings!" she cried with another outburst of admiration. "*Yah-yah-yah-bellah-vitah-yah!* That's Italian, Carmina." The door opened again while the performer was in full vigour—and Miss Minerva appeared.

When she entered the room, Carmina at once saw that Zo had correctly observed her governess. Miss Minerva's heavy eyebrows lowered; her lips were pale; he head was held angrily erect. "Carmina!" she said sharply, "you shouldn't encourage that child." She turned round, in search of the truant pupil. Incurably stupid at her lessons, Zo's mind had its gleams of intelligence, in a state of liberty. One of those gleams had shone propitiously, and had lighted her out of the room.

Miss Minerva took a chair: she dropped into it like a person worn out with fatigue. Carmina spoke to her gently. Words of sympathy were thrown away on that self-tormenting nature.

"No; I'm not ill," she said. "A night without sleep; a perverse child to teach in the morning; and a detestable temper at all times—that's what is the matter with me." She looked at Carmina. "You seem to be wonderfully better to-day. Has stupid Mr. Null really done you some good at last?" She noticed the open writing-desk, and discovered the letter. "Or is it good news?"

"I have heard from Ovid," Carmina answered. The photograph was still in her hand; but her inbred delicacy of feeling kept the portrait hidden.

The governess's sallow complexion turned little by little to a dull greyish white. Her hands, loosely clasped in her lap, tightened when she heard Ovid's name. That slight movement over, she stirred no more. After waiting a little, Carmina ventured to speak. "Frances," she said, "you have not shaken hands with me yet." Miss Minerva slowly looked up, keeping her hands still clasped on her lap.

"When is he coming back?" she asked. It was said quietly.

Carmina quietly replied, "Not yet—I am sorry to say."

"I am sorry too."

"It's good of you, Frances, to say that."

"No: it's not good of me. I'm thinking of myself—not of you." She suddenly lowered her tone. "I wish you were married to him," she said.

There was a pause. Miss Minerva was the first to speak again.

"Do you understand me?" she asked.

"Perhaps you will help me to understand," Carmina answered.

"If you were married to him, even my restless spirit might be at peace. The struggle would be over."

She left her chair, and walked restlessly up and down the room. The passionate emotion which she had resolutely suppressed began to get beyond her control.

"I was thinking about you last night," she abruptly resumed. "You are a gentle little creature—but I have seen you show some spirit, when your aunt's cold-blooded insolence roused you. Do you know what I would do, if I were in your place? *I* wouldn't wait tamely till he came back to me— I would go to him. Carmina! Carmina! leave this horrible house!" She stopped, close by the sofa. "Let me look at you. Ha! I believe you have thought of it yourself?"

"I have thought of it."

"What did I say? You poor little prisoner, you *have* the right spirit in you! I wish I could give you some of my strength." The half-mocking tone in which she spoke, suddenly failed her. Her piercing eyes grew dim; the hard lines in her face softened. She dropped on her knees, and wound her lithe arms round Carmina, and kissed her. "You sweet child!" she said—and burst passionately into tears.

Even then, the woman's fiercely self-dependent nature asserted itself. She pushed Carmina back on the sofa. "Don't look at me! don't speak to me!" she gasped. "Leave me to get over it."

She stifled the sobs that broke from her. Still on her knees, she looked up, shuddering. A ghastly smile distorted her lips. "Ah, what fools we are!" she said. "Where is that lavender water, my dear—your favourite remedy for a burning head?" She found the bottle before Carmina could help her, and soaked her handkerchief in the lavender water, and tied it round her head. "Yes," she went on, as if they had been gossiping on the most commonplace subjects, "I think you're right: this is the best of all perfumes." She looked at the clock. "The children's dinner will be ready in ten minutes. I must, and will, say what I have to say to you. It may be the last poor return I can make, Carmina, for all your kindness."

She returned to her chair.

"I can't help it if I frighten you," she resumed; "I must tell you plainly that I don't like the prospect. In the first place, the sooner we two are parted—oh, only for a while!—the better for you. After what I went through, last night—no, I am not going to enter into any particulars; I am only going to repeat, what I have said already—don't trust me. I mean it, Carmina! Your generous nature shall not mislead you, if *I* can help it. When you are a happy married woman—when *he* is farther removed from me than he is even now—remember your ugly, ill-tempered friend, and let me come to you. Enough of this! I have other misgivings that are waiting to be confessed. You know that old nurse of yours intimately—while I only speak from a day or two's experience of her. To my judgment, she is a woman whose fondness for you might be turned into a tigerish fondness, on very small provocation. You write to her constantly. Does she know what you have suffered? Have you told her the truth?"

"Yes."

"Without reserve?"

"Entirely without reserve."

"When that old woman comes to London, Carmina—and sees you, and sees Mrs. Gallilee—don't you think the consequences may be serious? and your position between them something (if you were ten times stronger than you are) that no fortitude can endure?"

Carmina started up on the sofa. She was not able to speak. Miss Minerva gave her time to recover herself—after another look at the clock.

"I am not alarming you for nothing," she proceeded; "I have something hopeful to propose. Your friend Teresa has energies—wild energies. Make a good use of them. She will do anything you ask or her. Take her with you to Canada!"

"Oh, Frances!"

Miss Minerva pointed to the letter on the desk. "Does he tell you when he will be back?"

"No. He feels the importance of completely restoring his health—he is going farther and farther away—he has sent to Quebec for his letters."

"Then there is no fear of your crossing each other on the voyage. Go to Quebec, and wait for him there."

"I should frighten him."

"Not you!"

"What can I say to him?"

"What you *must* say, if you are weak enough to wait for him here. Do you think his mother will consider his feelings, when he comes back to marry you? I tell you again I am not talking at random. I have thought it all out: I know how you can make your escape, and defy pursuit. You have plenty of money; you have Teresa to take care of you. Go! For your own sake, for his sake, go!"

The clock struck the hour. She rose and removed the handkerchief from her head. "Hush!" she said. "Do I hear the rustling of a dress on the landing below?" She snatched up a bottle of Mr. Null's medicine—as a reason for being in the room. The sound of the rustling dress came nearer and nearer. Mrs. Gallilee (on her way to the schoolroom dinner) opened the door. She instantly understood the purpose which the bottle was intended to answer.

"It is *my* business to give Carmina her medicine," she said. "*Your* business is at the schoolroom table."

She took possession of the bottle, and advanced to Carmina. There were two looking-glasses in the room. One, in the usual position, over the fireplace; the other opposite, on the wall behind the sofa. Turning back, before she left the room, Miss Minerva saw Mrs. Gallilee's face, when she and Carmina looked at each other, reflected in the glass.

The girls were waiting for their dinner. Maria received the unpunctual governess with her ready smile, and her appropriate speech. "Dear Miss Minerva, we were really almost getting alarmed about you. Pardon me for noticing it, you look—" She caught the eye of the governess, and stopped confusedly.

"Well?" said Miss Minerva. "How do I look?"

Maria still hesitated. Zo spoke out as usual. "You look as if somebody had frightened you."

CHAPTER XXXVII.

After two days of rain, the weather cleared again.

It was a calm, sunshiny Sunday morning. The flat country round Benjulia's house wore its brightest aspect on that clear autumn day. Even the doctor's gloomy domestic establishment reflected in some degree the change for the better. When he rose that morning, Benjulia presented himself to his household in a character which they were little accustomed to see—the character of a good-humoured master. He astonished his silent servant by attempting to whistle a tune. "If you ever looked cheerful in your life," he said to the man, "look cheerful now. I'm going to take a holiday!"

After working incessantly—never leaving his laboratory; eating at his dreadful table; snatching an hour's rest occasionally on the floor—he had completed a series of experiments, with results on which he could absolutely rely. He had advanced by one step nearer towards solving that occult problem in brain disease, which had thus far baffled the investigations of medical men throughout the civilised world. If his present rate of progress continued, the lapse of another month might add his name to the names that remain immortal among physicians, in the Annals of Discovery.

So completely had his labours absorbed his mind that he only remembered the letters which Mrs. Gallilee had left with him, when he finished his breakfast on Sunday morning. Upon examination, there appeared no allusion in Ovid's correspondence to the mysterious case of illness which he had attended at Montreal. The one method now left, by which Benjulia could relieve the doubt that still troubled him, was to communicate directly with his friend in Canada. He decided to celebrate his holiday by taking a walk; his destination being the central telegraph office in London.[1]

But, before he left the house, his domestic duties claimed attention. He issued his orders to the cook.

At three o'clock he would return to dinner. That day was to witness the celebration of his first regular meal for forty-eight hours past; and he expected the strictest punctuality. The cook—lately engaged—was a vigourous little woman, with fiery hair and a high colour. She, like the man-servant, felt the genial influence of her master's amiability. He looked at her, for the first time since she had entered the house. A twinkling light showed itself furtively in his dreary gray eyes: he took a dusty old hand-screen[2] from the sideboard, and made her a present of it! "There," he said with his dry humour, "don't spoil your complexion before the kitchen fire." The cook possessed a sanguine temperament, and a taste to be honoured and encouraged—the taste for reading novels. She put her own romantic construction on the extraordinary compliment which the doctor's jesting humour had paid to her. As he walked out, grimly smiling and thumping his big stick on the floor, a new idea illumi-

---

1   *the central telegraph office in London*: By 1857, most cities in England were connected by telegraph, but the first trans-oceanic cable was not laid until 1866, so such correspondence, even to Canada, was still relatively exotic.

2   *a dusty old hand-screen*: The screen is a folding fan used by the cook to offset the heat and diffuse the smoke of the kitchen fire.

nated her mind. Her master admired her; her master was no ordinary man—it might end in his marrying her.

On his way to the telegraph office, Benjulia left Ovid's letters at Mrs. Gallilee's house.

If he had personally returned them, he would have found the learned lady in no very gracious humour. On the previous day she had discovered Carmina and Miss Minerva engaged in a private conference—without having been able even to guess what the subject under discussion between them might be. They were again together that morning. Maria and Zo had gone to church with their father; Miss Minerva was kept at home by a headache. At that hour, and under those circumstances, there was no plausible pretence which would justify Mrs. Gallilee's interference. She seriously contemplated the sacrifice of a month's salary, and the dismissal of her governess without notice.

When the footman opened the door, Benjulia handed in the packet of letters. After his latest experience of Mrs. Gallilee, he had no intention of returning her visit. He walked away without uttering a word.

The cable took his message to Mr. Morphew in these terms:—"Ovid's patient at Montreal. Was the complaint brain disease? Yes or no." Having made arrangements for the forwarding of the reply from his club, he set forth on the walk back to his house.

At five minutes to three, he was at home again. As the clock struck the hour, he rang the bell. The man-servant appeared, without the dinner. Benjulia's astonishing amiability—on his holiday—was even equal to this demand on its resources.

"I ordered roast mutton at three," he said, with terrifying tranquillity. "Where is it?"

"The dinner will be ready in ten minutes, sir."

"Why is it not ready now?"

"The cook hopes you will excuse her, sir. She is a little behindhand to-day."

"What has hindered her, if you please?"

The silent servant—on all other occasions the most impenetrable of human beings—began to tremble. The doctor had, literally, kicked a man out of the house who had tried to look through the laboratory skylight. He had turned away a female-servant at half an hour's notice, for forgetting to shut the door, a second time in one day. But what were these high-handed proceedings, compared with the awful composure which, being kept waiting for dinner, only asked what had hindered the cook, and put the question politely, by saying, "if you please"?

"Perhaps you were making love to her?" the doctor suggested, as gently as ever.

This outrageous insinuation stung the silent servant into speech. "I'm incapable of the action, sir!" he answered indignantly; "the woman was reading a story."

Benjulia bent his head, as if in acknowledgment of a highly satisfactory explanation. "Oh? reading a story? People who read stories are said to have excitable brains. Should you call the cook excitable?"

"I should, sir! Most cooks are excitable. They say it's the kitchen fire."

"Do they? You can go now. Don't hurry the cook—I'll wait."

He waited, apparently following some new train of thought which highly diverted him. Ten minutes passed—then a quarter of an hour—then another five minutes. When the servant returned with the dinner, the master's private reflections continued to amuse him: his thin lips were still widening grimly, distended by his formidable smile.

On being carved, the mutton proved to be underdone. At other times, this was an unpardonable crime in Benjulia's domestic code of laws. All he said now was, "Take it away." He dined on potatoes, and bread and cheese. When he had done, he was rather more amiable than ever. He said, "Ask the cook to come and see me!"

The cook presented herself, with one hand on her palpitating heart, and the other holding her handkerchief to her eyes.

"What are you crying about?" Benjulia inquired; "I haven't scolded you, have I?" The cook began an apology; the doctor pointed to a chair. "Sit down, and recover yourself." The cook sat down, faintly smiling through her tears. This otherwise incomprehensible reception of a person who had kept the dinner waiting twenty minutes, and who had not done the mutton properly even then (taken in connection with the master's complimentary inquiries, reported downstairs by the footman), could bear but one interpretation. It wasn't every woman who had her beautiful hair, and her rosy complexion. Why had she not thought of going upstairs first, just to see whether she looked her best in the glass? Would he begin by making a confession? or would he begin by kissing her?

He began by lighting his pipe. For a while he smoked placidly with his eye on the cook. "I hear you have been reading a story," he resumed. "What is the name of it?"

" 'Pamela; or Virtue Rewarded,' sir."[1]

Benjulia went on with his smoking. The cook, thus far demure and downcast, lifted her eyes experimentally. He was still looking at her. Did he want encouragement? The cook cautiously offered a little literary information.

"The author's name is on the book, sir. Name of Richardson."

The information was graciously received, "Yes; I've heard of the name, and heard of the book. Is it interesting?"

"Oh, sir, it's a beautiful story! My only excuse for being late with the dinner—"

---

1   *"Pamela, or Virtue Rewarded"*: *Pamela* (1740-41) was the first of three novels by
     Samuel Richardson (1689-1761). Its epistolary form must have been of interest
     to Collins, but the novel's mention here seems to serve primarily as a spring-
     board into some low comic relief.

"Who's Pamela?"

"A young person in service, sir. I'm sure I wish I was more like her! I felt quite broken-hearted when you sent the mutton down again; and you so kind as to overlook the error in the roasting—"

Benjulia stopped the apology once more. He pursued his own ends with a penitent cook, just as he pursued his own ends with a vivisected animal. Nothing moved him out of his appointed course, in the one or in the other. He returned to Pamela.

"And what becomes of her at the end of the story?" he asked.

The cook simpered. "It's Pamela who is the virtuous young person, sir. And so the story comes true—Pamela, or Virtue Rewarded."

"Who rewards her?"

Was there ever anything so lucky as this? Pamela's situation was fast becoming the cook's situation. The bosom of the vigourous little woman began to show signs of tender agitation—distributed over a large surface. She rolled her eyes amorously. Benjulia puffed out another mouthful of smoke. "Well," he repeated, "who rewards Pamela?"

"Her master, sir."

"What does he do?"

The cook's eyes sank modestly to her lap. The cook's complexion became brighter than ever.

"Her master marries her, sir."

"Oh?"

That was all he said. He was not astonished, or confused, or encouraged—he simply intimated that he now knew how Pamela's master had rewarded Pamela. And, more dispiriting still, he took the opportunity of knocking the ashes out of his pipe, and filled it, and lit it again. If the cook had been one of the few miserable wretches who never read novels, she might have felt her fondly founded hopes already sinking from under her. As it was, Richardson sustained her faith in herself; Richardson reminded her that Pamela's master had hesitated, and that Pamela's Virtue had not earned its reward on easy terms. She stole another look at the doctor. The eloquence of women's eyes, so widely and justly celebrated in poetry and prose, now spoke in the cook's eyes. They said, "Marry me, dear sir, and you shall never have underdone mutton again." The hearts of other savages have been known to soften under sufficient influences—why should the scientific savage, under similar pressure, not melt a little too? The doctor took up the talk again: he made a kind allusion to the cook's family circumstances.

"When you first came here, I think you told me you had no relations?"

"I am an orphan, sir."

"And you had been some time out of a situation, when I engaged you?"

"Yes, sir; my poor little savings were nearly at an end!" Could he resist that pathetic picture of the orphan's little savings—framed, as it were, in a delicately-designed reference to her fellow-servant in the story? "I was as poor as Pamela," she suggested softly.

"And as virtuous," Benjulia added.

The cook's eloquent eyes said, "Thank you, sir."

He laid down his pipe. That was a good sign, surely? He drew his chair nearer to her. Better and better! His arm was long enough, in the new position, to reach her waist. Her waist was ready for him.

"You have nothing in particular to do, this afternoon; and I have nothing particular to do." He delivered himself of this assertion rather abruptly. At the same time, it was one of those promising statements which pave the way for anything. He might say, "Having nothing particular to do to-day—why shouldn't we make love?" Or he might say, "Having nothing particular to do to-morrow—why shouldn't we get the marriage license?" Would he put it in that way? No: he made a proposal of quite another kind. He said, "You seem to be fond of stories. Suppose I tell you a story?"

Perhaps, there was some hidden meaning in this. There was unquestionably a sudden alteration in his look and manner; the cook asked herself what it meant.

If she had seen the doctor at his secret work in the laboratory, the change in him might have put her on her guard. He was now looking (experimentally) at the inferior creature seated before him in the chair, as he looked (experimentally) at the other inferior creatures stretched under him on the table.

His story began in the innocent, old-fashioned way.

"Once upon a time, there was a master and there was a maid. We will call the master by the first letter of the alphabet—Mr. A. And we will call the maid by the second letter—Miss B."

The cook drew a long breath of relief. There *was* a hidden meaning in the doctor's story. The unfortunate woman thought to herself, "I have not only got fine hair and a beautiful complexion; I am clever as well!" On her rare evenings of liberty, she sometimes gratified another highly creditable taste, besides the taste for reading novels. She was an eager play-goer. That notable figure in the drama—the man who tells his own story, under pretence of telling the story of another person—was no unfamiliar figure in her stage experience. Her encouraging smile made its modest appearance once more. In the very beginning of her master's story, she saw already the happy end.

"We all of us have our troubles in life," Benjulia went on; "and Miss B. had her troubles. For a long time, she was out of a situation; and she had no kind parents to help her. Miss B. was an orphan. Her little savings were almost gone."

It was too distressing. The cook took out her handkerchief, and pitied Miss B. with all her heart.

The doctor proceeded.

"But virtue, as we know when we read 'Pamela,' is sure of its reward.

Circumstances occurred in the household of Mr. A. which made it necessary for him to engage a cook. He discovered an advertisement in a newspaper, which informed him that Miss B. was in search of a situation. Mr. A. found her to be a young and charming woman. Mr. A. engaged her." At that critical part of the story, Benjulia paused. "And what did Mr. A. do next?" he asked.

The cook could restrain herself no longer. She jumped out of her chair, and threw her arms round the doctor's neck.

Benjulia went on with his story as if nothing had happened.

"And what did Mr. A. do next?" he repeated. "He put his hand in his pocket—he gave Miss B. a month's wages—and he turned her out of the house. You impudent hussy, you have delayed my dinner, spoilt my mutton, and hugged me round the neck! There is your money. Go."

With glaring eyes and gaping mouth, the cook stood looking at him, like a woman struck to stone. In a moment more, the rage burst out of her in a furious scream. She turned to the table, and snatched up a knife. Benjulia wrenched it from her hand, and dropped back into his chair completely overpowered by the success of his little joke. He did what he had never done within the memory of his oldest friend—he burst out laughing. "This *has* been a holiday!" he said. "Why haven't I got somebody with me to enjoy it?"

At that laugh, at those words, the cook's fury in its fiercest heat became frozen by terror. There was something superhuman in the doctor's diabolical joy. Even *he* felt the wild horror in the woman's eyes as they rested on him.

"What's the matter with you?" he asked. She muttered and mumbled—and, shrinking away from him, crept towards the door. As she approached the window, a man outside passed by it on his way to the house. She pointed to him; and repeated Benjulia's own words:

"Somebody to enjoy it with you," she said.

She opened the dining-room door. The man-servant appeared in the hall, with a gentleman behind him.

The gentleman was a scrupulously polite person. He looked with alarm at the ghastly face of the cook as she ran past him, making for the kitchen stairs. "I'm afraid I intrude on you at an unfortunate time," he said to Benjulia. "Pray excuse me; I will call again."

"Come in, sir." The doctor spoke absently, looking towards the hall, and thinking of something else.

The gentleman entered the room.

"My name is Mool," he said. "I have had the honour of meeting you at one of Mrs. Gallilee's parties."

"Very likely. I don't remember it myself. Take a seat."

He was still thinking of something else. Modest Mr. Mool took a seat in confusion. The doctor crossed the room, and opened the door.

"Excuse me for a minute," he said. "I will be back directly."

He went to the top of the kitchen stairs, and called to the housemaid. "Is the cook down there?"

"Yes, sir."

"What is she doing?"

"Crying her heart out."

Benjulia turned away again with the air of a disappointed man. A violent moral shock sometimes has a serious effect on the brain—especially when it is the brain of an excitable woman. Always a physiologist, even in those rare moments when he was amusing himself, it had just struck Benjulia that the cook—after her outbreak of fury—might be a case worth studying. But, she had got relief in crying; her brain was safe; she had ceased to interest him. He returned to the dining-room.

CHAPTER XXXVIII.

"You look hot, sir; have a drink. Old English ale, out of the barrel."[1]

The tone was hearty. He poured out the sparkling ale into a big tumbler, with hospitable good-will. Mr. Mool was completely, and most agreeably, taken by surprise. He too was feeling the influence of the doctor's good humour—enriched in quality by pleasant remembrances of his interview with the cook.

"I live in the suburbs, Doctor Benjulia, on this side of London," Mr. Mool explained; "and I have had a nice walk from my house to yours. If I have done wrong, sir, in visiting you on Sunday, I can only plead that I am engaged in business during the week—"

"All right. One day's the same as another, provided you don't interrupt me. You don't interrupt me now. Do you smoke?"

"No, thank you."

"Do you mind my smoking?"

"I like it, doctor."

"Very amiable on your part, I'm sure. What did you say your name was?"

"Mool."

Benjulia looked at him suspiciously. Was he a physiologist, and a rival? "You're not a doctor—are you?" he said.

"I am a lawyer."

One of the few popular prejudices which Benjulia shared with his inferior fellow-creatures was the prejudice against lawyers. But for his angry recollection of the provocation successfully offered to him by his despica-

---

1   *Old English ale, out of the barrel*: Ale was a preferred drink in Victorian England, and Benjulia lets Mool know that his stock is appropriately aged and packaged.

ble brother, Mrs. Gallilee would never have found her way into his confidence. But for his hearty enjoyment of the mystification of the cook, Mr. Mool would have been requested to state the object of his visit in writing, and would have gone home again a baffled man. The doctor's holiday amiability had reached its full development indeed, when he allowed a strange lawyer to sit and talk with him!

"Gentlemen of your profession," he muttered, "never pay visits to people whom they don't know, without having their own interests in view. Mr. Mool, you want something of me. What is it?"

Mr. Mool's professional tact warned him to waste no time on prefatory phrases.

"I venture on my present intrusion," he began, "in consequence of a statement recently made to me, in my office, by Mrs. Gallilee."

"Stop!" cried Benjulia. "I don't like your beginning, I can tell you. Is it necessary to mention the name of that old—?" He used a word, described in dictionaries as having a twofold meaning. (First, "A female of the canine kind." Second, "A term of reproach for a woman.") It shocked Mr. Mool; and it is therefore unfit to be reported.[1]

"Really, Doctor Benjulia!"

"Does that mean that you positively must talk about her?"

Mr. Mool smiled. "Let us say that it may bear that meaning," he answered.

"Go on, then—and get it over. She made a statement in your office. Out with it, my good fellow. Has it anything to do with me?"

"I should not otherwise, Doctor Benjulia, have ventured to present myself at your house." With that necessary explanation, Mr. Mool related all that had passed between Mrs. Gallilee and himself.

At the outset of the narrative, Benjulia angrily laid aside his pipe, on the point of interrupting the lawyer. He changed his mind; and, putting a strong constraint on himself, listened in silence. "I hope, sir," Mr. Mool concluded, "you will not take a hard view of my motive. It is only the truth to say that I am interested in Miss Carmina's welfare. I felt the sincerest respect and affection for her parents. You knew them too. They were good people. On reflection you must surely regret it, if you have carelessly repeated a false report? Won't you help me to clear the poor mother's memory of this horrid stain?"

Benjulia smoked in silence. Had that simple and touching appeal found its way to him? He began very strangely, when he consented at last to open his lips.

"You're what they call, a middle-aged man," he said. "I suppose you have had some experience of women?"

---

1   *He used a word ... unfit to be reported*: Collins flouts staid convention here, for in most circles mere allusion to such vulgar language was considered unsavoury, even in a late-century novel.

Mr. Mool blushed. "I am a married man, sir," he replied gravely.

"Very well; that's experience—of one kind.[1] When a man's out of temper, and a woman wants something of him, do you know how cleverly she can take advantage of her privileges to aggravate him, till there's nothing he won't do to get her to leave him in peace? That's how I came to tell Mrs. Gallilee, what she told you."

He waited a little, and comforted himself with his pipe.

"Mind this," he resumed, "I don't profess to feel any interest in the girl; and I never cared two straws about her parents. At the same time, if you can turn to good account what I am going to say next—do it, and welcome. This scandal began in the bragging of a fellow-student of mine at Rome. He was angry with me, and angry with another man, for laughing at him when he declared himself to be Mrs. Robert Graywell's lover: and he laid us a wager that we should see the woman alone in his room, that night. We were hidden behind a curtain, and we did see her in his room. I paid the money I had lost, and left Rome soon afterwards. The other man refused to pay."

"On what ground?" Mr. Mool eagerly asked.

"On the ground that she wore a thick veil, and never showed her face."

"An unanswerable objection, Doctor Benjulia!"

"Perhaps it might be. I didn't think so myself. Two hours before, Mrs. Robert Graywell and I had met in the street. She had on a dress of a remarkable colour in those days—a sort of sea-green. And a bonnet to match, which everybody stared at, because it was not half the size of the big bonnets then in fashion. There was no mistaking the strange dress or the tall figure, when I saw her again in the student's room. So I paid the bet."

"Do you remember the name of the man who refused to pay?"

"His name was Egisto Baccani."[2]

"Have you heard anything of him since?"

"Yes. He got into some political scrape, and took refuge, like the rest of them, in England; and got his living, like the rest of them, by teaching languages. He sent me his prospectus—that's how I came to know about it."

"Have you got the prospectus?"

"Torn up, long ago."

Mr. Mool wrote down the name in his pocket-book. "There is nothing more you can tell me?" he said.

---

1   *Very well; that's experience—of one kind*: This passage is clearly an inside joke with Collins, who never married and happily led a bohemian lifestyle that included fathering three children by one woman while living quite contentedly with another.

2   *Egisto Baccani*: An almost identical figure, the artist Mr. Pesca, also an Italian political refugee, appears in *The Woman in White*. Baccani, like Pesca, provides information that becomes crucial to the triumph of good over villainy by the novel's end.

"Nothing."

"Accept my best thanks, doctor. Good-day!"

"If you find Baccani let me know. Another drop of ale? Are you likely to see Mrs. Gallilee soon?"

"Yes—if I find Baccani."

"Do you ever play with children?"

"I have five of my own to play with," Mr. Mool answered.

"Very well. Ask for the youngest child when you go to Mrs. Gallilee's. We call her Zo. Put your finger on her spine—here, just below the neck. Press on the place—so. And, when she wriggles, say, With the big doctor's love."

Getting back to his own house, Mr. Mool was surprised to find an open carriage at the garden gate. A smartly-dressed woman, on the front seat, surveyed him with an uneasy look. "If you please, sir," she said, "would you kindly tell Miss Carmina that we really mustn't wait any longer?"

The woman's uneasiness was reflected in Mr. Mool's face. A visit from Carmina, at his private residence, could have no ordinary motive. The fear instantly occurred to him that Mrs. Gallilee might have spoken to her of her mother.

Before he opened the drawing-room door, this alarm passed away. He heard Carmina talking with his wife and daughters.

"May I say one little word to you, Mr. Mool?"

He took her into his study. She was shy and confused, but certainly neither angry nor distressed.

"My aunt sends me out every day, when it's fine, for a drive," she said. "As the carriage passed close by, I thought I might ask you a question."

"Certainly, my dear! As many questions as you please."

"It's about the law. My aunt says she has the authority over me now, which my dear father had while he was living. Is that true?"

"Quite true."

"For how long is she my guardian?"

"Until you are twenty-one years old."

The faint colour faded from Carmina's face. "More than three years perhaps to suffer!" she said sadly.

"To suffer? What do you mean, my dear?"

She turned paler still, and made no reply. "I want to ask one thing more?" she resumed, in sinking tones. "Would my aunt still be my guardian—supposing I was married?"

Mr. Mool answered this, with his eyes fixed on her in grave scrutiny.

"In that case, your husband is the only person who has any authority over you. These are rather strange questions, Carmina. Won't you take me into your confidence?"

In sudden agitation she seized his hand and kissed it. "I must go!" she said. "I have kept the carriage waiting too long already."

She ran out, without once looking back.

End of February 1883 *Belgravia* Serial Number

CHAPTER XXXIX.

Mrs. Gallilee's maid looked at her watch, when the carriage left Mr. Mool's house. "We shall be nearly an hour late, before we get home," she said.

"It's my fault, Marceline. Tell your mistress the truth, if she questions you. I shall not think the worse of you for obeying your orders."

"I'd rather lose my place, Miss, than get you into trouble."

The woman spoke truly, Carmina's sweet temper had made her position not only endurable, but delightful: she had been treated like a companion and a friend. But for that circumstance—so keenly had Marceline felt the degradation of being employed as a spy—she would undoubtedly have quitted Mrs. Gallilee's service.

On the way home, instead of talking pleasantly as usual, Carmina was silent and sad. Had this change in her spirits been caused by the visit to Mr. Mool? It was even so. The lawyer had innocently decided her on taking the desperate course which Miss Minerva had proposed.

If Mrs. Gallilee's assertion of her absolute right of authority, as guardian, had been declared by Mr. Mool to be incorrect, Carmina (hopefully forgetful of her aunt's temper) had thought of a compromise.

She would have consented to remain at Mrs. Gallilee's disposal until Ovid returned, on condition of being allowed, when Teresa arrived in London, to live in retirement with her old nurse. This change of abode would prevent any collision between Mrs. Gallilee and Teresa, and would make Carmina's life as peaceful, and even as happy, as she could wish.

But now that the lawyer had confirmed her aunt's statement of the position in which they stood towards one another, instant flight to Ovid's love and protection seemed to be the one choice left—unless Carmina could resign herself to a life of merciless persecution and perpetual suspense.

The arrangements for the flight were already complete.

That momentary view of Mrs. Gallilee's face, reflected in the glass, had confirmed Miss Minerva's resolution to interfere. Closeted with Carmina on the Sunday morning, she had proposed a scheme of escape, which would even set Mrs. Gallilee's vigilance and cunning at defiance. No pecuniary obstacle stood in the way. The first quarterly payment of Carmina's allowance of five hundred a year had been already made, by Mr. Mool's advice. Enough was left—even without the assistance which the nurse's resources would render—to purchase the necessary outfit, and to take the two women to Quebec. On the day after Teresa's arrival (at an hour of the morning while the servants were still in bed) Carmina and her companion could escape from the house on foot—and not leave a trace behind them.

Meanwhile, Fortune befriended Mrs. Gallilee's maid. No questions were put to her; no notice even was taken of the late return.

Five minutes before the carriage drew up at the house, a learned female friend from the country called, by appointment, on Mrs. Gallilee. On the coming Tuesday afternoon, an event of the deepest scientific interest was to take place. A new Professor had undertaken to deliver himself, by means of a lecture, of subversive opinions on "Matter." A general discussion was to follow; and in that discussion (upon certain conditions) Mrs. Gallilee herself proposed to take part.

"If the Professor attempts to account for the mutual action of separate atoms," she said, "I defy him to do it, without assuming the existence of a continuous material medium in space. And this point of view being accepted—follow me here!—what is the result? In plain words," cried Mrs. Gallilee, rising excitedly to her feet, "we dispense with the idea of atoms!"

The friend looked infinitely relieved by the prospect of dispensing with atoms.

"Now observe!" Mrs. Gallilee proceeded. "In connection with this part of the subject, I shall wait to see if the Professor adopts Thomson's theory.[1] You are acquainted with Thomson's theory? No? Let me put it briefly. Mere heterogeneity, together with gravitation, is sufficient to explain all the apparently discordant laws of molecular action. You understand? Very well. If the Professor passes over Thomson, *then*, I rise in the body of the Hall, and take my stand—follow me again!—on these grounds."

While Mrs. Gallilee's grounds were being laid out for the benefit of her friend, the coachman took the carriage back to the stables; the maid went downstairs to tea; and Carmina joined Miss Minerva in the schoolroom—all three being protected from discovery, by Mrs. Gallilee's rehearsal of her performance in the Comedy of Atoms.

The Monday morning brought with it news from Rome—serious news which confirmed Miss Minerva's misgivings.

Carmina received a letter, bearing the Italian postmark, but not addressed to her in Teresa's handwriting. She looked to the signature before she began to read. Her correspondent was the old priest—Father Patrizio. He wrote in these words:

"My dear child,—Our good Teresa leaves us to-day, on her journey to London. She has impatiently submitted to the legal ceremonies, rendered necessary by her husband having died without making a will. He hardly left anything in the way of money, after payment of his burial expenses,

---

1   *Thomson's theory*: Thomson's theory, which Mrs. Gallilee states excitedly for her friend, originated with Joseph John Thomson (1856-1940), the English physicist whose theories led to his discovery of the electron in 1895. Thomson was named professor of physics at Trinity College, Cambridge, as well as head of the College's Cavendish Laboratory, by the age of twenty-seven. He won the Nobel Prize for physics in 1906.

and his few little debts. What is of far greater importance—he lived, and died, a good Christian. I was with him in his last moments. Offer your prayers, my dear, for the repose of his soul.

'Teresa left me, declaring her purpose of travelling night and day, so as to reach you the sooner.

"In her headlong haste, she has not even waited to look over her husband's papers; but has taken the case containing them to England—to be examined at leisure, in your beloved company. Strong as this good creature is, I believe she will be obliged to rest on the road for a night at least. Calculating on this, I assume that my letter will get to you first. I have something to say about your old nurse, which it is well that you should know.

"Do not for a moment suppose that I blame you for having told Teresa of the unfriendly reception, which you appear to have met with from your aunt and guardian. Who should you confide in—if not in the excellent woman who has filled the place of a mother to you? Besides, from your earliest years, have I not always instilled into you the reverence of truth? You have told the truth in your letters. My child, I commend you, and feel for you.

"But the impression produced on Teresa is not what you or I could wish. It is one of her merits, that she loves you with the truest devotion; it is one of her defects, that she is fierce and obstinate in resentment. Your aunt has become an object of absolute hatred to her. I have combated—successfully, as I hope and believe—this unchristian state of feeling.

"She is now beyond the reach of my influence. My purpose in writing is to beg you to continue the good work that I have begun. Compose this impetuous nature; restrain this fiery spirit. Your gentle influence, Carmina, has a power of its own over those who love you—and who loves you like Teresa?—of which perhaps you are not yourself aware. Use your power discreetly; and, with the blessing of God and his Saints, I have no fear of the result.

"Write to me, my child, when Teresa arrives—and let me hear that you are happier, and better in health. Tell me also, whether there is any speedy prospect of your marriage. If I may presume to judge from the little I know, your dearest earthly interests depend on the removal of obstacles to this salutary change in your life. I send you my good wishes, and my blessing. If a poor old priest like me can be of any service, do not forget.

"FATHER PATRIZIO."

Any lingering hesitation that Carmina might still have felt, was at an end when she read this letter. Good Father Patrizio, like good Mr. Mool, had innocently urged her to set her guardian's authority at defiance.

CHAPTER XL.

When the morning lessons were over, Carmina showed the priest's letter to Miss Minerva. The governess read it, and handed it back in silence.

"Have you nothing to say?" Carmina asked.

"Nothing. You know my opinion already. That letter says what I have said—with greater authority."

"It has determined me to follow your advice, Frances."

"Then it has done well."

"And you see," Carmina continued, "that Father Patrizio speaks of obstacles in the way of my marriage. Teresa has evidently shown him my letters. Do you think he fears, as I do, that my aunt may find some means of separating us, even when Ovid comes back?"

"Very likely."

She spoke in faint weary tones—listlessly leaning back in her chair. Carmina asked if she had passed another sleepless night.

"Yes," she said, "another bad night, and the usual martyrdom in teaching the children. I don't know which disgusts me most—Zoe's impudent stupidity, or Maria's unendurable humbug."

She had never yet spoken of Maria in this way. Even her voice seemed to be changed. Instead of betraying the usual angry abruptness, her tones coldly indicated impenetrable contempt. In the silence that ensued, she looked up, and saw Carmina's eyes resting on her anxiously and kindly.

"Any other human being but you," she said, "would find me disagreeable and rude—and would be quite right, too. I haven't asked after your health. You look paler than usual. Have *you*, too, had a bad night?"

"I fell asleep towards the morning. And—oh, I had such a delightful dream! I could almost wish that I had never awakened from it."

"Who did you dream of?" She put the question mechanically—frowning, as if at some repellent thought suggested to her by what she had just heard.

"I dreamed of my mother," Carmina answered.

Miss Minerva raised herself at once in the chair. Whatever that passing impression might have been, she was free from it now. There was some little life again in her eyes; some little spirit in her voice. "Take me out of myself," she said; "tell me your dream."

"It is nothing very remarkable, Frances. We all of us sometimes see our dear lost ones in sleep. I saw my mother again, as I used to see her in the nursery at bedtime—tall and beautiful, with her long dark hair falling over her white dressing-gown to the waist. She stooped over me, and kissed me; and she looked surprised. She said, 'My little angel, why are you here in a strange house? I have come to take you back to your own cot, by my bedside.' I wasn't surprised or frightened; I put my arms round her neck; and we floated away together through the cool starry night; and we were at home again. I saw my cot, with its pretty white curtains and pink ribbons. I heard my mother tell me an English fairy story, out of a book which my father had given to her—and her kind voice grew fainter and fainter, while I grew more and more sleepy—and it ended softly, just as it used to end in the happy old days. And I woke, crying. Do *you* ever dream of your mother now?"

"I? God forbid!"

"Oh, Frances, what a dreadful thing to say!"

"Is it? It was the thought in me, when you spoke. And with good reason, too. I was the last of a large family—the ugly one; the ill-tempered one; the encumbrance that made it harder than ever to find money enough to pay the household expenses. My father swore at my mother for *being* my mother. She reviled him just as bitterly in return; and vented the rest of her ill-temper on my wretched little body, with no sparing hand. Bedtime was her time for beating me. Talk of your mother—not of mine! You were very young, were you not, when she died?"

"Too young to feel my misfortune—but old enough to remember the sweetest woman that ever lived. Let me show you my father's portrait of her again. Doesn't that face tell you what an angel she was? There was some charm in her that all children felt. I can just remember some of my playfellows who used to come to our garden. Other good mothers were with us—but the children all crowded round *my* mother. They would have her in all their games; they fought for places on her lap when she told them stories; some of them cried, and some of them screamed, when it was time to take them away from her. Oh, why do we live! why do we die! I have bitter thoughts sometimes, Frances, like you. I have read in poetry that death is a fearful thing. To me, death is a cruel thing,—and it has never seemed so cruel as in these later days, since I have known Ovid. If my mother had but lived till now, what happiness would have been added to my life and to hers! How Ovid would have loved her—how she would have loved Ovid!"

Miss Minerva listened in silence. It was the silence of true interest and sympathy, while Carmina was speaking of her mother. When her lover's name became mingled with the remembrances of her childhood—the change came. Once more, the tell-tale lines began to harden in the governess's face. She lay back again in her chair. Her fingers irritably platted and unplatted the edge of her black apron.

Carmina was too deeply absorbed in her thoughts, too eagerly bent on giving them expression, to notice these warning signs.

"I have all my mother's letters to my father," she went on, "when he was away from her on his sketching excursions. You have still a little time to spare—I should so like to read some of them to you. I was reading one, last night—which perhaps accounts for my dream? It is on a subject that interests everybody. In my father's absence, a very dear friend of his met with a misfortune; and my mother had to prepare his wife to hear the bad news—oh, that reminds me! There is something I want to say to you first."

"About yourself?" Miss Minerva asked.

"About Ovid. I want your advice."

Miss Minerva was silent. Carmina went on. "It's about writing to Ovid," she explained.

"Write, of course!"

The reply was suddenly and sharply given. "Surely, I have not offended you?" Carmina said.

"Nonsense! Let me hear your mother's letter."

"Yes—but I want you to hear the circumstances first."

"You have mentioned them already."

"No! no! I mean the circumstances, in my case." She drew her chair closer to Miss Minerva. "I want to whisper—for fear of somebody passing on the stairs. The more I think of it, the more I feel that I ought to prepare Ovid for seeing me, before I make my escape. You said when we talked of it—"

"Never mind what I said."

"Oh, but I do mind! You said I could go to Ovid's bankers at Quebec, and then write when I knew where he was. I have been thinking over it since—and I see a serious risk. He might return from his inland journey, on the very day that I get there; he might even meet me in the street. In his delicate health—I daren't think of what the consequences of such a surprise might be! And then there is the dreadful necessity of telling him, that his mother has driven me into taking this desperate step. In my place, wouldn't you feel that you could do it more delicately in writing?"

"I dare say!"

"I might write to-morrow, for instance. To-morrow is one of the American mail days.[1] My letter would get to Canada (remembering the roundabout way by which Teresa and I are to travel, for fear of discovery), days and days before we could arrive. I should shut myself up in an hotel at Quebec; and Teresa could go every day to the bank, to hear if Ovid was likely to send for his letters, or likely to call soon and ask for them. Then he would be prepared. Then, when we meet—!"

The governess left her chair, and pointed to the clock.

Carmina looked at her—and rose in alarm. "Are you in pain?" she asked.

"Yes—neuralgia, I think.[2] I have the remedy in my room. Don't keep me, my dear. Mrs. Gallilee mustn't find me here again."

The paroxysm of pain which Carmina had noticed, passed over her

---

1   *To-morrow is one of the American mail days*: Victorians had to time their overseas postings to catch a mail-steamer like the one that took Ovid to Quebec in chapter XXIII. The mail to the United States did not depart daily. *The Times* had a column titled "Mails" that informed readers about mail-steamer departures and arrivals.

2   *neuralgia, I think*: Miss Minerva here suffers some paroxysmal pain along a nerve.

face once more. She subdued it, and left the room. The pain mastered her again; a low cry broke from her when she closed the door. Carmina ran out: "Frances! what is it?" Frances looked over her shoulder, while she slowly ascended the stairs. "Never mind!" she said gently. "I have got my remedy."

Carmina advanced a step to follow her, and drew back.

Was that expression of suffering really caused by pain of the body? or was it attributable to anything that she had rashly said? She tried to recall what had passed between Frances and her self. The effort wearied her. Her thoughts turned self-reproachfully to Ovid. If *he* had been speaking to a friend whose secret sorrow was known to him, would he have mentioned the name of the woman whom they both loved? She looked at his portrait, and reviled herself as a selfish insensible wretch. "Will Ovid improve me?" she wondered. "Shall I be a little worthier of him, when I am his wife?"

Luncheon time came; and Mrs. Gallilee sent word that they were not to wait for her.

"She's studying," said Mr. Gallilee, with awe-struck looks. "She's going to make a speech at the Discussion to-morrow. The man who gives the lecture is the man she's going to pitch into. I don't know him; but— how do you feel about it yourself, Carmina?—I wouldn't stand in his shoes for any sum of money you could offer me. Poor devil! I beg your pardon, my dear; let me give you a wing of the fowl. Boiled fowl—eh? and tongue—ha? Do you know the story of the foreigner? He dined out fifteen times with his English friends. And there was boiled fowl and tongue at every dinner. The fifteenth time, the foreigner couldn't stand it any longer. He slapped his forehead, and he said, 'Ah, merciful Heaven, cock and bacon again!' You won't mention it, will you?—and perhaps you think as I do?—I'm sick of cock and bacon, myself."

Mr. Null's medical orders still prescribed fresh air. The carriage came to the door at the regular hour; and Mr. Gallilee, with equal regularity, withdrew to his club.

Carmina was too uneasy to leave the house, without seeing Miss Minerva first. She went up to the schoolroom.

There was no sound of voices, when she opened the door. Miss Minerva was writing, and silence had been proclaimed. The girls were ready dressed for their walk. Industrious Maria had her book. Idle Zo, perched on a high chair, sat kicking her legs. "If you say a word," she whispered, as Carmina passed her, "you'll be called an Imp, and stuck up on a chair. I shall go to the boy."

"Are you better, Frances?"

"Much better, my dear."

Her face denied it; the look of suffering was there still. She tore up the letter which she had been writing, and threw the fragments into the waste-paper basket.

"That's the second letter you've torn up," Zo remarked.

"Say a word more—and you shall have bread and water for tea!" Miss Minerva was not free from irritation, although she might be free from pain. Even Zo noticed how angry the governess was.

"I wish you could drive with me in the carriage," said Carmina. "The air would do you so much good."

"Impossible! But you may soothe my irritable nerves in another way, if you like."

"How?"

"Relieve me of these girls. Take them out with you. Do you mind?"

Zo instantly jumped off her chair; and even Maria looked up from her book.

"I will take them with pleasure. Must we ask my aunt's permission?"

"We will dispense with your aunt's permission. She is shut up in her study—and we are all forbidden to disturb her. I will take it on myself." She turned to the girls with another outbreak of irritability. "Be off!"

Maria rose with dignity, and made one of her successful exits. "I am sorry, dear Miss Minerva, if *I* have done anything to make you angry." She pointed the emphasis on "I," by a side-look at her sister. Zo bounced out of the room, and performed the Italian boy's dance on the landing. "For shame!" said Maria. Zo burst into singing. "*Yah yah-yah-bellah-vitah-yah!* Jolly! jolly! jolly!—we are going out for a drive!"

Carmina waited, to say a friendly word, before she followed the girls.

"You didn't think me neglectful, Frances, when I let you go upstairs by yourself!" Miss Minerva answered sadly and kindly. "The best thing you could do was to leave me by myself."

Carmina's mind was still not quite at ease. "Yes—but you were in pain," she said.

"You curious child! I am not in pain now."

"Will you make me comfortable, Frances? Give me a kiss."

"Two, my dear—if you like."

She kissed Carmina on one cheek and on the other. "Now leave me to write," she said.

Carmina left her.

The drive ought to have been a pleasant one, with Zo in the carriage. To Marceline, it was a time of the heartiest enjoyment. Maria herself condescended to smile, now and then. There was only one dull person among them. "Miss Carmina was but poor company," the maid remarked when they got back.

Mrs. Gallilee herself received them in the hall.

"You will never take the children out again without my leave," she said to Carmina. "The person who is really responsible for what you have done, will mislead you no more." With those words she entered the library, and closed the door.

Maria and Zo, at the sight of their mother, had taken flight. Carmina stood alone in the hall. Mrs. Gallilee had turned her cold. After awhile, she followed the children as far as her own room. There, her resolution failed her. She called faintly upstairs—"Frances!" There was no answering voice. She went into her room. A small paper packet was on the table; sealed, and addressed to herself. She tore it open. A ring with a spinel ruby in it dropped out:[1] she recognised the stone—it was Miss Minerva's ring.

Some blotted lines were traced on the paper inside.

"I have tried to pour out my heart to you in writing—and I have torn up the letters. The fewest words are the best. Look back at my confession—and you will know why I have left you. You shall hear from me, when I am more worthy of you than I am now. In the meantime, wear my ring. It will tell you how mean I once was. F. M."

Carmina looked at the ring. She remembered that Frances had tried to make her accept it as security, in return for the loan of thirty pounds.

She referred to the confession. Two passages in it were underlined: "The wickedness in me, on which Mrs. Gallilee calculated, may be in me still." And, again: "Even now, when you have found me out, I love him. Don't trust me."

Never had Carmina trusted her more faithfully than at that bitter moment!

CHAPTER XLI.[2]

The ordinary aspect of the schoolroom was seen no more.

Installed in a position of temporary authority, the parlour-maid sat silently at her needlework. Maria stood by the window, in the new character of an idle girl—with her handkerchief in her hand, and her everlasting book dropped unnoticed on the floor. Zo lay flat on her back, on the hearth-rug, hugging the dog in her arms. At intervals, she rolled herself over slowly from side to side, and stared at the ceiling with wondering eyes. Miss Minerva's departure had struck the parlour-maid dumb, and had demoralized the pupils.

Maria broke the silence at last. "I wonder where Carmina is?" she said.

"In her room, most likely," the parlour-maid suggested.

"Had I better go and see after her?"

The cautious parlour-maid declined to offer advice. Maria's well-balanced mind was so completely unhinged, that she looked with languid curiosity at her sister. Zo still stared at the ceiling, and still rolled slowly

---

1   *A ring with a spinel ruby in it dropped out*: A spinel is any kind of several hard and variously coloured minerals, the red variety (ruby) being valued as a gem.

2   *CHAPTER XLI*: Collins split chapter XLI of the *Belgravia* serial number (March 1883) for the volume edition of the novel. Chapter XLI of the *Belgravia* issue became chapters XLI and XLII in the Chatto & Windus edition.

from one side to the other. The dog on her breast, lulled by the regular motion, slept profoundly—not even troubled by a dream of fleas!

While Maria was still considering what it might be best to do, Carmina entered the room. She looked, as the servant afterwards described it, "like a person who had lost her way." Maria exhibited the feeling of the schoolroom, by raising her handkerchief in solemn silence to her eyes. Without taking notice of this demonstration, Carmina approached the parlourmaid, and said, "Did you see Miss Minerva before she went away?"

"I took her message, Miss."

"What message?"

"The message, saying she wished to see my mistress for a few minutes."

"Well?"

"Well, Miss, I was told to show the governess into the library. She went down with her bonnet on, ready dressed to go out. Before she had been five minutes with my mistress she came out again, and rang the hall-bell, and spoke to Joseph. 'My boxes are packed and directed,' she says; 'I will send for them in an hour's time. Good day, Joseph.' And she stepped into the street, as quietly as if she was going out shopping round the corner."

"Have the boxes been sent for?"

"Yes, Miss."

Carmina lifted her head, and spoke in steadier tones.

"Where have they been taken to?"

"To the flower-shop at the back—to be kept till called for."

"No other address?"

"None."

The last faint hope of tracing Frances was at an end. Carmina turned wearily to leave the room. Zo called to her from the hearth-rug. Always kind to the child, she retraced her steps. "What is it?" she asked.

Zo got on her legs before she spoke, like a member of parliament. "I've been thinking about that governess," she announced. "Didn't I once tell you I was going to run away? And wasn't it because of Her? Hush! Here's the part of it I can't make out—She's run away from Me. I don't bear malice; I'm only glad in myself. No more dirty nails. No more bread and water for tea. That's all. Good morning." Zo laid herself down again on the rug; and the dog laid himself down again on Zo.

Carmina returned to her room—to reflect on what she had heard from the parlour-maid.

It was now plain that Mrs. Gallilee had not been allowed the opportunity of dismissing her governess at a moment's notice: Miss Minerva's sudden departure was unquestionably due to Miss Minerva herself.

Thus far, Carmina was able to think clearly—and no farther. The confused sense of helpless distress which she had felt, after reading the few farewell words that Frances had addressed to her, still oppressed her mind. There were moments when she vaguely understood, and bitterly lamented, the motives which had animated her unhappy friend. Other moments followed, when she impulsively resented the act which had thrown her on her own resources, at the very time when she had most need of the encouragement that could be afforded by the sympathy of a firmer nature than her own. She began to doubt the steadiness of her resolution—without Frances to take leave of her, on the morning of the escape. For the first time, she was now tortured by distrust of Ovid's reception of her; by dread of his possible disapproval of her boldness; by morbid suspicion even of his taking his mother's part. Bewildered and reckless, she threw herself on the sofa—her heart embittered against Frances—indifferent whether she lived or died.

At dinner-time she sent a message, begging to be excused from appearing at the table. Mrs. Gallilee at once presented herself, harder and colder than ever, to inspect the invalid. Perceiving no immediate necessity for summoning Mr. Null, she said, "Ring, if you want anything," and left the room.

Mr. Gallilee followed, after an interval, with a little surreptitious offering of wine (hidden under his coat); and with a selection of tarts crammed into his pocket.

"Smuggled goods, my dear," he whispered, "picked up when nobody happened to be looking my way. When we are miserable—has the idea ever occurred to you?—it's a sign from kind Providence that we are intended to eat and drink. The sherry's old, and the pastry melts in your mouth. Shall I stay with you? You would rather not? Just my feeling! Remarkable similarity in our opinions—don't you think so yourself? I'm sorry for poor Miss Minerva. Suppose you go to bed?"

Carmina was in no mood to profit by this excellent advice.

She was still walking restlessly up and down her room, when the time came for shutting up the house. With the sound of closing locks and bolts, there was suddenly mingled a sharp ring at the bell; followed by another unexpected event. Mr. Gallilee paid her a second visit—in a state of transformation. His fat face was flushed: he positively looked as if he was capable of feeling strong emotion, unconnected with champagne and the club! He presented a telegram to Carmina—and, when he spoke, there were thrills of agitation in the tones of his piping voice.

"My dear, something very unpleasant has happened. I met Joseph taking this to my wife. Highly improper, in my opinion,—what do you say yourself?—to take it to Mrs. Gallilee, when it's addressed to you. It was no mistake; he was so impudent as to say he had his orders. I have reproved Joseph." Mr. Gallilee looked astonished at himself, when he made this latter statement—then relapsed into his customary sweetness of temper. "No bad news?" he asked anxiously, when Carmina opened the telegram.

"Good news! the best of good news!" she answered impetuously.

Mr. Gallilee looked as happy as if the welcome telegram had been addressed to himself. On his way out of the room, he underwent another relapse. The footman's audacious breach of trust began to trouble him once more: this time in its relation to Mrs. Gallilee. The serious part of it was, that the man had acted under his mistress's orders. Mr. Gallilee said—he actually said, without appealing to anybody—"If this happens again, I shall be obliged to speak to my wife."

The telegram was from Teresa. It had been despatched from Paris that evening; and the message was thus expressed:

"Too tired to get on to England by to-night's mail. Shall leave by the early train to-morrow morning, and be with you by six o'clock."

Carmina's mind was exactly in the state to feel unmingled relief, at the prospect of seeing the dear old friend of her happiest days. She laid her head on the pillow that night, without a thought of what might follow the event of Teresa's return.

END OF THE SECOND VOLUME

VOLUME THREE

CHAPTER XLII.

The next day—the important Tuesday of the lecture on Matter; the delightful Tuesday of Teresa's arrival—brought with it special demands on Carmina's pen.

Her first letter was addressed to Frances. It was frankly and earnestly written; entreating Miss Minerva to appoint a place at which they might meet, and assuring her, in the most affectionate terms, that she was still loved, trusted, and admired by her faithful friend. Helped by her steadier flow of spirits, Carmina could now see all that was worthiest of sympathy and admiration, all that claimed loving submission and allowance from herself, in the sacrifice to which Miss Minerva had submitted. How bravely the poor governess had controlled the jealous misery that tortured her! How nobly she had pronounced Carmina's friendship for Carmina's sake!

Later in the day, Marceline took the letter to the flower shop, and placed it herself under the cord of one of the boxes—still waiting to be claimed.

The second letter filled many pages, and occupied the remainder of the morning.

With the utmost delicacy, but with perfect truthfulness at the same time, Carmina revealed to her betrothed husband the serious reasons which had forced her to withdraw herself from his mother's care. Bound to speak at last in her own defence, she felt that concealments and compromises would be alike unworthy of Ovid and of herself. What she had already written to Teresa, she now wrote again—with but one modification. She expressed herself forbearingly towards Ovid's mother. The closing words of the letter were worthy of Carmina's gentle, just, and generous nature.

"You will perhaps say, Why do I only hear now of all that you have suffered? My love, I have longed to tell you of it! I have even taken up my pen to begin. But I thought of *you*, and put it down again. How selfish, how cruel, to hinder your recovery by causing you sorrow and suspense—to bring you back perhaps to England before your health was restored! I don't regret the effort that it has cost me to keep silence. My only sorrow in writing to you is, that I must speak of your mother in terms which may lower her in her son's estimation."

Joseph brought the luncheon up to Carmina's room.

The mistress was still at her studies; the master had gone to his club. As for the girls, their only teacher for the present was the teacher of music. When the ordeal of the lecture and the discussion had been passed, Mrs. Gallilee threatened to take Miss Minerva's place herself, until a new governess could be found. For once, Maria and Zo showed a sisterly similarity in their feelings. It was hard to say which of the two looked forward to her learned mother's instruction with the greatest terror.

Carmina heard the pupils at the piano, while she was eating her luncheon. The profanation of music ceased, when she went into the bedroom to get ready for her daily drive.

She took her letter, duly closed and stamped, downstairs with her—to be sent to the post with the other letters of the day, placed in the hall-basket. In the weakened state of her nerves, the effort that she had made in writing to Ovid had shaken her. Her heart beat uneasily; her knees trembled, as she descended the stairs.

Arrived in sight of the hall, she discovered a man walking slowly to and fro. He turned towards her as she advanced, and disclosed the detestable face of Mr. Le Frank.

The music-master's last reserves of patience had come to an end. Watch for them as he might, no opportunities had presented themselves of renewing his investigation in Carmina's room. In the interval that had passed, his hungry suspicion of her had been left to feed on itself. The motives for that incomprehensible attempt to make a friend of him remained hidden in as thick a darkness as ever. Victim of adverse circumstances, he had determined (with the greatest reluctance) to take the straightforward course. Instead of secretly getting his information from Carmina's journals and letters, he was now reduced to openly applying for enlightenment to Carmina herself.

Occupying, for the time being, the position of an honourable man, he presented himself at cruel disadvantage. He was not master of his own glorious voice; he was without the self-possession indispensable to the perfect performance of his magnificent bow. "I have waited to have a word with you," he began abruptly, "before you go out for your drive."

Already unnerved, even before she had seen him—painfully conscious that she had committed a serious error, on the last occasion when they had met, in speaking at all—Carmina neither answered him nor looked at him. She bent her head confusedly, and advanced a little nearer to the house door.

He at once moved so as to place himself in her way.

"I must request you to call to mind what passed between us," he resumed, "when we met by accident some little time since."

He had speculated on frightening her. His insolence stirred her spirit into asserting itself. "Let me by, if you please," she said; "the carriage is waiting for me."

"The carriage can wait a little longer," he answered coarsely. "On the occasion to which I have referred, you were so good as to make advances, to which I cannot consider myself as having any claim. Perhaps you will favour me by stating your motives?"

"I don't understand you, sir."

"Oh, yes—you do!"

She stepped back, and laid her hand on the bell which rang below stairs, in the pantry. "Must I ring?" she said.

It was plain that she would do it, if he moved a step nearer to her. He drew aside—with a look which made her tremble. On passing the hall-table, she placed her letter in the post-basket.[1] His eye followed it, as it left her hand: he became suddenly penitent and polite. "I am sorry if I have alarmed you," he said, and opened the house-door for her—without showing himself to Marceline and the coachman outside.

The carriage having been driven away, he softly closed the door again, and returned to the hall-table. He looked into the post-basket.

Was there any danger of discovery by the servants? The footman was absent, attending his mistress on her way to the lecture. None of the female servants were on the stairs. He took up Carmina's letter, and looked at the address: *To Ovid Vere, Esq.*

His eyes twinkled furtively; his excellent memory for injuries reminded him that Ovid Vere had formerly endeavoured (without even caring to conceal it) to prevent Mrs. Gallilee from engaging him as his music-master. By subtle links of its own forging, his vindictive nature now connected his hatred of the person to whom the letter was addressed, with his interest in stealing the letter itself for the possible discovery of Carmina's secrets. The clock told him that there was plenty of time to open the envelope, and (if the contents proved to be of no importance) to close it again, and take it himself to the post. After a last look round, he withdrew undiscovered, with the letter in his pocket.

On its way back to the house, the carriage was passed by a cab, with a man in it, driven at such a furious rate that there was a narrow escape of collision. The maid screamed; Carmina turned pale; the coachman wondered why the man in the cab was in such a hurry. The man was Mr. Mool's head clerk, charged with news for Doctor Benjulia.

CHAPTER XLIII.

The mind of the clerk's master had been troubled by serious doubts, after Carmina left his house on Sunday.

Her agitated manner, her strange questions, and her abrupt departure, all suggested to Mr. Mool's mind some rash project in contemplation—perhaps even the plan of an elopement. To most other men, the obvious

---

1   *she placed her letter in the post-basket.* The post-basket was a household receptacle into which letters were dropped for delivery to the post-office, usually by a domestic servant. The stealing of a letter from a post-basket (or post-bag) was not a new plot device for Collins. In *The Woman in White*, Marian Halcombe deposits a letter into the post-bag at Blackwater Park only to have it removed and confiscated by Count Fosco.

course to take would have been to communicate with Mrs. Gallilee. But the lawyer preserved a vivid remembrance of the interview which had taken place at his office. The detestable pleasure which Mrs. Gallilee had betrayed in profaning the memory of Carmina's mother, had so shocked and disgusted him, that he recoiled from the idea of holding any further intercourse with her, no matter how pressing the emergency might be. It was possible, after what had passed, that Carmina might feel the propriety of making some explanation by letter. He decided to wait until the next morning, on the chance of hearing from her.

On the Monday, no letter arrived.

Proceeding to the office, Mr. Mool found, in his business-correspondence, enough to occupy every moment of his time. He had purposed writing to Carmina, but the idea was now inevitably pressed out of his mind. It was only at the close of the day's work that he had leisure to think of a matter of greater importance—that is to say, of the necessity of discovering Benjulia's friend of other days, the Italian teacher Baccani. He left instructions with one of his clerks to make inquiries, the next morning, at the shops of foreign booksellers. There, and there only, the question might be answered, whether Baccani was still living, and living in London.

The inquiries proved successful. On Tuesday afternoon, Baccani's address was in Mr. Mool's hands.

Busy as he still was, the lawyer set aside his own affairs, in deference to the sacred duty of defending the memory of the dead, and to the pressing necessity of silencing Mrs. Gallilee's cruel and slanderous tongue. Arrived at Baccani's lodgings, he was informed that the language-master had gone to his dinner at a neighbouring restaurant. Mr. Mool waited at the lodgings, and sent a note to Baccani. In ten minutes more he found himself in the presence of an elderly man, of ascetic appearance; whose looks and tones showed him to be apt to take offence on small provocation, and more than half ready to suspect an eminent solicitor of being a spy.

But Mr. Mool's experience was equal to the call on it. Having fully explained the object that he had in view, he left the apology for his intrusion to be inferred, and concluded by appealing, in his own modest way, to the sympathy of an honourable man.

Silently forming his opinion of the lawyer, while he listened, Baccani expressed the conclusion at which he had arrived, in these terms:

"My experience of mankind, sir, has been a bitterly bad one. You have improved my opinion of human nature since you entered this room. That is not a little thing to say, at my age and in my circumstances."

He bowed gravely, and turned to his bed. From under it, he pulled out a clumsy tin box. Having opened the rusty lock with some difficulty, he produced a ragged pocket-book, and picked out from it a paper which looked like an old letter.

"There," he said, handing the paper to Mr. Mool, "is the statement which vindicates this lady's reputation. Before you open the manuscript I must tell you how I came by it."

He appeared to feel such embarrassment in approaching the subject, that Mr. Mool interposed.

"I am already acquainted," he said, "with some of the circumstances to which you are about to allude. I happen to know of the wager in which the calumny originated, and of the manner in which that wager was decided. The events which followed are the only events that I need trouble you to describe."

Baccani's grateful sense of relief avowed itself without reserve. "I feel your kindness," he said, "almost as keenly as I feel my own disgraceful conduct, in permitting a woman's reputation to be made the subject of a wager. From whom did you obtain your information?"

"From the person who mentioned your name to me—Doctor Benjulia."

Baccani lifted his hand with a gesture of angry protest.

"Don't speak of him again in my presence!" he burst out. "That man has insulted me. When I took refuge from political persecution in this country, I sent him my prospectus. From my own humble position as a teacher of languages, I looked up without envy to his celebrity among doctors; I thought I might remind him, not unfavourably, of our early friendship—I, who had done him a hundred kindnesses in those past days. He has never taken the slightest notice of me; he has not even acknowledged the receipt of my prospectus. Despicable wretch! Let me hear no more of him."

"Pray forgive me if I refer to him again—for the last time," Mr. Mool pleaded. "Did your acquaintance with him continue, after the question of the wager had been settled?"

"No, sir!" Baccani answered sternly. "When I was at leisure to go to the club at which we were accustomed to meet, he had left Rome. From that time to this—I rejoice to say it—I have never set eyes on him."

The obstacles which had prevented the refutation of the calumny from reaching Benjulia were now revealed. Mr. Mool had only to hear, next, how that refutation had been obtained. A polite hint sufficed to remind Baccani of the explanation that he had promised.

"I am naturally suspicious," he began abruptly; "and I doubted the woman when I found that she kept her veil down. Besides, it was not in my way of thinking to believe that an estimable married lady could have compromised herself with a scoundrel, who had boasted that she was his mistress. I waited in the street, until the woman came out. I followed her, and saw her meet a man. The two went together to a theatre. I took my place near them. She lifted her veil as a matter of course. My suspicion of foul play was instantly confirmed. When the performance was over, I traced her back to Mr. Robert Graywell's house. He and his wife were both absent at a party. I was too indignant to wait till they came back.

Under the threat of charging the wretch with stealing her mistress's clothes, I extorted from her the signed confession which you have in your hand. She was under notice to leave her place for insolent behaviour. The personation which had been intended to deceive me, was an act of revenge; planned between herself and the blackguard who had employed her to make his lie look like truth. A more shameless creature I never met with. She said to me, 'I am as tall as my mistress, and a better figure; and I've often worn her fine clothes on holiday occasions.' In your country Mr. Mool, such women—so I am told—are ducked in a pond.[1] There is one thing more to add, before you read the confession. Mrs. Robert Graywell did imprudently send the man some money—in answer to a begging letter artfully enough written to excite her pity. A second application was refused by her husband. What followed on that, you know already."

Having read the confession, Mr. Mool was permitted to take a copy, and to make any use of it which he might think desirable. His one remaining anxiety was to hear what had become of the person who had planned the deception. "Surely," he said, "that villain has not escaped punishment?"

Baccani answered this in his own bitter way.

"My dear sir, how can you ask such a simple question? That sort of man always escapes punishment. In the last extreme of poverty his luck provides him with somebody to cheat. Common respect for Mrs. Robert Graywell closed my lips; and I was the only person acquainted with the circumstances. I wrote to our club declaring the fellow to be a cheat—and leaving it to be inferred that he cheated at cards. He knew better than to insist on my explaining myself—he resigned, and disappeared. I dare say he is living still—living in clover on some unfortunate woman. The beautiful and the good die untimely deaths. *He*, and his kind, last and live."

Mr. Mool had neither time nor inclination to plead in favour of the more hopeful view, which believes in the agreeable fiction called "poetical justice." He tried to express his sense of obligation at parting. Baccani refused to listen.

"The obligation is all on my side," he said. "As I have already told you, your visit has added a bright day to my calendar. In our pilgrimage, my friend, through this world of rogues and fools, we may never meet again. Let us remember gratefully that we *have* met. Farewell."

So they parted.

Returning to his office, Mr. Mool attached to the copy of the confession a brief statement of the circumstances under which the Italian had become possessed of it. He then added these lines, addressed to

---

1   *such women ... are ducked in a pond*: Baccani refers to the long-abandoned practice of tying prostitutes and other people of questionable morals to a ducking, or cucking stool, and subjecting them to public ridicule by ducking them in a pond or stream.

Benjulia:—"*You* set the false report afloat. I leave it to your sense of duty, to decide whether you ought not to go at once to Mrs. Gallilee, and tell her that the slander which you repeated is now proved to be a lie. If you don't agree with me, I must go to Mrs. Gallilee myself. In that case please return, by the bearer, the papers which are enclosed."

The clerk instructed to deliver these documents, within the shortest possible space of time, found Mr. Mool waiting at the office, on his return. He answered his master's inquiries by producing Benjulia's reply.

The doctor's amiable humour was still in the ascendant. His success in torturing his unfortunate cook had been followed by the receipt of a telegram from his friend at Montreal, containing this satisfactory answer to his question:—"Not brain disease." With his mind now set completely at rest, his instincts as a gentleman were at full liberty to control him. "I entirely agree with you," he wrote to Mr. Mool. "I go back with your clerk; the cab will drop me at Mrs. Gallilee's house."

Mr. Mool turned to the clerk.

"Did you wait to hear if Mrs. Gallilee was at home?" he asked.

"Mrs. Gallilee was absent, sir—attending a lecture."

"What did Doctor Benjulia do?"

"Went into the house, to wait her return."

CHAPTER XLIV.

Mrs. Gallilee's page (attending to the house-door, in the footman's absence) had just shown Benjulia into the library, when there was another ring at the bell. The new visitor was Mr. Le Frank. He appeared to be in a hurry. Without any preliminary questions, he said, "Take my card to Mrs. Gallilee."

"My mistress is out, sir."

The music-master looked impatiently at the hall-clock. The hall-clock answered him by striking the half hour after five.

"Do you expect Mrs. Gallilee back soon?"

"We don't know, sir. The footman had his orders to be in waiting with the carriage, at five."

After a moment of irritable reflection, Mr. Le Frank took a letter from his pocket. "Say that I have an appointment, and am not able to wait. Give Mrs. Gallilee that letter the moment she comes in." With those directions he left the house.

The page looked at the letter. It was sealed; and, over the address, two underlined words were written:—"Private. Immediate." Mindful of visits from tradespeople, anxious to see his mistress, and provided beforehand with letters to be delivered immediately, the boy took a pecuniary view of Mr. Le Frank's errand at the house. "Another of them," he thought, "wanting his money."

As he placed the letter on the hall-table, the library door opened, and

Benjulia appeared—weary already of waiting, without occupation, for Mrs. Gallilee's return.

"Is smoking allowed in the library?" he asked.

The page looked up at the giant towering over him, with the envious admiration of a short boy. He replied with a discretion beyond his years: "Would you please step into the smoking-room, sir?"

"Anybody there?"

"My master, sir."

Benjulia at once declined the invitation to the smoking-room. "Anybody else at home?" he inquired.

Miss Carmina was upstairs—the page answered. "And I think," he added, "Mr. Null is with her."

"Who's Mr. Null?"

"The doctor, sir."

Benjulia declined to disturb the doctor. He tried a third, and last question.

"Where's Zo?"

"Here!" cried a shrill voice from the upper regions. "Who are You?"

To the page's astonishment, the giant gentleman with the resonant bass voice answered this quite gravely. "I'm Benjulia," he said.

"Come up!" cried Zo.

Benjulia ascended the stairs.

"Stop!" shouted the voice from above.

Benjulia stopped.

"Have you got your big stick?"

"Yes."

"Bring it up with you." Benjulia retraced his steps into the hall. The page respectfully handed him his stick. Zo became impatient. "Look sharp!" she called out.

Benjulia obediently quickened his pace. Zo left the schoolroom (in spite of the faintly-heard protest of the maid in charge) to receive him on the stairs. They met on the landing, outside Carmina's room. Zo possessed herself of the bamboo cane, and led the way in. "Carmina! here's the big stick, I told you about," she announced.

"Whose stick, dear?"

Zo returned to the landing. "Come in, Benjulia," she said—and seized him by the coat-tails. Mr. Null rose instinctively. Was this his celebrated colleague?

With some reluctance, Carmina appeared at the door; thinking of the day when Ovid had fainted, and when the great man had treated her so harshly. In fear of more rudeness, she unwillingly asked him to come in.

Still immovable on the landing, he looked at her in silence.

The serious question occurred to him which had formerly presented itself to Mr. Mool. Had Mrs. Gallilee repeated, in Carmina's presence, the lie which slandered her mother's memory—the lie which he was then in the house to expose?

Watching Benjulia respectfully, Mr. Null saw, in that grave scrutiny, an opportunity of presenting himself under a favourable light. He waved his hand persuasively towards Carmina. "Some nervous prostration, sir, in my interesting patient, as you no doubt perceive," he began. "Not such rapid progress towards recovery as I had hoped. I think of recommending the air of the seaside." Benjulia's dreary eyes turned on him slowly, and estimated his mental calibre at its exact value, in a moment. Mr. Null felt that look in the very marrow of his bones. He bowed with servile submission, and took his leave.

In the meantime, Benjulia had satisfied himself that the embarrassment in Carmina's manner was merely attributable to shyness. She was now no longer an object even of momentary interest to him. He was ready to play with Zo—but not on condition of amusing himself with the child, in Carmina's presence. "I am waiting till Mrs. Gallilee returns," he said to her in his quietly indifferent way. "If you will excuse me, I'll go downstairs again; I won't intrude."

Her pale face flushed as she listened to him. Innocently supposing that she had made her little offer of hospitality in too cold a manner, she looked at Benjulia with a timid and troubled smile. "Pray wait here till my aunt comes back," she said. "Zo will amuse you, I'm sure." Zo seconded the invitation by hiding the stick, and laying hold again on her big friend's coat-tails.

He let the child drag him into the room, without noticing her. The silent questioning of his eyes had been again directed to Carmina, at the moment when she smiled.

His long and terrible experience made its own merciless discoveries, in the nervous movement of her eyelids and her lips. The poor girl, pleasing herself with the idea of having produced the right impression on him at last, had only succeeded in becoming an object of medical inquiry, pursued in secret. When he companionably took a chair by her side, and let Zo climb on his knee, he was privately regretting his cold reception of Mr. Null. Under certain conditions of nervous excitement, Carmina might furnish an interesting case. "If I had been commonly civil to that fawning idiot," he thought, "I might have been called into consultation."

They were all three seated—but there was no talk. Zo set the example.

"You haven't tickled me yet," she said. "Show Carmina how you do it."

He gravely operated on the back of Zo's neck; and his patient acknowledged the process with a wriggle and a scream. The performance being so far at an end, Zo called to the dog, and issued her orders once more.

"Now make Tinker kick his leg!"

Benjulia obeyed once again. The young tyrant was not satisfied yet.

"Now tickle Carmina!" she said.

He heard this without laughing: his fleshless lips never relaxed into a smile. To Carmina's unutterable embarrassment, he looked at her, when *she* laughed, with steadier attention than ever. Those coldly-inquiring eyes exercised some inscrutable influence over her. Now they made her angry; and now they frightened her. The silence that had fallen on them again, became an unendurable infliction. She burst into talk; she was loud and familiar—ashamed of her own boldness, and quite unable to control it. "You are very fond of Zo!" she said suddenly.

It was a perfectly commonplace remark—and yet, it seemed to perplex him.

"Am I?" he answered.

She went on. Against her own will, she persisted in speaking to him. "And I'm sure Zo is fond of you."

He looked at Zo. "Are you fond of me?" he asked.

Zo, staring hard at him, got off his knee; retired to a little distance to think; and stood staring at him again.

He quietly repeated the question. Zo answered this time—as she had formerly answered Teresa in the Gardens. "I don't know."

He turned again to Carmina, in a slow, puzzled way. "I don't know either," he said.

Hearing the big man own that he was no wiser than herself, Zo returned to him—without, however, getting on his knee again. She clasped her chubby hands under the inspiration of a new idea. "Let's play at something," she said to Benjulia. "Do you know any games?"

He shook his head.

"Didn't you know any games, when you were only as big as me?"

"I have forgotten them."

"Haven't you got children?"

"No."

"Haven't you got a wife?"

"No."

"Haven't you got a friend?"

"No."

"Well, you *are* a miserable chap!"

Thanks to Zo, Carmina's sense of nervous oppression burst its way into relief. She laughed loudly and wildly—she was on the verge of hysterics, when Benjulia's eyes, silently questioning her again, controlled her at the critical moment. Her laughter died away. But the exciting influence still possessed her; still forced her into the other alternative of saying something—she neither knew nor cared what.

"I couldn't live such a lonely life as yours," she said to him—so loudly and so confidently that even Zo noticed it.

"I couldn't live such a life either," he admitted, "but for one thing."

"And what is that?"

"Why are you so loud?" Zo interposed. "Do you think he's deaf?"

Benjulia made a sign, commanding the child to be silent—without turning towards her. He answered Carmina as if there had been no interruption.

"My medical studies," he said, "reconcile me to my life."

"Suppose you got tired of your studies?" she asked.

"I should never get tired of them."

"Suppose you couldn't study any more?"

"In that case I shouldn't live any more."

"Do you mean that it would kill you to leave off?"

"No."

"Then what do you mean?"

He laid his great soft fingers on her pulse. She shrank from his touch; he deliberately held her by the arm. "You're getting excited," he said. "Never mind what I mean."

Zo, left unnoticed and not liking it, saw a chance of asserting herself. "I know why Carmina's excited," she said. "The old woman's coming at six o'clock."

He paid no attention to the child; he persisted in keeping watch on Carmina. "Who is the woman?" he asked.

"The most lovable woman in the world," she cried; "my dear old nurse!" She started up from the sofa, and pointed with theatrical exaggeration of gesture to the clock on the mantelpiece. "Look! it's only ten minutes to six. In ten minutes, I shall have my arms round Teresa's neck. Don't look at me in that way! It's your fault if I'm excited. It's your dreadful eyes that do it. Come here, Zo! I want to give you a kiss." She seized on Zo with a roughness that startled the child, and looked wildly at Benjulia. "Ha! you don't understand loving and kissing, do you? What's the use of speaking to *you* about my old nurse?"

He pointed imperatively to the sofa. "Sit down again."

She obeyed him—but he had not quite composed her yet. Her eyes sparkled; she went on talking. "Ah, you're a hard man! a miserable man! a man that will end badly! You never loved anybody. You don't know what love is."

"What is it?"

That icy question cooled her in an instant: her head sank on her bosom: she suddenly became indifferent to persons and things about her. "When will Teresa come?" she whispered to herself. "Oh, when will Teresa come!"

Any other man, whether he really felt for her or not, would, as a mere matter of instinct, have said a kind word to her at that moment. Not the vestige of a change appeared in Benjulia's impenetrable composure. She might have been a man—or a baby—or the picture of a girl instead of the girl herself, so far as he was concerned. He quietly returned to his question.

"Well," he resumed—"and what is love?"

Not a word, not a movement escaped her.

"I want to know," he persisted, waiting for what might happen.

Nothing happened. He was not perplexed by the sudden change. "This is the reaction," he thought. "We shall see what comes of it." He looked about him. A bottle of water stood on one of the tables. "Likely to be useful," he concluded, "in case she feels faint."

Zo had been listening; Zo saw her way to getting noticed again. Not quite sure of herself this time, she appealed to Carmina. "Didn't he say, just now, he wanted to know?"

Carmina neither heard nor heeded her. Zo tried Benjulia next. "Shall I tell you what we do in the schoolroom, when we want to know? His attention, like Carmina's attention, seemed to be far away from her. Zo impatiently reminded him of her presence—she laid her hand on his knee.

It was only the hand of a child—an idle, quaint, perverse child—but it touched, ignorantly touched, the one tender place in his nature, unprofaned by the infernal cruelties which made his life acceptable to him; the one tender place, hidden so deep from the man himself, that even his far-reaching intellect groped in vain to find it out. There, nevertheless, was the feeling which drew him to Zo, contending successfully with his medical interest in a case of nervous derangement. That unintelligible sympathy with a child looked dimly out of his eyes, spoke faintly in his voice, when he replied to her. "Well," he said, "what do you do in the schoolroom?"

"We look in the dictionary," Zo answered. "Carmina's got a dictionary. I'll get it."

She climbed on a chair, and found the book, and laid it on Benjulia's lap. "I don't so much mind trying to spell a word," she explained. "What I hate is being asked what it means. Miss Minerva won't let me off. She says, Look. *I* won't let *you* off. I'm Miss Minerva and you're Zo. Look!"

He humoured her silently and mechanically—just as he had humoured her in the matter of the stick, and in the matter of the tickling. Having opened the dictionary, he looked again at Carmina. She had not moved; she seemed to be weary enough to fall asleep. The reaction—nothing but the reaction. It might last for hours, or it might be at an end in another minute. An interesting temperament, whichever way it ended. He opened the dictionary.

"Love?" he muttered grimly to himself. "It seems I'm an object of compassion, because I know nothing about love. Well, what does the book say about it?"

He found the word, and ran his finger down the paragraphs of explanation which followed. "Seven meanings to Love," he remarked.[1] "First:

---

1   "*Seven meanings to Love,*" *he remarked*: Benjulia's dictionary remains unidentified, but the appropriateness of the cold-blooded doctor looking for love in a series of dry definitions should not be overlooked.

An affection of the mind excited by beauty and worth of any kind, or by the qualities of an object which communicate pleasure. Second: Courtship. Third: Patriotism, as the love of country. Fourth: Benevolence. Fifth: The object beloved. Sixth: A word of endearment. Seventh: Cupid, the god of love."

He paused, and reflected a little. Zo, hearing nothing to amuse her, strayed away to the window, and looked out. He glanced at Carmina.

"Which of those meanings makes the pleasure of her life?" he wondered. "Which of them might have made the pleasure of mine?" He closed the dictionary in contempt. "The very man whose business is to explain it, tries seven different ways, and doesn't explain it after all. And yet, there is such a thing." He reached that conclusion unwillingly and angrily. For the first time, a doubt about himself forced its way into his mind. Might he have looked higher than his torture-table and his knife? Had he gained from his life all that his life might have given to him?

Left by herself, Zo began to grow tired of it. She tried to get Carmina for a companion. "Come and look out of window," she said.

Carmina gently refused: she was unwilling to be disturbed. Since she had spoken to Benjulia, her thoughts had been dwelling restfully on Ovid. In another day she might be on her way to him. When would Teresa come?

Benjulia was too preoccupied to notice her. The weak doubt that had got the better of his strong reason, still held him in thrall. "Love!" he broke out, in the bitterness of his heart. "It isn't a question of sentiment: it's a question of use. Who is the better for love?"

She heard the last words, and answered him. "Everybody is the better for it." She looked at him with sorrowful eyes, and laid her hand on his arm. "Everybody," she added, "but you."

He smiled scornfully. "Everybody is the better for it," he repeated. "And who knows what it is?"

She drew away her hand, and looked towards the heavenly tranquillity of the evening sky.

"Who knows what it is?" he reiterated.

"God," she said.

Benjulia was silent.

End of March 1883 *Belgravia* Serial Number

CHAPTER XLV.

The clock on the mantelpiece struck six. Zo, turning suddenly from the window, ran to the sofa. "Here's the carriage!" she cried.

"Teresa!" Carmina exclaimed.

Zo crossed the room, on tiptoe, to the door of the bed-chamber. "It's mamma," she said. "Don't tell! I'm going to hide."

"Why, dear?"

The answer to this was given mysteriously in a whisper. "She said I wasn't to come to you. She's a quick one on her legs—she might catch me on the stairs." With that explanation, Zo slipped into the bedroom, and held the door ajar.

The minutes passed—and Mrs. Gallilee failed to justify the opinion expressed by her daughter. Not a sound was audible on the stairs. Not a word more was uttered in the room. Benjulia had taken the child's place at the window. He sat there thinking. Carmina had suggested to him some new ideas, relating to the intricate connection between human faith and human happiness. Slowly, slowly, the clock recorded the lapse of minutes. Carmina's nervous anxiety began to forecast disaster to the absent nurse. She took Teresa's telegram from her pocket, and consulted it again. There was no mistake; six o'clock was the time named for the traveller's arrival—and it was close on ten minutes past the hour. In her ignorance of railway arrangements, she took it for granted that trains were punctual. But her reading had told her that trains were subject to accident. "I suppose delays occur," she said to Benjulia, "without danger to the passengers?"

Before he could answer—Mrs. Gallilee suddenly entered the room.

She had opened the door so softly, that she took them both by surprise. To Carmina's excited imagination, she glided into their presence like a ghost. Her look and manner showed serious agitation, desperately suppressed. In certain places, the paint and powder on her face had cracked, and revealed the furrows and wrinkles beneath. Her hard eyes glittered; her laboured breathing was audible.

Indifferent to all demonstrations of emotion which did not scientifically concern him, Benjulia quietly rose and advanced towards her. She seemed to be unconscious of his presence. He spoke—allowing her to ignore him without troubling himself to notice her temper. "When you are able to attend to me, I want to speak to you. Shall I wait downstairs?" He took his hat and stick—to leave the room; looked at Carmina as he passed her; and at once went back to his place at the window. Her aunt's silent and sinister entrance had frightened her. Benjulia waited, in the interests of physiology, to see how the new nervous excitement would end.

Thus far, Mrs. Gallilee had kept one of her hands hidden behind her. She advanced close to Carmina, and allowed her hand to be seen. It held an open letter. She shook the letter in her niece's face.

In the position which Mrs. Gallilee now occupied, Carmina was hidden, for the moment, from Benjulia's view. Biding his time at the window, he looked out.

A cab, with luggage on it, had just drawn up at the house.

Was this the old nurse who had been expected to arrive at six o'clock?

The footman came out to open the cab-door. He was followed by Mr. Gallilee, eager to help the person inside to alight. The traveller proved to be a grey-headed woman, shabbily dressed. Mr. Gallilee cordially shook hands with her—patted her on the shoulder—gave her his arm—led her into the house. The cab with the luggage on it remained at the door. The nurse had evidently not reached the end of her journey yet.

Carmina shrank back on the sofa, when the leaves of the letter touched her face. Mrs. Gallilee's first words were now spoken, in a whisper. The inner fury of her anger, struggling for a vent, began to get the better of her—she gasped for breath and speech.

"Do you know this letter?" she said.

Carmina looked at the writing. It was the letter to Ovid, which she had placed in the post-basket that afternoon; the letter which declared that she could no longer endure his mother's cold-blooded cruelty, and that she only waited Teresa's arrival to join him at Quebec.

After one dreadful moment of confusion, her mind realised the outrage implied in the stealing and reading of her letter.

In the earlier time of Carmina's sojourn in the house, Mrs. Gallilee had accused her of deliberate deceit. She had instantly resented the insult by leaving the room. The same spirit in her—the finely-strung spirit that vibrates unfelt in gentle natures, while they live in peace—steadied those quivering nerves, roused that failing courage. She met the furious eyes fixed on her, without shrinking; she spoke gravely and firmly. "The letter is mine," she said. "How did you come by it?"

"How dare you ask me?"

"How dare *you* steal my letter?"

Mrs. Gallilee tore open the fastening of her dress at the throat, to get breath. "You impudent bastard!" she burst out, in a frenzy of rage.

Waiting patiently at the window, Benjulia heard her. "Hold your damned tongue!" he cried. "She's your niece."

Mrs. Gallilee turned on him: her fury broke into a screaming laugh. "My niece?" she repeated. "You lie—and you know it! She's the child of an adulteress! She's the child of her mother's lover!"

The door opened as those horrible words passed her lips. The nurse and her husband entered the room.

She was in no position to see them: she was incapable of hearing them. The demon in her urged her on: she attempted to reiterate the detestable falsehood. Her first word died away in silence. The lean brown fingers of the Italian woman had her by the throat—held her as the claws of a tigress might have held her. Her eyes rolled in the mute agony of an appeal for help. In vain! in vain! Not a cry, not a sound, had drawn attention to the attack. Her husband's eyes were fixed, horror-struck, on the victim of her rage. Benjulia had crossed the room to the sofa, when Carmina heard the words spoken of her mother. From that moment, he was watching the case. Mr. Gallilee alone looked round—when the nurse tightened her hold in a last merciless grasp; dashed the insensible woman on the floor; and, turning back, fell on her knees at her darling's feet.

She looked up in Carmina's face.

A ghastly stare, through half-closed eyes, showed death in life, blankly returning her look. The shock had struck Carmina with a stony calm. She had not started, she had not swooned. Rigid, immovable, there she sat; voiceless and tearless; insensible even to touch; her arms hanging down; her clenched hands resting on either side of her.

Teresa grovelled and groaned at her feet. Those ferocious hands that had laid the slanderer prostrate on the floor, feebly beat her bosom and her gray head. "Oh, Saints beloved of God! Oh, blessed Virgin, mother of Christ, spare my child, my sweet child!" She rose in wild despair—she seized Benjulia, and madly shook him. "Who are you? How dare you touch her? Give her to me, or I'll be the death of you. Oh, my Carmina, is it sleep that holds you? Wake! wake! wake!"

"Listen to me," said Benjulia, sternly.

She dropped on the sofa by Carmina's side, and lifted one of the cold clenched hands to her lips. The tears fell slowly over her haggard face. "I am very fond of her, sir," she said humbly. "I'm only an old woman. See what a dreadful welcome my child gives to me. It's hard on an old woman—hard on an old woman!"

His self-possession was not disturbed—even by this.

"Do you know what I am?" he asked. "I am a doctor. Leave her to me."

"He's a doctor. That's good. A doctor's good. Yes, yes. Does the old man know this doctor—the kind old man?" She looked vacantly for Mr. Gallilee. He was bending over his wife, sprinkling water on her deathly face.

Teresa got on her feet, and pointed to Mrs. Gallilee. "The breath of that She-Devil poisons the air," she said. "I must take my child out of it. To my place, sir, if you please. Only to my place."

She attempted to lift Carmina from the sofa—and drew back, breathlessly watching her. Her rigid face faintly relaxed; her eyelids closed, and quivered.

Mr. Gallilee looked up from his wife. "Will one of you help me?" he asked. His tone struck Benjulia. It was the hushed tone of sorrow—no more.

"I'll see to it directly." With that reply, Benjulia turned to Teresa. "Where is your place?" he said. "Far or near?"

"The message," she answered confusedly. "The message says." She signed to him to look in her hand-bag—dropped on the floor.

He found Carmina's telegram, containing the address of the lodgings. The house was close by. After some consideration, he sent the nurse into the bedroom, with instructions to bring him the blankets off the bed. In the minute that followed, he examined Mrs. Gallilee. "There's nothing to be frightened about. Let her maid attend to her."

Mr. Gallilee again surprised Benjulia. He turned from his wife, and looked at Carmina. "For God's sake, don't leave her here!" he broke out.

"After what she has heard, this house is no place for her. Give her to the old nurse!"

Benjulia only answered, as he had answered already—"I'll see to it." Mr. Gallilee persisted. "Is there any risk in moving her?" he asked.

"It's the least of two risks. No more questions! Look to your wife."

Mr. Gallilee obeyed in silence.

When he lifted his head again, and rose to ring the bell for the maid, the room was silent and lonely. A little pale frightened face peeped out through the bedroom door. Zo ventured in. Her father caught her in his arms, and kissed her as he had never kissed her yet. His eyes were wet with tears. Zo noticed that he never said a word about mamma. The child saw the change in her father, as Benjulia had seen it. She shared one human feeling with her big friend—she, too, was surprised.

CHAPTER XLVI.

The first signs of reviving life had begun to appear, when Marceline answered the bell. In a few minutes more, it was possible to raise Mrs. Gallilee, and to place her on the sofa. Having so far assisted the servant, Mr. Gallilee took Zo by the hand, and drew back. Daunted by the terrible scene which she had witnessed from her hiding-place, the child stood by her father's side in silence. The two waited together, watching Mrs. Gallilee.

She looked wildly round the room. Discovering that she was alone with the members of her family, she became composed: her mind slowly recovered its balance. Her first thought was for herself.

"Has that woman disfigured me?" she said to the maid.

Knowing nothing of what had happened, Marceline was at a loss to understand her. "Bring me a glass," she said. The maid found a hand-glass in the bedroom, and presented it to her. She looked at herself—and drew a long breath of relief. That first anxiety at an end, she spoke to her husband.

"Where is Carmina?"

"Out of the house—thank God!"

The answer seemed to bewilder her: she appealed to Marceline.

"Did he say, thank God?"

"Yes, ma'am."

"Can *you* tell me nothing? Who knows where Carmina has gone?"

"Joseph knows, ma'am. He heard Dr. Benjulia give the address to the cabman." With that answer, she turned anxiously to her master. "Is Miss Carmina seriously ill, sir?"

Her mistress spoke again, before Mr. Gallilee could reply. "Marceline! send Joseph up here."

"No," said Mr. Gallilee.

His wife eyed him with astonishment. "Why not?" she asked.

He said quietly, "I forbid it."

Mrs. Gallilee addressed herself to the maid. "Go to my room, and bring me another bonnet and a veil. Stop!" She tried to rise, and sank back. "I must have something to strengthen me. Get the sal volatile."[1]

Marceline left the room. Mr. Gallilee followed her as far as the door—still leading his little daughter.

"Go back, my dear, to your sister in the schoolroom," he said. "I am distressed, Zo; be a good girl, and you will console me. Say the same to Maria. It will be dull for you, I am afraid. Be patient, my child, and try to bear it for a while."

"May I whisper something?" said Zo. "Will Carmina die?"

"God forbid!"

"Will they bring her back here?"

In her eagerness, the child spoke above a whisper. Mrs. Gallilee heard the question, and answered it.

"They will bring Carmina back," she said, "the moment I can get out."

Zo looked at her father. "Do *you* say that?" she asked.

He shook his head gravely, and told her again to go to the schoolroom. On the first landing she stopped, and looked back. "I'll be good, papa," she said—and went on up the stairs.

Having reached the schoolroom, she became the object of many questions—not one of which she answered. Followed by the dog, she sat down in a corner. "What are you thinking about?" her sister inquired. This time she was willing to reply. "I'm thinking about Carmina."

Mr. Gallilee closed the door when Zo left him. He took a chair, without speaking to his wife or looking at her.

"What are you here for?" she asked.

"I must wait," he said.

"What for?"

"To see what you do."

Marceline returned, and administered a dose of sal volatile. Strengthened by the stimulant, Mrs. Gallilee was able to rise. "My head is giddy," she said, as she took the maid's arm; "but I think I can get downstairs with your help."

Mr. Gallilee silently followed them out.

At the head of the stairs the giddiness increased. Firm as her resolution might be, it gave way before the bodily injury which Mrs. Gallilee had received. Her husband's help was again needed to take her to her bedroom. She stopped them at the ante-chamber; still obstinately bent on following her own designs. "I shall be better directly," she said; "put me on the sofa." Marceline relieved her of her bonnet and veil, and asked

---

1   *Get the sal volatile*: Sal volatile are smelling salts.

respectfully if there was any other service required. She looked defiantly at her husband, and reiterated the order—"Send for Joseph." Intelligent resolution is sometimes shaken; the inert obstinacy of a weak creature, man or animal, is immovable. Mr. Gallilee dismissed the maid with these words: "You needn't wait, my good girl—I'll speak to Joseph myself, downstairs."

His wife heard him with amazement and contempt. "Are you in your right senses?" she asked.

He paused on his way out. "You were always hard and headstrong," he said sadly; "I knew that. A cleverer man than I am might—I suppose it's possible—a clear-headed man might have found out how wicked you are." She lay, thinking; indifferent to anything he could say to her. "Are you not ashamed?" he asked wonderingly. "And not even sorry?" She paid no heed to him. He left her.

Descending to the hall, he was met by Joseph. "Doctor Benjulia has come back, sir. He wishes to see you."

"Where is he?"

"In the library."

"Wait, Joseph; I have something to say to you. If your mistress asks where they have taken Miss Carmina, you mustn't—this is my order, Joseph—you mustn't tell her. If you have mentioned it to any of the other servants—it's quite likely they may have asked you, isn't it?" he said, falling into his old habit for a moment. "If you have mentioned it to the others," he resumed, "*they* mustn't tell her. That's all, my good man; that's all."

To his own surprise, Joseph found himself regarding his master with a feeling of respect. Mr. Gallilee entered the library.

"How is she?" he asked, eager for news of Carmina.

"The worse for being moved," Benjulia replied. "What about your wife?"

Answering that question, Mr. Gallilee mentioned the precautions that he had taken to keep the secret of Teresa's address.

"You need be under no anxiety about that," said Benjulia. "I have left orders that Mrs. Gallilee is not to be admitted. There is a serious necessity for keeping her out. In these cases of partial catalepsy,[1] there is no saying when the change may come. When it does come, I won't answer for her niece's reason, if those two see each other again. Send for you own medical man. The girl is his patient, and he is the person on whom the responsibility rests. Let the servant take my card to him directly. We can meet in consultation at the house."

He wrote a line on one of his visiting cards. It was at once sent to Mr. Null.

---

1   *In these cases of partial catalepsy, there is no saying when the change may come:*
Catalepsy, Benjulia's diagnosis of Carmina, involves muscular rigidity, a lack of awareness of environment, and a lack of response to external stimuli.

"There's another matter to be settled before I go," Benjulia proceeded. "Here are some papers, which I have received from your lawyer, Mr. Mool. They relate to a slander, which your wife unfortunately repeated—"

Mr. Gallilee got up from his chair. "Don't take my mind back to that—pray don't!" he pleaded earnestly. "I can't bear it, Doctor Benjulia—I can't bear it! Please to excuse my rudeness: it isn't intentional—I don't know myself what's the matter with me. I've always led a quiet life, sir; I'm not fit for such things as these. Don't suppose I speak selfishly. I'll do what I can, if you will kindly spare me."

He might as well have appealed to the sympathy of the table at which they were sitting. Benjulia was absolutely incapable of understanding the state of mind which those words revealed.

"Can you take these papers to your wife?" he asked. "I called here this evening—being the person to blame—to set the matter right. As it is, I leave her to make the discovery for herself. I desire to hold no more communication with your wife. Have you anything to say to me before I go?"

"Only one thing. Is there any harm in my calling at the house, to ask how poor Carmina goes on?"

"Ask as often as you like—provided Mrs. Gallilee doesn't accompany you. If she's obstinate, it may not be amiss to give your wife a word of warning. In my opinion, the old nurse is not likely to let her off, next time, with her life. I've had a little talk with that curious foreign savage. I said, 'You have committed, what we consider in England, a murderous assault. If Mrs. Gallilee doesn't mind the public exposure, you may find yourself in a prison.' She snapped her fingers in my face. 'Suppose I find myself with the hangman's rope round my neck,' she said, 'what do I care, so long as Carmina is safe from her aunt?' After that pretty answer, she sat down by her girl's bedside, and burst out crying."

Mr. Gallilee listened absently: his mind still dwelt on Carmina.

"I meant well," he said, "when I asked you to take her out of this house. It's no wonder if *I* was wrong. What I am too stupid to understand is—why *you* allowed her to be moved."

Benjulia listened with a grim smile; Mr. Gallilee's presumption amused him.

"I wonder whether there was any room left for memory, when nature furnished your narrow little head," he answered pleasantly. "Didn't I say that moving her was the least of two risks? And haven't I just warned you of what might have happened, if we had left your wife and her niece together in the same house? When I do a thing at my time of life, Mr. Gallilee—don't think me conceited—I know why I do it."

While he was speaking of himself in these terms, he might have said something more. He might have added, that his dread of the loss of Carmina's reason really meant his dread of a commonplace termination to an exceptionally interesting case. He might also have acknowledged, that he was not yielding obedience to the rules of professional etiquette, in confiding the patient to her regular medical attendant, but following the selfish suggestions of his own critical judgment.

His experience, brief as it had been, had satisfied him that stupid Mr. Null's course of action could be trusted to let the instructive progress of the malady proceed. Mr. Null would treat the symptoms in perfect good faith—without a suspicion of the nervous hysteria which, in such a constitution as Carmina's, threatened to establish itself, in course of time, as the hidden cause. These motives—not only excused, but even ennobled, by their scientific connection with the interests of Medical Research—he might have avowed, under more favourable circumstances. While his grand discovery was still barely within reach, Doctor Benjulia stood committed to a system of diplomatic reserve, which even included simple Mr. Gallilee.

He took his hat and stick, and walked out into the hall. "Can I be of further use?" he asked carelessly. "You will hear about the patient from Mr. Null."

"You won't desert Carmina?" said Mr. Gallilee. "You will see her yourself, from time to time—won't you?"

"Don't be afraid; I'll look after her." He spoke sincerely in saying this. Carmina's case had already suggested new ideas. Even the civilised savage of modern physiology (where his own interests are concerned) is not absolutely insensible to a feeling of gratitude.

Mr. Gallilee opened the door for him.

"By the-bye," he added, as he stepped out, "what's become of Zo?"

"She's upstairs, in the schoolroom."

He made one of his dreary jokes. "Tell her, when she wants to be tickled again, to let me know. Good-evening!"

Mr. Gallilee returned to the upper part of the house, with the papers left by Benjulia in his hand. Arriving at the dressing-room door, he hesitated. The papers were enclosed in a sealed envelope, addressed to his wife. Secured in this way from inquisitive eyes, there was no necessity for personally presenting them. He went on to the schoolroom, and beckoned to the parlour-maid to come out, and speak to him.

Having instructed her to deliver the papers—telling her mistress that they had been left at the house by Doctor Benjulia—he dismissed the woman from duty. "You needn't return," he said; "I'll look after the children myself."

Maria was busy with her book; and even idle Zo was employed!

She was writing at her own inky desk; and she looked up in confusion, when her father appeared. Unsuspicious Mr. Gallilee took if for granted that his favourite daughter was employed on a writing lesson—following Maria's industrious example for once. "Good children!" he said, looking affectionately from one to the other. "I won't disturb you; go on." He took a chair, satisfied—comforted, even—to be in the same room with the girls.

If he had placed himself nearer to the desk, he might have seen that Zo had been thinking of Carmina to some purpose.

What could she do to make her friend and playfellow well and happy again? There was the question which Zo asked herself, after having seen Carmina carried insensible out of the room.

Possessed of that wonderful capacity for minute observation of the elder persons about them, which is one among the many baffling mysteries presented by the minds of children, Zo had long since discovered that the member of the household, preferred to all others by Carmina, was the good brother who had gone away and left them. In his absence, she was always talking of him—and Zo had seen her kiss his photograph before she put it back in the case.

Dwelling on these recollections, the child's slowly-working mental process arrived more easily than usual at the right conclusion. The way to make Carmina well and happy again, was to bring Ovid back. One of the two envelopes which he had directed for her still remained—waiting for the letter which might say to him, "Come home!"

Zo determined to write that letter—and to do it at once.

She might have confided this design to her father (the one person besides Carmina who neither scolded her nor laughed at her) if Mr. Gallilee had distinguished himself by his masterful position in the house. But she had seen him, as everybody else had seen him, "afraid of mamma." The doubt whether he might not "tell mamma," decided her on keeping her secret. As the event proved, the one person who informed Ovid of the terrible necessity that existed for his return, was the little sister whom it had been his last kind effort to console when he left England.

When Mr. Gallilee entered the room, Zo had just reached the end of her letter. Her system of composition excluded capitals and stops; and reduced all the words in the English language, by a simple process of abridgment, to words of one syllable.

"dear ov you come back car is ill she wants you be quick be quick don't say I writ this miss min is gone I hate books I like you zo."

With the pen still in her hand, the wary writer looked round at her father. She had her directed envelope (sadly crumpled) in her pocket; but she was afraid to take it out. "Maria," she thought, "would know what to do in my place. Horrid Maria!"

Fortune, using the affairs of the household as an instrument, befriended Zo. In a minute more her opportunity arrived. The parlour-maid unexpectedly returned. She addressed Mr. Gallilee with the air of mystery in which English servants, in possession of a message, especially delight. "If you please, sir, Joseph wishes to speak to you."

"Where is he?"

"Outside, sir."

"Tell him to come in."

Thanks to the etiquette of the servants' hall—which did not permit Joseph to present himself, voluntarily, in the regions above the drawing-room, without being first represented by an ambassadress—attention was now diverted from the children. Zo folder her letter, enclosed it in the envelope, and hid it in her pocket.

Joseph appeared. "I beg your pardon, sir, I don't quite know whether I ought to disturb my mistress. Mr. Le Frank has called, and asked if he can see her."

Mr. Gallilee consulted the parlour-maid. "Was your mistress asleep when I sent you to her?"

"No, sir. She told me to bring her a cup of tea."

On those rare former occasions, when Mrs. Gallilee had been ill, her attentive husband never left it to the servants to consult her wishes. That time had gone by for ever.

"Tell your mistress, Joseph, that Mr. Le Frank is here."

CHAPTER XLVII.

The slander on which Mrs. Gallilee had reckoned, as a means of separating Ovid and Carmina, was now a slander refuted by unanswerable proof. And the man whose exertions had achieved this result, was her own lawyer—the agent whom she had designed to employ, in asserting that claim of the guardian over the ward which Teresa had defied.

As a necessary consequence, the relations between Mr. Mool and herself were already at an end.

There she lay helpless—her authority set at naught; her person outraged by a brutal attack—there she lay, urged to action by every reason that a resolute woman could have for asserting her power, and avenging her wrong—without a creature to take her part, without an accomplice to serve her purpose.

She got on her feet, with the resolution of despair. Her heart sank—the room whirled round her—she dropped back on the sofa. In a recumbent position, the giddiness subsided. She could ring the hand-bell on the table at her side. "Send instantly for Mr. Null," she said to the maid. "If he is out, let the messenger follow him, wherever he may be."

The messenger came back with a note. Mr. Null would call on Mrs. Gallilee as soon as possible. He was then engaged in attendance on Miss Carmina.

At that discovery, Mrs. Gallilee's last reserves of independent resolution gave way. The services of her own medical attendant were only at her disposal, when Carmina had done with him! At the top of his letter the address, which she had thus far tried vainly to discover, stared her in the face: the house was within five minutes' walk—and she was not even able to cross the room! For the first time in her life, Mrs. Gallilee's imperious spirit acknowledged defeat. For the first time in her life, she asked herself the despicable question: Who can I find to help me?

Someone knocked at the door.

"Who is it?" she cried.

Joseph's voice answered her. "Mr. Le Frank has called, ma'am—and wishes to know if you can see him."

She never stopped to think. She never even sent for the maid to see to her personal appearance. The horror of her own helplessness drove her on. Here was the man, whose timely betrayal of Carmina had stopped her on her way to Ovid, in the nick of time! Here was the self-devoted instrument, waiting to be employed.

"I'll see Mr. Le Frank," she said. "Show him up."

The music-master looked round the obscurely lit room, and bowed to the recumbent figure on the sofa.

"I fear I disturb you, madam, at an inconvenient time."

"I am suffering from illness, Mr. Le Frank; but I am able to receive you—as you see."

She stopped there. Now, when she saw him, and heard him, some perverse hesitation in her began to doubt him. Now, when it was too late, she weakly tried to put herself on her guard. What a decay of energy (she felt it herself) in the ready and resolute woman, equal to any emergency at other times! "To what am I to attribute the favour of your visit?" she resumed.

Even her voice failed her: it faltered in spite of her efforts to steady it. Mr. Le Frank's vanity drew its own encouraging conclusion from this one circumstance.

"I am anxious to know how I stand in your estimation," he replied. "Early this evening, I left a few lines here, enclosing a letter—with my compliments. Have you received the letter?"

"Yes."

"Have you read it?"

Mrs. Gallilee hesitated. Mr. Le Frank smiled.

"I won't trouble you, madam, for any more direct reply," he said; "I will speak plainly. Be so good as to tell me plainly, on your side, which I am—a man who has disgraced himself by stealing a letter? or a man who has distinguished himself by doing you a service?"

An unpleasant alternative, neatly defined! To disavow Mr. Le Frank or to use Mr. Le Frank—there was the case for Mrs. Gallilee's consideration. She was incapable of pronouncing judgment; the mere effort of decision, after what she had suffered, fatigued and irritated her. "I can't deny," she said, with weary resignation, "that you have done me a service."

He rose, and made a generous return for the confidence that had been placed in him—he repeated his magnificent bow, and sat down again.

"Our position towards each other seems too plain to be mistaken," he proceeded. "Your niece's letter—perfectly useless for the purpose with which I opened it—offers me a means of being even with Miss Carmina, and a chance of being useful to You. Shall I begin by keeping an eye on the young lady?"

"Is that said, Mr. Le Frank, out of devotion to me?"

"My devotion to you might wear out," he answered audaciously. "You may trust my feeling towards your niece to last—I never forget an injury. Is it indiscreet to inquire how you mean to keep Miss Carmina from joining her lover in Quebec? Does a guardian's authority extend to locking her up in her room?"

Mrs. Gallilee felt the underlying familiarity in these questions—elaborately concealed as it was under an assumption of respect.

"My niece is no longer in my house," she answered coldly.

"Gone!" cried Mr. Le Frank.

She corrected the expression. "Removed," she said, and dropped the subject there.

Mr. Le Frank took the subject up again. "Removed, I presume, under the care of her nurse?" he rejoined.

The nurse? What did he know about the nurse? "May I ask—?" Mrs. Gallilee began.

He smiled indulgently, and stopped her there. "You are not quite yourself to-night," he said. "Permit me to remind you that your niece's letter to Mr. Ovid Vere is explicit, and that I took the liberty of reading it before I left it at your house."

Mrs. Gallilee listened in silence, conscious that she had committed another error. She had carefully excluded from her confidence a man who was already in possession of her secrets! Mr. Le Frank's courteous sympathy forbade him to take advantage of the position of superiority which he now held.

"I will do myself the honour of calling again," he said, "when you are better able to place the right estimate on my humble offers of service. I wouldn't fatigue you, Mrs. Gallilee, for the world! At the same time, permit me to put one last question which ought not to be delayed. When Miss Carmina left you, did she take away her writing-desk and her keys?"

"No."

"Allow me to suggest that she may send for them at any moment."

Before it was possible to ask for an explanation, Joseph presented himself again. Mr. Null was waiting downstairs. Mrs. Gallilee arranged that he should be admitted when she rang her bell. Mr. Le Frank approached the sofa, when they were alone, and returned to his suggestion in a whisper.

"Surely, you see the importance of using your niece's keys?" he resumed. "We don't know what correspondence may have been going on, in which the nurse and the governess have been concerned. After we have already intercepted a letter, hesitation is absurd! You are not equal to the effort yourself. I know the room. Don't be afraid of discovery; I have a naturally soft footfall—and my excuse is ready, if somebody else has a soft footfall too. Leave it to me."

He lit a candle as he spoke. But for that allusion to the nurse, Mrs. Gallilee might have ordered him to blow it out again. Eager for any discovery which might, by the barest possibility, place Teresa at her mercy, she silently submitted to Mr. Le Frank. "I'll call to-morrow," he said— and slipped out of the room.

When Mr. Null was announced, Mrs. Gallilee pushed up the shade over the globe of the lamp. Her medical attendant's face might be worth observing, under a clear light.

His timid look, his confused manner, when he made the conventional apologies, told her at once that Teresa had spoken, and that he knew what had happened. Even he had never before been so soothing and so attentive. But he forgot, or he was afraid, to consult appearances by asking what was the matter, before he felt the pulse, and took the temperature, and wrote his prescription. Not a word was uttered by Mrs. Gallilee, until the medical formalities came to an end. "Is there anything more that I can do?" he asked.

"You can tell me," she said, "when I shall be well again."

Mr. Null was polite; Mr. Null was sympathetic. Mrs. Gallilee might be herself again in a day or two—or Mrs. Gallilee might be unhappily confined to her room for some little time. He had hope in his prescription, and hope in perfect quiet and repose—he would suggest the propriety of going to bed at once, and would not fail to call early the next morning.

"Sit down again," said Mrs. Gallilee.

Mr. Null turned pale. He foresaw what was coming.

"You have been in attendance on Miss Carmina. I wish to know what her illness is."

Mr. Null began to prevaricate at the outset. "The case causes us serious anxiety. The complications are formidable. Doctor Benjulia himself—"

"In plain words, Mr. Null, can she be moved?"

This produced a definite answer. "Quite impossible."

She only ventured to put her next question after waiting a little to control herself.

"Is that foreign woman, the nurse—the only nurse—in attendance?"

"Don't speak of her, Mrs. Gallilee! A dreadful woman; coarse, furious, a perfect savage. When I suggested a second nurse—"

"I understand. You asked just now if you could do anything for me. You can do me a great service—you can recommend me a trustworthy lawyer."

Mr. Null was surprised. As the old medical attendant of the family, he was not unacquainted with the legal adviser. He mentioned Mr. Mool's name.

"Mr. Mool has forfeited my confidence," Mrs. Gallilee announced. "Can you, or can you not, recommend a lawyer?"

"Oh, certainly! My own lawyer."

"You will find writing materials on the table behind me. I won't keep you more than five minutes. I want you to write from my dictation."

"My dear lady, in your present condition—"

"Do as I tell you! My head is quiet while I lie down. Even a woman in my condition can say what she means to do. I shall not close my eyes to-night, unless I can feel that I have put that wretch in her right place. Who are your lawyers?"

Mr. Null mentioned the names, and took up his pen.

"Introduce me in the customary form," Mrs. Gallilee proceeded; "and then refer the lawyers to my brother's Will. Is it done?"

In due time it was done.

"Tell them next, how my niece has been taken away from me, and where she has been taken to."

To the best of his ability, Mr. Null complied.

"Now," said Mrs. Gallilee, "write what I mean to do!"

The prospect of being revenged on Teresa revived her. For the moment, at least, she almost looked like herself again.

Mr. Null turned over to a new leaf, with a hand that trembled a little. The dictating voice pronounced these words:

"I forbid the woman Teresa to act in the capacity of nurse to Miss Carmina, and even to enter the room in which that young lady is now lying ill. I further warn this person, that my niece will be restored to my care, the moment her medical attendants allow her to be removed. And I desire my legal advisers to assert my authority, as guardian, to-morrow morning."

Mr. Null finished his task in silent dismay. He took out his handkerchief and wiped his forehead.

"Is there any very terrible effort required in saying those few words—even to a shattered creature like me?" Mrs. Gallilee asked bitterly. "Let me hear that the lawyers have got their instructions, when you come to-morrow; and give me the name and address of a nurse whom you can thoroughly recommend. Good-night!"

At last, Mr. Null got away. As he softly closed the dressing-room door, the serious question still dwelt on his mind: What would Teresa do?

CHAPTER XLVIII.

Even in the welcome retirement of the school-room, Mr. Gallilee's mind was not at ease. He was troubled by a question entirely new to him—the question of himself, in the character of husband and father.

Accustomed through long years of conjugal association to look up to his wife as a superior creature, he was now conscious that her place in his estimation had been lost, beyond recovery. If he considered next what ought to be done with Maria and Zo, he only renewed his perplexity and distress. To leave them (as he had hitherto left them) absolutely submitted to their mother's authority, was to resign his children to the influence of a woman, who had ceased to be the object of his confidence and respect. He pondered over it in the schoolroom; he pondered over it when he went to bed. On the next morning, he arrived at a conclusion in the nature of a compromise. He decided on applying to his good friend, Mr. Mool, for a word of advice.

His first proceeding was to call at Teresa's lodgings, in the hope of hearing better news of Carmina.

The melancholy report of her was expressed in two words: No change. He was so distressed that he asked to see the landlady; and tried, in his own helpless kindhearted way, to get a little hopeful information by asking questions—useless questions, repeated over and over again in futile changes of words. The landlady was patient: she respected the undisguised grief of the gentle modest old man; but she held to the hard truth. The one possible answer was the answer which her servant had already given. When she followed him out, to open the door, Mr. Gallilee requested permission to wait a moment in the hall. "If you will allow me, ma'am, I'll wipe my eyes before I go into the street."

Arriving at the office without an appointment, he found the lawyer engaged. A clerk presented to him a slip of paper, with a line written by Mr. Mool: "Is it anything of importance?" Simple Mr. Gallilee wrote back: "Oh, dear, no; it's only me! I'll call again." Besides his critical judgment in the matter of champagne, this excellent man possessed another accomplishment—a beautiful handwriting. Mr. Mool, discovering a crooked line and some ill-formed letters in the reply, drew his own conclusions. He sent word to his old friend to wait.

In ten minutes more they were together, and the lawyer was informed of the events that had followed the visit of Benjulia to Fairfield Gardens, on the previous day.

For a while, the two men sat silently meditating—daunted by the prospect before them. When the time came for speaking, they exercised an influence over each other, of which both were alike unconscious. Out of their common horror of Mrs. Gallilee's conduct, and their common interest in Carmina, they innocently achieved between them the creation of one resolute man.

"My dear Gallilee, this is a very serious thing."

"My dear Mool, I feel it so—or I shouldn't have disturbed you."

"Don't talk of disturbing me! I see so many complications ahead of us, I hardly know where to begin."

"Just my case! It's a comfort to me that you feel it as I do."

Mr. Mool rose and tried walking up and down his room, as a means of stimulating his ingenuity.

"There's this poor young lady," he resumed. "If she gets better—"

"Don't put it in that way!" Mr. Gallilee interposed. "It sounds as if you doubted her ever getting well—you see it yourself in that light, don't you? Be a little more positive, Mool, in mercy to me."

"By all means," Mr. Mool agreed. "Let us say, *when* she gets better. But the difficulty meets us, all the same. If Mrs. Gallilee claims her right, what are we to do?"

Mr. Gallilee rose in his turn, and took a walk up and down the room. That well-meant experiment only left him feebler than ever.

"What possessed her brother to make her Carmina's guardian?" he asked—with the nearest approach to irritability of which he was capable. The lawyer was busy with his own thoughts. He only enlightened Mr. Gallilee after the question had been repeated.

"I had the sincerest regard for Mr. Robert Graywell," he said. "A better husband and father—and don't let me forget it, a more charming artist—never lived. But," said Mr. Mool, with the air of one strong-minded man appealing to another: "weak, sadly weak. If you will allow me to say so, your wife's self-asserting way—well, it was so unlike her brother's way, that it had its effect on him! If Lady Northlake had been a little less quiet and retiring, the matter might have ended in a very different manner. As it was (I don't wish to put the case offensively) Mrs. Gallilee imposed on him—and there she is, in authority, under the Will. Let that be. We must protect this poor girl. We must act!" cried Mr. Mool with a burst of energy.

"We must act!" Mr. Gallilee repeated—and feebly clenched his fist, and softly struck the table.

"I think I have an idea," the lawyer proceeded; "suggested by something said to me by Miss Carmina herself. May I ask if you are in her confidence?"

Mr. Gallilee's face brightened at this. "Certainly," he answered. "I always kiss her when we say good-night, and kiss her again when we say good-morning."

This proof of his friend's claims as Carmina's chosen adviser, seemed rather to surprise Mr. Mool. "Did she ever hint at an idea of hastening her marriage?" he inquired.

Plainly as the question was put, it thoroughly puzzled Mr. Gallilee. His honest face answered for him—he was *not* in Carmina's confidence. Mr. Mool returned to his idea.

"The one thing we can do," he said, "is to hasten Mr. Ovid's return. There is the only course to take—as I see it."

"Let's do it at once!" cried Mr. Gallilee.

"But tell me," Mr. Mool insisted, greedy for encouragement—"does my suggestion relieve your mind?"

"It's the first happy moment I've had to-day!" Mr. Gallilee's weak voice piped high: he was getting firmer and firmer with every word he uttered.

One of them produced a telegraph-form; the other seized a pen. "Shall we send the message in your name?" Mr. Mool asked.

If Mr. Gallilee had possessed a hundred names he would have sent them (and paid for them) all. "John Gallilee, 14 Fairfield Gardens,

London, To —" There the pen stopped. Ovid was still in the wilds of Canada. The one way of communicating with him was through the medium of the bankers at Quebec, To the bankers, accordingly, the message was sent. "Please telegraph Mr. Ovid Vere's address, the moment you know it."

When the telegram had been sent to the office, an interval of inaction followed. Mr. Gallilee's fortitude suffered a relapse. "It's a long time to wait," he said.

His friend agreed with him. Morally speaking, Mr. Mool's strength lay in points of law. No point of law appeared to be involved in the present conference: he shared Mr. Gallilee's depression of spirits. "We are quite helpless," he remarked, "till Mr. Ovid comes back. In the interval, I see no choice for Miss Carmina but to submit to her guardian; unless—" He looked hard at Mr. Gallilee, before he finished his sentence. "Unless," he resumed, "you can get over your present feeling about your wife."

"Get over it?" Mr. Gallilee repeated.

"It seems quite impossible now, I dare say," the worthy lawyer admitted. "A very painful impression has been produced on you. Naturally! naturally! But the force of habit—a married life of many years—your own kind feeling—"

"What do you mean?" asked Mr. Gallilee, bewildered, impatient, almost angry.

"A little persuasion on your part, my good friend—at the interesting moment of reconciliation—might be followed by excellent results. Mrs. Gallilee might not object to waive her claims, until time has softened existing asperities. Surely, a compromise is possible, if you could only prevail on yourself to forgive your wife."

"Forgive her? I should be only too glad to forgive her!" cried Mr. Gallilee, bursting into violent agitation. "How am I to do it? Good God! Mool, how am I to do it? *You* didn't hear those infamous words. *You* didn't see that dreadful death-struck look of the poor girl. I declare to you I turn cold when I think of my wife! I can't go to her when I ought to go— I send the servants into her room. My children, too—my dear good children—it's enough to break one's heart—think of their being brought up by a mother who could say what she said, and do—What will they see, I ask you what will they see, if she gets Carmina back in the house, and treats that sweet young creature as she *will* treat her? There were times last night, when I thought of going away for ever—Lord knows where— and taking the girls with me. What am I talking about? I had something to say, and I don't know what it is; I don't know my own self! There, there; I'll keep quiet. It's my poor stupid head, I suppose—hot, Mool, burning hot. Let's be reasonable. Yes, yes, yes; let's be reasonable. You're a lawyer. I said to myself, when I came here, 'I want Mool's advice.' Be a dear good fellow—set my mind at ease. Oh, my friend, my old friend, what can I do for my children?"

Amazed and distressed—utterly at a loss how to interfere to any good purpose—Mr. Mool recovered his presence of mind, the moment Mr. Gallilee appealed to him in his legal capacity. "Don't distress yourself about your children," he said kindly. "Thank God, we stand on firm ground, there."

"Do you mean it, Mool?"

"I mean it. Where your daughters are concerned, the authority is yours. Be firm, Gallilee! be firm!"

"I will! You set me the example—don't you? *You're* firm—eh?"

"Firm as a rock. I agree with you. For the present at least, the children must be removed."

"At once, Mool!"

"At once!" the lawyer repeated.

They had wrought each other up to the right pitch of resolution, by this time. They were almost loud enough for the clerks to hear them in the office.

"No matter what my wife may say!" Mr. Gallilee stipulated.

"No matter what she may say," Mr. Mool rejoined, "the father is master."

"And *you* know the law."

"And I know the law. You have only to assert yourself."

"And *you* have only to back me."

"For your children's sake, Gallilee!"

"Under my lawyer's advice, Mool!"

The one resolute Man was produced at last—without a flaw in him anywhere. They were both exhausted by the effort. Mr. Mool suggested a glass of wine.

Mr. Gallilee ventured on a hint. "You don't happen to have a drop of champagne handy?" he said.

The lawyer rang for his housekeeper. In five minutes, they were pledging each other in foaming tumblers. In five minutes more, they plunged back into business. The question of the best place to which the children could be removed, was easily settled. Mr. Mool offered his own house; acknowledging modestly that it had perhaps one drawback—it was within easy reach of Mrs. Gallilee. The statement of this objection stimulated his friend's memory. Lady Northlake was in Scotland. Lady Northlake had invited Maria and Zo, over and over again, to pass the autumn with their cousins; but Mrs. Gallilee's jealousy had always contrived to find some plausible reason for refusal. "Write at once," Mr. Mool advised. "You may do it in two lines. Your wife is ill; Miss Carmina is ill; you are not able to leave London—and the children are pining for fresh air." In this sense, Mr. Gallilee wrote. He insisted on having the letter sent to the post immediately. "I know it's long before post-time," he explained. "But I want to compose my mind."

The lawyer paused, with his glass of wine at his lips. "I say! You're not hesitating already?"

"No more than you are," Mr. Gallilee answered.

"You will really send the girls away?"

"The girls shall go, on the day when Lady Northlake invites them."

"I'll make a note of that," said Mr. Mool.

He made the note; and they rose to say good-bye. Faithful Mr. Gallilee still thought of Carmina. "Do consider it again!" he said at parting. "Are you sure the law won't help her?"

"I might look at her father's Will," Mr. Mool replied.

Mr. Gallilee saw the hopeful side of this suggestion, in the brightest colours. "Why didn't you think of it before?" he asked.

Mr. Mool gently remonstrated. "Don't forget how many things I have on my mind," he said. "It only occurs to me now that the Will may give us a remedy—if there is any *open* opposition to the ward's marriage engagement, on the guardian's part."

There he stopped; knowing Mrs. Gallilee's methods of opposition too well to reckon hopefully on such a result as this. But he was a merciful man—and he kept his misgivings to himself.

On the way home, Mr. Gallilee encountered his wife's maid. Marceline was dropping a letter into the pillar-post-box at the corner of the Square;[1] she changed colour, on seeing her master. "Corresponding with her sweetheart," Mr. Gallilee concluded.

Entering the house with an unfinished cigar in his mouth, he made straight for the smoking-room—and passed his youngest daughter, below him, waiting out of sight on the kitchen stairs.

"Have you done it?" Zo whispered, when Marceline returned by the servants' entrance.

"It's safe in the post, dear. Now tell me what you saw yesterday, when you were hidden in Miss Carmina's bedroom."

The tone in which she spoke implied a confidential agreement. With honourable promptitude Zo, perched on her friend's knee, exerted her memory, and rewarded Marceline for posting her letter to Ovid.

CHAPTER XLIX.

It was past the middle of the day, before Mr. Le Frank paid his promised visit to Mrs. Gallilee. He entered the room with gloomy looks; and made his polite inquiries, as became a depressed musician, in the minor key.

"I am sorry, madam, to find you still on the sofa. Is there no improvement in your health?"

---

1   *Marceline was dropping a letter into the pillar-post-box at the corner of the Square:*
    Collins had acquaintance and fellow-novelist Anthony Trollope (1815-1882) to
    thank for Marceline's alternative to the dangerous Fairfield Gardens post-bas-
    ket. Trollope, who worked for the postal service for nearly thirty-five years,
    developed the pillar-post-boxes in 1852.

"None whatever."

"Does your medical attendant give you any hope?"

"He does what they all do—he preaches patience. No more of myself! You appear to be in depressed spirits."

Mr. Le Frank admitted with a sigh that appearances had not misrepresented him. "I have been bitterly disappointed," he said. "My feelings as an artist are wounded to the quick. But why do I trouble you with my poor little personal affairs? I humbly beg your pardon."

His eyes accompanied this modest apology with a look of uneasy anticipation: he evidently expected to be asked to explain himself. Events had followed her instructions to Mr. Null, which left Mrs. Gallilee in need of employing her music-master's services. She felt the necessity of exerting herself; and did it—with an effort.

"You have no reason, I hope, to complain of your pupils?" she said.

"At this time of year, madam, I have no pupils. They are all out of town."

She was too deeply preoccupied by her own affairs to trouble herself any further. The direct way was the easy way. She said wearily, "Well, what is it?"

He answered in plain terms, this time.

"A bitter humiliation, Mrs. Gallilee! I have been made to regret that I asked you to honour me by accepting the dedication of my Song. The music-sellers, on whom the sale depends, have not taken a tenth part of the number of copies for which we expected them to subscribe. Has some extraordinary change come over the public taste? My composition has been carefully based on fashionable principles—that is to say, on the principles of the modern German school. As little tune as possible; and that little strictly confined to the accompaniment. And what is the result? Loss confronts me, instead of profit—my agreement makes me liable for half the expenses of publication. And, what is far more serious in my estimation, your honoured name is associated with a failure! Don't notice me— the artist nature—I shall be better in a minute." He took out a profusely-scented handkerchief, and buried his face in it with a groan.

Mrs. Gallilee's hard common sense understood the heart-broken composer to perfection.

"Stupid of me not have offered him money yesterday," she thought: "this waste of time need never have happened." She set her mistake right with admirable brevity and directness. "Don't distress yourself, Mr. Le Frank. Now my name is on it, the Song is mine. If your publisher's account is not satisfactory—be so good as to send it to *me*." Mr. Le Frank dropped his dry handkerchief, and sprang theatrically to his feet. His indulgent patroness refused to hear him: to this admirable woman, the dignity of Art was a sacred thing. "Not a word more on that subject," she said. "Tell me how you prospered last night. Your investigations cannot have been interrupted, or I should have heard of it. Come to the result! Have you found anything of importance in my niece's room?"

Mr. Le Frank had again been baffled, so far as the confirmation of his own suspicions was concerned. But the time was not favourable to a confession of personal disappointment. He understood the situation; and made himself the hero of it, in three words.

"Judge for yourself," he said—and held out the letter of warning from Father Patrizio.

In silence, Mrs. Gallilee read the words which declared her to be the object of Teresa's inveterate resentment, and which charged Carmina with the serious duty of keeping the peace.

"Does it alarm you?" Mr. Le Frank asked.

"I hardly know what I feel," she answered. "Give me time to think."

Mr. Le Frank went back to his chair. He had reason to congratulate himself already: he had shifted to other shoulders the pecuniary responsibility involved in the failure of his Song. Observing Mrs. Gallilee, he began to see possibilities of a brighter prospect still. Thus far she had kept him at a certain distance. Was the change of mind coming, which would admit him to the position (with all its solid advantages) of a confidential friend?

She suddenly took up Father Patrizio's letter, and showed it to him.

"What impression does it produce on you," she asked, "knowing no more than you know now?"

"The priest's cautious language, madam, speaks for itself. You have an enemy who will stick at nothing."

She still hesitated to trust him.

"You see me here," she went on, "confined to my room; likely, perhaps, to be in this helpless condition for some time to come. How would you protect yourself against that woman, in my place?"

"I should wait."

"For what purpose?"

"If you will allow me to use the language of the card-table, I should wait till the woman shows her hand."

"She *has* shown it."

"May I ask when?"

"This morning."

Mr. Le Frank said no more. If he was really wanted, Mrs. Gallilee had only to speak. After a last moment of hesitation, the pitiless necessities of her position decided her once more. "You see me too ill to move," she said; "the first thing to do, is to tell you why."

She related the plain facts; without a word of comment, without a sign of emotion. But her husband's horror of her had left an impression, which neither pride nor contempt had been strong enough to resist. She allowed the music-master to infer, that contending claims to authority over Carmina had led to a quarrel which provoked the assault. The secret of the words that she had spoken, was the one secret that she kept from Mr. Le Frank.

"While I was insensible," she proceeded, "my niece was taken away from me. She has been suffering from nervous illness; she was naturally terrified—and she is now at the nurse's lodgings, too ill to be moved. There you have the state of affairs, up to last night."

"Some people might think," Mr. Le Frank remarked, "that the easiest way out of it, so far, would be to summon the nurse for the assault."

"The easiest way compels me to face a public exposure," Mrs. Gallilee answered. "In my position that is impossible."

Mr. Le Frank accepted this view of the case as a matter of course. "Under the circumstances," he said, "it's not easy to advise you. How can you make the woman submit to your authority, while you are lying here?"

"My lawyers have made her submit this morning."

In the extremity of his surprise, Mr. Le Frank forgot himself. "The devil they have!" he exclaimed.

"They have forbidden her, in my name," Mrs. Gallilee continued, "to act as nurse to my niece. They have informed her that Miss Carmina will be restored to my care, the moment she can be moved. And they have sent me her unconditional submission in writing, signed by herself."

She took it from the desk at her side, and read it to him, in these words:

"I humbly ask pardon of Mrs. Gallilee for the violent and unlawful acts of which I have been guilty. I acknowledge, and submit to, her authority as guardian of Miss Carmina Graywell. And I appeal to her mercy (which I own I have not deserved) to spare me the misery of separation from Miss Carmina, on any conditions which it may be her good will and pleasure to impose."

"Now," Mrs. Gallilee concluded, "what do you say?"

Speaking sincerely for once, Mr. Le Frank made a startling reply.

"Submit on your side," he said. "Do what she asks of you. And when you are well enough to go to her lodgings, decline with thanks if she offers you anything to eat or drink."

Mrs. Gallilee raised herself on the sofa. "Are you insulting me, sir," she asked, "by making this serious emergency the subject of a joke?"

"I never was more in earnest, madam, in my life."

"You think—you really think—that she is capable of trying to poison me?"

"Most assuredly I do."

Mrs. Gallilee sank back on the pillow. Mr. Le Frank stated his reasons; checking them off, one by one, on his fingers.

"Who is she?" he began. "She is an Italian woman of the lower orders. The virtues of the people among whom she had been born and bred, are not generally considered to include respect for the sanctity of human life. What do we know already that she has done? She has alarmed the priest, who keeps her conscience, and knows her well; and she has attacked you with such murderous ferocity that it is a wonder you have escaped with your life. What sort of message have you sent to her, after this experience of her temper? You have told the tigress that you have the power to separate her from her cub, and that you mean to use it. On those plain facts, as they stare us in the face, which is the soundest conclusion? To believe that she really submits—or to believe that she is only gaining time, and is capable (if she sees no other alternative) of trying to poison you?"

"What would you advise me to do?" In those words Mrs. Gallilee—never before reduced to ask advice of anybody—owned that sound reasoning was not thrown away on her.

Mr. Le Frank answered the demand made on him without hesitation.

"The nurse has not signed that act of submission," he said, "without having her own private reasons for appearing to give way. Rely on it, she is prepared for you—and there is at least a chance that some proof of it may be found. Have all her movements privately watched—and search the room she lives in, as I searched Miss Carmina's room last night."

"Well?" said Mrs. Gallilee.

"Well?" Mr. Le Frank repeated.

She angrily gave way. "Say at once that you are the man to do it for me!" she answered. "And say next—if you can—how it is to be done."

Mr. Le Frank's manner softened to an air of gentle gallantry.

"Pray compose yourself!" he said. "I am so glad to be of service to you, and it is so easily done!"

"Easily?"

"Dear madam, quite easily. Isn't the house a lodging-house; and, at this time of year, have I anything to do?" He rose, and took his hat. "Surely, you see me in my new character now? A single gentleman wants a bedroom. His habits are quiet, and he gives excellent references. The address, Mrs. Gallilee—may I trouble you for the address?"

CHAPTER L.

Towards seven o'clock on the evening of Thursday, Carmina recognised Teresa for the first time.

Her half-closed eyes opened, as if from a long sleep: they rested on the old nurse without any appearance of surprise. "I am so glad to see you, my dear," she said faintly. "Are you very tired after you journey?" None of the inquiries which might have been anticipated followed those first words. Not the slightest allusion to Mrs. Gallilee escaped her; she expressed no anxiety about Miss Minerva; no sign of uneasiness at finding herself in a strange room, disturbed her quiet face. Contentedly reposing, she looked at Teresa from time to time and said,"You will stay with me, won't you?" Now and then, she confessed that her head felt dull and heavy, and asked Teresa to take her hand. "I feel as if I was sinking away from you," she said; "keep hold of my hand and I shan't be afraid to go to sleep." The words were hardly spoken, before she sank into slumber. Occasionally, Teresa felt her hand tremble, and kissed it. She seemed to be conscious of the kiss, without waking—she smiled in her sleep.

But, when the first hours of the morning came, this state of passive repose was disturbed. A violent attack of sickness came on. It was repeated again and again. Teresa sent for Mr. Null. He did what he could to relieve the new symptom; and he despatched a messenger to his illustrious colleague.

Benjulia lost no time in answering personally the appeal that had been made to him.

Mr. Null said, "Serious derangement of the stomach, sir." Benjulia agreed with him. Mr. Null showed his prescription. Benjulia sanctioned the prescription. Mr. Null said, "Is there anything you wish to suggest, sir?" Benjulia had nothing to suggest.

He waited, nevertheless, until Carmina was able to speak to him. Teresa and Mr. Null wondered what he would say to her. He only said, "Do you remember when you last saw me?" After a little consideration, she answered, "Yes, Zo was with us; Zo brought in your big stick; and we talked—" She tried to rouse her memory. "What did we talk about?" she asked. A momentary agitation brought a flush to her face. "I can't remember it," she said; "I can't remember when you went away: does it matter?" Benjulia replied, "Not the least in the world. Go to sleep."

But he still remained in the room—watching her as she grew drowsy. "Great weakness," Mr. Null whispered. And Benjulia answered, "Yes; I'll call again."

On his way out, he took Teresa aside.

"No more questions," he said—"and don't help her memory if she asks you."

"Will she remember, when she gets better?" Teresa inquired.

"Impossible to say, yet. Wait and see."

He left her in a hurry; his experiments were waiting for him. On the way home, his mind dwelt on Carmina's case. Some hidden process was at work there: give it time—and it would show itself. "I hope that ass won't want me," he said, thinking of his medical colleague, "for at least a week to come."

The week passed—and the physiologist was not disturbed.

During that interval, Mr. Null succeeded in partially overcoming the attacks of sickness: they were less violent, and they were succeeded by longer intervals of repose. In other respects, there seemed (as Teresa persisted in thinking) to be some little promise of improvement. A certain mental advance was unquestionably noticeable in Carmina. It first showed itself in an interesting way: she began to speak of Ovid.

Her great anxiety was, that he should know nothing of her illness. She forbade Teresa to write to him; she sent messages to Mr. and Mrs. Gallilee, and even to Mr. Mool, entreating them to preserve silence.

The nurse engaged to deliver the messages—and failed to keep her word. This breach of promise (as events had ordered it) proved to be harmless. Mrs. Gallilee had good reasons for not writing. Her husband and Mr. Mool had decided on sending their telegram to the bankers. As for

Teresa herself, she had no desire to communicate with Ovid. His absence remained inexcusable, from her point of view. Well or ill, with or without reason, it was the nurse's opinion that he ought to have remained at home, in Carmina's interests. No other persons were in the least likely to write to Ovid—nobody thought of Zo as a correspondent—Carmina was pacified.

Once or twice, at this later time, the languid efforts of her memory took a wider range.

She wondered why Mrs. Gallilee never came near her; owning that her aunt's absence was a relief to her, but not feeling interest enough in the subject to ask for information. She also mentioned Miss Minerva. "Do you know where she has gone? Don't you think she ought to write to me?" Teresa offered to make inquiries. She turned her head wearily on the pillow, and said, "Never mind!" On another occasion, she asked for Zo, and said it would be pleasant if Mr. Gallilee would call and bring her with him. But she soon dropped the subject, not to return to it again.

The only remembrance which seemed to dwell on her mind for more than a few minutes, was her remembrance of the last letter which she had written to Ovid.

She pleased herself with imagining his surprise, when he received it; she grew impatient under her continued illness, because it delayed her in escaping to Canada; she talked to Teresa of the clever manner in which the flight had been planned—with this strange failure of memory, that she attributed the various arrangements for setting discovery at defiance, not to Miss Minerva, but to the nurse.

Here, for the first time, her mind was approaching dangerous ground. The stealing of the letter, and the events that had followed it, stood next in the order of remembrance—if she was capable of a continued effort. Her weakness saved her. Beyond the writing of the letter, her recollections were unable to advance. Not the faintest allusion to any later circumstances escaped her. The poor stricken brain still sought its rest in frequent intervals of sleep. Sometimes, she drifted back into partial unconsciousness; sometimes, the attacks of sickness returned. Mr. Null set an excellent example of patience and resignation. He believed as devoutly as ever in his prescriptions; he placed the greatest reliance on time and care. The derangement of the stomach (as he called it) presented something positive and tangible to treat: he had got over the doubts and anxieties that troubled him, when Carmina was first removed to the lodgings. Looking confidently at the surface—without an idea of what was going on below it—he could tell Teresa, with a safe conscience, that he understood the case. He was always ready to comfort her, when her excitable Italian nature passed from the extreme of hope to the extreme of despair. "My good woman, we see our way now: it's a great point gained, I assure you, to see our way."

"What do you mean by seeing your way?" said the downright nurse. "Tell me when Carmina will be well again."

Mr. Null's medical knowledge was not yet equal to this demand on it. "The progress is slow," he admitted, "still Miss Carmina is getting on."

"Is her aunt getting on?" Teresa asked abruptly. "When is Mistress Gallilee likely to come here?"

"In a few days—" Mr. Null was about to add "I hope;" but he thought of what might happen when the two women met. As it was, Teresa's face showed signs of serious disturbance: her mind was plainly not prepared for this speedy prospect of a visit from Mrs. Gallilee. She took a letter out of her pocket.

"I find a good deal of sly prudence in you," she said to Mr. Null. "You must have seen something, in your time, of the ways of deceitful Englishwomen. What does that palaver mean in plain words?" She handed the letter to him.

With some reluctance he read it.

"Mrs. Gallilee declines to contract any engagement with the person formerly employed as nurse, in the household of the late Mr. Robert Graywell. Mrs. Gallilee so far recognises the apology and submission offered to her, as to abstain from taking immediate proceedings. In arriving at this decision, she is also influenced by the necessity of sparing her niece any agitation which might interfere with the medical treatment. When the circumstances appear to require it, she will not hesitate to exert her authority."

The handwriting told Mr. Null that this manifesto had not been written by Mrs. Gallilee herself. The person who had succeeded him, in the capacity of that lady's amanuensis,[1] had been evidently capable of giving sound advice. Little did he suspect that this mysterious secretary was identical with an enterprising pianist, who had once prevailed on him to take a seat at a concert; price five shillings.

"Well?" said Teresa.

Mr. Null hesitated.

The nurse stamped impatiently on the floor. "Tell me this! When she does come here, will she part me from Carmina? Is that what she means?"

"Possibly," said prudent Mr. Null.

Teresa pointed to the door. "Good-morning! I want nothing more of you. Oh, man, man, leave me by myself!"

The moment she was alone, she fell on her knees. Fiercely whispering, she repeated over and over again the words of the Lord's Prayer: " 'Lead us not into temptation, but deliver us from evil.' Christ, hear me! Mother of Christ, hear me! Oh, Carmina! Carmina!"

---

1 *The person who succeeded him ... lady's amanuensis*: Collins was quite familiar with the use of an amanuensis, or copier of manuscripts. His own daughters, first Marian and later Constance Harriet, both served him well as general secretaries and copy-writers during his long periods of extended and debilitating illness.

She rose and opened the door which communicated with the bedroom. Trembling pitiably, she looked for a while at Carmina, peacefully asleep—then turned away to a corner of the room, in which stood an old packing-case, fitted with a lock. She took it up; and, returning with it to the sitting-room, softly closed the bedroom door again.

After some hesitation, she decided to open the case. In the terror and confusion that possessed her, she tried the wrong key. Setting this mistake right, she disclosed—strangely mingled with the lighter articles of her own dress—a heap of papers; some of them letters and bills; some of them faded instructions in writing for the preparation of artists' colours.

She recoiled from the objects which her own act had disclosed. Why had she not taken Father Patrizio's advice? If she had only waited another day; if she had only sorted her husband's papers, before she threw the things that her trunk was too full to hold into that half-empty case, what torment might have been spared to her! Her eyes turned mournfully to the bedroom door. "Oh, my darling, I was in such a hurry to get to You!"

At last, she controlled herself, and put her hand into the case. Searching it in one corner, she produced a little tin canister. A dirty label was pasted on the canister, bearing this quaint inscription in the Italian language:

"If there is any of the powder we employ in making some of our prettiest colours, left in here, I request my good wife, or any other trustworthy person in her place, to put a seal on it, and take it directly to the manufactory, with the late foreman's best respects. It looks like nice sugar. Beware of looks—or you may taste poison."

On the point of opening the canister she hesitated. Under some strange impulse, she did what a child might have done: she shook it, and listened.

The rustle of the rising and falling powder—renewing her terror—seemed to exercise some irresistible fascination over her. "The devil's dance," she said to herself, with a ghastly smile. "Softly up—and softly down—and tempting me to take off the cover all the time! Why don't I get rid of it?"

That question set her thinking of Carmina's guardian.

If Mr. Null was right, in a day or two Mrs. Gallilee might come to the house. After the lawyers had threatened Teresa with the prospect of separation from Carmina, she had opened the packing-case, for the first time since she had left Rome—intending to sort her husband's papers as a means of relief from her own thoughts. In this way, she had discovered the canister. The sight of the deadly powder had tempted her. There were the horrid means of setting Mrs. Gallilee's authority at defiance! Some women in her place, would use them. Though she was not looking into the canister now, she felt that thought stealing back into her mind. There was but one hope for her: she resolved to get rid of the poison.

How?

At that period of the year, there was no fire in the grate. Within the limits of the room, the means of certain destruction were slow to present themselves. Her own morbid horror of the canister made her suspicious of the curiosity of other people, who might see it in her hand if she showed herself on the stairs. But she was determined, if she lit a fire for the purpose, to find the way to her end. The firmness of her resolution expressed itself by locking the case again, without restoring the canister to its hiding-place.

Providing herself next with a knife, she sat down in a corner—between the bedroom door on one side, and a cupboard in an angle of the wall on the other—and began the work of destruction by scraping off the paper label. The fragments might be burnt, and the powder (if she made a vow to the Virgin to do it) might be thrown into the fire next—and then the empty canister would be harmless.

She had made but little progress in the work of scraping, when it occurred to her that the lighting of a fire, on that warm autumn day, might look suspicious if the landlady or Mr. Null happened to come in. It would be safer to wait till night-time, when everybody would be in bed.

Arriving at this conclusion, she mechanically suspended the use of her knife.

In the moment of silence that followed, she heard someone enter the bedroom by the door which opened on the stairs. Immediately afterwards, the person turned the handle of the second door at her side. She had barely time enough to open the cupboard, and hide the canister in it—when the landlady came in.

Teresa looked at her wildly. The landlady looked at the cupboard: she was proud of her cupboard.

"Plenty of room there," she said boastfully: "not another house in the neighbourhood could offer you such accommodation as that! Yes—the lock is out of order; I don't deny it. The last lodger's doings! She spoilt my tablecloth, and put the inkstand over it to hide the place. Beast! there's her character in one word. You didn't hear me knock at the bedroom door? I am so glad to see her sleeping nicely, poor dear! Her chicken broth is ready when she wakes. I'm late to-day in making my inquiries after our young lady. You see we have been hard at work upstairs, getting the bedroom ready for a new lodger. Such a contrast to the person who has just left. A perfect gentleman, this time—and so kind in waiting a week till I was able to accommodate him. My ground floor rooms were vacant, as you know—but he said the terms were too high for him. Oh, I didn't forget to mention that we had an invalid in the house! Quiet habits (I said) are indeed an essential qualification of any new inmate, at such a time as this. He understood. 'I've been an invalid myself' (he said); 'and the very reason I am leaving my present lodgings is that they are not quiet enough.' Isn't that just the sort of man we want? And, let me tell you, a handsome man too. With a drawback, I must own, in the shape of a bald head. But such a beard, and such a thrilling voice! Hush! Did I hear her calling?"

At last, the landlady permitted other sounds to be audible, besides the sound of her own voice. It became possible to discover that Carmina was now awake. Teresa hurried into the bedroom.

Left by herself in the sitting-room, the landlady—"purely out of curiosity," as she afterwards said, in conversation with her new lodger—opened the cupboard, and looked in.

The canister stood straight before her, on an upper shelf. Did Miss Carmina's nurse take snuff? She examined the canister: there was a white powder inside. The mutilated label spoke in an unknown tongue. She wetted her finger and tasted the powder. The result was so disagreeable that she was obliged to use her handkerchief. She put the canister back, and closed the cupboard.

"Medicine, undoubtedly," the landlady said to herself. "Why should she hurry to put it away, when I came in?"

CHAPTER LI.

In eight days from the date of his second interview with Mrs. Gallilee, Mr. Le Frank took possession of his new bedroom.

He had arranged to report his proceedings in writing. In Teresa's state of mind, she would certainly distrust a fellow-lodger, discovered in personal communication with Mrs. Gallilee. Mr. Le Frank employed the first day after his arrival in collecting the materials for a report. In the evening, he wrote to Mrs. Gallilee—under cover to a friend, who was instructed to forward the letter.

"Private and confidential. Dear Madam,—I have not wasted my time and my opportunities, as you will presently see.

"My bedroom is immediately above the floor of the house which is occupied by Miss Carmina and her nurse. Having some little matters of my own to settle, I was late in taking possession of my room. Before the lights on the staircase were put out, I took the liberty of looking down at the next landing.

"Do you remember, when you were a child learning to write, that one of the lines in your copy-books was, 'Virtue is its own reward'? This ridiculous assertion was actually verified in my case! Before I had been five minutes at my post, I saw the nurse open her door. She looked up the staircase (without discovering me, it is needless to say), and she looked down the staircase—and, seeing nobody about, returned to her rooms.

"Waiting till I heard her lock the door, I stole downstairs, and listened outside.

"One of my two fellow-lodgers (you know that I don't believe in Miss Carmina's illness) was lighting a fire—on such a warm autumn night, that the staircase window was left open! I am absolutely sure of what I say: I heard the crackle of burning wood—I smelt coal smoke.

"The motive of this secret proceeding it seems impossible to guess at. If they were burning documents of a dangerous and compromising kind, a candle would have answered their purpose. If they wanted hot water, surely a tin kettle and a spirit lamp must have been at hand in an invalid's bedroom? Perhaps, your superior penetration may be able to read the riddle which baffles my ingenuity.

"So much for the first night.

"This afternoon, I had some talk with the landlady. My professional avocations having trained me in the art of making myself agreeable to the sex, I may say without vanity that I produced a favourable impression. In other words, I contrived to set my fair friend talking freely about the old nurse and the interesting invalid.

"Out of the flow of words poured on me, one fact of very serious importance has risen to the surface. There is a suspicious canister in the nurse's possession. The landlady calls the powder inside, medicine. I say, poison.

"Am I rushing at a fanciful conclusion? Please wait a little.

"During the week of delay which elapsed, before the lodger in possession vacated my room, you kindly admitted me to an interview. I ventured to put some questions, relating to Teresa's life in Italy and to the persons with whom she associated. Do you remember telling me, when I asked what you knew of her husband, that he was foreman in a manufactory of artists' colours? and that you had your information from Miss Carmina herself, after she had shown you the telegram announcing his death?

"A lady, possessed of your scientific knowledge, does not require to be told that poisons are employed in making artists' colours. Remember what the priest's letter says of Teresa's feeling towards you, and then say—Is it so very unlikely that she has brought with her to England one of the poisons used by her husband in his trade? and is it quite unreasonable to suppose (when she looks at her canister) that she may be thinking of you?

"I may be right or I may be wrong. Thanks to the dilapidated condition of a lock, I can decide the question, at the first opportunity offered to me by the nurse's absence from the room.

"My next report shall tell you that I have contrived to provide myself with a sample of the powder—leaving the canister undisturbed. The sample shall be tested by a chemist. If he pronounces it to be poison, I have a bold course of action to propose.

"As soon as you are well enough to go to the house, give the nurse her chance of poisoning you.

"Dear madam, don't be alarmed! I will accompany you; and I will answer for the result. We will pay our visit at tea-time. Let her offer you a cup—and let me (under pretence of handing it) get possession of the poisoned drink. Before she can cry Stop!—I shall be on my way to the chemist.

"The penalty for attempted murder is penal servitude. If you still object to a public exposure, we have the chemist's report, together with your own evidence, ready for your son on his return. How will he feel about his marriage-engagement, when he finds that Miss Carmina's dearest friend and companion has tried—*perhaps, with her young lady's knowledge*—to poison his mother?

"Before concluding, I may mention that I had a narrow escape, only two hours since, of being seen by Teresa on the stairs.

"I was of course prepared for this sort of meeting, when I engaged my room; and I have therefore not been foolish enough to enter the house under an assumed name. On the contrary, I propose (in your interests) to establish a neighbourly acquaintance—with time to help me. But the matter of the poison admits of no delay. My chance of getting at it unobserved may be seriously compromised, if the nurse remembers that she first met with me in your house, and distrusts me accordingly. Your devoted servant, L. F."

Having completed his letter, he rang for the maid, and gave it to her to post.

On her way downstairs, she was stopped on the next landing by Mr. Null. He too had a letter ready: addressed to Doctor Benjulia. The fierce old nurse followed him out, and said, "Post it instantly!" The civil maid asked if Miss Carmina was better. "Worse!"—was all the rude foreigner said. She looked at poor Mr. Null, as if it was his fault.

Left in the retirement of his room, Mr. Le Frank sat at the writing-table, frowning and biting his nails.

Were these evidences of a troubled mind connected with the infamous proposal which he had addressed to Mrs. Gallilee? Nothing of the sort! Having sent away his letter, he was now at leisure to let his personal anxieties absorb him without restraint. He was thinking of Carmina. The oftener his efforts were baffled, the more resolute he became to discover the secret of her behaviour to him. For the hundredth time he said to himself, "Her devilish malice reviles me behind my back, and asks me before my face to shake hands and be friends." The more outrageously unreasonable his suspicions became, under the exasperating influence of suspense, the more inveterately his vindictive nature held to its delusion. After meeting her in the hall at Fairfield Gardens, he really believed Carmina's illness to have been assumed as a means of keeping out of his way. If a friend had said to him, "But what reason have you to think so?"—he would have smiled compassionately, and have given that friend up for a shallow-minded man.

He stole out again, and listened, undetected, at their door. Carmina was speaking; but the words, in those faint tones, were inaudible. Teresa's stronger voice easily reached his ears. "My darling, talking is not good for you. I'll light the night-lamp—try to sleep."

Hearing this, he went back to his bedroom to wait a little. Teresa's vigilance might relax if Carmina fell asleep. She might go downstairs for a gossip with the landlady.

After smoking a cigar, he tried again. The lights on the staircase were now put out: it was eleven o'clock.

She was not asleep: the nurse was reading to her from some devotional book. He gave it up, for that night. His head ached; the ferment of his own abominable thoughts had fevered him. A cowardly dread of the slightest signs of illness was one of his special weaknesses. The whole day, to-morrow, was before him. He felt his own pulse; and determined, in justice to himself, to go to bed.

Ten minutes later, the landlady, on *her* way to bed, ascended the stairs. She too heard the voice, still reading aloud—and tapped softly at the door. Teresa opened it.

"Is the poor thing not asleep yet?"

"No."

"Has she been disturbed in some way?"

"Somebody has been walking about, overhead," Teresa answered.

"That's the new lodger!" exclaimed the landlady. "I'll speak to Mr. Le Frank."

On the point of closing the door, and saying good-night, Teresa stopped, and considered for a moment.

"Is *he* your new lodger?" she said.

"Yes. Do you know him?"

"I saw him when I was last in England."

"Well?"

"Nothing more," Teresa answered. "Good-night!"

End of April 1883 *Belgravia* **Serial Number**

CHAPTER LII.

Watching through the night by Carmina's bedside, Teresa found herself thinking of Mr. Le Frank. It was one way of getting through the weary time, to guess at the motive which had led him to become a lodger in the house.

Common probabilities pointed to the inference that he might have reasons for changing his residence, which only concerned himself. But common probabilities—from Teresa's point of view—did not apply to Mr. Le Frank. On meeting him, at the time of her last visit to England, his personal appearance had produced such a disagreeable impression on her, that she had even told Carmina "the music-master looked like a rogue." With her former prejudice against him now revived, and with her serious present reasons for distrusting Mrs. Gallilee, she rejected the idea of his accidental presence under her landlady's roof. To her mind, the business of the new lodger in the house was, in all likelihood, the business of a spy.

While Mr. Le Frank was warily laying his plans for the next day, he had himself become an object of suspicion to the very woman whose secrets he was plotting to surprise.

This was the longest and saddest night which the faithful old nurse had passed at her darling's bedside.

For the first time, Carmina was fretful, and hard to please: patient persuasion was needed to induce her to take her medicine. Even when she was thirsty, she had an irritable objection to being disturbed, if the lemonade was offered to her which she had relished at other times. Once or twice, when she drowsily stirred in her bed, she showed symptoms of delusion. The poor girl supposed it was the eve or her wedding-day, and eagerly asked what Teresa had done with her new dress. A little later, when she had perhaps been dreaming, she fancied that her mother was still alive, and repeated the long-forgotten talk of her childhood. "What have I said to distress you?" she asked wonderingly, when she found Teresa crying.

Soon after sunrise, there came a long interval of repose.

At the later time when Benjulia arrived, she was quiet and uncomplaining. The change for the worse which had induced Teresa to insist on sending for him, was perversely absent. Mr. Null expected to be roughly rebuked for having disturbed the great man by a false alarm. He attempted to explain: and Teresa attempted to explain. Benjulia paid not the slightest attention to either of them. He made no angry remarks—and he showed, in his own impenetrable way, as gratifying an interest in the case as ever.

"Draw up the blind," he said; "I want to have a good look at her."

Mr. Null waited respectfully, and imposed strict silence on Teresa, while the investigation was going on. It lasted so long that he ventured to say, "Do you see anything particular, sir?"

Benjulia saw his doubts cleared up: time (as he had anticipated) had brought development with it, and had enabled him to arrive at a conclusion. The shock that had struck Carmina had produced complicated hysterical disturbance, which was now beginning to simulate paralysis. Benjulia's profound and practised observation detected a trifling inequality in the size of the pupils of the eyes, and a slightly unequal action on either side of the face—delicately presented in the eyelids, the nostrils, and the lips. Here was no common affection of the brain, which even Mr. Null could understand! Here, at last, was Benjulia's reward for sacrificing the precious hours which might otherwise have been employed in the laboratory! From that day, Carmina was destined to receive unknown honour: she was to take her place, along with the other animals, in his note-book of experiments.

He turned quietly to Mr. Null, and finished the consultation in two words.

"All right!"

"Have you nothing to suggest, sir?" Mr. Null inquired.

"Go on with the treatment—and draw down the blind, if she complains of the light. Good-day!"

"Are you sure he's a great doctor?" said Teresa, when the door had closed on him.

"The greatest we have!" cried Mr. Null with enthusiasm.

"Is he a good man?"

"Why do you ask?"

"I want to know if we can trust him to tell us the truth?"

"Not a doubt of it!" (Who could doubt it, indeed, after he had approved of Mr. Null's medical treatment?)

"There's one thing you have forgotten," Teresa persisted. "You haven't asked him when Carmina can be moved."

"My good woman, if I had put such a question, he would have set me down as a fool! Nobody can say when she will be well enough to be moved."

He took his hat. The nurse followed him out.

"Are you going to Mrs. Gallilee, sir?"

"Not to-day."

"Is she better?"

"She is almost well again."

CHAPTER LIII.

Left alone, Teresa went into the sitting-room: she was afraid to show herself at the bedside.

Mr. Null had destroyed the one hope which had supported her thus far—the hope of escaping from England with Carmina, before Mrs. Gallilee could interfere. Looking steadfastly at that inspiriting prospect, she had forced herself to sign the humble apology and submission which the lawyers had dictated. What was the prospect now? Heavily had the merciless hand of calamity fallen on that brave old soul—and, at last, it had beaten her down! While she stood at the window, mechanically looking out, the dreary view of the back street trembled and disappeared. Teresa was crying. Happily for herself, she was unable to control her own weakness; the tears lightened her heavy heart. She waited a little, in the fear that her eyes might betray her, before she returned to Carmina. In that interval, she heard the sound of a closing door, on the floor above.

"The music-master!" she said to herself.

In an instant, she was at the sitting-room door, looking through the keyhole. It was the one safe way of watching him—and that was enough for Teresa.

His figure appeared suddenly within her narrow range of view—on the mat outside the door. If her distrust of him was without foundation, he would go on downstairs. No! He stopped on the mat to listen—he stooped—*his* eye would have been at the keyhole in another moment.

She seized a chair, and moved it. The sound instantly drove him away. He went on, down the stairs.

Teresa considered with herself what safest means of protection—and, if possible, of punishment as well—lay within her reach. How, and where, could the trap be set that might catch him?

She was still puzzled by that question, when the landlady made her appearance—politely anxious to hear what the doctors thought of their patient. Satisfied so far, the wearisome woman had her apologies to make next, for not having yet cautioned Mr. Le Frank.

"Thinking over it, since last night," she said confidentially, "I cannot imagine how you heard him walking overhead. He has such a soft step that he positively takes me by surprise when he comes into my room. He has gone out for an hour; and I have done him a little favour which I am not in the habit of conferring on ordinary lodgers—I have lent him my umbrella, as it threatens rain. In his absence, I will ask you to listen while I walk about in his room. One can't be too particular, when rest is of such importance to your young lady—and it has struck me as just possible, that the floor of his room may be in fault. My dear, the boards may creak! I'm a sad fidget, I know; but, if the carpenter can set things right—without any horrid hammering, of course!—the sooner he is sent for, the more relieved I shall feel."

Through this harangue, the nurse had waited, with a patience far from characteristic of her, for an opportunity of saying a timely word. By some tortuous mental process, that she was quite unable to trace, the landlady's allusion to Mr. Le Frank had suggested the very idea of which, in her undisturbed solitude, she had been vainly in search. Never before, had the mistress of the house appeared to Teresa in such a favourable light.

"You needn't trouble yourself, ma'am," she said, as soon as she could make herself heard; "it *was* the creaking of the boards that told me somebody was moving overhead."

"Then I'm not a fidget after all? Oh, how you relieve me! Whatever the servants may have to do, one of them shall be sent instantly to the carpenter. So glad to be of any service to that sweet young creature!"

Teresa consulted her watch before she returned to the bedroom.

The improvement in Carmina still continued: she was able to take some of the light nourishment that was waiting for her. As Benjulia had anticipated, she asked to have the blind lowered a little. Teresa drew it completely over the window: she had her own reasons for tempting Carmina to repose. In half an hour more, the weary girl was sleeping, and the nurse was at liberty to set her trap for Mr. Le Frank.

Her first proceeding was to dip the end of a quill pen into her bottle of salad oil, and to lubricate the lock and key of the door that gave access to the bedroom from the stairs. Having satisfied herself that the key could now be used without making the slightest sound, she turned to the door of communication with the sitting-room next.

This door was covered with green baize.[1] It had handles but no lock; and it swung inwards, so as to allow the door of the cupboard (situated in the angle of the sitting-room wall) to open towards the bedroom freely. Teresa oiled the hinges, and the brass bolt and staple[2] which protected the baize door on the side of the bedroom. That done, she looked again at her watch.

Mr. Le Frank's absence was expected to last for an hour. In five minutes more, the hour would expire.

After bolting the door of communication, she paused in the bedroom, and wafted a kiss to Carmina, still at rest. She left the room by the door which opened on the stairs, and locked it, taking away the key with her.

Having gone down the first flight of stairs, she stopped and went back. The one unsecured door, was the door which led into the sitting-room from the staircase. She opened it and left it invitingly ajar. "Now," she said to herself, "the trap will catch him!"

The hall clock struck the hour when she entered the landlady's room.

The woman of many words was at once charmed and annoyed. Charmed to hear that the dear invalid was resting, and to receive a visit from the nurse: annoyed by the absence of the carpenter, at work somewhere else for the whole of the day. "If my dear husband had been alive, we should have been independent of carpenters; he could turn his hand to anything. Now do sit down—I want you to taste some cherry brandy of my own making."

As Teresa took a chair, Mr. Le Frank returned. The two secret adversaries met, face to face.

"Surely I remember this lady?" he said.

Teresa encountered him, on his own ground. She made her best curtsey, and reminded him of the circumstances under which they had formerly met. The hospitable landlady produced her cherry brandy. "We are going to have a nice little chat; do sit down, sir, and join us." Mr. Le Frank made his apologies. The umbrella which had been so kindly lent to him, had not protected his shoes; his feet were wet; and he was so sadly liable to take cold that he must beg permission to put on his dry things immediately.

Having bowed himself out, he stopped in the passage, and, standing on tiptoe, peeped through a window in the wall, by which light was conveyed to the landlady's little room. The two women were comfortably seated together, with the cherry brandy and a plate of biscuits on a table between them. "In for a good long gossip," thought Mr. Le Frank. "Now is my time!"

---

1   *This door was covered with green baize*: Baize is a cotton or woollen material napped to imitate felt.

2   *Teresa oiled ... the brass bolt and staple*: A staple is a U-shaped loop with pointed ends. It attaches to a surface, in this case a door, and holds the bolt in place.

Not five minutes more had passed, before Teresa made an excuse for running upstairs again. She had forgotten to leave the bell rope, in case Carmina woke, within the reach of her hand. The excellent heart of the hostess made allowance for natural anxiety. "Do it, you good soul," she said; "and come back directly!" Left by herself, she filled her glass again, and smiled. Sweetness of temper (encouraged by cherry brandy) can even smile at a glass—unless it happens to be empty.

Approaching her own rooms, Teresa waited, and listened, before she showed herself. No sound reached her through the half open sitting-room door. She noiselessly entered the bedroom, and then locked the door again. Once more she listened; and once more there was nothing to be heard. Had he seen her on the stairs?

As the doubt crossed her mind, she heard the boards creak on the floor above. Mr. Le Frank was in his room.

Did this mean that her well-laid plan had failed? Or did it mean that he was really changing his shoes and stockings? The last inference was the right one.

He had made no mere excuse downstairs. The serious interests that he had at stake, were not important enough to make him forget his precious health. His chest was delicate; a cold might settle on his lungs. The temptation of the half-open door had its due effect on this prudent man; but it failed to make him forget that his feet were wet.

The boards creaked again; the door of his room was softly closed—then there was silence. Teresa only knew when he had entered the sitting-room by hearing him try the bolted baize door. After that, he must have stepped out again. He next tried the door of the bedchamber, from the stairs.

There was a quiet interval once more. Teresa noiselessly drew back the bolt; and, opening the baize door by a mere hair's-breadth, admitted sound from the sitting-room. She now heard him turning the key in a chiffonier, which only contained tradesmen's circulars, receipted bills, and a few books.

(Even with the canister in the cupboard, waiting to be opened, his uppermost idea was to discover Carmina's vindictive motive in Carmina's papers!)

The contents of the chiffonier disappointed him—judging by the tone in which he muttered to himself. The next sound startled Teresa; it was a tap against the lintel of the door behind which she was standing. He had thrown open the cupboard.

The rasping of the cover, as he took it off, told her that he was examining the canister. She had put it back on the shelf, a harmless thing now—the poison and the label having been both destroyed by fire. Nevertheless, his choosing the canister, from dozens of other things scattered invitingly about it, inspired her with a feeling of distrustful surprise. She was no longer content to find out what he was doing by means of her ears. Determined to see him, and to catch him in the fact, she pulled open the baize door—at the moment when he must have discovered that the canister was empty. A faint thump told her he had thrown it on the floor. The view of the sitting-room was still hidden from her. She had forgotten the cupboard door.

Now that it was wide open, it covered the entrance to the bedroom, and completely screened them one from the other. For the moment she was startled, and hesitated whether to show herself or not. His voice stopped her.

"Is there another canister?" he said to himself. "The dirty old savage may have hidden it—"

Teresa heard no more. "The dirty old savage" was an insult not to be endured! She forgot her intention of stealing on him unobserved; she forgot her resolution to do nothing that could awaken Carmina. Her fierce temper urged her into furious action. With both hands outspread, she flew at the cupboard door, and banged it to in an instant.

A shriek of agony rang through the house. The swiftly closing door had caught, and crushed, the fingers of Le Frank's right hand, at the moment when he was putting it into the cupboard again.

Without stopping to help him, without even looking at him, she ran back to Carmina.

The swinging baize door fell to, and closed of itself. No second cry was heard. Nothing happened to falsify her desperate assertion that the shriek was the delusion of a vivid dream. She took Carmina in her arms, and patted and fondled her like a child. "See, my darling, I'm with you as usual; and I have heard nothing. Don't, oh, don't tremble in that way! There—I'll wrap you up in my shawl, and read to you. No! let's talk of Ovid."

Her efforts to compose Carmina were interrupted by a muffled sound of men's footsteps and women's voices in the next room.

She hurriedly opened the door, and entreated them to whisper and be quiet. In the instant before she closed it again, she saw and heard. Le Frank lay in a swoon on the floor. The landlady was kneeling by him, looking at his injured hand; and the lodgers were saying, "Send him to the hospital."

CHAPTER LIV.

On Monday morning, the strain on Mrs. Gallilee's powers of patient endurance came to an end. With the help of Mr. Null's arm, she was able to get downstairs to the library. On Tuesday, there would be no objection to her going out for a drive. Mr. Null left her, restored to her equable flow of spirits. He had asked if she wished to have somebody to keep her company—and she had answered briskly, "Not on any account! I prefer being alone."

On the morning of Saturday, she had received Mr. Le Frank's letter; but she had not then recovered sufficiently to be able to read it through. She could now take it up again, and get to the end.

Other women might have been alarmed by the atrocious wickedness of the conspiracy which the music-master had planned. Mrs. Gallilee was only offended. That he should think her capable—in her social position—of favouring such a plot as he had suggested, was an insult which she was determined neither to forgive nor forget. Fortunately, she had not committed herself in writing; he could produce no proof of the relations that had existed between them. The first and best use to make of her recovery would be to dismiss him—after paying his expenses, privately and prudently, in money instead of by cheque.

In the meantime, the man's insolence had left its revolting impression on her mind. The one way to remove it was to find some agreeable occupation for her thoughts.

Look at your library table, learned lady, and take the appropriate means of relief that it offers. See the lively modern parasites that infest Science, eager to invite your attention to their little crawling selves. Follow scientific inquiry, rushing into print to proclaim its own importance, and to declare any human being, who ventures to doubt or differ, a fanatic or a fool. Respect the leaders of public opinion, writing notices of professors, who have made discoveries not yet tried by time, not yet universally accepted even by their brethren, in terms which would be exaggerated if they were applied to Newton or to Bacon.[1] Submit to lectures and addresses by dozens which, if they prove nothing else, prove that what was scientific knowledge some years since; is scientific ignorance now—and that what is scientific knowledge now, may be scientific ignorance in some years more. Absorb your mind in controversies and discussions, in which Mr. Always Right and Mr. Never Wrong exhibit the natural tendency of man to believe in himself, in the most rampant stage of development that the world has yet seen. And when you have done all this, doubt not that you have made a good use of your time. You have discovered what the gentle wisdom of FARADAY saw and deplored, when he warned the science of his day in words which should live for ever: "The first and last step in the education of the judgment is—Humility."[2]

Having agreeably occupied her mind with subjects that were worthy of it, Mrs. Gallilee rose to seek a little physical relief by walking up and down the room.

Passing and repassing the bookcases, she noticed a remote corner

---

1 *Newton or ... Bacon*: The narrator, here serving as the voice of Mrs. Gallilee's conscience, names Sir Isaac Newton (1642-1727), English mathematician, scientist, and philosopher, and Francis Bacon (1561-1626), English philosopher and essayist.

2 *Humility*: See Note 7, p. 41, for information on Michael Faraday.

devoted to miscellaneous literature. A volume in faded binding of sky-blue, had been placed upside down. She looked at the book before she put it in its right position. The title was "Gallery of British Beauty."[1] Among the illustrations—long since forgotten—appeared her own portrait, when she was a girl of Carmina's age.

A faintly contemptuous smile parted her hard lips, provoked by the recollections of her youth.

What a fool she had been, at that early period of her life! In those days, she had trembled with pleasure at the singing of a famous Italian tenor; she had flown into a passion when a new dress proved to be a misfit, on the evening of a ball; she had given money to beggars in the street; she had fallen in love with a poor young man, and had terrified her weak-minded hysterical mother, by threatening to commit suicide when the beloved object was forbidden the house. Comparing the girl of seventeen with the matured and cultivated woman of later years, what a matchless example Mrs. Gallilee presented of the healthy influence of education, directed to scientific pursuits! "Ah!" she thought, as she put the book back in its place, "my girls will have reason to thank me when they grow up; they have had a mother who has done her duty."

She took a few more turns up and down the room. The sky had cleared again; a golden gleam of sunlight drew her to the window. The next moment she regretted even this concession to human weakness. A disagreeable association presented itself, and arrested the pleasant flow of her thoughts. Mr. Gallilee appeared on the door-step; leaving the house on foot, and carrying a large brown-paper parcel under his arm.

With servants at his disposal, why was he carrying the parcel himself?

The time had been, when Mrs. Gallilee would have tapped at the window, and would have insisted on his instantly returning and answering the question. But his conduct, since the catastrophe in Carmina's room, had produced a complete estrangement between the married pair. All his inquiries after his wife's health had been made by deputy. When he was not in the schoolroom with the children, he was at his club. Until he came to his senses, and made humble apology, no earthly consideration would induce Mrs. Gallilee to take the slightest notice of him.

She returned to her reading.

The footman came in, with two letters—one arriving by post; the other having been dropped into the box by private messenger. Communications of this latter sort proceeded, not unfrequently, from creditors. Mrs. Gallilee opened the stamped letter first.

It contained nothing more important than a few lines from a daily gov-

---

1   "*Gallery of British Beauty*": This book was an annual that featured portraits of ladies of fashion and was tremendously popular in the Victorian period. In Dickens's *Bleak House*, Tony Jobling rents a room at Krook's place and decorates the walls with "copperplate impressions from that truly national work, The Divinities of Albion, or Galaxy Gallery of British Beauties."

erness, whom she had engaged until a successor to Miss Minerva could be found. In obedience to Mrs. Gallilee's instructions, the governess would begin her attendance at ten o'clock on the next morning.

The second letter was of a very different kind. It related the disaster which had befallen Mr. Le Frank.

Mr. Null was the writer. As Miss Carmina's medical attendant, it was his duty to inform her guardian that her health had been unfavourably affected by an alarm in the house. Having described the nature of the alarm, he proceeded in these words: "You will, I fear, lose the services of your present music-master. Inquiries made this morning at the hospital, and reported to me, appear to suggest serious results. The wounded man's constitution is in an unhealthy state; the surgeons are not sure of being able to save two of the fingers. I will do myself the honour of calling to-morrow before you go out for your drive."

The impression produced by this intelligence on the lady to whom it was addressed, can only be reported in her own words. She—who knew, on the best scientific authority, that the world had created itself—completely lost her head, and actually said, "Thank God!"

For weeks to come—perhaps for months if the surgeons' forebodings were fulfilled—Mrs. Gallilee had got rid of Mr. Le Frank. In that moment of infinite relief, if her husband had presented himself, it is even possible that he might have been forgiven.

As it was, Mr. Gallilee returned late in the afternoon; entered his own domain of the smoking-room; and left the house again five minutes afterwards. Joseph officiously opened the door for him; and Joseph was surprised, precisely as his mistress had been surprised. Mr. Gallilee had a large brown paper parcel under his arm—the second which he had taken out of the house with his own hands! Moreover, he looked excessively confused when the footman discovered him. That night, he was late in returning from the club. Joseph (now on the watch) observed that he was not steady on his legs—and drew his own conclusions accordingly.

Punctual to her time, on the next morning, the new governess arrived. Mrs. Gallilee received her, and sent for the children.

The maid in charge of them appeared alone. She had no doubt that the young ladies would be back directly. The master had taken them out for a little walk, before they began their lessons. He had been informed that the lady who had been appointed to teach them would arrive at ten o'clock. And what had he said? He had said, "Very good."

The half-hour struck—eleven o'clock struck—and neither the father nor the children returned. Ten minutes later, someone rang the door bell. The door being duly opened, nobody appeared on the house-step. Joseph looked into the letter-box, and found a note addressed to his mistress, in his master's handwriting. He immediately delivered it.

Hitherto, Mrs. Gallilee had only been anxious. Joseph, waiting for events outside the door, heard the bell rung furiously; and found his mistress (as he forcibly described it) "like a woman gone distracted." Not without reason—to do her justice. Mr. Gallilee's method of relieving his wife's anxiety was remarkable by its brevity. In one sentence, he assured her that there was no need to feel alarmed. In another, he mentioned that he had taken the girls away with him for a change of air. And then he signed his initials—J. G.

Every servant in the house was summoned to the library, when Mrs. Gallilee had in some degree recovered herself.

One after another they were strictly examined; and one after another they had no evidence to give—excepting the maid who had been present when the master took the young ladies away. The little she had to tell, pointed to the inference that he had not admitted the girls to his confidence before they left the house. Maria had submitted, without appearing to be particularly pleased at the prospect of so early a walk. Zo (never ready to exert either her intelligence or her legs) had openly declared that she would rather stay at home. To this the master had answered, "Get your things on directly!"—and had said it so sharply that Miss Zoe stared at him in astonishment. Had they taken anything with them—a travelling bag for instance? They had taken nothing, except Mr. Gallilee's umbrella. Who had seen Mr. Gallilee last, on the previous night? Joseph had seen him last. The lower classes in England have one, and but one, true feeling of sympathy with the higher classes. The man above them appeals to their hearts, and merits their true service, when he is unsteady on his legs. Joseph nobly confined his evidence to what he had observed some hours previously: he mentioned the parcel. Mrs. Gallilee's keen perception, quickened by her own experience at the window, arrived at the truth. Those two bulky packages must have contained clothes—left, in anticipation of the journey, under the care of an accomplice. It was impossible that Mr. Gallilee could have got at the girls' dresses and linen, and have made the necessary selections from them, without a woman's assistance. The female servants were examined again. Each one of them positively asserted her innocence. Mrs. Gallilee threatened to send for the police. The indignant women all cried in chorus, "Search our boxes!"[1] Mrs. Gallilee took a wiser course. She sent to the lawyers who had been recommended to her by Mr. Null. The messenger had just been despatched, when Mr. Null himself, in performance of yesterday's engagement, called at the house.

He, too, was agitated. It was impossible that he could have heard what had happened. Was he the bearer of bad news? Mrs. Gallilee thought of Carmina first, and then of Mr. Le Frank.

"Prepare for a surprise," Mr. Null began, "a joyful surprise, Mrs. Gallilee! I have received a telegram from your son."

---

1   *"Search our boxes!"*: The scene echoes *The Moonstone*, where Cuff upsets the Verinder household domestics by demanding that their belongings be searched for the stolen diamond.

He handed it to her as he spoke.

"September 6th. Arrived at Quebec, and received information of Carmina's illness. Shall catch the Boston steamer, and sail to-morrow for Liverpool. Break the news gently to C. For God's sake send telegram to meet me at Queenstown."[1]

It was then the 7th of September. If all went well, Ovid might be in London in ten days more.

CHAPTER LV.

Mrs. Gallilee read the telegram—paused—and read it again. She let it drop on her lap; but her eyes still rested mechanically on the slip of paper. When she spoke, her voice startled Mr. Null. Usually loud and hard, her tones were strangely subdued. If his back had been turned towards her, he would hardly have known who was speaking to him.

"I must ask you to make allowances for me," she began, abruptly; "I hardly know what to say. This surprise comes at a time when I am badly prepared for it. I am getting well; but, you see, I am not quite so strong as I was before that woman attacked me. My husband has gone away—I don't know where—and has taken my children with him. Read his note: but don't say anything. You must let me be quiet, or I can't think."

She handed the letter to Mr. Null. He looked at her—read the few words submitted to him—and looked at her again. For once, his stock of conventional phrases failed him. Who could have anticipated such conduct on the part of her husband? Who could have supposed that she herself would have been affected in this way, by the return of her son?

Mrs. Gallilee drew a long heavy breath. "I have got it now," she said. "My son is coming home in a hurry, because of Carmina's illness. Has Carmina written to him?"

Mr. Null was in his element again: this question appealed to his knowledge of his patient. "Impossible, Mrs. Gallilee—in her present state of health."

"In her present state of health? I forgot that. There was something else. Oh, yes! Has Carmina seen the telegram?"

Mr. Null explained. He had just come from Carmina. In his medical capacity, he had thought it judicious to try the moral effect on his patient of a first allusion to the good news. He had only ventured to say that Mr. Ovid's agents in Canada had heard from him on his travels, and had reason to believe that he would shortly return to Quebec. Upon the whole, the impression produced on the young lady—

---

1   *Queenstown*: Ovid plans on steaming into Liverpool, but his ship will stop at Queenstown, on the southern coast of Ireland. It seems extravagant that Miss Minerva is sent, presumably by ferry, to meet him there.

It was useless to go on. Mrs. Gallilee was pursuing her own thoughts, without even the pretence of listening to him.

"I want to know who wrote to my son," she persisted. "Was it the nurse?"

Mr. Null considered this to be in the last degree unlikely. The nurse's language showed a hostile feeling towards Mr. Ovid, in consequence of his absence.

Mrs. Gallilee looked once more at the telegram. "Why," she asked, "does Ovid telegraph to You?"

Mr. Null answered with his customary sense of what was due to himself. "As the medical attendant of the family, your son naturally supposed, madam, that Miss Carmina was under my care."

The implied reproof produced no effect. "I wonder whether my son was afraid to trust us?" was all Mrs. Gallilee said. It was the chance guess of a wandering mind—but it had hit the truth. Kept in ignorance of Carmina's illness by the elder members of the family, at what other conclusion could Ovid arrive, with Zo's letter before him? After a momentary pause, Mrs. Gallilee went on. "I suppose I may keep the telegram?" she said.

Prudent Mr. Null offered a copy—and made the copy, then and there. The original (he explained) was his authority for acting on Mr. Ovid's behalf, and he must therefore beg leave to keep it. Mrs. Gallilee permitted him to exchange the two papers. "Is there anything more?" she asked. "Your time is valuable of course. Don't let me detain you."

"May I feel your pulse before I go?"

She held out her arm to him in silence.

The carriage came to the door while he was counting the beat of the pulse. She glanced at the window, and said, "Send it away." Mr. Null remonstrated. "My dear lady, the air will do you good." She answered obstinately and quietly, "No"—and once more became absorbed in thought.

It had been her intention to combine her first day of carriage exercise with a visit to Teresa's lodgings, and a personal exertion of her authority. The news of Ovid's impending return made it a matter of serious importance to consider this resolution under a new light. She had now, not only to reckon with Teresa, but with her son. With this burden on her enfeebled mind—heavily laden by the sense of injury which her husband's flight had aroused—she had not even reserves enough of energy to spare for the trifling effort of dressing to go out. She broke into irritability, for the first time. "I am trying to find out who has written to my son. How can I do it when you are worrying me about the carriage? Have you ever held a full glass in your hand, and been afraid of letting it overflow? That's what I'm afraid of—in my mind—I don't mean that my mind is a glass—I mean—" Her forehead turned red. "*Will* you leave me?" she cried.

He left her instantly.

The change in her manner, the difficulty she found in expressing her thoughts, had even startled stupid Mr. Null. She had herself alluded to results of the murderous attack made on her by Teresa, which had not perhaps hitherto sufficiently impressed him. In the shock inflicted on the patient's body, had there been involved some subtly-working influence that had disturbed the steady balance of her mind? Pondering uneasily on that question, he spoke to Joseph in the hall.

"Do you know about your master and the children?" he said.

"Yes, sir."

"I wish you had told me of it, when you let me in."

"Have I done any harm, sir?"

"I don't know yet. If you want me, I shall be at home to dinner at seven."

The next visitor was one of the partners in the legal firm, to which Mrs. Gallilee had applied for advice. After what Mr. Null had said, Joseph hesitated to conduct this gentleman into the presence of his mistress. He left the lawyer in the waiting-room, and took his card.

Mrs. Gallilee's attitude had not changed. She sat looking down at the copied telegram and the letter from her husband, lying together on her lap. Joseph was obliged to speak twice, before he could rouse her.

"To-morrow," was all she said.

"What time shall I say, ma'am?"

She put her hand to her head—and broke into anger against Joseph. "Settle it yourself, you wretch!" Her head drooped again over the papers. Joseph returned to the lawyer. "My mistress is not very well, sir. She will be obliged if you will call to-morrow, at your own time."

About an hour later, she rang her bell—rang it unintermittingly, until Joseph appeared. "I'm famished," she said. "Something to eat! I never was so hungry in my life. At once—I can't wait."

The cook sent up a cold fowl, and a ham. Her eyes devoured the food, while the footman was carving it for her. Her bad temper seemed to have completely disappeared. She said, "What a delicious dinner! Just the very things I like." She lifted the first morsel to her mouth—and laid the fork down again with a weary sigh. "No: I can't eat; what has come to me?" With those words, she pushed her chair away from the table, and looked slowly all round her. "I want the telegram and the letter." Joseph found them. "Can you help me?" she said. "I am trying to find out who wrote my son. Say yes, or no, at once; I hate waiting."

Joseph left her in her old posture, with her head down and the papers on her lap.

The appearance of the uneaten dinner in the kitchen produced a discussion, followed by a quarrel.

Joseph was of the opinion that the mistress had got more upon her mind than her mind could well bear. It was useless to send for Mr. Null; he had already mentioned that he would not be home until seven o'clock. There was no superior person in the house to consult. It was not for the servants to take responsibility on themselves. "Fetch the nearest doctor, and let *him* be answerable, if anything serious happens." Such was Joseph's advice.

The women (angrily remembering that Mrs. Gallilee had spoken of sending for the police) ridiculed the footman's cautious proposal—with one exception. When the others ironically asked him if he was not accustomed to the mistress's temper yet, Mrs. Gallilee's own maid (Marceline) said, "What do we know about it? Joseph is the only one of us who has seen her, since the morning."

This perfectly sensible remark had the effect of a breath of wind on a smouldering fire. The female servants, all equally suspected of having assisted Mr. Gallilee in making up his parcels, were all equally assured that there was a traitress among them—and that Marceline was the woman. Hitherto suppressed, this feeling now openly found its way to expression. Marceline lost her temper; and betrayed herself as her master's guilty confederate.

"I'm a mean mongrel—am I?" cried the angry maid, repeating the cook's allusion to her birthplace in the Channel Islands. "The mistress shall know, this minute, that I'm the woman who did it!"

"Why didn't you say so before?" the cook retorted.

"Because I promised my master not to tell on him, till he got to his journey's end."

"Who'll lay a wager?" asked the cook. "I bet half-a-crown she changes her mind, before she gets to the top of the stairs."

"Perhaps she thinks the mistress will forgive her," the parlour-maid suggested ironically.

"Or perhaps," the housemaid added, "she means to give the mistress notice to leave."

"That's exactly what I'm going to do!" said Marceline.

The women all declined to believe her. She appealed to Joseph. "What did I tell you, when the mistress first sent me out in the carriage with poor Miss Carmina? Didn't I say that I was no spy, and that I wouldn't submit to be made one? I would have left the house—I would!—but for Miss Carmina's kindness. Any other young lady would have made me feel my mean position. *She* treated me like a friend—and I don't forget it. I'll go straight from this place, and help to nurse her!"

With that declaration, Marceline left the kitchen.

Arrived at the library door, she paused. Not as the cook had suggested, to "change her mind;" but to consider beforehand how much she should confess to her mistress, and how much she should hold in reserve.

Zo's narrative of what had happened, on the evening of Teresa's arrival, had produced its inevitable effect on the maid's mind. Strengthening, by the sympathy which it excited, her grateful attachment to Carmina, it had necessarily intensified her dislike of Mrs. Gallilee—and Mrs. Gallilee's innocent husband had profited by that circumstance!

Unexpectedly tried by time, Mr. Gallilee's resolution to assert his paternal authority, in spite of his wife, had failed him. The same timidity which invents a lie in a hurry, can construct a stratagem at leisure. Marceline had discovered her master putting a plan of escape, devised by himself, to its first practical trial before the open wardrobe of his daughters—and had asked slyly if she could be of any use. Never remarkable for presence of mind in emergencies, Mr. Gallilee had helplessly admitted to his confidence the last person in the house, whom anyone else (in his position) would have trusted. "My good soul, I want to take the girls away quietly for change of air—you have got little secrets of your own, like me, haven't you?—and the fact is, I don't quite know how many petticoats—." There, he checked himself; conscious, when it was too late, that he was asking his wife's maid to help him in deceiving his wife. The ready Marceline helped him through the difficulty. "I understand, sir: my mistress's mind is much occupied—and you don't want to trouble her about this little journey." Mr. Gallilee, at a loss for any other answer, pulled out his purse. Marceline modestly drew back at the sight of it. "My mistress pays me, sir; I serve *you* for nothing." In those words, she would have informed any other man of the place which Mrs. Gallilee held in her estimation. Her master simply considered her to be the most disinterested woman he had ever met with. If she lost her situation through helping him, he engaged to pay her wages until she found another place. The maid set his mind at rest on that subject. "A woman who understands hairdressing as I do, sir, can refer to other ladies besides Mrs. Gallilee, and can get a place whenever she wants one."

Having decided on what she should confess, and on what she should conceal, Marceline knocked at the library door. Receiving no answer, she went in.

Mrs. Gallilee was leaning back in her chair: her hands hung down on either side of her; her eyes looked up drowsily at the ceiling. Prepared to see a person with an overburdened mind, the maid (without sympathy, to quicken her perceptions) saw nothing but a person on the point of taking a nap.

"Can I speak a word, ma'am?"

Mrs. Gallilee's eyes remained fixed on the ceiling. "Is that my maid?" she asked.

Treated—to all appearance—with marked contempt, Marceline no longer cared to assume the forms of respect either in language or manner. "I wish to give you notice to leave," she said abruptly; "I find I can't get on with my fellow-servants."

Mrs. Gallilee slowly raised her head, and looked at her maid—and said nothing.

"And while I'm about it," the angry woman proceeded, "I may as well own the truth. You suspect one of us of helping my master to take away the young ladies' things—I mean some few of their things. Well! you needn't blame innocent people. I'm the person."

Mrs. Gallilee laid her head back again on the chair—and burst out laughing.

For one moment, Marceline looked at her mistress in blank surprise. Then, the terrible truth burst on her. She ran into the hall, and called for Joseph.

He hurried up the stairs. The instant he presented himself at the open door, Mrs. Gallilee rose to her feet. "My medical attendant," she said, with an assumption of dignity; "I must explain myself." She held up one hand, outstretched; and counted her fingers with the other. "First my husband. Then my son. Now my maid. One, two, three. Mr. Null, do you know the proverb? 'It's the last hair that breaks the camel's back.'"[1] She suddenly dropped on her knees. "Will somebody pray for me?" she cried piteously. "I don't know how to pray for myself. Where is God?"

Bareheaded as he was, Joseph ran out. The nearest doctor lived on the opposite side of the Square. He happened to be at home. When he reached the house, the women servants were holding their mistress down by main force.

CHAPTER LVI.[2]

On the next day, Mr. Mool—returning from a legal consultation to an appointment at his office—found a gentleman, whom he knew by sight, walking up and down before his door; apparently bent on intercepting him. "Mr. Null, I believe?" he said, with his customary politeness.

Mr. Null answered to his name, and asked for a moment of Mr. Mool's time. Mr. Mool looked grave, and said he was late for an appointment already. Mr. Null admitted that the clerks in the office had told him so, and said at last, what he ought to have said at first: "I am Mrs. Gallilee's medical attendant—there is serious necessity for communicating with her husband."

Mr. Mool instantly led the way into the office.

The chief clerk approached his employer, with some severity of manner. "The parties have been waiting, sir, for more than a quarter of an hour." Mr. Mool's attention wandered: he was thinking of Mrs. Gallilee. "Is she dying?" he asked. "She is out of her mind," Mr. Null answered. Those words petrified the lawyer: he looked helplessly at the clerk—who, in his turn, looked indignantly at the office clock. Mr. Mool recovered himself. "Say I am detained by a most distressing circumstance; I will call on the parties later in the day, at their own hour." Giving those directions

---

1   *It's the last hair that breaks the camel's back*: The saying is proverbial.

2   *CHAPTER LVI*: Collins combined chapters LV and LVI in the *Belgravia* serial number (May 1883) to make chapter LVI of the Chatto & Windus volume edition.

to the clerk, he hurried Mr. Null upstairs into a private room. "Tell me about it; pray tell me about it. Stop! Perhaps, there is not time enough. What can I do?"

Mr. Null put the question, which he ought to have asked when they met at the house door. "Can you tell me Mr. Gallilee's address?"

"Certainly! Care of the Earl of Northlake—"

"Will you please write it in my pocket-book? I am so upset by this dreadful affair that I can't trust my memory."

Such a confession of helplessness as this, was all that was wanted to rouse Mr. Mool. He rejected the pocket-book, and wrote the address on a telegram. "Return directly: your wife is seriously ill." In five minutes more, the message was on its way to Scotland; and Mr. Null was at liberty to tell his melancholy story—if he could.

With assistance from Mr. Mool, he got through it. "This morning," he proceeded, "I have had the two best opinions in London. Assuming that there is no hereditary taint, the doctors think favourably of Mrs. Gallilee's chances of recovery."

"Is it violent madness?" Mr. Mool asked.

Mr. Null admitted that two nurses were required. "The doctors don't look on her violence as a discouraging symptom," he said. "They are inclined to attribute it to the strength of her constitution. I felt it my duty to place my own knowledge of the case before them. Without mentioning painful family circumstances—"

"I happen to be acquainted with the circumstances," Mr. Mool interposed. "Are they in any way connected with this dreadful state of things?"

He put that question eagerly, as if he had some strong personal interest in hearing the reply.

Mr. Null blundered on steadily with his story. "I thought it right (with all due reserve) to mention that Mrs. Gallilee had been subjected to—I won't trouble you with medical language—let us say, to a severe shock; involving mental disturbance as well as bodily injury, before her reason gave way."

"And they considered that to be the cause—?"

Mr. Null asserted his dignity. "The doctors agreed with Me, that it had shaken her power of self-control."

"You relieve me, Mr. Null—you infinitely relieve me! If our way of removing the children had done the mischief, I should never have forgiven myself."

He blushed, and said no more. Had Mr. Null noticed the slip of the tongue into which his agitation had betrayed him? Mr. Null did certainly look as if he was going to put a question. The lawyer desperately forestalled him.

"May I ask how you came to apply to me for Mr. Gallilee's address? Did you think of it yourself?"

Mr. Null had never had an idea of his own, from the day of his birth, downward. "A very intelligent man," he answered, "reminded me that you were an old friend of Mr. Gallilee. In short, it was Joseph—the footman at Fairfield Gardens."

Joseph's good opinion was of no importance to Mr. Mool's professional interests. He could gratify Mr. Null's curiosity without fear of lowering himself in the estimation of a client.

"I had better, perhaps, explain that chance allusion of mine to the children," he began. "My good friend, Mr. Gallilee, had his own reasons for removing his daughters from home for a time—reasons, I am bound to add, in which I concur. The children were to be placed under the care of their aunt, Lady Northlake. Unfortunately, her ladyship was away with my lord, cruising in their yacht. They were not able to receive Maria and Zoe at once. In the interval that elapsed—excuse my entering into particulars—our excellent friend had his own domestic reasons for arranging the—the sort of clandestine departure which did in fact take place. It was perhaps unwise on my part to consent—in short, I permitted some of the necessary clothing to be privately deposited here, and called for on the way to the station. Very unprofessional, I am aware. I did it for the best; and allowed my friendly feeling to mislead me. Can I be of any use? How is poor Miss Carmina? No better? Oh, dear! dear! Mr. Ovid will hear dreadful news, when he comes home. Can't we prepare him for it, in any way?"

Mr. Null announced that a telegram would meet Ovid at Queenstown—with the air of a man who had removed every obstacle that could be suggested to him. The kind-hearted lawyer shook his head.

"Is there no friend who can meet him there?" Mr. Mool suggested. "I have clients depending on me—cases, in which property is concerned, and reputation is at stake—or I would gladly go myself. You, with your patients, are as little at liberty as I am. Can't you think of some other friend?"

Mr. Null could think of nobody, and had nothing to propose. Of the three weak men, now brought into association by the influence of domestic calamity, he was the feeblest, beyond all doubt. Mr. Mool had knowledge of law, and could on occasion be incited to energy. Mr. Gallilee had warm affections, which, being stimulated, could at least assert themselves. Mr. Null, professionally and personally, was incapable of stepping beyond his own narrow limits, under any provocation whatever. He submitted to the force of events as a cabbage-leaf submits to the teeth of a rabbit.

After leaving the office, Carmina's medical attendant had his patient to see. Since the unfortunate alarm in the house, he had begun to feel doubtful and anxious about her again.

In the sitting-room, he found Teresa and the landlady in consultation. In her own abrupt way, the nurse made him acquainted with the nature of the conference.

"We have two worries to bother us," she said; "and the music-master is the worst of the two. There's a notion at the hospital (set agoing, I don't doubt, by the man himself), that I crushed his fingers on purpose. That's a lie! With the open cupboard door between us, how could I see him, or he see me? When I gave it a push-to, I no more knew where his hand was, than you do. If I meant anything, I meant to slap his face for prying about in my room. We've made out a writing between us, to show to the doctors. You shall have a copy, in case you're asked about it. Now for the other matter. You keep on telling me I shall fall ill myself, if I don't get a person to help me with Carmina. Make your mind easy—the person has come."

"Where is she?"

Teresa pointed to the bedroom.

"Recommended by me?" Mr. Null inquired.

"Recommended by herself. And we don't like her. That's the other worry."

Mr. Null's dignity declined to attach any importance to the "other worry." "No nurse has any business here, without my sanction! I'll send her away directly."

He pushed open the baize door. A lady was sitting by Carmina's bedside. Even in the dim light, there was no mistaking *that* face. Mr. Null recognised—Miss Minerva.

She rose, and bowed to him. He returned the bow stiffly. Nature's protecting care of fools supplies them with an instinct which distrusts ability. Mr. Null never liked Miss Minerva. At the same time, he was a little afraid of her. This was not the sort of nurse who could be ordered to retire at a moment's notice.

"I have been waiting anxiously to see you," she said—and led the way to the farther end of the room. "Carmina terrifies me," she added in a whisper. "I have been here for an hour. When I entered the room her face, poor dear, seemed to come to life again; she was able to express her joy at seeing me. Even the jealous old nurse noticed the change for the better. Why didn't it last? Look at her—oh, look at her!"

The melancholy relapse that had followed the short interval of excitement was visible to anyone now.

There was the "simulated paralysis," showing itself plainly in every part of the face. She lay still as death, looking vacantly at the foot of the bed. Mr. Null was inclined to resent the interference of a meddling woman, in the discharge of his duty. He felt Carmina's pulse, in sulky silence. Her eyes never moved; her hand showed no consciousness of his touch. Teresa opened the door, and looked in—impatiently eager to see the intruding nurse sent away. Miss Minerva invited her to return to her place at the bedside. "I only ask to occupy it," she said considerately, "when you want rest." Teresa was ready with an ungracious reply, but found no opportunity of putting it into words. Miss Minerva turned quickly to Mr. Null. "I must ask you to let me say a few words more," she continued; "I will wait for you in the next room."

Her resolute eyes rested on him with a look which said plainly, "I mean to be heard." He followed her into the sitting-room, and waited in sullen submission to hear what she had to say.

"I must not trouble you by entering into my own affairs," she began. "I will only say that I have obtained an engagement much sooner than I had anticipated, and that the convenience of my employers made it necessary for me to meet them in Paris. I owed Carmina a letter; but I had reasons for not writing until I knew whether she had, or had not, left London. With that object, I called this morning at her aunt's house. You now see me here—after what I have heard from the servants. I make no comment, and I ask for no explanations. One thing only, I *must* know. Teresa refers me to you. Is Carmina attended by any other medical man?"

Mr. Null answered stiffly, "I am in consultation with Doctor Benjulia; and I expect him to-day."

The reply startled her. "Dr. Benjulia?" she repeated.

"The greatest man we have!" Mr. Null asserted in his most positive manner.

She silently determined to wait until Doctor Benjulia arrived.

"What is the last news of Mr. Ovid?" she said to him, after an interval of consideration.

He told her the news, in the fewest words possible. Even he observed that it seemed to excite her.

"Oh, Mr. Null! who is to prepare him for what he will see in that room? Who is to tell him what he must hear of his mother?"

There was a certain familiarity in the language of this appeal, which Mr. Null felt it necessary to discourage. "The matter is left in my hands," he announced. "I shall telegraph to him at Queenstown. When he comes home, he will find my prescriptions on the table. Being a medical man himself, my treatment of the case will tell Mr. Ovid Vere everything."

The obstinate insensibility of his tone stopped her on the point of saying what Mr. Mool had said already. She, too, felt for Ovid, when she thought of the cruel brevity of a telegram. "At what date will the vessel reach Queenstown?" she asked.

"By way of making sure," said Mr. Null, "I shall telegraph in a week's time."

She troubled him with no more inquiries. He had purposely remained standing, in the expectation that she would take the hint, and go; and he now walked to the window, and looked out. She remained in her chair, thinking. In a few minutes more, there was a heavy step on the stairs. Benjulia had arrived.

He looked hard at Miss Minerva, in unconcealed surprise at finding her in the house. She rose, and made an effort to propitiate him by shaking hands. "I am very anxious," she said gently, "to hear your opinion."

"Your hand tells me that," he answered. "It's a cold hand, on a warm day. You're an excitable woman."

He looked at Mr. Null, and led the way into the bedroom.

Left by herself, Miss Minerva discovered writing materials (placed ready for Mr. Null's next prescription) on a side table. She made use of them at once to write to her employer. "A dear friend of mine is seriously ill, and in urgent need of all that my devotion can do for her. If you are willing to release me from my duties for a short time, your sympathy and indulgence will not be thrown away on an ungrateful woman. If you cannot do me this favour, I ask your pardon for putting you to inconvenience, and leave some other person, whose mind is at ease, to occupy the place which I am for the present unfit to fill." Having completed her letter in those terms, she waited Benjulia's return.

There was sadness in her face, but no agitation, as she looked patiently towards the bedroom door. At last—in her inmost heart, she knew it—the victory over herself was a victory won. Carmina could trust her now; and Ovid himself should see it!

Mr. Null returned to the sitting-room alone. Doctor Benjulia had no time to spare: he had left the bedroom by the other door.

"I may say (as you seem anxious) that my colleague approves of a proposal, on my part, to slightly modify the last prescription. We recognise the new symptoms, without feeling alarm." Having issued this bulletin, Mr. Null sat down to make his feeble treatment of his patient feebler still.

When he looked up again, the room was empty. Had she left the house? No: her travelling hat and her gloves were on the other table. Had she boldly confronted Teresa on her own ground?

He took his modified prescription into the bedroom. There she was, and there sat the implacable nurse, already persuaded into listening to her! What conceivable subject could there be, which offered two such women neutral ground to meet on? Mr. Null left the house without the faintest suspicion that Carmina might be the subject.

"May I try to rouse her?"

Teresa answered by silently resigning her place at the bedside. Miss Minerva touched Carmina's hand, and spoke. "Have you heard the good news, dear? Ovid is coming back in little more than a week."

Carmina looked—reluctantly looked—at her friend, and said, with an effort, "I am glad."

"You will be better," Miss Minerva continued, "the moment you see him."

Her face became faintly animated. "I shall be able to say good-bye," she answered.

"Not good-bye, darling. He is returning to you after a long journey."

"I am going, Frances, on a longer journey still." She closed her eyes, too weary or too indifferent to say more.

Miss Minerva drew back, struggling against the tears that fell fast over her face. The jealous old nurse quietly moved nearer to her, and kissed her hand. "I've been a brute and a fool," said Teresa; "you're almost as fond of her as I am."

A week later, Miss Minerva left London, to wait for Ovid at Queenstown.

CHAPTER LVII.

Mr. Mool was in attendance at Fairfield Gardens, when his old friend arrived from Scotland, to tell him what the cautiously expressed message in the telegram really meant.

But one idea seemed to be impressed on Mr. Gallilee's mind—the idea of reconciliation. He insisted on seeing his wife. It was in vain to tell him that she was utterly incapable of reciprocating or even of understanding his wishes. Absolute resistance was the one alternative left—and it was followed by distressing results. The kind-hearted old man burst into a fit of crying, which even shook the resolution of the doctors. One of them went upstairs to warn the nurses. The other said, "Let him see her."

The instant he showed himself in the room, Mrs. Gallilee recognised him with a shriek of fury. The nurses held her back—while Mr. Mool dragged him out again, and shut the door. The object of the doctors had been gained. His own eyes had convinced him of the terrible necessity of placing his wife under restraint. She was removed to a private asylum.

Maria and Zo had been left in Scotland—as perfectly happy as girls could be, in the society of their cousins, and under the affectionate care of their aunt. Mr. Gallilee remained in London; but he was not left alone in the deserted house. The good lawyer had a spare room at his disposal; and Mrs. Mool and her daughters received him with true sympathy. Coming events helped to steady his mind. He was comforted in the anticipation of Ovid's return, and interested in hearing of the generous motive which had led Miss Minerva to meet his stepson.

"I never agreed with the others when they used to abuse our governess," he said. "She might have been quick-tempered, and she might have been ugly—I suppose I saw her in some other light myself." He had truly seen her under another light. In his simple affectionate nature, there had been instinctive recognition of that great heart.

He was allowed to see Carmina, in the hope that pleasant associations connected with him might have a favourable influence. She smiled faintly, and gave him her hand when she saw him at the bedside—but that was all.

Too deeply distressed to ask to see her again, he made his inquiries for the future at the door. Day after day, the answer was always the same.

Before she left London, Miss Minerva had taken it on herself to engage the vacant rooms, on the ground floor of the lodging-house, for Ovid. She knew his heart, as she knew her own heart. Once under the same roof with Carmina, he would leave it no more—until life gave her back to him, or death took her away. Hearing of what had been done, Mr. Gallilee removed to Ovid's rooms the writing-desk and the books, the favourite music and the faded flowers, left by Carmina at Fairfield Gardens. "Anything that belongs to her," he thought, "will surely be welcome to the poor fellow when he comes back."

On one afternoon—never afterwards to be forgotten—he had only begun to make his daily inquiry, when the door on the ground floor was opened, and Miss Minerva beckoned to him.

Her face daunted Mr. Gallilee: he asked in a whisper, if Ovid had returned.

She pointed upwards, and answered, "He is with her now."

"How did he bear it?"

"We don't know; we were afraid to follow him into the room."

She turned towards the window as she spoke. Teresa was sitting there—vacantly looking out. Mr. Gallilee spoke to her kindly: she made no answer; she never even moved. "Worn out!" Miss Minerva whispered to him. "When she thinks of Carmina now, she thinks without hope."

He shuddered. The expression of his own fear was in those words—and he shrank from it. Miss Minerva took his hand, and led him to a chair. "Ovid will know best," she reminded him; "let us wait for what Ovid will say."

"Did you meet him on board the vessel?" Mr. Gallilee asked.

"Yes."

"How did he look?"

"So well and so strong that you would hardly have known him again—till he asked about Carmina. Then he turned pale. I knew that I must tell him the truth—but I was afraid to take it entirely on myself. Something Mr. Null said to me, before I left London, suggested that I might help Ovid to understand me if I took the prescriptions to Queenstown. I had not noticed that they were signed by Doctor Benjulia, as well as by Mr. Null. Don't ask me what effect the discovery had on him! I bore it at the time—I can't speak of it now."

"You good creature! you dear good creature! Forgive me if I have distressed you; I didn't meant it."

"You have not distressed me. Is there anything else I can tell you?"

Mr. Gallilee hesitated. "There is one thing more," he said. "It isn't about Carmina this time—"

He hesitated again. Miss Minerva understood. "Yes," she answered; "I spoke to Ovid of his mother. In mercy to himself and to me, he would hear no details. 'I know enough,' he said, 'if I know that she is the person to blame. I was prepared to hear it. My mother's silence could only be accounted for in one way, when I had read Zo's letter.'— Don't you know, Mr. Gallilee, that the child wrote to Ovid?"

The surprise and delight of Zo's fond old father, when he heard the story of the letter, forced a smile from Miss Minerva, even at that time of doubt and sorrow. He declared that he would have returned to his daughter by the mail train of that night, but for two considerations. He must see his stepson before he went back to Scotland; and he must search all the toy-shops in London for the most magnificent present that could be offered to a young person of ten years old. "Tell Ovid, with my love, I'll call again to-morrow," he said, looking at his watch. "I have just time to write to Zo by to-day's post." He went to his club, for the first time since he had returned to London. Miss Minerva thought of bygone days, and wondered if he would enjoy his champagne.

A little later Mr. Null called—anxious to know if Ovid had arrived.

Other women, in the position of Miss Minerva and Teresa, might have hesitated to keep the patient's room closed to the doctor. These two were resolved. They refused to disturb Ovid, even by sending up a message. Mr. Null took offence. "Understand, both of you," he said, "when I call to-morrow morning, I shall insist on going upstairs—and if I find this incivility repeated, I shall throw up the case." He left the room, triumphing in his fool's paradise of aggressive self-conceit.

They waited for some time longer—and still no message reached them from upstairs. "We may be wrong in staying here," Miss Minerva suggested; "he may want to be alone when he leaves her—let us go."

She rose to return to the house of her new employers. They respected her, and felt for her: while Carmina's illness continued, she had the entire disposal of her time. The nurse accompanied her to the door; resigned to take refuge in the landlady's room. "I'm afraid to be by myself," Teresa said. "Even that woman's chatter is better for me than my own thoughts."

Before parting for the night they waited in the hall, looking towards the stairs, and listening anxiously. Not a sound disturbed the melancholy silence.

CHAPTER LVIII.

Among many vain hopes, one hope had been realised: they had met again.

In the darkened room, her weary eyes could hardly have seen the betrayal of what he suffered—even if she had looked up in his face. She was content to rest her head on his breast, and to feel his arm round her. "I am glad, dear," she said, "to have lived long enough for this."

Those were her first words—after the first kiss. She had trembled and sighed, when he ran to her and bent over her: it was the one expression left of all her joy and all her love. But it passed away as other lesser agitations had passed away. One last reserve of energy obeyed the gentle persuasion of love. Silent towards all other friends, she was able to speak to Ovid.

"You used to breathe so lightly," she said. "How is it that I hear you now. Oh, Ovid, don't cry! I couldn't bear that."

He answered her quietly. "Don't be afraid, darling; I won't distress you."

"And you will let me say, what I want to say?"

"Oh, yes!"

This satisfied her. "I may rest a little now," she said.

He too was silent; held down by the heavy hand of despair.

The time had been, in the days of his failing health, when the solemn shadows of evening falling over the fields—the soaring song of the lark in the bright heights of the midday sky—the dear lost remembrances that the divine touch of music finds again—brought tears into his eyes. They were dry eyes now! Those once tremulous nerves had gathered steady strength, on the broad prairies and in the roving life. Could trembling sorrow, seeking its way to the sources of tears, overbear the robust vitality that rioted in his blood, whether she lived or whether she died? In those deep breathings that had alarmed her, she had indeed heard the struggle of grief, vainly urging its way to expression against the masterful health and strength that set moral weakness at defiance. Nature had remade this man—and Nature never pities.

It was an effort to her to collect her thoughts—but she did collect them. She was able to tell him what was in her mind.

"Do you think, Ovid, your mother will care much what becomes of me, when I die?"

He started at those dreadful words—so softly, so patiently spoken. "You will live," he said. "My Carmina, what am I here for but to bring you back to life?"

She made no attempt to dispute with him. Quietly, persistently, she returned to the thought that was in her.

"Say that I forgive your mother, Ovid—and that I only ask one thing in return. I ask her to leave me to you, when the end has come. My dear, there is a feeling in me that I can't get over. Don't let me be buried in a great place all crowded with the dead! I once saw a picture—it was at home in Italy, I think—an English picture of a quiet little churchyard in the country. The shadows of the trees rested on the lonely graves. And some great poet had written[1]—oh, such beautiful words about it. *The redbreast loves to build and warble there, And little footsteps lightly print the ground.*

---

1   *some great poet had written*: These rather bland lines of poetry are intriguingly problematic. The source of the first remains unidentified. The second of the two is employed by James Beattie in his "'The Battle of the Pigmies and Cranes,' from the Pygmæo-gerano-machia of Addison." The Joseph Addison poem mentioned in Beattie's title—"ΠΨΓΜΑΙΟ ΓΕΡΑΝΟΜΑΧΙΑ, sive, prælium inter Pygmæos et Grues commissum"—is a Latin piece written in 1698. Like Beattie, William Warburton also translated Addison's poem, titling it "ΠΨΓΜΑΙΟ ΓΕΡΑΝΟΜΑΧΙΑ, or, the Battle of the Cranes and Pigmies. From the Latin of Mr. Addison. In Imitation of Milton's Style," but the 1724 Warburton translation employs the line "Thick patters with his little Heels the Ground" instead of "Or little footsteps lightly print the ground." Evidently, then, Addison created a poem in Latin, and Beattie—as well as Warburton and perhaps others—translated the Addison, Warburton attempting to imitate Milton as he did so. By the time Carmina sees these lines attached to a picture, though, their history is obscure, and they have become what we might consider today to be fairly generic "calendar" or "post-card" expressions of sentimentality.

Promise, Ovid, you will take me to some place, far from crowds and noise—where children may gather the flowers on my grave."

He promised—and she thanked him, and rested again.

"There was something else," she said, when the interval had passed. "My head is so sleepy. I wonder whether I can think of it?"

After a while, she did think of it.

"I want to make you a little farewell present. Will you undo my gold chain? Don't cry, Ovid! oh, don't cry!"

He obeyed her. The gold chain held the two lockets—the treasured portraits of her father and her mother. "Wear them for my sake," she murmured. "Lift me up; I want to put them round your neck myself." She tried, vainly tried, to clasp the chain. Her head fell back on his breast. "Too sleepy," she said; "always too sleepy now! Say you love me, Ovid."

He said it.

"Kiss me, dear."

He kissed her.

"Now lay me down on the pillow. I'm not eighteen yet—and I feel as old as eighty! Rest; all I want is rest." Looking at him fondly, her eyes closed little by little—then softly opened again. "Don't wait in this dull room, darling; I will send for you, if I wake."

It was the only wish of hers that he disobeyed. From time to time, his fingers touched her pulse, and felt its feeble beat. From time to time, he stooped and let the faint coming and going of her breath flutter on his cheek. The twilight fell, and darkness began to gather over the room. Still, he kept his place by her, like a man entranced.

CHAPTER LIX.

The first trivial sound that broke the spell, was the sound of a match struck in the next room.

He rose, and groped his way to the door. Teresa had ventured upstairs, and had kindled a light. Some momentary doubt of him kept the nurse silent when he looked at her. He stammered, and stared about him confusedly, when he spoke.

"Where—where—?" He seemed to have lost his hold on his thoughts—he gave it up, and tried again. "I want to be alone," he said; recovering, for the moment, some power of expressing himself.

Teresa's first fear of him vanished. She took him by the hand like a child, and led him downstairs to his rooms. He stood silently watching her, while she lit the candles.

"When Carmina sleeps now," he asked, "does it last long?"

"Often for hours together," the nurse answered.

He said no more; he seemed to have forgotten that there was another person in the room.

She found courage in her pity for him. "Try to pray," she said, and left him.

He fell on his knees; but still the words failed him. He tried to quiet his mind by holy thoughts. No! The dumb agony in him was powerless to find relief. Only the shadows of thoughts crossed his mind; his eyes ached with a burning heat. He began to be afraid of himself. The active habits of the life that he had left, drove him out, with the instincts of an animal, into space and air. Neither knowing nor caring in what direction he turned his steps, he walked on at the top of his speed. On and on, till the crowded houses began to grow more rare—till there were gaps of open ground, on either side of him—till the moon rose behind a plantation of trees, and bathed in its melancholy light a lonely high road. He followed the road till he was tired of it, and turned aside into a winding lane. The lights and shadows, alternating with each other, soothed and pleased him. He had got the relief in exercise that had been denied him while he was in repose. He could think again; he could feel the resolution stirring in him to save that dear one, or to die with her. Now at last, he was man enough to face the terrible necessity that confronted him, and fight the battle of Art and Love against Death. He stopped, and looked round; eager to return, and be ready for her waking. In that solitary place, there was no hope of finding a person to direct him. He turned, to go back to the high road.

At that same moment, he became conscious of the odour of tobacco wafted towards him on the calm night air. Some one was smoking in the lane.

He retraced his steps, until he reached a gate—with a barren field behind it. There was the man, whose tobacco smoke he had smelt, leaning on the gate, with his pipe in his mouth.

The moonlight fell full on Ovid's face, as he approached to ask his way. The man suddenly stood up—stared at him—and said, "Hullo! is it you or your ghost?"

His face was in shadow, but his voice answered for him. The man was Benjulia.

"Have you come to see me?" he asked.

"No."

"Won't you shake hands?"

"No."

"What's wrong?"

Ovid waited to answer until he had steadied his temper.

"I have seen Carmina," he said.

Benjulia went on with his smoking. "An interesting case, isn't it?" he remarked.

"You were called into consultation by Mr. Null," Ovid continued; "and you approved of his ignorant treatment—you, who knew better."

"I should think I did!" Benjulia rejoined.

"You deliberately encouraged an incompetent man; you let that poor girl go on from bad to worse—for some vile end of your own."

Benjulia goodnaturedly corrected him. "No, no. For an excellent end—for knowledge."

"If I fail to remedy the mischief, which is your doing, and yours alone—"

Benjulia took his pipe out of his mouth. "How do you mean to cure her?" he eagerly interposed. "Have you got a new idea?"

"If I fail," Ovid repeated, "her death lies at your door. You merciless villain—as certainly as that moon is now shining over us, your life shall answer for hers."

Astonishment—immeasurable astonishment—sealed Benjulia's lips. He looked down the lane when Ovid left him, completely stupefied. The one imaginable way of accounting for such language as he had heard—spoken by a competent member of his own profession!—presented the old familiar alternative. "Drunk or mad?" he wondered while he lit his pipe again. Walking back to the house, his old distrust of Ovid troubled him once more. He decided to call at Teresa's lodgings in a day or two, and ascertain from the landlady (and the chemist) how Carmina was being cured.

Returning to the high road, Ovid was passed by a tradesman, driving his cart towards London. The man civilly offered to take him as far as the nearest outlying cabstand.

Neither the landlady nor Teresa had gone to their beds when he returned. Their account of Carmina, during his absence, contained nothing to alarm him. He bade them goodnight—eager to be left alone in his room.

In the house and out of the house, there was now the perfect silence that helps a man to think. His mind was clear; his memory answered, when he called on it to review that part of his own medical practice which might help him, by experience, in his present need. But he shrank—with Carmina's life in his hands—from trusting wholly to himself. A higher authority than his was waiting to be consulted. He took from his portmanteau the manuscript presented to him by the poor wretch, whose last hours he had soothed in the garret at Montreal.

The work opened with a declaration which gave it a special value, in Ovid's estimation.

"If this imperfect record of experience is ever read by other eyes than mine, I wish to make one plain statement at the outset. The information which is presented in these pages is wholly derived from the results of bedside practice; pursued under miserable obstacles and interruptions, and spread over a period of many years. Whatever faults and failings I may have been guilty of as a man, I am innocent, in my professional capacity, of ever having perpetrated the useless and detestable cruelties which go by the name of Vivisection. Without entering into any of the disputes on either side, which this practice has provoked, I declare my conviction that no asserted usefulness in the end, can justify deliberate cruelty in the means. The man who seriously maintains that any pursuit in which he can engage is independent of moral restraint, is a man in a state of revolt against God. I refuse to hear him in his own defense, on that ground."

Ovid turned next to the section of the work which was entitled "Brain Disease." The writer introduced his observations in these prefatory words:

"A celebrated physiologist,[1] plainly avowing the ignorance of doctors in the matter of the brain and its diseases, and alluding to appearances presented by post-mortem examination, concludes his confession thus: 'We cannot even be sure whether many of the changes discovered are the cause or the result of the disease, or whether the two are the conjoint results of a common cause.'

"So this man writes, after experience in Vivisection.

"Let my different experience be heard next. Not knowing into what hands this manuscript may fall, or what unexpected opportunities of usefulness it may encounter after my death, I purposely abstain from using technical language in the statement which I have now to make.

"In medical investigations, as in all other forms of human inquiry, the result in view is not infrequently obtained by indirect and unexpected means. What I have to say here on the subject of brain disease, was first suggested by experience of two cases, which seemed in the last degree unlikely to help me. They were both cases of young women; each one having been hysterically affected by a serious moral shock; terminating, after a longer or shorter interval, in simulated paralysis. One of these cases I treated successfully. While I was still in attendance on the other, (pursuing the same course of treatment which events had already proved to be right), a fatal accident terminated my patient's life, and rendered a post-mortem examination necessary. From those starting points, I arrived—by devious ways which I am now to relate—at deductions and discoveries that threw a new light on the nature and treatment of brain disease."

Hour by hour, Ovid studied the pages that followed, until his mind and the mind of the writer were one. He then returned to certain preliminary allusions to the medical treatment of the two girls—inexpressibly precious to him, in Carmina's present interests. The dawn of day found him prepared at all points, and only waiting until the lapse of the next few hours placed the means of action in his hands.

But there was one anxiety still to be relieved, before he lay down to rest.

He took off his shoes, and stole upstairs to Carmina's door. The faithful Teresa was astir, earnestly persuading her to take some nourishment. The little that he could hear of her voice, as she answered, made his heart ache—it was so faint and so low. Still she could speak; and still there was

---

1   *A celebrated physiologist:* The American doctor's manuscript quotes Sir David Ferrier. See Note 13, p. 42.

the old saying to remember, which has comforted so many and deceived so many: While there's life, there's hope.

End of May 1883 *Belgravia* Serial Number

CHAPTER LX.

After a brief interview with his step-son, Mr. Gallilee returned to his daughters in Scotland.

Touched by his fatherly interest in Carmina, Ovid engaged to keep him informed of her progress towards recovery. If the anticipation of saving her proved to be the sad delusion of love and hope, silence would signify what no words could say.

In ten days' time, there was a happy end to suspense. The slow process of recovery might extend perhaps to the end of the year. But, if no accident happened, Ovid had the best reasons for believing that Carmina's life was safe.

Freed from the terrible anxieties that had oppressed him, he was able to write again, a few days later, in a cheerful tone, and to occupy his pen at Mr. Gallilee's express request, with such an apparently trifling subject as the conduct of Mr. Null.

"Your old medical adviser was quite right in informing you that I had relieved him from any further attendance on Carmina. But his lively imagination (or perhaps I ought to say, his sense of his own consequence) has misled you when he also declares that I purposely insulted him. I took the greatest pains not to wound his self-esteem. He left me in anger, nevertheless.

"A day or two afterwards, I received a note from him; addressing me as 'Sir,' and asking ironically if I had any objection to his looking at the copies of my prescriptions in the chemist's book. Though he was old enough to be my father (he remarked) it seemed that experience counted for nothing; he had still something to learn from his junior, in the treatment of disease—and so on.

"At that miserable time of doubt and anxiety, I could only send a verbal reply, leaving him to do what he liked. Before I tell you of the use that he made of his liberty of action, I must confess something relating to the prescriptions themselves. Don't be afraid of long and learned words, and don't suppose that I am occupying your attention in this way, without a serious reason for it which you will presently understand.

"A note in the manuscript—to my study of which, I owe, under God, the preservation of Carmina's life—warned me that chemists, in the writer's country, had either refused to make up certain prescriptions given in the work, or had taken the liberty of altering the new quantities and combinations of some of the drugs prescribed.

"Precisely the same thing happened here, in the case of the first chemist to whom I sent. He refused to make up the medicine, unless I provided him with a signed statement taking the whole responsibility on myself.

"Having ascertained the exact nature of his objection, I dismissed him without his guarantee, and employed another chemist; taking care (in the interests of my time and my temper) to write my more important prescriptions under reserve. That is to say, I followed the conventional rules, as to quantities and combinations, and made the necessary additions or changes from my own private stores when the medicine was sent home.

"Poor foolish Mr. Null, finding nothing to astonish him in my course of medicine—as represented by the chemist—appears by his own confession, to have copied the prescriptions with a malicious object in view. 'I have sent them, (he informs me, in a second letter) to Doctor Benjulia; in order that he too may learn something in his profession from the master who has dispensed with our services.' This new effort of irony means that I stand self-condemned of vanity, in presuming to rely on my own commonplace resources—represented by the deceitful evidence of the chemist's book!

"But I am grateful to Mr. Null, notwithstanding: he has done me a service, in meaning to do me an injury.

"My imperfect prescriptions have quieted the mind of the man to whom he sent them. This wretch's distrust has long since falsely suspected me of some professional rivalry pursued in secret; the feeling showed itself again, when I met with him by accident on the night of my return to London. Since Mr. Null has communicated with him, the landlady is no longer insulted by his visits, and offended by his questions—all relating to the course of treatment which I was pursuing upstairs.

"You now understand why I have ventured to trouble you on a purely professional topic. To turn to matters of more interest—our dear Carmina is well enough to remember you, and to send her love to you and the girls. But even this little effort is followed by fatigue.

"I don't mean only fatigue of body: that is now a question of time and care. I mean fatigue of mind—expressing itself by defect of memory.

"On the morning when the first positive change for the better appeared, I was at her bedside when she woke. She looked at me in amazement. 'Why didn't you warn me of your sudden return?' she asked, 'I have only written to you to-day—to your bankers at Quebec! What does it mean?'

"I did my best to soothe her, and succeeded. There is a complete lapse in her memory—I am only too sure of it! She has no recollection of anything that has happened since she wrote her last letter to me—a letter which must have been lost (perhaps intercepted?), or I should have received it before I left Quebec. This forgetfulness of the dreadful trials through which my poor darling has passed, is, in itself, a circumstance which we must all rejoice over for her sake. But I am discouraged by it, at the same time; fearing it may indicate some more serious injury than I have yet discovered.

"Miss Minerva—what should I do without the help and sympathy of that best of true women?—Miss Minerva has cautiously tested her memory in other directions, with encouraging results, so far. But I shall not feel easy until I have tried further experiments, by means of some person who does not exercise a powerful influence over her, and whose memory is naturally occupied with what we older people call trifles.

"When you all leave Scotland next month, bring Zo here with you. My dear little correspondent is just the sort of quaint child I want for the purpose. Kiss her for me till she is out of breath—and say that is what I mean to do when we meet."

The return to London took place in the last week in October.

Lord and Lady Northlake went to their town residence, taking Maria and Zo with them. There were associations connected with Fairfield Gardens, which made the prospect of living there—without even the society of his children—unendurable to Mr. Gallilee. Ovid's house, still waiting the return of its master, was open to his step-father. The poor man was only too glad (in his own simple language) "to keep the nest warm for his son."

The latest inquiries made at the asylum were hopefully answered. Thus far, the measures taken to restore Mrs. Gallilee to herself had succeeded beyond expectation. But one unfavourable symptom remained. She was habitually silent. When she did speak, her mind seemed to be occupied with scientific subjects: she never mentioned her husband, or any other member of the family. Time and attention would remove this drawback. In two or three months more perhaps, if all went well, she might return to her family and her friends, as sane a woman as ever.

Calling at Fairfield Gardens for any letters that might be waiting there, Mr. Gallilee received a circular in lithographed writing; accompanied by a roll of thick white paper. The signature revealed the familiar name of Mr. Le Frank.

The circular set forth that the writer had won renown and a moderate income, as pianist and teacher of music. "A terrible accident, ladies and gentlemen, has injured my right hand, and has rendered amputation of two of my fingers necessary. Deprived for life of my professional resources, I have but one means of subsistence left—viz:[1]—collecting subscriptions for a song of my own composition. N.B.[2]—The mutilated musician leaves the question of terms in the hands of the art-loving public, and will do himself the honour of calling to-morrow."

---

1 *viz.*: viz. is an abbreviation of videlicet, a Latin word for "that is," "namely," or "it is easy to see."

2 *N.B.*: N.B. is an abbreviation of "nota bene," a Latin phrase meaning "note well."

Good-natured Mr. Gallilee left a sovereign to be given to the victim of circumstances—and then set forth for Lord Northlake's house. He and Ovid had arranged that Zo was to be taken to see Carmina that day.

On his way through the streets, he was met by Mr. Mool. The lawyer looked at the song under his friend's arm. "What's that you're taking such care of?" he asked. "It looks like music. A new piece for the young ladies—eh?"

Mr. Gallilee explained. Mr. Mool struck his stick on the pavement, as the nearest available means of expressing indignation.

"Never let another farthing of your money get into that rascal's pocket! It's no merit of his that the poor old Italian nurse has not made her appearance in the police reports."

With this preface, Mr. Mool related the circumstances under which Mr. Le Frank had met with his accident. "His first proceeding when they discharged him from the hospital," continued the lawyer, "was to summon Teresa before a magistrate. Fortunately she showed the summons to me. I appeared for her, provided with a plan of the rooms which spoke for itself; and I put two questions to the complainant. What business had he in another person's room? and why was his hand in that other person's cupboard? The reporter kindly left the case unrecorded; and when the fellow ended by threatening the poor woman outside the court, we bound him over to keep the peace.[1] I have my eye on him—and I'll catch him yet, under the Vagrant Act!"[2]

CHAPTER LXI.

Aided by time, care, and skill, Carmina had gained strength enough to pass some hours of the day in the sitting-room; reclining in an invalid-chair invented for her by Ovid. The welcome sight of Zo—brightened and developed by happy autumn days passed in Scotland—brought a deep flush to her face, and quickened the pulse which Ovid was touching, under pretence of holding her hand. These signs of excessive nervous sensibility warned him to limit the child's visit to a short space of time. Neither Miss Minerva nor Teresa were in the room: Carmina could have Zo all to herself.

---

1   *We bound him over to keep the peace*: By binding Mr. Le Frank over, Mr. Mool has required him to put up a sum of money at a local court, a sum he will forfeit if he fails to keep the peace.

2   *under the Vagrant Act*: There were several legislative attempts to deal with the problem of vagrancy and homelessness, but the Vagrant Act that Mool refers to here may be the Poor Law Amendment Act of 1834, a bitterly controversial attempt by William IV to limit relief to the poor by establishing workhouses for the able-bodied unfortunate.

"Now, my dear," she said, in a kiss, "tell me about Scotland."

"Scotland," Zo answered with dignity, "belongs to uncle Northlake. He pays for everything; and I'm Missus."

"It's true," said Mr. Gallilee, bursting with pride. "My lord says it's no use having a will of your own where Zo is. When he introduces her to anybody on the estate, he says, 'Here's the Missus.'"

Mr. Gallilee's youngest daughter listened critically to the parental testimony. "You see he knows," she said to Ovid. "There's nothing to laugh at."

Carmina tried another question. "Did you think of me, dear, when you were far away?"

"Think of you?" Zo repeated. "You're to sleep in my bedroom when we go back to Scotland—and I'm to be out of bed, and one of 'em, when you eat your first Scotch dinner.[1] Shall I tell you what you'll see on the table? You'll see a big brown steaming bag in a dish—and you'll see me slit it with a knife—and the bag's fat inside will tumble out, all smoking hot and stinking. That's a Scotch dinner. Oh!" she cried, losing her dignity in the sudden interest of a new idea, "oh, Carmina, do you remember the Italian boy, and his song?"

Here was one of those tests of her memory for trifles, applied with a child's happy abruptness, for which Ovid had been waiting. He listened eagerly. To his unutterable relief, Carmina laughed.

"Of course I remember it!" she said. "Who could forget the boy who sings and grins and says *Gimmee haypenny?*"

"That's it!" cried Zo. "The boy's song was a good one in its way. I've learnt a better in Scotland. You've heard of Donald, haven't you?"

"No."

Zo turned indignantly to her father. "Why didn't you tell her of Donald?"

Mr. Gallilee humbly admitted that he was in fault. Carmina asked who Donald was, and what he was like. Zo unconsciously tested her memory for the second time.

"You know that day," she said, "when Joseph had an errand at the grocer's and I went along with him, and Miss Minerva said I was a vulgar child?"

Carmina's memory recalled this new trifle, without an effort. "I know," she answered; "you told me Joseph and the grocer weighed you in the great scales."

Zo delighted Ovid by trying her again. "When they put me into the scales, Carmina, what did I weigh?"

"Nearly four stone, dear."

---

1   *That's a Scotch dinner.* Zoe has just described haggis, a mixture of the minced heart, lungs, and liver of a sheep or calf, all boiled in the stomach of the animal.

"Quite four stone. Donald weighs fourteen.[1] What do you think of that?"

Mr. Gallilee once more offered his testimony. "The biggest Piper on my lord's estate,"[2] he began, "comes of a Highland family, and was removed to the Lowlands by my lord's father. A great player—"

"And *my* friend," Zo explained, stopping her father in full career. "He takes snuff out of a cow's horn. He shovels it up his fat nose with a spoon, like this. His nose wags. He says, 'Try my sneeshin.' Sneeshin's Scotch for snuff. He boos till he's nearly double when uncle Northlake speaks to him. Boos is Scotch for bows. He skirls on the pipes—skirls means screeches. When you first hear him, he'll make your stomach ache. You'll get used to that—and you'll find you like him. He wears a purse and a petticoat; he never had a pair of trousers on in his life; there's no pride about him. Say you're my friend and he'll let you smack his legs—"

Here, Ovid was obliged to bring the biography of Donald to a close. Carmina's enjoyment of Zo was becoming too keen for her strength; her bursts of laughter grew louder and louder—the wholesome limit of excitement was being rapidly passed. "Tell us about your cousins," he said, by way of effecting a diversion.

"The big ones?" Zo asked.

"No; the little ones, like you."

"Nice girls—they play at everything I tell 'em. Jolly boys—when they knock a girl down, they pick her up again, and clean her."

Carmina was once more in danger of passing the limit. Ovid made another attempt to effect a diversion. Singing would be comparatively harmless in its effect—as he rashly supposed. "What's that song you learnt in Scotland?" he asked.

"It's Donald's song," Zo replied. "*He* taught me."

At the sound of Donald's dreadful name, Ovid looked at his watch, and said there was no time for the song. Mr. Gallilee suddenly and seriously sided with his step-son. "How she got among the men after dinner," he said, "nobody knows. Lady Northlake has forbidden Donald to teach her any more songs; and I have requested him, as a favour to me, not to let her smack his legs. Come, my dear, it's time we were home again."

Well intended by both gentlemen—but too late. Zo was ready for the performance; her hat was cocked on one side; her plump little arms were set akimbo; her round eyes opened and closed facetiously in winks worthy of a low comedian. "I'm Donald," she announced: and burst out with the song:[3] "*We're gayly yet, we're gayly yet; We're not very fou, but we're gayly*

---

1   *Nearly four stone ... Donald weighs fourteen*: A stone being fourteen pounds, Zoe weighs fifty-six pounds, Donald nearly two-hundred.

2   *The biggest Piper on my lord's estate*: Donald plays the bagpipes.

3   *burst out with song*: Zoe sings a traditional Scottish drinking song here.

yet: Then sit ye awhile, and tipple a bit; For we're not very fou, but we're gayly yet." She snatched up Carmina's medicine glass, and waved it over her head with a Bacchanalian screech. "Fill a brimmer, Tammie! Here's to Redshanks!"

"And pray who is Redshanks?" asked a lady, standing in the doorway. Zo turned round—and instantly collapsed. A terrible figure, associated with lessons and punishments, stood before her. The convivial friend of Donald, the established Missus of Lord Northlake, disappeared—and a polite pupil took their place. "If you please, Miss Minerva, Redshanks is nickname for a Highlander." Who would have recognised the singer of "We're gayly yet," in the subdued young person who made that reply?

The door opened again. Another disastrous intrusion? Yes, another! Teresa appeared this time—caught Zo up in her arms—and gave the child a kiss that was heard all over the room. "Ah, mia Giocosa!" cried the old nurse—too happy to speak in any language but her own. "What does that mean?" Zo asked, settling her ruffled petticoats. "It means," said Teresa, who prided herself on her English, "Ah, my Jolly." This to a young lady who could slit a haggis! This to the only person in Scotland, privileged to smack Donald's legs! Zo turned to her father, and recovered her dignity. Maria herself could hardly have spoken with more severe propriety. "I wish to go home," said Zo.

Ovid had only to look at Carmina, and to see the necessity of immediate compliance with his little sister's wishes. No more laughing, no more excitement, for that day. He led Zo out himself, and resigned her to her father at the door of his rooms on the ground floor.

Cheered already by having got away from Miss Minerva and the nurse, Zo desired to know who lived downstairs; and, hearing that these were Ovid's rooms, insisted on seeing them. The three went in together.

Ovid drew Mr. Gallilee into a corner. "I'm easier about Carmina now," he said. "The failure of her memory doesn't extend backwards. It begi. s with the shock to her brain, on the day when Teresa removed her to this house—and it will end, I feel confident, with the end of her illness."

Mr. Gallilee's attention suddenly wandered. "Zo!" he called out, "don't touch your brother's papers."

The one object that had excited the child's curiosity was the writing-table. Dozens of sheets of paper were scattered over it, covered with writing, blotted and interlined. Some of these leaves had overflowed the table, and found a resting-place on the floor. Zo was amusing herself by picking them up. "Well!" she said, handing them obediently to Ovid, "I've had many a rap on the knuckles for writing not half as bad as yours."

Hearing his daughter's remark, Mr. Gallilee became interested in looking at the fragments of manuscript. "What an awful mess!" he exclaimed. "May I try if I can read a bit?" Ovid smiled. "Try by all means;

you will make one useful discovery at least—you will see that the most patient men on the face of the civilised earth are Printers!"[1]

Mr. Gallilee tried a page—and gave it up before he turned giddy. "Is it fair to ask what this is?"

"Something easy to feel, and hard to express," Ovid answered. "These ill-written lines are my offering of gratitude to the memory of an unknown and unhappy man."

"The man you told me of, who died at Montreal?"

"Yes."

"You never mentioned his name."

"His last wishes forbade me to mention it to any living creature. God knows there were pitiable, most pitiable, reasons for his dying unknown! The stone over his grave only bears his initials, and the date of his death. But," said Ovid, kindling with enthusiasm, as he laid his hand on his manuscript, "the discoveries of this great physician shall benefit humanity! And my debt to him shall be acknowledged, with the admiration and the devotion that I truly feel!"

"In a book?" asked Mr. Gallilee.

"In a book that is now being printed. You will see it before the New Year."

Finding nothing to amuse her in the sitting-room, Zo had tried the bedroom next. She now returned to Ovid, dragging after her a long white staff that looked like an Alpen-stock.[2] "What's this?" she asked. "A broomstick?"

"A specimen of rare Canadian wood, my dear. Would you like to have it?"

Zo took the offer quite seriously. She looked with longing eyes at the specimen, three times as tall as herself—and shook her head. "I'm not big enough for it, yet," she said. "Look at it, papa! Benjulia's stick is nothing to this."

That name—on the child's lips—had a sound revolting to Ovid. "Don't speak of him!" he said irritably.

"Mustn't I speak of him," Zo asked, "when I want him to tickle me?"

Ovid beckoned to her father. "Take her away now," he whispered— "and never let her see that man again."

The warning was needless. The man's destiny had decreed that he and Zo were never more to meet.

---

1   *the most patient men ... are Printers!*: Collins pays homage to those who had the difficult job of deciphering his much-edited manuscripts (See Photograph 2 for assurance that Collins's compliment here was heartfelt).

2   *a long white staff that looked like an Alpenstock*: An alpenstock is a long staff used by mountain climbers.

CHAPTER LXII.

Benjulia's servants had but a dull time of it, poor souls, in the lonely house. Towards the end of December, they subscribed among themselves to buy one of those wonderful Christmas Numbers[1]—presenting year after year the same large-eyed ladies, long-legged lovers, corpulent children, snow landscapes, and gluttonous merry-makings—which have become a national institution: say, the pictorial plum puddings of the English nation.

The servants had plenty of time to enjoy their genial newspaper, before the dining-room bell disturbed them.

For some weeks past, the master had again begun to spend the whole of his time in the mysterious laboratory. On the rare occasions when he returned to the house, he was always out of temper. If the servants knew nothing else, they knew what these signs meant—the great man was harder at work than ever; and in spite of his industry, he was not getting on so well as usual.

On this particular evening, the bell rang at the customary time—and the cook (successor to the unfortunate creature with pretensions to beauty and sentiment) hastened to get the dinner ready.

The footman turned to the dresser, and took from it a little heap of newspapers; carefully counting them before he ventured to carry them upstairs. This was Doctor Benjulia's regular weekly supply of medical literature; and here, again, the mysterious man presented an incomprehensible problem to his fellow-creatures. He subscribed to every medical publication in England—and he never read one of them! The footman cut the leaves; and the master, with his forefinger to help him, ran his eye up and down the pages; apparently in search of some announcement that he never found—and, still more extraordinary, without showing the faintest sign of disappointment when he had done. Every week, he briskly shoved his unread periodicals into a huge basket, and sent them downstairs as waste paper.

The footman took up the newspapers and the dinner together—and was received with frowns and curses. He was abused for everything that he did in his own department, and for everything that the cook had done besides. "Whatever the master's working at," he announced, on returning to the kitchen, "he's farther away from hitting the right nail on the head

---

1   *Christmas Numbers*: Christmas Numbers were a common feature on the
    Victorian periodical landscape. Most weekly and monthly journals of the day
    offered their readers extra Christmas numbers in early or mid-December.
    Collins here refers to the various illustrated magazines that existed at the time
    and with which he was quite familiar, for he wrote for several of them, includ-
    ing *Belgravia*, the *Spirit of the Times*, the *Graphic, Arrowsmith's Christmas Annual*,
    and the *Illustrated London News*.

than ever. Upon my soul, I think I shall have to give warning! Let's relieve our minds. Where's the Christmas Number?"

Half an hour later, the servants were startled by a tremendous bang of the house-door which shook the whole building. The footman ran upstairs: the dining-room was empty; the master's hat was not on its peg in the hall; and the medical newspapers were scattered about in the wildest confusion. Close to the fender lay a crumpled leaf, torn out. Its position suggested that it had narrowly missed being thrown into the fire. The footman smoothed it out, and looked at it.

One side of the leaf contained a report of a lecture. This was dry reading. The footman tried the other side, and found a review of a new medical work.

This would have been dull reading too, but for an extract from a Preface, stating how the book came to be published, and what wonderful discoveries, relating to peoples' brains, it contained. There were some curious things said here—especially about a melancholy deathbed at a place called Montreal—which made the Preface almost as interesting as a story. But what was there in this to hurry the master out of the house, as if the devil had been at his heels?

Doctor Benjulia's nearest neighbour was a small farmer named Gregg. He was taking a nap that evening, when his wife bounced into the room, and said, "Here's the big doctor gone mad!" And there he was truly, at Mrs. Gregg's heels, clamouring to have the horse put to in the gig,[1] and to be driven to London instantly. He said, "Pay yourself what you please"—and opened his pocket-book, full of bank-notes. Mr. Gregg said, "It seems, sir, this is a matter of life or death." Whereupon he looked at Mr. Gregg—and considered a little—and, becoming quiet on a sudden, answered, "Yes, it is."

On the road to London, he never once spoke—except to himself—and then only from time to time.

It seemed, judging by what fell from him now and then, that he was troubled about a man and a letter. He had suspected the man all along; but he had nevertheless given him the letter—and now it had ended in the letter turning out badly for Doctor Benjulia himself. Where he went to in London, it was not possible to say. Mr. Gregg's horse was not fast enough for him. As soon as he could find one, he took a cab.

The shopman of Mr. Barrable,[2] the famous publisher of medical works, had just put up the shutters, and was going downstairs to his tea, when he heard a knocking at the shop door. The person proved to be a very tall man, in a violent hurry to buy Mr. Ovid Vere's new book. He said, by way

---

1   *have the horse put to in the gig*: A gig is a modest, one-horse, two-wheeled carriage.

2   *Mr. Barrable, the famous publisher of medical works*: Barrable is a fictional publisher.

of apology, that he was in that line himself, and that his name was Benjulia. The shopman knew him by reputation, and sold him the book. He was in such a hurry to read it, that he actually began in the shop. It was necessary to tell him that business hours were over. Hearing this, he ran out, and told the cabman to drive as fast as possible to Pall Mall.[1]

The library waiter at Doctor Benjulia's Club found him in the library, busy with a book.

He was quite alone; the members, at that hour of the evening, being generally at dinner, or in the smoking-room. The man whose business it was to attend to the fires, went in during the night, from time to time, and always found him in the same corner. It began to get late. He finished his reading; but it seemed to make no difference. There he sat—wide awake—holding his closed book on his knee, seemingly lost in his own thoughts. This went on till it was time to close the Club. They were obliged to disturb him. He said nothing; and went slowly down into the hall, leaving his book behind him. It was an awful night, raining and sleeting— but he took no notice of the weather. When they fetched a cab, the driver refused to take him to where he lived, on such a night as that. He only said, "Very well; go to the nearest hotel."

The night porter at the hotel let in a tall gentleman, and showed him into one of the bedrooms kept ready for persons arriving late. Having no luggage, he paid the charges beforehand. About eight o'clock in the morning, he rang for the waiter—who observed that his bed had not been slept in. All he wanted for breakfast was the strongest coffee that could be made. It was not strong enough to please him when he tasted it; and he had some brandy put in. He paid, and was liberal to the waiter, and went away.

The policeman on duty, that day, whose beat included the streets at the back of Fairfield Gardens, noticed in one of them, a tall gentleman walking backwards and forwards, and looking from time to time at one particular house. When he passed that way again, there was the gentleman still patrolling the street, and still looking towards the same house. The policeman waited a little, and watched. The place was a respectable lodging house, and the stranger was certainly a gentleman, though a queer one to look at. It was not the policeman's business to interfere on suspicion, except in the case of notoriously bad characters. So, though he did think it odd, he went on again.

Between twelve and one o'clock in the afternoon, Ovid left his lodgings, to go to the neighbouring livery stables, and choose an open carriage. The sun was shining, and the air was brisk and dry, after the stormy night. It was just the day when he might venture to take Carmina out for a drive.

On his way down the street, he heard footsteps behind him, and felt

---

1   *Pall Mall*: Pall Mall is a street North of St. James's Park and south of Piccadilly, noted for its gentlemen's clubs.

himself touched on the shoulder. He turned—and discovered Benjulia. On the point of speaking resentfully, he restrained himself. There was something in the wretch's face that struck him with horror.

Benjulia said, "I won't keep you long; I want to know one thing. Will she live or die?"

"Her life is safe—I hope."

"Through your new mode of treatment?"

His eyes and his voice said more than his words. Ovid instantly knew that he had seen the book; and that the book had forestalled him in the discovery to which he had devoted his life. Was it possible to pity a man whose hardened nature never pitied others? All things are possible to a large heart. Ovid shrank from answering him.

Benjulia spoke again.

"When we met that night at my garden gate," he said, "you told me my life should answer for her life, if she died. My neglect has not killed her—and you have no need to keep your word. But I don't get off, Mr. Ovid Vere, without paying the penalty. You have taken something from me, which was dearer than life. I wished to tell you that—I have no more to say."

Ovid silently offered his hand.

Benjulia's head drooped in thought. The generous protest of the man whom he had injured, spoke in that outstretched hand. He looked at Ovid.

"No!" he said—and walked away.

Leaving the street, he went round to Fairfield Gardens, and rang the bell at Mr. Gallilee's door. The bell was answered by a polite old woman—a stranger to him among the servants.

"Is Zo in the house?" he inquired.

"Nobody's in the house, sir. It's to be let, if you please, as soon as the furniture can be moved."

"Do you know where Zo is? I mean, Mr. Gallilee's youngest child."

"I'm sorry to say, sir, I'm not acquainted with the family."

He waited at the door, apparently hesitating what to do next. "I'll go upstairs," he said suddenly; "I want to look at the house. You needn't go with me; I know my way."

"Thank you kindly, sir!"

He went straight to the schoolroom.

The repellent melancholy of an uninhabited place had fallen on it already. The plain furniture was not worth taking care of: it was battered and old, and left to dust and neglect. There were two common deal writing desks,[1] formerly used by the two girls. One of them was covered with splashes of ink: varied here and there by barbarous caricatures of faces, in

---

1   *There were two common deal writing desks*: A deal desk is one constructed of fir or pine planks.

which dots and strokes represented eyes, noses, and mouths. He knew whose desk this was, and opened the cover of it. In the recess beneath were soiled tables of figures, torn maps, and dogseared writing books. The ragged paper cover of one of these last, bore on its inner side a grotesquely imperfect inscription:—*my cop book zo*. He tore off the cover, and put it in the breast pocket of his coat.

"I should have liked to tickle her once more," he thought, as he went down stairs again. The polite old woman opened the door, curtsying deferentially. He gave her half a crown. "God bless you, sir!" she burst out, in a gush of gratitude.

He checked himself, on the point of stepping into the street, and looked at her with some curiosity. "Do you believe in God?" he asked.

The old woman was even capable of making a confession of faith politely. "Yes, sir," she said, "if you have no objection."

He stepped into the street. "I wonder whether she is right?" he thought. "It doesn't matter; I shall soon know."

The servants were honestly glad to see him, when he got home. They had taken it in turn to sit up through the night; knowing his regular habits, and feeling the dread that some accident had happened. Never before had they seen him so fatigued. He dropped helplessly into his chair; his gigantic body shook with shivering fits. The footman begged him to take some refreshment. "Brandy, and raw eggs,"[1] he said. These being brought to him, he told them to wait until he rang—and locked the door when they went out.

After waiting until the short winter daylight was at an end, the footman ventured to knock, and ask if the master wanted lights. He replied that he had lit the candles for himself. No smell of tobacco smoke came from the room; and he had let the day pass without going to the laboratory. These were portentous signs. The footman said to his fellow servants, "There's something wrong." The women looked at each other in vague terror. One of them said, "Hadn't we better give notice to leave?" And the other whispered a question: "Do you think he's committed a crime?"

Towards ten o'clock, the bell rang at last. Immediately afterwards they heard him calling to them from the hall. "I want you, all three, up here."

They went up together—the two women anticipating a sight of horror, and keeping close to the footman.

The master was walking quietly backwards and forwards in the room: the table had pen and ink on it, and was covered with writings. He spoke to them in his customary tones; there was not the slightest appearance of agitation in his manner.

---

1   *Brandy, and raw eggs*: Eggs were a relatively common ingredient in alcoholic concoctions of the day, often finding their way into ale, rum, gin, and wine. A Victorian beverage known to some as "Cock-a-Doodle Broth" consisted of a mixture of brandy, water, sugar, and eggs, a variation of Benjulia's drink.

"I mean to leave this house, and go away," he began. "You are dismissed from my service, for that reason only. Take your written characters from the table; read them, and say if there is anything to complain of." There was nothing to complain of. On another part of the table there were three little heaps of money. "A month's wages for each of you," he explained, "in place of a month's warning. I wish you good luck." One of the women (the one who had suggested giving notice to leave) began to cry. He took no notice of this demonstration, and went on. "I want two of you to do me a favour before we part. You will please witness the signature of my Will." The sensitive servant drew back directly. "No!" she said, "I couldn't do it. I never heard the Death-Watch before in winter time—I heard it all last night."[1]

The other two witnessed the signature. They observed that the Will was a very short one. It was impossible not to notice the only legacy left; the words crossed the paper, just above the signatures, and only occupied two lines: "I leave to Zoe, youngest daughter of Mr. John Gallilee, of Fairfield Gardens, London, everything absolutely of which I die possessed." Excepting the formal introductory phrases, and the statement relating to the witnesses—both copied from a handy book of law, lying open on the table—this was the Will.

The female servants were allowed to go downstairs; after having been informed that they were to leave the next morning. The footman was detained in the dining-room.

"I am going to the laboratory," the master said; "and I want a few things carried to the door."

The big basket for waste paper, three times filled with letters and manuscripts; the books; the medicine chest; and the stone jar of oil from the kitchen—these, the master and the man removed together; setting them down at the laboratory door. It was a still cold starlight winter's night. The intermittent shriek of a railway whistle in the distance, was the only sound that disturbed the quiet of the time.

"Good night!" said the master.

The man returned the salute, and walked back to the house, closing the front door. He was now more firmly persuaded than ever that something was wrong. In the hall, the women were waiting for him. "What *does* it mean?" they asked. "Keep quiet," he said; "I'm going to see."

In another minute he was posted at the back of the house, behind the edge of the wall. Looking out from this place, he could see the light of the lamps in the laboratory streaming through the open door, and the dark figure of the master coming and going, as he removed the objects left out-

---

1   *I never heard the Death-Watch before in the winter time*: The cook refers to the sounds made by the so-called death-watch beetles, who were supposed to warn of a coming death.

side into the building. Then the door was shut, and nothing was visible but the dim glow that found its way to the skylight, through the white blind inside.

He boldly crossed the open space of ground, resolved to try what his ears might discover, now that his eyes were useless. He posted himself at the back of the laboratory, close to one of the side walls.

Now and then, he heard—what had reached his ears when he had been listening on former occasions—the faint whining cries of animals. These were followed by new sounds. Three smothered shrieks, succeeding each other at irregular intervals, made his blood run cold. Had three death-strokes been dealt on some suffering creatures, with the same sudden and terrible certainty? Silence, horrible silence, was all that answered. In the distant railway there was an interval of peace.

The door was opened again; the flood of light streamed out on the darkness. Suddenly the yellow glow was spotted by the black figures of small swiftly-running creatures—perhaps cats, perhaps rabbits—escaping from the laboratory. The tall form of the master followed slowly, and stood revealed watching the flight of the animals. In a moment more, the last of the liberated creatures came out—a large dog, limping as if one of its legs was injured. It stopped as it passed the master, and tried to fawn on him. He threatened it with his hand. "Be off with you, like the rest!" he said. The dog slowly crossed the flow of light, and was swallowed up in darkness.

The last of them that could move was gone. The death shrieks of the others had told their fate.

But still, there stood the master alone—a grand black figure, with its head turned up to the stars. The minutes followed one another: the servant waited, and watched him. The solitary man had a habit, well known to those about him, of speaking to himself; not a word escaped him now; his upturned head never moved; the bright wintry heaven held him spellbound.

At last, the change came. Once more the silence was broken by the scream of the railway whistle.

He started like a person suddenly roused from deep sleep, and went back into the laboratory. The last sound then followed—the locking and bolting of the door.

The servant left his hiding-place: his master's secret, was no secret now. He hated himself for eating that master's bread, and earning that master's money. One of the ignorant masses, this man! Mere sentiment had a strange hold on his stupid mind; the remembrance of the poor wounded dog, companionable and forgiving under cruel injuries, cut into his heart like a knife. His thought at that moment, was an act of treason to the royalty of Knowledge,—"I wish to God I could lame *him*, as he has lamed the dog!" Another fanatic! another fool! Oh, Science, be merciful to the fanatics, and the fools!

When he got back to the house, the women were still on the look-out for him. "Don't speak to me now," he said. "Get to your beds. And, mind this—let's be off to-morrow morning before *he* can see us."

There was no sleep for him when he went to his own bed.

The remembrance of the dog tormented him. The other lesser animals were active; capable of enjoying their liberty and finding shelter for themselves. Where had the maimed creature found a refuge, on that bitter night? Again, and again, and again, the question forced its way into his mind. He could endure it no longer. Cautiously and quickly—in dread of his extraordinary conduct being perhaps discovered by the women—he dressed himself, and opened the house door to look for the dog.

Out of the darkness on the step, there rose something dark. He put out his hand. A persuasive tongue, gently licking it, pleaded for a word of welcome. The crippled animal could only have got to the door in one way; the gate which protected the house-enclosure must have been left open. First giving the dog a refuge in the kitchen, the footman—rigidly performing his last duties—went to close the gate.

At his first step into the enclosure he stopped panic-stricken.

The starlit sky over the laboratory was veiled in murky red. Roaring flame, and spouting showers of sparks, poured through the broken skylight. Voices from the farm raised the first cry—"Fire! fire!"

At the inquest, the evidence suggested suspicion of incendiarism and suicide. The papers, the books, the oil betrayed themselves as combustible materials, carried into the place for a purpose. The medicine chest was known (by its use in cases of illness among the servants) to contain opium. Adjourned inquiry elicited that the laboratory was not insured, and that the deceased was in comfortable circumstances. Where were the motives? One intelligent man, who had drifted into the jury, was satisfied with the evidence. He held that the desperate wretch had some reason of his own for first poisoning himself, and then setting fire to the scene of his labours. Having a majority of eleven against him, the wise juryman consented to a merciful verdict of death by misadventure. The hideous remains of what had once been Benjulia, found Christian burial.[36] His brethren of the torture-table, attended the funeral in large numbers. Vivisection had been beaten on its own field of discovery. They honoured the martyr who had fallen in their cause.

---

36 *found Christian burial*: To insure a proper Church of England funeral service,
    and burial in a Church of England graveyard, a Victorian had to die properly. A
    suicide forfeited his right to such consecration. In fact, well into the nine-
    teenth century, suicides risked various degrees of post-mortem abuse, and
    until 1870, they had to relinquish their personal property to the crown.

CHAPTER LXIII.

The life of the New Year was still only numbered by weeks, when a modest little marriage was celebrated—without the knowledge of the neighbours, without a crowd in the church, and even without a wedding-breakfast.

Mr. Gallilee (honoured with the office of giving away the bride) drew Ovid into a corner before they left the house. "She still looks delicate, poor dear," he said. "Do you really consider her to be well again?"

"As well as she will ever be," Ovid answered. "Before I returned to her, time had been lost which no skill and no devotion can regain. But the prospect has its bright side. Past events which might have cast their shadow over all her life to come, have left no trace in her memory. I will make her a happy woman. Leave the rest to me."

Teresa and Mr. Mool were the witnesses; Maria and Zo were the bridesmaids: they had only waited to go to church, until one other eagerly expected person joined them. There was a general inquiry for Miss Minerva. Carmina astonished everybody, from the bride-groom downwards, by announcing that circumstances prevented her best and dearest friend from being present. She smiled and blushed as she took Ovid's arm. "When we are man and wife, and I am quite sure of you," she whispered, "I will tell *you*, what nobody else must know. In the meantime, darling, if you can give Frances the highest place in your estimation—next to me—you will only do justice to the noblest woman that ever lived."

She had a little note hidden in her bosom, while she said those words. It was dated on the morning of her marriage: "When you return from the honeymoon, Carmina, I shall be the first friend who opens her arms and her heart to you. Forgive me if I am not with you to-day. We are all human, my dear—don't tell your husband."

It was her last weakness. Carmina had no excuses to make for an absent guest, when the first christening was celebrated. On that occasion the happy young mother betrayed a conjugal secret to her dearest friend. It was at Ovid's suggestion that the infant daughter was called by Miss Minerva's christian name.

But when the married pair went away to their happy new life, there was a little cloud of sadness, which vanished in sunshine—thanks to Zo. Polite Mr. Mool, bent on making himself agreeable to everybody, paid his court to Mr. Gallilee's youngest daughter. "And who do you mean to marry, my little Miss, when you grow up?" the lawyer asked with feeble drollery.

Zo looked at him in grave surprise. "That's all settled," she said; "I've got a man waiting for me."

"Oh, indeed! And who may he be?"

"Donald!"

"That's a very extraordinary child of yours," Mr. Mool said to his friend, as they walked away together.

Mr. Gallilee absently agreed. "Has my message been given to my wife?" he asked.

Mr. Mool sighed and shook his head. "Messages from her husband are as completely thrown away on her," he answered, "as if she was still in the asylum. In justice to yourself, consent to an amicable separation, and I will arrange it."

"Have you seen her?"

"I insisted on it, before I met her lawyers. She declares herself to be an infamously injured woman—and, upon my honour, she proves it, from her own point of view. 'My husband never came near me in my illness, and took my children away by stealth. My children were so perfectly ready to be removed from their mother, that neither of them had the decency to write me a letter. My niece contemplated shamelessly escaping to my son, and wrote him a letter vilifying his mother in the most abominable terms. And Ovid completes the round of ingratitude by marrying the girl who has behaved in this way.' I declare to you, Gallilee, that was how she put it! 'Am I to blame,' she said, 'for believing that story about my brother's wife? It's acknowledged that she gave the man money—the rest is a matter of opinion. Was I wrong to lose my temper, and say what I did say to this so-called niece of mine? Yes, I was wrong, there: it's the only case in which there is a fault to find with me. But had I no provocation? Have I not suffered? Don't try to look as if you pitied me. I stand in no need of pity. But I owe a duty to my own self-respect; and that duty compels me to speak plainly. I will have nothing more to do with the members of my heartless family. The rest of my life is devoted to intellectual society, and the ennobling pursuits of science. Let me hear no more, sir, of you or your employers.' She rose like a queen, and bowed me out of the room. I declare to you, my flesh creeps when I think of her."

"If I leave her now," said Mr. Gallilee, "I leave her in debt."

"Give me your word of honour not to mention what I am going to tell you," Mr. Mool rejoined. "If she needs money, the kindest man in the world has offered me a blank cheque to fill in for her—and his name is Ovid Vere."

* * * * *

As the season advanced, two social entertainments which offered the most complete contrast to each other, were given in London on the same evening.

Mr. and Mrs. Ovid Vere had a little dinner party to celebrate their return. Teresa (advanced to the dignity of housekeeper) insisted on stuffing the tomatoes and cooking the macaroni with her own hand. The guests were Lord and Lady Northlake; Maria and Zo; Miss Minerva and Mr. Mool. Mr. Gallilee was present as one of the household. While he was in London, he and his children lived under Ovid's roof. When they went to Scotland, Mr. Gallilee had a cottage of his own (which he insisted on buying) in Lord Northlake's park. He and Zo drank too much champagne at dinner. The father made a speech; and the daughter sang, "We're gayly yet."

In another quarter of London, there was a party which filled the street with carriages, and which was reported in the newspapers the next morning.

Mrs. Gallilee was At Home to Science.[1] The Professors of the civilised universe rallied round their fair friend. France, Italy, and Germany bewildered the announcing servants with a perfect Babel of names—and Great Britain was grandly represented. Those three superhuman men, who had each had a peep behind the veil of creation, and discovered the mystery of life, attended the party and became centres of three circles—the circle that believed in "protoplasm," the circle that believed in "bioplasm," and the circle that believed in "atomized charges of electricity, conducted into the system by the oxygen of respiration." Lectures and demonstrations went on all through the evening, all over the magnificent room engaged for the occasion. In one corner, a fair philosopher in blue velvet and point lace,[2] took the Sun in hand facetiously. "The sun's life, my friends, begins with a nebulous infancy and a gaseous childhood." In another corner, a gentleman of shy and retiring manners converted "radiant energy into sonorous vibrations"—themselves converted into sonorous poppings by waiters and champagne bottles at the supper table. In the centre of the room, the hostess solved the serious problem of diet; viewed as a method of assisting tadpoles to develop themselves into frogs—with such cheering results that these last lively beings joined the guests on the carpet, and gratified intelligent curiosity by explorations on the stairs. Within the space of one remarkable evening, three hundred illustrious people were charmed, surprised, instructed, and amused; and when Science went home, it left a conversazione (for once) with its stomach well filled. At two in the morning, Mrs. Gallilee sat down in the empty room, and said to the learned friend who lived with her,

"At last, I'm a happy woman!"

THE END.

End of June 1883 *Belgravia* Serial Number

---

1 *Mrs. Gallilee was At Home to Science*: Mrs. Gallilee's late-season conversazione offers Collins the opportunity to remind us that his hero's mother remains lost to science; it also affords him a last chance to poke fun at the language of science.
2 *point lace*: Point lace is needlepoint.

Appendix A: *Reviews of* Heart and Science

1. Unsigned review, the *Academy*. April 28, 1883, Number 573, p. 290.

In several respects, which are too obvious to stand in need of being pointed out, the genius of Mr. Wilkie Collins resembles that of Edgar Poe; and, like Poe, Mr. Collins has invited the public into his workshop, exhibited his materials and tools, and affably expounded the methods by which the finished product comes to be what it is. Indeed, while the American story-teller wrote only one essay on "The Philosophy of Composition," the English novelist has written at least two or three Prefaces any one of which might put in a claim to the title. In the Preface to *Heart and Science*, Mr. Collins again takes his readers into his confidence, and gives them various pieces of information, of which the most important is his declaration that, while in all his works he had endeavoured to combine the character and humour which the British public love with the incident and dramatic situation for which he thinks the said public does not care, his latest work is one in which we are to "find the scales inclining, on the whole, in favour of character and humour." In spite of his Prefaces, however, it seems to me that we learn more of Mr. Wilkie Collins's methods from his books themselves than from what he has to tell us about them; and the reader who can distinguish any quality in *Heart and Science* which differentiates it from the majority of its numerous predecessors must be a reader whose critical perceptions have been refined to a pitch of rare subtlety. Certainly the plot, *qua* plot, is not nearly so complex as the plots of *The Woman in White* and *The Moonstone*, and it therefore absorbs a smaller proportion of the total interest of the story; but of the special interest of "character and humour: there is neither more nor less than in any of the writer's previous works. Even the fact that *Heart and Science* is in part polemical (being not merely a novel, but an anti-vivisection manifesto) does not set it in a place apart, for in one or two previous books Mr. Wilkie Collins has said his say concerning current controversies in as effective a manner as the limitations of the vehicle would allow; and here he is not less successful than in *Man and Wife* in the difficult task of mixing art and argument. That he is wholly successful cannot be said, for *Heart and Science* will be found more entertaining than convincing, save by those who do not need to be convinced. The vivisecting Dr. Benjulia is certainly repulsive enough, and it is quite possible that he may have his original in real life. But neither he nor the scientific Mrs. Gallilee, with her talk of "radiant energy" and "sonorous vibrations," can be accepted as a type; and, therefore, the conception, though interesting enough as an artistic product, has really no polemical value. The ordinary novel-reader will not, however, enjoy them less on this account; and, whatever else may be said of Benjulia, it must be declared that he is a singularly interesting and, in a way, fascinating creation. Mr. Wilkie Collins can deal strongly with a strong situation, but he has done nothing more powerful than his sketch of Benjulia's last hours, after his discovery that the one hope of his life had vanished, and that the loathsome labour of years had been in vain. For reasons which I have not space to give, Mrs. Gallilee is, I think, less successful. But Mr. Gallilee and the unscientific and illiterate Zoe are capital examples of genuine and unforced humour; and the book, as a whole, is thoroughly readable and enthralling from its first page to its last.

2. Unsigned review, the *Athenæum*. April 28, 1883, Number 2896, pp. 538-39.

The awkward sound of *Heart and Science*, the title of Mr. Wilkie Collins's new book, will perhaps help to make people remember it; but though it is better than some of the author's later works it is not equal to his best. He has hampered himself by trying to write with a purpose. Novel-readers as a rule are supposed to omit prefaces. It will be well if they do so in this case, for they will learn from the two prefaces to *Heart and Science* that the author's purpose is to help the cause of the anti-vivisectionists; that there is a good deal of science in the book; and that the physiological part of it is quite correct, the manuscript having been submitted to an eminent London surgeon. All this sounds depressing enough; but fortunately Mr. Wilkie Collins is far too experienced and too skilful a novelist to be able to allow himself to be dull. The reader who has read the prefaces soon forgets them and the threatened anti-vivisection and science when he finds himself quickly launched into the midst of a story which opens in the author's best manner. In the first preface, which is addressed "to readers in general," it is stated that the novel is one of character and humour rather than of incident and dramatic situation. Mr. Wilkie Collins seems to have misjudged his own work. The merits of it really are those which are the merits of so many of the author's books: that the plot is well contrived at starting; that coincidences are cleverly managed; that the reader's interest is seized at the outset and constantly roused again; that there is an air of mystery about the principal characters, and an uncertainty about what will happen which makes one guess for a solution as one goes along, and change one's mind over and over again; that the details are accurate; and that the dramatic effects are excellent. It may be readily admitted that Mr. Wilkie Collins is justified in saying that he has borne in mind the value of temperate advocacy, but the truth is that he is so much more an artist than an advocate that, on the whole, his novel is good enough to make one almost fail to notice that it was written against vivisection. Unfortunately the story has a weak ending. After imagining all sorts of strange possibilities the reader finds out at last that in truth there was very little plot at all. The second preface, "to readers in particular," points out the care that has been taken to have the science accurate. It is almost painful to think of the trouble that has been thrown away. Prof. Ferrier on the "Localization of Cerebral Disease," "Chambers's Encyclopædia," and a long list of books have been consulted, to say nothing of newspapers and magazines; but all that has been got from them is a phrase here and there to round off a sentence and raise a laugh at a learned lady. It seems almost a pity that a lawyer was not consulted too. One of the characters is a solicitor, and if accuracy in legal matters is as important as correctness in science, it would have been well to have avoided the mistake of sending a person to look for a will at Doctors' Commons instead of Somerset House. A lawyer could also have given some useful information on the subject of the guardianship of infants, a department of the law with which Mr. Wilkie Collins seems not to be familiar.

3. Unsigned review, the *Pall Mall Budget*. May 4, 1883, pp. 14-15.

"Mr. Wilkie Collins's New Novel"

Mr. Wilkie Collins begins his new novel with a quaint and characteristic preface, which may possibly seem to the youngest generation of this age of many generations a little old-fashioned. He is unquestionably right in saying that English and American readers of novels as a rule prefer character and humour to the other qualities of which the novel writer may avail himself. There would be nothing very noteworthy in the saying if it were not that plot (of which by implication, and indeed directly, Mr. Collins denies the attraction) used to be considered the special quality at which he himself aimed. There have been many different opinions as to his attainment of it; no difference, we think, as to his attempt to attain it. Therefore Mr. Wilkie Collins must be construed as saying in effect *do manus*. The rest of the preface amounts to a disclaimer of undue purpose, and to a vindication of the scientific correctness of the facts and opinions here put in the mouths of scientific persons. With this latter point we have very little to do, but Mr. Collins is on the whole justified in claiming that while dealing with such a very burning question as vivisection, and holding, as is evident, extremely strong opinions on that question, he has not attempted much, if any, harrowing of the feelings. His vivisector, Dr. Benjulia, is the chief attempt at character and humour in the book, but with rare exception Mr. Collins has bravely withstood the temptation to translate into words the pictorial representations which (as we now know) have so terribly disturbed poor Dr. M. de Cyon. It is true that Dr. Benjulia is six feet six high; but that is not libellous. He is also abnormally thin; but even the extreme sensitiveness of M. de Cyon himself can find no intolerable imputation here. He has a bamboo stick which is sometimes clotted with unpleasant stains: but this is almost the only transgression of strict equity of portraiture; for his brusqueness and sarcasm, his misanthropy and indifference, might be equally characteristic of a harmless grubber after Hebrew roots. And though he certainly comes to a very terrible end the reader is generously left to his choice to decide whether this is a special judgment or not. As far as the immediate cause of that end, is revealed, an equally sensitive mathematician might have been driven to it by discovering that some one had reached a solution by algebraical means while he was trying geometrical, and there is no public odium attached to either of these methods. That Mr. Collins has coloured his portrait of his vivisector in accordance with his own views on the subject is indisputable; but after considering the portrait with eyes as nearly achromatic as it is possible to use on such a subject, we do not know that he can be said to have coloured it unfairly.

Dr. Benjulia, though only remotely connected with the plot, is the most piquant and the most successful character in the book. The narrative, though in parts good, is somewhat spoiled by the affectations of the school of which Mr. Collins is the last considerable member now surviving. There might be nothing very strange in the name Benjulia, if a young surgeon of fortune and promise were not introduced with the certainly uncommon Christian name of Ovid, and there might be nothing noteworthy in the uncommon Christian name Ovid if a governess who has something to do with the plot did not bear the still more uncommon surname of Minerva. The subordinate doctor, and, so to speak, third villain, is Mr. Null; the heroine is named Carmina, her baleful aunt rejoices in the surname of Gallilee. All these things are individually less than nothing; collectively they amount to something. The errors of the school show themselves in other things besides nomenclature. It is, indeed, quite conceivable that a badhearted, extravagant, and vain woman, to whom her brother has with strangely foolish judgment left no immediate legacy worth speaking of, while he devises his whole fortune to her in case his daughter (whose guardian she is) dies unmarried, while she has power for some years to forbid her marriage under penalties, should scheme against her ward. But the conduct of the governess, Miss Frances Minerva, and that of Carmina's Italian nurse, Teresa, who is half inclined to defend her darling by poison, is wholly unnatural, forced, and superfluous. The parts of the book where these come in exhibit Mr. Wilkie Collins's old proclivity to the comedy of intrigue, in which the efforts and means used to produce a given result are wholly disproportionate to that result, and have, indeed, no effect upon it, except that of staving it off a little further.

Nevertheless *Heart and Science* is very far from being an uninteresting book. Dr. Benjulia (reduced a little) is not an unworthy brother of Count Fosco and Captain Wragge. It is difficult to believe that an experienced London surgeon like Ovid Vere would have had much doubt about the character of Benjulia's secret studies, but it is fair to say that he was very ill at the time. Carmina, the heroine, though given to fainting and brain fever to a more than eighteenth-century extent, is an amiable and attractive heroine enough. Her uncle, Mr. Gallilee, is an affectionate old imbecile, and his little child, Zo, the one being who makes Benjulia human, would have been agreeable if Mr. Collins had not introduced some strokes of perfectly unnecessary coarseness in her portrait. Mrs. Gallilee and her eldest child Maria are only caricatures of Maria Newcome and her family pushed into a region which the genius of Thackeray prevented his treading—the region of absolutely unnatural *charge*. Something of the same kind may be said of Miss Minerva. But these exceptions leave the writer something to boast himself of and the reader plenty to enjoy. The chief drawback of the book, one which it shares with most of its class, is that except the ill-conducted and ill-fated Benjulia there is scarcely anybody in whom it is possible to take much personal interest. Did Mr. Wilkie Collins mean to make his vivisector especially interesting?

4. Unsigned review, the *Spectator*. May 26, 1883 LVI, pp. 679-81.

"An Anti-Vivisection Novel"

Mr. Wilkie Collins, as his custom is, gives in the forefront of his latest book a semi-descriptive, semi-critical preface, which is, unlike the majority of such compositions, certain to be read. "In the abstract," as Sydney Smith's Scotch young lady would put it, a preface to a work of art is a work of supererogation, possibly an impertinence; for such a work ought not to need explanation or supplement, while, as for criticism, readers can supply *that* for themselves, and resent it as cordially as they resent unsolicited advice. Mr. Wilkie Collins, however, can do for a preface what Swift, according to Stella, could do for a broomstick,—he can make it entertaining, which he does partly by the sheer force of a bright and perfectly lucid style, pleasantly salted with the special kind of humour which never fails him, but mainly by his delightfully confidential manner, which probably leads some simple-minded readers to think that, having been told how the books are written, they could write them for themselves, "if they had a mind."

In this particular preface, Mr. Wilkie Collins returns to an old theory of his, and insists that the qualities in fiction which find most favour with the British public are character and humour, and that incident and dramatic situation only find a second place in their favour. He tells us that he has "always tried to combine the different merits of a good novel in one and the same book," but that he has "never succeeded in keeping an equal balance," and that in the present story we shall "find the scales inclining, on the whole, in favour of character and humour." Perhaps Mr. Wilkie Collins hardly states the case quite correctly. The ordinary novel-reader of the day does, indeed, value character and humour, but he values also incident and dramatic situation, as is amply proved by the continued popularity of the writer's own book, *The Woman in White*; and we are inclined to think that he values most of all the simple skill in the art of narration which is one of Mr. Wilkie Collins's strongest points. Whether there be much or little story in a novel, the reader demands that it shall be well told, and it is in this telling of a story that Mr. Wilkie Collins is supreme. There is less plot in *Heart and Science* than in many of the writer's previous works, but we do not find this out until we have closed the third volume; for what there is of story is so deftly managed, that we have in reading it the feeling of plot, just as in reading such an unrhymed poem as "Tears, Idle Tears," we have the feeling of rhyme.

When we began to speak about this preface we were, however, thinking not of such matters as these; but of the announcement that *Heart and Science* has been written partly as a contribution to the literature of the Anti-vivisection movement. We are not sure that this announcement is not a mistake, for if a novel have a distinct purpose apart from mere entertainment, it is, perhaps, better for several reasons that it should be left to reveal itself; but Mr. Collins has probably sufficient confidence both in himself and his cause to feel that he will lose little by thus showing his hand. We have never been able to see the force of an objection frequently brought against the polemical novel, that it attempts to substitute an appeal to the imagination and the feelings for the logical arguments which are asserted to be the only legitimate weapons in controversy. The heart, the conscience, and the imagination have their own arguments, not less than the reason; and when Mr. Collins traces in one of his characters "the result of the habitual practice of cruelty (no matter under what pretence) in fatally deteriorating the nature of man," he is making as genuine a contribution to the settlement of a vexed question as that made by the physiologist who proves, by hard fact, that vivisection has been misleading to science, as well as repulsive to morality.

Dr. Benjulia, the vivisecting surgeon, is not only an impressive figure, but a curiously interesting psychological study. Nothing could be truer to human nature than this picture of a man in whom the lust of knowledge has become as purely selfish and degrading as the lust of gold. Even granting, as in fairness we perhaps ought to grant, that a man like Benjulia begins his experiments with the desire of obtaining through them some knowledge which may be of use in relieving human suffering, it seems clear that indifference to suffering anywhere—say in a tortured dog or rabbit—must in the nature of things result in indifference to suffering everywhere; and knowledge which had been but a means to a beneficent end becomes an end in itself, and an end pursued in the manner which is purely selfish. Benjulia's supreme aim at the time when we make his acquaintance is not that a beneficent discovery should be made, but that he should be the man to make it; and he dissuades his friend Ovid Vere from visiting Italy, and sends him to Canada instead, because he fears that in Italy he may meet with physiologists who may put Vere on the scent which he himself has so long been following. This seems to us an entirely truthful conception, having behind it an irrefutable argument; nor does

Mr. Collins stray from the path of psychological certainty, when he goes still farther, and represents Benjulia, in the absorbing passion of his unhallowed quest, as allowing Carmina, the charming heroine of his book, to reach the very gates of death, in order that he may study, under favourable conditions, the phenomena of "simulated paralysis."

The portrait is rendered at once more truthful and more impressive by the fact that Mr. Collins does not yield, as an inferior artist would have yielded, to the temptation to make Benjulia wholly repulsive. There is something in the loveless solitude of his life, cut off as it is not only from human sympathy, but from the simple amenities of ordinary human intercourse, which irresistibly compels pity, even for a man who is himself pitiless; and the strongly-conceived picture of the last day of a wasted life— the day in which Benjulia discovers that the prize he has been seeking has slipped from his grasp—is an adequate and powerful realisation of Aristotle's often-quoted definition of the scope of tragedy. In one of the medical journals which are supplied to him every week, and which he examines, but never reads, Benjulia has at last found the thing that for years he has been fearing to find,—the review of a new book in which the problem upon which he has been working is solved. In the darkness of the winter evening, he starts for London, driving furiously, as if upon an errand of life and death—as indeed he is—and secures a copy of the fatal book. He drives to his club, and the library waiter finds him busily engaged in reading:—

> The man whose business it was to attend the fires went in during the night, from time to time, and always found him in the same corner. It began to get late. He finished his reading, but it seemed to make no difference. There he sat—wide awake—holding his closed book upon his knee, seemingly lost in his own thoughts. This went on till it was time to close the club. They were obliged to disturb him. He said nothing; and went slowly down into the hall, leaving his book behind him. It was an awful night, raining and sleeting; but he took no notice of the weather. When they fetched a cab, the driver refused to take him where he lived on such a night as that. He only said, 'Very well; go to the nearest hotel.'

The bed at the hotel is unslept in, and the next day Benjulia sallies forth, to return home for the last time, staying only to make an attempt to see once more the little girl, Zoe Gallilee, the only human creature who has ever stirred in him something like affection. The attempt is unsuccessful; the family has left the house; but the old woman in charge admits him, and nothing that Mr. Wilkie Collins has written is fuller of pathetic power than the story of how Benjulia visited the deserted school-room, bringing away from it as a relic of his little friend a torn paper cover, "which bore on its inner side a grotesquely-imperfect inscription,—'my cop book zo.'" Benjulia returns home, and until night he remains inactive. His pipe is unlit, the so-called laboratory outside the house where his mysterious experiments are made is unvisited, and only one demand is made upon the servants, that one being, however, sufficiently startling. They are called up to receive written characters and their wages in lieu of notice, and two of them are requested to witness the signature of their master's will. Then, when the darkness has fallen, Benjulia and his footman carry out into the still, cold starlight "the big basket for waste-paper, three times filled with letters and manuscripts, the books, the medicine-chest, and the stone jar of oil from the kitchen," and set them down at the door of the strange, dark building, the secret of which has been so well kept. Benjulia himself carries everything inside, and when the door is shut, the footman, bent upon discovery, posts himself close to one of the side walls:—

Now and then he heard—what had reached his ears when he had been listening on former occasions—the faint, whining cries of animals. These were followed by new sounds. Three smothered shrieks, succeeding one another at irregular intervals, make his blood run cold. Had three death-strokes been dealt on some suffering creatures, with the same sudden and terrible certainty? Silence, horrible silence, was all that answered. In the distant railway there was an interval of peace. The door was opened again, the flood of light streamed out on the darkness. Suddenly the yellow glow was spotted by the black figures of small, swiftly-running creatures—perhaps cats, perhaps rabbits—escaping from the laboratory. The tall form of the master followed slowly, and stood revealed, watching the flight of the animals. In a moment more, the last of the liberated creatures came out—a large dog—limping as if one of its legs was injured. It stopped as it passed the master, and tried to fawn on him. He threatened it with his hand. 'Be off with you, like the rest!' he said. The dog slowly crossed the flow of light, and was swallowed up in darkness. The last of them that could move was gone. The death-shrieks of the others had told their fate.

The footman sees his master retire into the building, and hears him bolt the door behind him. He goes back to the house, and to bed, but, horror-stricken at his discovery, he can get no sleep. The thought of the dog torments him, and he wonders if the maimed creature has found a refuge. He steals downstairs, and gently opens the house-door:—

Out of the darkness on the step there rose something dark. He put out his hand. A persuasive tongue, gently licking it, pleaded for a word of welcome. The crippled animal could only have got to the door in one way,— the gate which protected the house-enclosure must have been left open. First giving the dog a refuge in the kitchen, the footman, rigidly performing his last duties, went to close the gate. At his first step into the enclosure he stopped, panic-stricken. The starlit sky over the laboratory was veiled in murky red. Roaring flame and spouting showers of sparks poured through the broken skylight. Voices from the farm raised the first cry,— 'Fire! fire!'

Such is the end of Benjulia. The chapter in which the terrible story is told has a more powerful effect upon the imagination than anything we can remember in recent fiction; and vivid as the picture is, it cannot be said that it owes its vividness to partial or exaggerated presentation. Benjulia is consistent throughout,—consistent with himself, consistent with human nature, consistent with that law of conscious being the operation of which is seen in the reflex influence of action upon character. He is shown to us as a man utterly devoid of imagination, and this one fact alone suffices to account for his life and his death, and to give to the record of both a terrible homogeneity. We have heard it said that the portrait is drawn from life. We do not know whether this is so, and the question is not one of much interest. A picture so drawn is not necessarily lifelike; but whether Benjulia has or has not a living original, he is himself alive, we know him and understand him, and the conception owes its impressiveness to its imaginative veracity.

We have left ourselves without space in which to speak of the story itself, and of the subsidiary characters. The former is, it need hardly be said, thoroughly interesting, though a little slighter in conception than is usual with Mr. Wilkie Collins. The latter are, for the most part, average specimens of the writer's workmanship; but the delightful child, Zoe, represents the high average, while the more elaborately drawn portrait of her mother, Mrs. Gallilee, represents the low one. If we are intended to regard Mrs. Gallilee's devotion to science and her combined cunning and cruelty as standing in the relation of cause and effect,—and it seems to us that something like this *is* intended,—then Mr. Collins is guilty of the exaggeration which is so conspicuously absent from the portrait of Benjulia. Mr. Mool, the lawyer, is admirable, and Mr. Gallilee is very amusing, though not nearly so good as Zoe, whose reminiscences of her Scotch visit, in the third volume, are intensely funny. Quite apart from its special purpose, *Heart and Science* is a most fascinating story, and is certainly none the worse as a novel because, to quote the words of the preface, it "pleads the cause of the harmless and affectionate beings of God's creation."

5. Unsigned review, the *British Quarterly Review*. July and October 1883 LXXVIII, pp. 231-32.

"*Heart and Science*. A Story of the Present Time. By Wilkie Collins. In Three Vols. (Chatto and Windus.)"

Mr. Wilkie Collins has here presented us with a "novel with a purpose," and yet he has sacrificed none of his freedom and adroit resource of treatment. He has evidently, as he claims in the preface, devoted far more time and care to the study of character than in some former cases; but he is as ingenious as ever in managing his plot, in working one incident into another, and surprising us with developments which nevertheless have been well prepared for. His psychology in this case is closer and more realistic than we remember aforetime; though perhaps a certain section of the medical profession may feel a call to fight hard with him over some points. For he aims at exposing the dehumanizing effects of vivisection, believing with Dr. Haughton that persevered in without very effective checks on the side of ordinary sympathy, it may soon transform a man into a devil. But Mr. Wilkie Collins's great art is seen in tracing the purely psychological lines of the novel, a romance pure and simple, which cannot but affect the most ignorant and stolid. Readers who will not appreciate many of the points so cleverly made against vivisection, will sympathize with Hope (sic) Vere and Carmina in their sufferings and their final deliverance; with Miss Minerva, the governess, in her notable triumph over selfish passion; with poor Mr. Gallilee in his awkward position, and his noble decision though taken late; and with "Zo" in her *naïve* simplicities, and odd likings and dislikings, and her untainted healthy impulse, which enables her unconsciously to act with decision in a critical moment. It would not be fair for us to outline Mr. Wilkie Collins's well-laid plot: suffice it to say that in Mrs. Gallilee, the gradual ossification of the heart and healthy sympathies through excessive demand for knowledge and the power it is supposed to bring with it, is a most original study—the gradual slipping into crime itself seeming to be but a necessary outcome of the false theory of life she has sought to exhibit in practice. Dr. Benjulia, who isolates himself in his big laboratory, and is keen to wink at bad practice in poor practitioners like Null that he may carry on his own experiments in brain disease, is drawn with decisive pencil; and Mr. Le Frank forms as original a villain as Carmina's old Italian nurse does an attached dependant. Mr. Mool, the lawyer, is one of the weakest characters, but luckily very much does not depend on him. Mr. Collins expresses his thanks to Miss Power Cobbe and some others for aid given to him: he will doubtless furnish them with aid in their noble crusade against scientific cruelty. On the whole, Mr. Collins has secured success in a most difficult experiment; one chief cause of which is that he has dealt with results and general impressions, leaving detail of technicalities behind. The story is strong as a story; and only those who have dipped more or less deeply in the subject will be able to realize the labour Mr. Wilkie Collins has gone through by way of preparation for this work. He speaks of the warnings that come with advancing years, and "health that stands in need of improvement"—of which we are sorry to hear; but there is yet no token that his hand has lost its cunning in his own particular line of art, and Carmina is an admirable creation—sweet, tender, and true, whose touch converts nearly everything and everybody to show their best sides; only Mrs. Gallilee and Benjulia must for the novelist's purpose stand apart.

Appendix B: The vivisection debate of the 1870s and 1880s

1. Anti-vivisectionist George Hoggan's letter to the Editor of the *Morning Post*, reprinted in the *Spectator*, and prefaced by remarks from the editor. His letter, which some say offered the opening salvo in the vivisection battle of the mid-1870s, sparked weeks of debate in the "Letters to the Editor" section of the *Spectator*. From the *Spectator*. February 6, 1875, pp. 177-78.

"We republish with much reluctance the following painful letter to the Editor of Monday's *Morning Post*, as showing what the practice of Vivisection, when applied at least to the higher kinds of animals, really means. It has been conjectured, probably enough, that the laboratory referred to is not an English one. But whatever slight shades of difference the personal humanity of the physiologist who presides in such laboratories may make, the main characteristics of these vivisections, when performed on the higher orders of animals, like dogs and cats, cannot greatly differ, since they depend on the permanent conditions of the case. Let no one read the letter who has already made up his mind that the practice must be rigidly restricted or put an end to. For such a one it would be needless suffering.—Ed. *Spectator*."

To the Editor of the *Morning Post*

"Sir,—If the Society for the Prevention of Cruelty to Animals intend to give effect to the Memorial presented to it on Monday, and do its utmost to put down the monstrous abuses which have sprung up of late years in the practice of Vivisection, it will probably find that the greatest obstacle to success lies in the secrecy with which such experiments are conducted; and it is to the destruction of that secrecy that its best efforts should be directed, in the Legislature or elsewhere. It matters little what criminality the law may clearly attach to such practices. So long as the present privacy be maintained in regard to them, it will be found impossible to convict, from want of evidence. No student can be expected to come forward as a witness when he knows that he would be hooted, mobbed, and expelled from among his fellows for doing so, and any rising medical man would only achieve professional ruin by following a similar course. The result is that although hundreds of such abuses are being constantly perpetrated amongst us, the public knows no more about them than what the distant echo reflected from some handbook for the laboratory affords. On the other hand, if special knowledge be not forthcoming, and the public mind be alone left to carry on the crusade against unnecessary vivisection, feelings will be sure to take the place of facts, and the morbid, unreasoning excitement thereby created will either carry matters too far or fail altogether. As nothing will be likely to succeed so well as example in drawing forth information on these points from those capable but hesitating to give it, I venture to record a little of my own experience in the matter, part of which was gained as an assistant in the laboratory of one of the greatest living experimental physiologists. In that laboratory we sacrificed daily from one to three dogs, besides rabbits and other animals, and after four months' experience, I am of opinion that not one of those experiments on animals was justified or necessary. The idea of the good of humanity was simply out of the question, and would have been laughed at, the great aim being to keep up with, or get ahead of, one's contemporaries in science, even at the price of an incalculable amount of torture needlessly and iniquitously inflicted on the poor animals. During three campaigns I have witnessed many harsh sights, but I think the saddest sight I ever witnessed was when the dogs were brought up from the cellar to the laboratory for sacrifice. Instead of appearing pleased with the change from darkness to light, they seemed seized with horror as soon as they smelt the air of the place, divining apparently their approaching fate. They would make friendly advances to each of the three or four persons present, and as far as eyes, ears, and tail could make a mute appeal for mercy eloquent, they tried it in vain. Even when roughly grasped and thrown on the torture-trough, a low, complaining whine at such treatment would be all the protest made, and they would continue to lick the hand which bound them till their mouths were fixed in the gag, and they could only flap their tail in the trough as their last means of exciting compassion. Often when convulsed by the pain of their torture this would be renewed, and they would be soothed instantly on receiving a few gentle pats. It was all the aid and comfort I could give them, and I gave it often. They seemed to take it as an earnest of fellow-feeling that would cause their torture to come to an end—an end only brought by death.

Were the feelings of experimental physiologists not blunted, they could not long continue the practice of vivisection. They are always ready to repudiate any implied want of tender feeling, but I must say that they seldom show much pity; on the contrary, in practice they frequently show the reverse. Hundreds of times I have seen when an animal writhed in pain, and thereby deranged the tissues, during a deliberate dissection; instead of being soothed, it would receive a slap and an angry order to be quiet and behave itself. At other times, when an animal had endured great pain for hours without struggling or giving more than an occasional low whine, instead of letting the poor mangled wretch loose to crawl painfully about the place in reserve for another day's torture, it would receive pity so far that it would be said to have behaved well enough to merit death, and as a reward would be killed at once by breaking up the medulla with a needle, or "pithing," as this operation is called. I have often heard the professor say, when one side of an animal had been so mangled, and the tissues so obscured by clotted blood, that it was difficult to find the part search for, "Why don't you begin on the other side?" or, "Why don't you take another dog? What is the use of being so economical?" One of the most revolting features in the laboratory was the custom of giving an animal on which the professor had completed his experiment, and which had still some life left, to the assistants to practice the finding of arteries, nerves, &c., in the living animal, or for performing what are called fundamental experiments upon it,—in other words, repeating those which are recommended in the laboratory handbooks. I am inclined to look upon anæsthetics as the greatest curse to vivisectible animals. They alter too much the normal conditions of life to give accurate results, and they are therefore little depended upon. They indeed prove far more efficacious in lulling public feeling towards the vivisectors than pain in the vivisected. Connected with this there is a horrible proceeding that the public probably knows little about. An animal is sometimes kept quiet by the administration of a poison called "droorara," which paralyses voluntary motion while it heightens sensation, the animal being kept alive by means of artificial respiration until the effects of the poison have passed off.

On the Continent, I have often seen animals operated upon in this condition before an audience, who, as they were incapable of showing the pain they felt, were supposed by those present to be insensible to it, while all the time the poor brutes were suffering double torture that the feelings of the audience might be spared. To this recital I need hardly add that, having drunk the cup to the dregs, I cry off, and am prepared to see not only science, but even mankind, perish rather than have recourse to such means of saving it. I hope that we shall soon have a Government inquiry into the subject, in which experimental physiologists shall only be witnesses, not judges. Let all private vivisection be made criminal, and all experiments be placed under Government inspection, and we may have the same clearing-away of abuses that the Anatomy Act caused in similar circumstances.—I am, Sir, your obedient servant, George Hoggan, M.B. and C.M. 13 Granville Place, Portman Square,W.

2. Author and anti-vivisectionist Lewis Carroll's "Some Popular Fallacies about Vivisection." From the *Fortnightly Review*. XXIII (June 1875), pp. 847-54.

At a time when this painful subject is engrossing so large a share of public attention, no apology, I trust, is needed for the following attempt to formulate and classify some of the many fallacies, as they seem to me, which I have met with in the writings of those who advocate the practice. No greater service can be rendered to the cause of truth, in this fiercely contested field, than to reduce these shadowy, impalpable phantoms into definite forms, which can be seen, which can be grappled with, and which, when once fairly *laid*, we shall not need to exorcize a second time.

I begin with two contradictory propositions, which seem to constitute the two extremes, containing between them the golden mean of truth:—

1. *That the infliction of pain on animals is a right of man, needing no justification.*
2. *That it is in no case justifiable.*

The first of these is assumed in practice by many who would hardly venture to outrage the common feelings of humanity by stating it in terms. All who recognize the difference of right and wrong must admit, if the question be closely pressed, that the infliction of pain is in some cases wrong. Those who deny it are not likely to be amenable to argument. For what common ground have we? They must be restrained, like brute beasts, by physical force.

The second has been assumed by an Association lately formed for the total suppression of Vivisection, in whose manifesto it is placed in the same category with Slavery, as being an absolute evil, with which no terms can be made. I think I may assume that the proposition most generally accepted is an intermediate one, namely, that the infliction of pain is in some cases justifiable, but not in all.

3. *That our right to inflict pain on animals is coextensive with our right to kill, or even to exterminate a race (which prevents the existence of possible animals), all being alike infringements of their rights.*

This is one of the commonest and most misleading of all the fallacies. Mr. Freeman, in an article on Field Sports and Vivisection, which appeared in the *Fortnightly Review* for May, 1874, appears to countenance this when he classes death and pain together, as if they were admitted to be homogeneous. For example—

> By cruelty then I understand, as I have understood throughout, not all infliction of death or suffering on man or beast, but their wrongful or needless infliction. ... My positions then were two. First ... that certain cases of the infliction of death or suffering on brute creatures may be blameworthy. The second was, that all infliction of death or suffering for the purpose of mere sport is one of those blameworthy cases.

But in justice to Mr. Freeman I ought also to quote the following sentence, in which he takes the opposite view: "I must in all cases draw a wide distinction between mere killing and torture."

In discussing "the rights of animals," I think I may pass by, as needing no remark, the so-called right of a race of animals to be perpetuated, and the still more shadowy right of a non-existent animal to come into existence. The only question worth consideration is whether the killing of an animal is a real infringement of right. Once grant this, and a *reductio ad absurdum* is imminent, unless we are illogical enough to assign rights to animals in proportion to their size. Never may we destroy, for our convenience, some of a litter of puppies—or open a score of oysters when nineteen would have sufficed—or light a candle in a summer evening for mere pleasure, lest some hapless moth should rush to an untimely end! Nay, we must not even take a walk, with the certainty of crushing many an insect in our path, unless for really important business! Surely all this is childish. In the absolute hopelessness of drawing a line anywhere, I conclude (and I believe that many, on considering the point, will agree with me) that man has an *absolute* right to inflict death on animals, without assigning any reason, provided that it be a painless death, but that any infliction of pain needs its special justification.

4. *That man is infinitely more important than the lower animals, so that the infliction of animal suffering, however great, is justifiable if it prevent human suffering, however small.*

This fallacy can be assumed only when unexpressed. To put it into words is almost to refute it. Few, even in an age where selfishness has almost become a religion, dare openly avow a selfishness so hideous as this! While there are thousands, I believe, who would be ready to assure the vivisectors that, so far as their personal interests are concerned, they are ready to forego any prospect they may have of a diminution of pain, if it can only be secured by the infliction of so much pain on innocent creatures.

But I have a more serious charge than that of selfishness to bring against the scientific men who make this assumption. They use it dishonestly, recognising it when it tells in their favour, and ignoring it when it tells against them. For does it not presuppose the axiom that human and animal suffering differ *in kind*? A strange assertion this, from the lips of people who tell us that man is twin-brother to the monkey! Let them be at least consistent, and when they have proved that the lessening of *human* suffering is an end so great and glorious as to justify any means that will secure it, let them give the anthropomorphoid ape the benefit of the argument. Further than that I will not ask them to go, but will resign them in confidence to the guidance of an inexorable logic.

Had they only candour and the courage to do it, I believe that they would choose the other horn of the dilemma, and would reply, "Yes, man *is* in the same category as the brute; and just as we care not (you see it, so we cannot deny it) how much pain we inflict on the one, so we care not, unless when deterred by legal penalties, how much we inflict on the other. The lust for scientific knowledge is our real guiding principle. The lessening of human suffering is a mere dummy set up to amuse sentimental dreamers."

I come now to another class of fallacies—those involved in the comparison, so often made, between vivisection and field-sports. If the theory, that the two are essentially similar, involved no worse consequence than that sport should be condemned by all who condemn vivisection, I should be by no means anxious to refute it. Unfortunately the other consequence is just as logical, and just as likely, that vivisection should be approved of by all who approve of sport.

The comparison rests on the assumption that the main evil laid to the charge of vivisection is the pain inflicted on the animal. This assumption I propose to deal with, further on, as a fallacy: at present I will admit it for the sake of argument, hoping to show that, even on this hypothesis, the vivisectors have a very poor case. In making this comparison their first claim is—

5. *That it is fair to compare aggregates of pain.*

"The aggregate amount of wrong"—I quote from an article in the *Pall Mall Gazette* for February 13—"which is perpetrated against animals by sportsmen in a single year probably exceeds that which some of them endure from vivisectors in half a century." The best refutation of this fallacy would seem to be to trace it to its logical conclusion—that a very large number of trivial wrongs are equal to one great one. For instance, that man, who by selling adulterated bread inflicts a minute injury on the health of some thousands of persons, commits a crime equal to one murder. Once grasp this *reductio ad absurdum*, and you will be ready to allow that the only fair comparison is between individual and individual.

Supposing the vivisectors forced to abandon this position, they may then fall back on the next parallel—

6. *That the pain inflicted on an individual animal in vivisection is not greater than in sport.*

I am no sportsman, and so have no right to dogmatize, but I am tolerably sure that all sportsmen will agree with me that this is untrue in shooting, in which, whenever the creature is killed at once, it is probably as painless a form of death as could be devised; while the sufferings of one that escapes wounded ought to be laid to the charge of unskilful sport, not of sport in the abstract. Probably much the same might be said of fishing: for other forms of sport, and especially for hunting, I have no defence to offer, believing that they involve very great cruelty.

Even if the last two fallacies were granted to the advocates of vivisection, their use in the argument must depend on the following proposition being true:—

7. *That the evil charged against vivisection consists chiefly in the pain inflicted on the animal.*

I maintain, on the contrary, that it consists chiefly in the effect produced on the operator. To use the words of Mr. Freeman, in the article already quoted, "the question is not as to the aggregate amount of suffering inflicted, but as to the moral character of the acts by which the suffering is inflicted." We see this most clearly, when we shift our view from the act itself to its remoter consequences. The hapless animal suffers, dies, "and there an end:" but the man whose sympathies have been deadened, and whose selfishness has been fostered, by the contemplation of pain deliberately inflicted, may be the parent of others equally brutalised, and so bequeath a curse to future ages. And even if we limit our view to the present time, who can doubt that the degradation of a soul is a greater evil than the suffering of a bodily frame? Even if driven to admit this, the advocates of the practice may still assert—

8. *That vivisection has no demoralizing effect on the character of the operator.*

"Look at our surgeons!" they may exclaim. "Are they a demoralized or a brutalised class? Yet you must admit that, in the operations they have to perform, they are perpetually contemplating pain—aye, and pain deliberately inflicted by their own hands." The analogy is not a fair one; since the *immediate* motive—of saving the life, or diminishing the sufferings, of the person operated on—is a counteracting influence in surgery, to which vivisection, with its shadowy hope of some day relieving the sufferings of some human being yet unborn, has nothing parallel to offer. This, however, is a question to be decided by evidence, not by argument. History furnishes us with but too many examples of the degradation of character produced by the deliberate pitiless contemplation of suffering. The effect of the national bull-fights on the Spanish character is a case in point. But we need not go to Spain for evidence: the following extract from the *Echo*, quoted in the *Spectator* for March 20, will be enough to enable the reader to judge for himself what sort of effect this practice is likely to have on the minds of students:—

But if yet more be necessary to satisfy the public mind on this latter point (the effect on the operators), the testimony of an English physiologist, known to the writer, may be useful in conclusion. He was present some time past at a lecture, in the course of which demonstrations were made on living dogs. When the unfortunate creatures cried and moaned under the operations, many of the students *actually mimicked their cries in derision*! The gentleman who related this occurrence adds that the spectacle of the writhing animals and the fiendish behaviour of the audience so sickened him, that he could not wait for the conclusion of the lecture, but took his departure in disgust.

It is humiliating but an undeniable truth, that man has something of the wild beast in him, that a thirst for blood can be aroused in him by witnessing a scene of carnage, and that the infliction of torture, when the first instincts of horror have been deadened by familiarity, may become, first, a matter of indifference, then a subject of morbid interest, then a positive pleasure, then a ghastly and ferocious delight.

Here again, however, the analogy of sport is of some service to the vivisector, and he may plead that the influence we dread is already at work among our sportsmen. This I will now consider.

9. *That vivisection does not demoralise the character more than sport.*

The opponents' case would not, I think, suffer much even if this were admitted; but I am inclined to demur to it as a universal truth. We must remember that much of the excitement and interest of sport depend on causes entirely unconnected with the infliction of pain, which is rather ignored than deliberately contemplated; whereas in vivisection the painful effects constitute in many cases a part, in some cases the whole, of the interest felt by the spectator. And all they tell us of the highly developed intellect of the anatomical student, with which they contrast so contemptuously the low animal instincts of the foxhunter, is but another argument against themselves; for surely the nobler the being we degrade, the greater is the injury we inflict on society. *Corruptio optimi pessima.*

"But all this ignores the *motive* of the action," cry the vivisectors. "What is it in sport? Mere pleasure. In this matter we hold an impregnable position." Let us see.

10. *That, while the motive in sport is essentially selfish, in vivisection it is essentially unselfish.*

It is my conviction that the non-scientific world is far too ready to attribute to the advocates of science all the virtues they are so ready to claim; and when they put forward their favourite *ad captandum* argument that their labours are undergone for one pure motive—the good of humanity—society is far too ready to exclaim, with Mrs. Varden, "Here is a meek, righteous, thorough-going Christian, who, having dropped a pinch of salt on the tails of all the cardinal virtues, and caught them every one, makes light of their possession, and pants for more morality!" In other words, society is far too ready to accept the picture of the pale, worn devotee of science giving his days and nights to irksome and thankless toil, spurred on by no other motive than a boundless philanthropy. As one who has himself devoted much time and labour to scientific investigations, I desire to offer the strongest possible protest against this falsely coloured picture. I believe that any branch of science, when taken up by one who has a natural turn for it, will soon become as fascinating as sport to the most ardent sportsman, or as any form of pleasure to the most refined sensualist. The claim that hard work, or the endurance of privation, proves the existence of an unselfish motive, is simply monstrous. Grant to me that the miser is proved unselfish when he stints to himself of food and sleep to add one more piece of gold to his secret hoard, that the place-hunter is proved unselfish when he toils through long years to reach the goal of his ambition, and I will grant to you that the laborious pursuit of science is proof positive of an unselfish motive. Of course I do not assert, of even a single scientific student, that his real motive is merely that craving for more knowledge, whether useful or useless, which is as natural an appetite as the craving for novelty or any other form of excitement. I only say that the lower motive would account for the observed conduct quite as well as the higher.

Yet, after all, the whole argument, deduced from a comparison of vivisection with sport, rests on the following proposition, which I claim to class as a fallacy:—

11. *That the toleration of one form of an evil necessitates the toleration of all others.*

Grant this, and you simply paralyse all conceivable efforts at reformation. How can we talk of putting down cruelty to animals when drunkenness is rampant in the land? You would propose, then, to legislate in the interests of sobriety? Shame on you! Look at the unseaworthy ships in which our gallant sailors are risking their lives! What! Organize a crusade against dishonest shipowners, while our streets swarm with a population growing up in heathen ignorance! We can but reply, *non omnia possumus omnes.* And surely the man who sees his way to diminish in any degree even a single one of the myriad evils around him, may well lay to heart the saying of a wise man of old, "Whatsoever they hand findeth to do, do it with thy might."

The last parallel to which the advocates of vivisection may be expected to retreat, supposing all these positions to be found untenable, is the assertion—

12. *That legislation would only increase the evil.*

The plea, if I understand it aright, amounts to this,—that legislation would probably encourage many to go beyond the limit with which at present they are content, as soon as they found that a legal limit had been fixed beyond their own. Granting this to be the tendency of human nature, what is the remedy usually adopted in other cases? A stricter limit, or the abandonment of all limits? Suppose a case—that in a certain town it were proposed to close all taverns at midnight, and that the opponents of the measure urged, "At present some close at eleven—a most desirable hour: if you pass the law, all will keep open till midnight." What would the answer be? "Then let us do nothing," or "Then let us fix eleven, instead of twelve, as our limit"? Surely this does not need many words: the principle of doing evil that good may come is not likely to find many defenders, even in this modern disguise of forbearing to do good lest evil should come. We may safely take our stand on the principle of doing the duty which we see before us: secondary consequences are at once out of our control and beyond our calculation.

Let me now collect into one paragraph the contradictions of some of these fallacies (which I have here rather attempted to formulate and classify than to refute, or even fully discuss), and so exhibit in one view the case of the opponents of vivisection. It is briefly this—

That while we do not deny the absolute right of man to end the lives of the lower animals by a painless death, we require good and sufficient cause to be shown for all infliction of pain.

That the prevention of suffering to a human being does not justify the infliction of a greater amount of suffering on an animal.

That the chief evil of the practice of vivisection consists in its effect on the moral character of the operator; and that this effect is distinctly demoralising and brutalising.

That hard work and the endurance of privations are no proof of an unselfish motive.

That the toleration of one form of an evil is no excuse for tolerating another.

Lastly, that the risk of legislation increasing the evil is not enough to make all legislation undesirable.

We have now, I think, seen good reason to suspect that the principle of selfishness lies at the root of this accursed practice. That the same principle is probably the cause of the indifference with which its growth among us is regarded, is not perhaps so obvious. Yet I believe this indifference to be based on a tacit assumption, which I propose to notice as the last of this long catalogue of fallacies—

13. *That the practice of vivisection will never be extended so as to include human subjects.*

That is, in other words, that while science arrogates to herself the right of torturing at her pleasure the whole sentient creation up to man himself, some inscrutable boundary-line is there drawn, over which she will never venture to pass. "Let the galled jade wince, our withers are unwrung."

Not improbably, when that stately Levite of old was pacing with dainty step the road that led from Jerusalem to Jericho, "bemused with thinking of tithe-concerns," and doing his best to look unconscious of the prostrate form on the other side of the way, if it could have been whispered in his ear, "*Your* turn comes next to fall among the thieves!" some sudden thrill of pity might have been aroused in him: he might even, at the risk of soiling those rich robes, have joined the Samaritan in his human task of tending the wounded man. And surely the easy-going Levites of our own time would take an altogether new interest in this matter, could they only realise the possible advent of a day when anatomy shall claim, as legitimate subjects for experiment, first, our condemned criminals—next, per-

haps, the inmates of our refuges for incurables—then the hopeless lunatic, the pauper hospital-patient, and generally "him that hath no help-
er,"—a day when successive generations of students, trained from their
earliest years to the repression of all human sympathies, shall have developed a new and more hideous Frankenstein—a soulless being to whom
science shall be all in all. *Homo sum: quidvis humanum a me alienum puto.*

And when that day shall come, O my brother-man, you who claim for
yourself and for me so proud an ancestry—tracing our pedigree through
anthropomorphoid ape up to the primeval zoophyte—what potent spell
have *you* in store to win exemption from the common doom? Will you represent to that grim spectre, as he gloats over you, scalpel in hand, the
inalienable rights of man? He will tell you that this is merely a question
of relative expediency,—that, with so feeble a physique as yours, you
have only to be thankful that natural selection has spared you so long. Will
you reproach him with the needless torture he proposes to inflict on you?
He will smilingly assure you that the *hyperæsthesia*, which he hopes to
induce, is in itself a most interesting phenomenon, deserving much
patient study. Will you then, gathering up all your strength for one last
desperate appeal, plead with him as with a fellow-man, and with an ago-
nized cry for "Mercy!" seek to rouse some dormant spark of pity in that
icy breast? Ask it rather of the nether mill-stone.

3. Anti-vivisection advocate Lord Chief Justice Coleridge's "The
Nineteenth Century Defenders of Vivisection," a reply to Paget,
Owen, and Wilks. From the *Fortnightly Review.* XXXVIII (February
1882), pp. 225-36.

In the papers of Sir James Paget, Mr. Owen, and Dr. Wilks, on the subject of Vivisection published in the *Nineteenth Century* for December 1881,
more than one reference is made to a Judge or Judges. No other Judge has
spoken upon the subject, as far as I am aware; so that when a "Judge" or
"law officer" is mentioned by three gentlemen amongst those opponents
worthy at once of the contempt and anger which they express, or very
imperfectly conceal towards them, I cannot help applying some of the
censure to myself. I wish I could; partly because so to apply it may look
like vanity, as if in this regard I thought myself worthy of the notice of
such great people; but much more because the statements as to anything
I have ever said or written are so entirely inaccurate, that I must conclude
(want of apprehension in such distinguished men being out of the question), either that they have not read what they profess to notice, or that
they feel confident no one will read any reply.

I recognise, as much as any man can recognise it, the duty of a Judge
being in court and out of it a man *egregii altique silenti.* But there are occasions on which it is a duty to speak, and I think this is one. Sir James Paget
says that, "The only competent judges in such a case are those in whom

sentiment and intellectual power are fairly balanced, and who will dispassionately study the facts and compare the pain-giving and the utility of experiments on animals with those of any generally allowed or encouraged pursuit." Sir James Paget would deny, and I do not pretend to assert, that I am a "competent judge;" but I desire to state shortly and temperately, if I can, the reasons which lead me earnestly to support the Bill which Mr. Reid is about to submit to the House of Commons.

I should personally prefer in the abstract Regulation to Prohibition. I think it difficult to answer particular cases in which, without any unfair manipulation of circumstances, it may be shown, that total prohibition might or would stand in the way of justice, or even of humanity. But a practical matter cannot be thus dealt with. In the affairs of men it is hardly possible to lay down a general rule which will not produce hard cases. Probably no law was ever abolished which had not in its time done some good, for which, in particular instances, some defence could not be made. Probably no new law was ever enacted to which some exception could not be justly taken, and which did not in particular instances do some harm. Objections, as Dr. Arnold once said, do not bring us to the point; and nothing would ever be done if we waited till we had satisfied every possible object to the doing of what we propose. In all human action we have to choose and balance between opposing good and evil; and in any change of law to determine whether that which we propose, or that which exists, is *upon the whole* the best. On this principle I do not hesitate to support the absolute prohibition of what for shortness' sake, though with some verbal inaccuracy, I call, as others call it, vivisection.

The supporters of vivisection in this country are not in themselves content with the present state of things. As far as I know the repulsive literature of this subject, no defender of the practice, except Sir James Paget (and perhaps I misunderstand even his last sentence), has said or implied that he is satisfied with the present law. The repeal of it is to be at once attempted; and it is contended that even those (to my mind reasonable) restraints which it imposes so injuriously hamper the practice of vivisection, that little or no good can result from it, if these restraints are continued. But it seems to follow that if the present law is admitted to be as bad for vivisectors as total abolition, and if the present law is reasonable, they, at least, can have no strong motive for resisting an enactment in form of that which they say exists already in substance .

Is, then, the present law reasonable? It is the result of a most careful inquiry conducted by eminent men in 1875, men certainly neither weak sentimentalists nor ignorant and prejudiced humanitarians, men amongst whom are to be found Mr. Huxley and Mr. Erichsen, Mr. Hutton and Sir John Karslake. These men unanimously recommended legislation, and legislation, in some important respects, more stringent than Parliament thought fit to pass. They recommended it on a body of evidence at once interesting and terrible. Interesting indeed it is from the frank apathy to the sufferings of animals, however awful, avowed by some of the witnesses; for the noble humanity of some few; for the curious ingenuity with which others avoided the direct and verbal approval of horrible cruelties which yet they refused to condemn; and in some cases for the stern judgment passed upon men and practices, apparently now, after the lapse of six years, considered worthy of more lenient language. Terrible the evidence is for the details of torture, of mutilation, of life slowly destroyed in torment, or skilfully preserved for the infliction of the same or diversified agonies, for days, for weeks, for months, in some cases for more than a year. I want not to be, if I can help it, what Mr. Simon calls a "mere screamer;" nay, if possible, to avoid that yet more fatal imputation upon an Englishman which Dr. Wilks brings against his opponents, that we "lack a sense of the ludicrous." I wish to use quiet language, but I must, nevertheless, at all hazards own that, sharing probably the lower and less sensitive organizations of the monkey, the cat, and the dog, I fail altogether to see the joke which he sees, in any attempt to stay these tortures; and further that to read of them, not in the language of "paid scribes and hired agitators," but in the language of these humane and tender men who first inflict them and then describe them, makes me sick. True that the most exquisite and most prolonged tortures appear to have been inflicted out of England; true that, both before the Commission and since the Report, the broadest avowals of entire indifference to animal agony have come from foreign countries, or from foreigners in this. But our inferiority in this respect, the as yet unreasonable dislike of our medical classes to witnessing very painful experiments, are made the subject of earnest and repeated regret. It is hoped that we may be brought up to the foreign standard; that our insular prejudice may be purged away by degrees, and that in time we may feel the beauty and enter into the nobility of M. de Cyon's description of "the true vivisector." "He," says M. de Cyon, "must approach a difficult vivisection with the same joyful excitement, with the same delight, as the surgeon when he approaches a difficult operation from which he anticipates extraordinary consequences. He who shrinks from the section of a living animal, he who approaches a vivisection as an unpleasant necessity, may perhaps be able to repeat one or two particular vivisections, but will never become an artist in vivisection." *Principiis obsta.* I do not desire this result for my fellow-islanders. I think both that the Report of the Commission was at the time and has been since abundantly justified, and that the legislation founded on it did not go beyond very reasonable limits.

But that there exists a statute confining vivisection within reasonable limits, with which some people are dissatisfied, is not, it may be said, any ground for going beyond those limits, and prohibiting the practice altogether. By itself it is not. But the claims of the vivisectors have meanwhile become so large, the tone they take is so peremptory, the principles on which they base themselves are so alarming and (I think) so immoral, that I have become reluctantly convinced it is only by the strongest law, by absolutely forbidding the practice itself, that the grave mischief which follows from holding parley with these claims can be stayed or destroyed. Before the Commission, except by a witness or two of exceptional frankness or indiscretion, an apologetic tone was adopted, the duty of avoiding pain if possible was unreservedly at least in words admitted, of at least minimizing suffering, of never inflicting it except in pursuit of some reasonably probable discovery, of not torturing animals simply to show manual skill, or to illustrate acknowledged and ascertained truths. All this sort of thing has somehow disappeared. I am not conscious of any distorting influence on my judgment; I have no anti-scientific bias; I read as far as I can a good deal on both sides with a desire, I think sincere, to arrive at a sound conclusion, and I deliberately say that it seems to me no man can read the Blue Book of 1875, and these papers of Sir James Paget, Mr. Owen, and Dr. Wilks of 1881, without being conscious that, somehow or other, the whole atmosphere has changed. For example Magendie and his experiments are denounced before the Commission in language such as Robert Southey might have used, and did use, respecting them. Dr. Wilks's "world-famous Darwin" applies to experiments such as his what the Commission rightly call the "emphatic terms" "*detestation and abhorrence.*" Now in 1881 Sir James Paget speaks of them without a syllable of disapprobation, nay, I must say it seems to me, in a tone of absolute apology. What more cogent can be said? If here or elsewhere I seem to use language of blame or disrespect towards such a man as he is, a man whom in common with all the world I respect and admire with all my heart, it is only because in a grave matter I cannot help, after much reflection, being convinced that he is wrong. I admit the weight of his character; I recognise the moral force he brings to any side which he supports; and if I find that such a man as he cannot advocate his cause without what seems unfair reasoning, and an apparent disregard of or apology for hateful cruelty, it is the strongest possible argument to my mind that the cause itself should be done away with; for if even Sir James Paget cannot escape its evil influences, what will they not effect on the common run of men who have neither his head nor his heart to keep them right? I say, then, that the complete change of tone in the vivisectors, the open scoffing at laws of mercy which not so long ago were honoured at least in words, the broad claim that in pursuit of knowledge any cruelty may be inflicted on animals; these things not only startle me and shock my moral sense, but they convince that a practice which, according to the contention of its best and ablest advocates, involves these claims, is one which it is not longer safe to tolerate.

I do not say that vivisection is useless, and I am sure I never have said so. I do not know enough of the history of science to venture on any such statement. Dr. Wilks indeed asserts that he has looked in vain "for any speech delivered" (*inter alios*) "by a judge who has not made inutility the staple of his argument;" but he is absolutely inaccurate, and I contradict him as flatly as is consistent with courtesy. I should think it as foolish and presumptuous in me to say so, as it is presumptuous (I had almost said foolish) in the gentleman whom Dr. Wilks calls "the venerable Owen," to say of "One of our highest law officers" (meaning, I imagine, me), "that he *purposely*" (the word is the venerable gentleman's) "obstructs the best mode of admitting the light which the law looks for in cases of suspected poisoning." Mr. Owen is an old man, but I am no longer young; and I take leave to say that no age is venerable if a man has not learned to abstain from unmannerly imputations of motive, and from indulgence in mere scolding and abuse of opponents of whom (I do not speak of myself) he can know nothing but what is to their credit, and who at least at no time of their lives have ever been accused of endeavouring to crush a scientific adversary by means at once ungenerous and unfair. *Testa servat odorem*; but this is by the way. What I have said and do say is that very considerable men are not agreed as to the great utility of vivisection, or as to the value of the results which have followed from it. There are two sides to the question; which is the right one I do not pretend to say; but there are men of name, and statements which at least look authentic, upon both. There are certain stock cases, some of them very old, which reappear on every discussion; I have heard so often and so much of Mr. Spencer Wells's rabbits, that I will own to a suspicion that if the baked dogs, and mutilated cats, and gouged frogs, and nail-larded guinea-pigs, and brain-extracted monkeys, had resulted in anything worth hearing of, I should have heard of that too. But I do not say, and have never said, that vivisection is useless.

I must, however, be permitted to say how loose and vague are the notions of evidence which, as far as I know them, pervade the writings of men in science on this question. Sir James Paget once in my hearing, in the course of a very striking speech, not only with perfect candour admitted, but insisted on this defect. He said (and I think truly said) that men of science often (not, of course, always) arrive at conclusions on evidence which a lawyer would hardly admit to be evidence at all in a question of disputed fact. No fair man I think can fail to be struck with the uncertainty, a different point from inutility, of the conclusions to which vivisection has conducted those who practise it. The conclusions are doubted, are disputed, are contradicted, by the vivisectors themselves. So that it really is not experiment to verify or disprove theory, which one well-conducted and crucial experiment might do, but experiment *in vacuo*, experiment on the chance, experiment in pursuit of nothing in particular, but of anything which may turn up in the course of a hundred thousand vivisections, and during the course of a life devoted to them. This is the experiment for which liberty is claimed, and the unfettered pursuit of which we are called very hard names for objecting to. "Pseudo humanitarians," "ill-informed fanatics," "true pharisaical spirit," these are but specimens of the language—which the calm and serene men of science find it convenient to apply to their opponents. We may be wrong; but at least let our position be distinctly understood, and let the mode in which we are opposed be distinctly appreciated.

I deny altogether that it concludes the question to admit that vivisection enlarges knowledge. I do not doubt it does; but I deny that the pursuit of knowledge is in itself always lawful; still more do I deny that the gaining of knowledge justifies all means of gaining it. To begin with, proportion is forgotten. Suppose it capable of proof that by putting to death with hideous torment 3,000 horses you could find out the real nature of some feverish symptom, I should say without the least hesitation that it would be unlawful to torture the 3,000 horses. There is no proportion between the end and the means. Next, the moment you touch *man*, it is admitted that the formula breaks down; no one doubts that to cut up a hundred men and women would enlarge the bounds of knowledge as to the human frame more speedily and far more widely than to torture a thousand dogs or ten thousand cats. It is obvious; but it was admitted over and over again that experiments on animals were suggestive only, not conclusive, as to the human subject. Especially is this the case with poisons; some of the deadliest of which do not appreciably affect some animals, and as to all of which it is admitted that it is not safe to argue from their effects on animals to their effects on man. As to man himself, it was not so long ago that medical men met with a passion of disavowal, what they regarded as an imputation, viz. the suggestion that experiments were tried on patients in hospitals. I assume the disavowal to be true; but why, if all pursuit of knowledge is lawful, should the imputation be resented? The moment you come to distinguish between animals and man, you consent to limit the pursuit of knowledge by considerations not scientific but moral; and it is bad logic and a mere *petitio principii* to assume (which is the very point at issue), that these considerations avail for man but do not for animals. I hope that morals may always be too much for logic; it is permissible to express a fear that some day logic may be too much for morals.

An interesting illustration of this remark has just been given. Mr. Jonathan Hutchinson, the senior surgeon to the London Hospital, has recently been reported in the *British Medical Journal*, as avowing to his pupils that in fact a patient "in a miserable condition: had (1) not been cured, by a Dr. Tom Robinson, who had him under treatment and might easily have cured him, in order that the students at the hospital might be witnesses of the case; and (2) had been kept in the hospital "for a few days before using the magician's wand, in order that all might see that there was no natural tendency to amelioration." If this had been correct, it would certainly have been a curious and convincing proof of the reasonableness of the fear I have expressed that logic might now and then prove too much for morals; for if this is not experimenting upon a human subject, and putting him to needless suffering, in order to demonstrate an already known fact, I do not know what is. But Mr. Hutchinson says he has been, like Dr. Klein, misunderstood and misreported. There is no more said; but it is to be hoped that the practices of scientific men may not be so far misconstrued by their pupils who see them, it seems their language is misunderstood by those who hear it and report it.

It comes to this, that the *necessity* for vivisection, in order to attain the ends proposed, is not admitted by many persons of knowledge and authority; that its *practical* utility in alleviating human suffering, though not denied, is on the same authority said to be much exaggerated by those who practise or defend it; that even if it be admitted to be a means of gaining scientific knowledge, such knowledge is unlawful knowledge if it is pursued by means which are immoral; and that a disregard of all proportion between means and ends often makes both alike unlawful and indefensible. Meanwhile, if we turn to the other side, the positive evil engendered by the practice appears to me to be frightful. I do not speak only of sufferings of the tortured brutes. To dwell on these might be called "screaming," and I have said that the amount and intensity of these, as described by the vivisectors themselves, is absolutely sickening. In this world of pain and sorrow surely the highest of God's creatures should not wilfully increase a sum which seems too great already. I seem to hear those voices, and that wail, which the verse of Virgil, at once tender and majestic, has ascribed to infants, but which may come also from creatures hardly inferior to infants in intelligence, and not at all inferior to them in their capacity to suffer.

> Continuò auditæ voces, vagitus et ingens,
> Infantumque animæ flentes in limine primo,
> Quos dulcis vitæ exsortes, et ab ubere raptos,
> Abstulit atra dies et funere mersit acerbo.

Far worse I think in result are the practice and the principles on which it is defended upon the defenders and advocates of both. I should have expected this *à priori*. Where the infliction of pain is the special object of the experiment, where the power to endure it is the thing to be measured; nay, where the sensitiveness to pain and the liability to mortal or non-mortal injury of this or that organ, or set of organs, or nerves, or muscles is the matter of investigation, I should expect to find that a man who was an habitual vivisector, "an artist in vivisection," as M. de Cyon calls him, was one by nature callous to the sufferings of animals, or who in the course of these experiments had become so. Surely experience shows the justice of the expectation. Who, not a vivisector, can read without a shudder these papers in the *Nineteenth Century*, and Mr. Simon's address to the Medical Congress in 1881, a shudder at the utter and absolute indifference displayed to the terrible and widespread suffering which the practice the writers are defending entails upon helpless and harmless creatures? Yet who are these writers? Chosen men; bright examples (we are told) of the scientific class, persons whose names alone are to be arguments in their favour. If these men write thus, and it is incredible that merely as men of common sense they should affect an indifference they do not feel, what will be the temper of mind of the ordinary coarse, rough man, the common human being, neither better nor worse than his neighbours, of whom the bulk of the medical profession, like the bulk of every other profession, is made up? What is the effect of the familiarity with cruelty in other cases; what was it in the Slave States? What was it in the days of slavery and gladiators in Rome? What was it in England a hundred years ago? What is it now in places and amongst persons where and amongst whom cruelty and brutality is not the exception but the rule? Natural laws are not suspended in the case of vivisectors; and I will mention an instance within my own experience which I am sure cannot offend, because I am certain the person cannot be known. Some time since I met in society a very eminent man, a man of very high character, and for whom, in common with most men, I have a very great respect. He is certainly not an habitual vivisector, but I believe he has occasionally vivisected. I left his company shocked and disturbed to a degree difficult to express; not from any particular thing he said, or any particular experiment he described, for he said little on the subject, and I think described nothing; but from the assumption that underlay his conversation, that we had no duties to the lower creatures when science was in question, and that the animal world was to a man of science like clay to the potter, or marble to the sculptor, to be crushed or carved at his will with no more reference to pain in animals than if they were clay or marble. Yet this was almost gifted man, a man but for the taint of vivisection every way admirable, but a man whom that taint had made (I feel sure in his case, owing to the blessed inconsistency of humanity, to the animal world only) cruel and heartless.

This is a question not to be decided by an array of names. I know that great men are not all on one side about it. But we have great men, and those surely not weak or effeminate, on ours. In the single volume written by Sir Arthur Helps, entitled *Animals and their Masters*, there will be found a collection of authorities on this point, as well as other cognate to it, which may well bring to a pause these gentlemen, venerable and otherwise, who are so smart upon us with their sneers and sarcasms. I will not quote Montaigne, though a man less sentimental never lived; for he is old, and may be said to write only in the general. But what is to be said of Jeremy Bentham? "The question is," says he, "not, can they reason, or can they speak, but can they suffer?" What of Voltaire, who has passage after passage of trenchant scorn for the vivisectors of the faithful dog? What of Sir Arthur Helps himself, who "has a perfect horror of vivisection; the very word makes his flesh creep"? But why multiply examples? It is not true that fools and women and children are on one side, and wise men on the other. It is not true that we are Pharisees, or fanatics and shams. We know what we are about, and we think that Parliament will be moved, if it is moved at all, not by calling names, but by facts and arguments.

Now what besides this somewhat ostentatious contempt is the argument of these gentlemen? So far as it depends upon their frequent assertions of the practical value of vivisection, I have said already that I will not dispute with them as to the fact. A lawyer ought at any rate to know the folly of encountering an expert without the knowledge necessary for success in the conflict. I deny the practical conclusion sought to be drawn from it upon grounds of another sort which appear to me to be of overwhelming force, but which I will not repeat. There is, then, another line of argument which I am positively mortified to have to notice; it seems to me alike unworthy of the subject and of the men who use it. In substance it is this: it is hypocrisy, it is inconsistency, it is folly to attack vivisection, which, if it be cruel, is not more cruel than some, is not so cruel as many, sports or practices which all men follow, which you yourselves, the anti-vivisectors, either do not dare attack, or do not condemn. Then there is the inevitable Hudibras about "sins we have no mind to;" the equally inevitable Sydney Smith (distorted as inevitably from the context which made it sense), that all prohibitory acts contain principles of persecution; and so, because nature is cruel, because men are cruel, because there are hypocrites in the world, because the principle of prohibition may in some cases contain the principle of persecution—what then? Why something which, *consistently with all this argument*, may be horribly cruel and utterly useless, is to be let alone. As argument, nothing can be feebler; but are these statements fair? I think certainly not. It is true that there is much cruelty in the world as to which some men are careless, but a great many more are ignorant, and which, if they knew more or thought more, they would not permit. I do not believe that the gentle ladies and refined gentlemen who subject their horses to cruel pain, day by day or year by year, by means of gag-bits and bearing-reins, have ever seriously thought, or perhaps really know, what they are doing. They have not read Sir Francis Head, or Sir Arthur Helps, or Mr. Flower; they have not thought about it; they are in bondage to their coachmen. A man, a woman, who deliberately tortures a noble animal as we see hundreds, perhaps thousands, carelessly and ignorantly tortured day by day in London, is, I freely admit, open to the taunts of Mr. Owen and Dr. Wilks.

So again I should suppose that the vast majority of persons who have white veal brought into their houses have never seen, as I have seen, a calf still living hung up in a butcher's shop. If they had, and if they knew the process by which veal is made white, I think better of my countrymen than to believe that they would bear to see it at their tables. Most men do not reflect; nay, most men do not know these things. If they do, and the knowledge makes no difference in their practice, I leave them to the tender mercies of the gentlemen of the *Nineteenth Century*.

As to the mutilation of horses and bulls I do not know how they manage in other countries, but I am quite sure that in this it is, if these animals are to be kept in numbers at all, a matter of sheer necessity. If cruelty which can be prevented is used, it is wrong; and I at least do not defend it. Nor am I prepared to say that there is not much in our ordinary habits towards these and other animals which needs amending. But I think that Mr. Owen must be hard driven indeed if he can sincerely speak of mutilations "to enhance the charms of vocal music especially of the sacred kind," as things which his adversaries are interested, or are in consequence bound, to defend. I never heard of such a practice obtaining at any time in this country; and I imagine that his venerable age has led him for the moment to forget how long it is since it was tolerated even in the dominions of the Pope. Surely a man must be at his wits' end before he could gravely put forward such an argument as this in defense of a claim to vivisect by wholesale. If he is joking, I am sorry to say the humour has escaped me.

But sport? Well I am not ashamed to say that there are some sports which appear to me so cruel and so unmanly, that I wonder very much how any one can pleasure in them. Although in youth devoted to some kinds of manly exercise which inflicted pain only myself, and not quite unskilled in them, I own that at no time has the slaughter of pigeons out of cages, or of half-tame pheasants driven in thousands by beaters across the muzzles of guns, or some other forms of fashionable amusement in which the whole point is the wholesale destruction of terrified and unresisting creatures, ever appeared to me to be very distinguishable from duck-hunting, or cat-baiting, or the slaughter of cocks and hens in a poultry-yard. A fox, an otter, a stag (a wild one), die game; there is skill, there is courage, sometimes there is even danger at the end or in the course of the hunt which explain the enthusiasm of those devoted to it; and which make even one not devoted to it doubt whether Dr. Johnson was quite as wise as usual in saying "that it was only the paucity of human pleasures which persuaded us ever to call hunting one of them." But a hare! Certainly if to hunt down with hounds and horses one poor timid, trembling creature be manly, I am content on this matter to be unmanly all my life.

I do not defend everything that is done in sport. One I knew, a brave and high-spirited man, a keen and successful sportsman, gave it up in the prime of life because he could not face the cruelty. Another, almost the manliest man I ever came across, one of the best shots and finest riders in England, with whom I had many talks on these matters, did not give it up, for it had become a second nature to him, but laid down and enforced a set of rules for his shooting parties which, as he said, at least "reduced pain to a minimum." These men may have been exceptions, but, depend on it, they were not alone. Yet I do not doubt that there is a pain in sport; I do not question there is cruelty; if ever the general sentiment of mankind awakes to it I believe that either the cruelty will be indefinitely lessened, as it might be, or the sport itself put down, as bull-baiting has been in England, tried in vain in France, in spite of the patronage of the Empress. I should think, however, that Sir James Paget greatly overstates the pains of animals like the otters, which die fighting in hot blood. Moreover, at the worst as a rule they die quickly, and they and their pains end together. The slow torture, the exquisite agony, the suffering inflicted with scientific accuracy up to the point at which the frame can bear it without death, these things are unknown to sport. At least and at lowest sportsmen do not intend them.

These are the deductions which I think a fair man would make from

Sir James Paget's or Mr. Owen's facts. But grant them all, and what do they come to as an argument? I have already peremptorily denied that we defend or are indifferent to cruelty anywhere; and are we not to try to prevent one sort of cruelty which we can reach because there is much that we cannot? One can hardly suppose these gentlemen are in earnest. We are not to forbid larceny because there are many forms of dishonesty which the law cannot restrain; nor injury to life or limb from bodily violence because existence can be made miserable and life shortened by taunting, by temper, by a thousand means known to ingenious malignity and familiar to us all, which yet evade the law; not to punish rape because seduction, which may be more wicked, is dispunishable; not certain frauds and cheats, because a multitude of other frauds and cheats escape us. I waste time over such argument. Of two things, one—vivisection is right, and then there is an end of the matter; or, it is wrong. If it is wrong and can be prevented, it is none the less wrong, and ought none the less to be prevented, because other things are also wrong, but cannot be prevented, or cannot be prevented now. One thing at a time.

There is a sort of argument or mode of influence employed persistently on this question on which it is fit that I should say a word. The writers with whom I have been dealing, not content with the contumely they pour upon our "mature ignorance," "crude sentiments," and "pretences," are never tired of celebrating the moral and intellectual virtues of the men who agree with them. One man is "venerable," another "world famous," two more "most illustrious," and so forth. "The air broke into a mist with bells," says Mr. Browning; and it is well if the walls of our city do not tumble down and our own sense forsake us, with the blare of the trumpets which announce the arrival of each foe upon the field. But besides being surely a trifle weak, this trumpeting is nothing to the purpose. Why should a venerable osteologist, a world-famed naturalist, or a couple of most illustrious physicians, be any better judges than a man of average intellect, average education, and average fairness, when the question is what is the limit (it being I think certain that there is one) between lawful and unlawful knowledge, and lawful and unlawful means of gaining it; and what is the moral effect necessarily or probably, according to the common facts of human nature, of a certain course of practice? When the Factory Acts and the Mining Acts were passed, Parliament did not question the doctrines of the venerable Adam Smith, or the world-famous Mill, or the most illustrious Ricardo, but it decided that notwithstanding their doctrines, certain morally mischievous things, which could be prevented, should be.

I own I am not much moved by this appeal to authority. I remember the time when it was difficult even among cultivated men to get a hearing for the North, in the American civil war; and when the sympathies of society went with slavery. As far as I know the Church of England never raised a finger, and very few of its bishops ever raised a voice, to put down our own slave trade, or set free our own slaves. Sir Arthur Helps tells us, in the book already mentioned, that he never heard a single sermon, out of many hundreds he had attended, in which the duty of kindness to dumb animals had ever been alluded to. Yet amongst these preachers, or amongst the maintainers of slavery and the slave trade, were to be found I doubt not many who were venerable, some illustrious, a few world-famous.

Further, I have heard that the great Roman Communion holds that we have no duties to the animal creation; that it has been given to us in absolute subjection; that it is a Pagan view to hold otherwise; and that some clergymen sometimes deliberately bully animals before their pupils to show their despotic authority over them. I do not assert this; the name and known opinions of Cardinal Manning seem to show that at least it has never been so decided; but I have heard it on respectable evidence. If it be so, we must, with due responsibility, think and act for ourselves without authority, or, if need be, against it. But there is one authority, conclusive, no doubt, only to those who admit it, conclusive only to those who believe that they can read it, to which in conclusion I dare appeal. When a bishop in the Southern States had been defending slavery, he was asked what he thought our Lord would have said, what looks He who turned and looked upon St. Peter would have cast upon a slave mart in New Orleans, where husband was torn from wife, child from parent, and beautiful girls, with scarce a tinge of colour in them, were sold into prostitution. The answer of the bishop is not known, but I will venture on a kindred question. What would our Lord have said, what looks would He have bent, upon a chamber filled with "the unoffending creatures which He loves," dying under torture deliberately and intentionally inflicted, or kept alive to endure further torment, in pursuit of knowledge? Men must answer this question according to their consciences; and for any man to make himself in such a matter a rule for any other would be, I know, unspeakable presumption. But to any one who recognises the authority of our Lord, and who persuades himself that he sees which way that authority inclines, the mind of Christ must be the guide of life. "Shouldest thou not have had compassion upon these, even as I had pity on thee?" So He seems to me to say, and I shall act accordingly.

4. [From] Anti-vivisection movement spokesperson Frances Power Cobbe's "Vivisection and Its Two-Faced Advocates." From the *Contemporary Review*. XLI (April 1882), pp. 610-26.

The position in which we, the opponents of Vivisection, find ourselves at present is this:—

We seek to stop certain practices which appear to us to involve gross cruelty, and to be contrary to the spirit of English law. Our knowledge of them is derived almost exclusively from the published reports and treatises prepared and issued by the actual individual who carry out those practices; and our arguments are grounded upon *verbatim* citations from those published and accessible reports and treatises.

The persons whose practices we desire to stop, and their immediate associates, now meet our charges of cruelty by articles in the leading periodicals, wherein the proceedings in question are invested with a character not only diverse from, but opposite to, that which they wear in the scientific treatises and reports containing the original accounts.

I shall, in this paper, endeavour to indicate the outlines of these diversities and contradictions, premising that, from the nature of the case, the argument is a cumulative one, of which the full force can only be felt by those who have first perused the treatises and experienced the impression which they are calculated to produce. Afterwards, I shall deal with some subordinate matters respecting which my statements in a previous article (in the *Fortnightly Review*) have been called in question.

I. In the first place, the *purpose* of the great majority of experiments is differently described in the scientific treatises and in the popular articles. In the former, the *raison d'être* of most experiments appears to be the elucidation of points of purely scientific interest. It is only occasionally that we meet with allusions to diseases or their remedies, but the experiments are generally described as showing that one organ acts in one way and another in another—that such a lesion, or such an irritation, produces such and such results and reactions; and (especially) that Professor A.'s theory has been disproved and that of Professor B. (temporarily) established. In short, every page of these books corroborates the honest statement of Professor Hermann of Zurich: "The advancement of science, and not practical utility to medicine, is the true and straightforward object of all vivisection. No true investigator in his researches thinks of the practical utilization. Science can afford to despise this justification with which vivisection has been defended in England."—*Die Vivisectionfrage* p. 16.

We now turn to such articles as the six which have appeared in the *Nineteenth Century* and the two in the *Fortnightly Review* in defence of vivisection, and, *mirabile dictu!* not a solitary vivisection is mentioned of which the direct advancement of the healing art does not appear as the single-minded object.

2. Again, the *severity* of the experiments in common use, appears from the Treatises and Reports (always including the English "Handbook," *Transactions*, and *Journal of Physiology*) to be truly frightful. Sawing across the backbone, dissecting out and irritating all the great nerves, driving catheters along the veins and arteries, inoculating with the most dreadful diseases, cutting out pieces of the intestine, baking, stewing, pouring boiling water into the stomach, freezing to death, reducing the brain to the condition of a "lately-hoed potato field," these and similarly terrible experiments form the staple of some of them, and a significant feature in all.

But turning now to the popular articles, we find Dr. Lauder Brunton assuring the readers of the *Nineteenth Century* that "he has calculated that about twenty-four out of every 100 of the experiments (in the Parliamentary Returns), might have given pain. But of these twenty four, four-fifths are like vaccination, the pain of which is of no great moment. In about one-seventh of the cases the animal only suffered from the healing of a wound." Sir James Paget afforded us a still more *couleur de rose* view of the subject. He said: "I believe that, with these few exceptions, there are no physiological experiments which are not matched or far surpassed in painfulness by common practices permitted or encouraged by the most humane persons."

3. Again, in reading these terrible Treatises (the English "Handbook" included), we do not meet with one solitary appeal against the repetition of painful experiments, one caution to the student to forbear from the extremity of torture, one expression of pity or regret—even when the keenest suffering had been inflicted. On the contrary, we find frequent repetitions of such phrases as "interesting experiments," "very interesting experiments," "beautiful" (*schone*) cerebral inflammation, and so on. In short, the writers, frankly, seem pleased with their work, and exemplify Claude Bernard's description of the ideal vivisector—the man who "does not hear the animal's cries of pain, and is blind to the blood that flows, and who sees nothing but his idea and organisms which conceal from him the secrets he is resolved to discover." Or, still more advanced, they realized Cyon's yet stronger lecture in his great book of the "Methodik," of which, by the way, he has lately told us in the *Gaulois*, that when the book was coming out his English colleagues implored him not to allow it to be advertised in England.

In this great treatise M. Cyon Tells us:—

The true vivisector must approach a difficult vivisection with *joyful excitement*. ... He who shrinks from cutting into a living animal, he who approaches vivisection as a disagreeable necessity, may be able to repeat one or two vivisections, but he will never be an artist in vivisection. ... The sensation of the physiologist when, from a gruesome wound, full of blood and mangled tissue, draws forth some delicate nerve thread ... has much in common with that of a sculptor. (*Methodik* 15)

This is the somewhat startling self-revelation of the Vivisector, made by himself to his colleagues. The picture of him in the *Nineteenth Century* and *Fortnightly Review* is almost as different as one face of Janus from the other. We find him talking of the power of "controlling one's emotions," "disregarding one's own feelings at the sight of suffering," "subordinating feeling to judgment," and much more in the same strain, whereby the Vivisector is made to appear a martyr to the Enthusiasm of Humanity.

4. Again, as to the *number* of animals dissected alive, the Treatises make us suppose it to be enormous. M. Paul Bert gives cases of horrible experiments on dogs placed under the compression of eight atmospheres

and coming out stiffened, "so that the animal may be carried by one paw just as a piece of wood"—and cats which, when dissected after death, showed a "marrow which flowed like cream;" and of these experiments he gives the public instances up to No. 286. Schiff is calculated to have "used" 14,000 dogs and nearly 50,000 other animals during his ten years' work in Florence. Flourens told Blatin that Magendie had sacrificed 4,000 dogs to prove Bell's theory of the nerves, and 4,000 more to disprove the same; and that he, Flourens, had proved Bell was right by sacrificing some thousand more. Dr. Lauder-Brunton himself told the Royal Commission (Q 5,721) that in one series, out of three on one subject, he had sacrificed (without result) ninety cats in an experiment during which they lingered four or five hours after the chloroform (Q. 5,724), with their intestines "operated upon." He also carried on another series of 150 experiments on various animals, very painful, and notoriously without results (Q. 5, 748). This is the scale on which vivisections abroad and at home are carried on, if we are to be guided by the Treatises.

Turn we now to the popular Articles; and we find mention only of the very smallest numbers. Sir William Gull minimizes Bernard's stove-baked dogs to six (concerning the correction of which statement, see further, p. 616), and Professor Yeo brings down those of Professor Rutherford's victims to twelve (for which also see p. 622) every reference to numbers being apparently, like those of the Fuegians, limited to the digits of physiologists.

5. Again, as regards Anæsthetics, throughout the Treatises I cannot recall having once seen them mentioned as *means of allaying the sufferings of the animals*, but very often as convenient applications for *keeping them quiet*. Claude Bernard in his "Physiologie Opératoire," and Cyon in his great "Methodik," each devote a section to them as a MEANS OF RESTRAINT (*"contention"*), and describe their merits from that point of view. Morphia, for example Bernard recommends because it keeps the animal still, though "*il souffre la douleur;*" and of curare (which, he says, causes "the most atrocious sufferings which the imagination can conceive"), he remarks, without an expression of regret, that its use in vivisection is so universal that it may always be assumed to have been used in experiments not otherwise described. Nor can haste explain this omission to treat anæsthetics from the humanitarian point of view, for the Treatises contain long chapters of advice to the neophyte in vivisection, how he may ingeniously avoid being bitten by the dogs, or scratched by the yet more "*terrible*" cats, which are, Bernard pathetically complains, "*indocile*" when lifted on the torture trough.

Turning to our *Nineteenth Century* essayists, we find chloroform is everywhere, and curare nowhere.

6. Lastly, there is not as a trace in the Treatises—even in the English "Handbook"—of the supposed Wall of China which guards the Flowery Land of English Vivisection from the hordes of outer barbarians who prac-

tice in Paris, Leipsic, Florence, Strasbourg, and Vienna. We find, on the contrary, a frequent and cordial interchange of experiments and compliments. Our English vivisectionists study in the schools of the Continent, and in several cases have brought over foreigners to be their assistants at home. When Claude Bernard died, so little did English physiologists think of repudiating him, that a letter appeared in the *Times* of March 20, 1878, inviting subscriptions to raise as a monument to his honour, signed by Sir James Paget, Dr. Burdon-Sanderson, Professor Humphry, Professor Gerald Yeo, Mr. Ernest Hart, Mr. Romanes, and Dr. Michael Foster. Even last autumn, when Professors Goltz, Flint, Brown-Séquard, Béclard, and Chauveau joined the International Congress in London, they were received with the warmest welcome from their English colleagues, one hundred of whom accompanied Professors Goltz and Ferrier to inspect the dogs of the former and the monkeys of the latter (I beg pardon, of Professor Yeo); and when Professor Goltz returned to Germany, he published a volume containing beautiful coloured pictures of the mutilated brains of his dogs, and dedicated it—to whom does the reader think? To—

HIS ENGLISH FRIENDS!

All this does not look exactly like hearty disgust and repudiation of the foreign system.

But turn we to the *Nineteenth Century* and *Fortnightly Review*, and lo! The garments of our English physiologists are drawn closely around them, and we are assured they have "no connection whatever with the establishment over the way." I am even rebuked for placing on the same page (in my article "Four Replies") certain English experiments and "the disgusting details of foreign atrocities, which excite a persistent feeling of repugnance." Professor Yeo says he "regards with pain and loathing such work as that of Mantegazza," and asks me bitterly, "Why repeat the oft-told tale of horrors contained in the works of Claude Bernard, Paul Bert, Brown-Séquard, and Richet in France, of Goltz in Germany, Mantegazza in Italy, and Flint in America?" (p. 361.)

Surely this is a cargo of Jonahs thrown overboard together! Claude Bernard, the prince of physiologists, to whom this same Professor Gerald Yeo, four years ago, wished to raise a statue! Brown-Séquard, the honoured of Professor Huxley! Professor Flint, who, six months since, was the favoured guest of every scientific throng in London, and who, I presume, is of Anglo-Saxon race, only corrupted from human British vivisection by evil American communications! And lastly, Goltz!—poor Professor Goltz, who had so many cordial hand-shakes on quitting perfidious Albion, while the autumn leaves were falling, and who is now flung down the Gemonian stairs, as a sacrifice to the rabble of anti-vivisectors, even while the ink is scarcely dry on his touching dedication of his book:—

SEINEN
FREUDEN IN ENGLAND
GEWIDMET
VON DEM VERFASSER.

May not this new Raleigh fitly cry, not, "O the friendship of Princes!" but "O the friendship of Physiologists?"

Thus we see that, as a regards, first, the *purpose* of the majority of vivisections; second, their severity; third, their number; fourth, the caution of the experimenters; fifth, the use of anæsthetics; sixth, the difference between English and foreign vivisection,—in short, on every one of the points of importance in the controversy,—there is contradiction on the broadest scale between the scientific Treatises and Reports prepared for "brethren of the craft" and in the articles written in lay periodicals for the edification of the British public.

It is for the reader to judge which class of statement may, with the greater probability, be held to represent the genuine doings and feelings of the writers.

[The rest of F.P. Cobbe's lengthy rebuke of physiologists offers first an examination "of some minor points whereon my statements in the *Fortnightly Review* ... have been attacked" and then eleven consecutive pages of incriminating material taken directly from published descriptions (by physiologist Dr. Charles Roy) of actual vivisections.]

5. Physiologist Gerald F. Yeo's letter to the editor of the *Contemporary Review*, a defense of the practice of vivisection and a response to Frances Power Cobbe's "Vivisection and Its Two-Faced Advocates." From the *Contemporary Review*. XLI (May 1882), pp. 897-98.

Dear Sir,—In an article on "Vivisection and its Two-faced Advocates," which appears in the current number of the *Contemporary Review*, there are some inaccuracies which should be noticed, and as Miss Cobbe directly appeals to me to explain a point where she is in difficulty, I beg you will allow me an opportunity of gratifying her, and preventing your readers from being misled.

In page 611 Miss Cobbe says, "We find Dr. Brunton assuring the readers of the *Nineteenth Century* that 'he has calculated that about 24 out of every 100 of the experiments (in the Parliamentary Returns) might have given pain. But of these 24, four-fifths are like vaccination, the pain of which is of no great moment. In about one-seventh of the cases the animal only suffered from the healing of a wound.'"

Nothing resembling this occurs in Dr. Lauder Brunton's article in the *Nineteenth Century. But it is a tolerably accurate quotation of the sentence by which I introduced the following table in the Fortnightly Review* of last month, which shows the amount of pain inflicted in 100 vivisections:—

Absolutely painless. 75
As painful as vaccination 20
”   ” the healing of a wound 4
”   ” a surgical operation 1
                                                      ___
                                                      100

This is a perfectly correct statement of fact.

In page 614 Miss Cobbe refers to some remarks of mine about foreign physiologists; and, completely misinterpreting my meaning, makes it appear as if I accused a number of my foreign colleagues of perpetrating certain "horrors." I did not admit that the physiologists abroad are cruel, nor did I in the least intend to endorse the truth of the stories which I mentioned as having been "oft-told" *by Miss Cobbe.*

It never could have occurred to my mind to accuse the gentlemen named of anything like cruelty, because the one amongst them that I know best, and to whom Miss Cobbe refers with ironical pity, is a most kind and humane man, who never omits to give chloroform when it is possible to administer it, and is devotedly attached to the lower animals. I should be indeed sorry did any one imagine that I adopted Miss Cobbe's view of Professor Goltz's character, for I know him too well, and am proud to call him my friend. Perhaps I was premature in judging harshly of Mantegazza's operations—the one foreign experimenter I did "throw overboard"—because my knowledge of his work was derived solely from Miss Cobbe's writings, and may be quite incorrect. If she can attribute to Dr. Brunton words which I wrote one month ago, she may have put down to Signor Mantegazza the writings of some author of the old Italian school.

In page 622, Miss Cobbe, a second time, mistakes the total number of experiments done by Professor Rutherford for those done by him "under the express sanction of the law as it now stands." Professor Rutherford's experiments, though published in 1877-1878, extended over some ten or eleven years, and possibly were as numerous as is stated. All but twelve, however, were done without the "express sanction" of any special law, the Act not being in existence, and therefore Miss Cobbe's assertion that at least fifty dogs under the *express sanction of the law* as it now stands were used in experiments," is as far from the truth as when I contradicted it a month ago.

There is no want of accord between Professor Rutherford's reports and those of the Home Office such as Miss Cobbe infers. The scientific description does not say when or under what restrictions the experiments were made. If, instead of being absolutely accurate, the Parliamentary Reports be as "untrustworthy" as Miss Cobbe implies, they surely set forth all the experiments "done under the express sanction of the law," and thus must include those in question. It was only in the year 1878 that Professor Rutherford held this special certificate, and in it the number of experiments was limited to *twelve*. If Professor Rutherford did more than this number they were not "under the express sanction of the law as it now stands," and he must have acted illegally.

That he did not thus contravene the Act, and, further, that Miss Cobbe knows full well that he did not do so, I am thoroughly convinced by the fact that her vigilant Society has not instituted a prosecution.

The riddle Miss Cobbe so jocosely puts to me, "How twelve dogs can be killed thirty-one times over," now answers itself; and I venture to hope that the "little mistake of twelve dogs for thirty-one" now obviously appears—even to the meanest "lay intelligence"—to be of Miss Cobbe's manufacture, not mine.

I have received the following letter from Dr. Brunton, whose evidence is quoted by Miss Cobbe in refutation of what I said about the painlessness of Dr. Roy's experiments, and in support of the false assertion she makes (page 624), namely, "we absolutely deny the possibility of keeping an animal insensible by anæsthetics during curarization":—

"Dear Yeo,—I know of no reason whatever to prevent animals being kept perfectly insensible to pain by chloroform, during curarization, and I believe that any one who dogmatically denies the possibility of this is guilty either of gross ignorance or wilful misrepresentation.

The sentences from my evidence before the Royal Commission, quoted by Miss Cobbe, do not apply to Dr. Roy's experiments. I there expressly said, "in many instances" the administration of chloroform prevented satisfactory experiments from being made, knowing that this is *not* the case in all instances, but that some reflex actions, especially those connected with the vascular system, occur during the most profound chloroform narcosis.

Truly yours, T. Lauder Brunton"

From this it would appear that the "gentleman perfectly qualified to deal scientifically" with the matter (as Miss Cobbe states) knows little or nothing about it. It is a pity she should depend for her skilled information upon a person whose chief discretion seems to lie in his not disclosing his name. For it would be mere waste of time to expose the numerous fallacies of an anonymous authority. But I think it only fair to Miss Cobbe to let her know that, in the few places where this prolix statement bears at all on the point at issue, the opinions it contains are completely wrong, or, to use her own well-worn phrase, not even "accurate enough for scientific purposes." And I must repeat, in a most positive manner, my assertion that "the infliction of pain had no part in Dr. Roy's experiments."

I am, dear Sir, Yours obediently, Gerald F. Yeo

Appendix C: An Account of the Ferrier Trial

Frances Power Cobbe's account of the trial of Professor Ferrier, November 17, 1881. From *Life of Frances Power Cobbe as Told by Herself.* (London: Swan Sonnenschein, 1904) 672-75.

Among our undertakings on behalf of the victims of science was the prosecution of Prof. Ferrier at Bow Street on the 17th November, 1881, on the strength of certain reports in the two leading Medical Journals. We had ascertained that he had no license for Vivisection and yet we read as follows in a report of the proceedings at the International Medical Congress of 1881:—

"The members were shown two of the monkeys, a portion of whose cortex had been removed by Professor Ferrier."—*British Medical Journal*, 20th August, 1881.

"The interest attaching to the discussion was greatly enhanced by the fact that Professor Ferrier was willing to exhibit two monkeys which he had operated upon some months previously." ...

"In startling contrast to the dog were two monkeys exhibited by Professor Ferrier. One of them had been operated upon in the middle of January, the left motor area having been destroyed."—*Lancet*, October 8th, 1881.

When the reporters who had sent in their reports to the two journals were produced the following ludicrous examination took place in court:—

Dr. Charles Smart Roy (the Reporter for the *British Medical Journal*) was asked—

"Q. Did Professor Ferrier offer to exhibit two of the monkeys upon which he had so operated?
"A. At the Congress, no.
"Q. Did he subsequently?
"A. No; he showed certain of the members of the Congress two monkeys at King's College.
"Q. What two monkeys?
"A. Two monkeys upon which an operation had been performed.
"Q. By whom?
"A. By PROFESSOR YEO" (!!)

"The Editor of the Lancet, Dr. Wakeley, was next examined:—

"Dr. Wakeley, *sworn, examined by Mr. Waddy:*—

"Q. Are you the Editor of the *Lancet*?

"A. I am.

"Q Can you tell me who it was furnished his Report?

"A. I have the permission of the gentleman to give his name, Professor Gamgee, of Owen's College, Manchester.

"Mr. Waddy: What I should ask is that one might have an opportunity of calling Professor Gamgee.

"Mr. Gully (Counsel for the defendant): We have communicated with Professor Gamgee, and I know very well he will say precisely what was said by Dr. Roy."

—*Report of Trial*, November 17th, 1881.

The position of the Anti-vivisectionists on the occasion was, it must be confessed, like that of the simple countryman in the fair. "You lay your money that Professor Ferrier is under that cup?" "Yes, certainly! I saw both Professor Roy and Professor Gamgee put him there about five minutes ago." "Here then, see! Hay Presto! Hocus-pocus! There is only Professor Yeo!"

The group of Vivisectors and their allies, Dr. Michael Foster, Dr. Burdon-Sanderson, Dr. Ernest Hart, Prof. Ferrier, Dr. Roy and many more who filled the court, all evinced the utmost hilarity at the success of the device whereby (as a matter of necessity) the Anti-vivisection case collapsed.

At last, in the *Philosophical Transactions* of the Royal Society for 1884, the truth came to light. In the Prefatory Note to a record of Experiments by David Ferrier and Gerald Y. Yeo, M.D., occurs the statement:—

The facts recorded in this paper are partly the result of a research made conjointly by Drs. Ferrier and Yeo, aided by a grant from the British Medical Association, and partly of a research made by Dr. Ferrier alone, aided by a grant from the Royal Society.

The conjoint experiences are distinguished by an asterisk; and among them we find those of the two monkeys which formed the subject of the trial. Thus it stands confessed,—actually in the *Transactions of the Royal Society*,—that Professor Ferrier *had* the leading share (his name always appears first) in the experiments; and that, conjointly with Professor Yeo, he received a grant from the British Medical Association for performing the same!

If after this experience we have ceased to hope much from proceedings in Courts of Justice against our antagonists, it will not be thought surprising. The Society has been frequently twitted with the failure of this prosecution, "for which" our opponents say, we "had not a tittle of evidence." Elaborate reports in the two leading Medical journals do not, it appears, afford even "a tittle of evidence!"

Appendix D: Letters by Collins concerning or mentioning Heart and Science

1. Wilkie Collins's June 23, 1882 letter to Frances Power Cobbe, a leading anti-vivisection activist of the period, explaining to her his plans for his upcoming novel, *Heart and Science*. From *Life of Frances Power Cobbe as Told by Herself*. (London: Swan Sonnenschein, 1904) 558-59.

90 Gloucester Place, Portman Square, W.,
23rd June, 1882.

Dear Madam,

I most sincerely thank you for your kind letter and for the pamphlets which preceded it. The 'Address' seems to me to possess the very rare merit of forcible statement combined with a moderation of judgment which sets a valuable example, not only to our enemies, but to some of our friends. As to the "Portrait," I feel such a strong universal interest in it that I must not venture on criticism. You have given me exactly what I most wanted for the purpose that I have in view—and you have spared me time and trouble in the best and kindest of ways. If I require further help, you shall see that I am gratefully sensible of the help that has been already given.

I am writing to a very large public both at home and abroad; and it is quite needless (when I am writing to *you*) to dwell on the importance of producing the right impression by means which keep clear of terrifying and revolting the ordinary reader. I shall leave the detestable cruelties of the laboratory to be merely inferred, and, in tracing the moral influence of those cruelties on the nature of the man who practices them, and the result as to his social relations with the persons about him, I shall be careful to present him to the reader as a man not infinitely wicked and cruel, and to show the efforts made by his better instincts to resist the inevitable hardening of the heart, the fatal stupefying of all the finer sensibilities, produced by the deliberately merciless occupations of his life. If I can succeed in making him, in some degree, an object of compassion as well as of horror, my experience of readers of fiction tells me that the right effect will be produced by the right means.

Believe me, very truly yours,
Wilkie Collins

2. Wilkie Collins's July 13, 1882 letter to Surgeon General C.A. Gordon. Reprinted with the kind permission of Barry Pike.

90, Gloucester Place, Portman Square, W.,
13th July 1882

Dear Sir,

Permit me to thank you for the kindness which has favoured me with a copy of your "Remarks on Experimental Pharmacology." I am reading your work with the greatest of interest, and with a very sincere admiration of the clearness and impartiality with which the case is stated.

I am endeavouring to add my small contribution in aid of the good cause, by such means as Fiction will permit—and I am especially obliged to you for valuable "facts" which I could never have discovered for myself.

Believe me, dear sir,
Faithfully yours,
Wilkie Collins

The morsel of paper enclosed will show that this little I may be able to do will at least have a large audience.

3. Wilkie Collins's July 5, 1882 letter to Augustus Frederick Lehmann, a close friend. From the Harry Ransom Research Center, Austin, Texas.

90, Gloucester Place, Portman Square, W.,
5th July 1882

My dear Fred,

My absence from Berkeley Square will have told you my gouty story— and my silence (when I ought long since to have thanked you for you most kind letter) only means that I am too weary of myself to write about myself. It has been a milder attack this time—and I am going to leave off my patch.

When you write to the Padrona—give her my best love—and tell her to be as happy in Scotland as the happiest woman living. When she comes back to London, she will completely fulfil my aspirations, if she will let me know of it.

I have nothing else to say. My life is my new book [*Heart and Science*]. Some critic said *The Woman in White* "was written in blood and vitriol." This book is being written in blood and dynamite.

Yours affectionately,
WC

4. Wilkie Collins's February 24, 1883 letter to W.M. Laffan, a Harper Brothers' representative in London. From the Harry Ransom Research Center, Austin, Texas.

> 90, Gloucester Place, Portman Square, W.,
> 24th February 1883

Dear Sir,

I have been too thoroughly disgusted with the thefts committed on *Heart and Science* during its periodical publication in the United States to make any arrangements for its publication there in book-form. Under the sanction of the President and Congress, the honest American citizen who purchased my advance-sheets for Frank Leslie's newspaper was robbed of them three days afterward, in each week, by the publication of another New York newspaper—to say nothing of other thefts committed in other places.

However, as an act of courtesy to Messrs. Harper, I very gladly send, by today's registered bank post, the corrected revises of the 1st volume of the contemplated book republication in civilized countries. The remaining proofs of volumes 2 and 3 shall follow as soon as they reach me.

> Believe me, Dear Sir,
> Faithfully yours
> Wilkie Collins

5. Wilkie Collins's February 25, 1883 letter to Mrs. Augustus Frederick Lehmann, a close friend. From the Harry Ransom Research Center, Austin, Texas.

> 90, Gloucester Place, Portman Square, W.,
> 25th February 1883

Dearest Padrona:

The sight of your handwriting was delightful—and the sight of you will be better still. Anybody who says there is no such thing as luck—lies. Last year, I was too ill to get to you at all. This year, I am only not well enough to get out to dinner at nights. But I might come to lunch—when you have no company—if you will choose from one day and hour, and make travel allowances for Wilkie's infirmities. For six months—while I was writing furiously, without cessation, one part sane and three parts mad—I had no gout. I finished my story [*Heart and Science*]—discovered one day that I was half dead with fatigue—and the next day that the gout was in my right eye.

No more of that! I am nearly well—and I pull off my black patch indoors. But I am forbidden night air—like old Rogers. But *he* was only eighty—I am a hundred.

With love to you particularly—and to everybody else generally—your always affectionately,

WC

Weak brandy and water—and *no* wholesome joints.

6. Wilkie Collins's March 9, 1883 letter to the editor of *Belgravia* magazine. From the Harry Ransom Research Center, Austin, Texas.

90, Gloucester Place, Portman Square, W.,
9th March 1883

Heart and Science

Note to the Editor:

The end of the Second Volume of the Book-reprint here has been altered. In order to save time, I am obliged to send the printers copy corrected of chapters 39-41, instead of the book revises.

While I am about it, I may perhaps add that there is hardly a page of this *periodical* publication which has not been revised, altered, abridged, in one place, or enlarged in another, for the English reprint. The "Author's Edition" is, in this case, really the only complete edition. As to the *exact* date of publication here, I will write again next week.

Wilkie Collins

7. Wilkie Collins's March 24, 1883 letter to W.M. Laffan. From the Harry Ransom Research Center, Austin, Texas.

90, Gloucester Place, Portman Square, W.,
24th March 1883

Dear Sir,

Since I last wrote, the publishers have decided to hasten the book-publication here of *I*. The new date will be the 10th or 12th of April next. The supply of most of Volume III will be quickened next week—and duplicates shall be sent to you as soon as they are corrected.

Faithfully yours
Wilkie Collins

Appendix E: An excerpt from A.C. Swinburne's obituary commentary on Collins.

From the Fortnightly Review. CCLXXV, November 1, 1889, pp. 589-99.

Swinburne began his discussion of *Heart and Science* by quoting from the novel at length and discussing his opinions of various characters. At one point in the essay, he writes of Ovid Vere's half-sister, Zo Gallilee, "There is a capital child in it, for one thing; her experiences of Scottish life and character, as related on the occasion of her last appearance, are nothing less than delicious." Here he discusses Benjulia and provides his opinion of "thesis" novels:

Not quite so much can be said against the leading character of the story: the relentless lover of knowledge who lives for that love alone is at least *un succès manqué*. Now and then he becomes a really living, interesting, and rather memorable figure. The cynomaniacs with whom the death or the suffering of "that beast man" is less of account than the death or the suffering of a rabbit or a dog must naturally, one would think, have disapproved of a story in which the awkward champion of their preposterous cause has contrived somehow so to concentrate the serious interest of his book on the person of a vivisector, whom he meant to be an object of mere abhorrence, as to leave him an object of something like sympathy and admiration as well as compassion and respect; none the less deserved if he did once feel a desire to vivisect his vicious and thankless idiot of a brother. The cynical sentimentality—cynical in the metaphorical no less than in the literal sense of the word—which winces and whines at the thought of a benefit conferred on mankind at the price of experiments made on the vile or at any rate the viler body of a beast is worth exactly as much as the humanity and sympathy which inspire the advocates of free trade in the most unspeakable kind of pestilence. And it strikes me that Mr. Godfrey Ablewhite (of *The Moonstone*) would have been a fitter champion of free and independent hydrophobia than the creator of that distinguished philanthropist; who would certainly have been a quite ideal chairman at a meeting of the Ladies' Society for the Propagation of the—well, let us say for the Dissemination of Contagious Disease (Unlimited).

> What brought Sir Visto's ill-got wealth to waste?
> Some demon whispered—"Visto! Have a taste."

A slight change in that famous couplet will express and condense the truth about Wilkie Collins the teacher and preacher more happily and aptly than many pages of analysis.

What brought good Wilkie's genius nigh perdition?
Some demon whispered—"Wilkie! Have a mission."

Nothing can be more fatuous than to brand all didactic or missionary fiction as an illegitimate or inferior form of art: the highest works in that line fall short only of the highest ever achieved by man. Many of the very truest and noblest triumphs achieved by the matchless genius of Charles Dickens were achieved in this field: but Collins, I must be allowed to repeat, was no more a Dickens that Dickens was a Shakespeare; and if the example of his illustrious friend misled him into emulation or imitation of such labours, we can only regret that he was thus misguided: remembering nevertheless that "the light which led astray was light from" Dickens.

Appendix F: A Notice in The Times of Professor Helmholtz's Visit to London, April 12, 1881.

(Collins refers to this notice in the Preface to *Heart and Science* and uses some of the language contained within it in the novel itself.)

Professor Helmholtz.—The President (Professor G.C. Foster, F.R.S.), and members of the Society of Telegraph Engineers and of Electricians gave a *conversazione* last night in the library of University College, Gower-street, in honour of the visit of Professor Helmholtz to this country. The fine building and the large quadrangle in front were illuminated by one of the Crompton arc lamps placed above the pediment. Another in the circular Flaxman gallery brought out the lines of the beautiful rilievi with perfect distinctness. Among those who were present to meet the guest of the evening were Lord Claud J. Hamilton, M.P., Professor Kuhn (successor of Professor Helmholtz in the University of Heidelberg), Professor Klein, Professor Burdon Sanderson, Mr. Norman Lockyer, Dr. Frankland, Professor Ray Lunkester, Professor Alexander J. Ellis, Dr. Tidy, Mr. Busk, Professor Kennedy, Professor Adam, Professor Corneld, Professor Hughes, Mr. Le Fevre (President of the Balloon Society of Great Britain), Mr. J.H. Gilbert, and Mr. Alexander Siemens. Many of the members of the society and others had lent instruments and apparatus showing some of the purposes to which electricity has recently been applied, and, also, the means by which electrical research is still being carried on. The telephotographic machine of Mr. Shelford Bidwell was exhibited, and the process by which a picture might be produced at a distance of many miles from the object to be photographed. The outline of a butterfly with the markings on the wings was in this way very distinctly reproduced last night. The President showed some interesting electrical instruments; Mr. W.H. Preece sent some apparatus by which the conversion of radiant energy into sonorous vibrations and the diathermancy of ebonite were illustrated; and Mr. Alfred J. Frost, the secretary of the society, had made a selection of old and rare books on electricity and magnetism from the Ronalds collection in the society's library. Mr. A. Stroh exhibited some ingenious instruments designed to illustrate Professor Helmholtz's vowel theory. The library was partly lighted by electric incandescent lamps, made on Swan's system. Professor Helmholtz ends to-day his visit to London, and goes with Mr. Spottiswoode, President of the Royal Society, to his country house at Coombe Bank, Sevenoaks. From thence he will proceed to Dublin, to receive an honorary doctor's degree from the University of that city. During his stay in London, Professor Helmholtz has visited the laboratories of Mr. Crookes, F.R.S., Mr. de la Rue, F.R.S., Mr. Spottiswoode, P.R.S., and that of the Royal Institution.

Appendix G: Serial Parts Divisons

Belgravia serial part divisions and the corresponding page numbers in this edition are as follows:

August 1882 — Chapters I-VI (pp. 45-69)

September 1882 — Chapters VII- X (pp. 70-90)

October 1882 — Chapters XI-XV (pp. 90-116)

November 1882 — Chapters XVI-XX (pp. 116-139)

December 1882 — Chapters XXI-XXVI (pp. 143-166)

January 1883 — Chapters XXVII-XXXII (pp. 166-191)

February 1883 — Chapters XXXIII-XXXVIII (pp. 191-220)

March 1883 — Chapters XXXIX-XLIV (pp. 221-247)

April 1883 — Chapters XLV-LI (pp. 247-279)

May 1883 — Chapters LII-LIX (pp. 279-309)

June 1883 — Chapters LX-LXIII (pp. 309-327)

Appendix H: Robert Browning's anti-vivisection poetry

1. "Tray" (from *Dramatic Idylls*, First Series, 1879)

> Sing me a hero! Quench my thirst
> Of souls, ye bards!
>
>   Quoth Bard the first:
> Sir Olaf, the good knight, did don
> His helm and eke his habergeon ...
> Sir Olaf and his bard—!
>
> That sin-scathed brow (quoth Bard the second),
> That eye wide ope as though Fate beckoned
> My hero to some steep, beneath
> Which precipice smiled tempting death ...
> You too without your host have reckoned!
>
> A beggar-child (let's hear this third!)
> Sat on a quay's edge: like a bird
> Sand to herself at careless play,
> And fell into the stream. 'Dismay!
> Help, you the standers-by!' None stirred.
>
> Bystanders reason, think of wives
> And children ere they risk their lives.
> Over the balustrade has bounced
> A mere instinctive dog, and pounced
> Plumb on the prize. 'How well he dives!
>
> 'Up he comes with the child, see, tight
> In mouth, alive too, clutched from quite
> A depth of ten feet—twelve, I bet!
> Good dog! What, off again? There's yet
> Another child to save? All right!
>
> How strange we saw no other fall!
> It's instinct in the animal.
> Good dog! But he's a long while under:
> If he got drowned I should not wonder—
> Strong current, that against the wall!

'Here he comes, hold in mouth this time
—What may the thing be? Well, that prime!
Now, did you ever? Reason reigns
In man alone, since all Tray's pains
Have fished—the child's doll from the slime!'

And so, amid the laughter gay,
Trotted my hero off,—old Tray,—
Till somebody, prerogatived
With reason, reasoned: 'Why he dived,
His brain would show us, I should say.

'John, go and catch—or, if needs be,
Purchase—that animal for me!
By vivisection, at expense
Of half-an-hour and eighteenpence,
How brain secretes dog's soul, we'll see!'

2. "Arcades Ambo" (from *Asolando*, 1889)

A. You blame me that I ran away?
    Why, Sir, the enemy advanced:
Balls flew about, and—who can say
    But one, if I stood firm, had glanced
In my direction? Cowardice?
I only know we don't live twice,
Therefore—shun death, is my advice.

B. Shun death at all risks? Well, at some?
    True, I myself, Sir, though I scold
The cowardly, by no means come
    Under reproof as overbold
—I, who would have no end of brutes
Cut up alive to guess what suits
My case and saves my toe from shoots.

Select Bibliography

Bibliography: Wilkie Collins

Andrew R. V. "A Wilkie Collins Check-List." *English Studies in Africa* 3 (March 1960): 79-98.

Ashley, Robert. "Wilkie Collins." *Victorian Fiction: A Second Guide to Research*, ed. George H. Ford. New York: Modern Lanuguage Association, 1978.

Beetz, Kirk H. *Wilkie Collins: An Annotated Bibliography, 1889-1976*. Metuchen, NJ: Scarecrow, 1976.

——. "Wilkie Collins Studies, 1972-83," *Dickens Studies Annual*, XIII, 1984, 333-55.

Edwards, P.D., I.G. Sibley, and Margaret Versteeg. *Indexes to Fiction in Belgravia*. Department of English, U of Queensland: *Victorian Fiction Research Guides*, XIV, 1988.

Gasson, Andrew. "Wilkie Collins: A Collector's and Bibliographer's Challenge." *The Private Library* (Summer 1980): 51-77.

Parrish, M.L. *Wilkie Collins and Charles Reade: First Editions, Described with Notes*. London: Constable, 1940.

Wolff, Robert L., "Wilkie Collins." *Nineteenth-Century Fiction: A Bibliographical Catalogue*, Vol. I. New York: Garland, 1981: 254-272.

Biography: Wilkie Collins

Ashley, Robert. *Wilkie Collins*. London: Arthur Barker, 1952.

Clarke, William. *The Secret Life of Wilkie Collins*. London: Allison & Busby, 1988.

Davis, Nuel Pharr. *The Life of Wilkie Collins*. Urbana, Illinois: U of Illinois P, 1956.

Marshall, William. *Wilkie Collins*. New York: Twayne, 1970.

Peters, Catherine. *The King of Inventors: A Life of Wilkie Collins*. London: Secker & Warburg, 1991.

Robinson, Kenneth. *Wilkie Collins: A Biography*. London: Bodley Head, 1951.

Sayers, Dorothy. *Wilkie Collins: A Biographical and Critical Study*. Ed. E.R. Gregory. Toledo, Ohio: Friends of the U of Toledo Libraries, 1977.

Critical Studies, General Studies, Letters

Altick, R. D. *The English Common Reader: A Social History of the Mass Reading Public, 1800-1900*. Chicago: U of Chicago P, 1957.

——. *Victorian Studies in Scarlet*. New York: Norton, 1970.

Andrew, R. V. *Wilkie Collins: A Critical Survey of his Prose Fiction, With a bibliography*. New York: Garland, 1979.

Coleman, Ronald, ed. *The University of Texas Collections of the Letters of Wilkie Collins, Victorian Novelist*. Austin, TX.: University of Texas, 1975.

Heller, Tamar. *Dead Secrets: Wilkie Collins and the Female Gothic.* New Haven, CT: Yale UP, 1992.

Lonoff, Sue. *Wilkie Collins and His Victorian Readers: A Study in the Rhetoric of Authorship.* New York: A.M.S., 1982.

Lynd, H. M. *England in the Eighteen-Eighties: Toward a Social Basis for Freedom.* London: Frank Cass, 1945.

MacEachen, Dougald. "Wilkie Collins' *Heart and Science* and the Vivisection Controversy." *The Victorian Newsletter* (Spring 1966): 22-25.

———. "Wilkie Collins and British Law." *Nineteenth Century Fiction* 5 (September 1950): 121-36.

Milley, H.J.W. "The Achievement of Wilkie Collins and His Influence on Dickens and Trollope." Diss. Yale, 1941.

O'Neill, Philip. *Wilkie Collins: Women, Property and Propriety.* London: Macmillan, 1988.

Page, Norman, ed. *Wilkie Collins: The Critical Heritage.* London: Routledge & Kegan Paul, 1974.

Reed, John R. *Victorian Conventions.* Athens, Ohio: Ohio UP, 1975.

Smith, Nelson, and R.C. Terry. *Wilkie Collins to the Forefront: Some Reassessments.* New York: AMS Press, 1995.

Taylor, Jenny Bourne. *In the Secret Theatre of Home: Wilkie Collins, Sensation, Narrative and Nineteenth-Century Psychology.* London: Routledge, 1988.

Vivisection: Critical Studies, General Studies, Bibliographies

Cobbe, Frances Power. *Life of Frances Power Cobbe as Told by Herself.* London: Swan Sonnenschein, 1904.

Coleridge, Stephen. *Vivisection: A Heartless Science.* Edinburgh: Turnball & Spears, 1916.

Fairholme, Edward, G., and Wellesley Pain. *A Century of Work for Animals: The History of the R.S.P.C.A., 1824-1924.* New York: E.P. Dutton, 1924.

Finsen, Lawrence, and Susan Finsen. *The Animal Rights Movement in America: From Compassion to Respect.* New York: Twayne, 1994.

French, Richard D. *Antivivisection and Medical Science in Victorian Society.* Princeton, NJ: Princeton UP, 1975.

Lansbury, Coral. *The Old Brown Dog: Women, Workers, and Vivisection in Edwardian England.* Madison, WI: The U of Wisconsin P, 1985.

Leahy, Michael. *Against Liberation: Putting Animals in Perspective.* New York: Routledge, 1991.

Magel, Charles R. *A Bibliography on Animal Rights and Related Matters.* Washington, D.C.: UP of America, 1981.

Rupke, Nicolaas, ed. *Vivisection in Historical Perspective.* London: Croom Helm, 1987.

Swain, John. *Brutes and Beasts.* London: Noel Douglas, 1933.

Vyvyan, John. *In Pity and in Anger: A Study of the Use of Animals in Science.* London: Michael Joseph, 1969.

broadview literary texts

"Broadview's series format is inviting. Clearly printed on good paper, with distinctive photographs on the covers, the books provide the physical pleasure that is so often a component of enticing one to pick up a book in the first place....And, by providing a broad context, the editors have done us a great service."
Eighteenth-Century Fiction

"These very useful and well-edited texts are to be welcomed. The inclusion of lesser-known works is a series feature worthy of support. The volumes are a delight to handle and offer useful background material for reading and discussion."
Angus Ross, Sussex University

"These editions [*Frankenstein, Hard Times, Heart of Darkness*] are top-notch—far better than anything else in the market today."
Craig Keating, Langara College

The Broadview Literary Texts series represents an important effort to see the ever-changing canon of English literature from new angles. The series brings together texts that have long been regarded as classics with lesser-known texts that offer a fresh light—and that in many cases may also claim to be of real importance in our literary tradition.

Each volume in the series presents the text together with a variety of documents from the period, enabling readers to get a fuller, richer sense of the world out of which it emerged. Samples of the science available for Mary Shelley to draw on in writing *Frankenstein*; stark reports from the Congo in the late nineteenth century that help to illuminate Conrad's Heart of Darkness; late eighteenth-century statements on the proper roles for women and men that help contextualize the feminist themes of the late eighteenth-century novels *Millenium Hall* and *Something New*—these are the sorts of fascinating background materials that round out each Broadview Literary Texts edition.

Each volume also includes a full introduction, chronology, bibliography, and explanatory notes. Newly typeset and produced on high-quality paper in an attractive Trade paperback format, Broadview Literary Texts are a delight to handle as well as to read.

The distinctive cover images for the series are also designed (like the duotone process itself) to combine two slightly different perspectives. Early photographs inevitably evoke a sense of pastness, yet the images for most volumes in the series involve a conscious use of anachronism. The covers are thus designed to draw attention to social and temporal context, while suggesting that the works themselves may also relate to periods other than that from which they emerged—including our own era.